FLIGHTS

EXTREME VISIONS OF FANTASY

FLIGHTS

EXTREME VISIONS OF FANTASY

EDITED BY

AL SARRANTONIO

A ROC BOOK

ROC
Published by New American Library, a division of
Penguin Group (USA) Inc., 375 Hudson Street,
New York, New York 10014, U.S.A.
Penguin Books Ltd, 80 Strand,
London WC2R 0RL, England
Penguin Books Australia Ltd, 250 Camberwell Road,
Camberwell, Victoria 3124, Australia
Penguin Books Canada Ltd, 10 Alcorn Avenue,
Toronto, Ontario, Canada M4V 3B2
Penguin Books (N.Z.) Ltd, Cnr Rosedale and Airborne Roads,
Albany, Auckland 1310, New Zealand

Penguin Books Ltd, Registered Offices: 80 Strand, London WC2R 0RL, England

First published by Roc, an imprint of New American Library,
a division of Penguin Group (USA) Inc.

ISBN 0-451-45977-6

Set in Sabon
Designed by Ginger Legato

Printed in the United States of America

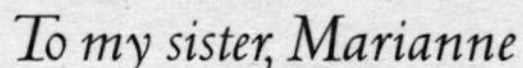

To my sister, Marianne

ACKNOWLEDGMENTS

Every time I edit a book, I say the same thing on the acknowledgments page: No book is an island. It's no less true this time. My heartfelt thanks to

Beth, always there, who put up with yet *another* one;

Laura Anne Gilman, editor supreme;

Kathleen Bellamy, whose gentle perseverance paid off;

Chris Lotts, for (lots of) help;

And, once more (and always), the editors, quiet linchpins of the field who, almost always without fanfare, got or get it done: Terry Carr, Damon Knight, Ellen Datlow, David G. Hartwell, Betsy Mitchell, Gordon Van Gelder, Gardner Dozois, Susan Allison, Ginjer Buchanan, Melissa Singer, Jennifer Brehl, John Douglas, Stan Schmidt, Scott Edelman, Patrick Nielsen Hayden, Shawna McCarthy . . .

Ever too many to name.

CONTENTS

INTRODUCTION

PART ONE: *The Meal*

We sit, you and I, at a long and festooned wooden table. Candles burn in sconces on the walls. Servants attend. There is the sound of music: finger bells, a deep thumping drum, the rasp of a krummhorn.

I rise and, as designated host, propose a toast: "My friends, we gather here for nothing less than a feast—partake!"

At which time, there is a trumpet fanfare (silence from the krummhorn!), the entry of a procession, waiters bearing a great meal.

I command, and the feast is set down before you:

This book.

PART TWO: *The Recipe*

Flights: Extreme Visions of Fantasy is a direct descendant of my two previous original anthologies, *Redshift* and *999*. All three were inspired by Harlan Ellison's groundbreaking *Dangerous Visions,* in that I told the contributors not to be concerned with taboos (if they could find any these days). More specifically, and important, I told them not to feel constrained in any way, to write whatever fantasy tales they wanted. And most important of all, I asked them to write really good stories, which, in the end, is how any original anthology is judged.

How did they do?

I think they did splendidly. At over two hundred thousand words, and weighing in with one novella, ten novelettes, seventeen short stories, and one short-short, *Flights* is easily one of the largest anthologies of original short fantasy fiction ever published. I also pray it's one of the best. One measure of how easy my job was on this project is the amount of good material I had to turn away. It would have filled another volume.

PART THREE: *The Definition*

My first original anthology, *999,* presented horror and suspense stories. The second, *Redshift,* concerned speculative fiction stories, with an emphasis on science fiction. *Flights* is filled to the edges with new fantasy stories.

How did I define fantasy?

Well, luckily, I found someone who defined it for me. In an essay in a recent issue of *Locus,* Charles Brown's excellent and indispensable monthly magazine of the science fiction and fantasy field, Ed Bryant wrote:

> I tend to see the overall umbrella of virtually all fiction as fantasy. The tradition of attempting to grasp, grapple with, and interpret both the internal and the external universe through speculation goes back far beyond the written word, deep into the oral tradition. When speculation attempted to restrict itself to the rational, to the likelihood of what might be explained according to the rules as we knew them, then that's essentially science fiction. But go for explanations that are innately irrational, contradicting the way things work as we understand the rules—that's what most of us these days think of as fantasy.

Sorry, folks, I can't do better than that, since it pretty much defines what you'll find between these two covers. And the umbrella here is a wide one. You'll find plenty of princes and princesses, retold fairy tales, fables—but also strange stories that would have been right at home on *The Twilight Zone,* and a few stories unlike anything you've ever read, including a children's book written (definitely) for adults.

PART FOUR: *Back to the Feast*

So is *Flights* one of the best original fantasy anthologies ever published? That's for you to decide, of course. But, because of the wonderful writers involved, it surely is one heck of a good book of new stories.

A maid or manservant stands behind you, gently tying your bib around your neck.

The book sits before you.

Pick up your knife and fork, and turn the page.

Dig in.

Al Sarrantonio
July 2003

In a way, it's comforting to start out a huge anthology like this with a familiar title. But there's nothing familiar about **Robert Silverberg***'s tale itself, which is exactly why it's leading off. It's beautifully told, visually picturesque, apt, thoroughly enjoyable—all attributes of Silverberg's long and distinguished career.*

Not too long ago (and this is a sidebar) I plucked one of Bob's novels from the 1970s off my shelves, The Book of Skulls. *I remembered it fondly, but was afraid that if I reread it, it would have lost the magic it wove from those long-ago late New Wave days. I was wrong. It was just as fresh as the day I first read it.*

Silverberg's entire career has been like that: he's shown a restless and laser-sharp mind that transforms anything it focuses on into something special.

Like what follows, familiar title or no.

The Sorcerer's Apprentice

Robert Silverberg

Gannin Thidrich was nearing the age of thirty and had come to Triggoin to study the art of sorcery, a profession for which he thought he had some aptitude, after failing at several others for which he had none. He was a native of the Free City of Stee, that splendid metropolis on the slopes of Castle Mount, and at the suggestion of his father, a wealthy merchant of that great city, he had gone first into meat-jobbing, and then, through the good offices of an uncle from Dundilmir, he had become a dealer in used leather. In neither of these occupations had he distinguished himself, nor in the desultory projects he had undertaken afterward. But from childhood on, he had pursued sorcery in an amateur way, first as a boyish hobby, and then as a young man's consolation for shortcomings in most of the other aspects of his life—helping out friends even unluckier than he with an uplifting spell or two, conjuring at parties, earning a little by reading palms in the marketplace—and at last, eager to attain more arcane skills, he had taken himself to Triggoin, the capital city of sorcerers, hoping to apprentice himself to some master in that craft.

Triggoin came as a jolt, after Stee. That great city, spreading out magnificently along both banks of the river of the same name, was distinguished for its huge parks and game preserves, its palatial homes, its towering riverfront buildings of reflective gray-pink marble. But Triggoin, far up in the north beyond the grim Valmambra Desert, was a closed, claustrophobic place, dark and unwelcoming, where Gannin Thidrich found himself confronted with a bewildering tangle of winding medieval streets lined by ancient mustard-colored buildings with blank facades and gabled roofs. It was winter here. The trees were leafless and the air was cold. That was a new thing for him, winter: Stee was seasonless, favored all the year round by the eternal springtime of Castle Mount. The sharp-edged air was harsh with the odors of stale cooking oil and unfamiliar spices; the faces of the few people he encountered in the streets just within the gate were guarded and unfriendly.

He spent his first night there in a public dormitory for wayfarers, where in a smoky, dimly lit room he slept, very poorly, on a tick-infested straw mat among fifty other footsore travelers. In the morning, waiting in a long line for the chance to rinse his face in icy water, he passed the time by scanning the announcements on a bulletin board in the corridor and saw this:

APPRENTICE WANTED

Fifth-level adept offers instruction for serious student, plus lodging. Ten crowns per week for room and lessons. Some household work required, and assistance in professional tasks.

Apply to V. Halabant,
7 Gapeligo Boulevard,
West Triggoin.

That sounded promising. Gannin Thidrich gathered up his suitcases and hired a street-carter to take him to West Triggoin. The carter made a sour face when Gannin Thidrich gave him the address, but it was illegal to refuse a fare, and off they went. Soon Gannin Thidrich understood the sourness, for West Triggoin appeared to be very far from the center of the city; a suburb, in fact, perhaps even a slum, where the buildings were so old and dilapidated, they might well have dated from Lord Stiamot's time and a cold, dusty wind blew constantly down out of a row of low, jagged hills. Number 7 Gapeligo Boulevard proved to be a ramshackle lopsided structure, three asymmetrical floors behind a weather-beaten stone wall that showed sad signs of flaking and spalling. The ground floor housed what seemed to be a tavern, not open at this early hour; the floor above it greeted him with a padlocked door; Gannin Thidrich struggled upward with his luggage and at the topmost landing was met with folded arms and hostile glance by a tall, slender woman of about his own age, auburn haired, dusky skinned, with keen, unwavering eyes and thin, savage-looking lips. Evidently she had heard his bumpings and thumpings on the staircase and had come out to inspect the source of the commotion. He was struck at once, despite her chilly and even forbidding aspect, with the despairing realization that he found her immensely attractive.

"I'm looking for V. Halabant," Gannin Thidrich said, gasping a little for breath after his climb.

"I am V. Halabant."

That stunned him. Sorcery was not a trade commonly practiced by women, though evidently there were some who did go in for it. "The apprenticeship—?" he managed to say.

"Still available," she said. "Give me these." In the manner of a porter she swiftly separated his bags from his grasp, hefting them as though they were weightless, and led him inside.

Her chambers were dark, cheerless, cluttered, and untidy. The small room to the left of the entrance was jammed with the apparatus and paraphernalia of the professional sorcerer: astrolabes and ammatepilas, alembics and crucibles, hexaphores, ambivials, rohillas and verilistias, an armillary sphere, beakers and retorts, trays and metal boxes holding blue powders and pink ointments and strange seeds, a collection of flasks containing mysterious colored fluids, and much more that he was unable to identify. A second room adjacent to it held an overflowing bookcase, a couple of chairs, and a swaybacked couch. No doubt this room was for consultations. There were cobwebs on the window, and he saw dust beneath the couch and even a few sandroaches, those ubiquitous nasty scuttering insects that infested the parched Valmambra and all territories adjacent to it, were roaming about. Down the hallway lay a small dirty kitchen, a tiny room with a toilet and tub in it, storeroom piled high with more books and pamphlets, and beyond it the closed door of what he supposed—correctly, as it turned out—to be her own bedroom. What he did not see was any space for a lodger.

"I can offer one hour of formal instruction per day, every day of the week, plus access to my library for your independent studies, and two hours a week of discussion growing out of your own investigations," V. Halabant announced. "All of this in the morning; I will require you to be out of here for three hours every afternoon, because I have private pupils during that time. How you spend those hours is unimportant to me, except that I will need you to go to the marketplace for me two or three times a week, and you may as well do that then. You'll also do sweeping, washing, and other household chores, which, as you surely have seen, I have very little time to deal with. And you'll help me in my own work as required, assuming, of course, your skills are up to it. Is this agreeable to you?"

"Absolutely," said Gannin Thidrich. He was lost in admiration of her lustrous auburn hair, her finest feature, which fell in a sparkling cascade to her shoulders.

"The fee is payable four weeks in advance. If you leave after the first week, the rest is refundable, afterward not." He knew already that he was not going to leave. She held out her hand. "Sixty crowns, that will be."

"The notice I saw said it was ten crowns a week."

Her eyes were steely. "You must have seen an old notice. I raised my rates last year."

He would not quibble. As he gave her the money, he said, "And where am I going to be sleeping?"

She gestured indifferently toward a rolled-up mat in a corner of the room that contained all the apparatus. He realized that that was going to be his bed. "You decide that. The laboratory, the study, the hallway, even. Wherever you like."

His own choice would have been her bedroom, with her, but he was wise enough not to say that, even as a joke. He told her that he would sleep in the study, as she seemed to call the room with the couch and books. While he was unrolling the mat, she asked him what level of instruction in the arts he had attained, and he replied that he was a self-educated sorcerer, strictly a novice, but with some apparent gift for the craft. She appeared untroubled by that. Perhaps all that mattered to her was the rent; she would instruct anyone, even a novice, so long as he paid on time.

"Oh," he said as she turned away. "I am Gannin Thidrich. And your name is—?"

"Halabant," she said, disappearing down the hallway.

Her first name, he discovered from a diploma in the study, was Vinala, a lovely name to him, but if she wanted to be called Halabant, then Halabant was what he would call her. He would not take the risk of offending her in any way, not only because he very much craved the instruction that she could offer him, but also because of the troublesome and unwanted physical attraction that she held for him.

He could see right away that that attraction was in no way reciprocated. That disappointed him. One of the few areas of his life where he had generally met with success was in his dealings with women. But he knew that romance was inappropriate, anyway, between master and pupil, even if they were of differing sexes. Nor had he asked for it: it had simply smitten him at first glance, as had happened to him two or three times earlier in his life. Usually such smitings led only to messy difficulties, he had discovered. He wanted no such messes here. If these feelings of his for Halabant became a problem, he supposed, he could go into town and purchase whatever the opposite of a love-charm was called. If they sold love-charms here, and he had no doubt that they did, surely they would sell antidotes for love, as well. But he wanted to remain here, and so he would do whatever she asked of him, call her by whatever name she requested, and so forth, obeying her in all things. In this ugly, unfriendly city, she was the one spot of brightness and warmth for him, regardless of the complexities of the situation.

But his desire for her did not cause any problems, at first, aside from the effort he had to make in suppressing it, which was considerable but not insuperable.

On the first day he unpacked, spent the afternoon wandering around the unprepossessing streets of West Triggoin during the stipulated three hours for her other pupils, and, finding himself alone in the flat when he returned, he occupied himself by browsing through her extensive collection of texts on sorcery until dinnertime. Halabant had told him that he was free to use her little kitchen, and so he had purchased a few things at the corner market to cook for himself. Afterward, suddenly very weary, he lay down on his mat in the study and fell instantly asleep. He was vaguely aware, sometime later in the night, that she had come home and had gone down the hallway to her room.

In the morning, after they had eaten, she began his course of instruction in the mantic arts.

Briskly she interrogated him about the existing state of his knowledge. He explained what he could and could not do, a little surprised himself at how much he knew, and she did not seem displeased by it either. Still, after ten minutes or so, she interrupted him and set about an introductory discourse of the most elementary sort, beginning with a lecture on the three classes of demons, the untamable valisteroi, the frequently useful kalisteroi, and the dangerous and unpredictable irgalisteroi. Gannin Thidrich had long ago encompassed the knowledge of the invisible beings, or at least thought he had; but he listened intently, taking copious notes, exactly as though all this were new to him, and after a while he discovered that what he thought he knew was shallow indeed, that it touched only on the superficialities.

Each day's lesson was different. One day it dealt with amulets and talismans, another with mechanical conjuring devices, another with herbal remedies and the making of potions, another with interpreting the movements of the stars and how to cast spells. His mind was awhirl with new knowledge. Gannin Thidrich drank it all in greedily, memorizing dozens of spells a day. ("To establish a relationship with the demon Ginitiis: *Iimea abrasax iabe iarbatha chramne*" . . . "To invoke protection against aquatic creatures: *Loma zath aioin acthase balamaon*" . . . "Request for knowledge of the Red Lamp: *Imantou lantou anchomach*" . . .) After each hour-long lesson, he flung himself into avid exploration of her library, searching out additional aspects of what he had just been taught. He saw, ruefully, that while he had wasted his life in foolish and abortive business ventures, she had devoted her years, approximately the same number as his, to a profound and comprehensive study of the magical arts, and he admired the breadth and depth of her mastery.

On the other hand, Halabant did not have much in the way of a paying practice, skillful though she obviously was. During Gannin Thidrich's first week with her, she gave just two brief consultations: one to a shopkeeper who had been put under a geas by a commercial rival, one to an elderly man who lusted after a youthful niece and wished to be cured of his obsession. He assisted her in both instances, fetching equipment from the laboratory as requested. The fees she received in both cases, he noticed, were minimal: a mere handful of coppers. No wonder she lived in such dismal quarters and was reduced to taking in private pupils like himself and whoever it was who came to see her in the afternoons while he was away. It puzzled him that she remained here in Triggoin, where sorcerers swarmed everywhere by the hundreds or the thousands and competition had to be brutal, when she plainly would be much better off setting up in business for herself in one of the prosperous cities of the Mount, where a handsome young sorceress with skill in the art would quickly build a large clientele.

It was an exciting time for him. Gannin Thidrich felt his mind opening outward day by day, new knowledge flooding in, the mastery of the mysteries beginning to come within his grasp.

His days were so full that it did not bother him at all to pass his nights on a thin mat on the floor of a room crammed with ancient, acrid-smelling books. He needed only to close his eyes, and sleep would come up and seize him as though he had been drugged. The winter wind howled outside, and cold drafts broke through into his room, and sandroaches danced all around him, making sandroach music with their little scraping claws, but nothing broke his sleep until dawn's first blast of light came through the library's uncovered window. Halabant was always awake, washed and dressed, when he emerged from his room. It was as if she did not need sleep at all. In these early hours of the morning, she would hold her consultations with her clients in the study, if she had any that day, or else retire to her laboratory and putter about with her mechanisms and her potions. He would breakfast alone—Halabant never touched food before noon—and set about his household chores, the dusting and scrubbing and all the rest, and then would come his morning lesson and after that, until lunch, his time to prowl in the library. Often he and she took lunch at the same time, though she maintained silence throughout and ignored him when he stole the occasional quick glance at her across the table from him.

The afternoons were the worst part, when the private pupils came and he was forced to wander the streets. He begrudged them, whoever they were, the time they had with her, and he hated the grimy taverns and bleak gaming-halls where he spent these winter days when the weather was too grim to allow him simply to walk about. But then he would return to the flat, and if he found her there, which was not always the case, she would allow him an hour or so of free discourse about matters magical, not a lesson but simply a conversation, in which he brought up issues that fascinated or perplexed him and she helped him toward an understanding of them. These were wonderful hours, during which Gannin Thidrich was constantly conscious not just of her knowledge of the arts but also of Halabant's physical presence, her strange off-center beauty, the warmth of her body, the oddly pleasing fragrance of it. He kept himself in check, of course. But inwardly he imagined himself taking her in his arms, touching his lips to hers, running his fingertips down her lean, lithe back, drawing her down to his miserable thin mat on the library floor, and all the while some other part of his mind was concentrating on the technical arcana of sorcery that she was offering him.

In the evenings, she was usually out again—he had no idea where—and he studied until sleep overtook him, or, if his head was throbbing too fiercely with newly acquired knowledge, he would apply himself to the unending backlog of housekeeping tasks, gathering up what seemed like the dust of decades from under the furniture, beating the rugs, oiling the kitchen pots, tidying the books, scrubbing the stained porcelain of the sink, and on and on, all for her, for her, for love of her.

It was a wonderful time.

But then in the second week came the catastrophic moment when he awoke too early, went out into the hallway, and blundered upon her as she was heading into the bathroom for her morning bath. She was naked. He saw her from the rear, first, the long lean back and the narrow waist and the flat, almost boyish buttocks, and then, as a gasp of shock escaped his lips and she became aware that he was there, she turned and faced him squarely, staring at him as coolly and unconcernedly as though he were a cat, or a piece of furniture. He was overwhelmed by the sight of her breasts, so full and close-set that they almost seemed out of proportion on such a slender frame, and of her flaring sharp-boned hips, and of the startlingly fire-hued triangle between them, tapering down to the slim thighs. She remained that way just long enough for the imprint of her nakedness to burn its way fiercely into Gannin Thidrich's soul, setting loose a conflagration that he knew would be impossible for him to douse. Hastily he shut his eyes as though he had accidentally stared into the sun; and when he opened them again, a desperate moment later, she was gone and the bathroom door was closed.

The last time Gannin Thidrich had experienced such an impact, he had been fourteen. The circumstances had been somewhat similar. Now, dizzied and dazed as a tremendous swirl of adolescent emotion roared through his adult mind, he braced himself against the hallway wall and gulped for breath like a drowning man.

For two days, though neither of them referred to the incident at all, he remained in its grip. He could hardly believe that something as trivial as a momentary glimpse of a naked woman, at his age, could affect him so deeply. But of course there were other factors—the instantaneous attraction to her that had afflicted him at the moment of meeting her; and their proximity in this little flat, where her bedroom door was only twenty paces from his; and the whole potent master-pupil entanglement that had given her such a powerful role in his lonely life here in the city of the sorcerers. He began to wonder whether she had worked some sorcery on him herself as a sort of amusement, capriciously casting a little lust-spell over him so that she could watch him squirm, and then deliberately flaunting her nakedness at him that way. He doubted it, but, then, he knew very little about what she was really like, and perhaps—how could he say?—there was some component of malice in her character, something in her that drew pleasure from tormenting a poor fish like Gannin Thidrich, who had been cast upon her shore. He doubted it, but he had encountered such women before, and the possibility always was there.

He was making great progress in his studies. He had learned now how to summon minor demons, how to prepare tinctures that enhanced virility, how to employ the eyebrow of the sun, how to test for the purity of gold and silver by the laying on of hands, how to interpret weather omens, and much more. His head was swimming with his new knowledge. But also he remained dazzled by the curious sort of beauty that he saw in her, by the closeness in which they lived in the little flat, by the memory of that one luminous encounter in the dawn. And when in the fourth week it seemed to him that her usual coolness toward him was softening—she smiled at him once in a while now, she showed obvious delight at his growing skill in the art, she even asked him a thing or two about his life before coming to Triggoin—he finally mistook diminished indifference for actual warmth and, at the end of one morning's lesson, abruptly blurted out a confession of his love for her.

An ominous red glow appeared on her pale cheeks. Her dark eyes flashed tempestuously. "Don't ruin everything," she warned him. "It is all going very well as it is. I advise you to forget that you ever said such a thing to me."

"How can I? Thoughts of you possess me day and night!"

"Control them, then. I don't want to hear any more about them. And if you try to lay a finger on me, I'll turn you into a sandroach, believe me."

He doubted that she really meant that. But he abided by her warning for the next eight days, not wanting to jeopardize the continuation of his course of studies. Then, in the course of carrying out an assignment she had given him in the casting of auguries, Gannin Thidrich inscribed her name and his in the proper places in the spell, inquired as to the likelihood of a satisfactory consummation of desire, and received what he understood to be a positive prognostication. This inflamed him so intensely with joy that when Halabant came into the room a moment later, Gannin Thidrich impulsively seized her and pulled her close to him, pressed his cheek against hers, and frantically fondled her from shoulder to thigh.

She muttered six brief, harsh words of a spell unknown to him in his ear and bit his earlobe. In an instant he found himself scrabbling around amidst gigantic dust grains on the floor. Jagged glittering motes floated about him like planets in the void. His vision had become eerily precise down almost to the microscopic level, but all color had drained from the world. When he put his hand to his cheek in shock, he discovered it to be an insect's feathery claw, and the cheek itself was a hard thing of chitin. She had indeed transformed him into a sandroach.

Numb, he considered his situation. From this perspective, he could no longer see her—she was somewhere miles above him, in the upper reaches of the atmosphere—nor could he make out the geography of the room, the familiar chairs and the couch, or anything else except the terrifyingly amplified details of the immensely small. Perhaps in another moment her foot would come down on him, and that would be that for Gannin Thidrich. Yet he did not truly believe that he had become a sandroach. He had mastered enough sorcery by this time to understand that that was technically impossible, that one could not pack all the neurons and synapses, the total intelligence of a human mind, into the tiny compass of an insect's head. And all those things were here with him inside the sandroach, his entire human personality, the hopes and fears and memories and fantasies of Gannin Thidrich of the Free City of Stee, who had come to Triggoin to study sorcery and was a pupil of the woman V. Halabant. So this was all an illusion. He was not really a sandroach; she had merely made him *believe* that he was. He was certain of that. That certainty was all that preserved his sanity in those first appalling moments.

Still, on an operational level, there was no effective difference between thinking you were a six-legged chitin-covered creature one finger-joint in length and actually *being* such a creature. Either way, it was a horrifying condition. Gannin Thidrich could not speak out to protest against her treatment of him. He could not restore himself to human shape and height. He could not do anything at all except the things that sandroaches did. The best he could manage was to scutter in his new six-legged fashion to the safety to be found underneath the couch, where he discovered other sandroaches already in residence. He glared at them balefully, warning them to keep their distance, but their only response was an incomprehensible twitching of their feelers. Whether that was a gesture of sympathy or one of animosity, he could not tell.

The least she could have done for me, he thought, was to provide me with some way of communicating with the others of my kind, if this is to be my kind from now on.

He had never known such terror and misery. But the transformation was only temporary. Two hours later—it seemed like decades to him, sandroach time, all of it spent hiding under the couch and contemplating how he was going to pursue the purposes of his life as an insect—Gannin Thidrich was swept by a nauseating burst of dizziness and a sense that he was exploding from the thorax outward, and then he found himself restored to his previous form, lying in a clumsy sprawl in the middle of the floor. Halabant was nowhere to be seen. Cautiously he rose and moved about the room, reawakening in himself the technique of two-legged locomotion, holding his outspread fingers up before his eyes for the delight of seeing fingers again, prodding his cheeks and arms and abdomen to confirm that he was once again a creature of flesh. He was. He felt chastened and immensely relieved, even grateful to her for having relented.

They did not discuss the episode the next day, and all reverted to as it had been between them, distant, formal, a relationship of pure pedagogy and nothing more. He remained wary of her. When, now and then, his hand would brush against hers in the course of handling some piece of apparatus, he would pull it back as if he had touched a glowing coal.

Spring now began to arrive in Triggoin. The air was softer; the trees grew green. Gannin Thidrich's desire for his instructor did not subside, in truth it grew more maddeningly acute with the warming of the season, but he permitted himself no expression of it. There were further occasions when he accidentally encountered her going to and fro, naked, in the hall in earliest morning. His response each time was instantly to close his eyes and turn away, but her image lingered on his retinas and burrowed down into his brain. He could not help thinking that there was something intentional about these provocative episodes, something flirtatious, even. But he was too frightened of her to act on that supposition.

A new form of obsession now came over him, that the visitors she received every afternoon while he was away were not private pupils at all, but a lover, rather, or perhaps several lovers. Since she took care not to have her afternoon visitors arrive until he was gone, he had no way of knowing whether this was so, and it plagued him terribly to think that others, in his absence, were caressing her lovely body and enjoying her passionate kisses while he was denied everything on pain of being turned into a sandroach again.

But of course he *did* have a way of knowing what took place during those afternoons of hers. He had progressed far enough in his studies to have acquired some skill with the device known as the Far-Seeing Bowl, which allows an adept to spy from a distance. Over the span of three days, he removed from Halabant's flat one of her bowls, a supply of the pink fluid that it required, and a pinch of the grayish activating powder. Also he helped himself to a small undergarment of Halabant's—its fragrance was a torment to him—from the laundry basket. These things he stored in a locker he rented in the nearby marketplace. On the fourth day, after giving himself a refresher course in the five-word spell that operated the bowl, he collected his apparatus from the locker, repaired to a tavern where he knew no one would intrude on him, set the bowl atop the garment, filled it with the pink fluid, sprinkled it with the activating powder, and uttered the five words.

It occurred to him that he might see scenes now that would shatter him forever. No matter: he had to know.

The surface of the fluid in the bowl rippled, stirred, cleared. The image of V. Halabant appeared. Gannin Thidrich caught his breath. A visitor was indeed with her: a young man, a boy, even, no more than twelve or fifteen years old. They sat chastely apart in the study. Together they pored over one of Halabant's books of sorcery. It was an utterly innocent hour. The second student came soon after: a short, squat fellow wearing coarse clothing of a provincial cut. For half an hour Halabant delivered what was probably a lecture—the bowl did not provide Gannin Thidrich with sound—while the pupil, constantly biting his lip, scribbled notes as quickly as he could. Then he left, and after a time was replaced by a sad, dreamy-looking fellow with long shaggy hair, who had brought some sort of essay or thesis for Halabant to examine. She leafed quickly through it, frequently offering what no doubt were pungent comments.

No lovers, then. Legitimate pupils, all three. Gannin Thidrich felt bitterly ashamed of having spied on her, and aghast at the possibility that she might have perceived, by means of some household surveillance spell of whose existence he knew nothing, that he had done so. But she betrayed no sign of that when he returned to the flat.

A week later, desperate once again, he purchased a love-potion in the sorcerers' marketplace—not a spell to free himself from desire, though he knew that was what he should be getting, but one that would deliver her into his arms. Halabant had sent him to the marketplace with a long list of professional supplies to buy for her—such things as elecamp, golden rue, quicksilver, brimstone, goblin-sugar, mastic, and thekka ammoniaca. The last item on the list was maltabar, and the same dealer, he knew, offered potions for the lovelorn. Rashly Gannin Thidrich purchased one. He hid it among his bundles and tried to smuggle it into the flat, but Halabant, under the pretext of offering to help him unpack, went straight to the sack that contained it and pulled it forth. "This was nothing that I requested," she said.

"True," he said, chagrined.

"Is it what I think it is?"

Hanging his head, he admitted that it was. She tossed it angrily aside. "I'll be merciful and let myself believe that you bought this to use on someone else. But if I was the one you had in mind for it—"

"No. Never."

"Liar. Idiot."

"What can I do, Halabant? Love strikes like a thunderbolt."

"I don't remember advertising for a lover. Only for an apprentice, an assistant, a tenant."

"It's not my fault that I feel this way about you."

"Nor mine," said Halabant. "Put all such thoughts out of your mind, if you want to continue here." Then, softening, obviously moved by the dumbly adoring way in which he was staring at her, she smiled and pulled him toward her and brushed his cheek lightly with her lips. "Idiot," she said again. "Poor hopeless fool." But it seemed to him that she said it with affection.

Matters stayed strictly business between them. He hung upon every word of her lessons as though his continued survival depended on committing every syllable of her teachings to memory, filled notebook after notebook with details of spells, talismans, conjurations, and illusions, and spent endless hours rummaging through her books for amplifying detail, sometimes staying up far into the night to pursue some course of study that an incidental word or two from her had touched off. He was becoming so adept, now, that he was able to be of great service to her with her outside clientele, the perfect assistant, always knowing which devices or potions to bring her for the circumstances at hand; and he noticed that clients were coming to her more frequently now, too. He hoped that Halabant gave him at least a little credit for that.

He was still aflame with yearning for her, of course—there was no reason for that to go away—but he tried to burn it off with heroic outpourings of energy in his role as her housekeeper. Before coming to Triggoin, Gannin Thidrich had bothered himself no more about household work than any normal bachelor did, doing simply enough to fend off utter squalor and not going beyond that, but he cared for her little flat as he had never cared for any dwelling of his own, polishing and dusting and sweeping and scrubbing, until the place took on an astonishing glow of charm and comfort. Even the sandroaches were intimidated by his work and fled to some other apartment. It was his goal to exhaust himself so thoroughly between the intensity of his studies and the intensity of his housework that he would have no shred of vitality left over for further lustful fantasies. This did not prove to be so. Often, curling up on his mat at night after a day of virtually unending toil, he would be assailed by dazzling visions of V. Halabant, entering his weary mind like an intruding succubus, capering wantonly in his throbbing brain, gesturing lewdly to him, beckoning, offering herself, and Gannin Thidrich would lie there sobbing, soaked in sweat, praying to every demon whose invocations he knew that he be spared such agonizing visitations.

The pain became so great that he thought of seeking another teacher. He thought occasionally of suicide, too, for he knew that this was the great love of his life, doomed never to be fulfilled, and that if he went away from Halabant, he was destined to roam forever celibate through the vastness of the world, finding all other women unsatisfactory after her. Some segment of his mind recognized this to be puerile romantic nonsense, but he was not able to make that the dominant segment, and he began to fear that he might actually be capable of taking his own life in some feverish attack of nonsensical frustration.

The worst of it was that she had become intermittently quite friendly toward him by this time, giving him, intentionally or otherwise, encouragement that he had become too timid to accept as genuine. Perhaps his pathetic gesture of buying that love-potion had touched something in her spirit. She smiled at him frequently now, even winked, or poked him playfully in the shoulder with a finger to underscore some point in her lesson. She was shockingly casual, sometimes, about how she dressed, often choosing revealingly flimsy gowns that drove him into paroxysms of throttled desire. And yet at other times she was as cold and aloof as she had been at the beginning, criticizing him cruelly when he bungled a spell or spilled an alembic, skewering him with icy glances when he said something that struck her as foolish, reminding him over and over that he was still just a blundering novice who had years to go before he attained anything like the threshold of mastery.

So there always were limits. He was her prisoner. She could touch him whenever she chose, but he feared becoming a sandroach again should he touch her, even accidentally. She could smile and wink at him, but he dared not do the same. In no way did she grant him any substantial status. When he asked her to instruct him in the great spell known as the Sublime Arcanum, which held the key to many gates, her reply was simply, "That is not something for fools to play with."

There was one truly miraculous day when, after he had recited an intricate series of spells with complete accuracy and had brought off one of the most difficult effects she had ever asked him to attempt, she seized him in a sudden joyful congratulatory embrace and levitated them both to the rafters of the study. There they hovered, face-to-face, bosom against bosom, her eyes flashing jubilantly before him. "That was wonderful!" she cried. "How marvelously you did that! How proud I am of you!"

This is it, he thought, the delirious moment of surrender at last, and slipped his hand between their bodies to clasp her firm round breast, and pressed his lips against hers and drove his tongue deep into her mouth. Instantly she voided the spell of levitation and sent him crashing miserably to the floor, where he landed in a crumpled heap with his left leg folded up beneath him in a way that sent the fiercest pain through his entire body.

She floated gently down beside him.

"You will always be an idiot," she said, and spat, and strode out of the room.

Gannin Thidrich was determined now to put an end to his life. He understood completely that to do such a thing would be a preposterous overreaction to his situation, but he was determined not to allow mere rationality to have a voice in the decision. His existence had become unbearable, and he saw no other way of winning his freedom from this impossible woman.

He brooded for days about how to go about it, whether to swallow some potion from her storeroom or to split himself open with one of the kitchen knives or simply to fling himself from the study window, but all of these seemed disagreeable to him on the aesthetic level and fraught with drawbacks besides. Mainly what troubled him was the possibility that he might not fully succeed in his aim with any of them, which seemed even worse than succeeding would be.

In the end he decided to cast himself into the dark, turbulent river that ran past the edge of West Triggoin on its northern flank. He had often explored it, now that winter was over, in the course of his afternoon walks. It was wide and probably fairly deep, its flow during this period of springtime spate was rapid, and an examination of a map revealed that it would carry his body northward and westward into the grim uninhabited lands that sloped toward the distant sea. Since he was unable to swim—one did not swim in the gigantic River Stee of his native city, whose swift current swept everything and everyone willy-nilly downstream along the mighty slopes of Castle Mount—Gannin Thidrich supposed that he would sink quickly and could expect a relatively painless death.

Just to be certain, he borrowed a rope from Halabant's storeroom to tie around his legs before he threw himself in. Slinging it over his shoulder, he set out along the footpath that bordered the river's course, searching for a likely place from which to jump. The day was warm, the air sweet, the new leaves yellowish green on every tree, springtime at its finest—what better season for saying farewell to the world?

He came to an overlook where no one else seemed to be around, knotted the rope about his ankles and, without a moment's pause for regret, sentimental thoughts, or final statements of any sort, hurled himself down headlong into the water.

It was colder than he expected it to be, even on this mild day. His plummeting body cut sharply below the surface, so that his mouth and nostrils filled with water and he felt himself in the imminent presence of death, but then the natural buoyancy of the body asserted itself, and despite his wishes, Gannin Thidrich turned upward again, breaching the surface, emerging into the air, spluttering and gagging. An instant later he heard a splashing sound close beside him and realized that someone else had jumped in, a would-be rescuer, perhaps.

"Lunatic! Moron! What do you think you're doing?"

He knew that voice, of course. Apparently V. Halabant had followed him as he made his doleful way along the riverbank and was determined not to let him die. That realization filled him with a confused mixture of ecstasy and fury.

She was bobbing beside him. She caught him by the shoulder, spun him around to face her. There was a kind of madness in her eyes, Gannin Thidrich thought. The woman leaned close and in a tone of voice that stung like vitriol, she said, *"Iaho ariaha . . . aho ariaha . . . bakaksikhekh! Ianian! Thatlat! Hish!"*

Gannin Thidrich felt a sense of sudden forward movement and became aware that he was swimming, actually swimming, moving downstream with powerful strokes of his entire body. Of course that was impossible. Not only were his legs tied together, but he had no idea of how to swim. And yet he was definitely in motion: he could see the riverbank changing from moment to moment, the trees lining the footpath traveling upstream as he went the other way.

There was a river otter swimming beside him, a smooth sleek beautiful creature, graceful and sinuous and strong. It took Gannin Thidrich another moment to realize that the animal was V. Halabant, and that in fact he was an otter also, that she had worked a spell on them both when she had jumped in beside them, and had turned them into a pair of magnificent aquatic beasts. His legs were gone—he had only flippers down there now, culminating in small webbed feet—and gone, too, was the rope with which he had hobbled himself. And he could swim. He could swim like an otter.

Ask no questions, Gannin Thidrich told himself. Swim! Swim!

Side by side they swam for what must have been miles, spurting along splendidly on the breast of the current. He had never known such joy. As a human, he would have drowned long ago, but as an otter he was a superb swimmer, tireless, wondrously strong. And with Halabant next to him, he was willing to swim forever: to the sea itself, even. Head down, nose foremost, narrow body fully extended, he drilled his way through the water like some animate projectile. And the otter who had been V. Halabant kept pace with him as he moved along.

Time passed and he lost all sense of who or what he was, or where, or what he was doing. He even ceased to perceive the presence of his companion. His universe was only motion, constant forward motion. He was truly a river otter now, nothing but a river otter, joyously hurling himself through the cosmos.

But then his otter senses detected a sound to his left that no otter would be concerned with, and whatever was still human in him registered the fact that it was a cry of panic, a sharp little gasp of fear, coming from a member of his former species. He pivoted to look and saw that V. Halabant had reverted to human form and was thrashing about in what seemed to be the last stages of exhaustion. Her arms beat the air, her head tossed wildly, her eyes were rolled back in her head. She was trying to make her way to the riverbank, but she did not appear to have the strength to do it.

Gannin Thidrich understood that in his jubilant onward progress, he had led her too far down the river, pulling her along beyond her endurance, that as an otter he was far stronger than she and by following him she had exceeded her otter abilities and could go no farther. Perhaps she was in danger of drowning, even. Could an otter drown? But she was no longer an otter. He knew that he had to get her ashore. He swam to her side and pushed futilely against her with his river otter nose, trying in vain to clasp her with the tiny otter flippers that had replaced his arms. Her eyes fluttered open and she stared into his and smiled, and spoke two words, the counterspell, and Gannin Thidrich discovered that he, too, was in human form again. They were both naked. He found that they were close enough now to the shore that his feet were able to touch the bottom. Slipping his arm around her, just below her breasts, he tugged her along, steadily, easily, toward the nearby riverbank. He scrambled ashore, pulling her with him, and they dropped down gasping for breath at the river's edge under the warm spring sunshine.

They were far out of town, he realized, all alone in the empty but not desolate countryside. The bank was soft with mosses. Gannin Thidrich recovered his breath almost at once; Halabant took longer, but before long she, too, was breathing normally. Her face was flushed and mottled with signs of strain, though, and she was biting down on her lip as though trying to hold something back, something that Gannin Thidrich understood, a moment later, to be tears. Abruptly she was furiously sobbing. He held her, tried to comfort her, but she shook him off. She would not or could not look at him.

"To be so weak—" she muttered. "I was going under. I almost drowned. And to have you see it—you—*you*—"

So she was angry with herself for having shown herself, at least in this, to be inferior to him. That was ridiculous, he thought. She might be a master sorcerer and he only a novice, yes, but he was a man, nevertheless, and she a woman, and men tended to be physically stronger than women, on the average, and probably that was true among otters, too. If she had displayed weakness during their wild swim, it was a forgivable weakness, which only exacerbated his love for her. He murmured words of comfort to her and was so bold to put his arm about her shoulders, and then, suddenly, astonishingly, everything changed—she pressed her bare body against him, she clung to him, she sought his lips with a hunger that was almost frightening, she opened her legs to him, she opened everything to him, she drew him down into her body and her soul.

Afterward, when it seemed appropriate to return to the city, it was necessary to call on her resources of sorcery once more. They both were naked, and many miles downstream from where they needed to be. She seemed not to want to risk returning to the otter form again, but there were other spells of transportation at her command, and she used one that brought them instantly back to West Triggoin, where their clothing and even the rope with which Gannin Thidrich had bound himself were lying in damp heaps near the place where he had thrown himself into the river. They dressed in silence and in silence they made their way, walking several feet apart, back to her flat.

He had no idea what would happen now. Already she appeared to be retreating behind that wall of untouchability that had surrounded her since the beginning. What had taken place between them on the riverbank was irreversible, but it would not transform their strange relationship unless she permitted it to do so, Gannin Thidrich knew, and he wondered whether she would. He did not intend to make any new aggressive moves without some sort of guidance from her.

And indeed it appeared that she intended to pretend that nothing had occurred at all, neither his absurd suicide attempt nor her foiling of it by following him to the river and turning them into otters nor the frenzied, frenetic, almost insane coupling that had been the unexpected climax of their long swim. All was back to normal between them as soon as they were at the flat: she was the master, he was the drudge, they slept in their separate rooms, and when during the following day's lessons he bungled a spell, as even now he still sometimes did, she berated him in the usual cruel, cutting way that was the verbal equivalent of transforming him once again into a sandroach. What, then, was he left with? The taste of her on his lips, the sound of her passionate outcries in his ears, the feel of the firm ripe swells of her breasts against the palms of his hands?

On occasions over the next few days, though, he caught sight of her studying him surreptitiously out of the corner of her eye, and he was the recipient of a few not-so-surreptitious smiles that struck him as having genuine warmth in them, and when he ventured a smile of his own in her direction, it was met with another smile instead of a scowl. But he hesitated to try any sort of follow-up maneuver. Matters still struck him as too precariously balanced between them.

Then, a week later, during their morning lesson, she said briskly, "Take down these words: *Psakerba enphnoun orgogorgoniotrian phorbai.* Do you recognize them?"

"No," said Gannin Thidrich, baffled.

"They are the opening incantation of the spell known as the Sublime Arcanum," said Halabant.

A thrill rocketed down his spine. The Sublime Arcanum at last! So she had decided to trust him with the master spell, finally, the great opener of so many gates! She no longer thought of him as a fool who could not be permitted knowledge of it.

It was a good sign, he thought. Something was changing.

Perhaps she was still trying to pretend even now that none of it had ever happened, the event by the riverbank. But it had, it had, and it was having its effect on her, however hard she might be battling against it, and he knew now that he would go on searching, forever if necessary, for the key that would unlock her a second time.

I love this story.

And can I tell you why, exactly?

No.

A lot of **Kit Reed**'*s work is like that—there's some mojo subtext working on you while you're reading the tale that you're really not aware of: clockwork just out of your peripheral vision, strange tugs and whispers that you don't understand even as you read the words so cleanly laid out on the page.*

Her stuff is special, has always been special, and will always be special.

Kit was having trouble coming up with something for this book early on. If I remember what she told me correctly, she was on a train either coming from or going to New York City, when something began to click (or clack?).

Lucky us.

Perpetua

Kit Reed

We are happy to be traveling together in the alligator. To survive the crisis in the city outside, we have had ourselves made *very small.*

To make our trip more pleasant, the alligator herself has been equipped with many windows, cleverly fitted between the armor plates so we can look out at the disaster as we ride along. The lounge where we are riding is paneled in mahogany and fitted with soft leather sofas and beautifully sculpted leather chairs where we recline until seven, when the chef Father engaged calls us to a sit-down dinner in the galley lodged at the base of our alligator's skull. Our vehicle is such a technical masterpiece that our saurian hostess zooms along unhampered, apparently at home in the increasingly treacherous terrain. If she knows we're in here, and if she guesses that tonight we will be dining on Boeuf Wellington and asparagus terrine with Scotch salmon and capers while she has to forage, she rushes along as though she doesn't care. We hear occasional growls and sounds of rending and gnashing over the Vivaldi track Father has chosen as background for this first phase of our journey; she seems to be finding plenty to eat outside.

Inside, everything is arranged for our comfort and happiness, perhaps because Father knows we have reservations about being here. My sisters and I can count on individualized snack trays, drugs of choice and our favorite drinks, which vary from day to day. Over our uniform jumpsuits, we wear monogrammed warm-up jackets in our favorite colors—a genteel lavender for Lily, which Ella apes because she's too young to have her own ideas; jade for Stephanie and, it figures, my aggressively girlish sister Anna is in Passive Pink; Father doesn't like it, but I have chosen black.

"Molly, that color doesn't become you."

"Nobody's going to see me, what difference does it make?"

"I like my girls to look nice."

I resent this because we all struggled to escape the family and made it, too. We'd still be out there if it wasn't for this. "Your girls, your girls—we haven't been your girls in years."

Father: "You will always be my girls." That smile.

OK, I am the family gadfly. "This crisis. Is there something funny going on that we don't know about?"

"Molly," he thunders. "Look out the windows. Then tell me if you think there's anything funny about this."

"I mean, is this a trick to get us back?"

"If you think I made this up, send a goddamn e-mail. Search the Web or turn on the goddamn TV!"

The chairs are fitted with wireless connections so we can download music and e-mail our loved ones, although we never hear back, and at our fingertips are multimedia remotes. We want for nothing here in the alligator. Nothing material, that is. I check my sources, and Father is right. It is a charnel house out there while in here with Father, we are pampered and well fed and snug.

It is a velvet prison, but look at the alternative! Exposure to thunderstorms and fires in collision, vulnerability to mudslides and flooding of undetermined origin; our alligator slithers through rivers of bloody swash, and our vision is obscured by the occasional collision with a severed limb. We can't comprehend the nature or the scope of the catastrophe, only that it's all around us, while here inside the alligator, we are safe.

Her name is Perpetua. Weird, right? Me knowing? But I do.

So we are safe inside Perpetua, and I guess we have Father to thank. Where others ignored the cosmic warnings, he took them to heart. Got ready. Spared no expense. I suppose we should be glad.

If it weren't for the absence of certain key loved ones from our table and from our sumptuous beds in the staterooms aft of the spiny ridge, we probably would.

It's Father's fault. Like a king summoning his subjects, he brought us back from the corners of the earth, where we strayed after we grew up and escaped the house. He brought us in from West Hollywood (Stephanie) and Machu Picchu (Lily) and (fluffy Anna) Biarritz and Farmington, for our baby sister Ella attends the exclusive Miss Porter's School. And Father reached me . . . where? When Father wants you, it doesn't matter how far you run, you will come back.

Emergency, the message said, *Don't ask. Just come,* and being loyal daughters, we did. With enormous gravity, he sat us down in the penthouse.

"My wandering daughters." He beamed. Then he explained. He even had charts. The catastrophe would start here, he said, pointing to the heart of the city. Then it would blossom, expanding until it blanketed the nation and finally, the world. Faced with destruction, would you dare take your chances outside? Would we?

He was not asking. "You will come."

"Of course, Father," we said, although even then I was not sure.

Anna the brownnose gilded the lily with that bright giggle. "Anything you say, Father. Anything to survive."

Mother frowned. "What makes you think you'll survive?"

"Erna!"

"What if this is the Last Judgment?" she had Father's Gutenberg Bible in her lap.

He shouted: "Put that thing down!"

She looked down at the book and then up at him. "What makes you think anybody will survive?"

"That's enough!"

"More than enough, Richard." She raked him with a smile. "I think I'll take my chances here."

He and Mother have never been close. He shrugged. "As you wish. But, you girls . . ."

Anna said, "Daddy, can we bring our jewelry?"

Stephanie laid her fingertip in the hollow of Father's throat. "I'm fresh out of outfits—can I go to Prada and pick up a few things?"

I said, "It's not like we'll be going out to clubs."

"Daddy?"

"Molly, watch your tone." Stephanie is Father's favorite. He told her, "Anything you want, sweet, but be back by four."

Little Ella asked if she could bring all her pets—a litter of kittens and a basset hound. The cat is the natural enemy of the alligator, Father explained; even in miniature—and we were about to be miniaturized—the cats would be an incipient danger, but the dog's all right. Ella burst into tears.

"Can I bring my boyfriend?" Lily said.

Our baby sister punched her in the breast so hard, she yelled. "Not if I can't take Mittens."

"Boyfriends?" We girls chorused, "Of course."

Father shook his head.

You see, because we are traveling in elegant but close quarters, there's no room for anybody else. This meant no boyfriends, which strikes me as thoughtless if not a little small. When we protested, Father reminded us of our choices: death in the disaster or life in luxury with concomitant re-knotting of family ties. He slammed his fist on the hunt table his decorator brought from Colonial Williamsburg at great expense. "Cheap at the price."

I was thinking of my boyfriend, whom I had left sleeping in Rangoon. Never guessing I was leaving forever, I stroked his cheek and slipped out. "But Derek!"

"Don't give it another thought."

"Daddy, what's going to happen to Derek?"

"He'll keep."

Stephanie, Anna and Lily said, "What's going to happen to Jimmy/David/Phil!"

"Oh, they'll keep," he said. Perceiving that he had given the wrong answer, he added, "Trust me. It's being taken care of."

"But, Daddy!"

Perceiving that he still hadn't said enough, he explained that although we were being miniaturized, his technicians would see to it that all our parts would match when we and our boyfriends were reunited, although he did not make clear whether we would be restored to normal size or the men we loved would be made extremely small. He said whatever it took to make us do what he wanted, patting us each with that fond, abstracted smile.

"I've got my best people on it. Don't worry. They'll be fine."

Anna did her loving princess act. "Promise?"

Now Father became impatient. "Girls, I am sparing no expense on this. Don't you think I have covered every little thing?"

None of us dares ask him what this all cost. Unlike most people in the city outside, we are, after all, still alive, but the money! How much will be left for us when Father dies?

Of course in normal times, the brass fixtures, the ceiling treatment and luxurious carpeting that line our temporary home would be expensive, but the cost of miniaturizing all these priceless objects and embedding them in our alligator? Who can guess!

One of us began to cry.

"Stop that," Father roared. "Enough is enough."

It probably is enough for him, riding along in luxury with his five daughters, but what about Stephanie and Anna and Lily and Ella and me?

The first few days, I will admit, passed pleasantly as we settled into our quarters and slipped into our routines. Sleep as late as we like and if we miss breakfast Chef leaves it outside our doors in special trays that keep the croissants moist, the juice cold and the coffee hot. There's even a flower on the tray. Late mornings in the dayroom, working puzzles or reading or doing needlework, a skill Father insisted we learn when we were small. Looking at what he's made of us, I have to wonder: five daughters at his beck and call, making a fuss over him and doing calligraphy that would have pleased blind old Milton; we all nap after lunch. We spend our afternoons in the music room followed by cocktails in the lounge and in the evening we say grace over a delicious meal at the long table, with Father like the Almighty at the head. Is this what he had in mind for us from the first?

I have never seen him happier.

This poses a terrible problem. Is the catastrophe outside a real unknitting of society and the city as we know it and, perhaps, the universe, or is it something Father manufactured to keep us in his thrall?

My sisters may be happy, but I am uncertain. I'm bored and dubious. I'm bored and suspicious and lonely as hell.

The others are in the music room with Father at the piano, preparing a Donizetti quartet. I looked in and saw them together in the warm light; with his white hair sparkling in the halogen glow of the piano lamp, he looked exalted. As if there were a halo around his head. Now, I love Father, but I was never his favorite. There's no part in the Donizetti piece for me. Why should I go in there and play along? Instead I have retreated to the lounge, where I strain at the window in hope. For hours I look out, staring in a passion of concentration because Derek is out there somewhere, whereas I . . . If I keep at this, I think, if I press my face to the glass and stare intently, if I can *just keep my mind on what I want,* then maybe I can become part of the glass or pass through it and find Derek.

With my head pressed against the fabric of our rushing host, I whisper: "Oh, please."

Outside it is quite simply desolate. Mud and worse things splash on my window as the giant beast that hosts us lunges over something huge, snaps at some adversary in her path, worries the corpse and takes a few bites before she rushes on. God, I wish she'd slow down. I wish she would stop! I want her to lurch onto a peak and let me out!

Can't. On autopilot.

Odd. The glass is buzzing. Vibration or what? I brush my face, checking for bees. If I knew how, I'd run to the galley at the base of her skull and thump on the brushed steel walls until she got my message. Crucial question: Do alligators know Morse code?

No need.

"What?"

My God. She and I are in communication.

"Lady!"

The windowpane grows warm, as though I have made her blush. *It's Perpetua.*

"I know!"

I thought you did.

"Oh, lady, can you tell me what's going on?"

Either more or less than you think.

In a flash I understand the following: We are not, as I suspected—hoped!—being duped. Father has his girls back, all right—he has us at his fingertips in a tight space where he has complete control—but this is his response to the warnings, not something he made up. Although my best-case scenario would confirm my suspicions and make it easy to escape, we are not captive inside a submarine in perfectly normal New York City, witlessly doing his bidding while our vehicle sloshes around in a total immersion tank.

There really is a real disaster out there.

Soon enough, tidal waves will come crashing in our direction, to be followed by meteorite showers, with volcanic eruptions pending and worse to come. As for Father's contrivances, I am correct about one thing: the cablevision we watch and the Web we surf aren't coming in from the world outside; they are the product of the database deep in the server located behind our alligator's left eye.

"But what about Derek?"

I don't know.

"Can you find out?"

You have to promise to do what I want.

I whisper into the window set into her flank: "What do you want?"

Promise?

"Of course I promise!"

Then all that matters is your promise. It doesn't matter what I want.

"I need to know what's happening! Maybe Mother is right—maybe it really is the hand of God. Wouldn't you get sick of people like us and want to clean house?"

Not clear.

"Whether God is sick of us?"

Any of it. The only clear thing is what we have to do.

"What? What!"

She lets me know that although I left him in Rangoon, Derek is adrift somewhere in New York. Don't ask me whether he flew or came by boat or what I'm going to do. Just ask me what I think, and then ask me how I know.

You have to help me.

"You have to stop and let me out!"

I know what's out there because, my God, Perpetua is showing me. Images spill into my head and cloud my eyes: explosions mushrooming, tornadoes, volcanic geysers, what? In seconds I understand how bad it is, although Perpetua can't tell me whether we are in the grip of terrorists or space aliens or a concatenation of natural disasters or what; she shows me Derek standing in the ruins of our old building with his hand raised as if to knock on the skeletal door, I see looters and carnivores and all the predictable detritus of a disaster right down to the truck with the CNN remote, and I see that they won't be standing there much longer because the roiling clouds are opening for a fresh hailstorm unless it's a firestorm or a tremendous belching of volcanic ash.

You won't last a minute out there, not the way you are.

She's right. To survive the crisis in the city outside, we have had ourselves made very small.

You got it. You don't stand a chance.

"Oh God," I cry.

Not God, not by a long shot.

"Oh, lady!" I hear Father and the others chattering as they come in from the music room. I whisper into the glass. My mouth leaves a wet lip print frosted by my own breath. "What am I going to do?"

Our saurian hostess exits my consciousness so quickly that I have to wonder whether she was ever there. My only proof? I have her last words imprinted; *Find out how.*

Chef brings our afternoon snack trays, and my sisters and I graze, browsing contentedly, like farm animals. Father nods, and he and Chef exchange looks before Chef bows and backs out of the room.

It comes to me like a gift.

Passionately, I press my lips to the glass. "It's in the food."

Find the antidote. Take it when you get out.

"Are you? Are you, Perpetua?" I am wild with it. "Are you really going to stop and let me out?"

She doesn't answer. The whole vehicle that encloses our family begins to thrash. I hear magnified snarling and terrible rending noises as she snaps some enemy's spine and over Vivaldi I hear her giant teeth clash as she worries it to death.

We bide our time then, Perpetua and I, at least I do. What choice do I have?

But while I am waiting, her history is delivered to me whole. It is not so much discovered as remembered, as though it happened to me. Sleeping or waking, I can't say when or how she reaches me; her story seeps into my mind, and as it unfolds I understand why she and I are bonded. Rather, why she chose me. Rushing along through the night while Father plots and my sisters sleep, our alligator somehow drops me into the tremendous ferny landscape of some remote, prehistoric dawn, where I watch, astonished, as her early life unfolds under a virgin sun that turns the morning sky pink. Although I am not clear whether it is her past or a universal past that Perpetua is drawing, at some level I understand. She shows me the serpentine tangle of clashing reptiles and the emergence of a king, and she takes me beyond that to deliver me at the inevitable: that all fathers of daughters are kings. I see Perpetua's gigantic, armored father with his flaming jaws and his great teeth, and I join his delicate, scaly daughters as they slither here and there in the universe, apparently free but always under his power.

So you see.

I have the context, if not the necessity.

Then over the next few days while we float along in our comfortable dream world, she encourages me to explore.

While the others nap, I feel my way along the flexible vinyl corridors that snake through Perpetua's sinuous body, connecting the chambers where we sleep and the rooms where we eat and the ones where we entertain ourselves. The tubing is transparent, and I see Perpetua's vitals pulsing wherever I flash my light. Finally I make my way to the galley—quietly, because Chef sleeps nearby. It's a hop, skip and a jump to the medicine chest, where I find unmarked glass capsules sealed in a case. I slip one into my pocket, in case. From the galley, I discover, there are fixed passageways leading up and a flexible one leading down. I open the hatch and descend.

Yes, Perpetua says inside my head and as I get closer to her destination, repeating like an orgasmic lover, *Yes, yes, yes!*

I have found the Destruct button.

It is located at the bottom of the long stairway that circumvents her epiglottis; opening the last hatch I find my way into the control center, which is lodged in her craw. And here it is. Underneath there is a neatly printed plate put there by Father's engineers: IN CASE OF EMERGENCY, BREAK GLASS.

Perpetua's great body convulses. *Yes.*

Trembling, I press my mouth to the wall: "Is this what you want?" I can't afford to wait for an answer. "It would be suicide!"

We have a deal.

"But what about me?"

When it's time, you'll see.

The next few days are extremely hard. Perpetua rushes on without regard for me while Chef bombards us with new delicacies and Father and my sisters rehearse Gilbert and Sullivan in the music room. I can't help but think of Mother, alone in the ruins of our penthouse. Is she all right, is she maybe in some safe place with my lover Derek, or did she die holding the Gutenberg Bible in an eternal *I told you so?* Mother! Is that the Last Judgment shaping up out there, or is it simply the end of the world? Whatever it is, I think, she and Derek are better off than I am, trapped in here.

Father asks, "What's the matter with you?"

"Nothing. I'm fine."

My sisters say, "Is it Derek? Are you worried about Derek? This is only the beginning, so get over it."

"I'm fine."

"Of course you are—we're terribly lucky," they say. Father has given them jewels to match their eyes. "We're lucky as hell, and everything's going to be fine."

I can hardly bear to be with them. "Whatever you want," I whisper to Perpetua, "Let's do it."

When it's time.

Relief comes when you least expect it, probably because you aren't expecting it. Perpetua and I are of the Zen Archer school of life. She summons me out of a stone sleep.

It's time.

The alligator and I aren't one now, but we are thinking as one. Bending to her will, I pad along the corridors to the galley and descend to the control room. She doesn't have to explain. Predictably, the Destruct button is red. At the moment, it is glowing. I use the hammer to break the glass.

Now.

I push the button that sets the timer. The bottom falls out of the control room, spilling me into her throat, and she vomits me out. I crunch down on the breakable capsule that will bring me back to normal size.

My God, I'm back in the world! I'm back in the world, and it is terrible.

As I land in the muck, Perpetua rushes on like an express train roaring over me while I huddle on the tracks or the Concorde thundering close above as I lie on my back on the runway, counting the plates in its giant belly as it takes off. I have pushed the Destruct button. Is the timer working? Did it abort? Our alligator hostess is traveling at tremendous speeds, and as she slithers on, she whips her tail and opens her throat in a tremendous cry of grief that comes out of her in a huge, reptilian groan: *Noooooooo.*

Rolling out of her wake, I see the stars spiraling into the Hudson; in that second I think I see the proliferation and complexity of all creation dividing into gold and dross, unless it is light and dark, but which is which I cannot tell. A black shape on the horizon advances at tremendous speeds; it resolves into a monstrous reptile crushing everything in its path. The great mouth cracks wide as the huge beast approaches, blazing with red light that pours out from deep inside, and all at once I understand. This vast, dark shape is the one being Perpetua hates most, but she is helpless and rushing toward it all the same, and the terror is that she has no choice.

This is by no means God jerking her along; it is a stupendous alligator with its greedy jaws rimmed with blood, summoning Perpetua and its thousand other daughters into its path, preparing to devour them.

The thought trails after her like a pennant of fire. *The father is gathering us in.*

So I understand why the alligator helped me.

And I understand as well the scope of her gift to me: in another minute, I will become an orphan, as the monster alligator lunges for Perpetua and she stops it in its tracks, destructing in an explosion that lights up the apocalyptic skies. And because I am about to be free, and free of Father forever. . . .

I understand why I had to help her die.

Scared now.

It's OK.

I'll be fine.

***Catherine Asaro** is, as I write this in the summer of 2003, now the president of the Science Fiction and Fantasy Writers of America. Her work has been nominated for Hugo and Nebula Awards and has earned many other honors, including the* Analog *readers' poll and the National Readers Choice Award.*

She writes both space adventure and SF romantic thrillers. Her story for Flights *is neither, a strange and wonderful hybrid of fantasy and weird science.*

The Edges of Never-Haven

Catherine Asaro

Straight edges could take your soul.

The city of Never-Haven encircled a central plaza, where a circular fountain spewed up arches of water. Orb-houses filled the city, all round. Tonight, three moons lit the sky, as white as bone, casting ghostly light over the city of curves. Denric Windward Valdoria ran hard, gasping, his feet pounding on a path that spiraled from the outskirts of the city to its center.

He ran to stay alive.

Edger-demons pursued him, flitting from shadow to shadow. From edge to edge. In this city, straight edges brought the spells of cruelty, but only if they appeared in inanimate objects or drawings. A chance straight edge on a rock, a vertical cliff face, a stately tree trunk: none caused a threat. But build a house with straight walls or a road without turns and twists, and you invited the demons of Never-Haven.

Denric had been far from the city, wandering in the flats, or so he had thought. He hadn't realized he had reached the city outskirts. He had done no more than draw a line in the sand with his toe. Just a line. Always absentminded, he hadn't even realized what he had done—until it was too late.

His hosts in the sand flats had warned him: Avoid the city. If he was imprudent enough to enter, he must create no straight edges. Never-Haven offered a better life than the harsh sand flats where he had come to live a few days ago. The inhabitants of a long-vanished civilization had raised the original city. Its purpose: to cage Edgers. The demons were forever confined within its limits, never able to leave. They hadn't been able to stop humans from settling their city, but they made sure the trespassers lived on the edge of fear. As long as the humans created no straight lines, they remained free, but if ever they made a mistake—as had Denric tonight—they became prey to the Edgers.

So now he ran.

Denric gulped in breaths, his hand clamped over the stitch in his side. He was no athlete; he couldn't keep this pace much longer. His fear roiled. He had no idea how many Edgers were chasing him. Their wings rustled behind him. He didn't know what kept them from overtaking him; perhaps the curves in this path he followed. But they were drawing nearer. Their breath rasped, and their razor-claws clacked in the night.

"Help! Someone!" His yell echoed through the city—and the words bounced back to him like solid objects. The spell-enhanced echoes rained over him, buffeting his body until he stumbled. Catching his balance, he clamped his mouth shut, terrified by the unnatural echoes.

And he ran in silence, while Edgers pursued.

Desperate for a refuge, Denric veered toward a plaza on his left. No water arched out of its round fountain. Infuriated hisses erupted from the Edgers close on his heels, and he redoubled his efforts, running even harder. The fountain loomed before him, one and a half times his height. Jumping up, he grabbed its upper edge, hauled himself over, and tumbled into the bowl. He hit the bottom with a jarring thump.

Wails arose in the plaza, accompanied by frenzied clicking. He squeezed his eyes shut as if that could hold off his tormentors, but a grating noise immediately spurred him to open them. Silhouetted against the night sky, thorny heads appeared around the rim of the bowl, human-size but triangular. Edgers peered down at him, glinting in the moonlight, each with three glittering eyes. Huddled in the bottom of the fountain, Denric wrapped his arms around his knees and shivered.

The bowl was too deep for them to reach him even with their long arms. They might have slid down, if they could have endured the fountain. But his hope proved sound; they seemed unable to tolerate its curved bowl.

"Go away," he said in a low voice, afraid to speak louder and restart the echoes. He traced curves in the air, on the fountain, even on himself, but nothing warded away the Edgers.

His heart was beating fast from his run. He hadn't realized how out of shape he had become at the university, where he had earned his doctorate in literature. Although he was healthy and hale, he no longer regularly exercised. All highborn youths among his people learned to use a sword and bow; as a prince, even the seventh of ten children, he had been no exception. But he had always preferred reading to swordplay, and he had stopped training years ago.

Unfortunately, books wouldn't help him now. How long would his pursuers wait up there? Edgers slept during the day, shunning the sunlight that bedeviled their translucent eyes and gnarly skin. They and the humans of Never-Haven maintained an uneasy truce; at night, humans stayed within their round houses while Edgers left their straight-edged dunes and prowled the city. But surely by morning, people would be out and about. Whether or not they would help him, if he survived until then, was another question altogether.

He had known, in theory, that people sometimes lived in places where they would never willingly stay if they had other prospects or a means to leave. But it had never seemed real before he came here, to Sandstorm, which included the sand flats, Never-Haven, the deserts, and the stark mountains beyond, a region with few resources, industries, or jobs. He had wanted to establish a school, teaching children to read and write.

Denric shivered, wondering if he would ever meet his students now. He loved teaching. After his graduation last year, several universities had offered him professorships, mostly because of his credentials, though his title as a Ruby Prince hadn't hurt. He had come here instead, for almost no pay, because he wanted to make a difference with his life, which until now had been one of privileges he had inherited rather than earned.

He had just meant to explore Sandstorm. But as often happened, he had become preoccupied with his thoughts, and so he hadn't realized he had crossed the invisible boundary around Never-Haven. Now he was trapped in a bowl, with Edgers after his absentminded royal hide.

The clank of metal awoke Denric. He wouldn't have believed he could sleep now, yet here he was, waking up, groggy and disoriented. The moons were gone from overhead, but he could make out Edgers around the rim of the bowl above him. More silhouettes had gathered.

Metal hit stone again—and something struck his leg, what felt like a heavy chain. He jumped to his feet, holding in his yell. Another chain whacked his knee.

"No!" Backing away, he came up against the side of the bowl. When a chain swung into his shoulder, he put up his arm to ward it off—and a link caught his hand.

A square.

By the time Denric comprehended the shape, it was too late; his direct contact with the chain had counteracted the bowl's protective spell. The link snapped around his wrist, and he gasped at the shock of cold iron. Nausea surged in him.

The Edgers pulled on the chain, yanking him against the bowl, stretching his arm over his head. As he struggled, close to panic, they dragged him up the fountain. Bu the longer he slid on its curving surface, the more the link around his wrist weakened. His hope surged; if he could just work free—

Then a second chain swung into him. He tried to twist away, but he couldn't manage it. One of its square links caught his other wrist, and the Edgers pulled his arm above his head, towing him by both wrists now.

So they hauled him out of the fountain.

Denric had a sudden memory from years ago: climbing in the mountains with his older brothers Vyrl and Del-Kurj. He had fallen into a hollow and broken his leg. Only ten years old at the time, he had been terrified. Then Vyrl had scrambled down to him while Del ran for help. Their presence and concern had pushed back his fear. He had help: he would survive. He wished fiercely now for such assurance, but no rescue was coming tonight.

When Denric reached the top of the bowl, he was ready to scream. Edgers loomed around him like giant praying mantises, their skin glistening darkly. Each had three triangular nostrils below three eyes, and a hexagonal mouth with teeth hanging over the lips. Instead of forearms, razor-claws extended from their elbows, two blades like a double sword. The metal glinted as his captors hauled him over the edge of the bowl.

"No!" Denric whispered. Those claws could slice him into pieces. None of his hosts had been able to tell him what happened to a person captured by Edgers; apparently no one had returned to offer the story.

But instead of cutting him, an Edger used its long arm like a rope, wrapping the upper part around Denric's torso, leaving the razor-claw free.

Then it jumped.

Denric grunted when they hit the ground. He lost his balance and would have fallen, but the Edger caught him. With a groan, Denric doubled over its arm. The Edger yanked him upright, wrenching his chained arms in front of his body. The links around his wrists opened, but before he could react, the Edger pulled his arms behind his back and chained him again. He felt shell-shocked, unable to absorb it all. The thought of dying terrified him.

An Edger planted its elbow against Denric's back and shoved. He stumbled forward, his hair swinging around his face. The Edger pushed again, driving him in a straight line.

So they took him away.

No light filtered into the cellar. The blackness had an oppressive quality, like a blanket of nothing. The Edgers had pushed Denric on his knees with his back to a large pipe, then pulled his arms back and shackled his wrists behind the pipe. His muscles ached, and cold seeped from the floor through his trousers. Whispers tugged at the edges of his hearing.

Denric fought his dismay. He was a scholar, ill suited to the escapes of an adventurer, but he couldn't just wait here. He yanked on his chains, gauging their strength. They felt unbreakable. The pipe rose up against his back, straight and hard, and the stone floor was flat under his knees. Nor did he doubt this room had straight walls.

A rustle came from the darkness.

"Who is it?" Denric hated the tremor in his voice. Steeling himself, he spoke more firmly. "Who walks there?"

Another rustle.

"*Who is it?*" The words escaped before he could stop them.

A creak came in front of him, like the bending of a rusty hinge. He pressed into the pole against his back, straining to pull his hands up or down, anything to free himself.

A cough.

"Gods, no." He tried to slide around the pole, but a rectangular duct blocked his way.

Light flared.

Denric jerked back and hit his head on the pipe. His vision swam, making it hard to focus on the glowing blur in front of him. As his sight cleared, he realized he was staring into a face—a human face—eerily lit from below by a boxy lamp. The man had gaunt features, with skin that stretched too tightly over his skull. His eyes, shadowed and dark, were deeply set and overhung by his eyebrows, giving his gaze a hooded aspect. Only a few feet away, he was crouching so his gaze was level with his prisoner's. Darkness hid his body.

He spoke in a shadowed voice. "My greetings, Teacher."

Denric hunched his shoulders. "How did you know I teach?"

"All here know. You are new to Sandstorm." He lifted his lamp, causing the sleeve of his robe to fall back.

Denric knew then that his first impression had been wrong. This creature had a man's face, yes, but instead of a forearm, two blades extended from his elbow, glinting in the light of his lamp.

"What do you want with me?" Denric asked hoarsely.

"Only this." The Edger-man reached forward with his razor-claw. Denric tried to duck, but he could go nowhere. The blades reached to his neck, closer, closer—

And snapped.

A scream caught in Denric's throat. It took him several moments to comprehend that the Edger-man hadn't just sliced open his jugular vein. Instead, he had cut Denric's . . . *hair?* It was true: a curl of gold hair lay balanced on the man's claw.

"So." The man studied the curl. "I wonder if you could calculate an equation for this."

Denric swallowed the bile in his throat. "I've no idea."

"Your hair protects you."

He gave a shaky laugh. "The ol' hair trick, eh?"

"Don't make fun of me, human."

Denric shut his mouth, fast.

The man's voice grated. "Were it my choice, you would die miserably for violating Never-Haven with your straight line. But your curls have stopped whatever I might have done."

Denric had no idea what he meant; he had thought only inanimate curves countered the Edger spells. And if they could cut off one of his curls, why not all of them? He didn't ask, lest he misspeak again and stir his captor's anger. He could feel the man's simmering rage like a tangible presence.

"No matter." The stranger stood, holding up his light. He traced lines in the air, speaking an arcane language Denric had never heard. But he recognized one phrase in the spell: *Prince Denricson Windward Valdoria.*

"What is that?" Denric's voice cracked. "What are you doing?"

The Edger-man didn't answer; he just continued his incantation. Shadows overcame Denric, shrouding his mind.

Silence. No whispers. Denric groggily opened his eyes into a white blur. Brightness surrounded him. He had been in a cellar; now he was . . .

Lying on a bed?

He squinted, confused. It was true. He lay sprawled facedown on a white quilt. Gauzy white curtains hung from ceiling to floor on all sides, enclosing the bed. The drapes were translucent, but they hung in many layers, enough so he couldn't see through them.

He pushed up on his hands, relieved to find himself mobile. But when he tried to pull his legs under him, he discovered his left ankle was chained to a squared bedpost. Gritting his teeth, he slid over to the bedpost and sat up, his ankle pulling the chain tight as his legs hung off the bed. He tried to push aside the curtains, but instead of cloth, they felt like a solid wall. The vertical drapes penned him as securely as any prison.

"Awake, I see," a woman said.

He turned with a start. Across the bed, a woman stood in the narrow space between the mattress and the curtains. Tall, with shimmering black hair, she had slanted eyes and a porcelain face that gave her an eerie, exotic beauty. A dark robe covered her from shoulder to wrist to ankle. Her hand showed beneath the hem of one sleeve, but the blades of a razor-claw glinted in her other sleeve.

"Who—?" Denric would have finished his sentence, except *Who are you?* sounded so trite.

She didn't answer. Instead, she sat at the head of the bed and stretched out her razor-claw. Even knowing she was too far away to reach him, he jerked back. This felt like another of his dreams, the one where he found himself armed with a sword much too heavy to use, facing opponents who handled theirs with ease, faceless creatures who could destroy him with barely a thought.

Those fears had stalked Denric throughout his youth, living as he did in a world that valued a man's prowess in battle far more than book learning. He just wanted to teach. He had never been strong enough to wield a sword well or interested enough to learn strategies that would compensate for his lack of muscle. Nor was his perpetually tousled mop of hair and his face, which too many people called "angelic," likely to inspire dread in his enemies. He was only a little less than average height, and in reasonably good shape, but compared with his brawny, towering brothers and their natural skill at weapons, he had always felt lacking.

"Ruby Prince." The woman had a voice like whiskey, smooth and husky. If he listened too long, it would inebriate him.

"What do you want?" He tried to ignore her bladed arm.

"What do you think, hmm?" Leaning forward, she brought her claw arm to within a finger-span of his face. Sweat beaded on his forehead, but he didn't back down.

She touched his curls with the tip of a blade. "These do seem to protect you."

"How?" He hadn't meant to speak, but the word came out before he could stop it.

A smile, cool and perfect, touched her cultured lips. "Because I find them too attractive to destroy." She sat back, her lashes lowering over her tilted eyes. Then she crooked the finger of her human hand. "Come here, pretty human."

Ah, hell. Being a demon's plaything ranked about as high on his list of preferred activities as catching pneumonia.

"No," he said.

"I think yes." She traced a straight line in the air, from high to low, and a shudder went through Denric. When she drew a line from left to right, he felt pulled forward. He resisted, leaning back. Then she made a line from low to high, and he couldn't stop from tilting toward her. When she completed her rectangle in the air, with a line from right to left, he began to slide toward her despite his efforts to hold back.

Ironically, the chain came to his rescue, pulling him up short as it stretched his leg out behind him. With her spell drawing him, he had to brace his hands on the bed so he wouldn't keel over onto his face. The awkward position annoyed him so much, he momentarily forgot to be terrified. Instead, he scowled. "Are you done playing?"

"Should I be?" As she traced a curve in the air, the pulling sensation stopped, and he jerked back in compensation. With no warning, she slashed the bed with her claw, cutting the quilt in a line. Clinks rattled behind Denric, and he swung around to see the chain fall apart. He pulled his leg under him fast, before the chain could catch it again. Then he turned back to the woman, afraid to ask what she planned next.

"Come here," she murmured.

Alarmed, he tried to back away. It did no good; against his will, he slid forward those last few hand-spans to where she sat. When he raised his arm to defend himself, she caught it in her human hand. In reflex, he jerked back his other fist, ready to strike. She reacted just as fast, opening her razor-claw around his wrist.

Denric froze, staring at the blades. Light glinted on their edges. If she snapped the claw, she would slice his fist off at the wrist. Slowly, and ever so carefully, he drew his hand back and lowered his arm.

"What do you want with me?" he asked.

"Your children are heirs to an empire, eh?"

He felt as if his stomach had dropped. Of course she knew. A memory jumped in his mind from several years ago, a processional of the Imperialate nobility, the wealthy and powerful, those with lives such as most people never witnessed, except at such parades meant to entertain a weary public. Members of each noble House had walked down a great concourse, going to their seats in an amphitheatre, where they would watch the day's entertainment, plays and such.

Denric's family had entered last, as befitted their royal status, with lesser members coming first, then those with higher rank. The parade ended with his aunt, the Ruby Pharaoh. As the seventh child of the Pharaoh's sister, Denric had gone before most of his other kin. But it still placed him higher in rank than the most powerful nobles. Unlike many of his siblings, who took their status for granted, it troubled him that he inherited rather than earned his standing. He wanted his achievements to arise from hard work. Regardless, one fact remained: Any legitimate child he fathered would have the rights, privileges, and power of a Ruby Dynasty heir.

"So quiet," the Edger-woman said.

"You can't have my child," Denric said.

Never taking her gaze from him, she traced her claw on the curtains. The spell that made them rigid walls to Denric had no effect on her blades. She neatly sliced the cloth into a hexagon, and a six-sided piece of gauze drifted onto the bed.

Denric blinked. "How did you do that?" He pressed the curtains nearest to him, but they remained solid.

She indicated her human hand. "Once I was all like this. No longer."

"You deliberately changed into an Edger?" What would possess a person to such insanity?

"For the spells. They are the reward of transformation."

"How could you?"

Her voice hardened. "You've never needed for anything, princeling. Never lived the edges of life, only its sweet fullness. Here we have nothing but edges. *Nothing.*" With deadly calm, she added, "Now you learn the other side."

Her words plucked a wire within him, one drawn tight by his fear that she spoke the truth, that he had no right to his life. He knew how his aunt, the pharaoh, would respond: *Our privileges are small compensation for the responsibilities we carry.* By the Ruby Dynasty, an empire rose or fell; if they faltered, untold populations could suffer.

At times Denric felt the weight of those duties crushing him, and he carried less than many members of his family. He couldn't defend the Imperialate as an officer; he lacked the military brilliance of his siblings. But he could teach, perhaps an even more effective defense for an empire. Educate her people. Help them learn to help themselves. Or so he had believed. Now, faced with someone who had given up her humanity just to survive, his idealistic views seemed hollow.

The Edger-woman was scrutinizing him as if trying to read his thoughts from his face. When she touched the hexagon of gauze on the bed, a shudder went through Denric, starting in his shoulders and shaking down his torso into his legs. Pushed by this new spell, he drew her into his arms. Inside he was shouting, fighting the compulsion she laid on him. The muscles in his arms and legs spasmed. Yet still he held her.

Her body felt human in his embrace. *Curved.* She put her human arm around his waist and laid her head on his shoulder. "I am pleased."

Unwilling but unable to stop, he leaned his head against hers. "Why are you doing this? No child I have with you would be legitimate." She threatened to scorch his heart. He came from a close, devoted family; they were his world. Over the years he had begun to long for his own. In that, legitimacy made no difference; he would acknowledge and love any offspring he sired. One of his deepest fears was that he would become a father but lose his child. It would kill him.

"By the time of its birth," she murmured, "it will be legitimate."

Denric stiffened. Good gods, could they force his marriage? Surely not. A vow made under duress wasn't valid. "My family would never believe I consented to such a union."

She pressed her lips against his cheek. "What do you think they would do to have you back? And your baby, hmmm? But the child could stay here. That would be messy for you."

His panic sparked. *No.* Clenching his fists, he made circles on her back, pressing with his knuckles. It didn't help counter her spell; he continued to hold her as if they were lovers.

Denric drew in a deep breath. Damn it all, he wouldn't let the Edgers terrorize him. If the worst happened, he would deal with it, somehow. Some way.

He spoke in a quieter voice. "I don't understand how you could give up being human."

"Surely you see." She released him from her spell enough so she could lean back to look at him. "I have powers I could only imagine before."

"How much of you has changed?"

She hesitated, then seemed to make a decision. Pulling aside her robe, she revealed her leg where it hung off the bed. It was also a razor-claw, longer and deadlier than her arm, ending in a metal pad that would allow her to walk.

Denric touched the metal knee. "What transformed you?"

"The Edgers."

He looked up at her. "How?"

"They know spells."

"What spells?"

"Equations."

He grimaced. "Lots of people know equations." It didn't make the infernal things any more palatable.

"Edgers use them in ways humans cannot." She drew a line in the air. "Linear equations, those that make lines, are Edger spells. The equation of a curve can counter such spells because it is of a higher order. Nonlinear."

He didn't recall enough mathematics to understand fully, but he did remember what "higher order" meant. Linear equations had their variables raised only to the first power; curves had their variables raised to higher powers.

He tilted his head, curious despite himself. "Why would only linear spells do magic?" He wasn't convinced Edger spells really were the magic of demons rather than the ancient technology of a vanished alien race.

"Straight lines are unyielding." She shrugged. "Curves are softer."

It didn't tell him much. He wondered if she was thinking of herself more than the spells. He was almost certain curves were stronger than straight lines. Wasn't that why chain links were round instead of square? Edger chains needed spells to strengthen them. But her comment made sense in another way; in giving up part of her humanity, she had gained the unyielding edges she needed to survive.

She was watching him closely. "You are a complicated man, I think. Too complex for simple straight edges."

"Most people are." He shifted his weight, wanting to move away but unable to counter the remnants of her spell. He had never been good at equations. He wished he had the ability of his teenaged brother, Kelric, his youngest sibling. Kelric would have been a superb theorist, except he had been talked into attending a military academy instead. He would also marry in a few years, a dynastic union arranged with a noblewoman, an officer in the Imperial Fleet. Denric had almost ended up betrothed to her himself, but in the end she had chosen Kelric, whose military interests more closely matched her own.

An idea came to him. "You and I can't marry. I already have a wife."

She frowned. "We know you don't."

"It's a betrothal."

"You're lying."

"Check. Kelricson Valdoria is to wed Corey Majda, the Matriarch of Majda."

"Your name is Denric."

"That's a nickname." If she investigated, she would find references to both his and Kelric's possible betrothals, and it might not be immediately obvious he and his brother weren't the same person.

Her scowl deepened. "We will check this lie."

"Good." Perhaps it would buy him time.

"Even if it is true, you are still a valuable hostage." She studied him. "Perhaps even more so, if a powerful matriarch wants her golden-haired prince back."

Damn. "What is it you want from me?"

"You will see."

Concentrating on her, Denric realized the truth: They would never let him go. They had too much to lose. As soon as his family knew he was free, they would seek vengeance against his kidnappers. He had far more use as a hostage; his parents would give much to ensure his safety, all the more so because war, assassination, and politics had so often torn his family apart. He had been able to come here to teach only because he was the seventh child of the Pharaoh's sister; had he been closer to the throne, the government would have forbidden him this post. His parents worried for him regardless. He hated knowing he had fulfilled their worst fears.

Stop it, Denric thought. He had to live his own life. Yes, danger existed. But he had to face it, not hide in the protected shadow of his heredity.

"What deal did you make with the demons?" he asked. "What did you trade to them for this power of spells?"

Her shoulders hunched. "You ask too much."

"It's me, isn't it?" He watched for her reaction. "You promised to increase their sway over humans. Right now they have Never-Haven. But the more of us they control, the more their influence extends into human realms. Perhaps someday they will escape Never-Haven, yes? Those of you who have transformed must bring them valuable humans."

She clenched her fist. "We do as we please."

"I don't believe you. I think you have no choice."

Her voice was low. "Nor do you."

"No! I would never transform."

"Perhaps." She slid her arm around his neck and brushed her lips across his.

Clamping his mouth shut, he thought of circles, waves, parabolas, anything curved. Nothing helped: she continued to kiss him, and he continued to let her.

But then she drew back, her expression pensive. "Before the Edgers took me in, I had no home. Nowhere to go." Tightly, she added, "Men took advantage of that."

Denric felt ill, understanding her implication. "And now?"

Her eyes glinted. "No one touches me unless I allow it." Then she added, "It seems I cannot make myself force another."

Although she said no more, he sensed her inner struggle. The Edgers hadn't taken all her humanity: she had a conscience. "Then surely you see you must let me go."

"The time will come, Ruby Prince, when you want me of your own free will." She flicked her fingers in a curve through the air, and the force holding him released. "The spells work on your mind as well as your body. It just takes longer."

With that, she rose to her feet, her robe falling over her leg, hiding the blades. Then she left, easily pushing aside the curtains. He tried to grab them, but they billowed away from his hand and fell into place, once again becoming a solid wall.

Denric sat cross-legged on the bed, thinking. The people of Never-Haven paid a devastating price to escape their harsh existence. It was true, Edgers offered them better lives, but only if the humans indentured themselves. They were still trapped, now by a pact with demons rather than by poverty. He had a responsibility here, but his becoming an Edger wasn't the solution. He wanted to help, not constrain these people in a life worse than what they already suffered.

He wondered, too, if Edger-humans had to remain in Never-Haven. If

Edgers left, they faded away into nothing. But transformed humans weren't fully Edgers, at least not those he had seen. Did they have more freedom? The prospect of their leaving to prey on their untransformed brethren chilled Denric.

Edger motivations were alien to him. What would they do, alter every human in Never-Haven? Yes, apparently, if they could. And then? He was beginning to see the answer. They would lure in more humans. No wonder they wanted him as a hostage. He would draw people here: would-be rescuers, covert agents, and the curious, come to see the city that ensorcelled a Ruby Prince. Humans were safe as long as they avoided straight edges, but no one could keep that up forever. One by one, the Edgers would transform them. It was a bizarre scenario, a city packed with demons. If they reached a critical number, they could push out the boundaries of Never-Haven, making it larger and larger until it overran all Sandstorm.

Denric shuddered. He had to escape. The Edger-woman claimed he couldn't use their magic—if it really was magic and not an esoteric, ancient technology his people no longer understood. He wasn't even sure the two possibilities were that different. This had started when he drew a line in the sand, so obviously he could have an effect, if only he knew how. It all centered on equations. They did indeed seem like arcane spells to him, an unknowable language only its acolytes could comprehend. His drawing curves hadn't countered any spells, but perhaps that was because he didn't understand the math.

Denric struggled to remember the equation for a curve, *any* curve. He recalled only one, a parabola. Visualizing it in his mind, he imagined the curtains giving way to his push. But when he pushed, they still felt solid. What was he missing? Scowling, he slashed his hand across the drapes in a parabola.

They gave along the curve.

"Hey!" Denric grinned. Pushing the cloth, he dented its surface. No matter how hard he tried, though, he could achieve nothing more. Within seconds, the dent vanished. Disappointed, he concentrated and drew a bigger parabola. The drapes gave again, but no more than before.

His elation faded. He needed something more. What? A more complicated equation perhaps. Years ago he had known the formula for a circle, but he no longer remembered, besides which, he had never understood it anyway.

Try, he thought. He guessed at the equation and drew a circle on the curtains. Nothing happened. He changed the math in his mind and tried again, still with no luck. On his third try, the cloth gave a little, but no more than for the parabola.

Denric exhaled. Scanning his prison, he pondered what he could do. The hexagon the Edger-woman had cut from the drapes lay close to where he was sitting. With a frown, he scooted across the bed and tried his counterspell on the curtains farthest from the hexagon. The drapes dented—

And billowed out from his hand. Caught off guard, he froze. By the time he had gathered his wits enough to touch the curtains, they had settled down and become rigid again.

With his heart beating hard, Denric stood up between the bed and drapes. He repeated his spell, and this time when the drapes billowed, he shoved them aside and ran out—

Into darkness.

Cold.

Denric shivered. Darkness surrounded him. He reached out, but found nothing. Nor did he see any sign of his prison, no light, nothing.

Turning in a circle, he thought of the equation that had led him here—and light flickered in the distance. He stopped, blinking. He hadn't been trying a spell, but apparently the procedure worked regardless. Or more accurately, it negated a spell, in this case one of darkness.

He headed for the light, crossing his arms against the cold, rubbing his palms on his elbows for warmth. Soon he was walking down a rough-hewn tunnel of old stone blocks. Up ahead, an archway framed the corridor, coming to a triangular point high overhead. Light poured through it, so bright he could see nothing within the brilliance. Rattles, cracks, and clinks came from beyond the arch.

He stopped at the opening and bit his lip. This could be a gate to freedom or a path deeper into captivity. What to do: Enter the light or retreat into the dark? His inclination was to think of light as good, but that instinct might have little basis here.

Well, he had to do something, and he really, really didn't want to stay in the dark. Steeling himself, he walked forward. Light poured everywhere, blinding him. A voice keened, a lament of grief so great, it threatened to break his heart.

Gradually the light dimmed, until he could make out the surroundings. He was in a room of a castle.

His room.

Denric shook his head, trying to clear the vision. But it persisted. He recognized everything: the fresh atmosphere of home, so unlike the dusty air of Never-Haven; the distant voices of the castle waking in the morning; the aromas of breakfast. He also knew the person standing by the window alcove across the room, staring out at the Plains of Dalavador.

His mother.

When he realized she was crying, he strode over to her. "Mother? What is wrong? Why are you sad?"

She gave no sign she heard, only continued to gaze out the window, her face streaked with tears, her hair tumbling down her back in a gold mane, a much longer version of his own curls. She had a shawl around her shoulders and was wearing a long robe. Dawn was just lighting the sky outside.

"Mother?" He stopped next to her, reaching out—and his hand went through her arm.

Denric stared at his hand. "No, it can't be."

She continued to cry, oblivious of him. He spun around, intent on a counterspell—and froze. His body was laid out on the bed in a shroud of mourning. His mother was weeping for him. For his death.

"It's not true." He raised his voice. "Do you hear me?" He didn't know who he was challenging: the Edgers, fate, himself? "I'm *alive!*"

He turned back to his mother, the queen of Skyfall. It tore at him, seeing her grieve. Family, home, hearth—they mattered to him more than anything else. He was just a simple man who wanted to sit by the fire with a wife and children. His passing would be inauspicious, mourned by only a few, for unlike his brothers he was no great hero. His sister, Soz, had also entered the military, distinguishing herself far better than he ever could.

Denric mentally shook himself. No he wasn't a great officer. That didn't make him any less. He spoke gently to his mother, even knowing she couldn't hear. "If I truly have died, or soon will, please know I love you, Father, and the family. Remember that, feel it somehow, even if you never know I was here."

Unexpectedly, her lips formed a word: *Denric?* His heart leapt, but he had no chance to ask if she heard him. A mist was rising around them. It thickened until the world became formless and dim, with nothing but the ground beneath his feet. He called to her, but the fog muffled his words into silence.

Denric pushed his hands through his hair, his arms shaking. Had he died? He clenched his fists, pressing them against his head. "I won't give in." Then he shouted, "Do you hear me? I won't become an Edger."

Silence.

Denric lowered his arms, his muscles so tense he couldn't unclench his hands. He wanted to run, but he didn't dare, lest he become lost. He tried his counterspells, but nothing worked. His universe remained formless.

"It doesn't matter what you do," he told the mist, the spells, anyone who could hear. "It doesn't matter what you show me. I won't consent to become an Edger."

"Bravado," a voice hissed.

Denric swung around. "Who is that?"

"Mother," it whispered. "Father. Brother. Sister. Transform them."

"You're lying." It couldn't be true. They couldn't have brought his family here.

"No lie," the voice murmured.

The sibilant words lifted the hairs on Denric's neck. He opened his mouth to shout another denial. Then he stopped. Yelling at a formless voice wouldn't achieve anything.

Suddenly the Edger-woman spoke out of the mist. "Pretty boy. Will you die?"

"If I do, it will be as a human. I won't transform."

Silence.

Sweat beaded on Denric's forehead. "Is anyone there?"

No answer.

It took a conscious effort for him to stay put, to keep from calling in a panic. He had always thought of himself as an unruffled sort, but waiting now, in this nothingness, took every bit of control he could muster. Inside, he was terrified. But somehow he managed to keep from running like a maniac.

After a while, he realized the mist was thinning. As his surroundings became clearer, puzzlement set in. He was outside Never-Haven, farther out in the sand flats even than when he had traced a line in the ground with his toe.

Denric stepped back, away from the city. From the direction of Never-Haven, a dark figure was approaching, forming out of the thinning mist. It took a moment for him to recognize her as the Edger-woman. She stopped a few paces away, the wind blowing her hair around her face.

"I won't go back," Denric said.

Her voice came like gusts over a distant plain. "Not many escape."

"Escape?" He wasn't certain he had heard correctly.

She indicated the sand flats around them. "You are outside the boundaries of Never-Haven."

"You're letting me go?"

"No. You have left despite us."

He didn't believe it. "How?"

"Do you not wonder how someone as untutored in mathematics as yourself could evade our spells? If you can, surely anyone can manage it."

So much for her confidence in his intellect. "And can they?"

"No."

"Then why me?"

"Equations are only a framework. Fear makes the spell." Her voice was a chill wind. "The only way to escape Never-Haven is to face your fears."

"That's it?" He couldn't hold back his incredulity.

She raised her eyebrow. "You consider it easy?"

He thought of what he had been through. "No, not easy."

"You are one of only a few to escape."

"What happened to the others?"

Her hair blew across her face. "They became like us."

Denric shuddered. "I should go now."

"Don't return, beautiful prince. I would take you before any other." Her voice was barely audible now, as her body began to thin, like mist. "I cannot follow you outside the city; I must stay in Never-Haven now that I am transformed. But if ever you become trapped here again, I will find a spell to hold you forever."

Denric spoke softly. "I cannot change what made your life hell. But perhaps I can help others."

"Perhaps."

He swallowed. "Good-bye."

"Good-bye," she whispered.

Then she faded from sight.

Grit blew across the sand flats. Denric stood alone, outside his rounded house. The fates willing, he would build a home here.

He looked toward Never-Haven in the distance, with its curved towers. *Fierce, beautiful city.* It demanded an abysmal price of its people, that they lose their humanity to survive. He thought of the woman, terrible in her beauty. Forever trapped. Denrick knew he would live every moment in the shadow of Never-Haven, aware of its presence. It would never let him forget he owed these people a debt.

And yet—in dealing with the Edgers, he had found an inner core of his character, one that would help him survive. He would offer what he could to the children here, that they might find a better way to escape their crushing lives than the path chosen by their kin in the city.

Perhaps he could give them hope.

Until he clued me in, I had no idea **Tim Powers** *was born in New York (Buffalo), but I did know he was born in a leap year the same calendar year as me, which makes me in my fifties and Tim just into his teens. He is the author of many wonderful novels, among them the award winners* The Anubis Gates *(Philip K. Dick Award and Prix Apollo),* Dinner at Deviant's Palace *(another Phil Dick award),* Last Call *(World Fantasy Award), and* Declare *(ditto).*

Pat Moore

Tim Powers

"Is it okay if you're one of the ten people I send the letter to," said the voice on the telephone, "or is that redundant? I don't want to screw this up. 'Ear repair' sounds horrible."

Moore exhaled smoke and put out his Marlboro in the half-inch of cold coffee in his cup. "No, Rick, don't send it to me. In fact, you're screwed—it says you have to have ten friends."

He picked up the copy he had got in the mail yesterday, spread the single sheet out flat on the kitchen table and weighted two corners with the dusty salt and pepper shakers. It had clearly been photocopied from a photocopy, and originally composed on a typewriter.

> This has been sent to you for good luck. The original is in San Fransisco. You must send it on to ten friend's, who, you think need good luck, within 24 hrs of receiving it.

"I could use some luck," Rick went on. "Can you loan me a couple of thousand? My wife's in the hospital, and we've got no insurance."

Moore paused for a moment before going on with the old joke; then, "Sure," he said, "so we won't see you at the lowball game tomorrow?"

"Oh, I've got money for *that*." Rick might have caught Moore's hesitation, for he went on quickly, without waiting for a dutiful laugh, "Mark 'n' Howard mentioned it this morning on the radio. You're famous."

> The luck is now sent to you—you will receive Good Luck within three days of receiving this, provided you send it on. Do not send money, since luck has no price.

On a Wednesday dawn five months ago now, Moore had poured a tumbler of Popov Vodka at this table, after sitting most of the night in the emergency room at—what had been the name of the hospital in San Mateo, not Saint Lazarus, for sure—and then he had carefully lit a Virginia Slims from the orphaned pack on the counter and laid the smoldering cigarette in an ashtray beside the glass. When the untouched cigarette had burned down to the filter and gone out, he had carried the full glass and the ashtray to the back door and set them in the trash can, and then washed his hands in the kitchen sink, wondering if the little ritual had been a sufficient good-bye. Later he had thrown out the bottle of vodka and the pack of Virginia Slims too.

> A young man in Florida got the letter, it was very faded, and he resolved to type it again, but he forgot. He had many troubles, including expensive ear repair. But then he typed ten copy's and mailed them, and he got a better job.

"Where you playing today?" Rick asked.

"The Garden City in San Jose, probably," Moore said, "the six- and twelve-dollar Hold 'Em. I was just about to leave when you called."

"For sure? I could meet you there. I was going to play at the Bay on Bering, but if we were going to meet there, you'd have to shave—"

"And find a clean shirt, I know. But I'll see you at Larry's game tomorrow, and we shouldn't play at the same table anyway. Go to the Bay."

"Naw, I wanted to ask you about something. So you'll be at the Garden City. You take the 280, right?"

> Pat Moore put off mailing the letter and died, but later found it again and passed it on, and received threescore and ten.

"Right."

"If that crapped-out Dodge of yours can get up to freeway speed."

"It'll still be cranking along when your Saturn is a planter somewhere."

"Great, so I'll see you there," Rick said. "Hey," he added with forced joviality, "you're famous!"

> Do not ignore this letter
> ST LAZARUS

"Type up ten copies with your name in it, you can be famous too," Moore said, standing up and crumpling the letter. "Send one to Mark 'n' Howard. See you."

He hung up the phone and fetched his car keys from the cluttered table by the front door. The chilly sea breeze outside was a reproach after the musty staleness of the apartment, and he was glad he'd brought his denim jacket.

He combed his hair in the rearview mirror while the old slant-six engine of the Dodge idled in the carport, and he wondered if he would see the day when his brown hair might turn gray. He was still thirty years short of threescore and ten, and he wasn't envying the Pat Moore in the chain letter.

The first half hour of the drive down the 280 was quiet, with a Gershwin CD playing the *Concerto in F* and the pines and green meadows of the Fish and Game Refuge wheeling past on his left under the gray sky, while the pastel houses of Hillsborough and Redwood City marched across the eastern hills. The car smelled familiarly of Marlboros and Doublemint gum and engine exhaust.

Just over those hills, on the 101 overlooking the Bay, Trish had driven her Ford Grenada over an unrailed embankment at midnight, after a Saint Patrick's Day party at the Bayshore Meadows. Moore was objectively sure he would drive on the 101 one day, but not yet.

Traffic was light on the 280 this morning, and in his rearview mirror he saw the little white car surging from side to side in the lanes as it passed other vehicles. Like most modern cars, it looked to Moore like a computer mouse. He clicked up his turn signal lever and drifted over the lane-divider bumps and into the right lane.

The white car—he could see the blue Chevy cross on its hood now—swooped up in the lane Moore had just left, but instead of rocketing on past him, it slowed, pacing Moore's old Dodge at sixty miles an hour.

Moore glanced to his left, wondering if he knew the driver of the Chevy—but it was a lean-faced stranger in sunglasses, looking straight at him. In the moment before Moore recognized the thing as a shotgun viewed muzzle-on, he thought the man was holding up a microphone; but instantly another person in the white car had blocked the driver—Moore glimpsed only a purple shirt and long dark hair—and then with squealing tires the car veered sharply away to the left.

Moore gripped the hard green plastic of his steering wheel and looked straight ahead; he was braced for the sound of the Chevy hitting the center-divider fence, and so he didn't jump when he heard the crash—even though the seat rocked under him and someone was now sitting in the car with him, on the passenger side against the door. For one unthinking moment he thought someone had been thrown from the Chevrolet and had landed in his car.

He focused on the lane ahead and on holding the Dodge Dart steady between the white lines. Nobody could have come through the roof, or the windows or the doors. Must have been hiding in the backseat all this time, he thought, and only now jumped over into the front. What timing. He was panting shallowly, and his ribs tingled, and he made himself take a deep breath and let it out.

He looked to his right. A dark-haired woman in a purple dress was grinning at him. Her hair hung in a neat pageboy cut, and she wasn't panting.

"I'm your guardian angel," she said. "And guess what my name is."

Moore carefully lifted his foot from the accelerator—he didn't trust himself with the brake yet—and steered the Dodge onto the dirt shoulder. When it had slowed to the point where he could hear gravel popping under the tires, he pressed the brake; the abrupt stop rocked him forward, though the woman beside him didn't shift on the old green upholstery.

"And guess what my name is," she said again.

The sweat rolling down his chest under his shirt was a sharp tang in his nostrils. "Hmm," he said, to test his voice; then he said, "You can get out of the car now."

In the front pocket of his jeans was a roll of hundred-dollar bills, but his left hand was only inches away from the .38 revolver tucked into the open seam at the side of the seat. But both the woman's hands were visible on her lap, and empty.

The engine was still running, shaking the car, and he could smell the hot exhaust fumes seeping up through the floor. He sighed, then reluctantly reached forward and switched off the ignition.

"I shouldn't be talking to you," the woman said in the sudden silence. "*She* told me not to. But I just now saved your life. So don't tell me to get out of the car."

It had been a purple shirt or something, and dark hair. But this was obviously not the person he'd glimpsed in the Chevy. A team, twins?

"What's your name?" he asked absently. A van whipped past on the left, and the car rocked on its shock absorbers.

"Pat Moore, same as yours," she said with evident satisfaction. He noticed that every time he glanced at her, she looked away from something else to meet his eyes; as if whenever he wasn't watching her, she was studying the interior of the car, or his shirt, or the freeway lanes.

"Did you—get threescore and ten?" he asked. Something more like a nervous tic than a smile was twitching his lips. "When you sent out the letter?"

"That wasn't me, that was *her*. And she hasn't got it yet. And she won't, either, if her disciples kill all the available Pat Moores. You're in trouble every which way, but I like you."

"Listen, when did you get into my car?"

"About ten seconds ago. What if he had backup, another car following him? You should get moving again."

Moore called up the instant's glimpse he had got of the thing in front of the driver's hand—the ring had definitely been the muzzle of a shotgun, twelve-gauge, probably a pistol grip. And he seized on her remark about a backup car because the thought was manageable and complete. He clanked the gearshift into Park, and the Dodge started at the first twist of the key, and he levered it into Drive and gunned along the shoulder in a cloud of dust until he had got up enough speed to swing into the right lane between two yellow Stater Bros. trucks.

He concentrated on working his way over to the fast lane, and then when he got there, his engine roaring, he just watched the rearview mirror and the oncoming exit signs until he found a chance to make a sharp right turn across all the lanes and straight into the exit lane that swept toward the southbound 85. A couple of cars behind him honked.

He was going too fast for the curving interchange lane, his tires chirruping on the pavement, and he wrestled with the wheel and stroked the brake.

"Who's getting off behind us?" he asked sharply.

"I can't see," she said.

He darted a glance at the rearview mirror and was pleased to see only a slow-moving old station wagon, far back.

"A station wagon," she said, though she still hadn't looked around. Maybe she had looked in the passenger-side door mirror.

He had got the car back under control by the time he merged with the southbound lanes, and then he braked, for the 85 was ending ahead, at a traffic signal by the grounds of some college.

"Is your neck hurt?" he asked. "Can't twist your head around?"

"It's not that. I can't see anything you don't see."

He tried to frame an answer to that, or a question about it, and finally just said, "I bet we could find a bar fairly readily. Around here."

"I can't drink. I don't have any ID."

"You can have a Virgin Mary," he said absently, catching a green light and turning right just short of the college. "Celery stick to stir it with." Raindrops began spotting the dust on the windshield.

"I'm not so good at touching things," she said. "I'm not actually a living person."

"Okay, see, that means what? You're a *dead* person, a ghost?"

"Yes."

Already disoriented, Moore flexed his mind to see if anything in his experience or philosophies might let him believe this; and there was nothing that did. This woman, probably a neighbor, simply knew who he was, and she had hidden in the back of his car back at the apartment parking lot. She was probably insane. It would be a mistake to get further involved with her.

"Here's a place," he said, swinging the car into a strip-mall parking lot to the right. "Pirate's Cove. We can see how well you handle popcorn before you try a drink."

He parked around behind the row of stores, and the back door of the Pirate's Cove led them down a hallway stacked with boxes before they stepped through an arch into the dim bar. There were no other customers in the place at this early hour, and the long room smelled more like bleach than like beer; the teenaged-looking bartender barely gave them a glance and a nod as Moore led the woman across the worn carpet and the parquet square to a table under a football poster. There were four low stools instead of chairs.

The woman couldn't remember any movies she'd ever seen, and claimed not to have heard about the war in Iraq, so when Moore walked to the bar and came back with a glass of Budweiser and a bowl of popcorn, he sat down and just stared at her. She was easier to see in the dim light from the jukebox and the neon bar signs than she had been out in the gray daylight. He would guess that she was about thirty—though her face had no wrinkles at all, as if she had never laughed or frowned.

"You want to try the popcorn?" he asked as he unsnapped the front of his denim jacket.

"Look at it so I know where it is."

He glanced down at the bowl, and then back at her. As always, her eyes fixed on his as soon as he was looking at her. Either her pupils were fully dilated, or else her irises were black.

But he glanced down again when something thumped the table and a puff of hot salty air flicked his hair, and some popcorn kernels spun away through the air.

The popcorn still in the bowl had been flattened into little white jigsaw-puzzle pieces. The orange plastic bowl was cracked.

Her hands were still in her lap, and she was still looking at him. "I guess not, thanks."

Slowly he lifted his glass of beer and took a sip. That was a powerful raise, he thought, forcing himself not to show any astonishment—though you should have suspected a strong hand. Play carefully here.

He glanced toward the bar; but the bartender, if he had looked toward their table at all, had returned his attention to his newspaper.

"Tom Cruise," the woman said.

Moore looked back at her and after a moment raised his eyebrows.

She said, "That was a movie, wasn't it?"

"In a way." *Play carefully here.* "What did you—? Is something wrong with your vision?"

"I don't have any vision. No retinas. I have to use yours. I'm a ghost."

"Ah. I've never met a ghost before." He remembered a line from a Robert Frost poem: *There's something the dead are keeping back.*

"Well, not that you could see. You can see me only because . . . I'm like the stamp you get on the back of your hand at Disneyland; you can't see me unless there's a black light shining on me. *She's* the black light."

"You're in her field of influence, like."

"Sure. There's probably dozens of Pat Moore ghosts in the outfield, and *she's* the whole infield. I'm the shortstop."

"Why doesn't . . . *she* want you to talk to me?" He never drank on days he intended to play, but he lifted his glass again.

"She doesn't want me to tell you what's going to happen." She smiled, and the smile stayed on her smooth face like the expression on a porcelain doll. "If it were up to me, I'd tell you."

He swallowed a mouthful of beer. "But."

She nodded, and at last let her smile relax. "It's not up to me. She'd kill me if I told you."

He opened his mouth to point out a logic problem with that, then sighed and said instead, "Would she know?" She just blinked at him, so he went on, "Would she know it, if you told me?"

"*Oh* yeah."

"How would she know?"

"You'd be doing things. You wouldn't be sitting here drinking, for sure."

"What would I be doing?"

"I think you'd be driving to San Francisco. If I told you—if you asked—" For an instant she was gone, and then he could see her again; but she seemed two-dimensional now, like a projection on a screen—he had the feeling that if he moved to the side, he would just see this image of her get narrower, not see around the other side of her.

"What's in San Francisco?" he asked quickly.

"Well if you asked me about Maxwell's Demon-n-n-n—"

She was perfectly motionless, and the drone of the last consonant slowly deepened in pitch to silence. Then the popcorn in the cracked bowl rattled in the same instant that she silently disappeared like the picture on a switched-off television set, leaving Moore alone at the table, his face suddenly chilly in the bar's air-conditioning. For a moment *air-conditioning* seemed to remind him of something, but he forgot it when he looked down at the popcorn—the bowl was full of brown BBs, unpopped dried corn. As he watched, each kernel slowly opened in white curls and blobs until all the popcorn was as fresh looking and uncrushed as it had been when he had carried it to the table. There hadn't been a sound, though he caught a strong whiff of gasoline. The bowl wasn't cracked anymore.

He stood up and kicked his stool aside as he backed away from the table. She was definitely gone.

The bartender was looking at him now, but Moore hurried past him and back through the hallway to the stormy gray daylight.

What if she had backup? he thought as he fumbled the keys out of his pocket; and, *She doesn't want me to tell you what's going to happen.*

He realized that he'd been sprinting only when he scuffed to a halt on the wet asphalt beside the old white Dodge, and he was panting as he unlocked the door and yanked it open. Rain on the pavement was a steady textured hiss. He climbed in and pulled the door closed, and had rammed the key into the ignition—

—when the drumming of rain on the car roof abruptly went silent, and a voice spoke in his head: *Relax. I'm you. You're me.*

And then his mouth had opened and the words were coming out of his mouth: "We're Pat Moore, there's nothing to be afraid of." His voice belonged to someone else in this muffled silence.

His eyes were watering with the useless effort to breathe for himself.

He knew this wasn't the Pat Moore he had been in the bar with. This was the *her* she had spoken of. A moment later the thoughts had been wiped away, leaving nothing but an insistent pressure of *all-is-well.*

Though nothing grabbed him, he found that his head was turning to the right, and with dimming vision he saw that his right hand was moving toward his face.

But *all-is-well* had for some time been a feeling that was alien to him, and he managed to resist it long enough to make his infiltrated mind form a thought—she's crowding me out.

And he managed to think too: Alive or dead, stay whole. He reached down to the open seam in the seat before he could lose his left arm too, and he snatched up the revolver and stabbed the barrel into his open mouth. A moment later he felt the click through the steel against his teeth when he cocked the hammer back. His belly coiled icily, as if he were standing on the coping of a very high wall and looking up.

The intrusion in his mind paused, and he sensed confusion, and so he threw at it the thought, *One more step, and I blow my head off.* He added, *Go ahead and call this bet, please. I've been meaning to drive the 101 for a while now.*

His throat was working to form words that he could only guess at, and then he was in control of his own breathing again, panting and huffing spit into the gun barrel. Beyond the hammer of the gun, he could see the rapid distortions of rain hitting the windshield, but he still couldn't hear anything from outside the car.

The voice in his head was muted now: *I mean to help you.*

He let himself pull the gun away from his mouth, though he kept it pointed at his face, and he spoke into the wet barrel as if it were a microphone. "I don't want help," he said hoarsely.

I'm Pat Moore, and I want help.

"You want to . . . take over, possess me."

I want to protect you. A man tried to kill you.

"That's your pals," he said, remembering what the ghost woman had told him in the car. "Your disciples, trying to kill all the Pat Moores—to keep you from taking one over, I bet. Don't joggle me now." Staring down the rifled barrel, he cautiously hooked his thumb over the hammer and then pulled the trigger and eased the hammer down. "I can still do it with one pull of the trigger," he told her as he lifted his thumb away. "So you—what, you put off mailing the letter, and died?"

The letter is just my chain mail. The only important thing about it is my name, and the likelihood that people will reproduce it and pass it on. Bombers evade radar by throwing clouds of tinfoil. The chain mail is my name, scattered everywhere so that any blow directed at me is dissipated.

"So you're a ghost too."

A prepared ghost. I know how to get outside of time.

"Fine, get outside of time. What do you need me for?"

You're alive, and your name is mine, which is to say your identity is mine. I've used too much of my energy saving you, holding you. And you're the most compatible of them all—you're a Pat Moore identity squared, by marriage.

"Squared by—" He closed his eyes and nearly lowered the gun. "Everybody called her Trish," he whispered. "Only her mother called her Pat." He couldn't feel the seat under him, and he was afraid that if he let go of the gun, it would fall to the car's roof.

Her mother called her Pat.

"You can't have me." He was holding his voice steady with an effort. "I'm driving away now."

You're Pat Moore's only hope.

"You need an exorcist, not a poker player." He could move his right arm again, and he started the engine and then switched on the windshield wipers.

Abruptly the drumming of the rain came back on, sounding loud after the long silence. She was gone.

His hands were shaking as he tucked the gun back into its pocket, but he was confident that he could get back onto the 280, even with his worn-out windshield wipers blurring everything, and he had no intention of getting on the 101 any time soon; he had been almost entirely bluffing when he told her, *I've been meaning to drive the 101 for a while now.* But like an alcoholic who tries one drink after long abstinence, he was remembering the taste of the gun barrel in his mouth: That was easier than I thought it would be, he thought.

He fumbled a pack of Marlboros out of his jacket pocket and shook one out.

As soon as he had got onto the northbound 85, he became aware that the purple dress and the dark hair were blocking the passenger-side window again, and he didn't jump at all. He had wondered which way to turn on the 280, and now he steered the car into the lane that would take him back north, toward San Francisco. The grooved interchange lane gleamed with fresh rain, and he kept his speed down to forty.

"One big U-turn," he said finally, speaking around his lit cigarette. He glanced at her; she looked three-dimensional again, and she was smiling at him as cheerfully as ever.

"I'm your guardian angel," she said.

"Right, I remember. And your name's Pat Moore, same as mine. Same as everybody's, lately." He realized that he was optimistic, which surprised him; it was something like the happy confidence he had felt in dreams in which he had discovered that he could fly and leave behind all earthbound reproaches. "I met *her,* you know. She's dead too, and she needs a living body, and so she tried to possess me."

"Yes," said Pat Moore. "That's what's going to happen. I couldn't tell you before."

He frowned. "I scared her off, by threatening to shoot myself." Reluctantly he asked, "Will she try again, do you think?"

"Sure. When you're asleep, probably, since this didn't work. She can wait a few hours—a few days, even, in a pinch. It was just because I talked to you that she switched me off and tried to do it right away, while you were still awake. *Jumped the gun,*" she added, with the first laugh he had heard from her. It sounded as if she were trying to chant in a language she didn't understand.

"Ah," he said softly. "That raises the ante." He took a deep breath and let it out. "When did you . . . die?"

"I don't know. Some time besides now. Could you put out the cigarette? The smoke messes up my reception; I'm still partly seeing that bar, and partly a hilltop in a park somewhere."

He rolled the window down an inch and flicked the cigarette out. "Is this how you looked, when you were alive?"

She touched her hair as he glanced at her. "I don't know."

"When you were alive—did you know about movies, and current news? I mean, you don't seem to know about them now."

"I suppose I did. Don't most people?"

He was gripping the wheel hard now. "Did your mother call you Pat?"

"I suppose she did. It's my name."

"Did your . . . friends, call you Trish?"

"I suppose they did."

I suppose, I suppose! He forced himself not to shout at her. She's dead, he reminded himself, she's probably doing the best she can.

But again he thought of the Frost line: *There's something the dead are keeping back.*

They had passed under two gray concrete bridges, and now he switched on his left turn signal to merge with the northbound 280. The pavement ahead of him glittered with reflected red brake lights.

"See, my wife's name was Patricia Moore," he said, trying to sound reasonable. "She died in a car crash five months ago. Well, a single-car accident. Drove off a freeway embankment. She was drunk." He remembered that the popcorn in the Pirate's Cove had momentarily smelled like spilled gasoline.

"I've been drunk."

"So has everybody. But—you might be her."

"Who?"

"My wife. Trish."

"I might be your wife."

"Tell me about Maxwell's Demon."

"I would have been married to you, you mean. We'd *really* have been Pat Moore then. Like mirrors reflecting each other."

"That's why *she* wants me, right. So what's Maxwell's Demon?"

"It's . . . She's dead, so she's like a smoke ring somebody puffed out in the air, if they were smoking. Maxwell's Demon keeps her from disappearing like a smoke ring would, it keeps her . . ."

"Distinct," Moore said when she didn't go on. "Even though she's got no right to be distinct anymore."

"And me. Through her."

"Can I kill him? Or make him stop sustaining her?" And you, he thought; it would stop him sustaining you. Did I stop sustaining you before? Well, obviously.

Earthbound reproaches.

"It's not a *him,* really. It looks like a sprinkler you'd screw onto a hose, to water your yard, if it would spin. It's in her house, hooked up to the air-conditioning."

"A sprinkler." He was nodding repeatedly, and he made himself stop. "Okay. Can you show me where her house is? I'm going to have to sleep sometime."

"She'd kill me."

"Pat—Trish—" Instantly he despised himself for calling her by that name. "—you're already dead."

"She can get outside of time. Ghosts aren't really in time anyway. I'm wrecking the popcorn in that bar in the future as much as in the past, it's all just cards in a circle on a table, none in front. None of it's really now or not-now. She could make me not ever—she could take my thread out of the carpet—you'd never have met me, even like this."

"Make you never have existed."

"Right. Never was any me at all."

"She wouldn't dare—Pat." Just from self-respect, he couldn't bring himself to call her Trish again. "Think about it. If you never existed, then I wouldn't have married you, and so I wouldn't be the Pat Moore squared that she needs."

"If you *did* marry me. *Me,* I mean. I can't remember. Do you think you did?"

She'll take me there, if I say yes, he thought. She'll believe me if I say it. And what's to become of me, if she doesn't? That woman very nearly crowded me right out of the world five minutes ago, and I was wide awake.

The memory nauseated him.

What becomes of a soul that's pushed out of its body, he thought, as *she* means to do to me? Would there be *anything* left of *me,* even a half-wit ghost like poor Pat here?

Against his will came the thought, You always did lie to her.

"I don't know," he said finally. "The odds are against it."

There's always the 101, he told himself, and somehow the thought wasn't entirely bleak. Six chambers of it, hollow-point .38s. Fly away.

"It's possible, though, isn't it?"

He exhaled, and nodded. "It's possible, yes."

"I think I owe it to you. Some Pat Moore does. We left you alone."

"It was my fault." In a rush he added, "I was even glad you didn't leave a note." It's true, he thought. I was grateful.

"I'm glad she didn't leave a note," this Pat Moore said.

He needed to change the subject. "*You're* a ghost," he said. "Can't you make *her* never have existed?"

"No. I can't get far from real places or I'd blur away, out of focus, but she can go way up high, where you can look down on the whole carpet, and—twist out strands of it; bend somebody at right angles to *everything,* which means you're gone without a trace. And anyway, she and her students are all blocked against that kind of attack, they've got ConfigSafe."

He laughed at the analogy. "You know about computers?"

"No," she said emptily. "Did I?"

He sighed. "No, not a lot." He thought of the revolver in the seat, and then thought of something better. "You mentioned a park. You used to like Buena Vista Park. Let's stop there on the way."

Moore drove clockwise around the tall, darkly wooded hill that was the park, while the peaked roofs and cylindrical towers of the old Victorian houses were teeth on a saw passing across the gray sky on his left. He found a parking space on the eastern curve of Buena Vista Avenue, and he got out of the car quickly to keep the Pat Moore ghost from having to open the door on her side; he remembered what she had done to the bowl of popcorn.

But she was already standing on the splashing pavement in the rain, without having opened the door. In the ashy daylight, her purple dress seemed to have lost all its color, and her face was indistinct and pale; he peered at her, and he was sure the heavy raindrops were falling right through her.

He could imagine her simply dissolving on the hike up to the meadow. "Would you rather wait in the car?" he said. "I won't be long."

"Do you have a pair of binoculars?" she asked. Her voice too was frail out here in the cold.

"Yes, in the glove compartment." Cold rain was soaking his hair and leaking down inside his jacket collar, and he wanted to get moving. "Can you . . . *hold* them?"

"I can't hold anything. But if you take out the lens in the middle you can catch me in it, and carry me."

He stepped past her to open the passenger-side door and bent over to pop open the glove compartment, and then he knelt on the seat and dragged out his old leather-sleeved binoculars and turned them this way and that in the wobbly gray light that filtered through the windshield.

"How do I get the lens out?" he called over his shoulder.

"A screwdriver, I guess," came her voice, barely audible above the thrashing of the rain. "See the tiny screw by the eyepiece?"

"Oh. Right." He used the small blade from his pocketknife on the screw in the back of the left barrel, and then had to do the same with a similar screw on the forward side of it. The eyepiece stayed where it was, but the big forward lens fell out, exposing a metal cross on the inside; it was held down with a screw that he managed to rotate with the knife tip—and then a triangular block of polished glass fell out into his palm.

"That's it—that's the lens," she called from outside the car.

Moore's cell phone buzzed as he was stepping backward to the pavement, and he fumbled it out of his jacket pocket and flipped it open. "Moore here," he said. He pushed the car door closed and leaned over the phone to keep the rain off it.

"Hey Pat," came Rick's voice, "I'm sitting here in your Garden City Club in San Jose, and I could be at the Bay. Where are you, man?"

The Pat Moore ghost was moving her head, and Moore looked up at her. With evident effort, she was making her head swivel back and forth in a clear *no* gesture.

The warning chilled Moore. Into the phone he said, "I'm—not far, I'm at a bar off the 85. Place called the Pirate's Cove."

"Well, don't chug your beer on my account. But come over here when you can."

"You bet. I'll be out of here in five minutes." He closed the phone and dropped it back into his pocket.

"They made him call again," said the ghost. "They lost track of your car after I killed the guy with the shotgun." She smiled, and her teeth seemed to be gone. "That was good, saying you were at that bar. They can tell truth from lies, and that's only twenty minutes from being true."

Guardian angel, he thought. "You killed him?"

"I think so." Her image faded, then solidified again. "Yes."

"Ah. Well—good." With his free hand he pushed the wet hair back from his forehead. "So what do I do with this?" he asked, holding up the lens.

"Hold it by the frosted sides, with the long edge of the triangle pointed at me; then look at me through the two other edges."

The glass thing was a blocky right-triangle, frosted on the sides but polished smooth and clear on the thick edges; obediently he held it up to his eye and peered through the two slanted faces of clear glass.

He could see her clearly through the lens—possibly more clearly than when he looked at her directly—but this was a mirror image: the dark slope of the park appeared to be to the left of her.

"Now roll it over a quarter turn, like from noon to three," she said.

He rotated the lens ninety degrees—but her image in it rotated a full 180 degrees, so that instead of seeing her horizontal, he saw her upside down.

He jumped then, for her voice was right in his ear. "Close your eyes, and put the lens in your pocket."

He did as she said, and when he opened his eyes again, she was gone—

the wet pavement stretched empty to the curbstones and green lawns of the old houses.

"You've got me in your pocket," her voice said in his ear. "When you want me, look through the lens again and turn it back the other way."

It occurred to him that he believed her. "Okay," he said, and sprinted across the street to the narrow stone stairs that led up into the park.

His leather shoes splashed in the mud as he took the path to the left. The city was gone now, hidden behind the dense overhanging boughs of pine and eucalyptus, and the rain echoed under the canopy of green leaves. The cold air was musky with the smells of mulch and pine and wet loam.

Up at the level playground lawn, the swing sets were of course empty, and in fact he seemed to be the only living soul in the park today. Through gaps between the trees, he could see San Francisco spread out below him on all sides, as still as a photograph under the heavy clouds.

He splashed through the gutters that were made of fragments of old marble headstones—keeping his head down, he glimpsed an incised cross filled with mud in the face of one stone, and the lone phrase IN LOVING MEMORY on another—and then he had come to the meadow with the big old oak trees he remembered.

He looked around, but there was still nobody to be seen in the cathedral space, and he hurried to the side and crouched to step in under the shaggy foliage and catch his breath.

"It's beautiful," said the voice in his ear.

"Yes," he said, and he took the lens out of his pocket. He held it up and squinted through the right-angle panels, and there was the image of her, upside down. He rotated it counterclockwise ninety degrees, and the image was upright, and when he moved the lens away from his eye, she was standing out in the clearing.

"Look at the city some more," she said, and her voice now seemed to come from several yards away. "So I can see it again."

One last time, he thought. Maybe for both of us; it's nice that we can do it together.

"Sure." He stepped out from under the oak tree and walked back out into the rain to the middle of the clearing and looked around.

A line of trees to the north was the panhandle of Golden Gate Park, and past that he could see the stepped levels of Alta Vista Park; more distantly to the left he could just make out the green band that was the hills of the Presidio, though the two big piers of the Golden Gate Bridge were lost behind miles of rain; he turned to look southwest, where the Twin Peaks and the TV tower on Mount Sutro were vivid above the misty streets; and then far away to the east the white spike of the Transamerica Pyramid stood up from the skyline at the very edge of visibility.

"It's beautiful," she said again. "Did you come here to look at it?"

"No," he said, and he lowered his gaze to the dark mulch under the trees. Cypress, eucalyptus, pine, oak—even from out here he could see that mushrooms were clustered in patches and rings on the carpet of wet black leaves, and he walked back to the trees and then shuffled in a crouch into the aromatic dimness under the boughs.

After a couple of minutes, "Here's one," he said, stooping to pick a mushroom. Its tan cap was about two inches across, covered with a patch of white veil. He unsnapped his denim jacket and tucked the mushroom carefully into his shirt pocket.

"What is it?" asked Pat Moore.

"I don't know," he said. "My wife was never able to tell, so she never picked it. It's either *Amanita lanei,* which is edible, or it's *Amanita phalloides,* which is fatally poisonous. You'd need a real expert to know which this is."

"What are you going to do with it?"

"I think I'm going to sandbag *her*. You want to hop back into the lens for the hike down the hill?"

He had parked the old Dodge at an alarming slant on Jones Street on the south slope of Russian Hill, and then the two of them had walked steeply uphill past close-set gates and balconies under tall sidewalk trees that grew straight up from the slanted pavements. Headlights of cars descending Jones Street reflected in white glitter on the wet trunks and curbstones, and in the wakes of the cars the tire tracks blurred away slowly in the continuing rain.

"How are we going to get into her house?" he asked quietly.

"It'll be unlocked," said the ghost. "She's expecting you now."

He shivered. "Is she. Well, I hope I'm playing a better hand than she guesses."

"Down here," said Pat, pointing at a brick-paved alley that led away to the right between the Victorian-gingerbread porches of two narrow houses.

They were in a little alley now, overhung with rosebushes and rosemary, with white-painted fences on either side. Columns of fog billowed in the breeze, and then he noticed that they were human forms—female torsos twisting transparently in the air, blank-faced children running in slow motion, hunched figures swaying heads that changed shape like water balloons.

"The outfielders," said the Pat Moore ghost.

Now Moore could hear their voices: *Goddam car—I got yer unconditional right here—Excuse me, you got a problem?—He was never there for me—So I told him, you want it, you come over here and take it—Bless me, Father, I have died—*

The acid smell of wet stone was lost in the scents of tobacco and jasmine perfume and liquor and old, old sweat.

Moore bit his lip and tried to focus on the solid pavement and the fences. "Where the hell's her place?" he asked tightly.

"This gate," she said. "Maybe you'd better—"

He nodded and stepped past her; the gate latch had no padlock, and he flipped up the catch. The hinges squeaked as he swung the gate inward over flagstones and low-cut grass.

He looked up at the house the path led to. It was a one-story 1920s bungalow, painted white or gray, with green wicker chairs on the narrow porch. Lights were on behind stained glass panels in the two windows and the porch door.

"It's unlocked," said the ghost.

He turned back toward her. "Stand over by the roses there," he told her, "away from the . . . the outfielders. I want to take you in in my pocket, okay?"

"Okay."

She drifted to the roses, and he fished the lens out of his pocket and found her image in the right-angle faces, then twisted the lens and put it back into his pocket.

He walked slowly up the path, stepping on the grass rather than on the flagstones, and stepped up to the porch.

"It's not locked, Patrick," came a woman's loud voice from inside.

He turned the purple-glass knob and walked several paces into a high-ceilinged kitchen with a black-and-white tiled floor; a blond woman in jeans and a sweatshirt sat at a Formica table by the big old refrigerator. From the next room, beyond an arch in the white-painted plaster, a steady whistling hiss provided an irritating background noise, as if a tea kettle were boiling.

The woman at the table was much more clearly visible than his guardian angel had been, almost aggressively three-dimensional—her breasts under the sweatshirt were prominent and pointed, and her nose and chin stood out perceptibly too far from her high cheekbones, and her lips were so full that they looked distinctly swollen.

A bottle of Wild Turkey bourbon stood beside three *Flintstones* glasses on the table, and she took it in one hand and twisted out the cork with the other. "Have a drink," she said, speaking loudly, perhaps in order to be heard over the hiss in the next room.

"I don't think I will, thanks," he said. "You're good with your hands." His jacket was dripping on the tiles, but he didn't take it off.

"I'm the solidest ghost you'll ever see."

Abruptly she stood up, knocking her chair against the refrigerator, and then she rushed past him, her Reeboks beating on the floor—and her body seemed to rotate as she went by him, as if she were swerving away from him, though her course to the door was straight. She reached out one lumpy hand and slammed the door.

She faced him again and held out her right hand. "I'm Pat Moore," she said, "and I want help."

He flexed his fingers, then cautiously held out his own hand. "I'm Pat Moore too," he said.

Her palm touched his, and though it was moving very slowly, his own hand was slapped away when they touched.

"I want us to become partners," she said. Her thick lips moved in ostentatious synchronization with her words.

"Okay," he said.

Her outlines blurred for just an instant; then she said, in the same booming tone, "I want us to become one person. You'll be immortal, and—"

"Let's do it," he said.

She blinked her black eyes. "You're—agreeing to it," she said. "You're accepting it, now?"

"Yes." He cleared his throat. "That's correct."

He became aware that a figure was sitting at the table. He looked past her and saw that it was a transparent old man in an overcoat, hardly more visible than a puff of smoke.

"Is he Maxwell's Demon?" Moore asked.

The woman smiled, baring huge teeth. "No, that's . . . a soliton. A poor little soliton who's lost its way. I'll show you Maxwell's Demon."

She lunged and clattered into the next room, and Moore followed her, trying simultaneously not to slip on the floor and to keep an eye on her and on the misty old man.

He stepped into a parlor, and the hissing noise was louder in here. Carved dark wood tables and chairs and a modern exercise bicycle had been pushed against a curtained bay window in the far wall, and a vast carpet had been rolled back from the dusty hardwood floor and humped against the chair legs. In the high corners of the room and along the fluted top of the window frame, things like translucent cheerleaders' pom-poms grimaced and waved tentacles or locks of hair in the agitated air. Moore warily took a step away from them.

"Look over here," said the alarming woman.

In the near wall, an air-conditioning panel had been taken apart, and a red rubber hose hung from its machinery and was connected into the side of a length of steel pipe that lay on a TV table. Nozzles on either end of the pipe were making the loud whistling sound.

Moore looked more closely at it. It was apparently two sections of pipe, one about eight inches long and the other about four, connected together by a blocky fitting where the hose was attached, and a stove stopcock stood half-open near the end of the longer pipe.

"Feel the air," the woman said.

Moore cupped a hand near the end of the longer pipe and then yanked it back—the air blasting out of it felt hot enough to light a cigar. More cautiously he waved his fingers over the nozzle at the end of the short pipe; and then he rolled his hand in the air jet, for it was icy cold.

"*It's* not supernatural," she boomed, "even though the air conditioner's set for seventy. A spiral washer in the connector housing sends air spinning up the long pipe; the hot molecules spin out to the sides of the little whirlwind in there, and it's them that the stopcock lets out. The cold molecules fall into a smaller whirlwind inside the big one, and they move the opposite way and come out at the end of the short pipe. Room-temperature air is a mix of hot and cold molecules, and this device separates them out."

"Okay," said Moore. He spoke levelly, but he was wishing he had brought his gun along from the car. It occurred to him that it was a rifled pipe that things usually come spinning out of, but which he had been ready to dive into. He wondered if the gills under the cap of the mushroom in his pocket were curved in a spiral.

"But this is counterentropy," she said, smiling again. "A Scottish physicist named Maxwell p-postulay-postul—guessed that a Demon would be needed to sort the hot molecules from the cold ones. If the Demon is present, the effect occurs, and vice versa—if you can make the effect occur, you've summoned the Demon. Get the effect, and the cause has no choice but to be present." She thumped her chest, though her peculiar breasts didn't move at all. "And once the Demon is present, he—he—"

She paused, so Moore said, "Maintains distinctions that wouldn't ordinarily stay distinct." His heart was pounding, but he was pleased with how steady his voice was.

Something like an invisible hand struck him solidly in the chest, and he stepped back.

"You don't touch it," she said. Again there was an invisible thump against his chest. "Back to the kitchen."

The soliton old man, hardly visible in the bright overhead light, was still nodding in one of the chairs at the table.

The blond woman was slapping the wall, and then a white-painted cabinet, but when Moore looked toward her, she grabbed the knob on one of the cabinet drawers and yanked it open.

"You need to come over here," she said, "and look in the drawer."

After the things he'd seen in the high corners of the parlor, Moore was cautious; he leaned over and peered into the drawer—but it contained only a stack of typing paper, a felt-tip laundry-marking pen, and half a dozen yo-yos.

As he watched, she reached past him and snatched out a sheet of paper and the laundry marker; and it occurred to him that she hadn't been able to see the contents of the drawer until he was looking at them.

I don't have any vision, his guardian angel had said. *No retinas. I have to use yours.*

The woman had stepped away from the cabinet now. "I was prepared, see," she said loudly enough to be heard out on Jones Street, "for my stupid students killing me. I knew they might. We were all working to learn how to transcend time, but I got there first, and they were afraid of what I would do. So *boom-boom-boom* for Mistress Moore. But I had already set up the Demon, and I had Xeroxed my chain mail and put it in addressed envelopes. Bales of them, the stamps cost me a fortune. I came back strong. And I'm going to merge with you now and get a real body again. You accepted the proposal—you said 'Yes, that's correct'—you didn't put out another bet this time to chase me away."

The cap flew off the laundry marker, and then she had slapped the paper down on the table next to the Wild Turkey bottle. "Watch me!" she said, and when he looked at the piece of paper, she began vigorously writing on it. Soon she had written *Pat* in big sprawling letters and was embarked on *Moore.*

She straightened up when it was finished. "Now," she said, her black eyes glittering with hunger, "you cut your hand and write with your blood, tracing over the letters. Our name is us, and we'll merge. Smooth as silk through a goose."

Moore slowly dug the pocketknife out of his pants pocket. "This is new," he said. "you didn't do this name-in-blood business when you tried to take me in the car."

She waved one big hand dismissively. "I thought I could sneak up on you. You resisted me, though—you'd probably have tried to resist me even in your sleep. But since you're accepting the inevitable now, we can do a proper contract, in ink and blood. Cut, cut!"

"Okay," he said, and unfolded the short blade and cut a nick in his right forefinger. "*You've* made a new bet now, though, and it's to me." Blood was dripping from the cut, and he dragged his finger over the *P* in her crude signature.

He had to pause halfway through and probe again with the blade tip to get more freely flowing blood; and as he was painfully tracing the *R* in *Moore,* he began to feel another will helping his hand to push his finger along, and he heard a faint drone like a radio carrier wave starting up in his head. Somewhere he was crouched on his toes on a narrow, outward-tilting ledge with no handholds anywhere, with vast volumes of emptiness below him—and his toes were sliding—

So he added quickly, "And I raise back at you."

By touch alone, looking up at the high ceiling, he pulled the mushroom out of his shirt pocket and popped it into his mouth and bit down on it. Check and raise, he thought. Sandbagged. Then he lowered his eyes, and in an instant her gaze was locked on to his.

"What happened?" she demanded, and Moore could hear the three syllables of it chug in his own throat. "What did you do?"

"*Amanita,*" said the smoky old man at the table. His voice sounded like nothing organic—more like sandpaper on metal. "It was time to eat the mushroom."

Moore had resolutely chewed the thing up, his teeth grating on bits of dirt. It had the cold-water taste of ordinary mushrooms, and as he forced himself to swallow it, he forlornly hoped, in spite of all his bravura thoughts about the 101 freeway, that it might be the *lanei* rather than the deadly *phalloides.*

"He ate a mushroom?" the woman demanded of the old man. "You never told me about any mushroom! Is it a poisonous mushroom?"

"I don't know," came the rasping voice again. "It's either poisonous or not, though, I remember that much."

Moore was dizzy with the first twinges of comprehension of what he had done. "Fifty-fifty chance," he said tightly. "The death-cap *Amanita* looks just like another one that's harmless, both grown locally. I picked this one today, and I don't know which it was. If it's the poison one, we won't know for about twenty-four hours, maybe longer."

The drone in Moore's head grew suddenly louder, then faded until it was imperceptible. "You're telling the truth," she said. She flung out an arm toward the back porch, and for a moment her bony forefinger was a foot long. "Go vomit it up, now!"

He twitched, like someone mistaking the green left-turn arrow for the green light. No, he told himself, clenching his fists to conceal any trembling. Fifty-fifty is better than zero. You've clocked the odds and placed your bet. Trust yourself.

"No good," he said. "The smallest particle will do the job, if it's the poisonous one. Enough's probably been absorbed already. That's why I chose it." This was a bluff, or a guess, anyway, but this time she didn't scan his mind.

He was tense, but a grin was twitching at his lips. He nodded toward the old man and asked her, "Who *is* the lost sultan, anyway?"

"Soliton," she snapped. "He's you, you—dumb-brain." She stamped one foot, shaking the house. "How can I take you now? And I can't wait twenty-four hours just to see if I *can* take you!"

"Me? How is he me?"

"My name's Pat Moore," said the gray silhouette at the table.

"Ghosts are solitons," she said impatiently, "waves that keep moving all-in-a-piece after the living push has stopped. Forward or backward doesn't matter to them."

"I'm from the *future,*" said the soliton, perhaps grinning.

Moore stared at the indistinct thing, and he had to repress an urge to run over there and tear it apart, try to set fire to it, stuff it in a drawer. And he realized that the sudden chill on his forehead wasn't from fright, as he had at first assumed, but from profound embarrassment at the thing's presence here.

"I've blown it all on you," the blond woman said, perhaps to herself even though her voice boomed in the tall kitchen. "I don't have the . . . sounds like *courses* . . . I don't have the energy reserves to go after another living Pat Moore *now*. You were perfect, Pat Moore squared—why did you have to be a die-hard suicide fan?"

Moore actually laughed at that—and she glared at him in the same instant that he was punched backward off his feet by the hardest invisible blow yet.

He sat down hard and slid, and his back collided with the stove; and then, though he could still see the walls and the old man's smoky legs under the table across the room and the glittering rippled glass of the windows, he was somewhere else. He could feel the square tiles under his palms, but in this other place he had no body.

In the now-remote kitchen, the blond woman said, "Drape him," and the soliton got up and drifted across the floor toward Moore, shrinking as it came so that its face was on a level with Moore's.

Its face was indistinct—pouches under the empty eyes, drink-wrinkles spilling diagonally across the cheekbones, petulant lines around the mouth—and Moore did not try to recognize himself in it.

The force that had knocked Moore down was holding him pressed against the floor and the stove, unable to crawl away, and all he could do was hold his breath as the soliton ghost swept over him like a spiderweb.

You've got a girl in your pocket, came the thing's raspy old voice in his ear.

Get away from me, Moore thought, nearly gagging.

Who get away from who?

"I can get another living Pat Moore," the blond woman was saying, "if I never wasted any effort on you in the first place, if there was never a *you* for me to notice." He heard her take a deep breath. "I can do this."

Her knee touched his cheek, slamming his head against the oven door. She was leaning over the top of the stove, banging blindly at the burners and the knobs, and then Moore heard the triple click of one of the knobs turning, and the faint thump of the flame coming on. He peered up and saw that she was holding the sheet of paper with the ink and blood on it, and then he could smell the paper burning.

Moore became aware that there was still the faintest drone in his head only a moment before it ceased.

"Up," she said, and the ghost was a net surrounding Moore, lifting him up off the floor and through the intangible roof and far away from the rainy shadowed hills of San Francisco.

He was aware that his body was still in the house, still slumped against the stove in the kitchen, but his soul, indistinguishable now from his ghost, was in some vast region where *in front* and *behind* had no meaning, where the once-apparent dichotomy between *here* and *there* was a discarded optical illusion, where comprehension was total but didn't depend on light or sight or perspective, and where even *ago* and *to come* were just compass points; everything was in stasis, for motion had been left far behind with sequential time.

He knew that the long braids or vapor trails that he encompassed and that surrounded him were lifelines, stretching from births in that direction to deaths in the other—some linked to others for varying intervals, some curving alone through the non-sky—but they were more like long electrical arcs than anything substantial even by analogy; they were stretched across time and space, but at the same time, they were coils too infinitesimally small to be perceived, if his perception had been by means of sight; and they were electrons in standing waves surrounding an unimaginable nucleus, which also surrounded them—the universe, apprehended here in its full volume of past and future, was one enormous and eternal atom.

But he could feel the tiles of the kitchen floor beneath his fingertips. He dragged one hand up his hip to the side pocket of his jacket, and his fingers slipped inside and touched the triangular lens.

No, said the soliton ghost, a separate thing again.

Moore was still huddled on the floor, still touching the lens—but he and his ghost were sitting on the other side of the room at the kitchen table too, and the ghost was holding a deck of cards in one hand and spinning cards out with the other. It stopped when two cards lay in front of each of them. The Wild Turkey bottle was gone, and the glow from the ceiling lamp was a dimmer yellow than it had been.

"Hold 'Em," the ghost rasped. "Your whole lifeline is the buy-in, and I'm going to take it away from you. You've got a tall stack there, birth to now, but I won't go all-in on you right away. I bet our first seven years—Fudgsicles, our dad flying kites in the spring sunsets, the star decals in constellations on our bedroom ceiling, our mom reading the Narnia books out loud to us. Push 'em out." The air in the kitchen was summery with the pink candy smell of Bazooka gum.

Hold 'Em, thought Moore. I'll raise.

Trish killed herself, he projected at his ghost, *rather than live with us anymore. Drove her Granada over the embankment off the 101. The police said she was doing ninety, with no touch of the brake.* Again he smelled spilled gasoline—

—and so, apparently, did his opponent; the pouchy-faced old ghost flickered but came back into focus. "I make it more," said the ghost. "The next seven. Bicycles, the Albert Payson Terhune books, hiking with Joe and

Ken in the oil fields, the Valentine from Theresa What's-her-name. Push 'em out, or forfeit."

Neither of them had looked at their cards, and Moore hoped the game wouldn't proceed to the eventual arbitrary showdown—he hoped that the frail ghost wouldn't be able to keep sustaining raises.

I can't hold anything, his guardian angel had said.

It hurt Moore, but he projected another raise at the ghost: *When we admitted we had deleted her poetry files deliberately, she said "You're not a nice man." She was drunk, and we laughed at that when she said it, but one day after she was gone, we remembered it, and then we had to pull over to the side of the road because we couldn't see through the tears to drive.*

The ghost was just a smoky sketch of a midget or a monkey now, and Moore doubted it had enough substance even to deal the next three cards. In a faint birdlike voice it said, "The next seven. College, and our old motorcycle, and—"

And Trish at twenty, Moore finished, grinding his teeth and thinking about the mushroom dissolving in his stomach. *We talked her into taking her first drink. Pink gin, Tanqueray with Angostura bitters. And we were pleased when she said, "Where has this been all my life?"*

"All my life," whispered the ghost, and then it flicked away like a reflection in a dropped mirror.

The blond woman was sitting there instead. "What did you have?" she boomed, nodding toward his cards.

"The winning hand," said Moore. He touched his two facedown cards. "The pot's mine—the raises got too high for him." The cards blurred away like fragments left over from a dream.

Then he hunched forward and gripped the edge of the table, for the timeless vertiginous gulf, the infinite atom of the lifelines, was a sudden pressure from outside the world, and this artificial scene had momentarily lost its depth of field.

"I can twist your thread out, even without his help," she told him. She frowned, and a vein stood out on her curved forehead, and the kitchen table resumed its cubic dimensions and the light brightened. "Even dead, I'm more potent than you are."

She whirled her massive right arm up from below the table and clanked down her elbow, with her forearm upright; her hand was open.

Put me behind her, Pat, said the Pat Moore ghost's remembered voice in his ear.

He made himself feel the floor tiles under his hand and the stove at his back, and then he pulled the triangular lens out of his pocket; and when he held it up to his eye, he was able to see himself and the blond woman at the table across the room, and the Pat Moore ghost was visible upside down behind the woman. He rotated the glass a quarter turn, and she was now upright.

He moved the lens away and blinked, and then he was gripping the edge of the table and looking across it at the blond woman, and at her hand only a foot away from his face. The fingerprints were like comb-tracks in clay. Peripherally he could see the slim Pat Moore ghost, still in the purple dress, standing behind her.

"Arm wrestling?" he said, raising his eyebrows. He didn't want to let go of the table, or even move—this localized perspective seemed very frail.

The woman only glared at him out of her irisless eyes. At last he leaned back in the chair and unclamped the fingers of his right hand from the table edge; and then he shrugged and raised his right arm and set his elbow beside hers. With her free hand she picked up his pocketknife and hefted it. "When this thing hits the floor, we start." She clasped his hand, and his fingers were numbed as if with a hard impact.

Her free hand jerked, and the knife was glittering in a fantastic non-euclidean parabola through the air, and though he was braced all the way through his torso from his firmly planted feet, when the knife clanged against the tiles, the massive power of her arm hit his palm like a falling tree.

Sweat sprang out on his forehead, and his arm was steadily bending backward—and the whole world was rotating too, narrowing, tilting away from him to spill him, all the bets he and his ghost had made, into zero.

In the car, the Pat Moore ghost had told him, *She can bend somebody at right angles to* everything, *which means you're gone without a trace.*

We're not sitting at the kitchen table, he told himself; we're still dispersed in that vaster comprehension of the universe.

And if she rotates me ninety degrees, he was suddenly certain, I'm gone.

And then the frail Pat Moore ghost leaned in from behind the woman and clasped her diaphanous hand around Moore's; and together they were Pat Moore squared, their lifelines linked still by their marriage, and he could feel her strong pulse in supporting counterpoint to his own.

His forearm moved like a counterclockwise second hand in front of his squinting eyes as the opposing pressure steadily weakened. The woman's face seemed in his straining sight to be a rubber mask with a frantic animal trapped inside it, and when only inches separated the back of her hand from the Formica tabletop, the resistance faded to nothing, and his hand was left poised empty in the air.

The world rocked back to solidity with such abruptness that he would have fallen down if he hadn't been sitting on the floor against the stove.

Over the sudden pressure-release ringing in his ears, he heard a scurrying across the tiles on the other side of the room, and a thumping on the hardwood planks in the parlor.

The Pat Moore ghost still stood across the room, beside the table; and the Wild Turkey bottle was on the table, and he was sure it had been there all along.

He reached out slowly and picked up his pocketknife. It was so cold that it stung his hand.

"Cut it," said the ghost of his wife.

"I can't cut it," he said. Barring hallucinations, his body had hardly moved for the past five or ten minutes, but he was panting. "You'll die."

"I'm dead already, Pat. This"—she waved a hand from her shoulder to her knee—"isn't any good. I should be gone." She smiled. "I think that was the *lanei* mushroom."

He knew she was guessing. "I'll know tomorrow."

He got to his feet, still holding the knife. The blade, he saw, was still folded out.

"Forgive me," he said awkwardly. "For everything."

She smiled, and it was almost a familiar smile. "I forgave you in midair. And you forgive me too."

"If you ever did anything wrong, yes."

"Oh, I did. I don't think you noticed. Cut it."

He walked back across the room to the arch that led into the parlor, and he paused when he was beside her.

"I won't come in with you," she said, "if you don't mind."

"No," he said. "I love you, Pat."

"Loved. I loved you too. That counts. Go."

He nodded and turned away from her.

Maxwell's Demon was still hissing on the TV table by the disassembled air conditioner, and he walked to it one step at a time, not looking at the forms that twisted and whispered urgently in the high corners. One seemed to be perceptibly more solid than the rest, but all of them flinched away from him.

He had to blink tears out of his eyes to see the air hose clearly, and when he did, he noticed a plain ON-OFF toggle switch hanging from wires that were still connected to the air-conditioning unit. He cut the hose and switched off the air conditioner, and the silence that fell then seemed to spill out of the house and across San Francisco and into the sky.

He was alone in the house.

He tried to remember the expanded, timeless perspective he had participated in, but his memory had already simplified it to a three-dimensional picture, with himself floating like a bubble in one particular place.

Which of the . . . jet trails or arcs or coils was mine? He wondered now. How long is it?

I'll be better able to guess tomorrow, he thought. At least I know it's there, forever—and even though I didn't see which one it was, I know it's linked to another.

If there's anything in the literary world that **Joyce Carol Oates** *hasn't done, I'd like to know what it is.*

Recent things of hers I've read, stumbled across, noted: We Were the Mulvaneys *(an* Oprah *selection);* The Tattooed Girl, *a new novel; an introduction to* The Best of the Kenyon Review; *another introduction to a paperback edition of Conrad's* The Heart of Darkness and The Secret Sharer. *Believe me, that's only a taste of what she's been up to.*

For us, though, she's in familiar territory, writing a Gothic with Lovecraftian overtones, a dark fantasy that made the hair on the back of my head stand up.

[illegible]: Six Hypotheses

Joyce Carol Oates

The child Fitzie was the first to succumb to what could not yet have been named the [illegible] contagion in the Loving household. It was therefore taken for granted that the [illegible] contagion began with Fitzie, or began in Fitzie. (The linguistic distinction *with/in* is crucial to our understanding of the tragedy.) Yet it's possible to think—and this theory is the most attractive as it is the most impersonal, absolving any individual member of the Loving family of wittingly or unwittingly introducing disaster into their household—it started in Fitzie's small room off the first-floor landing of the Lovings' eighteenth-century stone farmhouse on the Delaware River, Upper Black Eddy, Pennsylvania.

Sometime soon after the March thaw of 1999, when the child was seven years old.

Hypothesis #1: *The Room*

Because, according to witnesses who'd entered Fitzie's room, during and after the time of the [illegible] contagion, the room was *not right*. Just a sensation you had, a visceral sense something is *not right*. The room wasn't on the ground floor of the house, and it wasn't on the second floor with the other bedrooms. It was a dwarf room off the landing, at the rear of the house. Overlooking the bog.

Dwarf room! Why dwarf!

A crude pejorative with a sinister connotation. Dwarf!

The ceiling was at least two inches lower than the ceilings of the other bedrooms. And it was a beamed ceiling, so the beams made it appear even lower. The room used to be a servant's room. Long ago, in the years 1845 to 1863, it was (possibly) used as a stop on the legendary Underground Railway.* When you step through the doorway to enter the room, instinctively you duck your head. If you're an adult, you do. Big Fitzie bumped his head on the damned doorframe more than once, stumbling inside in the night to rescue Little Fitzie from one of the nightmares. Momma Kat, who wasn't nearly so tall as her six-foot-three husband, would instinctively stoop when she entered the room, flinching. Yet it was a cozy room. It was a hideaway kind of room that would appeal to a seven-year-old eager for a room of his own. But there was something about its cramped dimensions that stole your breath like a cave in which oxygen is slowly and irrevocably being depleted.

Not a cave! Not a dwarf room, and not a cave.

Walls, beamed ceiling, woodplank floor, and a dormer window.

Overlooking the bog.

HYPOTHESIS #2: *The Bog*

Swampy rank-smelling profusion of cattails and tall snaky-sinuous rushes that sway, writhe, undulate in the wind as if stroked by a gigantic hand and those beautiful upright deep-purple cluster flowers that begin to bloom in midsummer and continue until the first frost—

Loosestrife.

In early spring coming alive with peepers—a frantic singing/mating of myriad tiny frogs. In summer, thrumming with bullfrogs, nocturnal insects of every species. In the muck in the fecundity of the rank-smelling bog a cascade, a waterfall, ceaseless trill of life seeking blindly to—

Reproduce!

The Lovings. Of whom it would be repeatedly said that they had been, before the disaster, the ideal American family. And that their name was "ironic."

* A number of private residences in Bucks County have been authenticated as stops on the legendary Underground Railway, which provided runaway slaves of the antebellum South hiding places, provisions, and moral support on their way north. The property owned by the Lovings has been designated "historic" by the Bucks County Historical Preservation Society, and the "strong likelihood" is that it was a stop on the Underground Railway.

Big Fitzie a.k.a. Dad-*dy*
Momma Kat a.k.a. Mom-*my*
Dee-Dee a.k.a. Grump
Ray-Ray a.k.a. Awesome Possum
Little Fitzie a.k.a. Tickle
Baby Ceci

More objectively, the Lovings would be identified in the media:

Fritz Loving, 39
Katherine Donahue Loving, 36
Deirdre Loving, 12
Raymond Loving, 10
Fritz Loving Jr., 7
Ceci Loving, 9 months

Hypothesis #3: *Baby Ceci*

That it was not Fitzie but his infant sister who was the (unconscious, unwitting) agent of the contagion. For, who knows what dreams drift through an infant's soft brain? Who knows what (accidental, unrecorded) bumps to an infant's soft skull might provoke such dreams? According to all reports, this youngest and most vulnerable of the Lovings was a "colicky" baby who cried incessantly. Especially in the night. A bundle of frantic shorted-out neurons. Kicking and shrieking red-faced gasping for breath like a tiny pig being smothered and both parents exhausted and sleep-deprived staggering through their daytime lives like somnambulists. Only Momma Kat's heavy milk-filled breasts could quench Baby Ceci's ravenous hunger, temporarily.

Colic. A commonplace medical condition in infants, usually outgrown after three or four months.

Sometime after the March thaw, 1999. In the night, the otherwise healthy, normal seven-year-old began to feel what he called something—some things—that were "tight"—"tighttight"—pulse beats in his head coming "fastfast"—"fastfastfaster"—close to bursting. Nights in succession he whimpered in his sleep, sweated through his pajamas, dampening sheets and mattress. Poor Fitzie who had not wet his bed in years now began again to lose control of his bladder out of agitation. Poor Fitzie terrified by bad dreams. Deeply ashamed of being such a baby. Crying Mom-*my*! Dad-*dy*! in the night so that sleep-dazed Big Fitzie would bump his forehead entering, Momma Kat would stumble barefoot, stubbing a toe, hurrying to hug the frightened child in his bed, Fitzie sweetie it's only a bad dream, only a dream sweetie, your lamp hasn't been turned off, your lamp is on honey, nobody will turn it off, Daddy and Mommy are here now honey, the bad things can't get you, there are no bad things sweetie, nothing to be afraid of nothing trying to squeeze through the window, nothing in the ceiling, see sweetie nothing beneath your bed no alligator or crocodile or Gila monster Mommy and Daddy promise!

When Fitzie's nightmares first began, Momma Kat would remain with him for what remained of the night, cuddling beside the shaken child and dozing off, as sometimes, reassured by his mother, Fitzie would also. As the nightmares continued, Momma Kat had a harder time dozing off in Fitzie's bed, or anywhere.

The change in Fitzie. Fearful now of falling asleep anywhere, not just in his room. For the Up-and-Down Black Things as he'd begun to call them followed him anywhere. Overnight at Grandma's house, the Up-and-Down Things were waiting for him, and angry knowing he'd tried to escape them. Nasty Up-and-Down Things aiming for his eyes, his nostrils. Aiming for his opened mouth as he sucked for air.

Needle Things.

Things.

Trying to explain to his parents how they were tighttight things. Crowded together and going fastfastfaster so it was awful, like his head was on fire.

Fitzie, sweetie, can you draw them for me? Can you?

Momma Kat gave Fitzie a black Crayola and a sheet of construction paper.

Fitzie was frightened at first. Hunched over the paper, panting. As if running. Running uphill. Panting, perspiring. They could see the terror glistening in his eyes. Looking up at Momma Kat and saying finally the crayon was not right, he needed a pencil or a pen, so Momma Kat gave him a felt-tip pen. Fitzie, try!

Momma Kat was astonished: *Musical notes?*

Dee-Dee had begun piano lessons a few months before. Momma Kat, who'd been a fairly serious piano student as a girl, often drifted to the spinet in the living room, battered old Chickering from another era, a few snatched minutes of piano-playing, just fooling around as Katherine called it. Often a child would clamber up on Mommy's lap or cuddle cozily beside her on the piano bench. At seven, Fitzie was a little too big for Momma Kat's lap, but he would cuddle beside her on the bench when she sat down to run her capable hands up and down the keyboard, making the living room windows vibrate and quiver as if with the passing of marching men, making whichever children were within earshot giggle in delight as Momma Kat shifted from one of her prissy-boring old Mozart rondos/Chopin études to boogie-woogie, "Chopsticks," "Battle Hymn of the Republic." For a spell when he was three or four, Fitzie was intrigued by the musical notes, always black, always upright like fishhooks or sea horses on the always-black staves for "treble" and "bass" that were always five lines each never six, never four, never ten, never one hundred and ten, *Why is that, Mommy?* and Mommy laughed saying as she did in reply to many of her children's unanswerable questions *Just is, honey.*

And a wet little kiss.

Having the distraught, sleep-deprived child draw the Things was a mistake. The first of several (unconscious, unwitting) parental mistakes made by the Lovings.

For now the Things acquired shape, visual identity. Once seen, they could not be forgotten. They'd acquired a way *in.*

A way into—what?

A way into Momma Kat.

Poor Dee-Dee!

A healthy pretty girl of twelve. One of the most popular girls in her seventh grade class at Upper Black Eddy Middle School. Always good-natured, smiling. (Calling Dee-Dee "Grump" was a Loving family joke begun when Dee-Dee was a toddler.) Always a good eater, a good sleeper. With her mother's serene disposition, hazel eyes, fair freckled skin. About two weeks after Fitzie began to have trouble sleeping, Dee-Dee began to wake from anxious shallow dreams in which needlelike things were jabbing at her: eyes, nostrils, ears, mouth. Insomnia struck Dee-Dee like a virulent strain of measles. Within a few nights she was desperate. Night fevers, sweating through her pajamas and bedclothes. For most of her young life, Dee-Dee had loved to read, sat up now in bed in the night trying to read but could not concentrate though knowing that the Needle Things were not really in the room with her (she'd checked, every square inch) but could not concentrate embarked upon her journey as Fitzie was embarked upon his unable to comprehend what had happened or was happening or would happen for if you don't sleep Dee-Dee was shortly to discover at home at school at friends' houses if you don't sleep the [illegible] Things being to stalk you in daytime too if you don't sleep you begin to shatter into pieces at mealtimes in the Lovings' spacious country kitchen the [illegible] Things pushing boldly near writhing, undulating turn your head and they leap back out of sight, you see just the afterimage not the [illegible] Things themselves. Like her little brother Fitzie who gagged when he tried to eat, now Dee-Dee who'd always had a healthy appetite began to gag and vomit after a few mouthfuls, and Momma Kat and Big Fitzie were becoming desperate for what was happening to their happy family? What was happening to their happy lives? They had been such devoted parents! They were such devoted parents! Worse yet their insomniac children were not the children they knew. Dee-Dee who'd been such a sweet-natured child had changed by quick degrees into a short-tempered girl grimacing at her family as if she couldn't bear to see them let alone be loved by them, or approached—"Don't touch!" And there was Fitzie sullen and indifferent his teeth glistening with saliva as if he'd have liked to tear out somebody's throat. *These are not our beautiful children, what has happened to our beautiful children?*

Pediatricians, child psychiatrists, and psychotherapists. Some wished to prescribe tranquilizers, barbiturates; some cautioned against powerful psychotropic drugs especially for a seven-year-old. As for Baby Ceci—"She'll grow out of it."

Hypothesis #4: *Demons*

Demons?

There are none.

Ray-Ray, ten years old. For most of his life the "middle" child. Quiet, watchful. Even in his bassinet. With an air of something brooding and withheld. A slender boy, with an olive-pale complexion. Unlike his fair freckled parents who laughed that Ray-Ray was smarter than either of them, must be the emergence of "genius" genes from an obscure ancestor. Ten years old in sixth grade at Upper Black Eddy Elementary, Ray-Ray was allowed to take ninth grade math at the adjoining Middle School; his science teacher was encouraging him to work on a Time Travel project for the upcoming Bucks County School Science Fair, which Ray-Ray was doing with such concentration, you'd think that he believed in time travel. (Did he? Ray-Ray was evasive answering.) Precocious child, you could tell by the eyes. Dreamy theorizing, not very practical minded. Known as the Awesome Possum within the family the reason wasn't clear why, possibly Ray-Ray's dreamy slow-blinking manner at mealtimes lost in his own thoughts while the others are noisy, laughing and teasing one another and in their midst there's Ray-Ray frowning calculating how Time Travel might be achieved. And so when the Things began to invade Ray-Ray's sleep, he had difficulty waking, lacked the capacity to be jolted out of a nightmare by sheer fright into wakefulness. Poor Ray-Ray, only ten years old, enduring nightmares of stress/tension/things-pulling-at-things/vertical things intersecting with horizontal things producing static electricity and these things tightly impacted as if (was this the explanation?) the linear medium of Time that prevents all things from happening simultaneously had begun to fray and buckle, and soon allthingswouldbehappeningatonceintheuniverse and a gigantic black hole would swallow it all. Unlike the other children, Ray-Ray seemed incapable of screaming for his parents to come rescue him. Suffered soaring blood pressure, in danger of blood vessels bursting in his brain. The pediatrician's nurse was stunned taking a reading of the child's blood pressure so much higher than the blood pressure of any child in her experience. Ray-Ray suffered from migraine headaches, eyes leaking tears so he was nearly blind. In school lapsing into a light doze so his teachers despaired of him. A thousand pulses beating in his brain he said as in halting speech tried to explain the emergence of the

Things a door opens in the earth swings upward like an old-fashioned cellar door built slantwise across a flight of crumbling stone steps (like the cellar door at the rear of the old part of the Lovings' house), at once you are drawn down, and inside. At once! No choice but to OBEY! For such doors swing upward opening a kind of vacuum (or BLACK HOLE to use the commonplace metaphor) and always you are swept inside a BLACK HOLE the definition of which is if there could be a single instant when you are conscious of the malevolent presence of a BLACK HOLE it would be the identical instant you are sucked inside the BLACK HOLE, to oblivion.

Ray-Ray began to laugh explaining. Ray-Ray was so much smarter than his bumbling parents. Well-intentioned dummies. In the crude jargon of middle-school assholes. But hey, Ray-Ray loved them. Certainly he loved them. Momma Kat he loved, Big Fitzie his daddy he loved. Drawing on a sheet of paper to show them the BLACK HOLE exerts such a powerful suction it drags into its (limitless, uncharted and unchartable) depths even the memory of an entity. Where/when the entity CEASES TO EXIST its history is simultaneously SUCKED INTO OBLIVION with it.

Ray-Ray was really laughing now. Wiping at his eyes that were looking gluey. The kid's old-young eyes, teachers at the middle school would speak of after his death. Refuting Ray-Ray's terror of forgetfulness, instant oblivion. Ray-Ray rocking with laughter as his anxious parents try to calm him.

Dee-Dee who'd been listening sucking her thumb standing barefoot in the middle of the kitchen smelling of scorched food saying Mom-*my*, Dad-*dy* it's what the Things have come to tell us we will forget each other, too.

Third month of the contagion. Humid midsummer. The bog is fraught with reptilian/insect life. Thrumming through the night and much of the day. A drunk-looking moon swings overhead. Big Fitzie isn't going to abandon his family, spends nights away in Philly the two-hour commute to and from is treacherous when you're sleep-deprived, can't keep your fucking eyes open. Can't sleep at the Dream House but can't sleep anywhere else, either. Shattering into pieces is Big Fitzie. He'd begun to see the things, too. Awake-seeming he has seen. Flying/pecking/jabbing/stabbing black fissures in the air like tears in fabric. Can't focus on the things directly only elliptically. Afterimage not the things themselves. In the corner of Big Fitzie's disintegrating brain.

His doctor has prescribed a barbiturate. Taking this barbiturate leaves Big Fitzie dehydrated and stunned sleeping for nine, twelve, fourteen hours on weekends sleep of the dead, delicious!

High blood pressure, though. Big Fitzie must take beta blockers now, blood thinners, not yet forty years old. One night realizing stone cold sober thinking is not worth the terrible effort required like running through a bog into ever deeper muck sucksucksucking at your clumsy feet. Big Fitzie's secret is he blames himself for the distress of his household. Blames blames himself! For a husband and father may be unfaithful to his family in black moods of doubt hidden from others. In fact since age fifteen Fritz Loving has been weak, vicious. Finding in a culvert amid stinky semi-rotting things a naked rubber doll-baby, at first he'd thought it might be an actual baby but it was not, only a rubbery doll-baby he'd kicked across the culvert *No life matters, no life matters shit.* He'd been relieved. He'd been anxious before worrying about his soul but relieved now. The memory swung at him like an elbow. Hey asshole it's *you.* It ain't your children it's *you.*

Nobody knew. Kat certainly did not know. Pregnant with Deirdre years ago unsuspecting gorgeous-glowing Kat with the radiant skin and manelike red-gold hair had not known. Her husband who adored her yet *If they die it would be easier.* Not a thought Big Fitzie had actually "had" but a thought that sailed into his head like a tune. Desperate with love for his wife and the baby-to-be. Most adoring father after Dee-Dee was born. (He'd assisted in the birth. He'd been there trying not to faint.) Heart torn from his chest as in one of those Aztec ceremonies, nearly. Love came so strong for that beautiful baby girl. Yet there was the next, Raymond. Thinking *Another baby! But I am her baby.* Crazy about his son, though. An American dad requires a son. Catcher's mitt, tossing a softball. Backyard. Bicycle with training wheels, then without. Repeat when the next one was born. What's-his-name: Fritzie Jr. Little Fitzie. (Ray-Ray had trouble pronouncing *r* as in Fritzie so his baby brother came to be, inside the family, Fitzie. Logical?) This last baby another girl, forget the name, colic-baby, no one's fault certainly not the baby's fault, who knows what severe abdominal pains a colic-suffering baby endures, unable to speak, able only to scream, kick, cry, pierce her parents' hearts with stabbing needles, no one's fault he wishes her frenzied little heartbeat would simply cease, her lungs pumping away like a miniature bellows would simply collapse, *Christ let me sleep.*

* * *

Momma Kat (Oh, she's come to hate that silly name: Why did her husband start calling her that, when Dee-Dee was a toddler grasping at speech) continues of course to seek professional help. It's what you do if you're an affluent American. So ashamed! Her family so afflicted! You're the mommy, you must know it's your fault. Certainly it's your fault. As "Katherine Loving" making an appointment with a psychiatrist on the staff of Penn medical school, older Caucasian male suggests that the entire Loving family seems to have succumbed to mass hysteria possibly provoked by some unconscious, unwitting remark/action of hers. Very likely. (But Katherine can't remember. Her memory has become a sieve, she's only thirty-six years old.) The psychiatrist prescribes a tranquilizer, a mood-elevator, a barbiturate. Momma Kat returns racked with guilt, she believes in holistic medicine, holistic healing, she and Dee-Dee both, now she's a hypocrite, takes the barbiturate just once dropping into a trancelike sleep that becomes a nightmare she can't wake from groaning and writhing in her sleep, has to sleep naked since she sweats through her nightgowns, assailed by Things like savage perforations in her optic nerves. Trapped in such a delirium in midafternoon her children come rushing to her Mom*my*! Mom*my*! Wake up Mom*my* but Mommy sleeps for fourteen hours.

HYPOTHESIS #5: "MASS HYSTERIA"

Mass is an extreme adjective applied to only six individuals of whom one is a baby less than a year old. "Mass hysteria" is a matter of *Whether God's archangels or only just wayward roaming demons the revelation received by the afflicted children's mother is she must not allow the Things to comprehend that she is aware of them for their mission is to destroy her through her children as her children are to be destroyed/cleansed through her.*

Mommy help me Dee-Dee begged. The shattered things inside her head, hurting. Only when she splashed cold—icy cold!—water onto her face were her eyes truly *awake*. Then the vagueness sifted back.

Dee-Dee's seventh grade homeroom. She could manage to stay awake by pinching/poking/digging at herself with her already broken nails. Yet at the back of the room the beige rough-textured wall fell away into depthless darkness no one else seemed to notice except Dee-Dee Loving.

Her underarms were beginning to sprout hairs. Between her legs, too. And she was breathless, and hot. Fever-hot. Sweaty. And there were thoughts careening and stabbing like deranged knitting needles. So (she knew) she could never be clean again. Never pure again. She knew.

She'd read sixty-nine Nancy Drew novels (of which she could not recall a single plot!) since she'd begun reading the series at the age of ten.

Doomed not only to forget but also to be forgotten.

Big Fitzie was home often now. Did his work via e-mail, fax, telephone. Spared himself the treacherous commute to and from Philly. Was Big Fitzie on sick leave from the brokerage, or had Big Fitzie been "terminated"? Momma Kat kept meaning to ask him but kept forgetting.

In the bog amid the twittering cries of late summer, slow unfurling coils of water snakes. Licorice black, with creamy-pale bellies and eyes unperturbed as glass.

Big Fitzie understood that his place was at home. Momma Kat had Baby Ceci, and Little Fitzie, and Ray-Ray, and Dee-Dee, these children in their afflictions were her responsibility but could not be hers alone. Big Fitzie could not desert her in this time of crisis, and would not. Momma Kat speaking in her cracked ruined voice of God's archangels. Unless she was speaking to God's archangels. Avengers of error and sin. Punishers. Executioners.

It was possible to see, as Momma Kat was beginning to see, that the Things were not a contagion after all but a gift of God to those beloved of Him.

Hypothesis #6: *Time Travel*

Through a tear in the fabric of time, precipitated by Ray-Ray in all innocence, the contagion rushed into the Loving family.

For Ray-Ray alone of the Lovings knew: the universe is a four-dimensional nexus of (simultaneous) events perceived and experienced as chronological. Already at the age of ten, Ray-Ray understood what mathematics would one day have assured him (had he lived just a few years beyond September 30, 1999): Time moves at an unvarying rate, Time is a warm current in a stream so uniform as to be unnoticed so long as you are moved along with the current you have no idea you are moving. "Clock time" can instruct you that you are in fact moving—or being moved. But you are not conscious of this movement, because it is so slow no consciousness of the terrible stream moving you from "birth" to "death" from the first burst of blinding daylight to the final occluded spasm of extinction.

Children! Breakfast!

Ray-Ray ignored his mother's call. Possibly, Ray-Ray did not hear his mother's call. Already with the clarity of hallucination he was stepping into his Time Machine. Already he'd constructed his Time Machine. No one was welcome to ride with Ray-Ray on his risky journey. He loved Dee-Dee; he loved poor Little Fitzie. He would not wish to endanger them. Ray-Ray was an explorer into the Unknown. The upright rods parted shivering, and Ray-Ray stepped through. Too late to put on his cyclist's crash helmet, Mommy would not know. Too late to say good-bye to her and Daddy. At first it wasn't clear in which direction Ray-Ray was traveling: Past? Future? (Since all events happen simultaneously, the distinction remained mysterious to him.) He shut his eyes, he was in sudden dizzying motion. Hurtling backward, against the current of Time therefore into the "past." Emerging exhausted and confused clawing his way out of the Time Machine and into a hallway it was the upstairs hallway he was just outside his room hadn't left the house blinking and dry-mouthed hearing footsteps on the back stairs and seeing his mirror reflection lurching toward him except it was no mirror *it was Ray-Ray himself.*

Quickly Ray-Ray stumbled into his parents' bedroom. He had made a terrible mistake, he'd journeyed only a few days into the past, nearly confronted his own self of the previous week, what an asshole! What a joke! Ray-Ray waited for his "younger" self to pass by the bedroom door, saw the "younger" self dreamy and preoccupied yawning/scratching at his head/at his crotch imagining no one could see him. Ray-Ray felt a sense of loss so profound, his heart seemed to turn to wet sand, so ashamed. He had assumed he'd travel back farther into the past before his own birth certainly, perhaps into the previous century, instead he has traveled such a trifling distance, as if his desire to time-travel has been mocked, and now he must hide from his own "self" and from the others in his family not wishing to astonish and terrify them, makes his way down the back stairs quietly as he can pushes out the screen door runs floating across the lawn crashing into cattails erect and sharp as swords flailing at his face, he is determined to hide in the bog until dark at least, must spare his family the shock of seeing a second Ray-Ray in their midst, hurtled into the not-distant past by a crude miscalculation, in the bog the soft wet spongy earth begins to suck at his feet, he loses his balance, falls and cuts his hands, the six-foot rushes writhing and undulating in what seems like agitation, unease, his face is being slapped, slashed, he's down on hands and knees, struggling to breathe, [illegible] rushing at him as water snakes to their prey that struggling desperately cannot struggle desperately enough.*

Not that Big Fitzie is so convinced as Momma Kat. The news of the archangels. Revelation! Interior of Big Fitzie's head isn't so sparkly as Momma Kat's. In Big Fitzie's head confused clusters of [illegible] dense as gnats on a humid summer night in the vicinity of the bog. [illegible] growing bolder each day. Moving freely about the Dream House. As if the Dream House is their house. Relatives of the family concerned about Fritz and Katherine's "increasingly strange, uncommunicative" behavior over the summer will speak of coming to the house knocking at the door peeking through windows seeing no human figures but wraithlike sticks? Rods? Floating in the air of certain of the rooms careening in sunshine like motes so the assumption is that you are "seeing things" and not seeing "things" and so out of a natural fear of incipient madness you wish to see nothing further.

Big Fitzie wishes to see nothing further! Big Fitzie has seen enough. A man must protect his family against all danger but Big Fitzie cannot. Big Fitzie is shutting down. Breakfast! is the clarion call. Breakfast, my darlings! I love you calls Momma Kat forlorn and hopeful come to breakfast please *please*.

Except for Momma Kat's quivering voice the house is strangely quiet. Though no one has noticed, Baby Ceci has gradually ceased her terrible crying. She lies upstairs in her reeking bassinet, feebly kicking. For some days Dee-Dee has been changing the infant's soaked diapers, gingerly washing her and dabbing baby powder on her inflamed skin but now Dee-Dee too in her exhaustion has forgotten Baby Ceci.

More frantically now Momma Kat calls her family to breakfast. Slowly they obey her: Big Fitzie shirtless, in unironed khaki shorts and barefoot;

* In theory, Raymond Loving's body, which was not among the bodies recovered from the house fire, is somewhere in the bog. There is also the slim possibility that somehow Ray-Ray escaped, and is still alive somewhere, having wandered off amnesiac.

Dee-Dee in a soiled nightgown, stumbling down the stairs; Little Fitzie drifting into the kitchen like a wraith. No one notices, or will notice, that Ray-Ray is not among them.

Ray-Ray come back, Ray-Ray we love you they would have called to the ten-year-old tears streaking their baffled faces but all memory of "Raymond Loving" seems to have faded from them.

Blueberry pancakes, scrambled eggs and little pork sausages and whole grain toast, luscious feast of a breakfast no one is hungry to eat not even Momma Kat nodding off, falling asleep open-eyed at the grill seeing Big Fitzie chewing sausage with slow-grinding jaws and forcing himself to swallow, Dee-Dee yawning pushing at her plate, Fitzie steeling himself trying not to gag as he lifts a forkful of scrambled eggs slowly tremulously to his mouth. Momma Kat has ground up each of her numerous barbiturate/tranquilizer/mood-elevator capsules and sprinkled the mixture into the food and into tall brimming-white glasses of milk set out for Big Fitzie and the children but she sees now that this phase of God's mission isn't going to work, no one will be eating more than a few desultory mouthfuls of their final meal together including Momma Kat herself in a dream nostalgic mood recalling the lavish Sunday brunches she'd prepared for herself and her young husband when they'd been newlyweds, in that long-ago years before the storm of fecundity burst upon them, how happy they'd been she is smiling to recall.

My darlings. I love you.

Momma Kat has prepared the next step. She has brought into the kitchen a two-gallon can of gasoline from the garage, gasoline used for Big Fitzie's tractor lawn mower, now she sprinkles it about her groggy family seated in the kitchen nook, Dee-Dee's sensitive nostrils twitch, Little Fitzie's eyelids quiver, Big Fitzie scratches at his fatty-muscled chest as if bewildered but it's too late, Momma Kat has drawn a deep breath, lighted a match, and tossed it.

Come to us! Sleep. We love you.

***Elizabeth A. Lynn** has two World Fantasy Awards to her credit, for "The Woman Who Loved the Moon" (Best Short Story, 1980) and* Watchtower *(Best Novel, same year). She has published two story collections, as well as a bunch of novels besides* Watchtower *(which is the first book in a trilogy that also includes* The Dancers of Arun *and* The Northern Girl*), in both fantasy and SF. Next up is* Dragon's Treasure, *which should be published in the U.K. and the U.S. by the time you read this.*

The Silver Dragon

Elizabeth A. Lynn

This is a story of Iyadur Atani, who was master of Dragon Keep and lord of Dragon's Country a long, long time ago.

At this time, Ryoka was both the same as and different than it is today. In Issho, in the west, there was peace, for the mages of Ryoka had built the great wall, the Wizards' Wall, and defended it with spells. Though the wizards were long gone, the power of their magic lingered in the towers and ramparts of the wall. The Isojai feared it, and would not storm it.

In the east, there was no peace. Chuyo was not part of Ryoka, but a separate country. The Chuyokai lords were masters of the sea. They sailed the eastern seas in black-sailed ships, landing to plunder and loot and carry off the young boys and girls to make them slaves. All along the coast of Kameni, men feared the Chuyokai pirates.

In the north, the lords of Ippa prospered. Yet, having no enemies from beyond their borders to fight, they grew bored, and impatient, and quarrelsome. They quarreled with the lords of Issho, with the Talvelai, and the Nyo, and they fought among themselves. Most quarrelsome among them was Martun Hal, lord of Serrenhold. Serrenhold, as all men know, is the smallest and most isolated of the domains of Ippa. For nothing is it praised: not for its tasty beer or its excellence of horseflesh, nor for the beauty of its women, nor the prowess of its men. Indeed, Serrenhold is notable for only one thing: its inhospitable climate. *Bitter as the winds of Serrenhold,* the folk of Ippa say.

No one knew what made Martun Hal so contentious. Perhaps it was the wind, or the will of the gods, or perhaps it was just his nature. In the ten years since he had inherited the lordship from his father Owen, he had killed one brother, exiled another, and picked fights with all his neighbors.

His greatest enmity was reserved for Roderico diCorsini of Derrenhold. There had not always been enmity between them. Indeed, he had once asked Olivia diCorsini, daughter of Roderico diCorsini, lord of Derrenhold, to marry him. But Olivia diCorsini turned him down.

"He is old. Besides, I do not love him," she told her father. "I will not wed a man I do not love."

"Love? What does love have to do with marriage?" Roderico glared at his child. She glared back. They were very alike: stubborn and proud of it. "Pah. I suppose you *love* someone else."

"I do," said Olivia.

"And who might that be, missy?"

"Jon Torneo of Galva."

"Jon Torneo?" Roderico scowled a formidable scowl. "Jon Torneo? He's a shepherd's son! He smells of sheep fat and hay!" This, as it happened, was not true. Jon Torneo's father, Federico Torneo of Galva, did own sheep. But he could hardly be called a shepherd: he was a wool merchant, and one of the wealthiest men in the domain, who had often come to Derrenhold as Roderico diCorsini's guest.

"I don't care. I love him," Olivia said.

And the very next night she ran away from her father's house and rode east across the countryside to Galva. To tell you what happened then would be a whole other story. But since the wedding of Olivia diCorsini and Jon Torneo, while of great import to them, is a small part of this story, suffice it to say that Olivia married Jon Torneo and went to live with him in Galva. Do I need to tell you they were happy? They were. They had four children. The eldest—a boy, called Federico after his grandfather—was a friendly, sturdy, biddable lad. The next two were girls. They were also charming and biddable children, like their brother.

The fourth was Joanna. She was very lovely, having inherited her mother's olive skin and black, thick hair. But she was in no way biddable. She fought with her nurses and bullied her brother. She preferred trousers to skirts, archery to sewing, and hunting dogs to dolls.

"I want to ride. I want to fight," she said.

"Women do not fight," her sisters said.

"I do," said Joanna.

And her mother, recognizing in her youngest daughter the indomitable stubbornness of her own nature, said, "Let her do as she will."

So Joanna learned to ride, and shoot, and wield a sword. By thirteen she could ride as well as any horseman in her grandfather's army. By fourteen she could outshoot all but his best archers.

"She has not the weight to make a swordsman," her father's arms-master said, "but she'll best anyone her own size in a fair fight."

"She's a hellion. No man will ever want to wed her," Roderico diCorsini said, so gloomily that it made his daughter smile. But Joanna Torneo laughed. She knew very well whom she would marry. She had seen him, shining brighter than the moon, soaring across the sky on his way to his castle in the mountains, and had vowed—this was a fourteen-year-old girl, remember—that Iyadur Atani, the Silver Dragon, would be her husband. That he was a changeling, older than she by twelve years, and that they had never met disturbed her not a whit.

Despite his age—he was nearly sixty—the rancor of the lord of Serrenhold toward his neighbors did not cool. The year Joanna turned five, his war band attacked and burned Ragnar Castle. The year she turned nine, he stormed Voiana, the eyrie of the Red Hawks, hoping for plunder. But he found there only empty chambers and the rushing of wind through stone.

The autumn Joanna turned fourteen, Roderico diCorsini died: shot through the heart by one of Martun Hal's archers as he led his soldiers along the crest of the western hills. His son, Ege, inherited the domain. Ege diCorsini, though not the warrior his father had been, was a capable man. His first act as lord was to send a large company of troops to patrol his western border. His next act was to invite his neighbors to a council. "For," he said, "it is past time to end this madness." Couriers were sent to Mirrinhold and Ragnar, to Voiana and to far Mako. A courier was even sent to Dragon Keep.

His councilors wondered at this. "Martun Hal has never attacked the Atani," they pointed out. "The Silver Dragon will not join us."

"I hope you are wrong," said Ege diCorsini. "We need him." He penned that invitation with his own hand. And, since Galva lay between Derrenhold and Dragon Keep, and because he loved his sister, he told the courier, whose name was Ullin March, to stop overnight at the home of Jon Torneo.

Ullin March did as he was told. He rode to Galva. He ate dinner that night with the family. After dinner, he spoke quietly with his hosts, apprising them of Ege diCorsini's plan.

"This could mean war," said Jon Torneo.

"It will mean war," Olivia diCorsini Torneo said.

The next day, Ullin March took his leave of the Torneo family and rode east. At dusk he reached the tall stone pillar that marked the border between the diCorsini's domain and Dragon's Country. He was about to pass the marker, when a slender form leaped from behind the pillar and seized his horse's bridle.

"Dismount," said a fierce young voice, "or I will kill your horse." Steel glinted against the great artery in the gray mare's neck.

Ullin March was no coward. But he valued his horse. He dismounted. The hood fell back from his assailant's face, and he saw that it was a young woman. She was lovely, with olive-colored skin and black hair, tied back behind her neck in a club.

"Who are you?" he said.

"Never mind. The letter you carry. Give it to me."

"No."

The sword tip moved from his horse's neck to his own throat. "I will kill you."

"Then kill me," Ullin March said. Then he dropped, and rolled into her legs. But she had moved. Something hard hit him on the crown of the head.

Dazed and astonished, he drew his sword and lunged at his attacker. She slipped the blow and thrust her blade without hesitation into his arm. He staggered, and slipped to one knee. Again he was hit on the head. The blow stunned him. Blood streamed from his scalp into his eyes. His sword was torn from his grasp. Small hands darted into his shirt, and removed his courier's badge and the letter.

"I am sorry," the girl said. "I had to do it. I will send someone to help you, I promise." He heard the noise of hoofbeats, two sets of them. Cursing, he staggered upright, knowing there was nothing he could do.

Joanna Torneo, granddaughter of Roderico diCorsini, carried her uncle's invitation to Dragon Keep. As it happened, the dragon-lord was at home when she arrived. He was in his hall when a page came running to tell him that a courier from Ege diCorsini was waiting at the gate.

"Put him in the downstairs chamber, and see to his comfort. I will come," said the lord.

"My lord, it's not a him. It's a girl."

"Indeed?" said Iyadur Atani. "See to her comfort, then." The oddity of the event roused his curiosity. In a very short time he was crossing the courtyard to the little chamber where he was wont to receive guests. Within the chamber he found a well-dressed, slightly grubby, very lovely young woman.

"My lord," she said calmly, "I am Joanna Torneo, Ege diCorsini's sister's daughter. I bear you his greetings and a letter." She took the letter from the pocket of her shirt and handed it to him.

Iyadur Atani read her uncle's letter.

"Do you know what this letter says?" he asked.

"It invites you to a council."

"And it assures me that the bearer, a man named Ullin March, can be trusted to answer truthfully any questions I might wish to put to him. You are not Ullin March."

"No. I took the letter from him at the border. Perhaps you would be so kind as to send someone to help him? I had to hit him."

"Why?"

"Had I not, he would not have let me take the letter."

"Why did you take the letter?"

"I wanted to meet you."

"Why?" asked Iyadur Atani.

Joanna took a deep breath. "I am going to marry you."

"Are you?" said Iyadur Atani. "Does your father know this?"

"My mother does," said Joanna. She gazed at him. He was a handsome man, fair, and very tall. His clothes, though rich, were simple; his only adornment, a golden ring on the third finger of his right hand. It was fashioned in the shape of a sleeping dragon. His gaze was very direct, and his eyes burned with a blue flame. Resolute men, men of uncompromising courage, feared that fiery gaze.

When they emerged, first the girl, radiant despite her mud-stained clothes, and then the lord of the Keep, it was evident to all his household that their habitually reserved lord was unusually, remarkably happy.

"This is the lady Joanna Torneo of Galva, soon to be my wife," he said. "Take care of her." He lifted the girl's hand to his lips.

That afternoon he wrote two letters. The first went to Olivia Torneo, assuring her that her beloved daughter was safe in Dragon Keep. The second was to Ege DiCorsini. Both letters made their recipients very glad indeed. An exchange of letters followed: from Olivia Torneo to her headstrong daughter, and from Ege diCorsini to the lord of the Keep. Couriers wore ruts in the road from Dragon Keep to Galva, and from Dragon Keep to Derrenhold.

* * *

The council was held in the great hall of Derrenhold. Ferris Wulf, lord of Mirrinhold, a doughty warrior, was there, with his captains; so was Aurelio Ragnarin of Ragnar Castle and Rudolf diMako, whose cavalry was the finest in Ippa. Even Jamis Delamico, matriarch of the Red Hawk clan, had come, accompanied by six dark-haired, dark-eyed women who looked exactly like her. She did not introduce them: no one knew if they were her sisters, or her daughters. Iyadur Atani was not present.

Ege diCorsini spoke first.

"My lords, honored friends," he said, "for nineteen years, since the old lord of Serrenhold died, Martun Hal and his troops have prowled the borders of our territories, snapping and biting like a pack of hungry dogs. His people starve, and groan beneath their taxes. He has attacked Mirrinhold, and Ragnar, and Voiana. Two years ago, my lord of Mirrinhold, his archers killed your son. Last year they killed my father.

"My lords and captains, nineteen is too long. It is time to muzzle the dogs." The lesser captains shouted. Ege diCorsini went on. "Alone, no one of us has been able to prevail against Martun Hal's aggression. I suggest we unite our forces and attack him."

"How?" said Aurelio Ragnarin. "He hides behind his walls, and attacks only when he is sure of victory."

"We must go to him, and attack him where he lives."

The leaders looked at one another, and then at diCorsini as if he had lost his mind. Ferris Wulf said, "Serrenhold is unassailable."

"How do you know?" Ege diCorsini said. "For nineteen years no one has attacked it."

"You have a plan," said Jamis Delamico.

"I do." And Ege diCorsini explained to the lords of Ippa exactly how he planned to defeat Martun Hal.

At the end of his speech, Ferris Wulf said, "You are sure of this?"

"I am."

"I am with you."

"And I," said Aurelio Ragnarin.

"My sisters and my daughters will follow you," Jamis Delamico said.

Rudolf diMako stuck his thumbs in his belt. "Martun Hal has stayed well clear of my domain. But I see that he needs to be taught a lesson. My army is yours to command."

* * *

Solitary in his fortress, Martun Hal heard through his spies of his enemies' machinations. He summoned his captains to his side. "Gather the troops," he ordered. "We must prepare to defend our borders. Go," he told his spies. "Watch the highways. Tell me when they come."

Sooner than he expected, the spies returned. "My lord, they come."

"What are their forces?"

"They are a hundred mounted men, and six hundred foot."

"Archers?"

"About a hundred."

"Have they brought a ram?"

"Yes, my lord."

"Ladders? Ropes? Catapults?"

"They have ladders and ropes. No catapults, my lord."

"Pah. They are fools, and overconfident. Their horses will do them no good here. Do they think to leap over Serrenhold's walls? We have three hundred archers, and a thousand foot soldiers," Martun Hal said. His spirits rose. "Let them come. They will lose."

The morning of the battle was clear and cold. Frost hardened the ground. A bitter wind blew across the mountain peaks. The forces of the lords of Ippa advanced steadily upon Serrenhold castle. On the ramparts of the castle, archers strung their bows. They were unafraid, for their forces outnumbered the attackers, and besides, no one had ever besieged Serrenhold and won. Behind the castle gates, the Sererenhold army waited. The swordsmen drew their swords and taunted their foes: "Run, dogs! Run, rabbits! Run, little boys! Go home to your mothers!"

The attackers advanced. Ege diCorsini called to the defenders, "Surrender, and you will live. Fight, and you will die."

"We will not surrender," the guard captain said.

"As you wish," diCorsini said. He signaled to his trumpeter. The trumpeter lifted his horn to his lips and blew a sharp trill. Yelling, the attackers charged. Despite the rain of arrows coming from the castle walls, a valiant band of men from Ragnar Castle scaled the walls, and leaped into the courtyard. Back to back, they fought their way slowly toward the gates. Screaming out of the sky, a flock of hawks flew at the faces of the amazed archers. The rain of arrows faltered.

A second group of men smashed its way through a postern gate and battled in the courtyard with Martun Hal's men. Ferris Wulf said to Ege diCorsini, "They weaken. But still they outnumber us. We are losing too many men. Call him."

"Not yet," Ege DiCorsini said. He signaled. Men brought the ram up. Again and again they hurled it at the gates. But the gates held. The men in the courtyard fought and died. The hawks attacked the archers, and the archers turned their bows against the birds and shot them out of the sky. A huge red hawk swooped to earth and became Jamis Delamico.

"They are killing my sisters," she said, and her eyes glittered with rage. "Why do you wait? Call him."

"Not yet," said Ege diCorsini. "Look. We are through." The ram broke through the gate. Shouting, the attackers flung themselves at the breach, clawing at the gate with their hands. Fighting with tremendous courage, the attackers moved them back from the gates, inch by inch.

But there were indeed many more defenders. They drove the diCorsini army back, and closed the gate, and braced it with barrels and wagons and lengths of wood.

"Now," said Ege diCorsini. He signaled the trumpeter. The trumpeter blew again.

Then the dragon came. Huge, silver, deadly, he swooped upon the men of Serrenhold. His silver claws cut the air like scythes. He stooped his head, and his eyes glowed like fire. Fire trickled from his nostrils. He breathed upon the castle walls, and the stone hissed and melted like snow in the sun. He roared. The sound filled the day, louder and more terrible than thunder. The archers' fingers opened, and their bows clattered to the ground. The swordsmen trembled, and their legs turned to jelly. Shouting, the men of Ippa stormed over the broken gates and into Serrenhold. They found the lord of the castle sitting in his hall, with his sword across his lap.

"Come on," he said, rising. "I am an old man. Come and kill me."

He charged them then, hoping to force them to kill him. But though he fought fiercely, killing two of them, and wounding three more, they finally disarmed him. Bruised and bloody, but whole, Martun Hal was bound and marched at swordpoint out of his hall to the courtyard where the lords of Ippa stood. He bowed mockingly into their unyielding faces.

"Well, my lords. I hope you are pleased with your victory. All of you together, and still it took dragonfire to defeat me."

Ferris Wulf scowled. But Ege diCorsini said, "Why should more men of Ippa die for you? Even your own people are glad the war is over."

"Is it over?"

"It is," diCorsini said firmly.

Martun Hal smiled bleakly. "Yet I live."

"Not for long," someone cried. And Ferris Wulf's chief captain, whose home Martun Hal's men had burned, stepped forward and set the tip of his sword against the old man's breast.

"No," said Ege diCorsini.

"Why not?" said Ferris Wulf. "He killed your father."

"Whom would you put in his place?" Ege diCorsini said. "He is Serrenhold's rightful lord. His father had three sons, but one is dead, and the other gone, who knows where. He has no children to succeed him. *I* would not reign in Serrenhold. It is a dismal place. Let him keep it. We will set a guard about his border, and restrict the number of soldiers he may have, and watch him."

"And when he dies?" said Aurelio Ragnarin.

"Then we will name his successor."

Glaring, Ferris Wulf fingered the hilt of his sword. "He should die *now*. Then we could appoint a regent. One of our own captains, someone honorable and deserving of trust."

Ege diCorsini said, "We could do that. But that man would never have a moment's peace. *I* say, let us set a watch upon this land, so that Martun Hal may never trouble our towns and people again, and let him rot in this lifeless place."

"The Red Hawk clan will watch him," Jamis Delamico said.

And so it came to pass. Martun Hal lived. His weapons were destroyed; his war band, all but thirty men, was disbanded and scattered. He was forbidden to travel more than two miles from his castle. The lords of Ippa, feeling reasonably secure in their victory, went home to their castles, to rest and rebuild and prepare for winter.

Ege di Corsini, riding east amid his rejoicing troops, made ready to attend a wedding. He was fond of his niece. His sister had assured him that the girl was absolutely determined to wed Iyadur Atani, and as for the flame-haired, flame-eyed dragon-lord, he seemed equally eager for the match. Remembering stories he had heard, Ege diCorsini admitted, though only to himself, that Joanna's husband was not the one he would have chosen for her. But no one had asked his opinion.

The wedding was held at Derrenhold and attended by all the lords of Ippa, except, of course, Martun Hal. Rudolf diMako attended, despite the distance, but no one was surprised; there was strong friendship between the diMako and the Atani. Jamis Delamico came. The bride was pronounced to be astonishingly beautiful, and the bride's mother almost as beautiful. The dragon-lord presented the parents of his bride with gifts: a tapestry, a mettlesome stallion and a breeding mare from the Atani stables, a sapphire pendant, a cup of beaten gold. The couple drank the wine. The priestess said the blessings.

The following morning, Olivia diCorsini Torneo said farewell to her daughter. "I will miss you. Your father will miss you. You must visit often. He is older than he was, you know."

"I will," Joanna promised. Olivia watched the last of her children ride away into the bright autumnal day. The two older girls were both wed, and Federico was not only wed but twice a father, as well.

I don't feel like a grandmother, Olivia Torneo thought. Then she laughed at herself and went inside to find her husband.

And so there was peace in Ippa. The folk of Derrenhold and Mirrinhold and Ragnar ceased to look over their shoulders. They left their daggers sheathed and hung their battle-axes on the walls. Men who had spent most of their lives fighting put aside their shields and went home, to towns and farms and wives they barely remembered. More babies were born the following summer than had been born in the previous three years put together. The midwives were run ragged trying to attend the births. Many of the boys, even in Ragnar and Mirrinhold, were named Ege or Roderico. A few of the girls were even named Joanna.

Martun Hal heard the tidings of his enemies' good fortune, and his hatred of them deepened. Penned in his dreary fortress, he took count of his gold. Discreetly, he let it be known that the lord of Serrenhold, although beaten, was not without resources. Slowly, cautiously, some of those who had served him before his defeat crept across the border to his castle. He paid them and sent them out again to Derrenhold and Mirrinhold, and even—cautiously—into Iyadur Atani's country.

"Watch," he said, "and when something happens, send me word."

As for Joanna Torneo Atani, she was as happy as she had known she would be. She adored her husband and was unafraid of his changeling nature. The people of his domain had welcomed her. Her only disappointment, as the year moved from spring to summer and to the crisp cold nights of autumn again, was that she was childless.

"Every other woman in the world is having a baby," she complained to her husband. "Why can't I?"

He smiled and drew her into the warmth of his arms. "You will."

Nearly three years after the surrender of Martun Hal, with the Hunter's Moon waning in the autumn sky, Joanna Atani received a message from her mother.

Come, it said. *Your father needs you.* She left the next morning for Galva, accompanied by her maid and escorted by six of Dragon Keep's most experienced and competent soldiers.

"Send word if you need me," her husband said.

"I will."

The journey took two days. Outside the Galva gates, a beggar warming his hands over a scrap of fire told Joanna what she most wanted to know.

"Your father still lives, my lady. I heard it from Viksa the fruit-seller an hour ago."

"Give him gold," Joanna said to her captain as she urged her horse through the gate. Word of her coming hurried before her. By the time Joanna reached her parents' home, the gate was open. Her brother stood before it.

She said, "Is he dead?"

"Not yet." He drew her inside.

Olivia diCorsini Torneo sat at her dying husband's bedside, in the chamber they had shared for twenty-nine years. She still looked young, nearly as young as the day she had left her father's house behind for good. Her dark eyes were clear, and her skin smooth. Only her lustrous thick hair was no longer dark; it was shot through with white, like lace.

She smiled at her youngest daughter and put up her face to be kissed. "I am glad you could come," she said. "Your sisters are here." She turned back to her husband.

Joanna bent over the bed. "Papa?" she whispered. But the man in the bed, so flat and still, did not respond. A plain white cloth wound around Jon Torneo's head was the only sign of injury: otherwise, he appeared to be asleep.

"What happened?"

"An accident, a week ago. He was bringing the herd down from the high pasture when something frightened the sheep: they ran. He fell among them and was trampled. His head was hurt. He has not woken since. The physician Phylla says there is nothing she can do."

Joanna said tremulously, "He always said sheep were stupid. Is he in pain?"

"Phylla says not."

That afternoon, Joanna wrote a letter to her husband, telling him what had happened. She gave it to a courier to take to Dragon Keep.

Do not come, she wrote. *There is nothing you can do. I will stay until he dies.*

One by one his children took their turns at Jon Torneo's bedside. Olivia ate her meals in the chamber and slept on a pallet laid by the bed. Once each day she walked outside the gates, to talk to the people who thronged day and night outside the house, for Jon Torneo was much beloved. Solemn strangers came up to her weeping. Olivia, despite her own grief, spoke kindly to them all.

Joanna marveled at her mother's strength. She could not match it: she found herself weeping at night and snapping by day at her sisters. She was even, to her shame, sick one morning.

A week after Joanna's arrival, Jon Torneo died. He was buried, as was proper, within three days. Ege diCorsini was there, as were the husbands of Joanna's sisters, and all of Jon Torneo's family, and half Galva, or so it seemed.

The next morning, in the privacy of the garden, Olivia Torneo said quietly to her youngest daughter, "You should go home."

"Why?" Joanna said. She was dumbstruck. "Have I offended you?" Tears rose to her eyes. "Oh, Mother, I'm so sorry. . . ."

"Idiot child," Olivia said, and put her arms around her daughter. "My treasure, you and your sisters have been a great comfort to me. But you should be with your husband at this time." Her gaze narrowed. "Joanna? Do you not know that you are pregnant?"

Joanna blinked. "What makes you—? I feel fine," she said.

"Of course you do," said Olivia. "DiCorsini women never have trouble with babies."

Phylla confirmed that Joanna was indeed pregnant.

"You are sure?"

"Yes. Your baby will be born in the spring."

"Is it a boy or a girl?" Joanna asked.

But Phylla could not tell her that.

So Joanna Atani said farewell to her family, and, with her escort about her, departed Galva for the journey to Dragon Keep. As they rode toward the hills, she marked the drifts of leaves on the ground and the dull color on the hills, and rejoiced. The year was turning. Slipping a hand beneath her clothes, she laid her palm across her belly, hoping to feel the quickening of life in her womb. It seemed strange to be so happy, so soon after her father's untimely death.

Twenty-one days after the departure of his wife from Dragon Keep, Iyadur Atani called one of his men to his side.

"Go to Galva, to the house of Jon Torneo," he said. "Find out what is happening there."

The courier rode to Galva. A light snow fell as he rode through the gates. The steward of the house escorted him to Olivia Torneo's chamber.

"My lady," he said, "I am sent from Dragon Keep to inquire after the well-being of the lady Joanna. May I speak with her?"

Olivia Torneo's face slowly lost its color. She said, "My daughter Joanna left a week ago to return to Dragon Keep. Soldiers from Dragon Keep were with her."

The courier stared. Then he said, "Get me fresh horses."

He burst through the Galva gates as though the demons of hell were on his horse's heels. He rode through the night. He reached Dragon Keep at dawn.

"He's asleep," the page warned.

"Wake him," the courier said. But the page would not. So the courier himself pushed open the door. "My lord? I am back from Galva."

The torches lit in the bedchamber.

"Come," said Iyadur Atani from the curtained bed. He drew back the curtains. The courier knelt on the rug beside the bed. He was shaking with weariness, and hunger, and also with dread.

"My lord, I bear ill news. Your lady left Galva to return home eight days ago. Since then, no one has seen her."

Fire came into Iyadur Atani's eyes. The courier turned his head. Rising from the bed, the dragon-lord said, "Call my captains."

The captains came. Crisply their lord told them that their lady was missing somewhere between Galva and Dragon Keep, and that it was their task, their only task, to find her. "You *will* find her," he said, and his words seemed to burn the air like flames.

"Aye, my lord," they said.

They searched across the countryside, hunting through hamlet and hut and barn, through valley and cave and ravine. They did not find Joanna Atani.

But midway between Galva and the border between the diCorsini land and Dragon's Country, they found, piled in a ditch and rudely concealed with branches, the bodies of nine men and one woman.

"Six of them we know," Bran, second-in-command of Dragon Keep's archers, reported to his lord. He named them: they were the six men who Joanna Atani's escort had comprised. "The woman is my lady Joanna's maid. My lord, we have found the tracks of many men and horses, riding hard and fast. The trail leads west."

"We shall follow it," Iyadur Atani said. "Four of you shall ride with me. The rest shall return to Dragon Keep, to await my orders."

They followed that trail for nine long days across Ippa, through bleak and stony hills, through the high reaches of Derrenhold, into Serrenhold's wild, windswept country. As they crossed the borders, a red-winged hawk swept down upon them. It landed in the snow, and became a dark-eyed woman in a gray cloak.

She said, "I am Madelene of the Red Hawk sisters. I watch this land. Who are you, and what is your business here?"

The dragon-lord said, "I am Iyadur Atani. I am looking for my wife. I believe she came this way, accompanied by many men, perhaps a dozen of them, and their remounts. We have been tracking them for nine days."

"A band of ten men rode across the border from Derrenhold into Serrenhold twelve days ago," the watcher said. "They led ten spare horses. I saw no women among them."

Bran said, "Could she have been disguised? A woman with her hair cropped might look like a boy, and the lady Joanna rides as well as any man."

Madelene shrugged. "I did not see their faces."

"Then you see ill," Bran said angrily. "Is this how the Red Hawk sisters keep watch?" Hawk-changeling and archer glared at one another.

"Enough," Iyadur Atani said. He led them onto the path to the fortress. It wound upward through the rocks. Suddenly they heard the clop of horses' hooves against the stone. Four horsemen appeared on the path ahead of them.

Bran cupped his hands to his lips. "What do you want?" he shouted.

The lead rider shouted back, "It is for us to ask that! You are on our land!"

"Then speak," Bran said.

"Your badges proclaim that you come from Dragon Keep. I bear a message to Iyadur Atani from Martun Hal."

Bran waited for the dragon-lord to declare himself. When he did not, the captain said, "Tell me, and I will carry it to him."

"Tell Iyadur Atani," the lead rider said, "that his wife will be staying in Serrenhold for a time. If any attempt is made to find her her, then she will die, slowly and in great pain. That is all." He and his fellows turned their horses and bolted up the path.

Iyadur Atani said not a word, but the dragon rage burned white hot upon his face. The men from Dragon Keep looked at him, once. Then they looked away, holding their breaths.

Finally he said, "Let us go."

When they reached the border, they found Ege diCorsini, with a large company of well-armed men, waiting for them.

"Olivia sent to me," he said to Iyadur Atani. "Have you found her?"

"Martun Hal has her," the dragon-lord said. "He says he will kill her if we try to get her back." His face was set. "He may kill her anyway."

"He won't kill her," Ege diCorsini said. "He'll use her to bargain with. He will want his weapons and his army back, and freedom to move about his land."

"Give it to him," Iyadur Atani said. "I want my wife."

So Ege deCorsini sent a delegation of his men to Martun Hal, offering to modify the terms of Serrenhold's surrender, if he would release Joanna Atani unharmed.

But Martun Hal did not release Joanna. As diCorsini had said, he used her welfare to bargain with, demanding first the freedom to move about his own country, and then the restoration of his war band, first to one hundred, then to three hundred men.

"We must know where she is. When we know where she is, we can rescue her," diCorsini said. And he sent spies into Serrenhold, with instructions to discover where in that bleak and barren country the lady of Ippa was. But Martun Hal, ever crafty, had anticipated this. He sent a message to Iyadur Atani, warning that payment for the trespass of strangers would be exacted upon Joanna's body. He detailed, with blunt and horrific cruelty, what that payment would be.

In truth, despite the threats, he did nothing to hurt his captive. For though years of war had scoured from him almost all human feeling save pride, ambition, and spite, he understood quite well that if Joanna died, and word of that death reached Dragon Keep, no power in or out of Ryoka could protect him.

* * *

As for Joanna, she had refused even to speak to him from the day his men had brought her, hair chopped like a boy's, wrapped in a soldier's cloak, into his castle. She did not weep. They put her in an inner chamber, and placed guards on the door, and assigned two women to care for her. They were both named Kate, and since one was large and one not, they were known as Big Kate and Small Kate. She did not rage, either. She ate the meals the women brought her and slept in the bed they gave her.

Winter came early, as it does in Serrenhold. The wind moaned about the castle walls, and snow covered the mountains. Weeks passed, and Joanna's belly swelled. When it became clear beyond any doubt that she was indeed pregnant, the women who served her went swiftly to tell their lord.

"Are you sure?" he demanded. "If this is a trick, I will have you both flayed!"

"We are sure," they told him. "Send a physician to her, if you question it."

So Martun Hal sent a physician to Joanna's room. But Joanna refused to let him touch her. "I am Iyadur Atani's wife," she said. "I will allow no other man to lay his hands on me."

"Pray that it is a changeling, a dragon-child," Martun Hal said to his captains. And he told the two Kates to give Joanna whatever she needed for her comfort, save freedom.

The women went to Joanna and asked what she wanted.

"I should like a window," Joanna said. The rooms in which they housed her had all been windowless. They moved her to a chamber in a tower. It was smaller than the room in which they had been keeping her, but it had a narrow window, through which she could see sky and clouds, and on clear nights, stars.

When her idleness began to weigh upon her, she said, "Bring me books." They brought her books. But reading soon bored her.

"Bring me a loom."

"A loom? Can you weave?" Big Kate asked.

"No," Joanna said. "Can you?"

"Of course."

"Then you can teach me." The women brought her the loom, and with it, a dozen skeins of bright wool. "Show me what to do." Big Kate showed her how to set up the threads, and how to cast the shuttle. The first thing she made was a yellow blanket, a small one.

Small Kate asked, "Who shall that be for?"

"For the babe," Joanna said.

Then she began another: a scarlet cloak, a large one, with a fine gold border.

"Who shall that be for?" Big Kate asked.

"For my lord, when he comes."

One gray afternoon, as Joanna sat at her loom, a red-winged hawk alighted on her windowsill.

"Good day," Joanna said to it. It cocked its head and stared at her sideways out of its left eye. "There is bread on the table." She pointed to the little table where she ate her food. She had left a slice of bread untouched from her midday meal, intending to eat it later. The hawk turned its beak and stared at her out of its right eye. Hopping to the table, it pecked at the bread.

Then it fluttered to the floor and became a dark-eyed, dark-haired woman wearing a gray cloak. Crossing swiftly to Joanna's seat, she whispered, "Leave the shutter ajar. I will come again tonight." Before Joanna could answer, she turned into a bird and was gone.

That evening Joanna could barely eat. Concerned, Big Kate fussed at her. "You have to eat. The babe grows swiftly now; it needs all the nourishment you can give it. Look, here is the cream you wanted, and here is soft ripe cheese, come all the way from Merigny in the south, where they say it snows once every hundred years."

"I don't want it." Big Kate reached to close the window shutter. "Leave it!"

"It's freezing."

"I am warm."

"You might be feverish." Small Kate reached to feel her forehead.

"I am not. I'm fine."

At last they left her. She heard the bar slide across the door. She lay down on her bed. As was their custom, they had left her but a single candle, but light came from the hearth log. The babe moved in her belly. "Little one, I feel you," she whispered. "Be patient. We shall not always be in this loathsome place."

Then she heard the rustle of wings. A human shadow sprang across the walls of the chamber. A woman's voice said softly, "My lady, do you know me? I am Madelene of the Red Hawk sisters. I was at your wedding."

"I remember." Tears—the first she had shed since the start of her captivity—welled into Joanna's eyes. She knuckled them away. "I am glad to see you."

"And I you," Madelene said. "Since first I knew you were here, I have looked for you. I feared you were in torment, or locked away in some dark dungeon, where I might never find you."

"Can you help me to escape this place?"

Madelene said sadly, "No, my lady. I have no power to do that."

"I thought not." She reached beneath her pillow and brought out a golden brooch shaped like a full-blown rose. It had been a gift from her husband on their wedding night. "Never mind. Here. Take this to my husband."

In Dragon Keep, Iyadur Atani's mood grew grimmer and more remote. Martun Hal's threats obsessed him: he imagined his wife alone, cold, hungry, confined to darkness, perhaps hurt. His appetite vanished; he ceased to eat, or nearly so.

At night he paced the castle corridors, silent as a ghost, cloakless despite the winter cold, his eyes like white flame. His soldiers and his servants began to fear him. One by one, they vanished from the castle.

But some, more resolute or more loyal, remained. Among them was Bran the archer, now captain of the archery wing, since Jarko, the former captain, had disappeared one moonless December night. When a strange woman appeared among them, claiming to bear a message to Iyadur Atani from his captive wife, it was to Bran the guards brought her.

He recognized her. Leading her to Iyadur Atani's chamber, he pounded on the closed door. The door opened. Iyadur Atani stood framed in the doorway. His face was gaunt.

Madelene held out the golden brooch.

Iyadur Atani knew it at once. The grief and rage and fear that had filled him for four months eased a little. Lifting the brooch from Madelene's palm, he touched it to his lips.

"Be welcome," he said. "Tell me how Joanna is. Is she well?"

"She bade me say that she is, my lord."

"And—the babe?"

"It thrives. It is your child, my lord. Your lady charged me to say that, and to tell you that no matter what rumors you might have heard, neither Martun Hal nor any of his men has touched her. Indeed, no torment has been offered her at all. Only she begs you to please, come quickly to succor her, for she is desperate to be home."

"Can you visit her easily?"

"I can."

"Then return to her, of your kindness. Tell her I love her. Tell her not to despair."

"She will not despair," Madelene said. "Despair is not in her nature. But I have a second message for you. This one is from my queen." She meant the matriarch of the Red Hawks, Jamis Delamico. "She said to tell you, where force will not prevail, seek magic. She says, go west, to Lake Urai. Find the sorcerer who lives beside the lake, and ask him how to get your wife back."

Iyadur Atani said, "I did not know there were still sorcerers in the west."

"There is one. The common folk know him as Viksa. But that is not his true name, my queen says."

"And does your queen know the true name of this reclusive wizard?" For everyone knows that unless you know a sorcerer's true name, he or she will not even speak with you.

"She does. And she told me to tell it to you," said Madelene. She leaned toward the dragon-lord and whispered in his ear. "And she also told me to tell you, be careful when you deal with him. For he is sly, and what he intends to do, he does not always reveal. But what he says he will do, he will do."

"Thank you," Iyadur Atani said, and he smiled, for the first time in a long time. "Cousin, I am in your debt." He told Bran to see to her comfort and to provide her with whatever she needed—food, a bath, a place to sleep. Summoning his servants, he asked them to bring him a meal and wine.

Then he called his officers together. "I am leaving," he said. "You must defend my people and hold the borders against outlaws and incursions. If you need help, ask for aid from Mako or Derrenhold."

"How long will you be gone, my lord?" they asked him.

"I do not know."

Then he flew to Galva.

"I should have come before," he said. "I am sorry." He assured Olivia that despite her captivity, Joanna was well, and unharmed. "I go now to get her," he said. "When I return, I shall bring her with me. I swear it."

Issho, the southeastern province of Ryoka, is a rugged place. Though not so grim as Ippa, it has none of the gentle domesticated peace of Nakase. Its plains are colder than those of Nakase, and its rivers are wilder. The greatest of those rivers is the Endor. It starts in the north, beneath that peak which men call the Lookout, Mirrin, and pours ceaselessly south, cutting like a knife through Issho's open spaces to the border where Chuyo and Issho and Nakase meet.

It ends in Lake Urai. Lake Urai is vast, and even on a fair day, the water is not blue, but pewter gray. In winter, it does not freeze. Contrary winds swirl about it; at dawn and at twilight gray mist obscures its contours, and at all times the chill bright water lies quiescent, untroubled by even the most violent wind. The land about it is sparsely inhabited. Its people are a hardy, silent folk, not particularly friendly to strangers. They respect the lake and do not willingly discuss its secrets. When the tall, fair-haired stranger appeared among them, having come, so he said, from Ippa, they were happy to prepare his food and take his money, but were inclined to answer his questions evasively, or not at all.

The lake is as you see it. The wizard of the lake? Never heard of him.

But the stranger was persistent. He took a room at The Red Deer in Jen, hired a horse—oddly, he seemed to have arrived without one—and roamed about the lake. The weather did not seem to trouble him. "We have winter in my country." His clothes were plain, but clearly of the highest quality, and beneath his quiet manner there was iron.

"His eyes are different," the innkeeper's wife said. "He's looking for a wizard. Maybe he's one himself, in disguise."

One gray March afternoon, when the lake lay shrouded in mist, Iyadur Atani came upon a figure sitting on a rock beside a small fire. It was dressed in rags and held what appeared to be a fishing pole.

The dragon-lord's heart quickened. He dismounted. Tying his horse to a tall reed, he walked toward the fisherman. As he approached, the hunched figure turned. Beneath the ragged hood he glimpsed white hair, and a visage so old and wrinkled that he could not tell if he was facing a man or a woman.

"Good day," he said. The ancient being nodded. "My name is Iyadur Atani. Men call me the Silver Dragon. I am looking for a wizard."

The ancient one shook its head and gestured, as if to say, Leave me alone. Iyadur Atani crouched.

"Old One, I don't believe you are as you appear," he said in a conversational tone. "I believe you are the one I seek. If you are indeed"—and then he said the name that Madelene of the Red Hawks had whispered in his ear—"I beg you to help me. For I have come a long way to look for you."

An aged hand swept the hood aside. Dark gray eyes stared out of a withered, wrinkled face.

A feeble voice said, "Who told you my name?"

"A friend."

"Huh. Whoever it was is no friend of *mine*. What does the Silver Dragon need a wizard for?"

"If you are truly wise," Iyadur Atani said, "you know."

The sorcerer laughed softly. The hunched figure straightened. The rags became a silken gown with glittering jewels at its hem and throat. Instead of an old man, the dragon-lord faced a man in his prime, of princely bearing, with luminous chestnut hair and eyes the color of a summer storm. The fishing pole became a tall staff. Its crook was carved like a serpent's head. The sorcerer pointed the staff at the ground and said three words.

A doorway seemed to open in the stony hillside. Joanna Torneo Atani stood within it. She wore furs and was visibly pregnant.

"Joanna!" The dragon-lord reached for her. But his hands gripped empty air.

"Illusion," said the sorcerer known as Viksa. "A simple spell, but effective, don't you think? You are correct, my lord. I know you lost your wife. I assume you want her back. Tell me, why do you not lead your war band to Serrenhold and rescue her?"

"Martun Hal will kill her if I do that."

"I see."

"Will you help me?"

"Perhaps," said the sorcerer. The serpent in his staff turned its head to stare at the dragon-lord. Its eyes were rubies. "What will you pay me if I help you?"

"I have gold."

Viksa yawned. "I have no interest in gold."

"Jewels," said the dragon-lord, "fine clothing, a horse to bear you wherever you might choose to go, a castle of your own to dwell in . . ."

"I have no use for those."

"Name your price, and I will pay it," Iyadur Atani said steadily. "I reserve only the life of my wife and my child."

"But not your own?" Viksa cocked his head. "You intrigue me. Indeed, you move me. I accept your offer, my lord. I will help you rescue your wife from Serrenhold. I shall teach you a spell, a very simple spell, I assure you. When you speak it, you will be able to hide within a shadow. In that way you may pass into Serrenhold unseen."

"And its price?"

Viksa smiled. "In payment, I will take—*you*. Not your life, but your service. It has been many years since I had someone to hunt for me, cook for me, build my fire, and launder my clothes. It will amuse me to have a dragon as my servant."

"For how long would I owe you service?"

"As long as I wish it."

"That seems *unfair*."

The wizard shrugged.

"When would this service start?"

The wizard shrugged again. "It may be next month, or next year. Or it may be twenty years from now. Do we have an agreement?"

Iyadur Atani considered. He did not like this wizard. But he could see no other way to get his wife back.

"We do," he said. "Teach me the spell."

So Viksa the sorcerer taught Iyadur Atani the spell which would enable him to hide in a shadow. It was not a difficult spell. Iyadur Atani rode his hired horse back to The Red Deer and paid the innkeeper what remained on his bill. Then he walked into the bare field beside the inn, and became the Silver Dragon. As the innkeeper and his wife watched openmouthed, he circled the inn once and then sped north.

"A dragon!" the innkeeper's wife said with intense satisfaction. "I wonder if he found the sorcerer. See, I told you his eyes were odd." The innkeeper agreed. Then he went up to the room Iyadur Atani had occupied and searched carefully in every cranny, in case the dragon-lord had chanced to leave some gold behind.

Now it was in Iyadur Atani's mind to fly immediately to Serrenhold Castle. But remembering Martun Hal's threats, he did not. He flew to a point just south of Serrenhold's southern border. And there, in a nondescript village, he bought a horse, a shaggy brown gelding. From there he proceeded to Serrenhold Castle. It was not so tedious a journey as he had thought it would be. The prickly stunted pine trees that grew along the slopes of the windswept hills showed new green along their branches. Birds sang. Foxes loped across the hills, hunting mice and quail and the occasional stray chicken. The journey took six days. At dawn on the seventh day, Iyadur Atani fed the brown gelding and left him in a farmer's yard. It was a fine spring morning. The sky was cloudless; the sun brilliant; the shadows sharp-edged as steel. Thorn-crowned hawthorn bushes lined the road to

Serrenhold Castle. Their shadows webbed the ground. A wagon filled with lumber lumbered toward the castle. Its shadow rolled beneath it.

"Wizard," the dragon-lord said to the empty sky, "if you have played me false, I will find you wherever you try to hide, and eat your heart."

In her prison in the tower, Joanna Torneo Atani walked from one side of her chamber to the other. Her hair had grown long again: it fell around her shoulders. Her belly was round and high under the soft thick drape of her gown. The coming of spring had made her restless. She had asked to be allowed to walk on the ramparts, but this Martun Hal had refused.

Below her window, the castle seethed like a cauldron. The place was never still; the smells and sounds of war continued day and night. The air was thick with soot. Soldiers drilled in the courtyard. Martun Hal was planning an attack on Ege diCorsini. He had told her all about it, including his intention to destroy Galva. *I will burn it to the ground. I will kill your uncle and take your mother prisoner,* he had said. *Or perhaps not. Perhaps I will just have her killed.*

She glanced toward the patch of sky that was her window. If Madelene would only come, she could get word to Galva, or to her uncle in Derrenhold. . . . But Madelene would not come in daylight; it was too dangerous.

She heard a hinge creak. The door to the outer chamber opened. "My lady," Big Kate called. She bustled in, bearing a tray. It held soup, bread, and a dish of thin sour pickles. "I brought your lunch."

"I'm not hungry."

Kate said, troubled, "My lady, you have to eat. For the baby."

"Leave it," Joanna said. "I will eat." Kate set the tray on the table and left.

Joanna nibbled at a pickle. She rubbed her back, which ached. The baby's heel thudded against the inside of her womb. "My precious, my little one, be still," she said. For it was her greatest fear that her babe, Iyadur Atani's child, might in its haste to be born arrive early, before her husband arrived to rescue them. That he would come, despite Martun Hal's threats, she had no doubt. "Be still."

Silently, Iyadur Atani materialized from the shadows.

"Joanna," he said. He put his arms about her. She reached her hands up. Her fingertips brushed his face. She leaned against him, trembling.

She whispered into his shirt, "How did you—?"

"Magic." He touched the high mound of her belly. "Are you well? Have they mistreated you?"

"I am very well. The babe is well." She seized his hand and pressed his palm over the mound. The baby kicked strongly. "Do you feel?"

"Yes." Iyadur Atani stroked her hair. A scarlet cloak with an ornate gold border hung on a peg. He reached for it and wrapped it about her. "Now, my love, we go. Shut your eyes, and keep them shut until I tell you to open them." He bent and lifted her into his arms. Her heart thundered against his chest.

She breathed into his ear, "I am sorry. I am heavy."

"You weigh nothing," he said. His human shape dissolved. The walls of the tower shuddered and burst apart. Blocks of stone and splintered planks of wood toppled into the courtyard. Women screamed. Arching his great neck, the Silver Dragon spread his wings and rose into the sky. The soldiers on the ramparts threw their spears at him and fled. Joanna heard the screaming and felt the hot wind. The scent of burning filled her nostrils. She knew what must have happened. But the arms about her were her husband's, and human. She did not know how this could be, yet it was. Eyes tight shut, she buried her face against her husband's shoulder.

Martun Hal stood with a courier in the castle hall. The crash of stone and the screaming interrupted him. A violent gust of heat swept through the room. The windows of the hall shattered. Racing from the hall, he looked up and saw the dragon circling. His men crouched, sobbing in fear. Consumed with rage, he looked about for a bow, a spear, a rock . . . Finally he drew his sword.

"Damn you!" he shouted impotently at his adversary.

Then the walls of his castle melted beneath a white-hot rain.

In Derrenhold, Ege diCorsini was wearily, reluctantly preparing for war. He did not want to fight Martun Hal, but he would, of course, if troops from Serrenhold took one step across his border. That an attack would be mounted he had no doubt. His spies had told him to expect it. Jamis of the Hawks had sent her daughters to warn him.

Part of his weariness was a fatigue of the spirit. *This is all my fault. I should have killed him when I had the opportunity. Ferris was right.* The other part of his weariness was physical. He was tired much of the time, and none of the tonics or herbal concoctions that the physicians prescribed seemed to help. His heart raced oddly. He could not sleep. Sometimes in the night he wondered if the Old One sleeping underground had dreamed of him. When the Old One dreams of you, you die. But he did not want to die and leave his domain and its people in danger, and so he planned a war, knowing all the while that he might die in the middle of it.

"My lord," a servant said, "you have visitors."

"Send them in," Ege diCorsini said. "No, wait." The physicians had said he needed to move about. Rising wearily, he went into the hall.

He found there his niece Joanna, big with child, and with her, her flame-haired, flame-eyed husband. A strong smell of burning hung about their clothes.

Ege diCorsini drew a long breath. He kissed Joanna on both cheeks. "I will let your mother know that you are safe."

"She needs to rest," Iyadur Atani said.

"I do not need to rest. I have been doing absolutely nothing for the last six months. I need to go home," Joanna said astringently. "Only I do not wish to ride. Uncle, would you lend us a litter and some steady beasts to draw it?"

"You may have anything I have," Ege diCorsini said. And for a moment he was not tired at all.

Couriers galloped throughout Ippa, bearing the news: Martun Hal was dead; Serrenhold Castle was ash, or nearly so. The threat of war was—after twenty years—truly over. Martun Hal's captains—most of them—had died with him. Those still alive hid, hoping to save their skins.

Two weeks after the rescue and the burning of Serrenhold, Ege diCorsini died.

In May, with her mother and sisters at her side, Joanna gave birth to a son. The baby had flame-colored hair and eyes like his father's. He was named Avahir. A year and a half later, a second son was born to Joanna Torneo Atani. He had dark hair, and eyes like his mother's. He was named Jon. Like the man whose name he bore, Jon Atani had a sweet disposition and a loving heart. He adored his brother, and Avahir loved his younger brother fiercely. Their loyalty to each other made their parents very happy.

Thirteen years almost to the day from the burning of Serrenhold, on a bright spring morning, a man dressed richly as a prince, carrying a white birch staff, appeared at the front gate of Atani Castle and requested audience with the dragon-lord. He refused to enter or even to give his name, saying only, "Tell him the fisherman has come for his catch."

His servants found Iyadur Atani in the great hall of his castle.

"My lord," they said, "a stranger stands at the front gate, who will not give his name. He says. 'The fisherman has come for his catch.' "

"I know who it is," their lord replied. He walked to the gate of his castle. The sorcerer stood there, leaning on his serpent-headed staff, entirely at ease.

"Good day," he said cheerfully. "Are you ready to travel?"

And so Iyadur Atani left his children and his kingdom to serve Viksa the wizard. I do not know—no one ever asked her, not even their sons—what Iyadur Atani and his wife said to one another that day. Avahir Atani, who at twelve was already full-grown, as changeling children are wont to be, inherited the lordship of Atani Castle. Like his father, he gained the reputation of being fierce but just.

Jon Atani married a granddaughter of Rudolf diMako and went to live in that city.

Joanna Atani remained in Dragon Keep. As time passed and Iyadur Atani did not return, her sisters and her brother, even her sons, urged her to remarry. She told them all not to be fools; she was wife to the Silver Dragon. Her husband was alive and might return at any time, and how would he feel to find another man warming her bed? She became her son's chief minister, and in that capacity could often be found riding across Dragon's Country, and elsewhere in Ippa, to Derrenhold and Mirrinhold and Ragnar, and even to far Voiana, where the Red Hawk sisters, one in particular, always welcomed her. She would not go to Serrenhold.

But always she returned to Dragon Keep.

As for Iyadur Atani: he traveled with the wizard throughout Ryoka, carrying his bags, preparing his oatcakes and his bathwater, scraping mud from his boots. Viksa's boots were often muddy, for he was a great traveler, who walked, rather than rode, to his many destinations. In the morning, when Iyadur Atani brought the sorcerer his breakfast, Viksa would say, "Today we go to Rotsa"—or Ruggio, or Towena. "They have need of magic." He never said how he knew this. And off they would go to Vipurri or Rotsa or Talvela, to Sorvino, Ruggio, or Rowena.

Sometimes the need to which he was responding had to do directly with magic, as when a curse needed to be lifted. Often it had to do with common disasters. A river had swollen in its banks and needed to be restrained. A landslide had fallen on a house or barn. Sometimes the one who needed them was noble, or rich. Sometimes not. It did not matter to Viksa. He could enchant a cornerstone, so that the wall it anchored would rise straight and true; he could spell a field, so that its crop would thrust from the soil no matter what the rainfall.

His greatest skill was with water. Some sorcerers draw a portion of their power from an element: wind, water, fire, or stone. Viksa could coax a spring out of earth that had known only drought for a hundred years. He could turn stagnant water sweet. He knew the names of every river, stream, brook, and waterfall in Issho.

In the first years of his servitude, Iyadur Atani thought often of his sons, and especially Avahir, and of Joanna, but after a while his anxiety for them faded. After a longer while, he found he did not think of them so often—rarely at all, in fact. He even forgot their names. He had already relinquished his own. *Iyadur is too grand a name for a servant,* the sorcerer had remarked. *You need a different name.*

And so the tall, fair-haired man became known as Shadow. He carried the sorcerer's pack and cooked his food. He rarely spoke.

"Why is he so silent?" women, bolder and more curious than their men, asked the sorcerer.

Sometimes the sorcerer answered, "No reason. It's his nature." And sometimes he told a tale, a long, elaborate fantasy of spells and dragons and sorcerers, a gallant tale in which Shadow had been the hero, but from which he had emerged changed—broken. Shadow, listening, wondered if perhaps this tale was true. It might have been. It explained why his memory was so erratic, and so vague.

His dreams, by contrast, were vivid and intense. He dreamed often of a dark-walled castle flanked by white-capped mountains. Sometimes he dreamed that he was a bird, flying over the castle. The most adventurous of the women, attracted by Shadow's looks and, sometimes, by his silence, tried to talk with him. But their smiles and allusive glances only made him shy. He thought that he had had a wife, once. Maybe she had left him. He thought perhaps she had. But maybe not. Maybe she had died.

He had no interest in the women they met, though as far as he could tell, his body still worked as it should. He was a powerful man, well formed. Shadow wondered sometimes what his life had been before he had come to serve the wizard. He had skills: he could hunt and shoot a bow, and use a sword. Perhaps he had served in some noble's war band. He bore a knife now, a good one, with a bone hilt, but no sword. He did not need a sword. Viksa's reputation, and his magic, shielded them both.

Every night, before they slept, wherever they were, half speaking, half chanting in a language Shadow did not know, the sorcerer wove spells of protection about them and their dwelling. The spells were very powerful. They made Shadow's ears hurt.

Once, early in their association, he asked the sorcerer what the spell was for.

"Protection," Viksa replied. Shadow had been surprised. He had not realized Viksa had enemies.

But now, having traveled with the sorcerer as long as he had, he knew that even the lightest magic can have consequences, and Viksa's magic was not always light. He could make rain, but he could also make drought. He could lift curses or lay them. He was a man of power, and he had his vanity. He enjoyed being obeyed. Sometimes he enjoyed being feared.

Through spring, summer, and autumn, the wizard traveled wherever he was called to go. But in winter they returned to Lake Urai. He had a house beside the lake, a simple place, furnished with simple things: a pallet, a table, a chair, a shelf for books. But Viksa rarely looked at the books; it seemed he had no real love for study. Indeed, he seemed to have no passion for anything, save sorcery itself—and fishing. All through the Issho winter, despite the bitter winds, he took his little coracle out upon the lake and sat there with a pole. Sometimes he caught a fish, or two, or half a dozen. Sometimes he caught none.

"Enchant them," Shadow said to him one gray afternoon, when his master had returned to the house empty-handed. "Call them to your hook with magic."

The wizard shook his head. "I can't."

"Why not?"

"I was one of them once." Shadow looked at him, uncertain. "Before I was a sorcerer, I was a fish."

It was impossible to tell if he was joking or serious. It might have been true. It explained, at least, his affinity for water.

While Viksa fished, Shadow hunted. The country around the lake was rich with game; despite the winter, they did not lack for meat. Shadow hunted deer and badger and beaver. He saw wolves, but did not kill them. Nor would he kill birds, though birds there were; even in winter, geese came often to the lake. Their presence woke in him a wild, formless longing.

One day he saw a white bird, with wings as wide as he was tall, circling over the lake. It had a beak like a raptor. It called to him, an eerie sound. Something about it made his heart beat faster. When Viksa returned from his sojourn at the lake, Shadow described the strange bird to him, and asked what it was.

"A condor," the wizard said.

"Where does it come from?"

"From the north," the wizard said, frowning.

"It called to me. It looked—noble."

"It is not. It is scavenger, not predator." He continued to frown. That night he spent a long time over his nightly spells.

In spring, the kingfishers and guillemots returned to the lake. And one April morning, when Shadow laid breakfast upon the table, Viksa said, "Today we go to Dale."

"Where is that?"

"In the White Mountains, in Kameni, far to the north." And so they went to Dale, where a petty lordling needed Viksa's help in deciphering the terms and conditions of an ancient prophecy, for within it lay the future of his kingdom.

From Dale they traveled to Secca, where a youthful hedge-witch, hoping to shatter a boulder, had used a spell too complex for her powers and had managed to summon a stone demon, which promptly ate her. It was an old, powerful demon. It took a day, a night, and another whole day until Viksa, using the strongest spells he knew, was able to send it back into the Void.

They rested that night at a roadside inn, south of Secca. Viksa, exhausted from his battle with the demon, went to bed right after his meal, so worn that he fell asleep without taking the time to make his customary incantations.

Shadow considered waking him to remind him of it, and decided not to. Instead, he, too, slept.

And there, in an inn south of Secca, Iyadur Atani woke.

He was not, he realized, in his bed, or even in his bedroom. He lay on the floor. The coverlet around his shoulders was rough, coarse wool, not the soft quilt he was used to. Also, he was wearing his boots.

He said, "Joanna?" No one answered. A candle sat on a plate at his elbow. He lit it without touching it.

Sitting up soundlessly, he gazed about the chamber, at the bed and its snoring occupant, at the packs he had packed himself, the birchwood staff athwart the doorway. . . . Memory flooded through him. The staff was Viksa's. The man sleeping in the bed was Viksa. And he—*he* was Iyadur Atani, lord of Dragon Keep.

His heart thundered. His skin coursed with heat. The ring on his hand glowed, but he could not feel the burning. Fire coursed beneath his skin. He rose.

How long had Viksa's magic kept him in thrall—five years? Ten years? More?

He took a step toward the bed. The serpent in the wizard's staff opened its eyes. Raising its carved head, it hissed at him.

The sound woke Viksa. Gazing up from his bed at the bright shimmering shape looming over him, he knew immediately what had happened. He had made a mistake. *Fool,* he thought, *Oh, you fool.*

It was too late now.

The guards on the walls of Secca saw a pillar of fire rise into the night. Out of it—so they swore, with such fervor that even the most skeptical did not doubt them—flew a silver dragon. It circled the flames, bellowing with such power and ferocity that all who heard it trembled.

Then it beat the air with its wings and leaped north.

In Dragon Keep, a light powdery snow covered the garden. It did not deter the rhubarb shoots breaking through the soil, or the fireweed, or the buds on the birches. A sparrow swung in the birch branches, singing. The clouds that had brought the snow had dissipated; the day was bright and fair, the shadows sharp as the angle of the sparrow's wing against the light.

Joanna Atani walked along the garden path. Her face was lined, and her hair, though still lustrous and thick, was streaked with silver. But her step was as vigorous, and her eyes as bright, as they had been when first she came to Atani Castle, over thirty years before.

Bending, she brushed a snowdrop free of snow. By midday, she judged, the snow would be gone. A clatter of pans arose in the kitchen. A clear voice, imperious and young, called from within. She smiled. It was Hikaru, Avahir's firstborn and heir. He was only two years old, but had the height and grace of a lad twice that age.

A woman answered him, her voice soft and firm. That was Geneva Tuolinnen, Hikaru's mother. She was an excellent mother, calm and unexcitable. She was a good seamstress, too, and a superb manager; far better at running the castle than Joanna had ever been. She could scarcely handle a bow, though, and thought swordplay was entirely men's work.

She and Joanna were as friendly as two strong-willed women can be.

A black, floppy-eared puppy bounded across Joanna's feet, nearly knocking her down. Rup the dog-boy scampered after it. They tore through the garden and raced past the kitchen door into the yard.

A man walked into the garden. Joanna shaded her eyes. He was quite tall. She did not recognize him. His hair was nearly white, but he did not move like an old man. Indeed, the height of him and the breadth of his shoulder reminded her of Avahir, but she knew it was not Avahir. He was hundreds of miles away, in Kameni.

She said, "Sir, who are you?"

The man came closer. "Joanna?"

She knew that voice. For a moment she ceased to breathe. Then she walked toward him.

It was her husband.

He looked exactly as he had the morning he had left with the wizard, sixteen years before. His eyes were the same, and his scent, and the heat of his body against hers. She slid her palms beneath his shirt. His skin was warm. Their lips met.

I do not know—no one ever asked them—what Iyadur Atani and his wife said to one another that day. Surely there were questions, and answers. Surely there were tears, of sorrow and of joy.

He told her of his travels, of his captivity, and of his freedom. She told him of their sons, particularly of his heir, Avahir, who ruled Dragon's Country.

"He is a good lord, respected throughout Ryoka. His people fear him and love him. He is called the Azure Dragon. He married a girl from Issho. She is cousin to the Talvela; we are at peace with them, and with the Nyo. She and Avahir have a son, Hikaru. Jon, too, is wed. He and his wife live in Mako. They have three children, two boys and a girl. You are a grandfather."

He smiled at that. Then he said, "Where is my son?"

"In Kameni, at a council called by Rowan Imorin, the king's war leader, who wished to lead an army against the Chuyo pirates." She stroked his face. It was not true, as she had first thought, that he was unchanged. The years had marked him. Still, he looked astonishingly young. She wondered if she seemed old to him.

"Never leave me again," she said.

A shadow crossed his face. He lifted her hands to his lips and kissed them, front and back. Then he said, "My love, I would not. But I must go. I cannot stay here."

"What are you saying?"

"Avahir is lord of this land now. You know the dragon-nature. We are jealous of power, we dragons. It would go ill were I to stay."

Joanna's blood chilled. She did know. The history of the dragon-folk is filled with tales of rage and rivalry: sons strive against fathers, brothers against brothers, mothers against their children. They are bloody tales. For this reason, among others, the dragon kindred do not live very long.

She said steadily, "You cannot hurt your son."

"I would not," said Iyadur Atani. "Therefore I must leave."

"Where will you go?"

"I don't know. Will you come with me?"

She locked her fingers through his huge ones and smiled through tears. "I will go wherever you wish. Only give me time to kiss my grandchild and write a letter to my son. For he must know that I have gone of my own accord."

And so, Iyadur Atani and Joanna Torneo Atani left Atani Castle. They went quietly, without fuss, accompanied by neither man nor maidservant. They went first to Mako, where Iyadur Atani greeted his younger son and met his son's wife, and their children.

From there they went to Derrenhold, and from Derrenhold, west, to Voiana, the home of the Red Hawk sisters. From Voiana, letters came to Avahir Atani and to Jon Atani from their mother, assuring them, and particularly Avahir, that she was with her husband, and that she was well.

Avahir Atani, who truly loved his mother, flew to Voiana. But he arrived to find them gone.

"Where are they?" he asked Janis Delamico, who was still matriarch of the Red Hawk clan. For the Red Hawk sisters live long.

"They left."

"Where did they go?"

Jamis Delamico shrugged. "They did not tell me their destination, and I did not ask."

There were no more letters. Over time, word trickled back to Dragon Keep that they had been seen in Rowena, or Sorvino, or Secca, or the mountains north of Dale.

"Where were they going?" Avahir Atani asked, when his servants came to him to tell him these stories. But no one could tell him that.

Time passed; Ippa prospered. In Dragon Keep, a daughter was born to Avahir and Geneva Atani. They named her Lucia. She was small and dark-haired and feisty. In Derrenhold and Mako and Mirrinhold, memories of conflict faded. In the windswept west, the folk of Serrenhold rebuilt their lord's tower.

In the east, Rowan Imorin, the war leader of Kameni, summoned the lords of all the provinces to unite against the Chuyo pirates. The lords of Ippa, instead of quarreling with each other, joined the lords of Nakase and Kameni. They fought many battles. They gained many victories.

But in one battle, not the greatest, an arrow shot by a Chuyo archer sliced into the throat of Avahir Atani, and killed him. Grimly, his mourning soldiers made a pyre and burned his body. For the dragon-kindred do not lie in earth.

Hikaru, the Shining Dragon, became lord of Dragon Keep. Like his father and his grandfather before him, he was feared and respected throughout Ippa.

One foggy autumn, a stranger arrived at the gates of Dragon Keep, requesting to see the lord. He was an old man with silver hair. His back was stooped, but they could see that he had once been powerful. He bore no sword, but only a knife with a bone hilt.

"Who are you?" the servants asked him.

"My name doesn't matter," he answered. "Tell him I have a gift for him."

They brought him to Hikaru. Hikaru said, "Old man, I am told you have a gift for me."

"It is so," the old man said. He extended his palm. On it sat a golden brooch, fashioned in the shape of a rose. "It is an heirloom of your house. It was given by your grandfather, Iyadur, to his wife Joanna, on their wedding night. She is dead now, and so it comes to you. You should give it to your wife, when you wed."

Frowning, Hikaru said, "How do you come by this thing? Who are you? Are you a sorcerer?"

"I am no one," the old man replied, "a shadow."

"That is not an answer," Hikaru said, and he signaled to his soldiers to seize the stranger.

But the men who stepped forward to hold the old man found their hands passing through empty air. They hunted through the castle for him, but he was gone. They decided that he was a sorcerer, or perhaps the sending of a sorcerer. Eventually they forgot him. When the shadow of the dragon first appeared in Atani Castle, rising like smoke out of the castle walls, few thought of the old man who had vanished into shadow one autumnal morning. Those who did kept it to themselves. But Hikaru Atani remembered. He kept the brooch and gave it to his wife upon their wedding night. And he told his soldiers to honor the shadow-dragon when it came, and not to speak lightly of it.

"For clearly," he said, "it belongs here."

The shadow of the dragon still lives in the walls of Atani Castle. It comes as it chooses, unsummoned. And still, in Dragon's Country, and throughout Ippa and Issho, and even into the east, the singers tell the story of Iyadur Atani, of his wife, Joanna, and of the burning of Serrenhold.

***L. E. Modesitt** is equally at home in the worlds of fantasy and science fiction. Recent books include* Ecolitan Prime *and* The Ethos Effect. *His* Spellsong Cycle, *which numbered five books, concerned wizardry emerging from music.*

For the present project he contributes a nifty tale concerning . . . well, read the title.

Fallen Angel

L. E. Modesitt, Jr.

Jaweau was sitting in the big white chair behind his desk when I walked in. The desk is white. Everything is, except for some of the chairs, and yet it's not blinding. "You are always welcome, Lucian, even if you never bother knocking. . . .

"Stow it. You always know I'm coming."

He nodded in that phony sad manner of his, like he wanted to be the forgiving male counterpart of the Maid. "We know, Lucian."

I took the black oak chair, the one he kept for me. Two others were gray, the rest white. All sorts came to see Jaweau, but not many who weren't white. That was why I was there. "What's the job?"

"Real estate. We need an attraction spell for the new villas beyond the Elysian Gardens. Aesthetic and ecological balance, you know?"

"An attraction spell for what angels should want to do naturally?"

"Goodness does not equal wisdom, Lucian," he pointed out. "Nor, as you have repeatedly proved, does wisdom equate to goodness."

"So you're calling me in?"

"I thought we should have something with depth and staying power. I even thought you might reconsider—"

"Never." Once had been enough. More than enough.

"Never is a long time."

I ignored that possibility. "An appeal to young angels, cherubim, mothers, that sort of thing?" I had to sneer. Even saints and angels retained some cupidity.

"No . . . the full spectrum. Draw in the seraphim, too." Jaweau shrugged as only an angel could shrug, resigned without being cynical.

"Muckin' Maid!" An attraction spell for cherubim and seraphim, and Jaweau and his crew of goody-goodies looked down on me?

"Don't swear. If I have to clean the place, it comes off your fee. I told you—"

I was still pissed. A full-spectrum attraction spell, for the dark's due! "You want to pay for that? Do you know what that means? You need a priestess—twice—stable holy water, a virgin singer, and I'll have to be celibate the whole time until I write the song. I can't do crap else if I take the job. That's a thousand golds, minimum."

"Well . . . that would just about take care of what you owe. . . ." Jaweau smiled sweetly, the white creep. "Besides, you're always celibate here, unless you do a resonance spell. What choice do you have?"

He was stating a fact, and I ignored it. "Owe! Maid be damned . . ."

He raised his right hand, and the light gathered at his fingertips. "I warned you."

"I'm sorry." The bastard had me. One dose of his goody-goodies, and I'd be worthless for days. I can't afford that much of what everyone else calls holiness, not and remain sane. How Jaweau does it is beyond me. I mean, how can a guy who looks like an angel, and *is* one, run both Ciudad Eternidad and the only ad agency in the city? Well, someone has to, and it has to be an angel. All they let us do is be consultants. There are some things they just can't do. Like disease-killing . . . they can't even destroy a tiny bacterium . . . or deep attraction spells.

I shifted my weight in the black chair and looked toward him. He was waiting for me to talk. Of course, I couldn't stare him down. That would have set the whole place on fire, and I couldn't afford to pay that off, either. And I'd have a headache for months, after I lost the job and woke up a month later. The opposites bit, again. "All right. How good does it have to be?"

"You do this one right, and we'll call it even. You can stay away from here forever, if you want."

"I occasionally like to come up here and look around. It's worth seeing to understand why I prefer Hel." I paused. "Besides, it upsets you. You really don't want me around, do you? Gets them asking questions."

Jaweau shrugged again. He didn't have to admit anything, but I could tell I was getting on his nerves. Maybe I reminded him of the old days too much.

"Give me a couple of days," I finally said. "I didn't plan on two songs."

"You can do the dark side in a couple of hours." Jaweau let a halo circle that golden hair. He always did have an eye for effects.

"That's the easy part. You think it's easy for me to write a virgin song, even for a fallen angel?"

"I always admitted you were an artist, Lucian deNoir—"

"Don't say it."

"You comprehend the fallen. I still don't understand. . . ."

"You never will." I stood up. "You'll know when the songs are ready."

He nodded. "The skies will weep . . . again."

Such dragon crap, and he believes it. All the damned angels and saints do because he does.

I left as quickly as I could, and I sure as Hel didn't look in his eyes. Once I had trusted him, but you know where trusting an angel leads. I'm sure the bastard used his web of light to remove any traces of skepticism I'd left behind.

My villa was the same as always, the same low hill, the same as when—I try not to think about it, but I'm sure Jaweau leaves it that way just to remind me. The painting of the Maid still hangs over the couch in the workroom. The harps are gone, but I don't need them anyway. I poured a goblet of water—that's the one drink I can have in Ciudad Eternidad without risk. Then I sat down, the Maid looking over my shoulder.

Writing the song for the dark side of the resonance spell took a couple of hours. That was after it took me three days to write the piece for the singer, and the white song had to come first. With all the crap about grace, they have to turn to me to write a true white song. The Maid has a sense of irony, all right.

I have to finish on the dark side, or I'd start believing in all that crap about grace and forgiveness, and I don't ever want to believe that again.

It was cloudy when I finished, but that was my legacy. Jaweau can be a real bastard. At least it was done. I sealed both folios, one with white wax, the other with black, and made my way back to Jaweau's. I walked deliberately.

He met me outside the big chamber, and I suppose his eyes were sad, but I didn't look.

"Who's the singer?" Not that I really cared, though I'd have to before the spell was set and twisted.

"Name's Kyralyn. The blonde by the pentagram."

"All right." I didn't look at her or at the three angels who carried the harps. The singer carried her own. She had to, of course, since the strings were different.

The dark drummer was Khango. I'd worked with him before. Solid, but really didn't care much so long as he could work. He was naturally dark. Some are.

"Are you going to check her out?" Jaweau held the web between his hands, and the light cascaded along the strings.

I lifted a hand, and he stepped back.

"Keep your black hands off my webs, Lucian."

"Then don't tell me when to check out the singers." I grinned, but he didn't grin back. I took a deep breath and looked at the singer, really looked, and not through his web, either.

She stared back with eyes as blue and deep as Eden, blue over the tears of a fallen angel. I almost wanted to turn away, but, what the Hel, it was her choice. No one had made her do what she had, and, if she wanted to sing the spell, that was her choice, too.

Except it wasn't, and we both knew it. And neither of us could say so. In some ways, Jaweau is an angelic sadist.

One of the angels smiled sadly over a golden harp, and I wanted to paste him, not that it would have done any good, just would have confirmed his opinion of me.

People think working a resonance spell is like similarity or contagion. That's dragon crap, not that there've ever been dragons, but dark mages—that's what I think of myself as, anyway, no matter what the holies call me—are supposed to believe in the unbelievable. More crap.

A resonance spell is a lot trickier, because you've got to have a virgin song, sung by a virgin singer—not pure, but virgin—and then you've got to twist it so that it resonates. The twist's the thing, a betrayal of the first two. I didn't like it, but we all do things we don't like.

"Let's get on with it."

"As you wish." Jaweau moved the web, and a line of fire flared around the pentagram.

I stepped into the pentagram, and Jaweau closed the gap with the light web. Kyralyn stood at the focal point of the pentagram, on the lines, but not breaking them, and opened the folio. White wax crumpled to the floor. No one else had seen the song, and she couldn't even open the folder until I was held inside the pentagram, not if the spell were to resonate properly.

Khango sat on a black stool between the two base points of the pentagram. After Kyralyn broke the seal on her folder, he opened his. The black wax melted in dark flames. His black sticks hovered above the drums, waiting for Kyralyn to begin.

She studied at the notes, and time froze. Finally, her fingers touched the silver harp strings. The angels used gold, but Kyralyn was still a fallen angel and only a virgin technically, thanks to Jaweau. He'll bend the rules when he wants to, the sanctimonious bastard.

I waited behind the white lines of the pentagram.

Kyralyn began.

Hel, could she sing! I might have heard better in the time since . . . but I didn't recall when. She was so good that the faint cloak of darkness that had surrounded her, the one that probably only Jaweau and I could see, seemed to lighten as she sang, almost vanishing. As she shimmered toward the white, Khango continued weaving the counterpoint, and the darkness gathered around the base of the pentagram. Even before she finished, the chamber was resonating.

Although I had written the notes and words, when Kyralyn sang them, I forgot them, and that was as it should be. No one else would remember them either, nor the black counterpoint sung by the dark drummer.

As the song and countersong shivered to a close, I wiped my forehead. It was hot in the pentagram, damned hot, as always.

Outside the pentagram, Jaweau and the others squirmed, as if the resonance were the beat of an unheard dance that picked at them. The whole chamber echoed with the unheard songspell, the resonance lingering, waiting for the next phase, and for the priestess. We all waited. I certainly couldn't do anything else.

The good mothers like to make you wait and squirm, to realize exactly what you've done. That unset resonance even twisted my guts as I watched for the door to open. Finally, the priestess stepped into the chamber. Actually, it was a chapel, since you don't mess with things like resonance spells in any other place, not if you want to keep a whole soul in your body. I might belong to the depths, but even I don't like the thought of spending eternity rent into burning fragments, and the Maid has never been that merciful to those of us who harbor darkness.

The priestess didn't waste any time, either, starting right out with the familiar words. "Dearly beloved . . ." When she got to the part about redemption through love, I looked down. After that, she avoided looking at me, and her eyes kept straying to Kyralyn.

I watched Kyralyn's eyes, too. They were a deep open blue, the honest kind you don't associate with fallen angels, and I wondered how exactly she had betrayed herself, not that what I was doing was any better, even if everyone knew it was necessary. I mean, you do have to set the spell, and no one was going to let me out of the pentagram unbound. The ceremony binds the power between us, and the twist locks it back into the rune rods that Jaweau had already placed out beyond the Elysian Gardens.

The good mother did the shortest ceremony possible, ending up with the traditional pronouncement about not putting asunder what the Maid hath joined, and once our hands touched across the pentagram, and the silver rings flared their linked fires, Jaweau opened the pentagram. I shivered. I couldn't help it.

Kyralyn didn't. Those open blue eyes held so much pain that I had to look away. Me . . . I had to look away. Figure that, and over a resonance spell.

I swallowed, and stepped across the pentagram. It still hurt, even after Jaweau erased the light.

Kyralyn turned to me. Tears should have been falling from those eyes, but they were as clear as old-time skies. She actually stepped toward me until we were perhaps three paces apart. She licked her lips, but her eyes met mine.

"You're Lucian—"

"Please don't say it. You don't have to."

"All right." Her speaking voice was a trace husky, unlike the silver tones that had set the spell.

I drew her to me, gently, with both hands. Her hands touched my waist, and my fingers traced the fine line of her chin. In time, I looked her full in the face, and my eyes burned as they met hers. Even if she were just a singer, that made her, after all, a fallen angel, and that's hard. Especially for me, no matter what anyone says.

I took her arm, and we made our way from the chapel toward my villa. We had to walk, because nothing in Ciudad Eternidad would carry me.

Her eyes widened as we neared the open gate, and the villa beyond, far more graceful and beautiful, still, than any other structure in the city. "I didn't . . . realize. . . ."

"He was merciful . . ." I temporized.

"I wouldn't call it that." Her tone was thoughtful, but her steps matched mine as we crossed the line of black marble between the gateposts and walked to the low steps leading to the portico.

Once we reached the room with the balcony, I offered her water. That was all. I didn't want to tempt her, although it would have been technically fair. She could have refused, but I like to play it straight, unlike Jaweau.

She took the water, looked at it, and then slowly sipped it.

In time, she let me undress her, and I was gentle.

For a while, I even forgot.

Later, I told her, "I do love you."

"You can't." Her words were sad, even as her hands drew me closer. "You belong to . . ."

I forced myself to meet her eyes. "I can't lie here. Everything I say in Ciudad Eternidad must be true." That is absolutely true, so far as it goes. I cannot lie in any city of the saints or angels. And I did love her, absolutely, as those deep, innocent eyes cut through me. Not that it mattered. Nothing had changed, except for those moments when I held a fallen angel, and they came to an end too soon.

When she finally slept, I eased away from her crumpled form and watched the boreali. Then I went down to my workroom and looked at the Bucelli painting for a long time. Maybe there were other universes where it had turned out differently. Maybe.

Morning came, and eventually Kyralyn walked down the stairs, wearing the white gown. She deserved that, and it looked good on her.

I didn't let her say a word. "You can pick up the papers at the priestess's after the Sabbath. I even paid gold for an annulment, not a lousy twenty pieces of silver for a divorce." I had to be the one who paid for the betrayal, of course, or the resonance wouldn't stay set.

Her eyes glistened for a moment, like silver, I'd say . . . if I were the poetic sort. Then she looked at the painting of the Maid, the one by Bucelli that shows Her before the judges, just before they crucified Her. I had Merleno duplicate it. The spell cost a good ten golds, but it was worth it then, more so now. He captured the innocence in her eyes, the way no one else did. Sort of like Kyralyn's, I guess.

"You don't mean it." Kyralyn looked at me again, like the first time after the resonance set in us, and my eyes still burned.

"You were a great lay, Kyralyn, and we did one Hel of a resonance spell. But that's all I can give you." I looked down at the black tabletop—all the furniture got darker when I stayed at the villa for very long. She was already shimmering a bit, and the annulment hadn't even been entered. I knew I'd never do another resonance as good. Too bad the spell doesn't work unless there's betrayal.

"You don't mean it," she repeated. "You don't have to do this."

But I did. Or Jaweau would have everything. "Like I said, you were a great lay." I didn't meet her eyes. Instead I looked back at the copy of the Bucelli. Damn, Merleno had done a fine job.

The workroom was silent, but I refused to look into those eyes. If I had, I'd have been thinking about . . . never mind.

When I finally looked up, Kyralyn was gone.

You've redeemed your soul, Kyralyn. The saints will be pleased. I wasn't sure Jaweau would be, and that pleased me.

Business is business, I guess. But I even envied the pain in Kyralyn's eyes.

I sat down in the wooden chair at the oak table and looked at the portrait of the Maid for a long time. Perhaps I really looked at the Maid, but all I saw was Kyralyn. What else could I do? It was time to head back to Hel, until Jaweau or someone else needed me. Jaweau would, again, sooner or later.

He always does.

***Trish Cacek** has won both a Bram Stoker and World Fantasy Award for her short fiction, some of which has been collected in* Leavings, *as well as a mini-collection,* In the Spirit.

She is currently working on the second of four books called The New Hope Quartet, *set, she says, "in the very real and very haunted township of New Hope, Pennsylvania."*

The Following

P. D. Cacek

The stones moved.

The soft clatter of one stone tumbling over another was almost lost in the rustle of leaves. It was such an ordinary sound—the sound of feet walking on stone—and one she'd gotten used to over the years. So many years now that she didn't even bother to look back over her shoulder.

Besides, she knew what she'd see.

Nothing. The path would be empty, but the stones would still move as though shuffled by invisible feet.

It was amazing what a person could get used to, Lydia thought.

When they had to.

Crash. "Mitch!"

It was the tone of panic in her voice, more than the sound of shattering glass, that jerked Mitchell out of the last play of a doubleheader and sent him running toward the upstairs bedroom they'd shared for just over two months.

He'd been expecting something to happen. And hoping to God that it wouldn't.

The house had been quiet for almost four days—a new, all-time record—which was almost long enough to convince him that the thumps and moans and flickering lights, which couldn't be fixed no matter how many electricians checked the wiring, was just the house settling. Just the house getting used to being lived in again after standing empty for so long.

Thump—crash.

Just the house.

"Mitch!"

Mitchell bumped the doorjamb as he ran into the room, but the pain barely registered when he saw the remains of the antique-reproduction cheval mirror on the unmade bed. The rosewood frame was splintered in a half-dozen places and the glass shattered. Silvered fragments lay among the rumpled blankets like razor-sharp snowflakes.

"Damn," he whispered. He'd bought the mirror as a "Moving-In Day" present for the woman who was currently cowering in the narrow opening between the dresser and wall. "What did you do?"

He realized how stupid that question sounded right after he said it. She probably hadn't done anything.

Debra glared at him from over the top of her clasped, white-knuckled hands. The two Army Surplus duffle bags she'd moved in with were packed and sitting at her feet. There were shards of mirrored glass embedded in the faded olive-green canvas.

"I didn't touch it, Mitch," she said, anger replacing fear as she confirmed what he already suspected. "It just broke."

"Things just don't break, Debra. There's always a reason for everything that happens."

He tried to make himself believe that as he walked over to the bed and brushed the tips of his fingers lightly over a large shard of mirror that had remained in the frame. *Christ.* He wasn't aging well. Only thirty-seven, and he already looked like a man pushing fifty . . . and a nondescript man of fifty at that—gaunt, medium build, slightly stooped at the shoulders. Gray of hair and face and eyes, as unremarkable as air. Mitchell still couldn't understand what Debra had ever seen in him, except equity and a solid line of credit at most of the stores in town.

Mitchell shook his head at the bitter old man in the broken glass. That wasn't fair—Debra had stayed with him longer than any of his other lovers.

Two months and almost three weeks.

Another record.

It just wasn't fair.

He pressed down on the glass and felt a sharp sting. There was a smear of blood on the mirror when he moved his hand away.

"You don't believe me?"

Mitchell blinked as he looked up. It was strange, but he'd almost forgotten she was still there.

"Yeah, sure I do. I'm sorry. Look, I really don't want you to go, okay? I mean, it's . . . this, all of this has a reasonable explanation. Come on, I'll help you unpack."

She was about to say something poignant—they'd been together just long enough for him to be able to tell that by the way she sucked air into her mouth . . . but the house beat her to it.

There was a low rumble in the walls and then a flutter of air through the old heating ducts sounded like laughter. Mitchell looked down at the broken mirror and watched his reflection go a little grayer.

"Mitch?"

He didn't look up.

"Oh God, Mitch. Don't tell me you didn't hear that."

His reflection shrugged.

"It's just a draft. Old houses are drafty, you know that."

"And was it a draft that yanked the mirror out of my hands when I tried to move it?"

That finally made him look up. Debra's face was still pale, but there were growing spots of color in both her cheeks.

"I thought you said you didn't touch it."

The spots of color spread rapidly across her face, deepening it to a ghastly shade of red. She looked like she was about to have a stroke. Mitchell knew he should be worried about that. God knows he didn't want her to die . . . not in the house anyway.

He didn't have a choice.

"Look, maybe you're right, we're both on edge, so maybe it would be better if you left." He looked down at the duffle bags so he wouldn't have to look at her. "For a while. I'll carry these out to the car for you."

He was careful not to get any blood on the canvas handles when he picked up the bags.

"There are some things in the bathroom," Mitchell said, daring a peek as she stood up. He shouldn't have, but he stared at the interplay of muscles in her calves and thighs and remembered how her legs had felt wrapped around the small of his back when they made love. Just last night. "Do you need a box for those, or do you want to leave them?"

He wanted to add *"for when you come back"* but couldn't make himself say it. He hadn't been able to say it to any of his other lovers when they left.

The house settled, without warning, and the framed Georgia O'Keeffe print over the bed crashed to the floor.

"There!" She screamed as she ran out of the bedroom and down the hall, her voice trailing behind her like a contrail. "You saw that! You can't tell me you didn't see that. This place is haunted, Mitch! I kept telling you it's haunted, but you wouldn't listen!"

Her voice already sounded so far away.

Mitchell picked up the bags and followed the trail of sound to the front hall. She was standing just outside the open door, a video clutched in her hands, her natural hemp bag slung over one shoulder. The look in her eyes was almost as far away as the sound of her voice.

"I don't know why you just won't admit it, Mitch, but you know as well as I do that there's . . . something in this house. You've lived here longer than I have, you must know that."

Mitchell stood in the front hall of his house and rolled his shoulders. They were beginning to ache from the weight of the bags, and he wondered what of his, if anything, she may have packed. One of his other fiancées had *accidentally* taken one of his old sweatshirts when she moved out, and the house had been upset . . . noisy for a week after.

"It's just an old house," he repeated, low enough for the house to hear, "and old houses make noises and settle and sometimes things fall down and break."

"Goddamn it, Mitch, when are you going to wake up? You've living in a haunted house!" She thrust the video toward him, and Mitchell jerked back, expecting a blow. "Here, I bought this at the shop a week ago and was meaning to give it to you before I . . ." The spots of color on her cheeks deepened again. "You need to watch it. There's a number you can call at the end. Call her and then call me. I love you, Mitch, but I can't live like this."

He looked at the video's cover and chuckled. Done against a stark black-and-white background, the lurid red letters seemed to float a few inches above the plastic case: *A Step into the Unknown—Conversations with Lydia Light, Ghost Exterminator.* Mitchell tightened his grip on the handles so he wouldn't be tempted to take the video and toss it out the open door. Debra was always bringing things like this home from her job at the Crystalline Moon New Age Shoppe. Mitchell hadn't minded the scented candles or incense, and he was almost getting used to the mind-thawing tones she called music, but this was too much.

"You're kidding," he asked hopefully, "right?"

The color faded again, like someone throwing a switch, and she set the video down on the small hall table before walking out the front door and down the steps.

Mitchell followed, down the steps and out to her car, then stood there, bags in hand, and waited for her to unlock the trunk, waited for her to tell him she was kidding. When she didn't say anything, he hoisted the bags into the clutter of jumper cables, yellowed receipts and empty soda cans.

Debra's hand closed over his as he closed the trunk.

The front door of the house slammed shut. The wind was coming in the opposite direction. She pulled her hand away.

"Call me when it's gone," was all Debra said as she climbed into her dusty little economy car and drove away. Mitchell stood on the curb and watched until the taillights disappeared into the evening shadows. Like a ghost.

"Ghosts aren't real," he whispered.

And the air in the ducts laughed at him when he opened the door.

Lydia hadn't bothered to cut the grass at the edge of the path, hoping the hard, early frosts that had already reduced the tomato and pole bean vines to little more than tattered yellow scraps would do the job for her. And that had been a mistake.

With the stones, she could pretend it was just the wind, just errant gusts playing landscape designer. It was harder to pretend though, when the wall of autumn-dry grass was pushed aside, step by step by invisible step.

So many of them. There were so many of them.

For a moment as she climbed the stairs to the back porch, she thought she could almost see them. Almost recognize a face or two. Or twelve.

"I'm sorry," she whispered, letting the wind carry the words back to them. "I'm so sorry."

Mitchell jumped when the man answered the phone.

For some reason, even though he didn't know why, he thought she'd answer, saying: "Lydia Light, Ghost Exterminator." The first time he watched the video, he alternated between incredulous laughter and genuine bafflement that anyone could have actually believed any of the things the overly fawning host *("—our favorite guest—wonderful woman—emissary of light in the world of darkness—")* was saying about the flamboyant ebony-haired woman in flowing robes *("—I don't know why I can do this, but I capture souls—have all my life—extermination is guaranteed—")*. After the second view he wasn't laughing as much. And when he finished watching the video a third time, Mitchell wrote down the out-of-state Help Line Number and listened to the house thump the walls around him.

"Hello?"

Mitchell had no memory of either walking to the phone or dialing up the number on the piece of paper in his hand. It was stupid; he didn't believe in things like that. He was too rational, too sensible and living in a house that was just too old. That's all. Old houses creaked and thumped and sometimes things fell off walls. That's all it was. To think it was anything else was . . . pathetic.

But he still jumped when the man answered.

"Um, hello?"

"I think—" Mitchell took a deep breath. *This was so stupid, why am I doing this?* "I think I . . . I mean . . ."

"Yes?"

"Nothing. Sorry. Wrong number." *Which it probably is . . . the video is from a show that aired almost twenty years ago. Lydia Light could be dead now for all I know.*

"No problem."

The line went dead, and Mitchell stood there, the handset still to his ear—listening to the white noise static while the house moaned and gibbered and settled in for the night.

It's stupid to think that it might be something else.

So stupid.

Keith looked up when she opened the back door, smiling from ear to ear as he nodded to the mound of potato peels on the kitchen table in front of him. A long russet-colored curl unwound from the edge of the paring knife as he worked. It was a little game he liked to play, seeing how long a peel he could cut without it breaking.

He enjoyed his small victories.

It was one of the things she loved most about him.

One of the things she loved least, however, was his inability to judge quantity. It looked like he'd already peeled almost all of the ten-pound sack she thought she'd hidden well enough in the pantry.

"Oh, you've started dinner."

She hoped she sounded more pleased than surprised as she stepped over the sea salt that was laid across the threshold. There were other salt barriers at the threshold of the front door and along the inner ledge of each window. For eighteen years, the length of their marriage, she'd told him that it stopped ants from getting into the house, and he'd believed her.

Never questioned her once about it.

That was another thing she loved about him.

"Shoot," he said, and the smile lines around his mouth suddenly changed directions. "I guess I forgot to tell you."

Lydia Terrell unwound the knitted scarf from around her neck and draped it over the back of one of the kitchen chairs. She didn't want to spend the rest of the evening mentally adding and subtracting his faults and virtues, so she made herself think of nothing as she slipped out of her barn coat and rubbed her hands together to warm them.

"So tell me now."

"I said we'd bring the potato salad for the Friends of the Library potluck tomorrow night."

We? she wanted to ask. Looking at the hillock of peeled potatoes that still had to be cut, boiled, and lovingly mixed into the concoction of mayonnaise, brown mustard, paprika, diced onions, celery and pickles that had won her blue ribbons at every county fair within driving distance, Lydia unconsciously began flexing the stiffness out of her fingers. The early frost had been as hard on her arthritis as it had been on the tomato vines.

"I thought that was Saturday night."

Keith's frown deepened between his hazel-green eyes as the russet-colored peel broke and fell to the table. "No, I'm pretty sure it was Friday. I think."

Lydia had worked most of the stiffness out of her fingers by the time she reached the phone in the hall.

"I'll call Bernice and double-check," she called over her shoulder. "One nice thing about potato salad, it can't go bad as long as you keep it cold—Oh."

She cocked her head and pressed the phone closer to her ear. The normal bumblebee hum was missing, and in its place was the soft, but recognizable sound of someone breathing.

"Hello?"

The steady breathing changed into a ragged gasp.

"Hello?" she repeated. "Is someone there?"

Silence now, not even the hint of breath. Lydia shook her head. Every one of her instincts told her to hang up, hang up now—hang up right now and start making that potato salad. All the real-life police shows Keith watched on TV said the same thing when it came to suspicious phone calls: Hang up. *Do it. Hang up.*

"Um," a man's voice said, "I'm looking for a Lydia Light? I got this number from an old video."

Lydia sat down on the chair next to the phone. *Too late.* There was a rawness to the man's voice like an open wound; she couldn't hang up without at least hearing him out.

"This is the Terrell household," she said, hoping the truth would set her free, then added softly, "I'm Lydia."

A sigh whispered through the lines, and Lydia closed her eyes.

"I—uh, first let me just say that I don't believe in ghosts."

"Then why did you call?"

When the line went silent again, she opened her eyes and looked down the hall to the kitchen. Keith was still peeling potatoes, whistling a song that had been popular back in the Summer of Love, when they were both kids and reality was something that could be toyed with and changed if you believed hard enough and toked the right controlled substance. Lydia smiled when he looked up to wink and grab another potato. For Keith, reality lay on the table in front of him—she'd be up most of the night making potato salad. For her, reality was the phone in her hand.

"I called," the man finally said, "because . . . a friend of mine thinks there may be something . . . otherworldly going on in my house and I thought . . . my friend thought that you might be able to help. She, my friend, gave me a video of a show you did a while back and—Damn . . . sorry."

"That's all right," Lydia said, getting to her feet. "Anger's a powerful emotion. Stay angry and keep your disbelief. Sometimes that helps."

"But—the host of the show, the man who interviewed you said you can . . . that *if* a house is haunted you can—"

"He died."

"What?"

"Alan Wineberg, the interviewer. He died a few years ago." Lydia shook the memory away. She'd known he was dead before she read about it in the paper. He'd tapped at the kitchen window while she was drying dishes. "I'm sorry, that's an old video, and I'll tell you what I tell everyone: I don't do that sort of thing anymore. Good-bye and good luck."

The man was starting to say something, something beyond the "No, wait, please," when she replaced the receiver and walked back to the kitchen. She'd done those shows almost twenty-five years ago, back when she thought her talent was a blessing instead of a curse, and hadn't thought about them since . . . until, five Halloweens ago when she started getting calls. Some video junkie had found the old tapes of the *A Step into the Unknown* series and remastered them for modern equipment. Since then, for a week each year around Halloween, Lydia was again bombarded by requests for *ghost exterminations,* radio interviews and personal appearances at horror conventions and metaphysical bookstore openings. Could she appear on talk shows devoted to the paranormal? Would she be interested in being in a documentary about real-life hauntings? Could she *please* help?

Even if the caller, like the man she'd just hung up on, didn't believe in ghosts.

Kevin stopped whistling as he tossed the last peeled potato into the clear glass bowl. The ones on the bottom were already beginning to go brown. She'd have to soak them in cold water before boiling them.

"Well," he asked with the air of a man who'd just accomplished a great thing, "is the potluck tomorrow or Saturday?"

Lydia frowned until she realized what he was talking about. The phone call—she was supposed to have been on the phone with Bernice. She gave him one of her well-rehearsed befuddled looks, and it worked like a charm.

As it always did.

"You forgot to ask."

She shrugged her shoulders.

"Just like a woman, you start talking about one thing and forget the other. That's why it's men who go to war." He winked and she chuckled. It was a good marriage, all things considered. "Want me to call her back?"

"No," Lydia said, turning back toward the phone. "I'll do it. You start running cold water on those potatoes."

"Me?" He seemed genuinely shocked that she'd ask him to help beyond the peeling stage.

"You. And if I'm on the phone longer than five minutes, you come rescue me."

That he could do and he nodded.

Lydia waited until she heard the water running in the sink before picking up the receiver. She didn't know what she'd say if the man was still on the phone—*Go away, leave me alone, the video is ancient history. I don't do that anymore. What? All right, I'll be right there, but I have to warn you*—and almost felt faint with relief when she heard the bumblebee hum of an unconnected line.

Thank God.

Bernice answered on the second ring. "Ya-ho?"

"Hi, Bernice, it's Lydia. Is the potluck Friday or Satur—"

"Oh, Lydia! Wow, talk about ESP—I was just thinking about you. I know Keith said you two would be bringing potato salad, but I was wondering—oh, it's Saturday, hon, I tried to push for Friday since I have Melanie's dance recital Saturday morning and I know I'll be an absolute wreck even before the dinner, but the committee voted for Saturday—and, like I was saying, I know you and Keith want to bring potato salad, but I was wondering if I could persuade you into bringing something else? See, Nell, Jean and Steffie are *all* bringing potato salad—talk about not coordinating, huh—and frankly that's two too many, if you get my meaning. Not that I don't *love* potato salad but—"

Lydia sat down hard enough to make the back of the chair knock against the wall, but not loud enough for Keith to hear over the sound of running water and come to the rescue. She was doomed, doomed.

"So, you wouldn't mind, would you? I thought maybe something along the lines of finger food. Oh, you know the sort of thing, small things people can just—"

"Eat with their fingers," Lydia slipped in quickly, "like potato pancakes."

"Yes, or something with a little less starch. I mean we have all that potato salad, and I wouldn't want people to think—"

Lydia closed her eyes and prayed for release.

Mitchell was afraid to close his eyes, even though he knew it was foolish.

It was all Debra's fault. If she hadn't put the idea of ghosts into his head, he wouldn't be standing there right now, wondering about it.

And he sure as hell wouldn't have made that stupid call.

But there was something about the woman's voice on the phone . . . something that made me almost want to believe in—

No! It is stupid. So stupid.

He realized that the moment he'd hung up the phone. But at the same time, the noises he'd always been able to rationally explain away—*air in the pipes, loose floorboards, wind in the eaves*—had become louder, almost as if the house . . . or something inside the house had been listening to his side of the phone conversation and was angry at what he'd tried to do.

Even though he didn't believe in ghosts.

"There's nothing here," he said out loud to *the nothing* in the house. "It's just an old house and old houses settle."

Something, another picture or maybe the towel rack in the small downstairs half-bath crashed to the floor. Then, one by one, the lights downstairs began to blink out until only the desk lamp next to him remained on.

Mitchell didn't believe in ghosts, never had, but he leaned back in his chair and pressed his elbows hard against his belly as the lamp began to dim. "Stop it! Stop it! *Stop it!*"

Even though.

She can help me. She's the only one in the world who can.

He had to make sure. He had to.

It'd taken him less than twelve hours to find her.

Lydia knew it was her caller from the day before, the one who didn't believe in ghosts, but who nevertheless was slowly walking toward the house. She watched him through the lace pattern on the front curtains. It was impossible for her to tell his age; he looked as gray and ageless as the line of weathered granite stones that designated their property line from the neighboring field. His jeans were wrinkled at the crotch and knees, and there was a ghost image of the seat belt across the front of his windbreaker.

Another ghost, Lydia thought, and was glad Keith had already left for work when she opened the door.

"Mrs. Terrell?" His voice sounded weaker in person than it had over the phone.

Lydia nodded, keeping the salt-laced threshold between them. "How did you find me?"

The man seemed to appreciate the straightforward approach. He smiled his thanks as he exhaled.

"The Internet," he said with a one-shoulder shrug, the smile widening. "Something called switchboard-dot-com. All you have to do is supply a phone number, and it gives you an address. Maps, too."

"Big Brother really is watching," she said, and chuckled when she realized that the man standing in front of her, the man who didn't believe in ghosts, was probably too young to know that the term had once been a rallying cry for her generation, and not just a reference to some book on a high school required reading list. "Sorry, I don't have much use for computers."

The man licked his lips and shifted from one foot to the other like a child who'd had too much sugar or had waited too long to ask to use the bathroom. Lydia gripped the doorknob a little harder and looked over his shoulder. Behind him, the rocks along the edge of the sidewalk shifted ever so slightly. Not much, not even enough to make a sound—but just enough to get her attention.

Sensing an interloper.

"Look, I really don't know why I'm here," he said, "but after we spoke I got the feeling that . . . *if* any of this was real, you could tell me what to do."

The stones shifted again, clicking softly. The man heard it and started to turn around.

Forcing herself to smile, Lydia stepped back to let him enter. "I have fresh coffee and potato pancakes in the kitchen. Please come in. I'm Lydia."

"Mitchell," the man said, and didn't disturb so much as a grain of salt as he walked into her home.

The rocks tumbled over each other as she closed the door.

It was almost too incredible to believe it was really happening.

Here he was, three hours and almost two hundred miles away from everything he knew, or thought he knew, sitting in a stuffy, overheated kitchen with a woman he'd just met, a woman his mother's age, eating potato pancakes and talking about ghosts as if they were nothing more than stubborn laundry stains.

He couldn't remember ever being happier.

Lydia was an incredible woman.

"Another?" she asked, and although his stomach was frantically waving the white flag of surrender, he nodded and held out his plate. He'd eat until he burst if that's what she wanted.

Lydia was topping off both their coffee mugs as he forced another crisp forkful into his mouth.

"You either love potato pancakes or you're being incredibly gallant," she said as she set an old-fashioned burp-percolator down on the table between them. Mitchell studied her hands while she added milk and sugar to the blue stoneware mug on her side of the table. Her fingers were red and chapped, cold despite the room's stuffiness. It hurt him to see that and all he wanted to do was reach across the table and warm her hands.

But he didn't.

"They're great," he said instead and shoveled in another bite to prove it. "But I don't want to eat you out of house and home."

She laughed as she brought the mug to her lips.

"Believe me, you'd have to stay at least a week before that happened."

Mitchell's hand stopped halfway back to the plate, "What?"

"Nothing." Her smile lingered for a moment longer before fading. "I suppose you've already considered that the things happening in your house may be caused by natural phenomena. Houses settle and—"

"And old houses are notorious for having faulty wiring and air in the pipes, I know." Mitchell suddenly realized what he'd done and licked his lips, tasting salt and potatoes and cooking fat. "God, I'm sorry, I didn't mean for it to come out like that."

"Like what?" she asked, her smile once again obvious above the rim of her mug. He could see the beautiful young woman she'd been and grieved that he hadn't known her then.

"Insulting."

Mitchell held his breath until she shook her head. "You weren't, and it's good to be skeptical. In fact, sometimes it's the only thing that can save you. But you're right, old houses are full of sounds and troubles. This house you're sitting in has its share of sounds and thumps. It's been in my husband's family for seven generations, and there are so many loose timbers in the attic that when the wind comes out of the north you'd think you were standing in the middle of a Maine cornfield for all the rattling that goes on."

Mitchell chuckled politely even though he'd never been in Maine, let alone in a cornfield that he could remember.

"What about ghosts?" he asked, and immediately regretted it. She'd stopped laughing and age swept back over her face.

"You mean in the house?" He nodded. "No, there aren't any ghosts in the house. My husband doesn't believe in ghosts."

"Is that what keeps them out?"

Again, he'd meant it as a joke and, again, he failed. Her smile stayed hidden. She took one, two sips before lowering the mug, but she never moved her eyes away from the oily black-brown surface.

"No." She shook her head and a silver-brown curl danced across the top of one ear. He watched her hand as she brushed it back behind her ear. "But it helps, I think. My husband doesn't believe in anything that he can't see or taste or touch."

And this time Mitchell didn't stop himself. He reached out and took her hand, held it as if he was holding a tiny bird. She trembled once, but didn't pull away.

"It must be hard living with a man like that."

"No," she said, "it's very easy. In fact that's why I married him."

Mitchell shook his head. He didn't even know her husband's name, but he knew the man wasn't worthy of the woman sitting across from him.

"But doesn't he know what you do?"

"I don't *do* anything, Mitchell." She squeezed his hand and pulled away. "I walk into a house that's supposed to be haunted and then leave. There are no smoking mirrors, no incantations, no holy of holies recited."

"But in the interview you said—"

"I said I rid houses of ghosts, but that's not completely true. I don't get rid of ghosts, Mitchell, I collect souls and that's a very different thing, indeed."

It sounded as if she were confessing a terrible sin to him, and him alone. *God, why haven't I ever met a woman like her? Why haven't I met her before this? I can tell she feels comfortable with me.*

"I don't know why or how, but when I walk into a house that's supposed to be haunted, I attract the essence of whatever it is that remains when we die . . . the spirit or soul or . . ." She shrugged and folded her hands around her coffee mug. "A lot of the houses I *cleared* weren't haunted to begin with, but people believe what they want to believe, and see what they want to see. And some people, like you and my husband, don't believe in ghosts at all."

"No!" He suddenly didn't want to be anything like her husband. "I know that's what I said, but I was lying to myself.

"Please, Lydia. I believe in you."

Lydia tightened her grip on the mug, but it only made the small tremor in her hands worse. A drop of coffee sloshed over the rim. *It's started already.*

"Didn't you hear me, Mitchell? I don't exorcize ghosts. . . . I collect souls."

Her uncle's had been the first . . . at least, the first she'd been aware of.

It'd been the morning of her sixth birthday— Funny how she still could remember it. *Her mother had sent her out to the backyard to play while she baked the cake and finished decorating the house. Her mother had told her she wanted it to be a surprise, but Lydia—Liddie then—knew the real surprise was that her uncle Lydon was coming.*

She'd never met the man she was named for, but he was already a legend to her. Uncle Lydon was an "ambassador" and, as far back as Lydia could remember, his exploits and adventures had been her bedtime stories.

And he was coming to her *birthday party.*

Her friends, who also knew all about the time Brave Uncle Lydon had escaped a Bedouin horde by donning the robes of a humble shepherd, as well as the time Fearless Uncle Lydon had stayed in the embassy to answer the phones when everyone else had fled in terror after an earthquake destroyed most of the city. Lydia forgot the name of the city and what country it was in, but to her, Uncle Lydon was King Arthur, Zorro and Superman rolled into one.

And he *was coming to* her *party!*

Even though she wasn't supposed to know. And it was hard to pretend she didn't. But she tried, she really did.

Lydia was picking daisies to put around her cake when the screen door opened and a tall man in a sparkling white linen suit and bright red tie stepped out onto the patio. He was older than Lydia expected, and she was a little disappointed that he wasn't wearing shining armor or a cape, but she ran up to him, arms wide and hands filled with daisies to hug him fiercely around the knees.

"This is your uncle Lydon, Liddie," her mother said from the other side of the screen door. "Surprise."

Lydia squealed and giggled and pretended to be surprised. Until Uncle Lydon bent down and picked her up. And then she didn't have to act surprised. When their eyes met—his were dark like hers, almost the same shade of gray brown—he suddenly trembled and took a deep breath.

Uncle Lydon held his breath for a long time, so long that Lydia thought he'd gotten the hiccups and was holding his breath to make them go away. Having a full working knowledge of hiccups and what did and didn't work, Lydia was about tell him holding his breath would only make the hiccups louder, when Uncle Lydon exhaled.

And Lydia felt his ghost leave his body and brush past hers.

He was still alive, still holding her and smiling, but she knew part of him had gone.

Lydia knew as much about ghosts as she did about hiccups, maybe more. Her daddy had told her about ghosts when Bows, the cat that had been her companion since forever, had woken up dead one morning. It'd been scary to see him in his box, with his eyes wide open and not breath-

ing, but her daddy had told her that his soul was up in Kitty Heaven and he was happy. A soul was that part of a person or animal that you couldn't see, like a ghost but not scary.

So Lydia hadn't been scared of ghosts. Until that moment, when she felt her uncle's ghost leave his body to stand next to her.

And then she started to scream and kick and get as far away from the empty eyes and hollow body as she could.

"I don't know what's the matter with her," her mother said as she walked slowly across the patio, "she's usually a joy."

"Oh, she still is," empty Uncle Lydon said as his ghost shuffled up little dust devils in the dirt. Lydia howled at the top of her lungs and squeezed her eyes shut. "She's just not used to strangers, that's all it is. She's a love. A little love. And we're going to have wonderful times together. Don't cry, sweetheart. Don't cry, little angel."

"Yes, please don't cry, baby. Look, here's Daddy. If you cry, you'll make Daddy sad, and you don't want that, do you?"

And, unfortunately, Lydia did as she was told and looked at her daddy.

He was holding a yellow HAPPY BIRTHDAY GIRL *balloon in his hand and smiling at her through the screen door. His smile was the same as Uncle Lydon's. The same as her mother's. The same droopy half smile—like something, something important inside them had been taken away . . . or lost . . . or stolen.*

"What's the matter with my baby?" her father asked.

His smile looked just like Uncle Lydon's. And her mother's. Empty and hollow.

Lydia stopped crying and went limp.

"There." Uncle Lydon laughed. "See, all she needed was a minute to get used to me. Well, now, shall we go in and see what your favorite uncle has brought the birthday girl all the way from Morocco?"

Lydia dropped the daisies and nodded. "That's my girl," her uncle said. "She's such a good girl," her mommy said. "Happy Birthday to you," her daddy sang as he opened the screen door to let them in.

All *of them. Including the ghosts.*

It'd taken a long time to figure out why she was so "special," and by then it was too late.

"Did you hear what I said?" she asked. "I collect souls."

He nodded, his eyes never leaving her face.

"And you don't care."

He shook his head.

"No," she said, grabbing the percolator as she stood up, "I don't suppose you would now. Well, I'll make more coffee, and you can tell me about your ghost."

He smiled.

It *was* already too late.

Mitchell told her everything while the steady *plop, plop* of percolating coffee played a soft counterbalance in the background. It was easier than he'd thought it'd be, or maybe it was just the way she'd said it—almost as if she were asking about children. *"Tell me about your children." "Tell me about your ghost."*

It was just so easy to tell her everything, this wonderful woman.

He knew he was falling in love with her long before the coffee stopped perking.

"It sounds like your home is occupied by the ghost of a woman," she said with a certainty that left no room for question, "probably a jealous young woman who sees your girlfriend as a rival for your affections. Does that sound possible?"

Mitchell nodded and watched her hands. He'd discovered she had a habit of twisting the plain gold wedding band she wore when she talked. *Plain gold, unadorned. Probably cheap, probably the only thing her* husband *could afford when they were married. That was wrong—she deserved more than just a simple gold band and I would have bought her diamonds, if I were her husband.*

She needs a man who believes in her.

"My guess," Lydia said, twisting her ring, "is that as long as you don't have a girlfriend, your house will be quiet."

She needs someone like me.

"So, it's either learn to live alone or—?"

Mitchell reached out and took her hand. "I don't want to live alone."

She needs me.

Lydia unplugged the percolator and carefully dumped the steaming grounds, knowing Keith would forget to do that when he plugged it back in when he got home. He was always forgetting to do that, and then wondering why the coffee tasted bitter.

She smiled, thinking about that, and scribbled a quick note to tell him where she was and to remind him to take the tuna casserole out of the refrigerator unless he wanted potato pancakes for supper. Again.

"How long a drive did you say it was to your place?"

When he didn't immediately answer, Lydia turned to find him staring at her. His eyes were round, like a child's who knew he was about to be abandoned.

"You—you aren't going to spend the night?"

"That won't be necessary, Mitchell."

"But I thought—we could celebrate afterwards."

She shook her head and watched tears begin to form in his eyes. *God, why didn't I try harder to get those damned videos taken off the market?* But it seemed as if for every two video clearing houses she found, another three would spring up. She'd been rediscovered by the newest wave of paranormal enthusiasts. Her following was expanding yearly.

God help them. And her.

"Please?"

"I'm sorry," she whispered, and then tapped the pencil against the piece of paper. "Let's see, you said it was three hours to your house?"

He nodded.

"And three hours back, plus traffic would make it—" Lydia counted the numbers on her fingers to make sure, "five o'clock. I'll tell my husband six, so he won't worry."

Lydia didn't look at him again until she stuck the note to the refrigerator with the I ❤ YELLOWSTONE magnet Keith had found at a local garage sale. He wasn't big on traveling. Thank God.

Lydia looked straight ahead as she crossed the kitchen to take her coat down from the peg next to the door. Her car keys and wallet were in the left side pocket where they should be.

"All right," she said, opening the door, "shall we go?"

His body remained slumped at the table for a moment, but Lydia felt his spirit brush against her as it hovered at the door's threshold. When he finally stood up and stumbled out into the late morning, Lydia followed, carefully breaking the line of salt with the toe of her shoe so his spirit could follow.

Pretending to drop something, she mended the break and hoped it would be enough. She'd have to remember to fix it when she got home that night.

* * *

Keith looked up from his plate of potato pancakes as she stepped into the kitchen and he smiled.

"Hi! I made dinner."

Hanging up her coat, Lydia walked over to the refrigerator and took down the note, crumbling it into the trash before she got down the box of salt. She should have known he wouldn't see the note. He never did.

"Looks good," she said as she walked to the door. "Give me a minute, and I'll join you."

Keith grunted and slapped the bottom of the near-empty bottle of ketchup.

"You didn't go to the market, did you?" he asked.

"No, just visiting a friend."

"Oh. Hey, I got a call while you were out. Jack and Shirley's daughter Peggy just had a new baby."

"That's wonderful." Kneeling, Lydia pried open the metal spout and rebuilt the salt barrier across the doorway. "Is it a boy or girl?"

"Um."

She glanced at him over her shoulder. He shrugged. "Men. Did you at least ask the baby's name?"

"Terry? I think."

Lydia sighed and emptied out the rest of the salt.

"Ants, huh?"

"Yeah, thought I saw some this morning."

Keith smiled and lost interest. That was another thing she loved about him, his easy acceptance of everything she told him. If she'd suddenly decided to tell him the truth, that the salt was a protection against the souls that she's stolen throughout the years, he would have believed her . . . and then asked if she wanted to rent the new Jackie Chan movie at Blockbuster.

But what she loved most was the fact that she couldn't harm him. He'd lost his soul in the jungles of Vietnam, long before he'd met her.

Mitchell had almost died of embarrassment when they got back to the house. Debra had taped a note to the front door for the whole neighborhood, and Lydia, to see:

CALL ME THE MINUTE YOU GET RID OF GHOST!

I LOVE YOU—D

There was a phone number, to her sister's place, that she'd underlined three times.

He would have crumpled it up and shoved it into his pocket, forgetting it immediately, if Lydia hadn't commented about it. Told him, with a smile of infinite patience, that he was a very lucky young man.

He agreed with her, he said, but only because she was there with him.

And then her smile had gone away, and soon after that she did, too.

She stayed only a moment, no longer than it took to walk from the front door to the bottom of the staircase and back again, but she touched him on the cheek before she left and said, "I'm so sorry, Mitchell, but if it's any consolation, you won't feel any difference. The house is quiet now, dear. You can make that call now."

Mitchell had nodded, not hearing anything until she called him *dear*. Mitchell couldn't forget that or the touch of her hand against his cheek as he stood next to the phone in the quiet living room of the quiet house. The empty house. His house.

Mitchell twisted the note into a tight coil and used it to light the kindling in the fireplace.

Debra answered on the fourth ring. Breathless. Happy he'd called. Hopeful.

"Hi," he told her, "you can come home now. There's nothing here anymore."

While she yammered in his ear about how happy she was, Mitchell watched the flames curl the note to ash and touched the spot on his cheek where Lydia had touched him.

Lydia grabbed on to the doorjamb with her free hand, but she still heard her knees pop when she stood up. She was getting too old for this.

For *all* of this.

Holding the box of salt against the front of her sweater, Lydia took a deep breath and watched a leaf scurry across the path.

He pushed the others out of the way as she started to close the door. *Wait—don't go. Stay with me. Please.* And for a moment he thought she heard him. Just him, not any of the others who were all talking at once, trying to get her attention. Just him. Mitchell knew he was her favorite. He knew and she knew it, and that's all that mattered. *It's stupid . . . so stupid. Why don't the others go away and leave us alone?*

He would have made it to the porch before the door clicked shut, but he tripped.

And the stones moved.

***Dennis McKiernan** absolutely loves fantasy fiction—his first novels were inspired by J. R. R. Tolkein, and his work in that vein continues to this day with such books as* Once Upon a Winter's Night *and* Dragondoom.

The story that follows only solidifies his reputation as a modern master of fantasy fiction.

A Tower with No Doors

Dennis L. McKiernan

When passed from mouth to mouth,
a simple truth oft falls victim.

Once upon a time not so long ago—that is, if you are an immortal, but incredibly far back in the distant past if you happen to be a mayfly . . . and you, dear mayfly, flitting about as you are, I'll hurry my telling so that you might hear the end, too. Now let me see, where was I? Oh, yes, now I remember—there was a prince, a most handsome prince, who on a golden day went ahunting with his retinue, all of them splendidly arrayed in silks and satins and other such finery, and mounted upon high-stepping steeds, the most glorious of which was the prince's very own wonderful horse. With axes and lances and pearl-handled bows and gilded arrows fletched of peacock tail all glittering in the afternoon sun, toward the woodland they rode, some retainers with falcons awrist or other hooded hawking birds. And just as they entered the deep, dark forest, up jumped a snow-white hart.

" 'Tis mine," called the golden-haired prince, and sounding his silver-belled horn, he spurred swiftly after.

My lord!

My prince!

My liege! cried many, all leaping forward in pursuit as well. *'Ware, for white harts be enchanted!*

But the prince did not hear, and his horse was fleet, and soon the men hindward were lost arear.

But as fast as the prince did ride, the white hart was swifter still. And twisting and veering among the trees, the creature led the prince on a harrowing run. Over sunlit hill and through dimlit vale and up and down crystalline streams did the creature flee before the pursuit, and always just when the prince thought the hart was lost, a clear flash of white did he glimpse running among the dark trees. On they ran and on, and the sun did drift down the sky, until long shadows lay across the woodland as gathering evening drew nigh.

In the green distance behind, the retinue cast about quite 'wildered, for with the hart taking to stream upon stream and running up or down their lengths and emerging across rock ledges to come back among the trees, they had completely lost the track. And they were sore afraid, for men had been known to enter these darkling woods, never to be seen again. And whenever the hunt had run herein, they made certain to leave this sinister realm before twilight came on, and be back at the castle ere nightfall. "Come," said one of the noblemen, "let us return to the palace, for surely the prince is already there." And all the men did quickly agree to this course, saying it was exceedingly sensible. . . .

. . . Besides, it was getting dark.

As to the prince, at last the white hart was seen cresting a knoll to disappear beyond, and the prince reined his weary but wonderful horse to a halt along the bank of a clear-running stream. Dismounting, he let the steed take on water, while he himself drank, as well. And when he stood and looked about, nought did he recognize of the darkening 'scape. He was quite lost, his way back to the castle unknown. He set his silver-belled horn to his lips and blew a call to the air, yet only echoes sounded in response, to be swallowed in the leafy silence of the surround.

"Well, my friend," he said to his mount, "it seems we are fated to spend the night far from stable and bed." And he took up the reins and, afoot, led the horse up a long slope to camp upon high ground. Yet when he came to the crest of the knoll, there where the hart was last seen, what before him did he espy reaching skyward in the dying light of the day but a lone tower atop the next rise. Yet, what is this? On a golden rope up the side of the tower clambered a figure in black, striving to gain a candlelit window in the stonework high above.

"Come, old fellow," he said to his horse, "perchance our fortune has changed. Yon lies a refuge and mayhap a meal for each of us on this eve—oats for you and bread for me—and perhaps suitable quarters, as well. Rather would we beg shelter in a tower, secure from the beasts of the wood, than to lie in the open under night skies, with nought but a fire standing guard in the dark."

And so the prince took the reins of his steed and went down from the crest of the knoll and into the vale below, then up the long slope toward the base of the tower, twilight o'er the land. In mustering shadows as he neared the goal, he noted the golden rope was gone, perhaps drawn up to the candlelit window and in. Yet in its place a weeping drifted out and down, along with an argument in voice so low, he could not gather what was said, only that a conflict of wills was at hand. Yet when he reached the grey stone of the tower, one voice called out, "It is mine, not yours, and you must return it to me." And there followed a cruel laugh and additional weeping, but suddenly nothing more . . . and only mute silence reigned.

Around the base of the tower went the prince, leading his trusty mount, but no doors did he find whatsoever, and no other windows above. As he came full circle to the place where he began, he heard a scuttling among the boles of dark trees, and he just made out in the waning twilight the figure in black hieing down the slope and away from the tower with no doors. But, lo! the golden rope yet dangled, but it was now being drawn up.

The prince sprang forward and leapt as high as he could, and he just did catch the end, and up he clambered as the dark figure had done, his feet finding purchase as he went.

"Who's there?" called a lyrical voice, that of a lady, he was certain. "You cannot come back with your persistent demand unless you first set me free."

The prince did not answer as upward he scaled, to reach the window at last. And as he crossed the sill, his eyes did behold a creature most divine: 'twas a lady all unclothed, her hair as golden as his.

"Oh," she said, turning her back, and drawing her hair up and inward, for *that* was the golden rope he had climbed to reach this lofty place. Swiftly she unbraided the very long locks and loosened them afluff, and, covering herself in her own mane, at last she turned to the prince.

She was beautiful, incredibly beautiful, and the prince drew in a deep breath, trying to master his hammering heart, though he did wonder that he had a heart left, lost in her eyes as it was.

"My lord," she said, curtsying, the sweep of her hair parting here and there to reveal and then conceal, and she smiled quite knowingly.

"My lady," he responded, bowing, his quickening pulse in his ears, "I overheard: Are you trapped in this place? Mayhap I can set you free."

"Indeed I am trapped, by a magic spell, and I cannot hie from this tower. 'Twas most kind, your offer, but it simply cannot be."

Taken aback, the prince did frown, and he glanced at the window and said, "The one in black I saw climbing, is he at the root of your bane?"

" 'Tis a she," said the lady, "a terrible witch, who has set a geas 'pon me from which I cannot escape."

Reflexively the hand of the prince went to his belt, to rest on the pommel of his dagger, and he said, "Then mayhap I should slay her."

"Oh, no, my lord," cried the lady, falling to her knees, "you mustn't harm her at all, else I will be trapped evermore."

Quite distracted—for her hair had parted, revealing her plentiful charms—the prince cast about for aught to say, finally settling upon, "How came this to be?"

"Oh," she said, "oh," and paused, as if seeking a tale, and she settled back against the wall and smiled coyly up at him, with her snow-white legs slightly parted. After a moment when he made no move, she finally said, " 'Twas long ago when my mother was with child and she greatly desired the taste of parsley, and she begged my sire to gather some from the patch next door. Yet it was the garden of the witch, and when she caught him stealing the herb, she demanded the babe in return. He had no choice but to agree, and so when I was born I was given to the crone, and she placed me in this tower, and here I've been ever since, and if she should come to hurt, then here I'll ever remain."

"Then I'll discover another way to set you free," declared the prince, "mayhap destroy the tower."

" 'Tis magically warded," said the lady, standing and stepping toward the young man, her teeth a pearly white as she smiled. "Besides, let us not natter on about witches and freedom. Come and lie with me instead." And she took him in her embrace and thoroughly kissed him most deeply, and then began stripping him of his clothes.

A fire ran through his loins, and he did not resist, nor did he want to, but instead quickly wrenched off his spurred boots and doffed other garments, as well.

She looked at him admiringly, his desire apparent to the eye, and she reclined on the nearby bed and beckoned him to part her tresses and discover her treasures so hidden.

Revealed was a golden mound, and he quickly plunged himself within, and they both gasped in unbridled delight, their pleasure all-consuming, and she cast her locks over them both, and they coupled throughout the night, covered in a blanket of golden hair.

When dawn lay on the horizon, she took her gratification one last time, and, glowing, she said, "You must leave now, ere the witch comes again. But return on morrow eve, and once more we'll find joy in one another."

The prince donned his clothes as she braided her hair, and then he slid down her bound locks to the base of the grey stone tower, where he espied his steed quietly munching wild oats and tender green grass in the lush verdant dell below. As the prince wearily mounted up, he looked back at the edifice to catch a glimpse of the lady, but dark shutters now covered the window above, closing out the first rays of the sun. Sighing, he rode over the other knoll to come to the stream of the day before, and he and the horse took on deep draughts of clear water, and then set camp on the bank.

Exhausted, still the prince unsaddled the steed and curried him with twists of grass, then fell into a deep and dreamless sleep. When he awoke, 'twas midafternoon, and he was ravenously hungry. He took up his bow and stood along the bank and managed to impale a fish, and it was not more than half-cooked when he drew it from the small fire and consumed it whole.

Yet weary, he napped once more, and lavender twilight lay across the land when he wakened again. Taking a deep breath, he stood and saddled his steed and rode him back up the knoll, reaching the crown just in time to see the black-clad figure clambering once more up the side of the turret to the candlelit window above. Long did the prince pause, fingering his bow, thinking upon killing this evil being for trapping the lady in a stone tower with no doors.

Where he sat ahorse on the crest of the knoll, he once again could hear angry voices drifting out from the window and across the night air, yet what they said was not discernible, and it did not continue o'erlong. At last the black-clothed being slid down the golden braid to the ground below, and the prince then set an arrow to string and thought again that he should slay her. But then the words of the lady came back to him—*If she should come to hurt, then here I'll ever remain*—and he slipped the arrow back into his saddle quiver and unstrung his death-dealing bow.

When the crone was gone, the prince rode down through the vale then up to the base of the grey stone tower, and there did dangle the plait. Up he scaled, finding the climb rather difficult, for he was yet weary—drained, some might say.

As before, the lady unbound her braid and loosened her lengthy tresses, and again they coupled relentlessly, all the while covered in a glorious blanket of beautiful golden hair.

In the paling of dawn, at her insistence they mated once more, and then she bade him to leave—"The witch, if she finds you here, I don't know what she might do."

And so, the prince slid down the golden rope and wearily rode away, while behind, the dark shutters were closed against the bright rays of the just-risen sun.

And the next night found an exhausted prince barely able to climb the braid. Yet again did the golden-haired lady spark irresistible desire, and covered in auric tresses, they once more coupled away. Yet when the light of dawn came on the heels of the night, he knew he had not the strength to clamber down. "I'll simply wait for the witch," he said, drawing his dagger with a trembling hand, "and force her to set you free." And that was the moment he saw his reflection in the gleaming steel: white-haired and wrinkled and skin and bones he was, and he reeled back in horror and dropped the blade. And the lady laughed cruelly, and filled with an energy not her own, she took him up and flung him out the window, where he landed in a great clump of briars, and thorns did pierce his eyes.

He lay all day, but barely alive, bleeding from a hundred small punctures. And when the sun set, he felt hands take hold and drag him free of the thorns. And someone did bind his wounds and give him a draught of cool water. Even so, he could not speak nor sit nor stand, for he had no strength whatsoever. And then he heard a person nearby calling out: "Edwig, Edwig, let down my hair."

There came a sneer from on high, followed by, "So that I may climb without a stair?"

The prince simply lay without moving, and he could hear feet scrabbling against the stone, and he knew that someone was climbing the braid, feet against the tower.

Surely it's not the witch who aided me so.

Moments later there began a noisy quarrel, words drifting down from above, only this time the prince could hear what was being said, so loud and shrill were the voices:

"You trapped another man!"

"What of it?"

'Murderer! Murderer! Below lies another whom you have drawn to your tower and drained of his life essence."

There came that same cruel laugh, and then the lady—for the prince did recognize her voice—said, "The white hart, a good illusion, eh? And this man was especially potent: he lasted a day longer than most."

"Edwig, I shall see that no more victims come to your tower and—" Of a sudden the speaker stopped, then said, "Edwig, I am pregnant."

"What?" demanded the lady, Edwig most certainly. "That cannot be."

"Ah, but it is," said the other, "for well do I know my own being even though I am apart from it, and did you not say yourself that this man was especially potent."

"But I will lose all my power, should you be pregnant more than seven days. You must bring me the root of the—"

"Nay, I will not do so, Edwig. Instead, give me back my body, and the geas will be broken."

There came a shrill scream, and Edwig said, "But that means I will have to find another body, for you will not be a virgin if I give it back."

"So be it!" cried the one.

"So be it!" shouted Edwig, and there came a great lash of thunder, and then all fell into silence.

The prince lay without moving throughout the night, and the next day dawned and the sun rose on high, for he could feel it on his face. And as he lay in the warmth, he heard the sound of horns blowing, growing louder by the moment. He took hold of the strap on his own silver-belled horn and managed to bring the trump to his lips, and he blew a faint note, but he despaired, for it was so very weak. Yet it was enough, for within moments galloping horses drew near.

"Here's the prince's steed," a voice cried.

"And yon lies a body," shouted another.

The prince raised a hand.

"It's an old man," a third one called, "and he's alive."

Horses came nigh and someone dismounted, and the prince felt hands raising him to a sitting position. Water was pressed to his lips, and he drank thirstily.

"Where is my son, old man?"

It was his father's voice.

"Sire, it is I," said the prince, his words but a whisper, and he raised his hand so that his signet ring might be seen.

"You wear the sigil of my boy," said the king, "as well as his clothes, but you are an old man. You cannot be h—"

"Father, I have been bewitched by the lady of the tower."

"Tower? What tower?"

"The one at hand, Father."

"There is no tower at hand, only a barren knoll."

In that moment a great hunting hound came and lay down by the old man and licked his age-worn fingers, and all the king's retinue drew breaths in wonder, for well did they know that this hound loved no other than his very own master, the prince.

Too, the prince's magnificent horse nuzzled the oldster and softly whickered, and by this sign as well did all the men stir, for that splendid steed favored none else.

After long converse, with the prince reminding his father and the others of events in the past, at last they accepted him for who he was, though he was blind and aged. And they bore the frail old man back to the castle, bewitched though he might be.

When he recovered somewhat from his wounds, and had been fed substantial meals, he and his valet and his hunting hound and his noble set out to find the witch who had done this to him, for they would force her to reverse the spell and restore his drained-away youth.

They wandered the world for five years—an old blind man, a valet, a dog, and a most magnificent steed—seeking, but not finding.

Yet one eve, out in the waste, the prince heard a woman crooning a lullaby, and though he had not heard it in half a decade, he knew that it was the voice of the golden-haired lady.

"What is it you see?" he asked the valet.

Peering through the oncoming twilight, the valet replied, "A beautiful woman on a rug before a tent singing to two little golden-haired children."

"Take me to her," said the prince, and quickly it was done.

"My lady, do I know you? Did you once live in a tower?"

"Oh, my," she replied in the gathering dusk, "you must be him. Oh, you poor fellow, come to me, I have long-held in my body that which is rightfully yours."

And so he dismounted from his horse, and she bade him to lie down and place his head in her lap and, with her tears falling on his face, she said, "I have been saving this for you."

And she laid her right hand 'pon his brow and placed the left hand o'er his heart, and vigor flowed from her to him, as all the stolen vitality was restored. And, lo! his youth came back unto the prince in a burst of energy so intense that his eyes were healed and he could see again!

"You are not the one I met in the tower," said the prince, looking into her compassionate face.

"No," she replied. "I am the one whom you might have thought of as a dreadful crone, but that was *her* true form, not mine, for she stole my body from me."

"Ah then, it all comes clear," said the prince, and he sprang to his feet, renewed.

"My lady, you have made me that which I was. Could it be that you are a sorceress?"

"Nay, no mage am I, but a mere common girl."

"Then how did you trap the witch in the tower?"

"Ah, that," she said, nodding. "At the moment of exchange—my body for hers—then did some of her power become mine, and I had just enough to lay a geas on her from which she could not escape."

"She became a prisoner in her own tower," said the prince.

"Yes," said the lady. "And would remain so until I unto myself was restored."

"And when you changed back—?" asked the prince.

"I held on to your vitality and a bit of her power in case I would see you again . . . as has come about."

The prince smiled and settled back down at the side of the beautiful lady and took her hand in his, and he looked at the twin children, his hound licking the face of the laughing boy and his wonderful horse nuzzling the cooing girl.

"They are yours," the lady shyly said, when she saw where he did gaze.

He smiled back at her and they built a small fire and the valet brewed a fresh pot of tea and then discreetly withdrew. And the prince and the lady sat and sipped long into the night and spoke of all that had been.

And so ends my story of the tower with no doors, a story so distorted in the retelling by those who, unlike me, were not there, and so do not know the facts. And look at what has happened to the true tale: it has become a fable so entirely irrational that it makes no sense at all.

You, another immortal as am I, should be able to carry the genuine account forward and not inject too many errors in the retelling down through the years.

What of the pregnant mother and the yearning for parsley? Oh, that. Pfaa! It was a tale invented on the spot by the witch—a lamia, more like it, I deem—an outrageous fabrication to explain her presence in the tower, for the truth served not at all her ends. I ask you, what father and mother would ever agree to trade their newborn for a mere sprig of an herb? Oh, no. There was no parsley, nor the handing over of a babe by two nitwits. Instead, the lady's folks were common crofters who just happened to bear a beautiful, golden-haired daughter, who at sixteen caught the lamia's eye.

The hair? Though her own golden mane was quite magnificent, the lady herself did not have tresses that would reach from the window to the ground. Instead, that hair was brought about by a spell cast by the lamia, and she used it to get men up to her bed as well as to leech the vitality from them.

What's that? Oh, yes, the prince and the lady, they married and lived quite happily ever after.

What of the real witch, you ask? Well, I believe she is yet searching for a suitable virgin, but they are hard to come by these days.

Their names? Their human names? How should I know? Oh, "Edwig the Witch" I do remember, but as to the others—the lady, the prince? Pfaa! They all sound alike to me.

Oh my, but look, the mayfly is dead, though I told the tale in very little time. Ah me, such as the vagaries of extremely ephemeral lives. . . . Besides, 'twas his nature to land on my hide, and mine to swat him lifeless, as I did.

And now I must get back to my oats; I've gone some while without fare. Would you please place the feedbag over my nose? My hooves are *so* ill-suited to such a menial task.

The short-short story is a neat little creature: every single word counts, and if done correctly, it's a polished gem. I really wanted one for this collection, and **Larry Niven** *of all people—author of best-selling vast landscapes such as* Ringworld*—came through.*

Recent work from Larry includes a new collection, Scatterbrain, *which contains short stories and excerpts from novels.*

Boomerang

Larry Niven

There have been a succession of last gods. When an entity too powerful to exist goes mythical, lesser entities pull themselves out of their hiding places and rule for a time.

Daramulum ruled in Australia and New Zealand. Being less energetic than most, he survived longer than most. The magic of the Outback abos did not chew deeply into his reserves of manna, but invaders were another matter. They brought their own religions. They knew farming, and they bred. Humans are natural wizards, and their numbers grew too great.

The first boomerang was his. Daramulum had brought it to men at the beginning of time. They tried to throw it away, repeatedly, until Daramulum showed them how it could knock a behemoth off its feet. Men used a smaller version to hunt marsupials. The first boomerang was scaled to Daramulum himself.

When he chose to become mythical, Daramulum went to the farthest ends of the Earth. He stood hundreds of manheights tall, with a stride to match. Where the ocean was too deep to wade, he borrowed the ocean's manna and grew taller. He took with him certain books whose knowledge should be destroyed, and he took the archetype of the boomerang.

At the far end of the Earth, Daramulum found himself armpit deep in a tall forest. Somehow he hadn't expected that.

He hurled the first boomerang away from him.

It circled the world many times, then, as boomerangs do, it came back. Circling more narrowly the point where Daramulum waited, it flew lower. It began to cut down trees. Before it reached Daramulum, it had leveled whole forests. The latest of last gods died in a titanic blast of light and heat.

So Daramulum went myth—leaving his own myth and mystery, a puzzle for the entire civilized world—in Tunguska in 1906 CE.

***Elizabeth Hand**, besides being a heck of a short-story writer (her two collections to date:* Bibliomancy: Four Novellas *and* Last Summer at Mars Hill*), is also the author of seven novels, including her latest,* Mortal Love. *She lives on the coast of Maine.*

Here she writes about the nature of the beast: the beast, in this case, being the creative artist.

Wonderwall

Elizabeth Hand

A long time ago, nearly thirty years now, I had a friend who was waiting to be discovered. His name was David Baldanders; we lived with two other friends in one of the most disgusting places I've ever seen, and certainly the worst that involved me signing a lease.

Our apartment was a two-bedroom third-floor walkup in Queenstown, a grim brick enclave just over the District line in Hyattsville, Maryland. Queenstown Apartments were inhabited mostly by drug dealers and bikers who met their two-hundred-dollars-a-month leases by processing speed and bad acid in their basement rooms; the upper floors were given over to wasted welfare mothers from P. G. County and students from the University of Maryland, Howard, and the University of the Archangels and Saint John the Divine.

The Divine, as students called it, was where I'd come three years earlier to study acting. I wasn't actually expelled until the end of my junior year, but midway through that term, my roommate, Marcella, and I were kicked out of our campus dormitory, precipitating the move to Queenstown. Even for the mid-1970s, our behavior was excessive; I was only surprised the university officials waited so long before getting rid of us. Our parents were assessed for damages to our dorm room, which were extensive; among other things, I'd painted one wall floor-to-ceiling with the image from the cover of *Transformer*, surmounted by *JE SUIS DAMNE PAR L'ARC-EN-CIEL* scrawled in foot-high letters. Decades later, someone who'd lived in the room after I left told me that, year after year, Rimbaud's words would bleed through each successive layer of new paint. No one ever understood what they meant.

Our new apartment was at first an improvement on the dorm room, and Queenstown itself was an efficient example of a closed ecosystem. The bikers manufactured Black Beauties, which they sold to the students and welfare mothers upstairs, who would zigzag a few hundred feet across a wasteland of shattered glass and broken concrete to the Queenstown Restaurant, where I worked making pizzas that they would then cart back to their apartments. The pizza boxes piled up in the halls, drawing armies of roaches. My friend Oscar lived in the next building; whenever he visited our flat, he'd push open the door, pause, and then look over his shoulder dramatically.

"Listen—!" he'd whisper.

He'd stamp his foot, just once, and hold up his hand to command silence. Immediately we heard what sounded like surf washing over a gravel beach. In fact, it was the susurrus of hundreds of cockroaches clittering across the warped parquet floors in retreat.

There were better places to await discovery.

David Baldanders was my age, nineteen. He wasn't much taller than me, with long thick black hair and a soft-featured face: round cheeks, full red lips between a downy black beard and mustache, slightly crooked teeth much yellowed from nicotine, small well-shaped hands. He wore an earring and a bandanna that he tied, pirate-style, over his head; filthy jeans, flannel shirts, filthy black Converse high-tops that flapped when he walked. His eyes were beautiful—indigo, black-lashed, soulful. When he laughed, people stopped in their tracks—he sounded like Herman Munster, that deep, goofy, foghorn voice at odds with his fey appearance.

We met in the Divine's Drama Department and immediately recognized each other as kindred spirits. Neither attractive nor talented enough to be in the center of the golden circle of aspiring actors that included most of our friends, we made ourselves indispensable by virtue of being flamboyant, unapologetic fuckups. People laughed when they saw us coming. They laughed even louder when we left. But David and I always made a point of laughing loudest of all.

"Can you fucking believe that?" A morning, it could have been any morning: I stood in the hall and stared in disbelief at the Department's sitting area. White walls, a few plastic chairs and tables overseen by the glass windows of the secretarial office. This was where the other students chain-smoked and waited, day after day, for news: casting announcements for Department plays; cattle calls for commercials, trade shows, summer reps. Above all else, the Department prided itself on graduating Working Actors—a really successful student might get called back for a walk-on in *Days of Our Lives*. My voice rose loud enough that heads turned. "It looks like a fucking *dentist's* office."

"Yeah, well, Roddy just got cast in a Trident commercial," David said, and we both fell against the wall, howling.

Rejection fed our disdain, but it was more than that. Within weeks of arriving at the Divine, I felt betrayed. I wanted—hungered for, thirsted for, craved like drink or drugs—High Art. So did David. We'd come to the Divine expecting Paris in the 1920s, Swinging London, Summer of Love in the Haight.

We were misinformed.

What we got was elocution taught by the department head's wife; tryouts where tone-deaf students warbled numbers from *The Magic Show;* Advanced Speech classes where, week after week, the beefy department head would declaim Macduff's speech—*All my pretty ones? Did you say all?*—never failing to move himself to tears.

And there was that sitting area. Just looking at it made me want to take a sledgehammer to the walls: all those smug faces above issues of *Variety* and *Theatre Arts;* all those sheets of white paper neatly taped to white cinder block with lists of names beneath: callbacks, cast lists, passing exam results. My name was never there. Nor was David's.

We never had a chance. We had no choice.

We took the sledgehammer to our heads.

Weekends my suitemate visited her parents, and while she was gone, David and I would break into her dorm room. We drank her vodka and listened to her copy of *David Live*, playing "Diamond Dogs" over and over as we clung to each other, smoking, dancing cheek to cheek. After midnight we'd cadge a ride down to Southwest, where abandoned warehouses had been turned into gay discos—the Lost and Found, Grand Central Station, Washington Square, Half Street. A solitary neon pentacle glowed atop the old *Washington Star* printing plant; we heard gunshots, sirens, the faint bass throb from funk bands at the Washington Coliseum, ceaseless boom and echo of trains uncoupling in the rail yards that extended from Union Station.

I wasn't a looker. My scalp was covered with henna-stiffened orange stubble that had been cut over three successive nights by a dozen friends. Marcella had pierced my ear with a cork and a needle and a bottle of Gordon's gin. David usually favored one long drop earring, and sometimes I'd wear its mate. Other times I'd shove a safety pin through my ear, then run a dog leash from the safety pin around my neck. I had two-inch-long black-varnished fingernails that caught fire when I lit my cigarettes from a Bic lighter. I kohled my eyes and lips, used Marcella's Chloé perfume, shoved myself into Marcella's expensive jeans even though they were too small for me.

But mostly I wore a white poet's blouse or frayed striped boatneck shirt, droopy black wool trousers, red sneakers, a red velvet beret my mother had given me for Christmas when I was seventeen. I chain-smoked Marlboros, three packs a day when I could afford them. For a while I smoked clay pipes and Borkum Riff tobacco. The pipes cost a dollar apiece at the tobacconist's in Georgetown. They broke easily, and club owners invariably hassled me, thinking I was getting high right under their noses. I was, but not from Borkum Riff. Occasionally I'd forgo makeup and wear army khakis and a boiled wool navy shirt I'd fished from a Dumpster. I used a mascara wand on my upper lip and wore my bashed-up old cowboy boots to make me look taller.

This fooled no one, but that didn't matter. In Southeast, I was invisible—or nearly so. I was a girl, white, not pretty enough to be either desirable or threatening. The burly leather-clad guys who stood guard over the entrances to the L & F were always nice to me, though there was a scary dyke bouncer whom I had to bribe, sometimes with cash, sometimes with rough foreplay behind the door.

Once inside, all that fell away. David and I stumbled to the bar and traded our drink tickets for vodka and orange juice. We drank fast, pushing upstairs through the crowd until we reached a vantage point above the dance floor. David would look around for someone he knew, someone he fancied, someone who might discover him. He'd give me a wet kiss, then stagger off; and I would stand, and drink, and watch.

The first time it happened, David and I were tripping. We were at the L & F, or maybe Washington Square. He'd gone into the men's room. I sat slumped just outside the door, trying to bore a hole through my hand with my eyes. A few people stepped on me; no one apologized, but no one swore at me, either. After a while I stumbled to my feet, lurched a few feet down the hallway, and turned.

The door to the men's room was painted gold. A shining film covered it, glistening with smeared rainbows like oil-scummed tarmac. The door opened with difficulty because of the number of people crammed inside. I had to keep moving so they could pass in and out. I leaned against the wall and stared at the floor for a few more minutes, then looked up again.

Across from me, the wall was gone. I could see men, pissing, talking, kneeling, crowding stalls, humping over urinals, cupping brown glass vials beneath their faces. I could see David in a crowd of men by the sinks. He stood with his back to me, in front of a long mirror framed with small round lightbulbs. His head was bowed. He was scooping water from the faucet and drinking it, so that his beard glittered red and silver. As I watched, he slowly lifted his face, until he was staring into the mirror. His reflected image stared back at me. I could see his pupils expand like drops of black ink in a glass of water, and his mouth fall open in pure panic.

"David," I murmured.

Beside him, a lanky boy with dirty-blond hair turned. He, too, was staring at me, but not with fear. His mouth split into a grin. He raised his hand and pointed at me, laughing.

"Poseur!"

"Shit—shit . . ." I looked up, and David stood there in the hall. He fumbled for a cigarette, his hand shaking, then sank onto the floor beside me. "Shit, you, you saw—you—"

I started to laugh. In a moment David did, too. We fell into each other's arms, shrieking, our faces slick with tears and dirt. I didn't even notice that his cigarette scorched a hole in my favorite shirt till later, or felt where it burned into my right palm, a penny-size wound that got infected and took weeks to heal. I bear the scar even now, the shape of an eye, shiny white tissue with a crimson pupil that seems to wink when I crease my hand.

It was about a month after this happened that we moved to Queenstown. Me, David, Marcy, a sweet spacy girl named Bunny Flitchins, all signed the lease. Two hundred bucks a month gave us a small living room, a bathroom, two small bedrooms, a kitchen squeezed into a corner overlooking a parking lot filled with busted Buicks and shockshot Impalas. The place smelled of new paint and dry-cleaning fluid. The first time we opened the freezer, we found several plastic Ziploc bags filled with sheets of white paper. When we removed the paper and held it up to the light, we saw where rows of droplets had dried to faint grey smudges.

"Blotter acid," I said.

We discussed taking a hit. Marcy demurred. Bunny giggled, shaking her head. She didn't do drugs, and I would never have allowed her to: it would be like giving acid to your puppy.

"Give it to me," said David. He sat on the windowsill, smoking and dropping his ashes to the dirt three floors below. "I'll try it. Then we can cut them into tabs and sell them."

"That would be a *lot* of money," said Bunny delightedly. A tab of blotter went for a dollar back then, but you could sell them for a lot more at concerts, up to ten bucks a hit. She fanned out the sheets from one of the plastic bags. "We could make thousands and thousands of dollars."

"Millions," said Marcy.

I shook my head. "It could be poison. Strychnine. *I* wouldn't do it."

"Why not?" David scowled. "You do all kinds of shit."

"I wouldn't do it 'cause it's from *here*."

"Good point," said Bunny.

I grabbed the rest of the sheets from her, lit one of her gas jets on the stove, and held the paper above it. David cursed and yanked the bandanna from his head.

"What are you *doing?*"

But he quickly moved aside as I lunged to the window and tossed out the flaming pages. We watched them fall, delicate spirals of red and orange like tiger lilies corroding into black ash then grey then smoke.

"All gone," cried Bunny, and clapped.

We had hardly any furniture. Marcy had a bed and a desk in her room, nice Danish Modern stuff. I had a mattress on the other bedroom floor that I shared with David. Bunny slept in the living room. Every few days she'd drag a broken box spring up from the curb. After the fifth one appeared, the living room began to look like the interior of one of those pawnshops down on F Street that sold you an entire roomful of aluminum-tube furniture for fifty bucks, and we yelled at her to stop. Bunny slept on the box springs, a different one every night, but after a while she didn't stay over much. Her family lived in Northwest, but her father, a professor at the Divine, also had an apartment in Turkey Thicket, and Bunny started staying with him.

Marcy's family lived nearby, as well, in Alexandria. She was a slender, Slavic beauty with a waterfall of ice-blond hair and eyes like aqua headlamps, and the only one of us with a glamorous job—she worked as a model and receptionist at the most expensive beauty salon in Georgetown. But by early spring, she had pretty much moved back in with her parents, too.

This left me and David. He was still taking classes at the Divine, getting a ride with one of the other students who lived at Queenstown, or else catching a bus in front of Giant Food on Queens Chapel Road. Early in the semester he had switched his coursework: instead of theater, he now immersed himself in French language and literature.

I gave up all pretense of studying or attending classes. I worked a few shifts behind the counter at the Queenstown Restaurant, making pizzas and ringing up beer. I got most of my meals there, and when my friends came in to buy cases of Heineken, I never charged them. I made about sixty dollars a week, barely enough to pay the rent and keep me in cigarettes, but I got by. Bus fare was eighty cents to cross the District line; the newly opened subway was another fifty cents. I didn't eat much. I lived on popcorn and Reuben sandwiches from the restaurant, and there was a sympathetic waiter at the American Café in Georgetown who fed me ice cream sundaes when I was bumming around in the city. I saved enough for my cover at the discos and for the Atlantis, a club in the basement of a fleabag hotel at 930 F Street that had just started booking punk bands. The rest I spent on booze and Marlboros. Even if I was broke, someone would always spring me a drink and a smoke; if I had a full pack of cigarettes, I was ahead of the game. I stayed out all night, finally staggering out into some of the District's worst neighborhoods with a couple of bucks in my sneaker, if I was lucky. Usually I was broke.

Yet I really *was* lucky. Somehow I always managed to find my way home. At two or three or four a.m., I'd crash into my apartment, alone except for the cockroaches—David would have gone home with a pickup from the bars, and Marcy and Bunny had decamped to the suburbs. I'd be so drunk, I stuck to the mattress like a fly mashed against a window. Sometimes I'd sit cross-legged with the typewriter in front of me and write, naked because of the appalling heat, my damp skin grey with cigarette ash. I read *Tropic of Cancer*, reread *Dhalgen* and *A Fan's Notes* and a copy of *Illuminations* held together by a rubber band. I played Pere Ubu and Wire at the wrong speed, because I was too wasted to notice, and would finally pass out only to be ripped awake by the apocalyptic scream of the firehouse siren next door—I'd be standing in the middle of the room, screaming at the top of my lungs, before I realized I was no longer asleep. I saw people in my room, a lanky boy with dark-blond hair and clogs who pointed his finger at me and shouted *Poseur!* I heard voices. My dreams were of flames, of the walls around me exploding outward so that I could see the ruined city like a freshly tilled garden extending for miles and miles, burning cranes and skeletal buildings rising from the smoke to bloom, black and gold and red, against a topaz sky. I wanted to burn, too, tear through the wall that separated me from that other world, the *real* world, the one I glimpsed in books and music, the world I wanted to claim for myself.

But I didn't burn. I was just a fucked-up college student, and pretty soon I wasn't even that. That spring I flunked out of the Divine. All my other friends were still in school, getting boyfriends and girlfriends, getting cast in University productions of *An Inspector Calls* and *Arturo Roi*. Even David Baldanders managed to get good grades for his paper on Verlaine. Meanwhile I leaned out my third-floor window and smoked and watched the speed freaks stagger across the parking lot below. If I jumped, I could be with them: that was all it would take.

It was too beautiful for words, too terrifying to think this was what my life had shrunk to. In the mornings I made instant coffee and tried to read what I'd written the night before. Nice words but they made absolutely no sense. I cranked up Marcy's expensive stereo and played my records, compulsively transcribing song lyrics as though they might somehow bleed into something else, breed with my words and create a coherent storyline. I scrawled more words on the bedroom wall:

I HAVE BEEN DAMNED BY THE RAINBOW

I AM AN AMERICAN ARTIST, AND I HAVE NO CHAIRS

It had all started as an experiment. I held the blunt, unarticulated belief that meaning and transcendence could be shaken from the world, like unripe fruit from a tree; then consumed.

So I'd thrown my brain into the Waring blender along with vials of cheap acid and hashish, tobacco and speed and whatever alcohol was at hand. Now I wondered: Did I have the stomach to toss down the end result?

Whenever David showed up it was a huge relief.

"Come on," he said one afternoon. "Let's go to the movies."

We saw a double bill at the Biograph, *The Story of Adele H* and *Jules et Jim*. Torturously uncomfortable chairs, but only four bucks for four hours of air-conditioned bliss. David had seen *Adele H* six times already; he sat beside me, rapt, whispering the words to himself. I struggled with the French and mostly read the subtitles. Afterwards we stumbled blinking into the long ultraviolet D.C. twilight, the smell of honeysuckle and diesel, coke and lactic acid, our clothes crackling with heat like lightning and our skin electrified as the sugared air seeped into it like poison. We ran arm-in-arm up to the Café de Paris, sharing one of David's Gitanes. We had enough money for a bottle of red wine and a baguette. After a few hours, the waiter kicked us out, but we gave him a dollar anyway. That left us just enough for the Metro and the bus home.

It took us hours to get back. By the time we ran up the steps to our apartment, we'd sobered up again. It was not quite nine o'clock on a Friday night.

"Fuck!" said David. "What are we going to do now?"

No one was around. We got on the phone, but there were no parties, no one with a car to take us somewhere else. We riffled the apartment for a forgotten stash of beer or dope or money, turned our pockets inside out looking for stray seeds, Black Beauties, fragments of green dust.

Nada.

In Marcy's room we found about three dollars in change in one of her jeans pockets. Not enough to get drunk, not enough to get us back into the city.

"Damn," I said. "Not enough for shit."

From the parking lot came the low thunder of motorcycles, a baby crying, someone shouting.

"You fucking motherfucking fucker."

"That's a lot of fuckers," said David.

Then we heard a gunshot.

"Jesus!" yelled David, and yanked me to the floor. From the neighboring apartment echoed the *crack* of glass shattering. "They shot out a window!"

"I said, not enough money for *anything*." I pushed him away and sat up. "I'm not staying here all night."

"Okay, okay, wait . . ."

He crawled to the kitchen window, pulled himself onto the sill to peer out. "They *did* shoot out a window," he said admiringly. "Wow."

"Did they leave us any beer?"

David looked over his shoulder at me. "No. But I have an idea."

He crept back into the living room and emptied out his pockets beside me. "I think we have enough," he said after he counted his change for the third time. "Yeah. But we have to get there now—they close at nine."

"Who does?"

I followed him back downstairs and outside.

"Peoples Drug," said David. "Come on."

We crossed Queens Chapel Road, dodging Mustangs and blasted pickups. I watched wistfully as the 80 bus passed, heading back into the city. It was almost nine o'clock. Overhead the sky had that dusty gold-violet bloom it got in late spring. Cars raced by, music blaring; I could smell charcoal burning somewhere, hamburgers on a grill and the sweet far-off scent of apple blossom.

"Wait," I said.

I stopped in the middle of the road, arms spread, staring straight up into the sky and feeling what I imagined David must have felt when he leaned against the walls of Mr. P's and Grand Central Station: I was waiting, waiting, waiting for the world to fall on me like a hunting hawk.

"What the fuck are you *doing*?" shouted David as a car bore down and he dragged me to the far curb. "Come *on*."

"What are we getting?" I yelled as he dragged me into the drugstore.

"Triaminic."

I had thought there might be a law against selling four bottles of cough syrup to two messed-up looking kids. Apparently there wasn't, though I was embarrassed enough to stand back as David shamelessly counted pennies and nickels and quarters out onto the counter.

We went back to Queenstown. I had never done cough syrup before; not unless I had a cough. I thought we would dole it out a spoonful at a time, over the course of the evening. Instead David unscrewed the first bottle and knocked it back in one long swallow. I watched in amazed disgust, then shrugged and did the same.

"Aw, *fuck*."

I gagged and almost threw up, somehow kept it down. When I looked up, David was finishing off a second bottle, and I could see him eyeing the remaining one in front of me. I grabbed it and drank it, as well, then sprawled against the box spring. Someone lit a candle. David? Me? Someone put on a record, one of those Eno albums, *Another Green World*. Someone stared at me, a boy with long black hair unbound and eyes that blinked from blue to black and then shut down for the night.

"Wait," I said, trying to remember the words. "I. Want. You. To—"

Too late: David was out. My hand scrabbled across the floor, searching for the book I'd left there, a used New Directions paperback of Rimbaud's work. Even pages were in French; odd pages held their English translations.

I wanted David to read me "*Le lettre du voyant,*" Rimbaud's letter to his friend Paul Demeny; the letter of the seer. I knew it by heart in English and on the page but spoken French eluded me and always would. I opened the book, struggling to see through the scrim of cheap narcotic and nausea until at last I found it.

Je dis qu'il faut être voyant, se faire voyant.

Le Poète se fait voyant par un long, immense et raisonné dérèglement de tous les sens. Toutes les formes d'amour, de souffrance, de folie; il cherche lui-même . . .

I say one must be a visionary, one must become a seer.

The poet becomes a seer through a long, boundless and systematic derangement of all the senses. All forms of love, of suffering, of madness; he seeks them within himself . . .

As I read I began to laugh, then suddenly doubled over. My mouth tasted sick, a second sweet skin sheathing my tongue. I retched, and a bright-red clot exploded onto the floor in front of me; I dipped my finger into it then wrote across the warped parquet.

Dear Dav

I looked up. There was no light save the wavering flame of a candle in a jar. Many candles, I saw now; many flames. I blinked and ran my hand across my forehead. It felt damp. When I brought my finger to my lips, I tasted sugar and blood. On the floor David sprawled, snoring softly, his bandanna clenched in one hand. Behind him the walls reflected candles, endless candles; though as I stared I saw they were not reflected light after all but a line of flames, upright, swaying like figures dancing. I rubbed my eyes, a wave cresting inside my head then breaking even as I felt something splinter in my eye. I started to cry out but could not: I was frozen, freezing. Someone had left the door open.

"Who's there?" I said thickly, and crawled across the room. My foot nudged the candle; the jar toppled and the flame went out.

But it wasn't dark. In the corridor outside our apartment door, a hundred-watt bulb dangled from a wire. Beneath it, on the top step, sat the boy I'd seen in the urinal beside David. His hair was the color of dirty straw, his face sullen. He had muddy green-blue eyes, bad teeth, fingernails bitten down to the skin; skeins of dried blood covered his fingertips like webbing. A filthy bandanna was knotted tightly around his throat.

"Hey," I said. I couldn't stand very well, so slumped against the wall, slid until I was sitting almost beside him. I fumbled in my pocket and found one of David's crumpled Gitanes, fumbled some more until I found a book of matches. I tried to light one, but it was damp; tried a second time and failed again.

Beside me, the blond boy swore. He grabbed the matches from me and lit one, turned to hold it cupped before my face. I brought the cigarette close and breathed in, watched the fingertip flare of crimson then blue as the match went out.

But the cigarette was lit. I took a drag, passed it to the boy. He smoked in silence, after a minute handed it back to me. The acrid smoke couldn't mask his oily smell, sweat and shit and urine; but also a faint odor of green hay and sunlight. When he turned his face to me, I saw that he was older than I had first thought, his skin dark-seamed by sun and exposure.

"Here," he said. His voice was harsh and difficult to understand. He held his hand out. I opened mine expectantly, but as he spread his fingers only a stream of sand fell onto my palm, gritty and stinking of piss. I drew back, cursing. As I did, he leaned forward and spat in my face.

"Poseur."

"You *fuck*," I yelled. I tried to get up, but he was already on his feet. His hand was tearing at his neck; an instant later something lashed across my face, slicing upward from cheek to brow. I shouted in pain and fell back, clutching my cheek. There was a red veil between me and the world; I blinked and for an instant saw through it. I glimpsed the young man running down the steps, his hoarse laughter echoing through the stairwell; heard the clang of the fire door swinging open then crashing shut; then silence.

"Shit," I groaned, and sank back to the floor. I tried to staunch the blood with my hand. My other hand rested on the floor. Something warm brushed against my fingers: I grabbed it and held it before me: a filthy bandanna, twisted tight as a noose, one whip-end black and wet with blood.

I saw him one more time. It was high summer by then, the school year over. Marcy and Bunny were gone till the fall, Marcy to Europe with her parents, Bunny to a private hospital in Kentucky. David would be leaving soon, to return to his family in Philadelphia. I had found another job in the city, a real job, a GS-1 position with the Smithsonian; the lowest-level job one could have in the government, but it was a paycheck. I worked three twelve-hour shifts in a row, three days a week, and wore a mustard-yellow polyester uniform with a photo ID that opened doors to all the museums on the Mall. Nights I sweated away with David at the bars or the Atlantis; days I spent at the newly opened East Wing of the National Gallery of Art, its vast open white-marble space an air-conditioned vivarium where I wandered stoned, struck senseless by huge moving shapes like sharks spun of metal and canvas: Calder's great mobile, Miro's tapestry, a line of somber Rothko's, darkly shimmering waterfalls in an upstairs gallery. Breakfast was a Black Beauty and a Snickers bar; dinner whatever I could find to drink.

We were at the Lost and Found, late night early August. David as usual had gone off on his own. I was, for once, relatively sober: I was in the middle of my three-day workweek—normally I wouldn't have gone out, but David was leaving the next morning. I was on the club's upper level, an area like the deck of an ocean liner, where you could lean on the rails and look down onto the dance floor below. The club was crowded, the music deafening. I was watching the men dance with each other, hundreds of them, maybe thousands, strobe-lit beneath mirrorballs and shifting layers of blue and grey smoke that would ignite suddenly with white blades of laser light, strafing the writhing forms below so they let out a sudden single-voiced shriek, punching the air with their fists and blasting at whistles. I rested my arms on the rounded metal rail and smoked, thinking how beautiful it all was, how strange, how alive. It was like watching the sea.

And as I gazed, slowly it changed; slowly something changed. One song bled into another, arms waved like tendrils, a shadow moved through the air above them. I looked up, startled, glanced aside and saw the blond young man standing there a few feet from me. His fingers grasped the railing; he stared at the dance floor with an expression at once hungry and disdainful and disbelieving. After a moment, he slowly lifted his head, turned and stared at me.

I said nothing. I touched my hand to my throat, where his bandanna was knotted there, loosely. It was stiff as rope beneath my fingers: I hadn't washed it. I stared back at him, his green-blue eyes hard and somehow dull—not stupid, but with the obdurate matte gleam of unpolished agate. I wanted to say something, but I was afraid of him; and before I could speak, he turned his head to stare back down at the floor below us.

"Cela s'est passé," he said, and shook his head.

I looked to where he was gazing. I saw that the dance floor was endless, eternal: the cinder-block warehouse walls had disappeared. Instead, the moving waves of bodies extended for miles and miles until they melted into the horizon. They were no longer bodies but flames, countless flickering lights like the candles I had seen in my apartment, flames like men dancing; and then they were not even flames but bodies consumed by flame, flesh and cloth burned away until only the bones remained and then not even bone but only the memory of motion, a shimmer of wind on the water then the water gone and only a vast and empty room, littered with refuse: glass vials, broken plastic whistles, plastic cups, dog collars, ash.

I blinked. A siren wailed. I began to scream, standing in the middle of my room, alone, clutching at a bandanna tied loosely around my neck. On the mattress on the floor David turned, groaning, and stared up at me with one bright blue eye.

"It's just the firehouse," he said, and reached to pull me back beside him. It was five a.m. He was still wearing the clothes he'd worn to the Lost and Found. So was I: I touched the bandanna at my throat and thought of the young man at the railing beside me. "C'mon, you've hardly slept yet," urged David. "You have to get a little sleep."

He left the next day. I never saw him again.

A few weeks later my mother came, ostensibly to visit her cousin in Chevy Chase, but really to check on me. She found me spread-eagled on my bare mattress, screenless windows open to let the summer's furnace heat pour like molten iron into the room. Around me were the posters I'd shredded and torn from the walls; on the walls were meaningless phrases, crushed remains of cockroaches and waterbugs, countless rust-colored handprints, bullet-shaped gouges where I'd dug my fingernails into the drywall.

"I think you should come home," my mother said gently. She stared at my hands, fingertips netted with dried blood, my knuckles raw and seeping red. "I don't think you really want to stay here. Do you? I think you should come home."

I was too exhausted to argue. I threw what remained of my belongings into a few cardboard boxes, gave notice at the Smithsonian, and went home.

It's thought that Rimbaud completed his entire body of work before his nineteenth birthday; the last prose poems, *Illuminations,* indicate he may have been profoundly moved by the time he spent in London in 1874. After that came journey and exile, years spent as an arms trader in Abyssinia until he came home to France to die, slowly and painfully, losing his right leg to syphilis, electrodes fastened to his nerveless arm in an attempt to regenerate life and motion. He died on the morning of November 10, 1891, at ten o'clock. In his delirium, he believed that he was back in Abyssinia, readying himself to depart upon a ship called *Aphinar*. He was thirty-seven years old.

I didn't live at home for long—about ten months. I got a job at a bookstore; my mother drove me there each day on her way to work and picked me up on her way home. Evenings I ate dinner with her and my two younger sisters. Weekends I went out with friends I'd gone to high school with. I picked up the threads of a few relationships begun and abandoned years earlier. I drank too much but not as much as before. I quit smoking.

I was nineteen. When Rimbaud was my age, he had already finished his life work. I hadn't even started yet. He had changed the world; I could barely change my socks. He had walked through the wall, but I had only smashed my head against it, fruitlessly, in anguish and despair. It had defeated me, and I hadn't even left a mark.

Eventually I returned to D.C. I got my old job back at the Smithsonian, squatted for a while with friends in Northeast, got an apartment, a boyfriend, a promotion. By the time I returned to the city, David had graduated from the Divine. We spoke on the phone a few times: he had a steady boyfriend now, an older man, a businessman from France. David was going to Paris with him to live. Marcy married well and moved to Aspen. Bunny got out of the hospital and was doing much better; over the next few decades, she would be my only real contact with that other life, the only one of us who kept in touch with everyone.

Slowly, slowly, I began to see things differently. Slowly I began to see that there were other ways to bring down a wall: that you could dismantle it, brick by brick, stone by stone, over years and years and years. The wall would always be there—at least for me it is—but sometimes I can see where I've made a mark in it, a chink where I can put my eye and look through to the other side. Only for a moment; but I know better now than to expect more than that.

I spoke to David only a few times over the years, and finally not at all. When we last spoke, maybe fifteen years ago, he told me that he was HIV positive. A few years after that, Bunny told me that the virus had gone into full-blown AIDS, and that he had gone home to live with his father in Pennsylvania. Then a few years after that she told me no, he was living in France again, she had heard from him and he seemed to be better.

Cela s'est passé, the young man had told me as we watched the men dancing in the L & F twenty-six years ago. *That is over.*

Yesterday I was at Waterloo Station, hurrying to catch the train to Basingstoke. I walked past the new Eurostar terminal, the sleek Paris-bound bullet trains like marine animals waiting to churn their way back through the Chunnel to the sea. Curved glass walls separated me from them; armed security patrols and British soldiers strode watchfully along the platform, checking passenger IDs and waving people towards the trains.

I was just turning towards the old station when I saw them. They were standing in front of a glass wall like an aquarium's: a middle-aged man in an expensive-looking dark blue overcoat, his black hair still thick though greying at the temples, his hand resting on the shoulders of his companion. A slightly younger man, very thin, his face gaunt and ravaged, burned the color of new brick by the sun, his fair hair gone to grey. He was leaning on a cane; when the older man gestured he turned and began to walk, slowly, painstakingly down the platform. I stopped and watched: I wanted to call out, to see if they would turn and answer, but the blue-washed glass barrier would have muted any sound I made.

I turned, blinking in the light of midday, touched the bandanna at my throat and the notebook in my pocket, and hurried on. They would not have seen me anyway. They were already boarding the train. They were on their way to Paris.

Janny Wurts *is a triple threat, two of which I'll mention here (the other, as you'll see, later): She's a heck of a writer as well as a heck of an artist. Quite a combination.*

She's the best-selling author of Grand Conspiracy, *and* Peril's Gate *is a recent title in the huge* Wars of Light and Shadow *series.*

If you read fantasy, you've seen her artwork gracing many covers.

Enjoy the following.

Blood, Oak, Iron

Janny Wurts

The old King of Chaldir lay dying. Everyone knew. Scarcely anyone cared. He lay under quilts in a bed with gold posts and purple hangings, his waxy, cadaverous face throwing grotesque shadows by the guttering flare of the candles. Whole seconds passed, while his unsteady breath seemed to stop.

Such times the man who kept vigil at the bedside would lean close, a hand weathered brown from the bridle rein reaching out to clasp the skeletal wrist that rested limp on the coverlet. "I am here," he murmured softly. "I'll see you don't die in the dark."

More minutes would pass, while the candle flames bent in the drafts and the autumn winds rattled the casements. The trace scent of frost would knife through the close air, displacing its burden of unguents and tisanes, and the decayed must of age and sickness.

The old king never moved. His eggshell lids did not open.

Findlaire, who was the only legitimate royal son, would arise at measured intervals. Only lately aware that he was a prince in line for Chaldir's succession, he took no joy from the prospect. He was a tall man, long-strided, clothed still in a forester's leather, and his face wore the lines of a near-sighted squint. He replenished the wicks as they flickered and drowned. Then he laced patient knuckles in his salt-stranded hair and tried not to think of the dark that hemmed the wavering circles of light cast over the patterned carpet. The old king might have been unloved, but his suite was no less than lavish.

Throughout his long life, his attendants and councilors had served his needs out of fear. Now that he lay dying, they waited and whispered of uncanny powers, and the curse that held him in possession. Abroad in the fields, simple country folk gathered the grain shocks for threshing. The annual harvest would follow its rhythm, despite the imminent change in succession. The lands of Chaldir were reasonably prosperous. Its people were submissive but not starving. Kings were crowned, and kings passed away, but the shadow behind the power that governed the realm had not changed for three thousand years.

The ancient bargain with the fiend would prevail, folk said. Never mind that Prince Findlaire had been raised in lands far away, had never since he was a speechless infant inhabited the realm that his birthright destined him to inherit. Once the incumbent king died, and before the new one was crowned, the curse that burdened the royal line would claim its uncanny due. The heir was doomed to be claimed by the wraith, with the chancellor and the king's council of Chaldir left to keep what peace they could, under the terms of a horrific bargain.

Another dawn paled the sky through the casement. Crows soared across sunrise like scraps of black rag. They perched on the battlements and raised raucous complaint on the hour that Findlaire arose. He snuffed out all but four of the candles. Then he moved in his woodsman's quiet to the doorway, where he raised word to summon the servants. He stayed as they unlocked and unbarred the oak panel. A lean shadow braced against the armoire, he watched, his hands crossed at his belt, beside the empty scabbard of the knife he no longer wore at his hip. If the course his own fate must take was prescribed, he could still insist that his dying liege was attended with kindness and decency.

When the sheets had been changed and the king's withered flesh was resettled under the blankets in comfort, Findlaire returned to the bedside. He kissed the cheek of the father he had never known, who was now too far gone to exchange any word with a son born after the curse had overwhelmed his last human awareness. Then Findlaire left, to spend the day in the palace library poring over record scrolls and dusty piles of books.

In the afternoon, his uncle Guriman found him asleep, his cheek and the knuckles of one strong hand pillowed on the pages of Chaldir's bygone history. With his broad, outdoorsman's shoulders, and his forearms tucked like a cat's, Findlaire seemed relaxed but never innocuous.

"You aren't going to find any answers," Guriman said, his fish-pale elegance clothed in ribboned velvets and his girlish lisp a disquieting affectation for a man more than five decades old.

Findlaire opened his eyes, which were limpid as slate in a streambed. He straightened up. Not a muscle in his rangy frame tightened, but the stillness about him acquired the poise of a fully drawn bow. He regarded the soft uncle whose mounted henchmen had run him to earth like an animal, one day a fortnight past. The wrists underneath his chamois cuffs were still raw from his struggles, as men-at-arms he did not know had bundled him into a carriage and borne him to Chaldir, trussed and furious. They had hauled him into the palace and offered him meat and a bed, and called him "Your Grace," and "Prince." His bonds had been cut, since. But he was kept as close as a prisoner, and liveried crossbowmen flanked him wherever he went.

As they did now, in deferent quiet, one pair ranked at each end of the table. Others stood guard at the doorway. Their vigilance brightened like heat off stirred embers as Findlaire locked eyes with the uncle he had only just learned he possessed. Where another man might have railed or cursed, the forester preferred to say nothing. A lifetime of setting snares for shy animals had taught him unbreakable patience.

"Why trouble yourself?" Guriman ventured at last. He fingered a scroll with a pallid hand, his nails clean as a pampered woman's. "The king will die. As the closest male heir in line for the throne, the fiend of Chaldir will have you. Why waste your last days of awareness digging in vain through old books? You have little time. While your mind's still your own, I could send you a virgin girl to give you an hour of pleasure."

"You could unlock the doors," Findlaire said.

"Oh, no. To let you go would be utterly wasteful." Guriman gave the scroll a contemptuous flick. The parchment rolled the width of the table, and bumped against the jumble of manuscripts already searched and discarded. "I spent too many years keeping track of your whereabouts. Damn your mother to the nethermost hell pit for thinking to spare you from your fate. You will not escape, or shirk your crown, or hide in the obscurity of a commoner's lifestyle."

Findlaire glanced down, once more absorbed by the pages he had been reading. His stilled face suggested that antagonistic uncles and poised men-at-arms and locked doors were of little more moment than dust to the waters of a creek. Yet in the pale sunlight warming the table, his hands had closed into fists.

As though that small sign of frustration scratched an itch, Guriman shifted his weight from one slippered foot to the other. "I could recite you the history you're seeking. The bad bargain struck by your ancestor has granted the fiend a new body for each generation, in perpetuity. Its wraith will enslave the closest male relative as each possessed sovereign departs. You are the king's son. Your lot is cast. There will be no reprieve. Why should you not savor the time you have left? Trust me in this, each one of your forebears has searched this library before you. Not one in a hundred doomed generations found any means to keep the fiend from its promised binding."

Findlaire refused answer.

In baiting that blank wall of resistance, even Guriman found little sport.

If the books held no clues, *this* prince made it plain: he would comb through their pages again. He had no use for wealth or a ruler's inheritance. The crossbowmen watched his deliberate calm and did not find him complacent. Findlaire did not rage at his straits. Whatever vile promise his progenitor had made, whatever the downfall that claimed each descendent, the fiend's displaced wraith would not take him willing.

"You'll succumb," Guriman insisted at length. "You'll find no help for yourself in the past, though you blind yourself reading old manuscripts."

And sundown approached, like spite itself. Persistence wrung no secret from the crumbling books. Findlaire stood up to the prod of his jailers, and stretched aching shoulders, and longed for the grace of his yew bow, and his hunter's quiver of arrows. He was a man accustomed to venison roasted over an outdoor spit. The rich supper Guriman's lackeys brought did nothing but sour his stomach. Tonight, he spurned the overcooked meal. On a servant's brown bread and a pitcher of water, he would stand the night's vigil alongside his dying father.

The hours of darkness descended again, marked and measured by the arrhythmic whisper of the failing king's breath. Findlaire paced to stay wakeful. He tended the candles and leaned on the wall by the tower's iron barred casement. He had no sharp object to free the jammed catch. A crack in the glass let in the outdoors. Drawing in the chill autumn air, Findlaire listened to the mournful chime of a cowbell, windborne from some crofter's pasture. From the turret below, he caught snatches of coarse laughter, or yells of triumph as one of the soldiers on watch won at knucklebones or dice. The gusts sifted dry leaves across the starlit bailey, while the frost etched its hoary fingerprint over the runners of ivy latched to the outside sill.

Findlaire rested his forehead upon his closed fist. Weariness sucked him too hollow for sleep. He suffered the enclosed suffocation of walls with senses that felt silted and dull. Yet the passion burned in him, bright as pain itself. Longing seared every nerve to rebellion. There was an indelible part of his spirit that would not accept his imprisonment. The heart that belonged to the open forest could not be resigned to the usage of Chaldir's wraith.

Absorbed by the clean, white rise of the moon, Findlaire almost forgot his surroundings. If not for the hideous, ongoing need to keep track of the dying king's breaths, he might not have noticed the muted rasp, as furtive fingers lifted the door latch.

The brush of changed air against his nape aroused all his woodsman's instincts. Spurred to reaction, he whirled about. His reach for his knife met an empty sheath, and frustration. Past salvage, his peril was upon him.

The assassin launched through the bank of lit candles. Through the winnowed streamers of flame, Findlaire saw his form as a hurtling shadow the instant before he struck. Then a muscled, panting body slammed into him, bent on choking his life with a garrote.

Findlaire entangled his fist in the string before it looped tight round his throat. Slammed backward, he struck the wall. A tapestry ripped from its looped rings. His grunt mingled with the killer's snarl of frustration. Their locked struggle toppled them both to the floor. Rolling and kicking, and gouging for purchase, they tumbled across the rucked wool. Their battering progress swept over the rug and smashed through table and basin and towel racks. A scatter of overset candles crashed in a flying spray of spilled wax. Findlaire closed his hand on a billet of split wood, then used that at need to belabor his opponent. He knew where to strike to stun a trapped lynx. To subdue a man the same way fairly sickened him.

The assailant dropped, limp but unhurt. Findlaire recoiled back to his feet. Bent double, retching, he rushed the breached door. There, his armed sentries were now lying senseless, most likely drugged with a potion. Yet before he won clear, his chance to seize freedom was torn from his grasp once again. More men arrived and charged over the threshold. These bore him down with battering fists. The matchstick of wood he had snatched for a weapon proved no use against mail and steel helmets. Findlaire fought as the fox set upon by the pack, beyond every rational hope. Yet numbers prevailed. Slammed dizzy and bleeding, he lay under the weight of his captors, breathing hard. A man with a sword stepped into the corridor and dispatched the incapable bowmen. The ugly sound of their dying reached Findlaire. He shouted his astonished protest, the more horrified as he realized the unconscious assassin would be just as callously executed.

"Shut up, you!"

When he shouted again, he found himself served with a kick in the belly.

After that, Findlaire could do nothing at all but curl up and be wretchedly sick.

Later, propped up in a chair, with the abraded burns from the garrote a livid welt on his hand, he held his body tenderly still to quell the ache of his bruises. When Guriman arrived to inspect him and gloat, he had no inclination to speak. The smell of fresh death, and old incense, and medicine befouled the closed room, until he could wish to stop breathing.

On the bed, the dying king rasped, inhale to exhale, while beyond the barred glass, the stars slowly turned, serene in their timeless courses.

"Why did you not let the paid killer take you?" Guriman said, almost taunting. He approached in his beautiful brocade robe, careful to avoid the befouled carpet. "The creature was hired by my bitterest rival, or did you not know?"

Findlaire's quiet awareness itself framed reply. He might be a stranger unused to court ways, and the poisonous whispers of intrigue. Men might lie to themselves, caught up by ambition and their secretive, grasping desires. Yet a huntsman could recognize the hierarchy of wolf packs. Greed and avarice showed in the glitter of men's eyes. Such bitter jealousies could be sensed, and the smoldering envy of those who coveted Guriman's power as chancellor: the dominance and control that would divide all the world into the strong and the weak, with the forceful set over the cowed and the frightened.

"Poor craven," mused Guriman. "Too soft, or too simple to let go when you're beaten. If you had died before the old king, the fiend would be left to claim your next of kin. By default, the curse would have fallen on me. Where is your regret? Your hour of contrition? Your end could have bought a crude victory."

"No victory that matters," Findlaire rasped, his throat sore. No more would he say, beyond that. Eyes shut, he dreamed of green foliage, and of the roe deer grazing snug in their moonlit glens.

Guriman grew bored. He departed before long, appointing more trustworthy men-at-arms to redouble their guard at the doorway. Barred inside, Findlaire was left to his solitary vigil alongside the dying king. There was no sense of peace in the bony, stilled face on the pillow. No thoughts, in that skull, worth expressing. No work, for the hands that lay childishly soft, but age-spotted against silken coverlets. The oblivion inflicted by Chaldir's fiend did not instill beauty with quietude. Life expended its vigor, robbed of its self-awareness and without the innate, purposeful dignity alive in the simplest tree.

Findlaire tried, and failed, to encompass a concept that escaped definition of loss. His hurts kept him wakeful without need to pace. Throughout the crawling hours of night, he nursed his thrashed flesh, and attended the damaged stubs of the candles. The flames he kept burning shone bright and ephemeral, no less short-lived than the stifled existence he refused out of hand to accept.

Yet when the stars paled, the old king was still breathing. As though human will, through no mind of its own, fought the wraith's passage to its next host through the blank urge of bodily reflex.

When the raw, crimson dawn streaked the sky past the casement, Findlaire pinched out the wicks, one by one. As morning arrived, servants came and relieved him, to endure through the day until sundown.

By now gritty-eyed and aching tired, and wasted from the aftermath of nausea, Findlaire could not face another hour indoors. If he must sleep, he would choose a place where Guriman's penchant for comfort would be most inconvenienced, if he came to gloat.

The battlements between the wind-raked keeps were chilly enough, but the guardsmen blocked Findlaire's access. They refused him passage to the outer wall, no matter which portal he tried.

"Can't let you jump," the armed captain said gruffly. "We've got orders. Your life's to be guarded."

The bailey proved to be off-limits, as well, as too open a venue for assassins.

"Last night's attempt won't happen again," puffed the bowman who tagged at his heels, not pleased to be led on a pointless chase up and down tower stairwells. "Why not accept what can never be changed?"

Another man added, "The greater good of the kingdom demands that the fiend must be given its victim."

Findlaire stopped. He turned his head, his gray eyes wide open. "I'm no man's puppet," he told them.

His guardsmen exchanged dour glances and shrugged. The future was nothing if not inevitable. The terms of the curse would not be thwarted. The fiend would devour Findlaire's awareness and inhabit the shell of his body, while Guriman ruled, secure in his post as king's chancellor.

"You know the old fox has planned this for years. He's learned the hard way how to keep the fiend in a state of sated stupor. Why care, in the end? Your mind will be gone. If young children die screaming to feed your damned flesh, why should their suffering matter? The countryside will not be scourged through another reign of terror. For the sacrifice of an innocent few, the fiend's hunger can be constrained. For all our sakes, should your subjects not have the semblance of their prosperity?"

"Paid for, at what cost?" Findlaire shook his head.

But the guards, to a man, looked on without pity. "You don't realize the horrific bloodbath your destined end will prevent."

"I do," Findlaire rebutted. He had read the records. Year upon year, the graphic account had been kept by Chaldir's historians, a sorrowful toll of red slaughter set down in lines of immutable ink.

Findlaire descended another steep staircase, while his armed wardens crowded at his heels.

After a long bout of pacing through corridors and trying numerous forbidden doors, he encountered the cramped courtyard which adjoined the queen's abandoned apartments. The walled garden enclosed a cracked fountain, choked with the yellowed curls of willow leaves. Wind sifted a fine drizzle over the bent stems in the flower beds. Amid tangled weeds, a few hardy chrysanthemums raised blossoms of delicate purple. Half-smothered in snarls of bittersweet vine, the black stands of yew wore their poisonous yield of red berries.

While the men-at-arms grumbled and huddled under the arched portal to forestall the chance to escape, Findlaire walked the puddled pathways. He paused under the hulk of an ancient oak. The crabbed branches were tagged with bedraggled leaves, brown and sickened with galls. The scaled metal of a circular bench girdled the massive trunk. Time and age had expanded the tree's girth, until the collar of ornamental scrollwork had dug in like a shackle. The once graceful tracery of the wrought iron had been swallowed into the bulging, scabrous bark. Findlaire traced his straight fingers over the wound, moved to pity.

For how many generations had Chaldir's indifferent royal gardeners disregarded the tormented oak's plight?

"If I'd stood in my forefather's place with a chisel, I would have spared you this misery," Findlaire told the tree's hobbled spirit.

No remedy could lift the affliction now. The iron was too deeply embedded to excise without destroying the life of the tree.

A breeze ruffled through the leaves overhead. Droplets spilled down like cold tears. The morbid thought stirred within Findlaire's mind that his father suffered a similar blight. He had been throttled while still alive by the unnatural compulsions imposed by a fiend. Yet what axe in the world could cut through a binding curse, and what tool could rend the insubstantial blight of a wraith?

Distraught with sadness, Findlaire sat with his back braced against the wounded tree. For a helpless interval, he sought the illusion of oblivion behind his shuttered eyelids.

Exhaustion overcame him. He slept, while the rain fell and beaded his hair and slicked over his weathered features.

The dream came upon him unaware, its texture spun from the sorrowful thread that shaped his enclosed surroundings. He remained within the queen's ruined garden, amid the sere heads of dead flowers, while the drifts of dry-rotted leaves moldered under the tired oak. The rough bark rasped through the leathers on his back. His feet slowly chilled in his deer-hide boots, and his hands nestled loose in his lap.

Skin, bone, wood, and pith, he melted into the oak tree. The rusted bench kept its strangling grip on the bole, and gradually, over the passage of years, the metal artistry wrought by the smith came to fetter his ankles. He cried from the pain, perhaps as the tree had, voiceless and mute in its agony. None heard. No one came. His legs ached from the pressure. His shins gained weeping sores that scabbed over, transformed into welted scars that paralyzed tissue and tendon. Had he been a red-blooded animal, so deformed, a kind man would have dealt him a mercy stroke.

No such simple expedient was shown to the tree. Shackled in metal, impaired beyond healing, Findlaire ached beyond bearing for loss: the tree's and his own, for a natural freedom imprisoned and twisted by force.

Endurance remained. The tree had not died, though the iron bench girdled it.

For three thousand years, Chaldir's cursed royal line had bound over the lives of its sacrificed princes. Dreaming, Findlaire received the unfolding awareness: that the oak tree knew all their names. He shared the defeated vision of his predecessors, of strong men who had failed: of kings who had died by their own hand, and so condemned their sons, or their brothers. The kings who had tried blinding, or maiming a limb, on the chance that the wraith might reject a flawed vessel, and perhaps move on to roost elsewhere. He knew the fear of the desperately craven, and the seizing terror of others whose hearts had stopped, unable to withstand the uneasy nights of the vigil. He dreamed of men who had fled, and men who had killed their own fathers in ritual, seeking to destroy Chaldir's fiend. He knew the wise men, and their desperate seeking, reduced to vanquished despair. One after the next, Findlaire saw the sad ghosts whose joy and whose laughter had been robbed by the curse that hounded Chaldir's royal lineage.

"You will follow in our footsteps," they said, weeping the tears of the ages. "Like us, you will have no choice at the end. Your sire will die, and you will be left to suffer the next chapter of a blighted legacy."

Bound to the oak's memory, Findlaire saw the changing loom of the garden spin its tapestry of four seasons. Under spring moonlight, he watched generations of Chaldir's jeweled courtiers dance by torchlight or embrace as young lovers under the tree. Their lives seemed more fleeting than those of the moths, which circled the torch flames in blinded frenzy. He witnessed the night when his mother had given her promise to his lost father: that she would flee the realm and bear the king's child in secret, then foster him into a commoner's home to be raised in nameless obscurity.

"There is endurance in oak, and cold iron, and blood." The voice was a woman's, and faint as the whisper of leaves brushed by a passing breeze. "A seed's urge to grow is rooted and fixed. But a man is born gifted with movement and choice. Why has your lineage begotten its sons? Why has each one bequeathed a doomed child, one generation after another?"

"Hope," Findlaire murmured in dreaming reply. The one word contained all the treasure he knew: the green scent of balsam, which had infused the peace and boundless beauty that lived in the summer wood. He offered that grave like a flawless jewel, to the heart of the crippled tree.

Soon after that he opened his eyes to gray mist. His leathers had soaked in the icy drizzle. He felt gritty, used up, and the chill of the rainfall had sunk through to his bones. The neglected garden held nothing but puddles, each reflecting the moss-grown walls, the cracked stone of the fountain, and the tangle of weed-choked flower beds.

Yet standing, attuned to a forester's instincts, Findlaire sensed that he was no longer alone.

An oak leaf winnowed down and feathered his cheek like the brush of a withered finger.

He followed its spiraling flight toward the ground, then noticed the acorn he had missed before, on the flagstone next to his boot. He picked it up. Hope lay within its hardened shell: the unfulfilled promise of a fresh start, and the latent dream of a seedling that might sprout and grow without any hindrance or boundary. Findlaire tucked the acorn into his pocket.

While his uncle's vigilant guards barred the door, the withered leaf settled, trembling.

"The king will die tonight," Guriman said, while outside the glass casement, clouds banked and gathered, and lightning flared on the horizon.

"The vigil has lasted for seven days, and the fiend has taken your measure. Are you certain you don't wish me to send you a woman? This may be the last chance you have in this world to savor a human comfort."

"No." Findlaire stood with his back to the wall while the candles around the king's bed were lit, one by one, by a liveried servant. "I will get you no heir." In his hardened fist, clenched over the acorn, he had all the comfort he wanted.

Guriman shrugged. "Such scruple you have! But the gesture is meaningless. I have sons aplenty. The unlucky eldest will inherit the curse. He, or one of his grandsons, will be alive to receive the fiend's wraith when you finally succumb to old age."

Findlaire had nothing to say.

"No last wishes?" prodded Guriman. "No bequests? No noble words for your subjects?" His lightless pale eyes flicked over the tall forester, who held his stilled ground in the corner. "Well, then. Suit yourself. Once the old king is dead and you are possessed, I will return with a living child. You won't be so calm or so reticent then, as you murder to satisfy the fiend's appetite."

Findlaire gripped the acorn. Unlike a man, an unquickened seed could not know the cruelty of anticipation. Its natural being did not encompass the concept of futility or abject despair. A man, trapped to face the descent of the dark, could do little but cling to the undefiled stillness of silence.

Soon enough, Guriman grew restless, and he left. Findlaire remained behind the locked door, with the dying king and the flames of the candles, and the wind-driven rain, beating the barred glass of the casements. Darkness descended, thick as a pall, while the storm gathered force and the gusts shrilled over the tower stonework.

Thunder growled and hammered the air, and lightning cracked over the battlements. Inside the locked chamber, like the hush of held breath, the dread hour approached, when the fiend would spin free of its housing of flesh and lay claim to its next hapless bearer. The release that drew nigh brought the old king no peace. He thrashed, moaning, and plucked at his sheets, as though fighting the wraith that had ravaged him. As though he knew his ending approached, with the spirit left holding its vile burden of murder and the cheated waste of a lifetime.

Findlaire moved, then. He could not ignore suffering. He collected the frail, icy hands of his father. Using the tone that had gentled hurt deer, he sat and spoke quiet reassurance.

"You are not alone. No matter how dreadful the evil inside, someone who cares sits beside you." With no decent shred of comfort to give, Findlaire closed his strong fingers over the old man's and abided. As he had for the tree, he offered up all he owned: the undying renewal that clothed the green glens, steeped in patience to outlast all strife.

In time, the king quieted. His raucous breaths slowed. The fidgeting tremors released his aged limbs. He lay like a figure of chalk on the pillows, while the rhythm of his labored heart missed its beat and finally wearied and stopped.

Findlaire looked up. He saw the glassy stare of dead eyes and understood that Chaldir's doom was upon him. He released the slack hands, stood up, then stepped back, while the jaw of the corpse gaped open. The last wisp of breath sighed out of slack lungs, disgorging the wraith of the fiend.

It emerged as a pallid, luminous mist, writhing like smoke through the darkness. Aware, all at once, that the candles had snuffed, Findlaire gave ground before it. He retreated until he slammed into the wall, as no doubt his victimized forebears had done, on countless nights before this one.

The wraith winnowed toward him. He watched it advance; his pulse raced with dread. Yet where others had shouted or screamed curses, or whimpered in paralyzed fear, his own lips stayed sealed. Findlaire made no sound. With every last fiber of will he possessed, he clung to determined silence.

The fiend came on, an animate, swirling mist that bridged the black air in between. Findlaire pressed against stone, as helpless as his predecessors, while the abhorrent coils snaked in to claim him.

The touch, when it came, was numbingly cold.

Here, many another royal victim had quieted. Battered past all resistance, a man might let go in surrender, grateful for the discovery that his defeat would be softly painless. The wraith's entry would sear out all feeling sensation and seal the mind in dreamless oblivion.

Others fought, hammering their fists bloody in useless rage that their struggle bought no last salvation.

Still others wept blinding tears of self-pity and cried out in wounded loss.

Findlaire held still, without fight, without sound. Yet his calm held no shred of acceptance. The denial he shaped as Chaldir's wraith enveloped him was not the outrage born of defeat. He held nothing else but the flame of his love: for life, for freedom, for the unassailable dignity wrapped up in his memory of balsam.

Eyes closed, lips shut, lungs clamped against the need to inhale, he clasped the acorn and cherished its limitless promise of hope.

Yet a man can stop breathing for only so long. Wrung dizzy, sucked into the blank ebb toward faintness, Findlaire knew the urge to survive must eventually compel his starving lungs to seek air. When consciousness faltered and reflex resurged, the wraith of the fiend would seize entry. Its freezing draught would flow into his chest, then lace through his blood, and savage his heart.

This, a forester who lived by his traps understood. Like the constricted oak in the garden, he must honor life. He would pay the price of a twisted existence, but that ending would not be eternal. *There would be a seed sometime,* that would find new ground; a king's son who survived to win freedom.

Left nothing else, he must concede that his single failure did not bring defeat for all time. He hung his last thought on that chance for renewal: the heart's-peace of the wood, that did not own strife or acknowledge destruction as final.

While his mind dimmed and the wraith twined about him, and the storm cracked and slammed with unbridled fury, he remembered the maimed tree choked in the garden, and its fathomless strength of endurance.

Hope was an acorn, enclosed in his hand.

As his will broke and his burning chest shuddered, and the wraith's poisoned presence swirled in on the air drawn through his contorted throat, the oak tree gave him, like a perfect jewel, the rooted acceptance of its own being.

Man and tree melded. Human flesh acquired the staid hardiness of wood, and blood flowed, sap slow, thick as syrup. The girdling pain of cold iron-cased ankles that forgot every quickened sensation of movement. Thought froze, and awareness knew only itself, a spiraling force that flowed with the seasons, to grow, and to reach for the light.

The awareness of a tree did not know terror. It did not feel passion or rage or discontent. It tendered no coin but the gift of its ongoing right to existence.

There, the wraith found no pain to exploit, no raw nerve to torment, no desire to balk. However it groped, it encountered no restless need to haze into submission. Stuck fast, nailed still, encircled by life that stayed true to itself within a strangling ring of cold iron, the fiend's hunger could find no resistance to grapple. Man and tree joined for the space of one breath, no more than the gap between heartbeats. On that crystalline instant, the wraith was pinned down. It howled, imprisoned in calm. It battered against the unbreakable dignity held in the latent spark in an acorn.

Life for life's sake framed the only defense its destructive will could not breach.

Given nothing to dominate, the wraith that had fed upon Chaldir's princes lost its power and faded, and finally snuffed out of existence.

Outside the king's palace, the storm reached its peak. Lightning flickered and cracked. The darkness blazed white, seared across by the wild force of the elements. The shaft that spread down struck and split the old oak. Its untamed might splintered bark and limb and warped wood, and unleashed an explosion of blazing fragments. The iron bench glowed sullen red, and then steamed in the quench of the deluge.

Within the closed bedchamber, Findlaire collapsed. He sprawled motionless under the shadow of night, the acorn still cradled within the palm of his defiant hand.

He lay so, as dawn broke and the early light pierced through the clouds and flooded the glass of the casements. Voices approached from the corridor outside, strident over the wails of a child.

Findlaire woke to that sound. He stirred and beheld the corpse of his father, settled at peace on the bed. Then the door was wrenched open. As Guriman strode through with the terrified offering to further his wicked alliance, the prince who was forester was up on his feet. Nor was he calm any longer.

Guriman quailed before the bared face of his rage. Cowering, he stepped back and hastily passed off the child to one of the guardsmen. "The fiend's wraith," he stammered. "Chaldir's curse on our lineage—"

"Broken!" snapped Findlaire, a man of few words. "You are left with your conscience and with a brother you owe the right of a decent funeral."

At Guriman's back, the henchman who was left clutching the child dropped, shaken, onto his knees. His submission was followed, shamefaced, by others, until not a guard was left standing. "Long live the king."

Findlaire stared at them, startled. Then he shook his head. "Choose someone else worthy. I've already worn the only crown that has any natural meaning."

While Guriman regarded him, speechlessly stupefied, Findlaire let go and laughed. Freed to walk out, he would leave for the forest and fulfill a promise by planting an acorn.

***Charles de Lint** has quietly, gently, inevitably, become a major name in the fantasy field. His reflective, pastoral stories and novels have won him a following and many awards, including the World Fantasy Award for* The Onion Girl.

For Flights, *he looks into a thing familiar to his fiction: the prism of human love.*

Riding Shotgun

Charles de Lint

I

I wasn't surprised to learn that my father had died. He would have been seventy-two this winter, and he'd always lived hard—I doubted that had changed after I left the farm. What surprised me was that I was in his will. We hadn't spoken in twenty-five years. I hadn't thought of him, except in passing, for maybe half that time. If you'd asked me, I would have said he'd leave his estate to a charity like MADD, considering how it was drunk driving that changed all of our lives.

I missed the funeral. There are a lot of Coes in the phone book, so it took the lawyers a while to track me down.

When they told me he'd left everything to me, I authorized them to put the farm up for sale, with the proceeds to be split between MADD and the local animal shelter. Dad never much cared for me, but he always did have a soft spot for strays.

I could have used the money. I'm a half-owner of a vintage clothing and thrift shop in Lower Foxville, and there always seems to be more money going out than coming in. But I knew it wouldn't be right to keep this unexpected inheritance.

Alessandra was good about it. There are things we argue about, but how we deal with family isn't one of them.

We're not exactly a couple, but we don't see other people either. It's hard to explain. We met in AA, and we're good for each other. Neither of us have had a drink in fifteen years—sixteen for me, actually.

We have a pair of bachelor apartments in the same building as the store.

Ours isn't a platonic relationship, but neither of us can sleep with someone else. Alessandra gets panic attacks if she wakes and there's someone in bed with her.

For me, it just makes the bad dreams worse.

2

We open late on Mondays, so one fall morning after the farm's sold but before the closing date, Alessandra and I drive out to have a look at the place. Alessandra wouldn't have come at all, but I don't drive anymore, and Newford's public transport system stops at the subdivisions that are still four or five miles south of the farm.

"I haven't been here in twenty-five years," I say as we pull into the lane.

I see the farmhouse ahead, surrounded by elms and maples in their fall colors. The barn and outbuildings lie behind the house, the fields yellow and brown, the hay tall. You know how they say you can never go back, or how everything looks smaller if you do?

As we drive up the lane, everything looks exactly the same.

"I hadn't spoken to him for that long either," I add. "To my father, I mean. Not once."

Alessandra nods. She knows. It's not like we haven't shared war stories a hundred times before. Late at night when the darkness closes in and a drink seems like the only thing that will let us sleep. Instead we talk.

She pulls up near the house and shuts off the engine.

"So what am I doing here?" I ask. "Why would he want me to have anything?"

"I wouldn't know, Marshall," she says. "I never met your father."

And wished she'd never met her own.

I nod. I wasn't really expecting an answer. The question had been pretty much rhetorical.

"Do you have the key for the house?" she asks.

That makes me smile. I'd forgotten about that. So some things have changed. Back when I lived here, I can't remember us ever locking our doors.

"I think I'll walk around a little outside first," I say.

"Sure. I'll wait in the car."

"I won't be long."

She touches the bag on the seat between us. "Don't worry. I've got a book."

She's always got a book. We pick them up by the boxful at garage and rummage sales, usually for free. You'd be surprised what people will just leave on the curb when the sale's done. Saves them carting it back inside the house and storing it, I guess.

At the rate we read, and considering our income, these books are a real windfall. Reading's another way to go somewhere else and keep the past at bay.

"Don't . . . you know," she says as I'm getting out of the car.

Get all wound up in what you can't change. She doesn't have to say it.

"I'm okay," I tell her.

But I'm not. I don't realize how *not* until about ten minutes later.

If the old man's last will and testament surprised me, what I find behind the barn pretty much takes all the strength from my legs. I find it hard to breathe. It's all I can do just to stand there at the corner of the barn, staring, my hand up on the greying barn wood to keep my balance.

I don't see the rusted junker, sitting in the tall grass on its wheel rims, the tires rotted away, the grille and right fender smashed in, windshield a spiderweb of cracks, side windows gone. I see the car I'd bought in 1977: a 1965 Chevy Impala two-door hardtop, with a 253 V-8 under the hood and 48,000 original miles on it. Black interior, crocus-yellow exterior, whitewalls. That long sleek slope of the rear window.

I'm dizzy looking at it. The wreck it is, the beauty and freedom it represented to the seventeen-year-old who'd worked his ass off for a whole summer and winter to be able to afford it. I see them both for a long time—the car that's there and the one in my head—until it finally settles back into the junker it is and I can breathe again. I push away from the wall, no longer needing it for support.

I had no idea that the old man had retrieved the car after the accident. Or that he'd stored it back here.

I was in police custody for the funeral because there was no one to put up my bail. When I got out of prison after doing my time, the last place I wanted to come was the farm. I wouldn't have been welcome anyway.

I walk over to the car and try the door, but it's rusted shut. I make a trip into the barn and come back with a crowbar to pry the door open. I don't know what all's been nesting in it, but it doesn't smell too bad.

I get in, and my foot bangs against a beer bottle. I remember that bottle, and the other half-dozen just like it I drank that long-ago afternoon.

I sit and stare at the spiderweb cracks that turn the view through the windshield into something like a finished jigsaw puzzle. My chest tightens again. Up on the dash, there's a baseball cap, half-eaten—by mice, I guess. I can make out the insignia. The Newford Hawks, from back when the city had a ball team. I used to listen to the games on a little transistor radio while I was doing my chores.

I'd dream about my car, listen to the games.

After the accident, I had different dreams about this car. About that day. About how it could all have been different.

I still do.

"Let me drive," Billy had said.

"You want to go to the quarry, little brother, you're staying in the shotgun seat."

I'd let him drive before, but I was feeling ornery that day. Too many beers.

Funny.

Alcohol was the problem.

And afterwards, alcohol was the only thing that had let me forget, allowing me the sweet taste of temporary oblivion. But that wasn't until I'd done my time and was back on the street again. When I was inside, I'd wake up two, three times a night, that afternoon still as fresh in my mind as when it happened.

I reach under my shirt and pull out a key on a string. I can't tell you why I've kept it all these years. I went through a lot of strings, lost pretty much all I ever had before I turned my life around again, but I've hung on to that key through the years.

We've got a jar of old keys in the store, and I've thought of tossing it in with the rest, but I never do.

Keys are funny things. They can unlock the cage and let you out, the way it was for me when I finally got that car. And they can lock you up and stand guard so that you'll never be free.

That key was both for me.

The string comes over my head easily, and that little flat piece of metal with its cut edge fits into the ignition just the way it's supposed to. I don't know why, but I put my foot on the clutch and turn the key to the right.

Of course nothing happens. It wasn't like I was actually expecting it to start up. But when you have the key that fits the lock, you have to try, right?

Then I turn it to the left. Backwards.

Nothing.

I smile to myself and start to turn it back, but it won't budge. I give it a harder turn, then back and forth, trying to loosen it.

Something like an electric charge runs up my arm.

That arm, my whole right side goes numb. There's a sharp pain in the center of my chest, radiating out. My vision blurs.

I think:

I'm having a heart attack.

No wonder the old man left the place to me in his will, left this old car just waiting for me.

He knew.

He just *knew* this would happen.

Crazy idea, but I'm not exactly thinking straight. And then I realize the pain's on the wrong side of my body for a heart attack.

Then what—?

The sharp hurt doesn't go away, but my vision clears. Vertigo hits me, deep and sudden, but at the same time I'm disassociated from it. I feel like the world's falling away below me, only it doesn't seem to concern me. Everything stays in focus. Preternaturally sharp.

I watch the cracks in the windshield disappear. They recede, leaving behind clear, uncracked glass. Weirder still, the view beyond the windshield is a flickering dance of images. It's like watching time-lapse photography. Seasons change. Weeds and scrub trees come and ago. Clouds strobe in the sky, here one moment—thick and woolly, or thin and long, or dark and pregnant with rain—gone the next.

And that's when I know I'm dreaming.

Or having some kind of attack.

Heart attack . . . panic attack . . .

It all stops so suddenly, it's as if I've suddenly run up against a wall. The last time I felt like that was twenty-five years ago, when the car was just about to hit the tree. When I put my arm out to stop Billy's forward motion, but there was too much momentum. He just about tore my arm out of its socket with the force of his forward motion. Went crashing into the windshield. Cracking it. Spraying blood . . .

The windshield's not cracked anymore.

There's a summer day on the other side of it, not the fall day that's supposed to be there.

"Al . . . aless . . ."

I can't get her name out.

"I'm definitely driving," a voice says from beside me. "You are totally wasted."

I turn so slowly, scared of what I'll see, scared of what I won't see. But he's there. My brother Billy.

Alive.

Alive!

I put out a hand to touch him. To see if he's real.

He can't be real.

He backs away from my hand.

"Whoa," he says. "What's with the groping, Marsh?"

And then I understand. Not how or why. I just understand that I've been given a second chance.

"Are you okay?" Billy asks. "You look a little like Patty Crawford, just before she puked all over the bleachers."

I let my hand drop.

"I . . . I'm okay," I tell him.

My voice sounds like a stranger's in my ears. Distant. No, it's just that it's from another time. Funny, I remember so much, a lot of it in painstaking detail, but not the sound of his voice. Not that mole, on his neck, right under his ear.

"I'm just feeling a little . . ."

"Out of it?" Billy finishes for me. "How many beers did you have, anyway?"

I look down at my feet. There's an empty bottle there. I don't see any others, but I remember I was starting in on my second half of a twelve-pack. I don't even know why. It's a beautiful summer's day. I'm alive. My *brother*'s alive. Why the hell would I be drinking?

"So can I drive?" Billy asks.

I need to explain something here. Billy was the golden boy in our family. The smart one who knew by the time he was fourteen that he was going to be a doctor. I, on the other hand, was unfocused. I liked cars. I liked girls. I liked to party. I had no idea what I wanted to do with my life beyond get off the farm.

The old man didn't get it—because it was different for his generation, I guess. You figured out what you wanted to be, what you *could* be, given your situation in life, and that's what you aimed for. He couldn't understand that not only did I not know, but I didn't care, either.

It was bad enough before Mom died. But after that, the friction between us got worse and worse. I could pretend that he favored my brother because Billy had Mom's blond hair, that his cherubic features reminded us of her, too. But the truth is, Billy was focused—something the old man could admire. He worked hard in school, aiming for scholarships. The money he got from his part-time jobs went into a college fund, not towards a car.

I couldn't begin to compete.

But the funny thing is, I never resented Billy for that. The old man, sure. But never Billy.

His dying was such a waste. See, that was the real heartbreak when he died. He was going to be somebody. A doctor. He was going to save lives.

I wasn't ever going to be anybody.

But I was the one who survived. The drunk driver. The one with nothing to lose.

Sitting here in my old Impala, looking at Billy, I know it doesn't have to be that way now. I can change what happened. I could just refuse to go anywhere, but Billy'd never let up. He was supposed to be meeting some girl at the quarry. So we have to go.

But so long as I'm not driving, it's not going to end the way it did the first time around.

"Sure," I say. "You can drive."

I open the driver's door and walk around the car while he scoots over to my seat. He grins at me when I get in, makes a show of putting on his seat belt. He wasn't wearing one the last time we did this. He takes off his ball cap and throws it onto the dashboard.

I fasten my seat belt, as well, and then we're off.

It's funny, considering how much I've thought of that moment, that day, but I can never remember what caused me to lose control of the car. I just know *where* it happened. I tense up as we start into the sharp turn on our local dead man's curve—more than one car's gone skidding off the gravel here. But Billy's got everything under control. He's driving fast, but not too fast.

And then it comes. Something, I still don't know what. A cat, a dog, a rabbit. It doesn't matter. Something small. Brown and fast.

Billy does the same thing I did—brakes—and the car starts to slide on the gravel. But he's not drunk, and he doesn't panic. He begins to straighten out, but we hit a pothole, and it startles him enough to momentarily lose his concentration. The back wheels skid on the gravel. He touches the brakes, remembers he shouldn't, and lifts his foot.

Too late.

We're going sideways.

He tries to straighten us again, touches the gas. The wheels catch on a bare patch of dirt along the side of the road. We shoot forward. Out of the curve, across the road.

We're going fast enough to clear the ditch.

We clear it.

I see the tree coming up. The same oak tree I hit.

We bottom out on the field—the shocks can't absorb this kind of an impact, but it doesn't slow our momentum.

Then we hit the tree, and the last thing I remember is my seat belt snapping and my face heading for the windshield.

3

"Hey, cowboy."

I blink at the unfamiliar voice. Open my eyes. The bright blue of the sky above me hurts too much to look at. It makes my eyes water, so I close them again and lie there for a long moment, trying to figure out where I am.

When it comes back to me, it's all in a rush: the crash. The same damn crash that killed Billy twenty-five years ago, repeating itself even though this time I wasn't driving.

And if I'm alive, then that means . . .

I sit up fast, and my head spins. I'm lying in tall, summer-green grass. The sky's clear above me; the sun's bright. I can hear the sound of bees and flies and June bugs. I don't hurt anywhere. I turn slowly, take in the big oak tree, the road. There's no car anywhere in sight. No Billy.

That's impossible. I'd think I was dreaming, but if I am, then I haven't stopped, because I'm not back in that old wrecked Impala of mine. I'm here, at the crash site, and it's still summer—not the autumn day when I pried open the Impala's door in back of the old man's barn.

Then I see the girl, the one whose voice brought me out of my blackout. She's standing on the side of the road, one hand on her hip. Her hair's so dark, it's black and she's wearing it pulled back in a ponytail. Her features are pretty, if a little hard. She's wearing bell-bottom jeans, fraying at the hems, and a white tube top. Cute little plastic see-through shoes.

"Welcome back to the world," she says. "Or what's left of it for us."

I realize I know her and dredge her name up from my memory. Ginny Burns. She used to live in the trailer park at the edge of town and ran away from home a couple of years ago—at least it was a couple of years ago if I'm still in the past. She was always a little wild, and her taking off like that didn't really surprise anybody.

Like about half the kids in school, I had a major crush on her, but she was unattainable. Three years older than me, and she didn't date kids.

I'm surprised she's come back.

"Ginny?" I say.

She studies me a little closer. "I know you," she says. "Marshall Coe—right? You've grown up some since the last time I saw you."

I may look like a kid, but I'm a middle-aged man inside this seventeen-year-old boy's body. Still, I feel a flush of pleasure at the thought of her actually knowing my name. I cover it up by standing and brushing the grass and dirt from my jeans.

"So when did you get back?" I ask, trying to be cool.

"What makes you think I ever left?"

"Well, you've been . . . gone."

She gives me a sad smile that softens her features and makes her look even prettier.

"Yeah," she says. "Just like you."

I'm confused for a minute. How could she know I left? Went to jail, moved to the city. That I had this whole life before I found myself back here in my seventeenth year, starting it over again.

"How—?" I start to ask her, but the next thing she says puts a stopper in my mouth that I can't talk around.

"Did I die?" she says. Her face goes hard again. "With a wire around my neck and some freak's dick up my ass."

"I . . ."

I don't know what to say. I'm focused on the word *die*. Then I remember her saying "just like you." And then . . .

"What . . . what do you mean? . . ."

She comes over to where I'm standing. "Sit down," she says, then lowers herself to the ground beside me, sitting cross-legged. "I forgot that it takes time for it all to sink in."

"What . . . seriously . . . what are you talking about?"

"The short of it," she says, "is we're dead. And I don't completely know the long of it."

"Dead? And my brother?"

She shrugs. "You're the only one who's been lying here."

"But we were together in the car. . . ."

"Look, I know it's confusing, but it gets easier. Just don't try to figure everything out at the same time—it's too much at first."

Easy for her to say.

"So I'm—we're dead."

She nods. "Yeah. It wasn't pretty for me, and I guess it wasn't for you either."

"What do you mean?"

"You've been lying here for a few days. Sometimes it takes the soul a while to wake up again—especially if they died hard."

I give a slow nod. "I guess I did. But all I really remember is that tree coming up on me . . . so fast. . . ."

"I wish I *didn't* remember," she says.

I think about the little she's already told me of how she died, and it's already too much. Time to change the subject.

"How do you know all this stuff?" I ask.

She shrugs. "Hanging around in boneyards. The dead have all kinds of things to tell you if you're willing to listen."

"So . . . this is it? This is what we get when we die?"

She shakes her head. "No. Most folks go on—don't ask me where, because I don't know and I haven't met anybody yet who can tell me."

"But these ghosts you've talked to—?"

"Well, like I said, most people go on. Then there's those you find in boneyards, or haunting the place they died. They won't accept that they're dead, so they just . . . linger. And finally there's the folks like us."

She paused a moment, but I don't say anything. I'm not so ready to be a part of her *us*. I don't know that I'm dead for sure. I don't know anything, really. For all I know, I'm still sitting in that junked-out car out behind my dad's barn, dreaming all this up. It would sure explain why I feel so damn calm.

But whether I believe or not, I find myself needing to know more.

"What about"—I still can't say *us,* so I settle for—"them?"

"We've still got unfinished business," she says. "We *can't* go on. Not till it's done."

I figure I know what her unfinished business is.

"You're waiting for your killer to be found," I say.

"Hell, no. I'm just waiting for somebody to find my body so that people know I'm dead."

I can't imagine that. Though I guess if I'm dreaming, I'm actually imagining *all* of this.

"I wonder why I'm still here?" I find myself saying.

"I couldn't tell you."

I give a slow nod. "I guess that's something we all have to work out for ourselves."

I look back at the oak tree, take in the fresh scars on its trunk. Ginny said I've been lying here in the field for days. I guess that explains why the car's not here. And why Billy's gone. I'm hoping it's because he got out of it okay. I'm also hoping that he's not going through what I did, but I don't see why he would. I was drunk, with a history of being picked up for one thing or another. Fighting, mostly, and drinking. But joyriding once. Vandalism a couple of times. By the time of the accident, the sheriff was looking for any excuse to put me away, and it's not like the old man ever stood up for me.

But Billy was about as clean-cut as they come. Dad would go pay his bail. He'd make sure Billy didn't spend an hour in jail, never mind the years in prison I did.

But I have to be sure.

"I need to see that he's all right," I say, and stand up.

"Your brother?"

"Yeah."

"Mind if I tag along? It gets lonesome sometimes."

"I don't mind," I say.

I start to walk down the road, back to the farm, and she falls into step beside me.

"So I guess you're stuck around here," I say.

She gives me a puzzled look, then smiles. "No, we can go anywhere we want. But I keep coming back, thinking there's some way I can get someone to notice me—you know, so I can steer them to my grave? People can see us, but not all the time, and not necessarily when we want them to. Pike says it's not impossible to interact with those we left behind, but that it's really hard. They have to be what he calls *sensitive*. The big problem is that, even if you do make contact, no one seems to get what you're trying to say—it comes out garbled, for some reason, or like a riddle—and it's not like you can write it out for them on a piece of paper, because the thing you can't do is have physical contact with the, you know, physical world."

"Because we're ghosts now."

She nods.

"Who's Pike?" I ask.

"John Pike," she says. "He lived at the end of Connell Road."

And then I remember. He was a real hermit, living in a tar-paper shack at the end of the road. Rumor was, he had a fortune in gold stashed away somewhere in that run-down excuse of a house of his, some kind of treasure, for sure. But he also had a couple of mean dogs and a shotgun loaded with salt that he wasn't afraid to use on trespassers. It did a bang-up job of keeping the curious away when he was alive.

"He died back in '75, '76," I say. "I was just a kid then."

"So was I. But I remember his picture in the paper."

I did, too. This scary wild man, long-haired and bearded. Kids used to dare each other to sneak into his place because everybody knew it was haunted.

"So he really was still hanging around," I say. "Like a ghost."

She nods. "At least he was when I died, and didn't that freak me out when I first met him. But he's gone on now."

She talks about it so easily, like still hanging around after you're dead is the most natural thing in the world. But the funny thing is, the longer we're walking along here, talking, the less unbelievable it seems. I mean, considering how this day's already gone for me . . .

"So he said, if we try really hard, we can contact the people we left behind?"

"Yeah," she says. "But that it's also really hard. You need a pretty strong connection between yourself and the person you left behind. And like I said, the time's got to be right and there's no way to guess that moment, so all you can do is keep trying. The world's not real for us anymore. All we can do is look at it. We can't be part of it anymore."

"It feels pretty real to me."

I scuff my shoes against the gravel and send bits of it flying into the ditch.

"It just feels real because you expect it to," she says. "But nothing really moved, and no one can see you. You can't really *affect* anything."

"I just kicked that gravel."

I do it again.

She shakes her head. "No, it just seems like you can. You'll see."

4

"Want to hear a weird story?" I say after we've been walking for a while.

She laughs. "What's weirder than the afterlife?"

I think of what happened about fifteen minutes ago when she stepped in front of this pickup that went barreling by us. How the driver never saw her. How I tried to grab her. How the pickup went right through both of us.

It's taken me most of those fifteen minutes for my legs to stop feeling so rubbery. Except if I'm dead, how come it still feels like I have a body?

"Earth to Marshall," she says.

I blink and give her a confused look.

"You said you had a weird story," she says. "But now you're just being weird."

"Sorry."

So I tell her about it all, my old Impala, how when I was trying to get the key out of the ignition, I found myself here, back in the past.

There's a long silence before she finally asks, "Is this on the level?"

I nod.

"So you're really how old?"

"Forty-three."

"Forty-three," she repeats, and she gets a look in her eyes that I can't describe. "Imagine having all those years."

I kind of glossed over the jail time and the years on skid row, and I don't expand on them now, because I know what she means. I might have had some tough times—doesn't matter that I brought them on myself—but at least I had them.

"Anything you'd go back and change if you could?" I ask instead.

She nods. "For starters, I wouldn't have gotten in the car with the freak that killed me. You know I had a funny feeling as soon as I opened his door, but I so wanted that ride. I was *so* ready to get away from here."

She shakes her head, and I don't know what to say. And then we're at the lane leading up to my old man's farm, and I can't think of anything but Billy and my need to know that he's okay.

She trails along behind as we walk up the lane, the same lane I drove up with Alessandra this morning, except that morning hasn't even happened yet. And I guess the way things have turned out, it never will.

I'm not sure what I expected to find here, but it wasn't the old man sitting on the front porch when he should be out in the back forty with his tractor. He's dressed for work: coveralls over a T-shirt, work boots on his feet, John Deere hat on the table beside him. But he doesn't look like he's ready to go anywhere. He looks deflated—defeated—and I get scared. Not for me, but for Billy. Because I know now: I died in that crash, but so did my brother. There's no other way to explain the old man's grief.

I can barely look at him, sitting there in the rocker, holding a framed picture loosely against his chest, gaze staring right through me as I come onto the porch. Ginny takes a seat on the stairs and doesn't follow me up.

I stand there looking at him for a long time. There's an unfamiliar emotion swelling inside me—unfamiliar so far as it concerns my feelings for the old man. I feel bad. For letting him down. For being such a shit. For not trying to be the man he wanted me to be. But especially for killing the son he loved.

"I . . . I'm so sorry, Dad."

I say the words I never got to say before.

He doesn't hear me, but he shifts in his chair as though he feels something. Then he lays the photo he's been holding against his chest down on his lap, and I find myself staring down at a school picture of my own seventeen-year-old self.

It's not Billy he's mourning.

It's me.

I back away and slowly make my way down the stairs until I'm sitting beside Ginny.

"What is it?" she says.

I shake my head. For a long time all I can do is stare out across the fields. Ginny puts a hand on my arm. Turns out we can touch each other. We just can't touch anything in the world we left behind.

"It's me," I finally say. "He's mourning me."

"Well, what did you expect? You're his son."

"No, you don't get it. He hated me. When . . . the other time . . . before I changed how it would turn out . . . when I got drunk and my brother died in the crash . . . he never spoke to me again. He never went my bail. He never tried to see me. He was never in the courtroom. . . ."

My voice trails off. It's impossible to catalog the enormity of the distance that lay between us.

"So what?" Ginny asks. "Now he hates your brother?"

"I . . ."

I realize I don't know.

I go back up the stairs. The front door's open, but the screen door's closed. I reach for the handle, but I can't get a grip on it.

"Just walk through," Ginny says, coming up behind me. "Maybe we can't touch the world, but it can't touch us either. At least not"—she looks at my father, grieving—"physically."

I need to go inside, to find Billy, but the business with the door is freaking me badly. I can't imagine walking through the screen. But I just can't seem to grab hold of the handle.

Ginny steps by me and walks right through the door—screen, wooden crossbars and all. It's like earlier on the road, when the truck went through us both. She reaches a hand back to me, and I take it. I let her lead me inside.

"Which way?" she asks.

I nod down the hallway towards the kitchen and take the lead, ignoring the closed doors of the parlor and the front sitting room. They haven't been used since my mother died.

When we find the kitchen empty, I lead us up the back stairs. My relief is immediate when we find Billy in his room, sitting at his desk, reading a book. I stay in the doorway, content to look at him, to know he's alive, but Ginny slips past me and walks over to the desk.

"Eeuw," she says as she looks at his book.

I join her and see that he's studying graphic black-and-white pictures of an autopsy. He's had that book for a while, and it *is* gross—I know, I've flipped through it before, but I can never take more than a few pictures.

"He's going to be a doctor," I tell Ginny. "He needs to know about this stuff."

"Yeah, but morbid much?"

I shrug. "He's always been interested in how people work. You know, muscle tissue and arteries and nerves and stuff."

Ginny nods. "All the things we don't have."

"I guess."

"He's a good-looking kid," she says.

"He takes after our mother."

I put my hand on Billy's head, trying to ruffle his hair, but my fingers go into his skull. I pull my hand back quickly.

It doesn't matter that I can't touch him, I tell myself. All that matters is that he's alive.

But I'd still like to give him a last hug before I go.

I settle for a look—drinking in the familiar sight of him, sitting at his desk and studying—then I leave the room.

"What was she like?" Ginny asks as she follows me out into the hall.

"Our mom? Everything the old man and I'm not: gentle, kind, thoughtful. And beautiful. She was like an angel, and now she's sleeping with them."

I want to hold that thought, but I can't. Not anymore.

"Unless she's like us," I add as we go down the stairs and step back through the screen door. "trapped in some kind of nonlife, able to see and hear the world go on around us, but unable to interact with it."

"Maybe heaven's where we end up when we go on," Ginny says.

"Maybe," I say, wanting to be convinced.

But Ginny lets my word hang, so if I'm going to believe Mom's safe and happy somewhere, I have to do my own convincing.

I give the old man a last glance before I step off the porch and head back up the lane. There's nothing left for me here now. I don't know what happens next, but at least I've accomplished this much: I've changed the past and made things right again.

But it's funny. I don't feel any better. Truth is, what I really want is a drink. Not a beer, like I was drinking before I died, but a stiff shot of whiskey.

I need some oblivion.

I almost ask Ginny if there's such a thing as ghost whiskey—maybe there's a reason another word for hard liquor is *spirits*—but I settle on stepping out of own head and getting Ginny to talk about her life instead.

"What was your mother like?" I ask her.

She shrugs. "I don't know. She left us not long after I was born."

I don't remember that from what I knew of her before, but I guess it's not so surprising. The kids I hung with only ever talked about how hot she was.

"That can't have been easy," I say.

"I never knew it to be any different. My dad was good to me—you know, he did his best. But he wasn't equipped to raise a kid, especially not the girl I turned out to be."

I can guess what she means, but I ask her anyway.

"A girl with a reputation," she explains. She shakes her head. "It's not something I ever asked for or wanted, but I sure as hell had one all the same."

"But you—"

I stop myself from saying it, but she nods and gives me a sad smile.

"Put out all the time, right?"

"It's just . . . I heard . . ."

She cups her hands on her breasts. They're not disproportionately huge, but you can't ignore them, either. Not in that tight little tube top.

"I got these the summer I turned twelve," she says, "and by Christmastime, everybody thought I was a slut. I got tired of arguing about it, so after a while, I just started acting like the trailer trash everybody'd already decided I was. But I'll tell you this, I was still a virgin when I died." Her features cloud over. "Well, right up to those last few minutes, I guess."

"I don't understand. Why would all these guys—?"

"Oh, please. Derek Kirkwood was the one who started it—said I'd done it with him under the bleachers during a football game. Now, I *was* down there with him, but only having one of his beers. And maybe I let him kiss me and have a little grope, but we never did it."

"Then why didn't you say something when he started telling people you did?"

"I'd already stopped caring. I had a lot of 'boyfriends,' all right. I was happy to have people take me to dances, to drink their beer and smoke their joints, but the most any of them got was a hand job." She gives me a sassy grin that never reaches her eyes. "But none of them was going to admit they didn't score when Kirkwood supposedly had. They might not ask me out again, but hell. If I *had* put out, they still probably wouldn't have."

"Jesus."

"If I'd've had any brains, I'd've put a stop to that long before it got to that point. But it was kind of fun at first—flattering that all these guys wanted me. And then it was too late."

We've reached the end of the lane, but neither of us makes a move to step onto the road.

"So that's why I took off," she says. "I wanted a new start. I wanted to go someplace where I could be who I decided I was, instead of letting other people decide it for me." She shakes her head. "And you can see what a good plan that was."

"I feel like a shit," I say.

"Why? Because you wanted to get into my pants as much as those other guys?"

I nod.

"Well, don't. I probably flirted with you like I did with any guy. I had a rep to uphold and all."

"It doesn't seem fair."

She shakes her head. "Nope. And neither does what we've got now, but we're stuck with it all the same."

She looks back down the lane at the farmhouse, then turns to look at me.

"So what are you going to do now, Marshall Coe?" she asks.

"I don't know."

"Ever been to Tibet?"

"I've never been any farther than the city—not in this life or the other one I had."

"So let's do a little traveling. Seeing the sights is about the only option left to us at this point."

Now it's my turn to take a last look at the old farmhouse.

I don't understand how my father could be grieving for me, but it's too late now to find out why he is.

I changed the past so that Billy's alive. Instead of the waste of a life I had, he can go out there and help people, make it a better world. But I can't be a part of that world.

So there's nothing left for me here except for the question of why I didn't go on after I died. Thinking about it, I realize I don't really care.

"Sure," I say when I turn back to her. "Why not?"

5

I think time moves differently when you're dead. You don't eat and you don't sleep, but there's always a little hunger in you, that's maybe got nothing to do with food, and while you don't lie down and take a nap, there are holes in your awareness all the same. The days don't seem to follow one after the other so much as jump around. When they don't slide by in a confusing blur.

I guess what I'm trying to say is that I lose track of time. I lose track of everything—the life I had that ended when I tried to start up that old Impala of mine, and the half-day or so of the second one I got.

It all just goes away.

We really do go to Tibet. We go to a lot of different countries, spending most of our time in the wild places. It's not like the big cities aren't interesting—and just as wild in their own way—but it gets old fast when people and vehicles keep going through you because no one knows you're there. That doesn't happen to you in the big empty places. The mountains of Nepal. The Australian outback. Out on the Arctic tundra. Deep in the Amazon jungles. The red rock canyons of southern Utah. The Mongolian steppes. The mountains of Peru. The Sahara.

Sometimes we're noticed there—by people sensitive to the spirit world—but we can't communicate with them, and we don't try. The only conversations we have are with the other dead, and we don't spend a lot of time with them either. The ones who stayed here are mostly a bitter, self-centered group, unable to understand why the world still goes on after they've died. I know I'm generalizing here, but unless one has unfinished business, why stay?

But the people with unfinished business aren't usually such great company either. Most of them died hard and unhappy, and they don't seem as resilient as Ginny in how they deal with it. They're focused on their deaths, determined to get their business done and move on.

No, that's not true. Most of them are just focused on their business. They don't even consider what will happen when it's done.

But they're not all like that, because some people's unfinished business isn't of a negative nature. Like the mother who's waiting for her son to graduate. The grandparent waiting for the birth of a grandchild. The husband waiting for his wife to stop mourning and fall in love again. They have stories I can appreciate—at least the first time around. By the third or fourth repetition, I'm ready to move on.

Ginny's not like that. She's good company, always ready for a laugh or an adventure, though the longer I get to know her, the more I'm aware of this streak of melancholy that runs under even her best moods. I'm also more than half in love with her, and that's just weird because, well, we're both dead, aren't we?

It's four years before we get back to this part of the world. I know that only because I remember when I died, and as we're walking by a newsstand, I happen to see the date on a newspaper, right above a heading that reads 3RD VICTIM FOUND. The headline depresses me. Seems there's some guy running around cutting up young women like they were meat at a butcher's. It's senseless and horrible, and I feel for the girls.

Ginny's looking in a store window and doesn't notice the headline, so I don't point it out to her. I don't want to remind her of her own terror time, starting out to find a new life and finding only an end in pain and horror.

We don't spend long in the city, but I want to look in on the old man before we head into some new wild place, so we head up into the country. I can't believe how far the city's spread in just four years.

The old man's changed, too. He seems to have aged ten years instead of four. He's still working the farm—on his own now. I check Billy's room, but he's moved out.

It takes me a while to track him down.

Turns out he made the dream come true. He's in pre-med at Butler U, on a scholarship, but he's working a job on the side that lets him keep a crummy little bachelor apartment in Lower Foxville, close to the campus. He's taking a shower when we drift into his apartment. I look around at all his books and things, waiting for him to come out when I realize that Ginny's not with me. I find her in the bathroom, checking Billy out.

"Jeez," I say. "Give him a little privacy."

She pulls her head out of the shower curtain and laughs. "We're ghosts, Marsh. What difference does it make what we see? Besides, he's got a nice butt."

I don't want to be having this conversation.

"Get away from there," I say.

But before she can respond, the shower stops and Billy opens the curtain. The first thing I think is, my little brother's all grown up. The second is, where'd he get the black eye?

But a funny thing happens when I see that bruise. It reminds me of . . .

It's like I suddenly wake up from a dream and my thoughts go flying to my other life, the one I had before the old Impala brought me back and put me into this one.

"Alessandra," I say softly.

Ginny turns to me. "What?"

I repeat the name. How could I have forgotten her? The same way I forgot all that other life, I guess.

"Oh, right," Ginny says. "Your old girlfriend."

She was way more than a girlfriend, but I'm not thinking about that right now. I'm thinking about how she was five years younger than me. How right now she'd be fifteen or sixteen, still living at home with her father—the drunk who used her as punching bag.

"I've got to see her," I say.

Ginny starts to say something, but I guess there's a look in my eyes that makes her just shrug instead.

"I'm proud of you, Billy," I tell my brother. "But what the hell are you doing fighting? You're going to be a doctor. You don't have time for crap like that."

He doesn't respond. Why should he? He can't hear me. He doesn't even know that we're here.

Then I lead the way out of his apartment, heading for where Alessandra is living at this time in her life.

"I guess you knew her for a long time," Ginny says when we're standing outside the brownstone where Alessandra and her father live.

I nod. "But not when she was a teenager."

"Then how'd you know to find this place?"

"She took me by here one time. Later, when we were together."

We stand on the pavement for a while, looking at the building. We're at the edge of the sidewalk where it meets the road so that we don't have people walking through us, but there's not much foot traffic anymore. It's almost dinnertime, and most people are home by now.

"So are we going in?" Ginny asks.

"I guess."

But I'm reluctant.

For one thing, I'm feeling this enormous guilt at having let all those years Alessandra and I were together just slip away out of my mind like they didn't mean anything. It was just the opposite. They meant everything. *She* meant everything.

For another, I'm nervous about what we'll find. If we've picked a time when her dad's drunk, it'll kill me to have to stand by, unable to step in and help.

"Marsh?" Ginny says.

I turn to look at her.

"You don't have to do this."

I shake my head. "Yeah, I do."

And I move forward, up the steps. Apartment 310, Alessandra told me. We walk through the front door and into the foyer—doing this has long since stopped bothering me—and head up to the third floor. We can hear yelling when we come out of the stairwell, and it gets louder as we go down the hall. Then there's the sound of breaking glass.

"Is her mother around?" Ginny asks, her voice hushed.

"No. She died when Alessandra was just a kid."

We step through the door, into the apartment. The noise is coming from down the hall, in the kitchen. I don't want to be here. I don't want to bear silent witness to Alessandra's terrors.

But I can't stop myself now.

Alessandra's stories were bad, but it's worse seeing it firsthand. She's lying on the floor, curled into a fetal position and bleeding from a cut on her head. Her father's standing over her, a broken bottle in his hand. That explains the cut.

Alessandra's crying—soundlessly, trying to be invisible. That's how she'd describe it to me. That all she was ever able to do was try to be invisible.

But it never helped.

Her father's yelling something, but I can't make out the words through the red rage that comes over me.

I've hated this man for a long, long time. In another, forgotten life, but it all comes back to me now in a rush. All those nights that Alessandra woke up crying. All those war stories she told, her voice flat, her eyes lost, looking off into the past.

Her father pulls back his foot, and I lose it.

I charge at him, hands flat in front of me.

I don't know what I'm thinking. What good will it do if I go running through him? But I can't do *nothing*.

And then the impossible happens.

My hands meet flesh. The force of my momentum knocks him backwards, off balance, and he goes down. The back of his head catches on the edge of the kitchen counter and makes an awful sound. A wet, *cracking* sound.

He twists as he falls. Lands on the floor. On his face.

And he doesn't move.

I stand there, stunned, then slowly step forward. I nudge him with my foot, but the toe of my shoe goes right through him.

I turn to Ginny. "What . . . what just happened? . . ."

She shakes her head, and we stand in the kitchen for what seems like a very long time. Staring at him, waiting for him to move.

He never does.

But Alessandra gets up. She holds her hand to her head, and blood seeps through her fingers. She shuffles over to him with the look of a scared dog, ready to bolt at a moment's notice. She does what I did, nudges him with a foot. Her shoe makes contact, but her father still doesn't move.

She stares at him, emotions playing across her features. Then she spits on him and slowly backs out of the kitchen.

I'm about to follow her—to do I don't know what—but Ginny grabs my arm.

"Marsh," she says, her voice strained.

I turn to see that the body on the floor has started to glow. Ginny and I exchange puzzled glances. When we look back, the glow is lifting from the body, separate from, but retaining the body's shape.

It's Alessandra's father. The *spirit* of her father. Sitting up.

Neither of us has ever seen somebody die before. We've never been right there when it happens. We don't know *what's* going to happen.

I'm thinking, I don't want to be here.

The spirit looks around, then pushes itself up from the floor until it's finally standing. Its face turns to us, but before I can tell if we register in its consciousness—if it even has a consciousness at this point—the spirit begins to diminish. I'm not quite sure how to describe it. It's as if there was a tiny pinprick hole in the fabric of the world, and the light that makes up the spirit just gets sucked away into it.

The last thing we see is that pinhole, shining a light so fierce that when it abruptly winks out, we have stars flashing in our gazes.

I clear my throat, then manage to say, "I guess it . . . went on."

Ginny gives a slow nod. "I guess."

I remember Alessandra, and we go looking for her, but she's left the apartment. I don't know if my killing her father is going to make things better or worse for her. If it's going to stop her slow descent into alcoholism that followed her finally getting away from the man in the life where I knew her, or if it's going to push her into a more radical plunge into I don't know what.

I can only hope she'll be all right.

"Was this my unfinished business?" I say, thinking aloud. "Helping Alessandra—maybe saving her life?"

"You're still here, aren't you?" Ginny says.

There's that.

I reach towards the nearest wall, and my hand goes through it. Just like it always has since I died.

"How could I have been able to push him like that?" I say. "I can't even pick up a pencil."

"I don't know. Maybe you just . . ."

"Just what?" I ask when she doesn't finish.

"Really needed to," she says. She seems reluctant. "Maybe if we need to do it badly enough . . . we can. You know, to help somebody or something like that."

I study her for a long moment.

"You've known this all along," I finally say. "Haven't you?"

She nods. "But it's nothing I've ever been able to do. Pike told me about it."

"Why didn't you tell *me*? Why were you so insistent on my believing that we can't affect the real world?"

"I was scared."

"Scared of what?"

"That you'd leave me."

"I don't understand," I say. "You told me that when we first met. You didn't even know me then."

She shrugs. "You just seemed so normal—and you were, too. You are. I'd been so lonely for so long. . . ."

I'm beginning to understand.

"You know how to deal with your own unfinished business, don't you?" I say.

She won't meet my gaze, but she nods.

"But you're scared to go on to . . . wherever it is we go next."

"I had so little time to be me," she says. "What happens when we cross over? Do we just disappear like your girlfriend's father did?"

"We don't know what happened to him. Where he went."

"I know. But I don't want to go yet. I'm not ready."

I can tell she hates saying it, because it groups her with all those losers hiding out in their graveyards, able to go on, but refusing to do so.

"Is there even such a thing as unfinished business?" I ask.

She nods.

"And when we do it—whatever it is—do we just get sucked away like Alessandra's old man did?"

"No. But, you know. You start feeling . . . thinner. Like there's nothing keeping you here anymore except your own need to stay."

"Did the graveyard ghosts tell you that?" I ask.

She shakes her head. "No, Pike did."

"Too bad he's not around anymore." I say. "I'd like to have asked him about all of this."

She told me he'd gone on, way back when we first met. But when I look at her now, I see from the expression on her face that that wasn't true either.

"He's still haunting that shack of his, isn't he?"

She nods.

We stand there for a while, neither of us speaking, uncomfortable with what's lying between us and too aware of the dead body in the kitchen, of what we both saw happen to the spirit that rose up from it.

I can't leave it like this.

"I won't leave you behind," I tell her. "When we go, we can go together."

"Promise?"

I nod.

But then everything changes again. Because when we go out looking for Alessandra, we find, instead, the ghost of a broken girl.

6

Her name's Sarah Hooper, and I recognize her from the picture in the newspaper that I saw earlier today. She's the third victim of whatever freak it is who's been going around killing young women over the past few weeks. She looks even smaller and frailer in person than she did in the photo. But she didn't go down easy.

"They say you shouldn't fight back," she tells us, "but I didn't care. I guess I knew he was going to kill me, and I just wanted to hurt him if I could. I hit him a few times—in the face, where I knew it'd show—but in the end, he was just . . . you know . . . too strong. . . ."

It's not too hard to figure out what her unfinished business is.

She was pretty messed up when we found her sitting on the ground in an alley not far from Alessandra's apartment, just staring at the brick wall across from her, but she's tougher than she looks.

"So I'm really dead," she says as we bring her up to speed on what she is now, why she's here. "I wasn't sure." She laughs, without any humor. "I know how that sounds, but you don't expect to still be around . . . after, you know? Not like this, where nothing seems any different except you can't touch anything. Nobody can hear or see you."

"Do you think you'd recognize the guy?" Ginny asks.

"Oh, yeah. We have—had a class together at the university. I never really talked to him except for this one time when he asked me out, but he caught me on a bad day and I just shot him down."

Ginny nods. "He gave you the creeps even then."

"Not really. He's just one of those guys with the choirboy good looks, and that's never appealed to me. But mostly I guess I was so hard on him because of the way he was always looking at me in class. He was, like, *always* watching me, it seemed."

"Do you know his name?" I ask.

"Coe," she says. "William Coe—don't try to call him Bill, or Billy. I called him Bill when I was turning him down, and he set me straight pretty quick."

Everything inside me goes still.

"Are . . . are you sure?" Ginny asks.

Sarah nods. "You don't forget the name of the guy who kills you." Her gaze goes from Ginny to me. "Do you know him?" she asks.

I give a slow nod. "He's my brother."

"Your brother. Jesus." She pauses for a heartbeat, then adds, "So did he kill you, too?"

I start to shake my head, but Ginny speaks up before I can.

"He was driving the car when Marsh died," she says.

I want to say he didn't do it on purpose, but I'm having too much trouble getting my head around the idea that Billy could be responsible for this woman's death. And at least two more.

Billy, who wanted to be a doctor. To help people.

Or maybe just to find out how they work so he'd know the best way to hurt them. To prolong their pain.

Because I'm thinking of that book with all the autopsy photographs in it. Maybe . . . maybe those pictures made him feel good. . . .

The idea of it makes me sick.

"So," Sarah's saying, "I just need to find a way to . . . what? Bring him to justice? Get my revenge on him?"

"Something like that," Ginny says.

"And then what?"

"You go on."

"Go on where?"

Ginny shrugs. "We don't know. Nobody on this side does."

Sarah gives a slow nod of her head. "I've got to think about this."

"You don't have to be alone," Ginny says as Sarah starts to walk away.

"Yeah, I do," she says. "I really do."

We watch her walk away, down the alley. Neither of us makes a move to stop her.

"So that's where he got the black eye," I say.

Ginny nods. "I'm so sorry, Marsh."

"You had nothing to do with it."

"I know. But . . ."

"And that damn book of his. It should have been a clue."

"There's no way you could have known."

A deep sadness has settled inside me. But riding on top of it is the same anger I felt a few hours ago when Alessandra's father was beating her. I have that need to hit something, and I kick at the nearest garbage bag. It goes flying across the alley and breaks against the far wall, spilling its contents.

"Don't be mad at me," Ginny says.

I know what she's thinking. First she disappointed me, and now my brother's hurt me even worse.

But I'm not mad—not at her. She wasn't deliberately trying to hurt me. She didn't tell me everything only because she was so lonely.

Maybe if I really was the seventeen-year-old I look to be . . . maybe I wouldn't understand. But I've seen things that kid never has and never will. Prison, living on the streets, the life of an alcoholic. I know that people mess up and get messed up by what life hands them.

Ginny had a fucked-up life and a worse death. And then she spent two years as a ghost, unable or unwilling to touch or be touched by anything or anybody. Is it any wonder she's clung to the first person who came along and treated her the way everybody deserves to be treated?

"I'm not mad," I tell her.

"How can you not be mad? I've lied to you about everything."

I shake my head. "No, just about the one thing."

"But maybe you could have stopped your brother *before* he started killing those girls."

Girls who died the way she did, alone and hard.

I hadn't even thought of that. That I could have stopped him.

"Maybe," I say. "But probably not. I'd've had to follow him around every day, just to know he was doing it. I'd have to *suspect* him first, and why would I do that? He was my little brother. You don't suspect your little brother of being a freak. So I'd've had to catch him in the act—or heard about it the way we just did—to believe."

And maybe that's my unfinished business. I came back and changed the way things were meant to be. Maybe my unfinished business is to fix this second mistake, because it looks like what I thought was my first mistake—drunk driving, killing my own brother—wasn't really a mistake at all.

Ginny's gaze goes to the garbage bag I kicked against the wall, then returns to me. I know what she's thinking. But she says it anyway.

"You have to kill him—like you did your girlfriend's dad."

Don't think I haven't already thought of that. But I shake my head.

"I don't know if I can just kill a person in cold blood," I say.

"What do you call what happened back in your old girlfriend's apartment?"

"An act of passion. Not something I planned to do like this would be." I sigh. "But it's not just that."

"Is it because he's your brother?"

I shake my head again, but I don't have any words for a while. I stare at the spill of garbage across the alley.

Ginny waits. Finally, I turn to look at her.

"I think I probably could do it," I say. "But I just can't stop thinking about the three girls that he's killed. How there might be even more—they just haven't found the other bodies yet."

"And if we don't do something now, he'll kill even more."

"I know. What I'm trying to figure out is a way to undo what I've done so that nobody ever got killed."

Understanding dawns in Ginny's eyes.

"You're going to try to get the car to bring you back again."

I nod.

"You're going to leave me."

I want to say, it's not like that. But we both know it is.

7

The old Impala's still out behind the barn. My dad saved it this time around, just as he did before. It's not in as bad shape as it was in my other life. The front end's still banged in, and the windshield's cracked. But it's still got all its windows, and it's not nearly as rusted out. There's not as much scrub and weeds growing around it either.

We get in the car and stare out through the cracks in the windshield. In this life I don't have a key hanging around my neck. But in this life there's a key still in the ignition.

I put my hand on it, but my fingers go right through.

I think about Billy, let the anger come back, but that doesn't help either.

"Maybe all I have to do is wake up," I say after about ten minutes of this. "Maybe all of this really is just a dream—right from when I first stuck that key in the ignition."

"Except I'm here," Ginny says.

I don't want to say, that doesn't make a difference. It could still be a dream.

"There's that," I tell her instead.

"You must be doing something wrong," she says.

Now that she's accepted that I'm doing this—or at least that I'm trying—she's been full of useful suggestions. Unfortunately, they aren't helping any more than my own efforts.

"What were you thinking about when it happened before?" she asks. "Were you really concentrating on the day of the crash . . . on your brother? . . ."

I shake my head, and her voice trails off.

"I wasn't thinking hard about anything," I say. "And for sure I wasn't looking for a way to live it all over again. I spent most of that other life of mine just trying to forget."

"Then I guess we need to go see Pike."

"I guess we do."

The funny thing is, this need of mine to stop Billy . . . I'm not even sure that this is my unfinished business. If I believe that, then I have to believe that life is preordained, and I don't buy that. We make a difference in the world. For good or bad, whether we want to or not, we make a difference. And I think it's our choices that make the difference.

But I'm not really looking for a Frank Capra moment here, though I'd love to wake up from this.

Instead I find myself at what's left of John Pike's ruin of a shack with the crazy-looking old man himself sitting there on a rocker, the ghost of an old bluetick hound asleep at his feet.

"Been a while," he says to Ginny.

She nods. "I want you to meet my friend," she says, and introduces me.

I can't help myself. I have to ask about the treasure, if it really exists.

"Sure, it does," he says. "Have a look inside."

So I do, but there's nothing there. Just a big mess of moldering books and magazines, old newspapers yellowed and chewed up by mice.

"I don't see it," I say.

"It's right in front of you, boy. The books. The *learning*. You won't find a bigger treasure than that."

The kid I look to be would have been disappointed. And I do feel a little twinge of disappointment myself, because like everybody else, I half believed those stories. But I understand what he means. I learned the worth of books and knowledge over the years. Mind you, I didn't use them to learn so much as to occupy my mind so that I wouldn't think of other things—things I used to wipe out of my mind with alcohol before I went on the wagon.

"We need your advice," Ginny says when I come back out onto the porch.

And then we tell him the whole sorry tale.

"Can't be done," he says when we finish up. "I've got some ideas about how you did it in the first place, but without a body, you're not going to be able to do it again."

"You're sure about that?"

"Sure as I'm dead, and I'm plenty damn sure about that."

I try not to let my frustration show, and I look out across the scrub brush lot that fronts what's left of his cabin.

"But that doesn't mean there isn't a solution to this problem of yours," he goes on.

I turn back to look at him, trying not to feel too much hope.

"I've heard stories," he says, "of spirits who ride a living person—take them over and make them do the things that are so hard for us ghosts to do. *Physical* things."

"You mean like possess them?"

He nods. "You just slip into their heads and take over. It works best with someone who's empty—you know, he's got nothing going in his life, nothing to look forward to. They're just waiting for any damn thing to come along and fill them up."

I start to understand what he's telling me, but that won't work with Billy. He's got too much to look forward to. All these other girls he's going to kill . . .

"But it also works on someone you were close to when you were alive," Pike adds. "Works better, maybe."

"Like my brother."

He nods. "But the way I heard it, you get only the one shot at riding somebody. You can't just jump from person to person."

"I'd only need the one shot." I hesitate, then add, "Except how do I know I can get the car to take me back again? I don't even know how it worked in the first place."

"It's not the car that's doing it," Pike says. "I think it's the key."

"What do you mean?"

"Sometimes, if you touch something often enough for luck, all those touches gather up inside the thing to become a real charm, the way riverbanks get beaches when sand drifts up in the curve of the watercourse. It's not planned—it just happens. And not all at once, but slowly, over the years."

"You think I made a charm out of that key?"

"Have you got a better explanation?"

I didn't.

"So," Pike goes on, "you just have to hope the key sitting there in the ignition of that car is the same one that you carried around with you for all those years."

"It probably is," Ginny says, "because you didn't get to take it away with you this last time."

Because this last time I died.

"And if that's the case," Pike says, "it's probably the same key you brought back with you from that other life of yours."

If, if, if . . .

"There's only way you're going to find out," he tells me.

Taking over Billy's easier than I think it will be. He's sitting in class at the university, and I just sidle up to him and slip right in. Then I get up and walk out of the lecture hall, leaving his books behind. Ginny falls in step beside me, and I turn to look at her.

"I can still see you," I say.

"I guess once you know how, it doesn't go away."

"You had a funny look on your face just now."

She nods. "I wasn't sure who it was inside."

She reaches out a hand to touch my arm, but it goes right through.

"We better get going," I say. "Before Sarah shows up with her own revenge in mind."

When we get outside, I check Billy's wallet. There's enough money in there to take a cab out to the farm, so that's what we do.

The old man's out in the back forty—we can hear his tractor from here—so we know we won't be disturbed. I get in behind the wheel, but I look at Ginny sitting beside me before I touch the key.

"I don't mean to break my promise," I start to say.

She shakes her head. "It's okay. I'm already dead. Saving these girls is way more important."

"I wish I could go back and save you."

"I wouldn't have listened to you anyway. You'd be just this kid, talking weird."

"If this works, I'm going to look for you when I'm done."

She gives me a sad look.

"I won't know who you are," she says. "All these years that we've been together won't have happened. Not for me."

"I'll remind you."

"Don't make any more promises."

There's no blame in her voice, but it hurts all the same.

"I can't even kiss you good-bye," I say.

She smiles, the sadness deepening in her eyes.

"I wouldn't want you to," she says. "Not looking like . . . him."

I nod. I reach for the key and turn it, waiting. But nothing happens.

"Do whatever you did the last time," Ginny says.

I think about it until it comes back to me. I turn the key right, then left twice, then quickly back and forth, and damned if the electric charge doesn't come rushing up my arm and the world around me starts to do its rewind thing again.

"Good-bye, Marshall Coe," I hear Ginny say. "I'm going to miss you."

Then she's gone and I'm back in time again, Billy and me, sitting in the car on that long ago afternoon.

8

Here's the thing that none of us considered: If I'm riding Billy, who's going to be inside my body?

I find out pretty quick.

I don't come back to the same moment I did before, where Billy was trying to convince me to let him drive. I come back to where he's already in the driver's seat, about to start up the car. I turn to look beside me and I'm sitting there—which, let me tell you, is freaky enough. But even freakier is, it's Billy looking out of my eyes.

"What the hell? . . ." he says.

His voice is slurred—from all the alcohol in my body that he's not used to, I guess—and he's totally confused. Well, who can blame him? But I don't give him time to adjust. I start up the car and pull out from behind the barn—my third time making this trip.

"Oh, Jesus," Billy says. "Stop the car, Marsh. I . . . I'm . . . something's wrong. . . ."

I just keep on driving.

He reaches out a hand to me, but I shove him against the passenger's door. Hard. His head bangs against the doorframe.

He's saying something else, voice rising in panic, but I tune him out because I need to work this through. I thought I'd go back to when I arrived the last time, before I let him get behind the wheel. I'd refuse to let him drive, and everything'd go back to the way it's supposed to be.

But obviously, I didn't.

It takes me a moment to figure out why I didn't. It's because when I worked the mojo this time, it was his body turning the key. This was the only point we could return to, when he had *his* hand on the key in the ignition.

What I have to do is figure out what happens next.

If the passenger always dies in the crash that's coming up, does that mean he'll die in my body? Or will we switch back and I'll die again?

I can't take that chance. It's not that I'm scared of dying—I've already been there. It's that I can't take the chance that *he'll* survive.

Then I realize what I have to do. I can't let the crash happen. I don't know how I'll stop him from becoming the killer he's going to be, but that's not something I should be trying to work out while driving this car.

On this road.

On this afternoon.

"Jesus Christ, Marsh!" he yells. "Stop the goddamn car!"

We're driving faster than I realized, but he's fumbling with the door handle anyway, trying to get it open. He's still got his seat belt on. But he could take it off. He could fall out. And at this speed, he could kill himself.

I keep one hand on the wheel, and grab at him.

Turn my gaze back to the road.

And realize we're already into the curve.

How'd we get here so fast?

Billy struggles in my grip. I stomp my foot on the brake but he pulls me at just that moment and I hit the gas pedal instead. I see the flash of the little animal darting out onto the road. I don't know if we run over it or not because right then we're leaving the road, heading straight for that damned oak tree again, and I realize I screwed it up this time, as well.

9

I get to go to the funeral this time.

My own funeral. In Billy's body. How weird is that?

Not half as weird as things are going to get, I guess. I have to deal with my father's grief. Then there's the whole business of being Billy, only I can't be Billy. I can't become the doctor he was going to be. I don't have it in me. I'm having enough trouble just *pretending* to be him these past few days.

To tell you the truth, I don't know how long I can deal with any of this. I mean, I can't even look in a mirror.

So I don't know what's going to happen, how long I'll last, but I know I have to hang on for a while because I still have some unfinished business. For one thing, there's a girl in the city who needs looking after. I have to get Alessandra away from her old man. But I can't just waltz in and sweep her away. She's only twelve or so at the moment.

Hell, I look to be only sixteen myself.

But there's something else I have to do before I deal with any of that.

After the funeral, I go back to the house with my father. He changes like he's going to work in the fields, but instead he takes down that photo of me and goes out and sits on the porch. Holding the photo. Staring across the fields.

I change, too. I walk around behind the barn to where my old Impala sits. I ask the old man why he had it towed here.

"It's all we've got left of him," he tells me.

There's no key in the ignition. I found it in my hand after the crash, and I put it in my pocket—just as I did the first time around. And just as in that other life, I'm wearing it on a string around my neck.

Don't ask me why. It just seems important.

I look at the car for a while longer, then walk away, across the fields alongside the house until I get to the country road. I follow it to the dead man's curve, leaving the road when I reach the old oak tree.

Anybody seeing me here is going to think I'm mourning my brother, but I'm not. I'm waiting for Ginny to show up.

I've come each afternoon since the crash.

I don't know if I'll be able to see her, but I call her name, and I talk out loud, hoping she's around, that she can at least hear and see me, even if I can't see her. I tell the story of the first time we met, and I urge her to stop living a half-life. To finish her business here and go on.

I can't tell if she hears me. I can't tell if she follows my advice or not. So I come back each day and do it all over again.

Today's no different. I walk up to the oak tree and lay my hands on the fresh scars that mar its bark. I say Ginny's name. Once. Twice.

And this time a voice answers me.

"Who are you?"

I turn, and there she is, standing on the side of the road, the same way she was the first time I met her.

"You're here," I say.

And I smile. It's the first time I've smiled in three days. It's so good to see her again.

"You can see me," she says. "You're alive and you can see me."

"Yeah, I can."

"And you can hear me."

I nod. "Come down and sit with me, Ginny. We need to talk."

She studies me for a long moment, then slowly comes down from the road and sits down under the oak. She puts out a hand to touch me, but her fingers go through my arm.

"I thought maybe . . . ," she says, but she lets her voice trail off.

Something I can't read moves in her eyes, and she looks away. I wait, patient, until she turns back to me.

"I know you," she says. "You're Marshall Coe's little brother."

It's such a small thing, but I'm pleased that she remembers me—remembers *me* by name—and not Billy.

"Yeah. Well sort of."

"What do you mean, 'sort of'?"

"It's a long story," I tell her.

"The one thing I have a lot of is time," she says.

"I know."

"*How* do you know?"

So I start to tell her, right from the beginning, the way I've just told you.

***A. A. Attanasio** has authored nineteen novels, which include* Radix, The Last Legends of Earth, The Moon's Wife: A Hystery, The Dragon and the Unicorn, *and a biker variation on the* Iliad, *written with Robert S. Henderson, titled* Silent.

He lives—and oh, how I envy him—in Hawaii.

Demons Hide Their Faces

A. A. Attanasio

Winterset in Egypt beside the rotting canal at Sidi Bishr, with the little, ceramic hashish pipe in her freckled hand, a thin thread of palpitant smoke twisting in the air before her, the professor faced her student and informed him seriously and with hollow impersonality, "The most avid collectors of books are demons. But they want only the old texts. The *oldest* texts."

The student, with his generous innocence, didn't take her meaning literally. "Yeah, I've heard tell that a smuggler in the stalls of Portobello Road can get thirty thousand pounds for even a small tablet from the dynasty of Nippur." He was a young man, with the look of a young man. "Those prices would make anybody a devil." Rufous hair cropped close to a round head, alert, brown, lemuroid eyes, and a lanky frame gave him the winsome aspect of a youth who had flourished as an antelope in another life.

That memory of ignorance traveled with him wherever he wandered across the floor of the damned. He never tired of recollecting his evening in Sidi Bishr and touching the pain of the nescience that had delivered him to this eerie netherworld. He never tired at all—for in hell, no one sleeps.

"Texts are more than you think they are," said the professor, and the sweet smoke from her pipe puzzled the air between them. "It's not for the money that demons want those ancient artifacts."

Again, he assumed that by demons the professor meant immoral collectors, people who would stop at nothing to acquire the rare cuneiform tablets and cylinder seals that commanded the highest prices at auctions. His misunderstanding was natural, for the professor did not seem a woman inclined to supernatural fantasies. She was known among the wealthiest families in both hemispheres as an antiquary of the highest erudition with postings as a bonded codex agent for Christie's and Sotheby's, credentialed as a bibliopole at the Museum of Antiquities in Berlin, and tenured as professor of historiography on faculty at the Sculo Normale Superiore in Pisa, where the student had met her.

His quest began at the Horned Gates of Goetia. Footed upon a lakebed of jagged lava and grouted with human bones, a colossal time-stained wall extended to the borders of sight, wide as the worldrim. The improbable rampart reared toward an indigo zenith and chimeric cloudscapes that ranged across the welkin with a disdainful and seraphic likeness of floating pagodas and blue tabernacles.

A round gateway stood unguarded. Corroded iron palings, wrought intricate as Gothic heraldry for devils, told him nothing. Nor did he recognize, at first, yon cinderland.

"I don't think we're going to find any valuable artifacts here." The student watched gnats spinning in the humid air above the putrid canal, where children dived into the ooze for coins. No bookstalls existed among the sprawling hovels of oyster-colored brick. "Why are we here?"

"The oldest texts are puissant talismans against evil." The professor sucked placidly on her ceramic pipe and watched light bleed from the citron sky. "Do you believe in evil?"

He squinted to see if she were teasing him. On the crowded tram out of Alexandria, which had forced them together among Bedouin with their chickens and vegetable baskets and improvident Egyptian families on their way to the dense Attarine Quarter or their steep littoral villages outside El Iskandariya, she had offered nothing. "Does it matter what I think?"

Does it matter? Had he actually said that to her? He could no longer be certain if that fateful evening in Sidi Bishr stamped his mind with memory or imagination. Since entering Goetia, mongrel speculations prospered.

The wind coughed like a lion in this gloomy world. Individual clouds hung low over slurry horizons and migrated lumberingly as herds of gray bison.

From out of the mists, a rider approached, a plum-blue African in a snowy turban. Upon the broken ground, his camel set down its large soft pads with serene elegance. The rider turned his flat profile toward the carbolic brink of the sky and spoke in Enochian, a language like the screaming of eagles.

"So, you cherish a modern sensibility?" Behind the professor, scarlet rays reached through clouds of mosquitoes and glimmered on the violet waterways and the goose-winged sails of dhows hurrying toward night. "You accept that we are infinitesimal creatures, our lives insignificant, our opinions of reality arbitrary and ultimately meaningless. Yes?"

"Reality itself is meaningless."

"Ah. Quite so." She laughed as abruptly as snapping a twig or plucking a flower. "Does that trouble you?"

"Should it?" The student felt annoyed. Love—or an alloy of carnal yearning and exotic allure that the student understood as love—had inspired him to follow her to Egypt on what she called a "book hunt." He had hoped that this trip would provide an opportunity for serious work by which he could demonstrate his skills and perhaps win her affection. But she seemed to be toying with his mind. And that stirred in him both gamey vexation and quirky arousal.

Was it the desperate moment of standing in a volcanic terrain the color of elephants—or the redolence of sandalwood lufting from the rider's black aba that inspired the student to take the large extended hand? No sooner was he hoisted atop the camel than they hurtled into formless fog.

The crying wind seethed. Eyes bleared by mist and speed, he pressed his face into the rider's back, breathed deeply of tawny incense. The wind's tormented cries writhed louder. He couldn't stop his ears for holding on to the rider, clasping with all his might not to be thrown by the jaunting beast.

The wind, shrieking through the crannies of his brain, buckled into voices. Schizoid whispers and shouts assailed him. Vaporous calls and responses feathered into ghostly conversations. And the cloven wind, like a vast living thing, uttered intimacies and obscene endearments that pinned his soul like a rape victim.

* * *

The professor said with sad resignation, as if imparting a fact stolen from the dead and costing her soul, "The measure of a mind has no other gauge than the significance that the mind endows upon the world."

"Then, my measure is pretty close to zero," he answered, allowing himself to sound nettled, "because I don't think the world has any significance whatsoever."

"Zero—" She smiled without mirth. He had never before seen a woman of such farouche beauty, and her unhappy smile stirred in him a scary and parlous thrill. "Zero is a most remarkable cipher—a figure of wonder second only to infinity."

"I was never much for math."

"And yet, math is all there is. Ever ponder that fact?" Behind wisps of sun-crayoned hair, her broad face—with its faceted cheekbones, violently askew nose, and proud, Byronic jaw—surveyed reality through eyes ice green and recessed as a pugilist's, with no farded upper lid. "Ever wonder why mathematics so precisely maps reality?"

"Never gave it any thought."

Sunrays slashed the fog of Goetia to summer haze. The camel bumped softly along a grassy hummock. Parkland sprawled before them, replete with chestnut avenues, flowery hedgerows, and high, peaceful fields tilted on slopes of emerald sward. The blue of the cumulus sky cut his heart with bliss.

They stopped, and the turbaned rider reached around, grabbed his passenger's arm, and deftly swung him to the ground. "You understand me now," he said in a chamois voice. "The wind has brought you to the Enochian language."

"Who are you?"

"I am the messenger sent to deliver you from the Goetic Gates." Behind him, a flock of doves flew into the beautiful sky. "This is where we part, I to the uplands and you—you go down there." The blue-black face gestured behind the traveler to a charred swamp of haggard briar, a smoldering garden of tormented trees hung with lichens and shag moss tattered and sere as rotted cerements.

* * *

"Of course. You're a bibliophile, as am I." The professor's remorseless gaze frightened and thrilled him. She looked simultaneously menacing and incomprehensibly lovely. "Words are your passion, yes?"

"Yes."

"You realize, of course, that words began as numbers. The first alphabets are alphanumeric systems. To the ancients, every letter possesses a unique number value. Every word equals the sum of the number values of that word's letters. And every phrase, sentence, page, and text exhibits an additive number value. Fundamentally, this ancient system constitutes a protoform of our own alphanumeric computers."

Watching her sitting in the vitreous light of day's end, her back against a rough thorn tree with Altair caught in the branches, he listened to the fluency of her voice without hearing her. When he realized that she had stopped and waited on his reply, he felt as though he was trying to retrieve a canceled dream. "I'm more interested in phonological studies in Akkadian."

In the Swamp of Goetia, the claggy mud pulled at each step and led him in a slow spiral among dolorous trees and rank weeds. At the center, he came to a black mere where nothing moved. Shawl moss hung still, gray as wizards' beards in the twisted cypresses. Cattails and reeds stood paralyzed. On a flat rock at the center of the glassy mere, the demon of the place sat.

He thought it was a turtle, head and limbs tucked out of sight. From inside its serried shell shaggy with green fungus, it addressed him in the Enochian tongue, "I am ancient proof alone, a voice not heard yet loved as the stillness in the black pearl. Who are you?"

"I am lost."

"You're not listening." The professor adjusted her silk puggaree scarf against the chill crepuscular wind. Night swelled quickly. The children who had been playing in the murky canal were gone. Above the fan palms, clear panels of starscapes glinted, and a few cirrus burned orange among the constellations. "The alphanumerics of writing originally served exclusively as a hieratic system."

"Hieratic—employed by priests. For what? To worship their gods?" He offered her a quiet smile. "Were Enku, Ani, and Ishtar big on ciphering?"

"The ciphering of writing manipulates the gods." She leaned forward with an almost deathly smirk. "The first texts are the software programs that direct the magic forces of the world. With them, the magic of Summer generated civilization—all the fundaments we take for granted: time defined in base sixty, agriculture, husbandry, architecture, cities—and, of course, money."

His attention had drifted into the smoky glitter of day's end among the closing fruit stands and the narrow shops crammed with clayware and lucky mirrors. "You or the hashish talking?"

From its craggy shell, the demon directed him—or banished him—out of the marsh, "You dreamcreature of a hotter world, come no closer. Turn your face of light toward the gleaming grass, and step away among amber horizon clouds. What you seek goes again shining into darkness, far from here. Begone, bright glance."

To his right, tule grass shimmered in a sudden breeze, glistening like fur. The windtrack swept toward a blighted horizon of bare trees in agonized poses. Beyond them, resinous clouds staggered low in the sky. He trudged toward them and at dusk mounted a scarp of poison ivy and clambered free of the leprous swamp.

The turtle in its painted shell awaited on a rock hob. "All things ended in their beginning end here."

The slant light leaning over his shoulder pierced the opaque murk he had traversed, and he glanced back as witness to mud-mired wraiths of miscarried life: clownish ruffles of condoms wavering like sea anemones in oily clouds of sperm, prawns of abortus, gilled gray clots, wrinkled death puppets roiling among small weightless skulls and quail-size briskets. In disgust, he yanked his attention away from that slithery soup. And the turtle chortled, "These kissed life on the mouth—and were eaten."

"Don't begrudge me my small pleasures." The professor drew languorously on her ceramic pipe and exhaled through her nostrils dragon jets of blue smoke. "Before the advent of writing—of spelling—there was no civilization. For over a hundred thousand years, humanity—people no different than you and I—wandered the surface of the earth as nomads, puny, dispossessed clans following wild herds and the seasons. Why did that change so abruptly? How have we come to find ourselves here in a world of jets and cell phones?" Her hard eyes softened to a suspiring gaze. "Magic."

"Right."

"Naturally, you're disinclined to believe me. But truth is not suspended because of your disbelief." She leaned back and averted her green gaze. A fire of carob-wood flapped on the strand, stirred by gusts from the dark sea on the other side of the canal, beyond slouching dunes. Silhouettes of robed figures passed before it. "The world we see around us is but a scrim to a vaster drama. Demons and the allies of life contend on a stage wide as all the universe, and the outcome of that conflict is entirely at hazard."

Beyond Goetia, tableland of scalloped salt glowed violet under starshine. He slogged all night toward crenulate mountains. At dawn, he toiled up a fuming esker and stood staring through mauve veils of blowing pumice at a mirage city. Thirst bulged in his thick face. He squinted against sundogs flaring from parabolic windows of art deco spires. Marble vaults and domes flamingo pink in early light, glittering steel cables, zeppelins big as August clouds moored to tower needles, and ribbon monorails hovered upon puma-hued sands.

Parched and haggard, he slumped into the Metropolis of Aethyrs. A fountain whose cubist segments smeared together in the blurry heat to an alabaster archer jetting prismatic water from her naked breasts slaked his thirst. Crowds coalesced out of the quaking air, their phantom forms sparkling like trout.

In the moil of the translucent crowd, he confronted an older doublegoer, an effigy of sadness, hair streaked with sun-pastels, and weathered countenance of immense world-weary serenity.

Himself?

"I brought you to Egypt to recruit you." The professor did not look at him as she spoke. She watched a kohl-limned moon rising, floating full in the dreamless gulf of night—newel bone ascending to the void above earth, to the celestial planes of the gods and the stairway of stars. "I myself was recruited long ago. I'm tired now. I want to live again in the quotidian world. But someone must take my place. Only in Egypt, where the magi built the most precise corridors into the demonworld, may we kindle a hope of retrieving the texts they are stealing. If we don't get them back, civilization will collapse."

"You realize how wack this sounds—professor?" It could only have been a joke, and he inclined his head backward, anticipating her laughter.

"I'm counting on your not believing me." On her breath, the phosphorus night of a desert Egypt. Moonlight moved in her hair like a lustrous fluid. "Deception is out of the question. But incredulity will serve, as well—as it did with me. So long ago."

"Well, okay." He waited till she looked at him, and in her fainéant eyes he fathomed she was not joking. "You've got my incredulity. What do you want to do with it?"

Above the Metropolis of Aethyrs, storm clouds towered like a cathedral. Before he could question his older self, a tornado of flies descended from those thunderheads and assailed the plaza. The ghost crowds stampeded down the boulevards, waving fists above their heads.

A frenzied horde of mounted lancers and archers, faces veiled with black head scarves, charged out of the maelstrom of flies. Robes bedighted with mirror shards and red tinsel, they rode standing, headlong horses eyes rolling, snarling and slavering, wild manes jet flames. He fled. The nightmare riders slashed through the vaporous denizens of the mirage city and bore down on him, yammering in Enochian voices high and far-carrying, "The dreaming fire! Stamp it out!"

Among purple billows of flies, he fled.

The student left behind the greasy canal at Sidi Bishr. Snagged in an invisible weave of curiosity, fantasy, and obdurate desire, he obeyed the odd instructions of his professor. "The demons have stolen a cuneiform tablet from the ancient dynasty of Sargon—the powerful *Lugal Zuqi-qi-pum Maqatum—Kings Thrown to the Scorpions*." Her face was tired and yet ferocious. Hard bits of moonlight shone in her eyes as though some prodigious activity in her brain had squeezed her thoughts to diamonds. "You'll find it in one of the 'prophets' tombs'—the first cave in the sea cliffs west of the canal. When you bring it back, you will have established your career, because the *Thrown Kings* has yet to be discovered. Hurry, though. Access is possible only on that final day of winter when the full moon rises. And watch your step. There'll be the usual litter of beer bottles underfoot."

* * *

Beneath the screaming horses, he fell. The trampling hooves pounded him flat, to a slant of three o'clock in the afternoon sunlight. Uncanny memories of boredom, soul ache, driftless solitude beyond rescue possessed him: weed precincts of railyards, gray rain leaning on windows, dangling husks in a spider's web, fronds of peeling wallpaper, neon shadows flickering onto cracked ceilings, aimless pollen dust bound for limbo across a vacant farmyard. This oppressive miscellany so saturated him with desuetude, he wanted to die.

Lugal Zuqi-qi-pum Maqatum stashed in a sea cave? He felt like a fool as he crossed the cobbled beach where the sponge-fleet harbored. The burnished faces of the crew glowed like copperware in the driftwood fires, watching him. Through zinc moonlight, he found his way past corrugated iron wharves and an irrigation trough from the canal choked with bramble. He breathed the windflung brine below the sea cliffs and the brassy kiss of nearby factories. A path of coral marl crunched under his shoes and led him to a gaunt cave.

The mournful horn of a barge sliding along the canal turned his attention to the distant sparkling skyline, coruscating minarets and skyscrapers beyond a dark headland and terraces of date palms with Betelgeuse peeking through. That the professor refused to accompany him, that she preferred the indolence of her ceramic pipe, assured him this was all a gruesome joke. But to what end?

He poked his head in the narrow opening. By reflected surf-glow, he spied the promised litter of beer bottles and fast-food cardboard, footprints in the sandspits at the cave entry, and names and dates scrawled in Arabic script upon the wall.

"Let her have her joke," he mumbled, and shoved into the cramped space, intending to turn about quickly and find her laughing in the moonlight under the pectoral curve of a dune.

Brisk sunlight and a bad smell crazed over him from the Horned Gates of Goetia. And his heart coughed with fear.

He wanted to die. Yet, something viscous and sticky in him cleaved to the world's brink. Not love, for all love's fabled glory. Nor hope, the soul's shuddering sickness. Willpower was a thing in a jar.

Rage alone upheld him. Fury at the absurdity. *Demons?* He violently rejected the idea that watchers in the dark could molest him with—what? Sadness? Desolation? The idea choked him with ire. He would not be squashed by ogres and monsters.

He would not let go. Like the stone refusal of Christ in the pietà's arms of Mary, like mountains welded to the planet's rim, he clung to life. With indomitable anger, his entire being quivered. And he rose up from the floor of creation.

He rose up through the scalloped salt flats. The barren pan wove shimmering illusions with the horizon's hot, blue thread. Platinum towers, glass high-rises, and office buildings with dirigibles moored to their steeples stood on planes of heat divorced from the ground. He turned his back upon the Metropolis of Aethyrs, contemptuous of its apparitions, and scanned the white expanse for the whirlwind of flies and the masked horsemen. The dry lake ranged empty under the fierce sun.

"Where am I?" he asked the fiery dream. "What's happened to me?" Throttled with dismay, he bawled a grotesque cry.

Days later, filthy and ragged, he shambled out of the desert. Swollen shapeless in a horror of agony, he shuffled into a magnolia forest. He collapsed among aloe spears crowding a pool of water clear as air, and he drank.

Gradually, sight returned. He sat up with a start. With stupefied brain, he squinted at the pool that had refreshed him and saw submerged bodies bloated and pale as dough. Their hair spread like smoke across the pebbly pond bed.

"Suicides," someone spoke in Enochian—a woman in maroon pajamas and black veil. She sat drenched in sunlight on the porphyry steps of a small temple. Onyx columns and copula of green chalcedony enclosed a marble pedestal. Atop the pedestal, a statue's gypsum head lay on its side wearing an ancient, enigmatic smile—and his face.

Spellbound, he stood and uttered in a voice hoarse with wonder, "You know me."

"Of course." The eyes above the veil, soft with dreams, susurrant as an addict's, were black honey. "You are a factory for the manufacture of excrement. You are a pylorus of endless hunger. I know you, you world of multiplying bacteria. Awe of maggots."

* * *

"Demons!" He groused and angrily departed the Temple of Himself. "Hell!" he spat derisively, finally accepting the absurd truth of his predicament. "Hell and demons! Damn it all!"

Behind him, the priestess from his temple yelled, "You will drink rats' tears! Do you hear me? You bile duct! You sphincter!"

"Yeah, yeah."

At the sandy verge of the magnolia forest, he paused. Inversions of heat stood the sky's tranquil lake upon the silicate plain of noon. Far off, he glimpsed the Metropolis of Aethyrs. But he was not bound there. His own ghost in that city had confided a longer journey and only silent speculation where he might retrieve the tutelary *Lugal Zuqi-qi-pum Maqatum.*

"The dreaming fire—" That was the name given him by the demon horsemen whose hooves could not kill him. *Dreaming this fiery hell . . . and dunes like slouching lions . . . an evil dream.*

Yet, a dream from which there was no waking—for he never slept. He felt his mind slip along fault lines of madness.

More deviltry . . .

He stared at a rock warped by heat until it disappeared. He provoked wind-feathered clouds out of sapphire emptiness. He inked night and stenciled the void with stars.

For the first time in hell, he smiled.

A hoarded mass of bougainvillea, palms, and giant ferns interrupted the magnetic haze of the wasteland. Morning sun spangled among mango trees isolated in an oasis backed by a salt lake and its further forevers of desert.

He breathed the jasmine air and strolled into the magnificent grove. A pool where he knelt to drink reflected how his wanderings as a dream-creature in the netherworld had reconfigured his hot atoms upon some grittier imagination deep in his psyche: sun-hued hair, curly as a heifer's, weathered face hollowed as an elk's, a taurine neck, and eyes, once reminiscent of a gazelle's, now tapered to the thin, pitiless gaze of a jinni.

At a watering trough shaded by acacia and sycamore, camels gnarred. Their dismounted riders, cowled figures in crimson robes trimmed in tinsel, loitered in a courtyard beyond large folding doors with pistol bolts and inscribed panels of sphinxes and griffins. They sat together on the raked sand of a rock garden and motioned for him to approach.

"*Lugal Zuqi-qi-pum Maqatum,*" an iron voice spoke. In the corrugated sand before them stood a clay tablet incised with cuneal scratchings. "Take it."

Over a carafe of date wine, he conversed with the demons in the rock garden. They wanted empathy. "We are part of each other," they explained in their basso-profundo voices. "You and we belong to the same universe, albeit at far extremes. And now that you know you are a dreaming fire, you can annoy us, but you cannot thwart us. You are too small. Try to understand. Here, at the dark limits of our expanding cosmos—in the googolth year of what you call time—each *atom* of our world is as large as the entire universe of your lifetime. Our reality is inherited from yours. Can you blame us for tinkering with our past—your world—to shape the contours of our experience?"

Butterflies, red as firecracker confetti, jittered around the sweet fumes of the carafe. "Why does your happiness require you to inflict suffering on my world?"

"We don't think that way, anymore than your carpenters think they are inflicting suffering on the forest when they carve a tree into a house."

"I've seen evil."

"Dreamcreature, you see what you dream. You see with human eyes. We sympathize. Our positron brains, like your carbon brains, perceive reality in selective ways. Truth is a fiction. Reality unknowable."

He peered into the darkness of their hooded faces with mutinous eyes. "I will return the *Thrown Kings* to my world. That magic will hold you at bay."

"You shall thwart only a portion of our efforts to design our own truth. We shall steal other texts."

"And I will return here and take them back."

"Some, yes. Others, no. You shall tire. Hot and compact as you are, as dazzling to us in your power as you are, your energy is finite."

"Others will join me."

"*Others?* No. You are alone, doomed to defend one small segment of time in your world. The texts you retrieve will preserve your civilization only for a while. We will steal them again. You will retrieve them again. We will steal and you retrieve. Again and again you will attack us and then circle back to that small tract of years that is yours and yours alone to protect, like a vicious guard dog—on a short leash."

The demons' words made his brain feel like a strange machine whose function eluded him. "I will tell others. Many will join me."

"The laws of information and entropy do not permit that."

"I don't understand."

"Of course not, else you would not speak such foolishness. The more information you spread, the greater the chaos you create. The more chaos you create, the easier for us to topple your civilization the way a lumberjack fells a tree for the sawmill. You will help us enormously if you do not hold this secret very close indeed."

Terror smoldered in him. "What are you saying?"

"Think of a house of cards. The information necessary to define the coordinates in space of those precisely ordered cards is much less by far than the information required to define the coordinates of those same cards scattered randomly. The greater the chaos, the more information. And *vice versa.*" The burly voice smote him. "The more people who know of us—or the more information you share with that one person who will replace you when you finally weary of this perpetual task—the greater the chaos by far—and the more material available for us to do our work."

Crushed breathless by this hopeless revelation, he could barely ask, "Why are you telling me this?"

They bellowed the answer in satanic chorus, "This is *information,* you benighted fool! The more you know, the greater the chaos that—"

He snatched the *Kings Thrown to the Scorpions* and ran wailing from the garden of demons, wailing as loud as he could to drown out those voices damning him with their hideous secrets.

A winged viper, tarry feathers a blur, eyes like fireflies, guided him across the badlands of hell to the Goetic Gates. Stepping past those slanderous iron palings, he found himself again in the sea cave at Sidi Bishr among strewn litter of empty bottles, of used condoms.

By some demonic temporal parallax, he had been returned to a time prior to his departure, antecedent even to his birth. *The demons' tight leash*. For weeks to come, he felt as one does in dreams. Imbrued with salty bereavement for the mundane reality departed from him forever, he proceeded in a daze. He carried heavily the silence inflicted on him and bridled in his heart the horror of madness.

As predicted by the professor who had damned him, *Lugal Zuqi-qipum Maqatum* earned him recognition in academic circles. He accepted a lecturer's chair in Sumerology at Trondheim in Norway, as far from Egypt as he could arrange. Yet, within a year, there appeared in the classroom a serenely tall man of blue-black skin wearing a black aba and white turban.

Among the sand cliffs and monument rocks of Egypt, secret corridors delivered him joylorn to the demonworld whenever the taciturn messenger summoned. He came and went frequently to that hallucinary demesne upon the universe's dark rim, recovering texts the demons stole. Each journey wore him closer to madness.

At last, he could take no more. In that sanctuary of memory anterior to aught of demons and their darkness beyond the crumbling stars, he recalled the professor who had recruited him. She would be of an age.

Winterset in Egypt at the opulent Shiraz teahouse, sitting under mirrored birdcages on a thistle-soft Baluchistan carpet, Hejaz incense twisting soft iridescent braids in the air behind him, the professor faced his student and informed her with a gentle, knowing smile. "The most avid collectors of books are demons. But they want only the old texts. The *oldest* texts."

***Nina Kiriki Hoffman** has been writing SF and fantasy for more than twenty years, and selling a heck of a lot of it. Her works have been finalists for the World Fantasy and Endeavor Awards.*

Novels include A Fistful of Sky *and* The Silent Strength of Stone; *her third short-story collection,* Time Travelers, Ghosts, and Other Visitors, *was published last year.*

Nina works in a bookstore, teaches writing, and sometimes carries tiny strange toys around in her bag.

Relations

Nina Kiriki Hoffman

Why did people always break?

Just when Sarah had them tenderized and sweet, trained to be just what she wanted, delicious and only the slightest bit resistant, the tiny tussle of kitten claws that excited her, something went wrong inside them and they broke.

This one, Jill, with her mountain cabin in the Idaho Sawtooths, her elegant ownership of a fantastic view and beautiful furniture, lovely music and imported foods, this one was a favorite, the best Sarah had found in a long time. Jill had lasted longer than the others, had kept her fighting spirit alive for quite a while. Sarah had loved Jill for months, and Jill had eventually loved Sarah. But now Jill's gray-green eyes were dead.

Sarah closed her eyes and kissed Jill. Jill still tasted sweet, and her lips responded to the kiss. Almost, Sarah could pretend they were at the beginning of capitulation, her favorite part of the relationship, where the other recognized that Sarah was powerful enough to force things, but didn't realize how powerful, how completely impossible to resist. That training was what Sarah loved. The tiny steps and occasional big ones toward the other's recognition that the other had no escape and no resources and no hope.

It was now, when the realization was complete, that Sarah lost interest.

She hugged Jill and stepped back, stared into Jill's eyes, looking for some last glimmer of fight to stamp out. All fight was gone. Jill stood silent, haunted, waiting.

"I won't be back," Sarah said. She touched Jill's lips with her first two fingers, watched Jill's pupils dilate, turned away before she saw anything that would hold her here. It was time to hunt for someone else.

Sarah loved the hunt.

There were rules to the hunting and ownership of humans. If she were going to bring someone home, where there were other people who had powers, some of them stronger than Sarah, she would have to follow the rules.

The new rule was: No more slaves. So, really, she couldn't bring anyone home anymore. At first she had fretted and raged, but then she realized she could own people away from home. Once she figured that out, she realized she need not follow any of the other rules, either, the ones about never take a person on their home ground, take only those who won't be missed or needed, only take another if you are in dire need of help. Life got much more interesting after Sarah threw out the rules, though she spent most of her time away from home now, and did the minimum amount of service for Family she could get away with.

She found Alonzo in a field.

She found him from above. Air was her sign, and air lifted her whenever she asked it to, carried her, even rendered her invisible as she desired. She hunted from air.

From above, Alonzo's dark red hair flamed in the sun, a weave of copper glints. His shirtless shoulders were wide. Sarah drifted down to look from the side, and she liked what she saw. He was young but full grown, dark from sun, strong with the slidy muscles of work, tall and perfect, focused on what he was doing. She even liked his face, with its deep-set brown eyes and long jaw.

She touched down in shadow, on a big rock under a maple tree at the edge of the field, then let air reveal her. She sat on the rock and watched Alonzo walk the furrows of the field. He was rangy and self-confident, stooping now and then to shift a clod of earth sideways, tamping down elsewhere. He was wearing wash-whitened jeans, but his feet were bare. What was he doing?

Singing.

Sarah cupped hands to her ears as Alonzo walked away from her. He was singing, but so softly she almost couldn't hear it. The tune almost sounded familiar. He stooped and touched the earth, smoothed something, patted something, sang, and wandered away. Presently he reached the far end of the field and turned back, walking another row, singing and stooping and working his way to her.

She waited. When he reached the near end of his row, five feet from her, she sent a breeze toward him. He glanced up.

"Oh," he said, in a rising tone, his voice warm and pleasant and low. "Who're you? How long you been there?"

"I'm Sarah."

"How'd you get way out here away from everything?"

She smiled at him and shrugged.

"I mean, this part of the farm isn't even on the road. Whatcha doing out here?"

"Watching you."

He rose and straightened, edged his shoulders back. He smiled at her.

She loved his eyes, deep under thick copper brows, their shadowed brown lightened by a few gold flecks. She loved his mouth. His smile stretched it wide. His full lower lip looked luscious.

"Why?" he asked.

"You're beautiful."

"Oh." Color flooded his face, and he turned away. "Don't you say that."

"Why not? It's true." She slid down the rock to stand before him. He was a head taller than she, his skin shades darker, sunbrowned, his chest lightly forested with red hair. His skin glistened with a sheen of perspiration. He smelled sweaty, and his hands were sheathed in dirt damped by sweat.

"Girls are beautiful. Men are handsome," he said, then in a lower voice, "You're beautiful."

Almost, she left. If he were an idiot, he wouldn't amuse her for long, no matter how fine his physical attributes were.

But she was here, face-to-face. Might as well give him a couple of other chances to impress her. "I introduced myself. Who are you?"

"Alonzo," he said.

"What were you doing, Alonzo?"

"Singing to the seeds."

A breeze brushed the back of her neck, raised prickles even in the hot, hot day. Seed singing? She remembered something about that. Something, but what? Nobody had brought it up in the course of normal events. There was a working farm at Chapel Hollow, but she left all that plant stuff to the others. For community service, she disciplined people and hunted and gathered.

"Bet that sounds funny, huh? Not many as does it anymore, but we always get a better crop when I do it."

"What song are you singing?" She stepped closer to him, and he smiled again, engaging and sweet. He smelled lovely, musky and male.

"Don't know, exactly. Nonsense, I s'pose. Whatever I think they need to hear."

"May I listen too?"

"Sure." He held out his hand, and she slid hers into it, wondering how long it had been since some trusting child had reached out to her, unafraid, unknowing. Fifteen years? Twenty? Not since she came into her gifts and talents, surely.

Alonzo was delicious. His hand was hard and hot in hers, callused and strong, though his grip was gentle. "Got three more rows to do," he said. He turned and tugged her with him along a furrow, and then his voice rose, eerie and strange, soft and stirring. "Time to wake, time to grow, time to change, time to send, find the water, find the sun, find the work your center holds," he sang. Knelt, touched ground, plunged a finger down into it, crooned something that made Sarah's cinnamon hair rise on its roots. *"Silla krella kalypta, miksash kooly tashypta."*

Her fingers clenched his. "What?" she whispered. "What? What are you saying?"

"Huh? I dunno. Probably something Mama sang to me when I was little."

She had never heard the lyrics before, but after she got over the shock of hearing her family language from this stranger—a language only used at home for rituals and curses—she worked out what he said. *Find your fertility, and I will protect you.*

"Where'd your mother come from?"

"Right here. Four generations we've worked this land. Put down roots, Mama said." Alonzo laughed.

"Four generations?" Sarah's family had been at Chapel Hollow for seven generations. Maybe this was some discarded offshoot of her family, or a tiny branch of the Southwater Clan, their split so long ago, she hadn't even heard rumors.

Family.

That was an added complication she hadn't anticipated. One could mistreat family in all kinds of ways, but one wasn't allowed to own them. On the other hand, if the waters were diluted enough, maybe Alonzo and his family had lost the powers that set Sarah and her family apart. Maybe they had different rules. Maybe she could own him anyway no matter what the rules were: So long as she overpowered him, how could he stop her?

What if she didn't overpower him? What if he had powers of his own?

Wouldn't that be terrific? She hadn't had a good fight in way too long.

"Four generations," Alonzo repeated. "We're not going anywhere. That's why I'm glad you came here." He tugged gently on her hand, and she went with him up the row as he sang to the things in the ground about sprouting, growing, strengthening, producing flowers and pollen and seed and fruit, ultimately providing and dying. Half the time he sang in English, and half in Ilmonish. Sarah fell into a light daze as she walked the earth with him. Something about his songs charmed and calmed her, made her think nothing mattered besides the sun on their heads, the scents of turned earth and nearby trees, the soft, rich soil under their feet, and the connection of their clasped hands. It was pleasant to walk along sweating with a boy. Every once in a while she summoned a breeze to breathe across their damp foreheads and the burning backs of their necks, tease their hair and brush over their arms. Alonzo smiled at her. Nice teeth.

She woke after they had walked the rest of the field, and the sun was straight above them. "You thirsty?" Alonzo asked.

Sarah licked her lips. What had she been thinking? She'd wasted an hour or two walking along beside this gentle idiot while he crooned to plants. Maybe she should get out of here, find someone more interesting to work on. Even if Alonzo *was* Family, that didn't make him automatically interesting.

"Actually, I'm *very* thirsty," Sarah said. She surprised herself. Usually if she was thirsty, she drank. Her throat was parched now. How had she come to this state without noticing?

"Come on up to the house. I'll get you some lemonade."

Go to his home place? No, that wasn't a good idea, not unless he lived alone. "Who else is at the house?"

"Everybody who's not out doing a job or at school. The three younger kids are off to school right now, but they'll be home after a bit. Mama's baking today, and Grandma is repairing. Grandpa's in the basement. He's always in the basement. Dad's plowing over in the east field, and my older brother Jacob, he's off with the cattle for the day."

Supposing any of them had powers, she'd rather not encounter several at once. First she needed to find out what Alonzo's skills were. "How about if I wait here and you go get the lemonade," Sarah said.

"Shy, are you?"

She smiled at him.

"That's so cute," he said. "Okay. You wait here. Don't you go away!"

When Sarah pulled her hand away from Alonzo's, it came slowly, which alarmed her. Had he been binding her to him? Those songs—

He leaned over and planted a kiss on her cheek, then ran across the field away from her. The kiss sizzled against her skin, a pleasant burn in the heat of the day. Her mouth tasted sweet now, a taste like the blood of bitten clover stems. She wandered back to the boulder under the maple where she had first watched Alonzo. She sat in the shade and brooded at her toes.

He was spelling her. Was he really spelling her? How could that be, without her noticing?

She muttered the chant for "Things Seen and Unseen," and saw that a downy blanket of green vines wrapped around her. She couldn't feel them or touch them. She didn't know what they were doing to her. But she knew she hadn't donned them on purpose, so they must be Alonzo's doing.

Oh, no. She said a prayer to air. Wind sprang up and blew the vines off her, and she woke up. Trapping her! Spelling her! Alonzo was hunting *her!* How dare he? Did he even know who she was? Well, she could show him. This *was* a fight, but he didn't fight fair.

Then again, neither did she.

The vines were easy to dispel. Once they were gone, and the mental fog that had calmed her with them, she said "Things Seen and Unseen" again, and realized that lines like thick, twisted ropes went from the soles of her feet to the earth below. She lifted her feet and felt the bottoms. She could see the ropes for the duration of the spell, but she couldn't feel them or break them. She raised her arms and asked air to lift her. It tugged her up into the sky, but before she got very high, the ropes on her feet stopped her. She tried going sideways and again was stopped.

What had he said about putting down roots?

She tried cutting spells, transforming spells, destroying spells. Nothing even nicked the ropes.

This couldn't be right. That dumb boy couldn't have trapped her this way. Or maybe he could. It might take major work to get out of this one.

Alonzo walked toward her across the field, carrying a wooden tray with a bottle, two glasses, and a plate of pastries on it. "Hey," he said. "You all right?"

He didn't know what she was. Best keep it that way as long as possible. Feign ignorance. "Thirsty," she said.

"Got your lemonade right here. You hungry? Mama sent along some brownies too. She wins prizes with these brownies at the county fair every year. She's looking forward to meeting you."

"Alonzo, I don't want to meet your mother."

"Sure you do. I bet she'll like you. You're way prettier than the girl Jacob got."

"What happened to the girl Jacob got?"

"Sissy? She's home now, waiting to have her first baby. Grandma's training her up in repairing work." He set the tray on the rock beside her, poured a tall glass of lemonade, and handed it to her.

The glass was cool and sweating in her hand. Sarah's mouth hungered for the lemonade. Her throat was so dry, just breathing hurt a little. What if this was another way he was binding her to this place, though? "Lemonade makes me thirsty," she whispered. "Can I have some water?"

"Well, sure. Wait here just a sec. There's a stream off a little ways. I'll get you a glassful." Alonzo took the empty glass and struck off into the forest.

Sarah set the glass of lemonade on the tray and rose to her feet. She couldn't transform the ropes at her soles into anything else, but what if she changed herself? She turned her face skyward and let herself melt into air, a transformation she feared, to utterly abandon herself to her element. She had had to demonstrate mastery in this skill before her great-aunt and teacher would lead her further into the dark disciplines, but she had never grown comfortable with it.

She had not tried it in years, but found that she still had this power. She became air and lifted free of the trap Alonzo had laid for her. Aahhhh. Good.

"Sarah?" Alonzo returned, calling her: she could feel his voice all through her. "Sarah, where'd you go? I got your water. Sarah?"

Now. Let's leave this place. Disperse utterly and go away, re-collect ourself somewhere else. She flung herself wide.

"Stop it," Alonzo said. He set down the glass of water, held out his hands, clenched them into fists.

Something flexed and jerked Sarah back into a person-sized and person-shaped package. She stood on the rock, suddenly herself again, terrified and shivering.

Alonzo leapt up onto the rock beside her and put his arms around her.

"I'm sorry. I didn't mean to scare you. I don't ever want to hurt you. But you're mine now, Sarah, and I don't want you all misty."

"I'm yours?"

"Didn't you give yourself to me? You came here and found me and walked with me while I was seed singing. Our earth knows you now. You're mine."

Her tears surprised her. He stroked her hair, then stooped and got the glass of water, held it to her lips. Little sobs shook her. She took the glass from his hand and sipped. The water was cool and sweet. She felt it in her mouth, her throat, her stomach, spreading out through her body, claiming her, another binding to this place, but she couldn't stop drinking, she was so thirsty. "I'm yours," she whispered. This stupid sweet boy had spelled her down tight. Set a trap for a sparrow, and caught a vulture. He didn't know yet.

He would learn.

"Let's have babies together." He took the empty glass from her hand, set it on the tray, held her and kissed her gently.

"No," she whispered. A baby. She had longed for a baby all her life. Ever since she was born, she had been told the greatest thing she could ever do was have a baby, but she had tried every spell she knew, every remedy, even ridiculous ones, and her womb had never quickened, no matter who she slept with. "We can't, Alonzo." Maybe he would free her now. She thought of little cinnamon-haired children with Alonzo-brown eyes, children who would love her just the way she was. If only.

She remembered when she was six and her youngest sister was born. She had loved holding the baby. She had even sought out other people's babies to hold and care for. She had grown, confident that someday she'd get her own baby and nobody would be able to take it away. She had made rules: Even when it cried, she wouldn't hit it. She would just hug it. She would always feed it when it was hungry. She would change it the instant it needed a new diaper. She would have the happiest baby in the world.

Then when she was twelve, her teacher, her great-aunt, did a foretelling, found she was barren. Something had soured in her then. She had tried to defy the foretelling. Later she had accepted it.

"We can't?" Alonzo asked. "Why not?"

"Something's wrong with me."

"No," he said. "You're perfect." He sat down on the rock and tugged her down too, pulled her into his lap. She relaxed into his embrace, wondering. He had already trapped her, when she hadn't known anyone could. What if he knew stronger spells than she did?

He set his hand on her stomach and closed his eyes. She felt warm power seep from his palm and into her like sunshine, strange and comforting, and then a blossom of heat inside her, spirals of heat in her breasts, a rising itch and readiness. "Perfect," he whispered.

She pulled his mouth to hers, tore his pants off, lifted her dress, sucked him inside.

The sun had gone west, the light changed to gold, the shadows lengthened, when she finally let him go. Her back itched and burned from the rough rock. She felt swollen and sore and strangely contented. Alonzo, scratched and bruised, was asleep now, facedown on the rocks beside her, his mouth half-open, his breathing quiet. He looked pale and exhausted. He didn't snore. Good. One thing she wouldn't have to fix.

She sat up, placed her hands over her stomach, sought inside herself, felt something she had given up hope she would ever feel. Tiny sparks.

Sparks. A future.

She set her palm on the rock. *How did you fix me?*

That is our skill, mine and Alonzo's, to make things ripe and ready, whispered the spirit of the place. *It was born in him, one in a long line of such people. It's one of the things this family has taught me.*

Thank you, Sarah thought, and then, *Am I trapped here forever?*

Do you want to leave?

For a moment she thought of her own branch of Family. She owed them duty, but would they really miss her? Probably not. Most of them hated her. Besides, technically, she was still with Family.

A fierce longing for open sky and infinite possibilities, the freedom of any direction, any new person she chose to play with, any possible next rose up in her, flooded her with regrets and frustrations.

She touched her stomach. It would be all right.

She could make her own people now.

***Neal Barrett, Jr.**, is buried treasure. His incredible repertoire of fantasy, science fiction, horror, western, and twenty other genres and mixtures of same have appeared in so many nooks and crannies for so long that it's only when you step way back to look at the whole picture that you realize what he's accomplished.*

Read everything by him you can get your hands on. Start with Pink Vodka Blues, Through Darkest America, *and his short-story collection,* Perpetuity Blues.

TOURISTS

Neal Barrett, Jr.

The bus wandered down through the morning countryside, down through gently rolling hills bright with lavender, pink and columbine blue. Down, down, plunging all of a sudden into cool, shady forests, the road flanked with columns of redwood, cedar and loblolly pine, giants that stretched up forever into a dazzling azure sky.

A chorus of *ooooh*s and *aaaah*s echoed through the bus. The morning was pleasant, and everyone rolled their windows down.

"My, how lovely," Mary Beth said. "Why, it's as lovely as can be."

"It is, indeed," said Liza Lee, leaning past her friend to see. "Oh, my, there's lily and rock moss and lady fern, too. And puttyroot and flag and merrybells by a little stream."

"Liza, I do not believe there's a flower you *don't* know, and that's as true as it can be."

"Yes, but you know birds, Mary Beth. You know birds a lot better than I."

"Oh, that's simply not so. Though I do know a few."

"More than a *few,* I'd say."

"Well, they go together, don't they? Flowers and birds? And little streams and trees? They are part of the beauty all around us, beauty for everyone to see."

The two grasped hands, and their cheery laughter echoed through the bus and made others grin, too.

As they talked, the bus broke through the trees and left the woods behind. The sun was hidden now, and the sky was a rather dreary green. Mary Beth noticed there didn't seem to be any flowers or birds—or, for that matter, anything pretty at all. Just rocks and dirt and clumps of blackened weeds.

"It's different outside, Liza Lee. There aren't any trees, and there's no little stream."

"Why, you're right, Mary Beth. There's hardly a thing out there to see."

The bus slowed then, and it turned down a very narrow road, past a dark pillar of stone, over a rattling bridge and a leaden river far below. Then, just up ahead, Mary Beth saw a man squatting by the side of the road. Great beads of tallowy sweat rolled down his corpulent flesh. His skin was swollen, pocked, severely inflamed, rife with ulcerations, lesions, blisters, pustules and boils of every sort. Two scabrous crows, birds with no feathers, were perched upon his head, pecking at his flesh. An enormous serpent was sliding, slipping, slicking from an orifice between the man's legs, dropping, slopping, without ever stopping, an endless stream of moist and steamy coils, oily convolutions, hideous piles that writhed and shivered on the ground.

All this clearly caused enormous discomfort in the man. His mouth was distorted in a scream, but no sound came out at all.

"I guess we're nearly there," said Mary Beth to Liza Lee.

"Yes," said Liza Lee, "I guess we likely are. . . ."

In a moment, a new sight appeared up ahead. At first, Mary Beth assumed it was part of the landscape that stretched out as far as the eye could see—rocks, rocks, and more rocks still, rocks scattered everywhere about, rocks of every shape and size. Rocks that only came in one color, smoked, singed, sizzled, burned to a dull and basic brick.

Then, closer, she saw the stones were formed into crude, disorderly piles, stacks, heaps, lumps and little mounds. Closer still, they appeared to be dwellings of a sort—shanties, hovels and shacks, some scarcely more than holes in the ground.

Yet, there were people there, people with curious features, people without any fingers, people with nothing where their mouths ought to be. People with toes where there should have been a nose. Hoppy, jerky, clumsy people with a head and a foot, and nothing more than that. On top of these gross distortions, many people were clearly plagued by toads.

"I don't know what I expected," Mary Beth said. "They didn't tell us it would be like this."

Well, not to tell a lie, she knew that wasn't quite so. The folder *had* said there were parts of the tour where one might expect to bring to mind, imagine, recall things they scarcely remembered anymore.

"And that," Mary Beth said to herself, "is exactly what's happening now."

Hot was one thing she suddenly recalled. Another was *something really smells bad here. . . .*

"Step over here, please, gather round me," said Bill Jim, the bus driver, and everyone did.

"I know you've all read the rules in your handouts, but I'd like to go over them now. Just bear with me a minute, and we'll get under way.

"First, stay with me at all times. That's a real important rule. There isn't any *harm* can come to you, I don't guess I have to say that."

Bill Jim showed them a cheery smile, and the passengers gave him smiles back. This showed Bill Jim people were getting in the spirit of things, and he liked to see that.

"The thing is, they've got rules here like everywhere else, and we're obliged to show 'em some respect. Okay, so don't wander off. Second is, there's going to be folks want to come up and talk. There isn't any rule against that, but I recommend you don't.

"Now. I guess we're all ready. Any questions before we start? You there, you go ahead."

"What we saw coming in?" asked Larry Lew. "Does that person *have* to do that?"

"Yes. Anyone else?"

"I was going to ask the same thing," said Mary Beth.

"Bill Jim, can I ask you why the sky's colored green?"

"Good question," Bill Jim said, for it was a question he liked a lot.

"They don't do blue. They don't do blue, lavender, lilac, any colors of the purple persuasion. No sapphires, violets or plum. They do a kind of lint, bone, tallow and whey; they don't do any white. Not much yellow. I've seen a little jaundice and flax.

"As I'm sure you've noticed, most every color is your burned-up brick. They do a kind of red, but it looks black to me. Black is big here, but the tour doesn't go as far as that. If you're ready—"

"Bill Jim," said Mary Beth, "this town we're in, I guess it's got a name."

Bill Jim showed her half a grin. "I'd tell you, but then you'd have to stay."

Mary Beth knew he didn't mean that at all, but she didn't ask another question, and neither did anyone else.

Mary Beth was quickly getting used to the fact that everywhere they went, everything looked much the same. Like Bill Jim said, if you didn't like brick, there weren't a lot of colors to see.

The *people* were different, though, in a way. And, in a way, they were really all the same. Like the drab, crumbly old buildings, like the hovels and little dark holes, one bodily affliction began to look much like the next. People tripped on their entrails, dropped a part or two, grew another head. It was, clearly, what everybody did.

Bill Jim led them around a dark corner, into a street exactly like the one they'd left behind. Not *exactly* the same, for this street boasted a small stone fountain, a sight that surprised Mary Beth, for they'd seen nothing like it on the tour.

Water bubbled up from the center and fell in a very pleasant spray, in a fine and sparkly mist, leaving circles of orderly ripples spreading out on every side.

A great many people were crowded about the fountain's edge, people of every shape and every size, people with every affliction you could name. Nobody moved; nobody spoke. No one did anything at all.

Bill Jim rushed them by, told them to hurry on along, told Mary Beth she was dragging behind. Mary Beth waited a moment, watching the people at the fountain, watching them stand there, gazing at the water as it bubbled and it sprayed. . . .

"You would think they could give these people something to do," Mary Beth told Liza Lee, not so loud that Bill Jim could hear. "All they do is stand around. I'm sure they would like to have jobs, or maybe take a class of some kind. I know it's not supposed to be *fun* or anything. Still . . ."

"Well, I don't think there's any chance of that," said Liza Lee.

A man wobbled by on his hands. His scabby legs walked clumsily behind him, held by a leash bound around the man's neck. He stuck out his tongue and said,

"Poke-drippy-slew . . ." or words to that effect.

"Don't answer him or anything—just look the other way," said Liza Lee, urging Mary Beth along. "You know what Bill Jim said."

"*I* think Bill Jim finds very little happy anywhere, and doesn't like us to either, Liza Lee."

"Oh, dear." Liza Lee brought her hand up to her mouth, somewhat astonished by what her friend had said. It simply wasn't like the Mary Beth she knew.

Mary Beth was quite surprised herself. She couldn't recall saying anything about anyone that wasn't as nice as it could be.

I think I know the reason for that, she decided. *Recalling* things was something the folder warned about. The word *cool* had come to her just as she passed the fountain. Now where did that come from? And there was *thirsty,* too, then *dry,* words rushing in like that, one on top of the next.

Remembering things was the reason she had strayed from happy for a while. Being here *did* make pictures and thoughts rise up in your head. Things you hadn't remembered before suddenly came to mind again.

And that could likely explain why she'd had a less than happy about Bill Jim. Bill Jim was a very good driver, and a very fine guide. He wasn't from Home, though, anyone could tell that. He wasn't from here, either. He came from somewhere in between. She didn't know how she knew that, but she did. It was one of the remember things again.

Which doesn't give me any right to say what I did, and I surely won't do it anymore.

"Come along now," Bill Jim said, as he did most any time they came on something new. "Nothing to stop for, nothing here to see."

There was, though, and Mary Beth wasn't the only member of the tour who didn't care to be hurried along.

"Bill Jim," said Jenny Cee, "would you tell us what they're doing there, please?"

"We do wish you would," put in Johnny Dee. "I think everyone would like to know."

Mary Beth was glad someone else has asked the question first. She didn't want Bill Jim to look at her funny again.

It was, truly, a curious sight indeed, even for the sights one came across here. A long, seemingly endless line stretched down the street and out of sight. As ever, there were people of every sort about. People with knobs, nubs, creases and folds. Wrinkles and crinkles and corrugated holes. Slits, splits, clots and gaping maws. People with people fronts, and animal behinds. People without any fronts. People with no behinds.

Many in the line were lying down, squatting, sprawling on the ground—those who had parts that allowed that sort of thing. Some had built hovels, crude piles of stone, or burrowed in the ground, as they waited in the line. Most of them weren't doing anything at all.

"There's nothing to see," Bill Jim said, "it's a line, that's all it is. Anyone can see that."

"What kind of line?" asked Jenny Cee.

"A long line, all right?"

"And where is the head of the line, Bill Jim?"

"Down there. Somewhere down the block."

"And what do they do when they get to the front, Bill Jim?"

"They go to the *back* of the line. Is that all? Can we move along now?"

Mary Beth wasn't sure when she'd drifted away. She was watching someone with a dozen heads, all of them bobbing, jerking about, none of them sure which way they ought to go. One minute the others were there; a moment later they were gone.

"Oh, my," Mary Beth said aloud, "Bill Jim is not going to like this at all."

She knew what had happened. She had started thinking again about the people in the line. One of the remember things happened, and it popped in her head there were two different kinds of people here. Well, there were no two *alike,* really, but she didn't mean that.

What she meant was, there were hangies and there were smooths. She hadn't noticed that before, and couldn't say why. When remember things were ready, they were simply there, and they weren't before that.

In that very same moment, she knew that once she had been a smooth, too. Somewhere. Before she'd come Home. Now where would *that* be? Wasn't that an odd thing to recall?

Maybe that's why you wore cloze on the tour. "We do because they *don't* do it here," she reasoned, pleased with herself for thinking something up something like that. She promised herself she'd tell the others, in case they didn't know. If, indeed, she could ever find them again.

"Goodness, I wonder just how I'm going to go about *that?*"

As ever, one street, one building, one wall looked like the ones she'd passed before. Maybe if she just stood there, Bill Jim and the others would somehow find *her?*

No, now that would never do. She had gotten into this mess, and she would find her way out.

She was doing just that, or doing the best she could, when she came upon the place with the fluttery, flickery lights. Mary Beth paused to get a better look. She knew she shouldn't, but she did. The lights came from a narrow alleyway, an alley so narrow, so tight, so terribly confined, it was hard to imagine anyone could squeeze inside.

Yet, there were people in there, people packed together, people side by side, watching the shadowy blink of black and white, watching the little gray windows in the wall. As the people watched, the pale lights danced across their faces, cast dull reflections in their eyes.

Some of the people were hangies, and some of them were smooths. Nobody looked at anyone else. Nobody spoke, nobody moved. No one did anything at all.

"Well, I am near certain this is where I ought to be," said Mary Beth. "I just know I have seen this place before."

The bus, she was sure, was parked just past the building ahead, the one where the squiggly crack ran up and down.

When she turned the corner, though, the bus wasn't there. What was there instead was a steep set of stairs. A sign above the stairs in scribbly black read,

DOWN

"My word," Mary Beth said aloud, "Down doesn't help a great deal. Down where?"

"First floor, Mary Beth. . . ," said a voice like a rattle, like a shriek, like a clatter, like a howl inside a din, a voice that cut and cleaved the very air. **". . . Pharts**
Phat
Phlegm
Phleas
Pestilence and Piss . . .

"Second floor,
Pigs
Puss
Puppy dogs and pain

"Third floor—"

"Please," said Mary Beth, "I don't even *know* what you're talking about. I *don't* know how you know my name."

"I'm good with people," said the voice. **"People are what I do."**

"I'm afraid I don't understand that, either."

"Hey, no problem. So how do you like the tour so far?"

Mary Beth wanted to be polite, but wasn't sure what she ought to say. Mostly, she was too surprised to say anything at all. This—*person* had simply appeared, in a blink, where the stairs ought to be.

That was quite peculiar, but the man himself was the strangest thing of all. He was gaunt, pale, not very tall, and he really had a very nice smile. His face and his bare and bony chest were covered in coils, whirls, swirls within whorls. When you tried to follow one pattern to the next, they did funny things to your head.

The eyes, though—Mary Beth had to blink twice—the eyes were two shiny bright coins, set in deep hollows in the maze, in the twisted patterns of his face. The eyes made Mary Beth want to look away, manners or not.

He sat there with a friend, sat behind a charred, scarred wooden table, sat there against something cloudy, something veiled, something dark and indistinct. The dark was hard to look at, like the man's eyes.

"Oh, just fine, thank you," Mary Beth answered finally. "The tour is really—quite nice."

"It is?" The man smiled, and he winked one silver eye. **"I'll have to speak to someone about that."**

Mary Beth wasn't good at funny, but she smiled anyway.

"I don't know your name," she said, knowing that was the proper thing to do, "though you seem to know mine."

"Bob. You can call me Bob."

"That's a very good name."

"You like Steve any better? Jack? George? How about Hampton Burke-Sykes III?"

"Really. Bob's just fine with me." She had to admit, though, he didn't seem very Bob at all. She wasn't sure what would really fit.

She didn't want to ask about the friend. That, again, was the right thing to do, unless Bob said something first. The friend was quite odd, even among the people she'd come across here. She had two pointies in front. You didn't have to see any more to know she was a smooth. Both of her eyes were sewn shut. Her ears and her nose had been cut with something sharp. Her mouth was torn in a wide and empty smile.

Mary Beth decided the smile wasn't real. This was a person who clearly didn't have any happy right now.

"Bill Jim's looking all over for you, Mary Beth. You're supposed to stay with the tour. No one ever comes here."

"I'm sorry, truly. I do apologize. I would never do anything on purpose to offend."

"Now I know that. You're a very, very good person, Mary Beth. But hey, I can overlook that."

Hoarse, cackly laughter came from the gloom, echoed from the dark behind Bob and the smooth. Mary Beth was sure she saw a host of shiny eyes before they vanished in the dark.

The man glanced over his shoulder with a smile that twisted the whorls and spirals in his face, twisted them all into something that wasn't there before. Then, he looked back at Mary Beth. Holding her in his gaze, he picked up a glass from the table, a glass so black, she couldn't guess what was inside. He drank the liquid down, smacked his lips and tossed the glass away, off into the black.

"Oh, my, manners," he said, in a voice that sounded just like Mary Beth. He turned politely to the smooth. **"You sure you won't have something? No? Not right now? Maybe later? Fine."**

The smooth didn't answer, of course. Didn't move, didn't do anything at all.

"Tell me about yourself," Bob said, though Mary Beth imagined there was much that he already knew. **"Tell me the things you like to do."**

"I like flowers and trees. I guess I like birds best of all. I guess I know the names of a zillion or two."

"That's a lot of birds, Mary Beth."

"It might not be that many. I really wouldn't know."

"What else, Mary Beth?"

"Oh, I do like to sing. I like to sing with Liza Lee. She's my best friend. I mean, I like everybody *else,* too."

"And you like being Home? You like it there, don't you, Mary Beth?"

"My, yes, I surely do."

"Better than you'd like being here, I suppose."

"Oh. Well . . ."

"Just teasing, Mary Beth. Bob's a big teaser, anyone'll tell you that. You ever see the Old Man? Ever talk to the Kid?"

"Who?" Mary Beth had to think about that for a moment; then she understood.

"Why, yes. Whenever I can, I surely do."

"When you see them, Mary Beth, will you give them this for me?"

"Now that's very nice, I—"

Bob's hand appeared in a blur, opened wide, and there was something smoky, something horrid, something vile.

"Oh. Oh—my goodness!" Mary Beth said.

Bob smiled, tried to catch her with his eyes, tried to snap her up, tried to draw her in, knew he couldn't do it, knew she was safe as safe can be, but he always had to try.

Mary Beth took a step back, felt a new remember, felt a new remember called *dread, shiver, quiver*, and *afraid,* felt it for a blink before it went away. Hoped, prayed she would never remember it again.

She was gone, then, gone as quickly as she could, and she never, ever, looked back the other way. . . .

The bus had never looked so bright, so clean and so white, so cool and inviting inside. Even in the thick and fevered air, under the drear and clotted sky, the bus was as shiny and new as it could be.

Bill Jim had clearly saved up a lot to say to Mary Beth, but when the time came, he sighed, gave her a What's the use? look and let the words just slide away.

Most of the group had picked up free souvenirs. Liza Lee had a cap with little horns. Johnny Dee had a scary paper mask. There were faded, raggedy shirts that read,

SURE, IT'S HOT.
BUT IT'S A *DRY* HEAT

I BEEN UP
AND I BEEN
D
O
W
N

Some of the shirts read HARVARD, YALE, and M.I.T. Mary Beth didn't understand the shirts at all, and didn't think anybody did.

When everyone was inside again, and Bill Jim had counted them twice, the door wheezed shut, and the bus began to roll out of town.

No one said a lot as they passed the same hovels and falling-down shacks, burrows and piles of bricky stone they'd passed coming in.

"Before we get to the bridge," Bill Jim called back, "you folks will have to toss out all those souvenirs. That's the rules. You can't take anything back out of here."

Everyone did as they were told. No one really seemed to mind. Now that they were on the way Home, people were starting to chatter and gather in little groups to sing. They began to get rid of their cloze—the folder said not to do that until they got past the bridge, but a lot of people did. Mary Beth and Liza Lee joined in, and they both felt better after that.

"I am not real sure I enjoyed the tour as much as I should," Liza Lee confided to her friend. "Do you know what I mean?"

Mary Beth had to smile. "I'm supposed to be the big grouchy face here. You caught me yourself, Liza Lee."

"Oh, now I didn't mean it *that* way. It just kind of slipped out. Really, I'm doing a happy right now."

"That's good. That's what we need to do."

Mary Beth understood how Liza Lee felt, for she still had remembers left, too. Not too many, and there weren't any big ones anymore.

"Everyone, listen up a minute, please," called out Bill Jim. "We're running a little late because we didn't *all* get back in time. Now, we're going to be seeing something up ahead. As your guide, I'd advise you to talk among yourselves while we're crossing the river and the bridge. This isn't something you folks need to see, I promise you that."

Of course, the minute Bill Jim said that, *everyone* ran to the left side of the bus. No one wanted to miss anything they really shouldn't see.

They made it just in time. The other bus was coming at them fast. You had to look quickly; it was there and it was gone, whining, rushing past in a blur, going the other way.

It was dark, scarred, dented. Bashed, mashed and wantonly trashed. It was covered with dust, grime, ages and eras, millennia of rust. And, as it passed, each broken window was filled with a bare and scrawny bottom, each bum, each cheek, each gluteal lump a gallery of ancient, forgotten whorls and swirls, convolutions and knotty coils. Then the bus and its odd, unnatural rumps were far behind, and they were over the bridge at last.

"Well," said Mary Beth, "I surely don't understand that."

"I don't see any reason why we should," said Liza Lee.

Past the high ridge of dark and ragged stone, up the narrow road. Once past the road, Mary Beth recalled, they would see the forest and the lovely hills again, and after that, Home.

What she hadn't remembered, hadn't recalled, was the pocked, ulcerated, quite uncomfortable man who was squatting by the side of the road.

He was there, just as he'd been before, screaming in silence as the hideous, never-ending piles slicked from his body to the ground.

Everyone quickly looked away. Everyone but Mary Beth. Why she kept looking, she really couldn't say. She didn't *want* to, but something made her stay. So she looked, and then she looked again. Looked at the man, watched him until she could scarcely see him anymore, until the bus was nearly past. Looked, looked into the twisted features, into the pale, lost and tortured eyes. And, though she knew it couldn't be, she imagined—for an instant—the man looked back.

"*William,*" she said, the word just suddenly there, rising out of nowhere at all.

"Oh, Will. Oh my, goodness me . . ."

The remember flickered in, flickered out again, and then it was gone, just as quickly as it came. . . .

Tom Disch *is a poet, novelist, short-story writer, book reviewer, critic (*The Dreams Our Stuff Is Made Of, *which won a Hugo), children's book author (*The Brave Little Toaster*), teacher (Wesleyan, the University of Minnesota), playwright, and, for all I know, astronaut and master chef. He has an acerbic wit and a mind like a steel trap.*

When he described to me over the phone the story you are about to read, I nearly dropped the receiver, I was laughing so hard.

The White Man

Thomas M. Disch

If human testimony, taken with every care and solemnity, judicially, before commissions innumerable, each consisting of many members, all chosen for integrity and intelligence, and constituting reports more voluminous perhaps than exist upon any other class of cases, is worth anything, it is difficult to deny, or even to doubt the existence of such a phenomenon as the vampire.

J. Sheridan Le Fanu,
Carmilla

It was the general understanding that the world was falling apart in all directions. Bad things had happened, and worse were on the way. Everyone understood that—the rich and the poor, old and young (although for the young it might be more dimly sensed, an intuition). But they also understood that there was nothing much anyone could do about it, and so you concentrated on having some fun while there was any left to have. Tawana chewed kwash, which the family grew in the backyard alongside the house, in among the big old rhubarb plants. Once they had tried to eat the rhubarb, but Tawana had to spit it out—and a lucky thing, too, because later on she learned that rhubarb is poison.

The kwash helped if you were hungry (and Tawana was hungry even when her stomach was full) but it could mess up your thinking at the same time. Once in the third grade when she was transferred to a different school closer to downtown and had missed the regular bus, she set off by herself on foot, chewing kwash, and the police picked her up, crying and shoeless, out near the old airport. She had no idea how she'd got there, or lost her shoes. That's the sort of thing the kwash could do, especially if you were just a kid. You got lost without even knowing it.

Anyhow, she was in high school now, and the whole system had changed. First, when there was the Faith Initiative, she'd gone to a Catholic school, where boys and girls were in the same room all day and things were very strict. You couldn't say a word without raising your hand, or wear your own clothes, only the same old blue uniform every day. But that lasted less than a year. Then the public schools got special teachers for the Somali kids with Intensive English programs, and Tawana and her sisters got vouchers to attend Diversitas, a charter school in what used to be a parking garage in downtown Minneapolis near the old football stadium that they were tearing down. *Diversitas* is the Latin word for "diversity," and all cultures were respected there. You could have your own prayer rug, or chant, or meditate. It was the complete opposite of Our Lady of Mercy, where everybody had to do everything at the same time, all together. How could you call that freedom of religion? Plus, you could wear pretty much anything you wanted at Diversitas, except for any kind of jewelry that was potentially dangerous. There were even prizes for the best outfits for the week, which Tawana won when she was in the sixth grade. The prize-winning outfit was a Swahili ceremonial robe with a matching turban that she'd designed herself with duct tape. Ms. McLeod asked her to wear it to the assembly when the prizes were given out, but that wasn't possible, since the towels had had to be returned to their container in the bathroom. She wasn't in fact Swahili, but at that point not many people (including Tawana) knew the difference between Somalia and other parts of Africa. At the assembly, instead of Tawana wearing the actual robe, they had shown a picture from the video on the school's surveillance camera. Up on the screen Tawana's smile must have been six feet from side to side. She was self-conscious about her teeth for the next week. (Kwash tends to darken teeth.)

Ms. McLeod had printed out a small picture from the same surveillance tape showing Tawana in her prize-winning outfit, all gleaming white with fuzzy pink flowers. But in the background of that picture there was another figure in white, a man. And no one who looked at the picture had any idea who he might have been. He wasn't one of the teachers, he wasn't in maintenance, and parents rarely visited the school in the daytime. At night there were remedial classes for adult refugees in the basement classrooms, and slams and concerts, sometimes, in the auditorium.

Tawana studied his face a lot, as though it were a puzzle to be solved. Who might he be, that white man, and why was he there at her ceremony? She taped the picture on the inside of the door of her hall locker, underneath the magnetic To Do list with its three immaculately empty categories: SHOPPING, SCHOOL, SPORTS. Then one day it wasn't there. The picture had been removed from her locker. Nothing else had been taken, just that picture of Tawana in her robe and the white man behind her.

That was the last year there were summer vacations. After that you had to go to school all the time. Everybody bitched about it, but Tawana wondered if the complainers weren't secretly glad if only because of the breakfast and lunch programs. With the new year-round schedule there was also a new music and dance teacher, Mr. Forbush, with a beard that had bleached tips. He taught junior high how to do ancient Egyptian dances, a couple of them really exhausting, but he was cute. Some kids said he was having a love affair with Ms. McLeod, but others said no, he was gay.

On a Thursday afternoon late in August of that same summer, when Tawana had already been home from school for an hour or so, the doorbell rang. Then it rang a second time, and a third time. Anyone who wanted to visit the family would usually just walk in the house, so the doorbell served mainly as a warning system. But Tawana was at home by herself, and she thought what if it was a package and there had to be someone to sign for it?

So she went to the door, but it wasn't a package; it was a man in a white shirt and a blue tie lugging a satchel full of papers. "Are you Miss Makwinja?" he asked Tawana. She should have known better than to admit that's who she was, but she said, yes, that was her name. Then he showed her a badge that said he was an agent for the Census Bureau, and he just barged into the house and took a seat in the middle of the twins' futon and started asking her questions. He wanted to know the name of everyone in the family, and how it was spelled and how old they all were and where they were born and their religion and did they have a job. An endless stream of questions, and it was no use saying you didn't know, 'cause then he would tell her to make a guess. He had a thermos bottle hanging off the side of his knapsack, all beaded with sweat the same as his forehead. The drops would run down the sides of the bottle and down his forehead and his cheeks in zigzags like the mice trying to escape from the laboratory in her brother's video game. "I have to do my homework now," she told him.

"That's fine," he said, and just sat there. Then after they both sat there for a while, not budging, he said, "Oh, I have some other questions here about the house itself. Is there a bathroom?"

Tawana nodded.

"More than one bathroom?"

"I don't know," she said, and suddenly she needed to go to the bathroom herself. But the man wouldn't leave, and he wouldn't stop asking his questions. It was like going to the emergency room and having to undress.

And then she realized that she had seen him before this. He was the man behind her in the picture. The picture someone had taken from her locker. The man she had dreamed of again and again.

She got up off the futon and went to stand on the other side of the wooden trunk with the twins' clothes in it. "What did you say your name was?" she asked warily.

"I don't think I did. We're not required to give out our names, you know. My shield number is K-384." He tapped the little plastic badge pinned to his white shirt.

"You know *our* names."

"True. I do. But that's what I'm paid for." And then he smiled this terrible smile, the smile she'd seen in stores and offices and hospitals all of her life, without ever realizing what it meant. It was the smile of an enemy, of someone sworn to kill her. Not right this moment, but someday maybe years later, someday for sure. He didn't know it yet himself, but Tawana did, because she sometimes had psychic powers. She could look into the future and know what other people were thinking. Not their ideas necessarily, but their feelings. Her mother had had the same gift before she died.

"Well," the white man said, standing up, with a different smile, "thank you for your time." He neatened his papers into a single sheaf and stuffed them back in his satchel.

Someday, somewhere, she would see him again. It was written in the Book of Fate.

All that was just before Lionel got in trouble with the INS and disappeared. Lionel had been the family's main source of unvouchered income, and his absence was a source of deep regret, not just for Lucy and the twins, but for all of them. No more pizzas, no more Hmong takeout. It was back to beans and rice, canned peas and stewed tomatoes. The cable company took away all the good channels, and there was nothing to look at but Tier One, with the law and shopping channels and really dumb cartoons. Tawana got very depressed and even developed suicidal tendencies, which she reported to the school medical officer, who prescribed some purple pills as big as your thumb. But they didn't help much more than a jaw of kwash.

Then Lucy fell in love with a Mexican Kawasaki dealer called Super Hombre and moved to Shakopee, leaving the twins temporarily with the family at the Twenty-sixth Avenue N.E. house. Except it turned out not to be that temporary. Super Hombre's Kawasaki dealership was all pretend. The bikes in the show window weren't for sale, they were just parked there to make it look like a real business. Super Hombre was charged with sale and possession of a controlled substance, and Lucy was caught in the larger sting and got five to seven. Minnesota had become very strict about even minor felonies.

Without Lucy to look after them, the niños became Tawana's responsibility, which was a drag not just in the practical sense that it meant curtailing her various extracurricular activities—the Drama Club, Muslim Sisterhood, Mall Minders—but because it was so embarrassing. She was at an age when she might have had niños of her own, but instead she'd preserved her chastity. And all for nothing because here she was just the same, wheeling the niños back and forth from day care, changing diapers, screaming at them to shut the fuck up. But she never smacked them, which was more than you could say for Lionel or Lucy. Super Hombre had been a pretty good care provider, too, when he had to, except the once when he laid into Kenny with his belt. But Kenny had been asking for it, and Super Hombre was stoned.

The worst thing about being a substitute mom were the trips to the County Health Center. Why couldn't people be counted on to look after their kids without a lot of government bureaucrats sticking their noses into it? All the paperwork, not to mention the shots every time there was some new national amber alert. Or the blood draws! What were they all about? If they did find out you were a carrier, what were they going to do about it anyhow? Empty out all the bad blood and pump you full of a new supply, like bringing a car in for a change of oil?

Basically Tawana just did not like needles and syringes. The sight of her own blood snaking into the little clouded plastic tube and slowly filling one cylinder after another made her sick. She would have nightmares. Sometimes just the sight of a smear of strawberry jam on one of the twin's bibs would register as a bloodstain, and she would feel a chill through her whole body, like diving into a pool. She *hated* needles. She hated the Health Center. She hated every store and streetlight along the way to the Health Center. And most of all she hated the personnel. Nurse Lundgren with his phony smile. Nurse Richardson with her orange hair piled up in an enormous bun. Dr. Shen.

But if someone didn't take the twins in to the Health Center, then there would be inspectors coming round to the house, perhaps even the INS. And more papers to fill out. And the possibility that the niños would be taken off to foster care and the child care stipends suspended or even canceled. So someone had to get them in to the Health Center and that someone was the person in the family with the least clout. Tawana.

Thanksgiving was the big holiday of the year for the Makwinjas, because of the turkeys. Back in the '90s, when the first Somalis had come to Minnesota, their grandfather among them, they'd all been employed by E. G. Harris, the biggest turkey processor in the country. Tawana had seen photographs of the gigantic batteries where the turkeys were grown. They looked like palaces for some Arabian sheikh, if you didn't know what they really were. One of the bonuses for E. G. Harris employees to this day was a supersize frozen bird on Thanksgiving and another at Christmas, along with an instruction DVD on making the most of turkey leftovers. There were still two members of the family working for E. G. Harris, so well into February there was plenty of turkey left for turkey potpie, turkey noodle casserole, and turkey up the ass (which was what Lucy used to call turkey à la king).

The older members of the family, who could still remember what life had been like in Somalia, had a different attitude toward all the food in America from that of Tawana and her sisters and cousins. Their lives revolved around cooking and grocery shopping and food vouchers. So when the neighborhood Stop & Shop was shut down and CVS took over the building, the older Makwinja women were out on the picket line every day to protest and chant and chain themselves to the awnings. (They were the only exterior elements that anything *could* be chained to: the doors didn't have knobs or handles.) Of course, the protests didn't accomplish anything. In due course CVS moved in, and once people realized there was nowhere else for fourteen blocks to buy basics like Coke and canned soup and toilet paper, they started shopping there. One of the last things that Tawana ever heard her grandfather say was after his first visit to the new CVS to fill his prescription for his diabetes medicine. "You know what," he said, "this city is getting to be more like Mogadishu every day." Aunt Bima protested vehemently, saying there was no resemblance at all, that Minneapolis was all clean and modern, while Mogadishu had always been a dump. "You think I'm blind?" Grandpa asked. "You think I'm stupid?" Then he just clamped his jaw shut and refused to argue. A week later he was dead. An embolism.

Half a block from the CVS, what used to be a store selling mattresses and pine furniture had subdivided into an All-Faiths Pentecostal Tabernacle (upstairs) and (downstairs) the Northeast Minneapolis Arts Cooperative. There was a sign over the entrance (which was always padlocked) that said IRON y MONGERS and under that what looked almost like an advertisement from *People* or *GQ* showing four fashion models with big dopey grins under a slogan in mustard-yellow letters: WELL-DRESSED PEOPLE WEAR CLEAN CLOTHES. In the display windows on either side of the locked door were mannequins dressed entirely in white. The two male mannequins sported white tuxedoes, and there were a number of female mannequins in stiff sheer white dresses and veils like bridal gowns but sexy. There were bouquets of paper flowers in white vases, and a bookcase full of books all painted white—like the hands and faces of the mannequins. The paint had been applied as carefully as makeup. The mannequins' eyes were realistically blue or green and their lips were bright red, even the two men.

The first time she saw them, Tawana thought the mannequins were funny, that the paint on their faces was like the makeup on clowns. But then, walking by the windows a few days later, during a late afternoon snow flurry, she was creeped out. The mannequins seemed half-alive, and threatening. Then, on a later visit, Tawana started feeling angry, as though the display in the windows was somehow a slur directed at herself and her family and all the African Americans in the neighborhood, at everyone who had to walk past the store (which wasn't really a store, since it was always closed) and look at the mannequins with their bright red lips and idiot grins. Why would anyone ever go to the trouble to fix up a window like that? They weren't selling the clothes. You couldn't go inside. If there was a joke, Tawana didn't get it.

She began to dream about the two mannequins in the tuxedos. In her dream, they were alive but mannequins at the same time. She was pushing the twins in their stroller along Twenty-seventh Avenue, and the two men, with their white faces and red lips, were following her, talking to each other in whispers and snickering. When Tawana walked faster, so would they, and when she paused at every curb to lift or lower the wheels of the stroller, the two men would pause, too. She realized they were following her in order to learn where she lived; that's why they always kept their distance.

The man in charge of the All-Faiths Pentecostal Tabernacle was a Christian minister by the name of Gospel Blantyre Blount, D.D., and he came from Malawi. "Malawi," the Reverend Blount explained to the seventh-grade class visiting the Tabernacle on the second Tuesday of Brotherhood Month, "is a narrow strip of land in the middle of Africa, in the middle of four *Z*s. To the west is Zambia and Zimbabwe, and to the east is Tanzania and Mozambique. I come from the town of Chiradzulu, which you may have read about or even seen on the news. The people there are mostly Zulus, and famous for being tall. Like me. How tall do you think I am?"

No one raised a hand.

"Don't be shy, children," said Ms. McLeod, who was wearing a traditional Zulu headress and several enormous copper earrings. "Take a guess. Jeffrey."

Jeffrey squirmed. "Six foot," he hazarded.

"Six foot ten inches," said Reverend Blount, getting up off his stool and demonstrating his full height, and an imposing gut, as well. "And I'm the short guy in the family."

This was greeted by respectful, muted laughter.

"Anyone here ever been to Africa?" Reverend Blount asked, in a rumbling, friendly voice, like the voice in the Verizon ads.

"I have!" said Tawana.

"Oh, Tawana, you have not!" Ms. McLeod protested with a rattle of earrings.

"I was born here in Minneapolis, but my family is from Somalia."

Reverend Blount nodded his head gravely. "I've been there. Somalia's a beautiful nation. But they got problems there. Just like Malawi, they got problems."

"Gospel," Ms. McLeod said, "you promised. We can't get into that with the children."

"Okay. But let me ask: How many of you kids has been baptized?"

Six of the children raised their hands. Jeffrey, who hadn't, explained: "We're Muslim, the rest of us."

"The reason I asked, is in the Tabernacle here, we don't think someone is a 'kid' if they been baptized. So the baptized are free to listen or not, as they choose."

"Gospel, this is not a religious matter."

"But what if it is? What it is, for sure, is a matter of life and death. And it's in the *newspapers*. I can show you! Right here." He took a piece of paper from an inside pocket of his dashiki, unfolded it, and held it up for the visitors to see. "This is from the *New York Times,* Tuesday, January fourteenth, 2003. Not that long ago, huh? And what it tells about is the *vampires* in Malawi. Let me just read you what it says at the end of the article, okay?

> In these impoverished rural communities [they're talking about Malawi], which lack electricity, running water, adequate

> food, education and medical care, peasant farmers are accustomed to being battered by forces they cannot control or fully understand.
>
> The sun burns crops, leaving fields withered and families hungry. Rains drown chickens and wash away huts, leaving people homeless. Newborn babies die despite the wails of their mothers and the powerful prayers of their elders.
>
> People here believe in an invisible God, but also in malevolent forces—witches who change into hyenas, people who can destroy their enemies by harnessing floods. So the notion of vampires does not seem far-fetched.

Reverend Blount laid the paper down on the pulpit and slammed his hand down over it, as though he were nailing it down. "And I'll just add this. It especially don't seem far-fetched if you seen them with your own eyes! If you had neighbors who was vampires. If you seen the syringes they left behind them when they was all full of blood and sleepy. 'Cause that's what these vampires use nowadays. They don't have sharp teeth like cats or wolves—they got syringes! And they know how to use them as well as any nurse at the hospital. Real fast and neat, they don't leave a drop of blood showing, just slide it in and slip it out." He pantomimed the vampires' expertise.

"Gospel, I'm sorry," Ms. McLeod admonished, "we are going to have to leave. Right now. Children, put your coats on. The reverend is getting into matters that we had agreed we wouldn't discuss in the context of Brotherhood Month."

"Vampires are real, kids," Reverend Blount boomed out, sounding more like Verizon than ever. "They are real, and they are living here in Minneapolis! If you just look around, you will see them in their white suits and their white dresses. And they are laughing at you cause you can't see what's there right under your nose."

Before she got up from her folding chair to follow Ms. McLeod out of the tabernacle, Tawana took one of the bulletins from the stack on the windowsill next to her. It was the first time in her life that she had taken up any kind of reading matter without being told to. Maybe she wasn't a kid anymore. Maybe the words of Gospel Blantyre Blount, D.D., had been the water of her baptism, just as they'd talked about at the Catholic school. They said if you were baptized and you died, your flesh would be raised incorruptible. That's how she felt leaving the All-Faith Tabernacle, incorruptible.

* * *

In April, the governor declared the ten counties of the Metro area a Disaster Area and called in the National Guard to help where the roads were washed away and in those areas that had security problems, especially East St. Paul and Duluth, where there had been massive demonstrations and looting. In Shakopee, six African-American teenagers were killed when their Dodge Ram pickup was swept off Route 19 by the reborn Brown Beaver River. An estimated twelve thousand acres of productive farmland were lost in that single inundation, and the president (who had vetoed the Emergency Land Reclamation Act) was widely blamed for the damage sustained throughout the state.

Despite all these tragedies, there hadn't been one school day canceled at Diversitas, though the bus service was now optional and rather expensive. Morning after soggy morning Tawana had trudged through the slush and the puddles in her leaky Nikes, which she had thrown such a scene to get when Aunt Bima had wanted to get her a cheaper alternative at the Mall of America. Now Tawana had no one but herself to blame for her misery, which made it a lot more of a misery than it would otherwise have been.

It was only the left Nike that leaked, so if she was careful where she stepped, her foot would stay dry for the whole thirty-four blocks she had to walk. Sometimes, if it wasn't raining too hard, she'd take a slightly longer route that passed by the CVS and other stores that had awnings she could walk under, making an umbrella unnecessary. Tawana hated umbrellas. That longer route also took her past the All-Faiths Tabernacle and the Northeast Minneapolis Arts Cooperative on the ground floor.

There, on the day after the governor's declaration, the "Well-Dressed People" display had been taken down and a new display mounted. The sign this time said

ENTERTAINMENT IS FUN—
FOR THE WHOLE FAMILY!

The same white-faced mannequins, in the same white clothes, were seated in front of an old-fashioned TV set with a dinky screen, and gazing at a tape loop that showed a part of a movie that they had all had to watch at school in the film-appreciation class. You could hear the music over an invisible speaker: "Singing in the rain . . ." The same snippet of the song over and over as the man on the TV whirled with his umbrella about a lamppost and splashed in the puddles on the street. Maybe it was supposed to be fun, like the sign in the window said, but it only made Tawana feel more miserably wet.

The next day it drizzled, and the same actor (Gene Kelly, it said at one point in the loop) was still whirling around the same lamppole to the same music. Then, to Tawana's astonishment, a door opened behind the TV set and a real man (but dressed in a white suit like the mannequins) stepped into the imaginary room behind the window. Tawana knew him. It was Mr. Forbush who had been the music and dance teacher at Diversitas two years earlier. His hair was shorter now and dyed bright gold. When he saw Tawana staring at him, he tripped his head to the side and smiled, and wiggled his fingers to say hello. Then he turned round to get hold of a gigantic, bright yellow baby chick, which he positioned next to the mannequins so it, too, would be looking at *Singin' in the Rain.*

When Mr. Forbush was satisfied with the baby chick's positioning, he began to fluff up its fake feathers with a battery-powered hair dryer. From time to time, when he saw Tawana still standing there under the awning, wavering between amusement and suspicion, he would aim the blow dryer at his own mop of wispy golden curls.

"Well, hello there," said a man's voice that seemed strangely familiar. "I believe we've met before."

Tawana looked to the side, where the Rev. Gospel Blantyre Blount, D.D., was standing in a black dashiki in the shadows of the entrance to the Tabernacle.

"You're Tawana, aren't you?"

She nodded.

"Would you like something to eat, Tawana?"

She nodded again and followed the minister up the dark stairway, leaving Gene Kelly singing and spinning around in the endless rain.

Reverend Blount poured some milk powder into a big mug and stirred it up with water from a plastic bottle, added a spoonful of Swiss Miss Diet Cocoa, and put the mug into a microwave to cook. After the bell dinged, he took it out and set it in front of Tawana on what would have been the kitchen table if this were a kitchen. It was more like an office or a library, with piles of paper on the table, and two desks, lots of bookcases. There was also a sink in one corner with a bathroom cabinet over it and a pile of firewood, though nowhere to burn any of it. A pair of windows let in some light from the back alley, but not a lot, since they were covered by pink plastic shower curtains, which were drawn almost closed so you could get only a peek at the back alley and the rain coming down.

"Nothing like a hot cup of cocoa on a rainy day," Reverend Blount declared in his booming voice. Tawana concurred with a wary nod and lifted the brim of the cup to her lips. It was more lukewarm than hot, but even so, she did not take a sip.

"I'll bet you're wondering why I called you here."

"You didn't call me here," Tawana said matter-of-factly. "I was looking at the crazy stuff inside that window downstairs."

"Well, I *was* calling, sending out a mental signal, and you *are* here, so figure that out. But you're right about that window. It's crazy, or something worse. Aren't you going to drink that cocoa?"

Tawana took a sip and then an actual swallow. Before she set the mug back down, she'd drunk down half the cocoa in it. All the while, Rev. Gospel Blantyre Blount kept his eyes fixed on her like a teacher expecting an answer to a question.

Finally he said, "It's the vampires, isn't it? You want to know about the vampires."

"I didn't say that."

"But that's what you was thinking." His large eyes narrowed to sly, knowing slits.

Tawana hooked her finger into the handle of the mug. It *was* the vampires. Ever since she'd read the stuff in the church bulletin that she'd taken home, she'd wanted to know more than just what was there in writing, most of it taken out of newspapers. She wanted the whole truth, the truth that didn't get into newspapers.

"You actually saw them yourself, the vampires?"

Reverend Blount nodded. His eyes looked sad, the lids all droopy, with yellowish scuzz in the corners. From time to time, he'd wipe the scuzz away with a fingertip, but it would be there again within a few blinks.

"What'd they look like?"

"Just the same as people you see on the street. Tall mostly, but then that's so for most us Malawis. They always wear white. That's how they get their name in Bantu. The White Man is what we call a vampire. It's not the same as calling someone a white man over here, though most vampires do have white skin. Not all, but the overwhelming majority."

Tawana pondered this. In the one movie she had ever seen about her own native country of Somalia, she had noticed the same thing. All the

American soldiers who went into the city of Mogadishu to kill the people there were white, with one exception. That one black soldier didn't have a name that she could remember, but she remembered him more clearly than all the white soldiers, because he behaved just the way they did, as though they'd turned him into one of them. If there could be black soldiers like him, why not black vampires?

"I saw the movie," she said, by way of offering her own credentials. And added (thinking he might not know which movie), "The one in black-and-white."

"*Dracula*!" said the Reverend Blount. "Yeah, that is one kind of vampire, all right. With those teeth. Don't mess with that mother. But the White Man is a different kind of vampire. He don't bite into your neck and suck the blood out, which must be a trickier business than they let on in the old movie. No, the White Man uses modern technology. He's got syringes. You know, like at the doctor's office. Big ones. He jabs them in anywheres, sometimes in the neck, or in the arm, wherever. Then when the thing is filled up with blood, he takes off the full test-tube-thing and wiggles in an empty one. As many times as he needs to. Sometimes he'll take all the blood they got, if he's hungry. Other times, but not that often, he'll only take a sip. Like you, with that cocoa. That's how new vampires get created. 'Cause there is some vampire blood inside the syringe, and it gets into the victim's bloodstream and turns them into vampires themselves. AIDS works just the same. You know about AIDS?"

Tawana nodded. "We have to study it at school. And you can't share needles."

"True! Especially with the White Man."

Tawana had a feeling she wasn't being told the whole story, just the way grown-ups never tell you the whole story about sex. Usually you had to listen to them when they thought you weren't there. Then you found out.

"The vampire you saw," she said, shifting directions, "was it just one? And was it a man or a woman?"

"Good question!" Reverend Blount said approvingly. "Because there can be lady vampires. Not as many as the men, but a lot. And to answer your question, the only ones I ever saw for sure was men. But I have met some ladies I thought might of been vampires—black ladies—but I cleared out before I could find out for certain. If I hadn't of, I might not be here now."

Tawana felt frustrated. Reverend Blount answered her questions honestly enough, but even so he seemed kind of . . . slippery. He wasn't telling her the *details*.

"You want to know the exact details, don't you?" he asked, reading her mind. "Okay, here's what happened. This was back in 1997, and I was studying theology at the All-Faiths Mission and Theological Seminary in Blantyre, which is the city in Malawi that has had the biggest vampire problem but which is also my middle name because I was born there. Well, one day Dr. Hopkins, who runs the Mission, assembled all the seminarians to the hall and told us we would be welcoming a guest from the United Nations health service, and he would be testing us for AIDS! Dr. Hopkins said how we should be cooperative and let the man from the UN do his job, because it was a humanitarian mission the same as ours, and there had to be someone to set an example. The health service, it seems, was having a problem with cooperation. People in Malawi don't like a stranger coming and sticking needles into them."

"I hate needles," Tawana declared fervently.

"Well, we all hate needles, sister. And why us? We had to wonder. Of course, at that time, no one in Blantyre really believed in AIDS. People got sick, yes, and they died, some of them, but there can be other explanations for that. Most people in Malawi thought AIDS was witchcraft. A witch can put a spell on someone and that someone starts feeling bad and he can't . . . do whatever he used to. And dies. Only this wasn't any ordinary kind of witchcraft."

"It was the White Man!"

Reverend Blount nodded gravely. "Exactly. Only we didn't know that then. So we agreed to go along with what Dr. Hopkins was asking us to do, and this 'guest' came to the Seminary, and we all lined up and let him take our blood. Only *I* refused to let him have any of mine, 'cause I had a funny feeling about the whole thing. Well, some time went by, and we more or less forgot about the visit we had. But then the guest returned and talked to Dr. Hopkins, and then he talked with four of the seminarians. But I think there was more than talk that went on. It was like he'd drained the blood right out of them. They were dead before they died. And within a month's time, they was genuinely dead, all four of them. It was all hushed up, but I was one of the people Dr. Hopkins asked to clean up their rooms after. And you know what I found? Syringes. I showed them to Dr. Hopkins, but he said just get rid of them, that is nothing to do with the Seminary. Well, what was it then? I wondered. They wasn't taking drugs in the Seminary. I don't think so! It wasn't AIDS, not them boys."

"It was the White Man," Tawana said.

Reverend Blount nodded. "It was the White Man. He tasted the different kinds of blood we sent him, and those boys had the taste the White Man liked best. So he kept coming back for more. And once a vampire has had his first taste, there's nothing you can do to stop him coming back for more. That old movie had it right there. I don't know how the vampires got to them, but those four boys sure as hell didn't commit suicide, which was what some of them at the Seminary was insinuating. Their whole religion is against suicide. No. No. The White Man got them, plain and simple."

"Tawana!" Ms. McLeod exclaimed with her customary excess of gusto. "Come in, come in!" The school's principal placed her wire-framed reading glasses atop a stack of multiple-choice Personnel Evaluation forms that had occupied the same corner of her desk since the start of the spring quarter, an emblem of her supervisory status and a clear sign that her rank as principal set her apart from graders of papers and monitors of lunchrooms.

Tawana entered the principal's office holding up the yellow slip that had summoned her from Numerical Thinking, her last class before lunch.

"Is this your essay, Tawana?" Ms. McLeod asked, producing three pages of ruled paper. The title—"Our Somali Brothers and Sisters: A Minnesota Perspective"—was written with orange Magic Marker in letters two inches high. Under it, on a more modest scale, was the author's name, Tawana Makwinja.

"Yes, Ms. McLeod."

"And the assignment was to write a letter about your family's cultural heritage. Is that right?"

Tawana dipped her head in agreement.

"Would you," purred Ms. McLeod, handing the paper to Tawana "read it aloud—so I can hear it in the author's own voice?"

Tawana looked down at the paper, then up at Ms. McLeod, whose thin, plucked eyebrows were lifted high to pantomime attentiveness and curiosity. "Just begin at the beginning."

Tawana began to read from her essay:

> It is difficult to determine exactly the number of Somalis living in the Twin Cities. Minnesota Department of Human Services has estimated as many as 15,000, but the Somalia Council of Minnesota maintains that these figures are greatly inflated. Over 95 percent of Somali people in Minnesota are refugees. Many So-

malis in Minnesota are single women with five or more children, because so many men were killed in the war.

According to Mohammed Essa, director of the Somali Community in Minnesota, the role of women as authority figures in U.S. society is different from Somalia, where few women work outside the home and men do not take instruction from women. For instance, the two sexes do not shake hands. Somalis practice corporal punishment, and many complain that the child protection workers are too quick to take away their children.

Somali religious tradition requires female circumcision at the youngest possible age, in order to ensure a woman's virginity, to increase a man's sexual pleasure, and promote marital fidelity. However, this practice is outlawed in Minnesota. Before the circumcision of an infant daughter, there is a 40-day period called the *afartanbah,* followed by important celebrations attended by friends and family members that involve the killing of a goat.

Somalis are proud of their heritage and lineage. Children and family are deeply valued by Somalis, who favor large families. Seven or more children are common. Due to resettlement and the inability to keep families together in refugee situations, few Somali children in Minnesota live with both parents. The availability of culturally appropriate childcare is a major issue in Minnesota.

Tawana looked up cautiously, as after a sustained punishment. Ms. McLeod had made her read the whole thing out loud. She would rather have been whipped with a belt.

"Thank you, Tawana," said Ms. McLeod, reaching out to take back the essay. "There were a *few* pronunciation problems along the way, but that often happens when we read words we know only from books. I'm sure you know what all the words *mean,* don't you?"

Tawana nodded, glowering.

"This one, for instance—*corporal*? What kind of punishment might that be? Hmm? Or *lineage*? Why exactly is that a source of pride, Tawana?"

Ms. McLeod went on with word after word. It really was not fair. Tawana wasn't stupid, but Ms. McLeod was trying to make her look stupid. Making her read her essay aloud had been a trap.

"Have *you* ever attended an *afartanbah,* Tawana?"

Tawana raised her eyes in despair. What kind of question was that! "What is a . . . the word you said?"

"You answered that question in your own essay, Tawana. It is a celebration forty days after the birth of a baby sister. Have you had such a celebration at your home, where there was goat?"

"Who eats goats in Minnesota?" Tawana protested. "You can't get goats with food stamps. I don't even *like* goat!"

With a thin smile Ms. McLeod conceded defeat in that line of interrogation and shifted back to pedagogic mode. "I want you to understand, Tawana, that there is nothing *wrong* with quoting from legitimate sources. All scholars do that. But note that I said *sources,* plural. To copy out someone else's work word for word is not scholarship, it is plagiarism, and that is simply against all the rules. Students are expelled from university classes for doing what you have done. So you will have to write your essay over, from scratch, and not just copy out . . . this!" She produced a printout of the same study from the Center for Cross-Cultural Health, "Somali Culture in Minnesota," that the school librarian had called up on the Internet for Tawana's use.

"That was the bad news," said Ms. McLeod with a sympathetic smile. "The *good* news is that you have really lovely handwriting!"

"I do?"

"Indeed. Firm, well-rounded, but not . . . childish. I don't know where you developed such a hand—not here at Diversitas, I'm sorry to say. The emphasis here has never been on fine penmanship."

"The nuns taught the Palmer method at my last school."

"Well, you must have been one of their best students. Now, penmanship is a genuine skill. And anyone with a skill is in a position to earn money! How would you like a *job,* Miss Makwinja?"

Tawana regarded the principal with ill-concealed dismay. "A job? But I'm just . . . a kid."

"Oh, I don't mean to send you off to a nine-to-five, full-time place of employment. No, this would be a part-time job, but it would pay more than you would earn by baby-sitting. And you could work as much or as little as you like, if you do a good job."

"What would I have to do?"

"Just copy out the words of a letter with your clear, bold penmanship. We can have an audition for the job right now. Here is the text of the letter I want you to copy. And here is the stationery to write on. You should be able to fit the whole letter on a single page, if you use both sides of the paper. Don't rush. Make it as neat as your essay."

Tawana regarded the letterhead on the stationery:

Holy Angels School of Nursing and Widwifery
4217 Ralph Bunche Boulevard Kampala
Uganda, East Africa.

"Here." Ms. McLeod placed a fat fountain pen on top of the Holy Angels stationery. "A real pen always makes a better impression than ball-point."

Tawana began to copy the letter, neatly and accurately, including all its mistakes.

Dear friend in Christ's Name,

I send you warm greeting hoping you are in a good-sounding health. I am so happy to write to you and I cry for your spiritual kindness to rescue me from this distressed moment.

I am Elesi Kuseliwa, a girl of 18 years old, and a first born in a family of 4 children. We are orphans.

I completed Ordinary level in 2003 and in 2004 I joined the above-mentioned school and took a course in midwifery. Unfortunately in October both our parents perished in a car accident on their way from church. We were left helpless in agony without any one to console or to take care of us. Life is difficult and unbearable.

This is my last and final year to complete my course of study. We study three terms a year and each term I am supposed to pay 450 UK pounds. The total fee for the year is 1350 pounds. I humbly request you to sympathize and become my sponsor so I may complete my course and to take my family responsibilities, most importantly, paying school fees for my younger sisters.

Enclosed is a photocopy of my end of third term school report. I pray and await your kind and caring response.

Yours faithfully,
Elisi Kuseliwa

"Very good," said Ms. McLeod when she had looked over the finished copy. "That took you just a little over fifteen minutes, which means that in an hour you should be able to make four copies just like this. Now I understand that girls your age can earn as much as two-fifty at baby-sitting. I'll do better than that. I'll pay four dollars an hour. Or one dollar for each letter you copy. Do we have a deal?"

What could Tawana say but yes.

Tawana still had one friend left from when she'd gone to Our Lady of Mercy, Patricia Brown. That was not her Somali name, of course. She'd become Patricia Brown when her mother died and she was adopted into the Brown family. She was a quiet, plodding bully of a girl, already two hundred pounds when Tawana had met her in fourth grade, and now lighting up the screen on the scale at 253. Tawana had won her friendship by patiently listening to Patricia's ceaseless complainings about her foster parents, her siblings, her teachers, and her classmates at Our Lady of Mercy, a skill she had learned from having sat still for Lucy's long whines and Grandpa's rants. In exchange for her nods and murmurs Tawana was able to see shows on the Browns' TV that Tawana couldn't get at home. That is how Tawana (and Patricia, as well) came to be a fan of *Buffy the Vampire Slayer.*

At first, the later afternoon reruns had been as hard to understand as if you arrived at a stranger's house in the middle of a complicated family quarrel that had been going on for years. You couldn't tell who was right and who was wrong. Or in this case who was the vampire and who wasn't. Buffy herself definitely wasn't, but she had her own superhuman powers. When she wanted to, she could zap one of the vampires to the other side of the room with just a tap of her finger. Sometimes she would walk up to a vampire and start talking to him and then without a word of warning whack him through the heart with a wooden stake. But other times, confusingly, she would fall in love with some guy who would turn out to be a vampire, but that didn't stop their being in love.

Patricia said there was a simple explanation. The vampires were able to confuse people by their good looks, and Buffy would eventually realize the mistake she was making with Spike and whack him just like the others. Tawana was not so sure. Spike might be a vampire, but he seemed to really love Buffy. Also, he looked a lot like Mr. Forbush, with the same bleached hair and thin face and sarcastic smile. Though, as Patricia had pointed out, what did that have to do with anything! It was all just a story like *Days of Our Lives,* only more so since it was about vampires and vampires are only make-believe. Tawana did not tell Patricia about the real vampires in Malawi. Everything that she had learned about the White Man was between her and Rev. Gospel Blount.

But in the course of watching many episodes of *Buffy* and thinking them over and discussing them with other kids at Diversitas, Tawana developed a much broader understanding of the nature of vampires and the powers they possessed than you could get from an out-of-date movie like *Dracula*. Or even from reading books, though Tawana had never actually tried to do that. She was not much interested in books. Even their smell could get her feeling queasy.

The main thing to be learned was that here in America, just the same as in Reverend Blount's native land of Malawi, there were vampires everywhere. Most people had no idea who the vampires were, but a few special individuals like Buffy, or Tawana, could recognize a vampire from the kind of fire that would flash from their eyes, or by other subtle signs.

The vampires in Minneapolis were usually white, and they tended to be on the thin side, and older, especially the men. And they would watch you when they thought you weren't looking. If you caught them at it, they would tilt their head backwards and pretend to be staring at the ceiling.

A lot of what people thought of as the drug problem was actually vampires. That was how they kept themselves out of the news. All the people who died from a so-called drug overdose? It was usually vampires.

Then one day in May toward the end of seventh grade, Tawana developed a major insight into vampires that was all her own. She was in the Browns' living room with Patricia and her younger brother Michael watching a rerun of *Buffy* that they all had seen before. Patricia and Michael were sitting side by side in the glider, spaced out on Michael's medication, and Tawana was sitting behind them, keeping the glider rocking real slow with her toe, the same as if they were the twins in their stroller. Instead of looking at the story on the TV, Tawana's attention was fixed on the big statue of Jesus on the wall. There were silver spikes through his hands and feet, and his naked body was twisting around and his neck stretched up, trying to escape the crucifix. Tawana realized that Jesus looked exactly like one of the vampires when Buffy had pounded a wooden stake into him. Their skin was the same clouded white, the same expression on their faces, a kind of holy pain. Not only that, but with Jesus, the same as with vampires, you might think you had killed him but then a day or two later he wasn't in the coffin where you thought. He was out on the street again, alive.

Jesus had been the first White Man!

Tawana kept rocking the two Brown children, and sneaking sideways glances at the crucifix, and wondering who in the world she could ever tell about her incredible insight, which kept making more and more sense.

The priests, the nuns, the missionaries! Hospitals and health clinics. The crucifixes in everybody's homes, just like the story of Moses when the Jews in Egypt marked their doors with blood to keep out the Angel of Death!

Everything was starting to connect. Here in America and there in Africa, for centuries and centuries, it was all the same ancient never-ending struggle of good against evil, human against vampire, Black against White.

On July 3, in preparation for the holidays, the Northeast Minneapolis Arts Cooperative once again changed its window display in the store that was never open underneath the All-Faiths Tabernacle. The old ENTERTAINMENT IS FUN—FOR THE WHOLE FAMILY! sign wasn't taken down. Instead WAR was pasted over ENTERTAINMENT, and the mannequins who had been sitting around the imaginary living room watching Gene Kelly on TV had been dismembered, their detached limbs and white clothes scattered around a cemetery made of cardboard tombstones and spray-on cobwebs. A big flag rippled in a breeze supplied by a standing fan at the side of the window, while the hidden sound system played the Jimi Hendrix version of "The Star-Spangled Banner."

Tawana's first reaction, as for the earlier displays, was a perplexed indignation, a sense of having been personally violated without knowing exactly how. But now that she had become more adept at unriddling such conundrums, the basic meaning of the display in the window slowly became clear, like a face on TV emerging from the green and grey sprinkles of static. This was the cemetery that the vampires lived in, only they weren't home. The White Man was hunting for more victims. The limbs beside the gravestones were the remnants of some earlier feast.

It actually helped to know what the real situation was. When there is a definite danger, it is possible to act. Tawana went round to the back of the building. The Arts Cooperative people always used their back door and kept their front door locked, and Reverend Blount did just the opposite. There was no doorbell, so Tawana knocked.

Mr. Forbush answered the inner door and stood behind the patched and sagging screen, blinking. "Yes?" he asked, stupid with sleep.

"Mr. Forbush, can I come in and talk with you?" When he seemed uncertain, she added, "It's about Reverend Blount, upstairs."

Tawana knew from Reverend Blount there were problems between the Arts Cooperative, who owned the building, and the Tabernacle, which was behind in its rent and taking its landlord to court for harassment and other reasons. And sure enough, Mr. Forbush forgot his suspicions and invited Tawana inside.

She was in a space almost as jumbled and crazy as the shop window out front, with some of the walls torn down, and drywall partitions painted to look like pictures, and rugs on top of rugs and piles of gigantic pillows and other piles of cardboard and plastic boxes and not much real furniture anywhere. Tawana had never been anywhere vampires lived, and this was nothing like she would have expected. She was fascinated, and a little dazed.

"What are you looking for?" Mr. Forbush asked. "The bathroom?"

"Are we by ourselves?" Tawana asked, running her fingers across the top of the gas stove as though it were a piano.

Before he could answer, the phone rang. All the tension inside Tawana relaxed away like a puff of smoke. The ring of the phone was the sound of heaven answering her prayers. Mr. Forbush swiveled round in the pile of cushions he'd settled down on, reaching for a cell phone on top of the CD player that sat on the bare floor.

Tawana grabbed hold of the cast-iron frying pan on the back burner of the stove, and before there was any answer to Mr. Forbush's "Hello?" she had knocked him over the head. The first blow didn't kill him, or the second. But they were solid enough that he was never able to fight back. He groaned some and waved his arms, but that did nothing to keep Tawana from slaying him.

Outside, along the driveway, there was an old, old wooden fence that hadn't been painted for years. That provided the stake she needed. She didn't even have to sharpen the end of it. She drove it through his heart with the same frying pan she'd used to smash his head in. She was amazed at the amount of blood that spilled out into the pile of pillows. Perhaps he had been feasting through the night.

There was no use trying to mop the floor, no way to hide the body. But she did change out of her bloody clothes, and found a white dress that must have belonged to one of the mannequins. She wore that to go home in, with her own dirty clothes stuffed in a plastic bag from CVS.

Mr. Forbush's death received a good deal of attention on WCCO and the other news programs, and Reverend Blount was often on the TV to answer questions and deny reports. But no charges were ever brought against him, or against any other suspect. However, it was not possible, after so much media attention, to deny that Minneapolis had a vampire problem just the same as Malawi. There were many who believed that Mr. Forbush had been a vampire, or at least had been associating with vampires, on the principle that where there is smoke there is fire. It was discovered by a reporter on the *Star* that the Arts Cooperative was a legal fiction designed to help Mr. Forbush evade state and local taxes, that he was, in effect, the sole owner, having inherited the property after the bankruptcy of his father's mattress store and the man's subsequent suicide. It was rumored that the father's death might not have been a suicide, and that he had been the first victim of the vampires—or, alternatively, that he had been the first of the vampires.

None of these stories ever received official media attention, but they were circulated widely enough that the All-Faiths Pentecostal Tabernacle became a big success story in the Twin Cities' Somali-American community. Reverend Blount received a special award for his contributions to Interfaith Dialogue from the Neighborhood Development Association, and even after the protests that followed the "Mall of America Massacre" and the effort by the police to close down the Tabernacle, he was saluted as a local hero and a possible candidate for the state senate.

Tawana was never to enjoy the same celebrity status, though as a member of All-Faiths' choir, she had her share of the general good fortune, including her own brief moment of glory in the spotlight. It was during the *NBC Special Report,* "The Vampires of Minnesota." She was in her red-and-white choir robes, standing outside the Tabernacle after a Sunday service. The camera had been pressed up to her face, close enough to kiss, and she'd stared right into it, no smile on her lips, completely serious, and said, "They said it could never happen here. They said it might happen somewhere *primitive* and *backwards* like Malawi, but never in Minneapolis."

Then she just lowered her eyes and turned her head sideways, and they started to roll the credits.

***Patricia A. McKillip** was born in Salem, Oregon—which isn't the witch one. She has published several YA novels, among them* The Forgotten Beasts of Eld, *which won the first World Fantasy Award in 1975.*

She's also written numerous novels for adults, including The Riddle-Master of Hed *trilogy and, most recently,* Ombria in Shadow.

She still lives in Oregon.

Out of the Woods

Patricia A. McKillip

The scholar came to live in the old cottage in the woods one spring. Leta didn't know he was there until Dylan told her of the man's request. Dylan, who worked with wood, cut and sold it, mended it, built with it, whittled it into toothpicks when he had nothing better to do, found the scholar under a bush, digging up henbane. From which, Dylan concluded, the young man was possibly dotty, possibly magical, but, from the look of him, basically harmless.

"He wants a housekeeper," he told Leta. "Someone to look after him during the day. Cook, wash, sew, dust, straighten. Buy his food, talk to peddlers, that sort of thing. You'd go there in the mornings, come back after his supper."

Leta rolled her eyes at her brawny, comely husband over the washtub as she pummeled dirt out of his shirts. She was a tall, wiry young woman with her yellow hair in a braid. Not as pretty or as bright as some, but strong and steady as a good horse, was how her mother had put it when Dylan came courting her.

"Then who's to do it around here?" she asked mildly, being of placid disposition.

Dylan shrugged, wood chips from a stick of kindling curling under his knife edge, for he had no more pressing work. "It'll get done," he said. He sent a couple more feathery chips floating to his feet, then added, "Earn a little money for us. Buy some finery for yourself. Ribbon for your cap. Shoe buckle."

She glanced down at her scuffed, work-worn clogs. Shoes, she thought with sudden longing. And so the next day she went to the river's edge and then took the path downriver to the scholar's cottage.

She'd known the ancient woman who had died there the year before. The cottage needed care; flowers and moss sprouted from its thatch; the old garden was a tangle of vegetables, herbs and weeds. The cottage stood in a little clearing surrounded by great oak and ash, near the river and not far from the road that ran from one end of the wood to the other. The scholar met her at the door as though he expected her.

He was a slight, bony young man with pale thinning hair and gray eyes that seemed to look at her, through her and beyond her, all at the same time. He reminded Leta of something newly hatched, awkward, its down still damp and all askew. He smiled vaguely, opened the door wider, inviting her in even before she explained herself, as though he already knew.

"Dylan sent me," she said, then gazed with astonishment at the pillars and piles of books, scrolls, papers everywhere, even in the rafters. The cauldron hanging over the cold grate was filthy. She could see a half-eaten loaf on a shelf in the open cupboard; a mouse was busily dealing with the other half. There were cobwebs everywhere, and unwashed cups, odd implements she could not name tossed on the colorful, wrinkled puddles of clothes on the floor. As she stood gaping, an old, wizened sausage tumbled out of the rafters, fell at her feet.

She jumped. The scholar picked up the sausage. "I was wondering what to have for breakfast." He put it into his pocket. "You'd be Leta, then?"

"Yes, sir."

"You can call me Ansley. My great-grandmother left me this cottage when she died. Did you know her?"

"Oh, yes. Everyone did."

"I've been away in the city, studying. I decided to bring my studies here, where I can think without distractions. I want to be a great mage."

"Oh?"

"It is an arduous endeavor, which is why I'll have no time for—" He gestured.

She nodded. "I suppose when you've become a mage, all you'll have to do is snap your fingers or something."

His brows rose; clearly, he had never considered the use of magic for housework. "Or something," he agreed doubtfully. "You can see for yourself what I need you for."

"Oh, yes."

He indicated the vast, beautifully carved table in a corner under a circular window from which the sunny river could be seen. Or could have been seen, but for the teetering pile of books blocking the view. Ansley must have brought the table with him. She wondered how he had gotten the massive thing through the door. Magic, maybe; it must be good for something.

"You can clear up any clutter in the place but that," he told her. "That must never be disturbed."

"What about the moldy rind of cheese on top of the books?"

He drew breath, held it. "No," he said finally, decisively. "Nothing on the table must be touched. I expect to be there most of the time anyway, learning spells and translating the ancient secrets in manuscripts. When," he asked a trifle anxiously, "can you start?"

She considered the various needs of her own husband and house, then yielded to his pleading eyes. "Now," she said. "I suppose you want some food in the place."

He nodded eagerly, reaching for his purse. "All I ask," he told her, shaking coins into her hand, "is not to be bothered. I'll pay whatever you ask for that. My father did well with the tavern he owned; I did even better when I sold it after he died. Just come and go and do whatever needs to be done. Can you manage that?"

"Of course," she said stolidly, pocketing the coins for a trip to the market in the village at the edge of the woods. "I do it all the time."

She spent long days at the cottage, for the scholar paid scant attention to time and often kept his nose in his books past sunset despite the wonderful smells coming out of his pots. Dylan grumbled, but the scholar paid very well, and didn't mind Leta taking leave in the late afternoons to fix Dylan's supper and tend for an hour to her own house before she went back to work. She cooked, scrubbed, weeded and washed, got a cat for the mice and fed it too, swept and mended, and even wiped the grime off the windows, though the scholar never bothered looking out. Dylan worked hard, as well, building cupboards and bedsteads for the villagers, chopping trees into cartloads of wood to sell in the market for winter. Some days, she heard his ax from dawn to dusk. On market days, when he lingered in the village tavern, she rarely saw his face until one or the other of them crawled wearily into bed late at night.

"We never talk anymore," she murmured once, surprisedly, to the dark when the warm, sweaty, grunting shape that was Dylan pushed under the bedclothes beside her. "We just work and sleep, work and sleep."

He mumbled something that sounded like "What else is there?" Then he rolled away from her and began to snore.

One day when Ansley had gone down to the river to hunt for the details of some spell, Leta made a few furtive passes with her broom at the dust under his worktable. Her eye fell upon a spiral of gold on a page in an open book. She stopped sweeping, studied it. A golden letter, it looked like, surrounded by swirls of gold in a frame of crimson. All that richness, she marveled, for a letter. All that beauty. How could a simple letter, this undistinguished one that also began her name, be so cherished, given such loving attention?

"One little letter," she whispered, and her thoughts strayed to earlier times, when Dylan gave her wildflowers and sweets from the market. She sighed. They were always so tired now, and she was growing thinner from so much work. They had more money, it was true. But she had no time to spend it, even on shoes, and Dylan never thought of bringing her home a ribbon or a bit of lace when he went to the village. And here was this letter, doing nothing more than being the first in a line of them, adorned in red and gold for no other reason than that it was itself—

She touched her eyes, laughed ruefully at herself, thinking, I'm jealous of a letter.

Someone knocked at the door.

She opened it, expecting Dylan, or a neighbor, or a tinker—anyone except the man who stood there.

She felt herself gaping, but could not stop. She could only think crazily of the letter again: how this man too must have come from some place where people as well as words carried such beauty about them. The young man wore a tunic of shimmering links of pure silver over black leather trousers and a pair of fine, supple boots. His cloak was deep blue black, the color of his eyes. His crisp dark curls shone like blackbirds' wings. He was young, but something, perhaps the long, jeweled sword he wore, made both Dylan and Ansley seem much younger. His lean, grave face hinted of a world beyond the wood that not even the scholar had seen.

"I beg your pardon," he said gently, "for troubling you." Leta closed her mouth. "I'm looking for a certain palace of which I've heard rumors all my life. It is surrounded by a deadly ring of thorns, and many men have lost their lives attempting to break through that ensorceled circle to rescue the sleeping princess within. Have you heard of it?"

"I—," Leta said, and stuck there, slack-jawed again. "I—I—"

Behind the man, his followers, rugged and plainly dressed, glanced at one another. That look, less courteous than the young man's, cleared Leta's head a bit.

"I haven't," she brought out finally. "But the man I work for is a—is trying to be—a mage; he knows a thousand things I don't."

"Then may I speak with him?"

"He's out—" She gestured, saw the broom still in her hand and hid it hastily behind her. "Down by the river, catching toads."

"Toads."

"For his—his magic."

She heard the faint snort. One of the followers pretended to be watching a crow fly; the other breathed, "My lord, perhaps we should ask farther down the road."

"We'll ride to the river," the young lord said, and turned to mount his horse again. He bowed graciously to Leta from his saddle. "Thank you. We are grateful."

Blinking at the light spangling off his harness and jewels, she watched him ride through the trees and toward the water. Then, slowly, she sat down, stunned and witless with wonder, until she heard Ansley's voice as he walked through the doorway and around her.

"I found five," he announced excitedly, putting a muddy bucket on his table. "One of them is pure white!"

"Did you see—?" Her voice didn't come. She was sitting on the floor, she realized then, with the broom across her knees. "Did you see the—? Them?"

"Who?" he asked absently, picking toads out of the bucket and setting them on his papers.

"The traveler. I sent him to talk to you." She hesitated, finally said the word. "I think he is a prince. He is looking for a palace surrounded by thorns, with a sleeping princess inside."

"Oh, him. No. I mean yes, but no I couldn't help him. I had no idea what he was talking about. Come here and look at this white one. You can do so many things with the white toads."

She had to wait a long time before Dylan came home, but she stayed awake so that she could tell him. As he clambered into bed, breathing a gust of beer at her, she said breathlessly, "I saw a prince today. On his way to rescue a princess."

He laughed and hiccuped at the same time. "And I saw the Queen of the Fairies. Did you happen to spot my knife too? I set it down yesterday when I was whittling, and it must have strolled away."

"Dylan—"

He kissed her temple. "You're dreaming, love. No princes here."

The days lengthened. Hawthorn blossoms blew everywhere like snow, leaving green behind. The massive oaks covered their tangled boughs with leaves. An early summer storm thundered through the woods one afternoon. Leta, who had just spread Ansley's washing to dry on the hawthorn bushes around the cottage, heard the sudden snarl of wind, felt a cold, hard drop of rain on her mouth. She sighed. The clothes were wet anyway; but for the wild wind that might steal them, she could have left them out. She began to gather them back into her basket.

She heard voices.

They sounded like wind at first, one high, pure, one pitched low, rumbling. They didn't seem human, which made Leta duck warily behind a bush. But their words were human enough, which made her strain her ears to listen. It was, she thought bewilderedly, like hearing what the winds had to say for themselves.

"Come into my arms and sleep, my lord," the higher voice crooned. "You have lived a long and adventurous life; you may rest now for a while."

"No," the deeper voice protested, half-laughing, half-longing, Leta thought. "It's not time for me to sleep, yet. There are things I still must teach you."

"What things, my heart?"

"How to understand the language of beetles, how to spin with spindrift, what lies hidden in the deepest place in the ocean and how to bring it up to light."

"Sleep a little. Teach me when you wake again."

"No, not yet."

"Sleep."

Leta crept closer to the voices. The rain pattered down now, great, fat drops the trees could not stop. Through the blur of rain and soughing winds stirring up the bracken, she saw two figures beneath an oak. They seemed completely unaware of the storm, as if they belonged to some enchanted world. The woman's long, fiery, rippling hair did not notice the wind, nor did the man's gray-white beard. He sat cradled in the oak roots, leaning back against the trunk. His face looked as harsh and weathered, as ancient and enduring as the wood. The woman stood over him, close enough for him to touch, which he did now and then, his hand caressing the back of her knee, coaxing it to bend. They were both richly dressed, he in a long, silvery robe flecked with tiny jewels like points of light along the sleeves, the hem. She wore silk the deepest green of summer, the secret green of trees who have taken in all the light they can hold, and feel, somewhere within them, summer's end. His eyes were half-closed. Hers were very wide as she stared down at him: pale amber encircling vivid points of black.

Leta froze. She did not dare move, lest those terrible eyes lift from his and search her out behind the bush with Ansley's trousers flapping on it.

"Sleep," the woman murmured again, her voice like a lightly dancing brook, like the sough of wind in reeds. "Sleep."

His hand dropped from her knee. He made an effort, half lifting his eyelids. His eyes were silver, metallic like a knife blade.

"Not yet, my sweet Nimue. Not yet."

"Sleep."

He closed his eyes.

There was a crack as though the world had been torn apart. Then came the thunder. Leta screamed as she felt it roll over her, through her, and down beneath her into the earth. The ancient oak, split through its heart, trailing limbs like shattered bone, loosed sudden, dancing streams of fire. Rain fell then in vast sheets as silvery as the sleeper's eyes. Leta couldn't see anything; she was drenched in a moment and sinking rapidly into a puddle. Rising, she glimpsed the light shining from the cottage windows. She stumbled out of the mysterious world toward it; wind blew her back through the scholar's door, then slammed the door behind her.

"I saw—I saw—," she panted.

But she did not know what she saw. Ansley, his attention caught at last by something outside his books—the thunder, maybe, or the lake she was making on his floor—looked a little pale in the gloom.

"You saw what?"

But she had only pieces to give him, nothing whole, nothing coherent. "I saw his eyes close. And then lightning struck the oak."

Ansley moved then. "Oh, I hope it won't topple onto my roof."

"His eyes closed—they were like metal—she put him to sleep with her eyes—"

"Show me the tree."

She led him eagerly through the rain. It had slowed a little; the storm was moving on. Somewhere else in the wood strange things were happening; the magic here had come and gone.

They stood looking at the broken heart of the oak, its wood still smoldering, its snapped boughs sagging, shifting dangerously in the wind. Only a stand of gnarled trunk was left, where the sleeper had been sitting.

"Come away," Ansley said uneasily. "Those limbs may still fall."

"But I saw two people—"

"They had sense enough to run, it seems; there are no bodies here. Just," he added, "a lot of wet clothes among the bushes. What exactly were those two doing?"

"They're your clothes."

"Oh."

She lingered, trying to find some shred of mystery left in the rain, some magic smoldering with the wood. "He closed his eyes," she whispered, "and lightning struck the oak."

"Well, he must have opened them fast enough then," Ansley said. "Come back into the house. Leave the laundry; you can finish all that later." His voice brightened as he wandered back through the dripping trees. "This will send the toads out to sun. . . ."

She did not even try to tell Dylan, for if the young scholar with all his books saw no magic, how could he?

Days passed, one very like the next. She cooked, washed, weeded in the garden. Flowers she had rescued from wild vines bloomed and faded; she picked herbs and beans and summer squashes. The scholar studied. One day the house was full of bats, the next full of crows. Another day he made everything disappear, including himself. Leta stepped, startled, into an empty cottage. Not a thing in it, not even a stray spider. Then she saw the scholar's sheepish smile forming in the air; the rest of his possessions followed slowly. She stared at him, speechless. He cleared his throat.

"I must have mistranslated a word or two in that spell."

"You might have translated some of the clutter out of the door while you were at it," she said. What had reappeared was as chaotic as ever. She could not imagine what he did at nights while she was at home. Invented whirlwinds, or made his pots and clothes dance in midair until they dropped, it looked like.

"Think of magic as an untamed creature," he suggested, opening a book while he rained crumbs on the floor chewing a crust he had found on his table. "I am learning ways to impose my will upon it, while it fights me with all its cunning for its freedom."

"It sounds like your garden," she murmured, tracking down her gardening basket, which was not on the peg where she hung it, but, for some reason, on a shelf, in the frying pan. The scholar made an absent noise, not really hearing her; she had gotten used to that. She went outside to pull up onions for soup. She listened for Dylan's ax while she dug; he had said he was cutting wood that day. But she didn't hear it, just the river and the birds and the breeze among the leaves.

He must have gone deeper than usual into the woods, she thought. But she felt the little frown between her brows growing tighter and tighter at his silence. For no reason her throat grew tight too, hurt her suddenly. Maybe she had misunderstood; maybe he had gone into the village to sell wood instead. That made the ache in her throat sharper. His eyes and voice were absent, those days. He looked at her, but hardly saw her; he kissed her now and then, brief, chuckling kisses that you'd give to a child. He had never gone to the village so often without her before; he had never wanted to go without her, before . . .

She asked him tentatively that night, as he rolled into bed in a cloud of beer fumes and wood smoke, "Will you take me with you, next time?"

He patted her shoulder, his eyes already closed. "You need your rest, working so hard for two houses. Anyway, it's nothing; I just have a quick drink and a listen to the fiddling, then I'm home to you."

"But it's so late."

He gave her another pat. "Is it? Then best get to sleep."

He snored; she stared, wide-eyed, back at the night.

She scarcely noticed when the leaves first began to turn. Suddenly there were mushrooms and berries and nuts to gather, and apples all over the little twisty apple tree in her own garden. The days were growing shorter, even while there seemed so much more to do. She pulled out winter garments to mend where the moths had chewed; she replenished supplies of soap and candles. Her hands were always red; her hair, it seemed, always slightly damp with steam from something. The leaves grew gold, began to fall, crackle underfoot as she walked from one house to the other and back again. She scarcely saw the two men: the scholar hunched over a book with his back to her, her husband always calling good-bye as he went to chop or sell or build. Well, they scarcely saw her either, she thought tiredly; that was the way of it.

She stayed into evening at the scholar's one day, darning his winter cloak while the stew she had made of carrots and potatoes and leeks bubbled over the fire. He was at his table, staring into what looked like a glass ball filled with swirling iridescent fires. He was murmuring to it; if it answered him, she didn't hear.

At least not for some time. When she began to hear the strange, crazed disturbance beneath the wind rattling at the door, she thought at first that the sound came from within the globe. Her needle paused. The noise seemed to be coming closer: a disturbing confusion of dogs barking, horns, faint bells, shouting, bracken and fallen limbs crackling under the pounding of many hooves. She stared at the glass ball, which was hardly bigger than the scholar's fist. Surely such an uproar couldn't be coming from that?

The wind shrieked suddenly. The door shook on its hinges. She froze, midstitch. The door sprang open as if someone had kicked it. All the confusion in the night seemed to be on the scholar's doorstep and about to roil into his cottage.

She leaped to her feet, terrified, and clung to the door, trying to force it shut against the wind. A dark current was passing the house: something huge and nameless, bewildering until her eyes began to find the shapes in the night. They appeared at random, lit by fires that seemed to stream from the nostrils of black horses galloping past her. The flames illumined great hounds with eyes like coals, upraised sword blades like broken pieces of lightning, cowled faces, harnesses strung with madly clamoring bells.

She stared, unable to move. One of the hooded faces turned toward her as his enormous horse, its hooves sparking fire, cleared her potato rows. The rider's face was gaunt, bony, his hair in many long braids, their ends secured around clattering bones. He wore a crown of gold; its great jewel reflected fire the color of a splash of blood. White moons in the rider's eye sockets flashed at Leta; he opened his jaws wide like a wolf and laughed.

She could not even scream, her voice was that shriveled with fear. She could only squeak. Then the door was taken firmly out of her hands, closed against the night.

The scholar grumbled, returning to his work, "I couldn't hear a thing with all that racket. Are you still here? Take a lamp with you when you go home."

She went home late, terrified at every step, every whine of wind and crackle of branch. Her cold hands woke Dylan as she hugged him close in their bed for warmth and comfort. He raised his head, breathing something that may have been a name, and maybe not. Then his voice came clear.

"You're late." He did not sound worried or angry, only sleepy. "Your hands are ice."

"Dylan, there was something wicked in the woods tonight."

"What?"

"I don't know—riders, dark riders, on horses with flaming breath—I heard horns, as if they were hunting—"

"Nobody hunts in the dark."

"Didn't you hear it?"

"No."

"Were you even here?" she asked incredulously. He turned away from her, settled himself again.

"Of course. You weren't, though, so I went to bed."

"You could have come to fetch me," she whispered. "You could have brought a lamp."

"What?"

"You could have wondered."

"Go to sleep," he murmured. "Sleep."

Winter, she thought as she walked to the scholar's cottage the next morning. There wouldn't be so much work then, with the snow flying. No gardens to tend, no trees to chop, with their wood damp and iron-clad. She and Dylan would see more of one another, then. She'd settle the scholar and come home before dark; they'd have long evenings together beside the fire. Leaves whirled around her. The brightly colored autumn squashes were almost the last things still unpicked in the garden, besides the root vegetables. One breath of frost, and the herbs would be gone, along with most of the green in the world.

"You'll need wood for winter," she reminded the scholar. "I'll have Dylan bring you some."

He grunted absently. She sighed a little, watching him, as she tied on her apron.

I've grown invisible, she thought.

Later, she caught herself longing for winter, and didn't know whether to laugh or cry.

Dylan stacked the scholar's wood under the eaves. The squashes grew fat as the garden withered around them. The air smelled of rain and sweet wood smoke. Now and then the sky turned blue; fish jumped into sunlight; the world cast a glance back at the season it had left. On one of those rare days Leta spread the washing on the bushes to dry. Drawn to the shattered oak, she left her basket and walked through the brush to look at it, search for some sign that she had truly seen—whatever she had seen.

The great, gnarled stump, so thick that two or maybe three of her might have ringed it with her arms, stood just taller than her head. Only this lower, rooted piece of trunk was left intact, though lightning had seared a black stain on it like a scar. It stood dreaming in the sunlight, revealing nothing of its secrets. Just big enough, she thought, to draw a man inside it, if one had fallen asleep against it. In spring, living shoots would rise like his dreams out of the trunk, crown it with leaves, this still-living heart big enough to hide a sleeping mage. . . .

Something moving down the river caught her eyes.

She went through the trees toward it, unable to see clearly what it was. An empty boat, it seemed, caught in the current, but that didn't explain its odd shape, and the hints of color about it, the drift of cloth that was not sail.

She ran down the river path a ways to get ahead of it, so that she could see it clearly as it passed. It seemed a fine, delicate thing, with its upraised prow carved into a spiral and gilded. The rest of it, except for a thin line of gold all around it, was painted black. Some airy fabric caught on the wind, drifted above it, and then fell back into the boat. Now the cloth was blue, now satiny green. Now colors teased at her: intricately embroidered scenes she could not quite make out, on a longer drift of linen. She waited, puzzled, for the boat to reach her.

She saw the face within and caught her breath.

It was a young woman. She lay in the boat as though she slept, her sleeves, her skirt, the tapestry work in her hands picked up by passing breezes, then loosed again. Her hair, the color of the dying leaves, was carefully coiled and pinned with gold. Leta started to call to her. Words stopped before they began. That lovely face, skin white as whitest birch, held nothing now: no words, no expressions, no more movement than a stone. She had nothing left to tell Leta but her silence.

The boat glided past. Golden oak leaves dropped gently down onto the still figure, as though the trees watched with Leta. She felt sorrow grow in her throat like an apple, a toad, a jewel. It would not come out in tears or words or any other shape. It kept growing, growing, while she moved because she still could—walk and speak and tell and even, with a reason, smile—down the river path. She followed the boat, not knowing where it was going, or what she was mourning, beginning to run after a while when the currents quickened and the trees thinned, and the high slender towers of a distant city gleamed in the light of the waning day.

***David Morrell** has been a monster presence in the thriller and suspense fields for the last few decades with titles like* The Brotherhood of the Rose, Burnt Sienna, *and especially* First Blood *and the other books concerning the Vietnam vet John Rambo.*

During that same time, he's also built monuments in the horror field and, when he turns his cool gaze on them, other fields, as well.

This time he provides a fantasy tale right out of the mind of Alfred Hitchcock.

Perchance to Dream

David Morrell

Dr. Baker.
Dr. Baker.

He came to my office on a Friday afternoon. Tall, slender, and sandy haired, he had a thin, aristocratic face that might have been handsome if it hadn't been so haggard. His eyes were puffy, their whites streaked with red. I was surprised when I later learned that he was forty. He looked at least ten years older.

He said his name was Jody Cooke—he emphasized the final *e*—and when I introduced myself as Dr. Gerald Baker, his brow tensed in a painful frown. "Baker. We're both in that nursery rhyme."

"Nursery rhyme?"

"The baker, the cook, and the candlestick maker."

"You've got it slightly wrong," I said.

"Wrong?"

"In the nursery rhyme, it's the butcher, the baker, and the candlestick maker."

"Ah, yes, the butcher," Jody said, his raw eyes going inward, in pain now.

When I asked him about his background, he answered, "I'm a professor at SCAD."

That's a harsh-sounding acronym for a beneficial organization: the Savannah College of Art and Design. He taught classes in architectural restoration, he explained, and had been instrumental in some of the more dramatic renovations in Savannah's once crumbling historic district.

The drawn look on his face emphasized what he said next. "I'm not sleeping well." He stared toward a pamphlet on my desk: the Savannah

Center for Sleep Disorders. It oddly occurred to me that there was only one letter's difference between SCSD and SCAD.

"Do you mean you have trouble falling asleep and you wake often during the night?" I asked.

"Insomnia? No." His forehead wrinkled in confusion. "I go to bed regularly at eleven, and I wake at seven. Eight hours ought to be enough, shouldn't it?"

"For most people," I answered. "There are rare cases of some people needing ten or twelve hours. A few others seem to need only three or four. But it's our opinion that almost everybody doesn't get enough."

"Sleep debt? Isn't that what they call it?"

"Yes."

"I don't think that's my problem. As near as I can tell, I sleep soundly. But I wake up exhausted. Every morning, I feel as though I never went to sleep. Look at me. From my face, you'd think I hadn't slept in weeks. For God's sake, can you help me get some rest?"

A sudden suspicion made me ask, "You came to me for tranquilizers?"

"No. I don't like taking pills. I don't even usually take aspirin. But I can't stand feeling this way. I have trouble concentrating. I've got so little energy, I can barely teach my classes. Can you help?"

I tested him further, emphasizing, "Medications are usually our last resort. If you do have a sleep disorder, behavior modification is sometimes all that's required."

"I'll do *anything*."

"Good. Here's a sleep questionnaire I need you to fill out. Basically, it's a diary. When and what you eat. When you sleep. How long you work. Whether you exercise."

"I play tennis every day."

"Whether you use caffeine or alcohol. They can interfere with sleep."

"I don't use either of them."

"That helps eliminate a possible explanation." I checked an appointment book on my desk. "We'll schedule some tests."

"Tests?"

"Yes, you'll have to make arrangements to come here to sleep. We have some comfortable, pleasant bedrooms. If you normally watch television before you go to sleep, we can provide one."

"Never. I like to read."

"You'll have to wear electrodes attached to various monitors. There'll also be a video camera."

"Electrodes?" Jody said. "A camera?"

"Our subjects feel somewhat self-conscious at first. But their sleep problems soon outweigh their self-consciousness. We require our subjects to spend at least two nights in the clinic. By the second night, they're much less distracted by the equipment."

Jody directed his red-streaked eyes toward the floor. The despair in them was profound. "When can we start?"

I scanned the appointment book. "Next Thursday."

"It can't be sooner?"

"I'm afraid not. We have a waiting list."

"Thursday can't come quickly enough."

I showed him one of the bedrooms, which resembled something in a nice hotel. He barely paid attention to the bedside tables, the lamp, the bureau, and the landscape paintings on the walls. I pointed out an adjacent bathroom and explained that if he had to relieve himself in the night, a technician would unclip his electrodes and then reclip them after he returned from the bathroom. But all Jody seemed to care about was the small camera at the top of a corner across from the bed.

"What time do you want me?" he asked.

"If your normal bedtime is eleven, get here at nine. The first night, it'll take a while to explain things and get you set up. The following night, you needn't be here until ten."

Dr. Baker.

Dr. Baker.

I long ago stopped spending my nights at the sleep-disorder center. Otherwise, I'd have acquired sleep disorders of my own. Instead, I rely on my researchers to monitor the subjects. Each morning, I go through the data and concentrate on any anomalies that have been recorded. It saves a lot of time.

But not that particular night. The telephone woke me at what I later realized was shortly after three. I'd been to a cocktail party that the Savannah Historical Society gave for its main supporters. Groggy, I pawed toward the receiver, fumbled it to my ear, and murmured, "What?"

"I'm sorry to wake you, but you'd better come back here," my top researcher said.

"Is something the matter with—?"

"Jody Cooke. You need to come back here."

In the middle of the night, there was hardly any traffic. It took me only fifteen minutes to reach the center's harshly lit parking garage, and as I stepped from my car, I heard an echoing bang. The building's exit door flew open. Jody Cooke stormed out. He wore loose-fitting pajama shorts. Electrode wires dangled from his head, throat, chest, and legs. His eyes were wild, even redder than when I'd last seen him. Fatigue lines ravaged his face.

"My car. Where's my car?" he demanded.

He held trousers in one hand while his other hand fumbled in them and came out with a set of keys.

"Professor Cooke?" I asked, startled.

His feet were bare. Agitated, he looked one way and then the other in the almost empty parking garage. *"Where's my car?"*

He saw a vehicle behind a van. "There!" He rushed toward it.

My researcher ran from the building, saw Jody unlocking the car, and hurried toward him. "Professor Cooke! Stop! Dr. Baker, help me!"

At that, my surprise wore off. I raced next to my researcher and reached Jody as he opened the car door.

"Stop!" the researcher said. "Dr. Baker, we can't let him drive! He's still asleep!"

"Jody," I shouted, hoping his first name would be more forceful. "Listen to me!"

He struggled.

"Jody, wake up!"

He pushed us away and scrambled into the driver's seat.

"He doesn't know what he's doing!" the researcher yelled. "He'll kill somebody."

Another researcher charged into the parking garage. Frantic, he held a hypodermic, but he would never have been able to get to the car before Jody drove away.

As Jody turned the ignition key, I pressed the center of the steering wheel. The horn's blare was amplified by the concrete in the cavernous garage. It was like an air-raid siren, nerve-torturing, deafening.

It made Jody freeze. As if he'd been punched in the stomach, he slumped forward, pressing his chest against my hand on the steering wheel. The horn kept blaring. He jerked his head up. His eyelids, which had barely moved earlier, now fluttered, confusion and shock coursing through him.

"I . . . What . . ."

"Try to relax. Take a deep breath. Calm yourself."

"What the hell am I doing here?"

Dr. Baker.

Dr. Baker.

"Sleepwalking?" He looked baffled. "Is *that* my problem?" In my office, Jody opened and closed his hands in dismay. Despite the clothes he'd put on, he looked chilled. "Is *that* why I'm always so tired?"

"Not sleepwalking."

He trembled. "But isn't that what I was doing?"

"In a manner of speaking. But that's only one of the symptoms. It appears that what's wrong with you is something we call *parasomnia*."

"What?"

"It's defined as unwilled and unwanted acts during sleep."

"I haven't the faintest idea what you're—"

"Watch this videotape."

Looking disoriented and afraid, he sat with me as I played it. A time counter on the bottom of the image showed that he'd gone to bed at 10:59. He'd read for a brief while—nothing sensational, only a book about renovating historic houses—and then had turned off the bedside lamp at 11:16. A faint night-light near the door to the bathroom was the only illumination, not enough for a normal camera, which was why ours was equipped with night-vision capability, giving the image a characteristic green tint. The camera gazed down from the right corner. Below it, lying under the covers, Jody appeared uncomfortable because of the electrodes attached to him, the wires dangling from under the covers. His eyes closed. In a while, printouts from the various monitors showed that he'd fallen asleep.

He tossed and turned a little, exhaled wearily (the camera had audio capability), and gradually seemed to be at rest. But then, at 2:47, he began fidgeting. "Dr. Baker," he murmured. "Dr. Baker." His movements became exaggerated until he rolled back and forth as if in great distress. Simultaneously, he kept talking to himself. "Where am I?" He repeated that numerous times. "Have to find me." His voice got louder. "Where *am* I? Need to find me!"

At 2:56, he threw off his covers and got out of bed. In a turmoil, he paced back and forth, trailing the electrode wires, clenching and unclenching his fists. "Where the hell have I gone?" His pacing became so violent that he tore some of the electrodes from his body while the wires attached to others were snapped from their monitors. "Damn it, where have I gone?"

At 2:59, a worried researcher entered the room and turned on the overhead lights. Jody showed no reaction either to the researcher's entrance or to the sudden glare. He just kept pacing violently, wanting to know what had become of himself. When the researcher tried to lead him back to the bed, Jody resisted, pushing the man's arms away, shoving him against the wall.

At that, the researcher hurried from the room and closed the door. What he did next wasn't on the tape, but it was part of the log of the event—he ran to a phone and woke me.

Meanwhile, Jody became more agitated. He paced forcefully to the limits of the room, slamming his hands against each wall. He yanked the bureau away from the wall. He tore the mattress and the box springs off the bed and stared at the floor under it. Then he jerked the door open and disappeared into the corridor. The time was now 3:08.

"We don't have cameras in other parts of the center, only in the bedrooms," I explained, "so we don't have any video of what happened next. From what the staff tells me, you stalked the halls, asking where you were. You barged into the four other bedrooms and woke the subjects we were studying. You became louder and more distressed. Just before I arrived, you grabbed your trousers from the bedroom and found your way to the parking garage."

"Asking where I was."

"Yes."

"I hadn't the faintest awareness of what I was doing."

"It doesn't appear so."

"My eyes were open."

"Yes. For sleepwalkers, that's rare. Most of them just stumble around, often injuring themselves."

"But *my* movements were purposeful." Jody looked ashen. "I have to assume I've been doing something similar at home for many nights in a row, searching the house. That's why I wake up feeling so tired. I've never torn the bedroom apart before. I'm getting worse. Does any of this make sense to you? What did you call it? Parasomnia?"

"Some subjects get down on all fours and howl like dogs. Others eat cigarettes or chew boxes of Kleenex, spitting out wads. Still others fight imaginary attackers, punching doors and walls, sometimes bloodying themselves or even breaking their hands."

Jody looked horrified. "But what *causes* this? Powerful dreams?"

I studied him. "Are you sure you want to discuss this now? If you don't feel alert, you might not be able to—"

"Talk to me, Dr. Baker. Help me understand what the hell's going on."

"Here's the short version of what happens when you sleep."

Jody leaned forward, concentrating.

"There are five stages," I explained. "The first is light sleep. The second is moderate sleep. The third and fourth are degrees of *deep* sleep. As well, there's the REM stage."

"Rapid eye movement."

"Yes. Vivid dreams are more likely to occur during this phase."

"Then that's when this must have happened, when I was going through a REM stage and responding to a dream."

"Not normally," I said.

"What do you mean?"

"One of the characteristics of the REM stage is that, while our eyes are darting back and forth behind our eyelids, our muscles lapse into a form of paralysis."

"Paralysis?" Jody asked.

"We can breathe and swallow and so forth. But our arms and legs aren't capable of functioning in a normal fashion. This seems to be a survival trait. Otherwise, if we dreamed that we were being attacked or that we were falling, our bodies might respond so violently that we'd injure ourselves."

"My God," he said.

"But some parasomniacs have a flaw in their sleep process that activates their muscles during the REM phase of sleep. Instead of being paralyzed, they react physically to dreams, often for the worse."

Jody sounded desperate. "Can you tell if I was in a REM phase when I started acting the way I did?"

"Before you tore the wires from the monitors?" I nodded and picked up the printouts, but what I saw made me frown. "The EEGs and EMGs for your brain wave and muscle-tone measurements indicate that you were not in a REM stage. Your muscles were perfectly functional. Your eyes weren't moving rapidly behind your lids. In fact, you weren't even in *deep* sleep. According to this, you were in stage two."

"Moderate sleep?"

"Yes."

"Does a person have vivid dreams in stage two?"

"No."

"Then what makes me act that way? *Every night.*"

"I'm sorry," I said. "Until we do more tests, I don't have an answer."

Jody groaned.

Dr. Baker.
Dr. Baker.

After testing subjects during a sleep period, we require them to return to the clinic four times during the next day. They interrupt their regular activities to lie down and try to nap while we monitor their brain waves, pulse, blood pressure, and so forth.

Jody arrived on schedule at ten a.m., but before I could ask him how he was feeling, I knew something was wrong. "Dr. Baker," he said. "Dr. Baker." He looked even more tired. His eyes were even more raw and haunted. But what troubled me was that his movements weren't only lethargic; they were clumsy, as if he wasn't conscious of them.

"Where am I?" he wanted to know.

But he wasn't talking about his location, as his next statement made clear. I was so caught by surprise, I couldn't speak.

"Have to find where I am," he told me.

My God, I thought, he's having another episode. He's asleep.

"Have to find myself."

He passed me as if he didn't see me.

"Professor Cooke," I managed to say.

He peered into one room, which fortunately was empty. He peered into another room and interrupted a subject who was doing her best to nap.

"Jody," I said, blocking his way.

The use of his first name worked.

"Please come with me," I said.

I feared that when I gripped his arm, he'd become violent as he had the night before. But in fact, he resisted only slightly when I led him into a bedroom and a researcher hooked him up to the monitors.

"Rest."

"Need to find me."

In my mind, there wasn't any doubt, but the printouts confirmed it—Jody was asleep. Phase two, the same as the night before.

But vivid dreams don't occur during that phase, so how could he be reacting to one? How could he be suffering from parasomnia?

Dr. Baker.
Dr. Baker.

We tested Jody for two further nights and the nap sessions on each subsequent day. His brain and body rhythms still provided no clues as to what was wrong with him. But during the nights, his fits were more extended and violent. As he destroyed each room, tearing apart the bed and looking under it, we were forced to lock his door lest he try to leave the building and possibly kill someone when he attempted to drive.

"Why do you suppose you keep saying that?" I asked as we watched a videotape of his previous night's behavior.

"That I need to find myself?" He seemed to have aged another year. His aristocratic cheeks looked pinched by invisible forceps. His red-streaked eyes were swollen. His sandy hair seemed to have hints of gray.

"Yes."

"Could it be I'm having some kind of, I don't know, out-of-body experience?" Jody asked, appalled by what he was seeing on the videotape. "Maybe, in my sleep, I'm so disoriented that I don't feel connected to myself. Maybe that's why I feel I have to find myself. Is that possible?"

"Let's take this a step at a time. You came here because your unsettled sleep made you exhausted."

"More exhausted every morning," Jody said, his haggard features proving the point.

"Then until I have enough data to understand what's causing this, I'm going to treat the exhaustion itself. When you and I first met, I told you medications were usually a last resort."

"I don't like taking—"

"So you said. But I'm going to prescribe one anyhow. It's called clonazepam."

"What is it?" Jody asked, dreading the answer.

"A sedative?"

"I knew it. I knew it. I hate feeling drugged."

"Do you hate it worse than the way you feel now?"

He seemed to stare right through me. "How is it going to solve my problem?"

"It relaxes the brain enough that the effect is almost the same as if your muscles were in paralysis during the REM phase of sleep. Basically, it'll stop you from doing what's on this videotape. It'll keep you in your bed."

"When I wake up, I won't feel exhausted?"

I nodded. "Because your body will have been able to rest."

"But what about my mind? What about the dreams I'm having that make me do this?"

"If they *are* dreams," I said. "As I told you, vivid dreams and phase two of sleep don't go together. This could be a basic hardwire problem. When you first noticed how exhausted you were in the morning, were you conscious of any major stresses you were going through? Trouble at work or in your personal life?"

He kept staring through me. "No," he finally answered. "Not at all."

"Of course, that doesn't mean you weren't stressed. It just means you weren't aware of it. There's a possibility that, because of stress or whatever, the portion of your brain that controls sleep began malfunctioning. Short circuits are occurring while you sleep. If we use clonazepam to make your brain relax, the short circuits might stop. Your brain might stop triggering the behavior we see on this tape."

Dr. Baker.

Dr. Baker.

It was one of the few times in my career when I'd tested a subject for a fourth night in a row. Jody swallowed a standard dose of clonazepam ninety minutes before going to bed. By the time he shut off the lamp, he was drowsy. I made an exception to my schedule and stayed at the clinic the entire night, watching the monitor printouts and the video screen. Around a quarter to three, the same as on the other nights, he squirmed beneath the covers. "Dr. Baker," he started saying. "Where am I? Have to find me." The tension in his body was obvious; something in him wanting to scramble from bed and begin searching. But the clonazepam had its intended effect. Gradually, his voice became less forceful. ". . . find me," he finally murmured. He lapsed into silence. His body stopped squirming.

"How do you feel?" I asked when he woke up in the morning.

"Groggy."

"That's because of the medication. But do you feel rested?"

Jody wiped a hand across his face. After considering for a moment, he said, "Thank heaven, yes."

"I think we've found a way to help you."

"But I'm still talking in my sleep. I'm still saying I need to find myself."

"If I'm right, as soon as your mind and body regain their energy, whatever synaptical problem in your brain causes these episodes will correct itself."

Dr. Baker.

Dr. Baker.

Jody lived in a splendid old house on Madison Square, one of the twenty-two small squares in Savannah's historical district. Almost a mansion actually, it was one of several whose restorations he'd told me he'd supervised. I didn't ask how he'd been able to buy it, given what I assumed was the modest salary he earned as a professor for the College of Art and Design.

Across from his home, the long limbs of live oaks drooped over the park. Spanish moss hung from them, seductively attractive. But its appeal was deceptive, as many tourists had discovered when they pulled some of the so-called moss from the trees, only to discover that it was infested with bugs.

Jody had given me permission to monitor his progress by installing a video camera in his bedroom and another in the corridor outside. As I assured him, these cameras wouldn't cause any damage to the house's interior. They could be set on tables, with no need for brackets. They could then be plugged into a wall and connected to tape machines placed next to them.

Exhausted from having watched Jody in the clinic all night, I could have arranged for an assistant to set up the cameras while I went home and slept, but my fascination with Savannah's history made me eager to see the two-hundred-year-old home's interior. I parked in the lane in back. Instead of entering from there, I walked along the house and admired the magnificent wrought-iron fence and the flower garden behind it. As with most historical Savannah homes, the front entrance was a floor above the street. At a time of dirt streets, this design had been intended to prevent dust from entering the house. Slaves and servants had occupied rooms on the ground floor. The kitchen and laundry facilities had been on the lower level, also.

Curved steps led up to a pillar on either side of Jody's huge front door. A gleaming black metal railing had a design of clusters of oak leaves. On one of the pillars, a plaque read, JODY COOKE, RESTORATIONS. The other pillar had the metal outline of a pineapple, the symbol for Southern hospitality.

I set down the cameras and pulled out a key that Jody had given me. As I inserted it into the lock, I heard a voice below and behind me:

"Excuse me. May I help you?"

The voice came from a tall blond woman, who was perhaps thirty-five and wore a somber gray suit. She had the high cheekbones and narrow chin of what the fashion magazines consider classical beauty.

"I'm installing some equipment," I said, and then turned the key.

"Why?" The woman came up the curved steps. Her tone was aggressive.

"Because the owner asked me to," I said, annoyed, and pushed the door open.

"Stop right there," the woman said. "Who *are* you?"

More annoyed, I told her, "Gerald Baker. Dr. Gerald Baker. From the Savannah Center for Sleep Disorders."

"Sleep disorders? What on earth are you talking about? *Where did you get that key*?"

"From a patient, who happens to be the house's owner," I said, hoping that would settle the matter and get this busybody out of my way so I could arrange the cameras and go home for a nap.

The woman took a step backward, as if she'd been pushed. For a moment, I feared that she would lose her balance and topple down the stairs. "Jody Cooke?" she asked.

"That's right. Now if you'll excuse us—"

"I'm his sister-in-law," the woman said. "I'm here to get some things I lent him."

That gave her sufficient authority that I decided to pause for a moment and explain. "If you think I don't belong here, use my cell phone"—I pulled it out—"and call him."

"There's nothing I'd like better," the woman said angrily. "Except that he's been dead for a month."

"What?"

"If you don't get out of here, I'll call the police."

"Dead? *No*. There's some mistake. I spoke to Professor Cooke this morning."

"Jody wasn't a professor. He was in real estate."

"I'm telling you, I've been treating a man named Professor Jody Cooke. He teaches at the College of Art and Design. The last time I spoke to him was this morning."

The woman stared at me as if she feared I was insane. "What did he look like?"

"Tall, thin, sandy hair, aristocratic features. He's extremely haggard from a sleep disorder."

Distraught, the woman opened her purse, pulled out a wallet, and removed a photograph.

What I saw made me off-balance enough that I had to grab the railing lest *I* topple down the stairs. In the photograph, two identical men matching Jody's description stood on either side of the blond woman who confronted me. "But . . ."

"This man on the left"—she gestured with a stiff finger—"is . . . was . . . Jody." Her voice thickened with emotion. "This man here on the right is

Jerod Cooke. He's my husband. *He* teaches at the College of Art and Design. I haven't seen him in ten days. Nobody at the college has, either. But the last time I *did* see him, he looked terrible because he hadn't been sleeping well ever since his twin brother had died."

Abruptly, she stiffened. "Sleeping? Oh, my God, you don't suppose . . ." As a startling thought seized her, she raced through the open door.

Hurrying after her, I barely noticed the huge rooms to the right and left of the large corridor. All I paid attention to was the pounding of her shoes on the wooden staircase as I rushed after her. On the upper level, she charged into the second room on the right and froze so quickly that I almost banged into her.

"No," she said.

The bedroom was a shambles. The bureau had been pulled down. The bed had been torn apart. The box spring lay in one corner, the mattress in another. Sheets and clothes were everywhere.

"My God," she said, "*this* is where he's been. Jerod's been living in Jody's bedroom!"

Dr. Baker.

Dr. Baker.

"Identical twins." The woman had finally introduced herself as Michelle Cooke. We sat in the drawing room, which was downstairs on the main floor, one floor above the street. The sounds of sporadic traffic passed below us, but the tops of the drooping trees in the park shielded us from what was underneath. Her voice sounded strained. "When their mother was still alive, she told me how inseparable Jerod and Jody were as children. From the moment they'd been born, they'd reached for one another, trying to embrace as their mother insisted they'd tried to embrace in the womb. As toddlers, they seemed to be able to communicate without speaking. When they did speak, it was often in a private language. They couldn't bear to be separated. Same preschool, grade school, high school, and college. They both played the piano beautifully. Duets." Michelle nodded toward a glinting grand piano in a corner of the room. "They both loved to sail. They both also . . ." A memory made her uncomfortable. "At one time, each of them dated *me* until I chose between them and married Jerod." More uncomfortable, she crossed her legs. "I guess I chose Jerod because he was steadier."

"How do you mean?" I asked.

Michelle indicated a well-stocked liquor cabinet opposite the piano.

"Ah," I said.

"About the only other noteworthy difference between them is that, while they both majored in architecture in college, Jerod chose to go into education while Jody used his knowledge of buildings to buy run-down historic houses, restore them, and sell them at a profit. As you can see from this property, he was very successful."

"How did Jody die?" It gave me an eerie feeling to use the name of a dead man to whom I thought I'd been talking for the past week and a half.

"One of his loves killed him."

I listened with growing apprehension.

"A month ago, Jerod and Jody took a sailboat they owned onto the Savannah River, heading toward the ocean. They did that a lot on weekends. It was something they really looked forward to, a chance to be together and share one of the things they most enjoyed. They'd checked the weather reports and knew there was a slight risk of a storm, but the probability seemed so remote, they decided to go through with their plans. That Saturday morning was glorious. By afternoon, the storm hit. By nightfall, Jody was dead."

"How?" I listened with greater uneasiness.

"Jerod told me how the storm came on so fast and strong, they couldn't get back to port. In fact, they had so little control of the sailboat, the wind threw it onto some rocks."

I leaned forward, listening more tensely.

"Jody injured his head and was pinned beneath wreckage inside the sailboat," Michelle said. "As it sank, Jerod tried to pull him free, but they were underwater, and when Jerod swam to the surface so he could breathe, a wave forced him away. As it was, *Jerod* almost died from being pounded on the rocks. After the storm moved on, some hikers found him unconscious on the shore. He spent two days in the hospital. I tried to assure him he had done everything possible to save Jody, but he wouldn't stop feeling guilty. The night after the funeral at Saint Bonaventure cemetery, Jerod began having sleep problems."

That explains why he was searching for himself, I thought. I must have said it out loud, because Michelle looked puzzled and asked, "What do you mean?"

I told her what had happened at the sleep clinic.

" 'Where am I? Have to find me'?" she asked.

"That's what he kept saying. 'Need to find me.' It was a persistent litany."

Michelle considered the significance. "In his subconscious, Jerod identified with Jody. Mentally, he was searching for him, trying to change places with his dead twin brother."

At once, I remembered something that Jody . . . I had to correct myself . . . that *Jerod* had told me. "He had the answer for what was happening to him. He just didn't know how true his words were."

Michelle moved her head from side to side in confusion.

"I was looking for an explanation in terms of sleep disorders," I said. "I should have realized that if he was in phase two of sleep and couldn't have vivid dreams that would prompt him to act as he did, then the solution had to lie somewhere else. In *psychological* disorders. He wondered if he was having an out-of-body experience. He said maybe he was so disoriented that he didn't feel connected to himself."

"I still don't . . ."

"Sleep therapists often receive training in psychology," I said. "Based on what you've told me, it's now clear that Jerod is dissociating. The memory of what happened has made him create a kind of half-wakeful dream in which he's trying to change reality. If he can only find himself, which I think means Jody, the name he insists on calling himself, then the accident never occurred."

"God help him," Michelle said.

"Oh, he needs help, all right," I said. "The sooner we find him, the better. I believe he's capable of hurting himself."

Michelle reached for the telephone. "I'm calling the police."

"No. We don't want to make him more disturbed."

"But you said we have to find him before he hurts himself."

"Yes," I said. "And I think I know exactly where he is."

Dr. Baker.

Dr. Baker.

We passed through the gates of Saint Bonaventure cemetery. Following Michelle's directions, I took various lanes past tombs, elaborate grave markers, and decaying headstones. The sky was gray from an approaching storm. The name of the trees—live oaks—was a cruel joke. Spanish moss hung from them, seeming almost to touch the roof of my car as we rounded a corner and saw a figure sprawled across a freshly sodded grave.

The figure was Jerod, of course, and the grave, as I'd anticipated, belonged to his twin brother, Jody, whom he'd convinced himself and me that he was. Lying facedown on the grave, he didn't seem to hear the car approach and stop. He didn't turn in our direction when we opened our doors and walked toward him. His back rose and fell spastically. At first, I thought the movement was from forceful breathing. Then I realized he was crying.

"Jerod," Michelle said, using his true name.

He didn't seem to hear, didn't look at us, didn't respond.

"Jerod," she repeated.

No response. His back kept heaving. His sobs were anguished. His fingers dug into the sod.

"Jerod," she tried again. "You have to believe I'm sorry. I didn't mean for it to happen. You've got to forgive me. *Please.*"

Whatever *that* meant. I didn't have time to try to understand. All that mattered was getting his attention.

"Jody," I said, using the name he wanted to assume.

His back stopped moving. His sobs froze. His hands stopped clawing at the dirt.

"Jody," I said, feeling the wind increase, the live oaks and the Spanish moss moving above us. "It'll soon rain. You have to go home."

"Please," Michelle said.

He shifted his gaze toward the name on the headstone: JODY COOKE.

"Go home, Jody," I said.

Tears clinging to his cheeks, he didn't resist when Michelle and I raised him to his feet. His clothes were streaked with dirt and grass stains.

Then he turned to me, and I recoiled, gaping at haggard features and raw red eyes that were mine.

Dr. Baker.

Dr. Baker.

I keep calling for you, but you don't come. Why won't you help me? Baker. Cooke. So close. Sometimes I need you so much, I see myself as you. It's raining. It's suddenly, inexplicably, unnervingly dark. The bug-infested Spanish moss hangs over me. I'm totally alone. I look at my watch. Almost three, the same as on every other night. My car's headlights cast my shadow over the grave, illuminating the name on the headstone. I sink to the ground and claw at the sod.

JODY COOKE.

The man who made a fortune restoring Savannah's crumbling historic houses. The man who loved alcohol as much as his twin avoided it. The man who once dated his brother's wife.

My wife.

And seduced her.

Put his candlestick in.

My wife.

Rub a dub dub.

I wanted to butcher the son of a bitch. SCAD. SCSD. One letter's difference. Slice off his . . . Stuff it in . . . Couldn't let anyone suspect. Lower level. Knocked him over the head. Sank the boat. Drowned him. The candlestick maker. Drowned the candlestick maker. Hidden beneath. Why did he have to . . . Why did she let him put his candlestick in . . . Bug-infested Spanish moss. Loved him more than . . . Reached for him in the salt water of the womb. Drowned him in the salt water of the . . . Out of body, out of mind. Restoration. Pineapple. Prick. Hospitality. Damn her, if Jody's who she wants, Jody's who I'll be!

Not Dr. Baker.

Headlights blazing.

A car roaring toward me.

Doors banging open.

Michelle shouting, "Jerod, I'm sorry!"

Dr. Baker shouting, "Jody!"

"Jerod!"

"Jody!"

"Jerod!"

Dr. Baker.

I swallowed clonazepam.

So how could I have reached this cemetery?

How could I be clawing at this grave?

How could it suddenly be night?

Not in the cemetery.

Lord help me, where *am* I?

In the sleep clinic.

Dr. Baker.

Dr. Baker.

I'm not Dr. Baker. I'm—

"Jerod!"

"Jody!"

Need to find myself.

"Wake up!"

Harry Turtledove's name is synonymous with alternate history. His many novels in that subgenre (such as recent titles American Empire: The Victorious Opposition, Ruled Britannia, *and* Gunpowder Empire*) are fascinating studies in "What if?"*

But by no means has he ever restricted himself to that branch of fantastic literature—and the following story is a prime example.

Coming Across

Harry Turtledove

Lingol dwelt in a land of quiet beauty. Forest and meadow, field and brook, all seemed part of something from the brush of a consummate master. Lingol's elven folk were in the habit of calling the One who had made their world the Artist, in tribute to Her excellence.

They did their best to add to the beauty they knew from their earliest moments. Castles rose white and gleaming. Even huts with thatched roofs were made with care and love, always clean, always comfortable. Elves were as glad to live in a hut as in a castle, especially when they had not done so for a century or two. For beings who lived as long as elves, doing something they had not done for a while was a precious boon.

Sooner or later, everything palled, even quiet beauty.

The lesser folk of that world—fairies and sprites, kobolds and imps—said elves lived forever. It was not quite true. There were times, though, when it seemed like forever. Elves *could* die: of boredom.

They fought it with elaborate games, and with even more elaborate love affairs. Sometimes it was hard to tell, even for them, where the one stopped and the other started. The games—and the affairs—had risks of their own. Elves could also die of accident or other violence, though they were anything but easy to kill.

Murder lay outside the law. Elfslayers faced the most terrible punishment of all: They were exiled to an island of eternal spring, where nothing ever changed. That way lay madness, slow to come but unending once it did.

Odds were that Lingol's people would softly and silently have vanished away, leaving the world richer for their memory, but for the Door. The

Door, without a doubt, was the Artist's greatest gift. For it linked *the* world with another, one as different as could be, one plainly shaped by a different Artist—if it was shaped at all, a point about which the elves argued endlessly. (But then, over what point, however small, did the elves *not* argue endlessly?)

Trips through the Door were rigidly rationed. How could it be otherwise? They would grow boring, too, if they came every year or even every century. Lingol had been waiting more than seven hundred years since his last journey to the other world. He had heard from others who'd gone through more recently that it had changed since his last visit.

Merely the idea of change was enough to make him eager. Again, in a world of eternal sameness, how could it be otherwise?

He'd traveled wisely on his last visit, from Constantinople to Rome to Paris to London. He'd admired all of them, not least because of the occasional bits of beauty lurking amidst the filth and squalor: a mosaic here, a ruined temple there, the tilt of a gargoyle's head somewhere else. And the mayfly lives of the folk in that other world struck him the same way. Even if they stayed healthy, they could not last long. And most of them did not; any one of them suffered more in a year than an elf did in an eternity.

Lingol had done what he could to help, casting spells of wellness over folk suffering from an unsavory assortment of horrifying maladies. But those charms, which would have done so much in his world (where they were so rarely needed), had no effect in the world to which the Door transported him (where they would have meant so much). Elves appreciated irony, as they appreciated all things that were not as they seemed at first glance, but the irony Lingol found there was too sharp, too piquant, even for his taste to savor.

When he came back to his own world, he spoke of what he'd done and how he'd failed. "Things are different there," agreed Belionora, an elf-woman who had visited that same part of the other world no more than a century before him. "Perhaps they have their own answers, for ours do not serve in that place."

"Perhaps they have no answers at all," Lingol said. The bare possibility excited him. Elves always had answers.

"If they do not, they try so hard to pretend they do," Belionora said.

"They do." Lingol nodded, remembering cathedrals and monasteries and nunneries and crosses by the side of the road. "Sometimes they find loveliness of a sort even in the pretense. Did you heard of the one called Francis of Assisi?"

Belionora shook her head; her white-gold locks, finer than spider silk, whipped back and forth. "He had not been born, I believe, when I traveled there."

"Ah." Lingol had to remind himself that births came as quick as deaths in the other world. "He was gone by the time I passed through, but not long gone, and the folk remembered him well and loved him well. By what they said of him, he understood all the troubles of that world and feared none of them."

"A rare spirit indeed," Belionora said.

Then they spoke of other things, but Lingol forgot neither the memories of Francis from the other world nor the conversation with someone he loved well—when the mood suited him, and her.

And when the Doorkeepers gave him as one of the choices for his next journey a city named for this Francis, he leaped at the chance to see it. "You will not find much resemblance," one of the Doorkeepers warned him.

Another Doorkeeper corrected the first: "You will not find *any* resemblance."

"I care not a bit," Lingol said. "Difference is to be cherished as much as resemblance. Difference is to be cherished more than resemblance, in fact, for it is less common. If not for the sake of difference, would the other world be so precious to us?"

The Doorkeepers looked at each other. They did not contradict Lingol, for they knew he had touched on truth. "Let it be as you wish, then," said the one who had corrected the other. "To the place called San Francisco you shall go. Step through the Door."

As Lingol obeyed, the Doorkeepers softly chanted the spells, refined over long millennia, that made the Door something more, something better, than a portal opening on the other world at random. The elf knew a timeless instant of dislocation, of disorientation, unlike anything else he had ever experienced. Then he breathed wild new air. A new sun shone in a new sky. He had come across.

San Francisco seemed all miracle and magic to Lingol. The last time he visited the other world, and all the times before that, the folk who lived there had had all they could do to survive from day to day. He'd pitied them even as he scorned them. They were trying to live like elves, and even the richest and wisest among them could achieve no more than the crudest parody—no, travesty—of the life he had temporarily left behind.

What they had in this city in the year they called 1979 was something else again. It was nothing like what Lingol had left, which only made it more intriguing. The folk remained short-lived, but most of them seemed far healthier than the ones Lingol had known before. They had done what they could with what they had.

And the things they had learned to do! They traveled in carriages that moved with no beasts to draw them, and that rolled swift as a galloping unicorn. They flew in metal birds, faster than any dragon. They knew nothing of crystal balls—which were as ineffective as spells of wellness here, in any case—but they could call to themselves sounds and pictures from around their world. They had even learned to freeze sounds in time somehow, so they might hear them whenever they pleased. Not the greatest elf-mage in Lingol's world could achieve such a marvel.

Lights burned through the night, burned with no smoke, burned with no stink, burned in a marvelous profusion of colors. Other elves had spoken of such things, but not taking travelers' tales seriously was a tradition in more than one land, more than one world.

Before Lingol went through the Door, the Doorkeepers had given him the pieces of paper that served as money in the other world. There was another marvel; on his last visit, only gold or silver would have passed current, as had always been true in his homeworld. The Artist who had made this one had had some very peculiar ideas indeed.

But, in their own context, they worked. The innkeeper's servant to whom he handed the papers took them without complaint and gave him the key to a room that boasted a soft bed, a bath, and hot and cold water that flowed at the turn of a tap: all the comforts of his own world, in other words, though the place was nothing like any he would have found there.

The room also boasted one of the boxes that called in pictures from across this country and across this world. Lingol watched in fascination. The pictures helped give him a better notion of what this quickly changing place was like these days. The words that went with them he took for his own. Like any elf, he had the gift of tongues. The folk here called this one English, but it bore scant resemblance to the language he'd used in London on his last visit here.

He listened to tales of turmoil: of murders, of robberies, of all sorts of violence and excess. He remembered such things from his earlier sojourns here; they were vanishingly rare in his world. For him, they had the thrill not so much of the forbidden but of the unimaginable. That folk made in an image not far removed from his own could do such things! . . .

And their pleasures seemed as outsized, as extravagant as their flaws. When he heard of the Castro district, a slow smile spread across his perfect features. He'd tried such variations before, of course. He knew—and knew of—no elf or elf-woman who had not tried them. Given the long, long span of years his people had to fill, who would *not* try anything, anything at all, to add variety?

But it was, or it had been, different here. When he last visited, men who coupled with men risked torment and death if they were found out. Maybe that had added an extra fillip to such couplings, for they'd gone on nonetheless. Here and now, they seemed accepted, even flaunted. That struck Lingol as very nearly civilized.

It also struck him as most intriguing.

The airline steward checked himself in the mirror in his hotel room before he headed for the bars. Here and in New York City, the competition was tougher than anywhere else in the world. But Gaetan knew he measured up.

"I *am* the prettiest one," he said to himself, first in English and then in the Quebecois French he'd grown up speaking. He started to laugh. He said that whenever he walked into a bar and checked out the scene. And even in San Francisco, a town crawling with the hottest men on the planet, he was right almost every time.

His T-shirt was tight over washboard abs, his jeans even tighter, the bulge in them everything anybody could hope for. He slid a comb out of his back pocket and ran it through his reddish-blond hair one more time. He wanted everything to be perfect. He smiled. It would be. His long face still looked young enough to be called boyish, but from the neck down he was all man.

He loved San Francisco. How could a gay man *not* love San Francisco? Here, you didn't have to pretend to be something you weren't. You could tell the world the truth. And the world, like as not, would invite you back to its apartment for a couple of drinks and whatever happened afterwards.

Or, if you didn't feel like waiting, you could go to the baths. No preliminaries there, no talk, no wasted time. Just right down to business.

Gaetan shook his head. He wanted something more than that tonight. Not something that would last forever, or even very long—he knew better. He wasn't going to find Mr. Right, stop cruising, and settle down. That didn't seem to be in the cards, not for him. But even little affairs were fun while they lasted.

Out he went, smiling to himself. He walked past the first bar he came to. The disco music blasting from the place was too loud to stand. He was a demon out on the dance floor, but if he wanted to make his head ring tonight, he'd do it with poppers, not with Donna Summer.

One of the innumerable Castro clones—muscles, mustache, clothes a lot like his—smiled at him as he walked down the street. He smiled back, but he kept walking. He didn't know exactly what he was looking for—he never did ahead of time—but this guy wasn't it.

Another bar. He nodded to himself. He remembered this place from the last time he'd been in town. They made good drinks, you could hear yourself think inside, and they had a crowd full of good-looking men. He opened the door and walked inside.

A bell over the door jangled. He liked that. It let the guys inside look up from their beers and Harvey Wallbangers and check out each new arrival. It let him pause, strike a pose, and get his first look at who was in the place.

"I am the prettiest—"

The words died unspoken in Gaetan's throat. He wasn't, not tonight. He gaped at the most gorgeous man he—or, he was sure, anybody else—had ever seen.

Gin and tonic was new to Lingol. He liked the taste. He liked what the drink did to him, too. He didn't get sodden, like an imp who'd guzzled too much wine and like more than a few of the men in the tavern with him, but he got happy. No two ways around that.

Folk here didn't do things the way elves did. In his own world, teasing and flirtation could last for years, sometimes decades. They were a pleasure in themselves. When you had all the time in the world, you weren't in a hurry about anything. Small pleasures had their places. They led up to the larger ones and made those sweeter.

When you didn't have all the time in the world, when your lifespan was sharply limited . . .

When you didn't have all the time in the world, you reached out and grabbed with both hands. However ignorant these folks were in other ways, they knew all about that. It was something different for Lingol, something new. Finding the different and the new was more precious to an elf than anything else, even patience. He wouldn't have cared to live like this all the time; he would have been utterly spent after a century or two.

But as long as he was here, why not live as these folk did? Why not revel in living as they did?

He sat in the tavern. He drank. He didn't even have to work to find companions. They came up to him. They came on to him. All he had to do was pick and choose.

When the bell over the door rang one more time, Lingol thought for a moment that another elf had come across and chosen this same tavern. He nearly laughed aloud, which proved how many gin and tonics he'd drunk. They might have blurred his sight a bit, too, for he realized almost at once it was only a man.

Lingol smiled a little. Yes, this fellow would have made a very homely elf. As a man, though, he wasn't bad at all. And he'd seen Lingol, too. There was no possible doubt of that. Lingol had noted the effect his looks had on this folk back in the time when Athens and Sparta fought for supremacy over Greece. That hadn't changed since, not in the slightest.

Well, well, the elf thought. *I wonder what happens next.* He smiled again.

Gaetan shook himself like a dog coming out of cold water. He didn't want to act like an idiot in front of this unbelievable man. Perfect build, sculptured features, platinum-blond hair that couldn't possibly have heard of peroxide, eyes a Siamese cat would have died for, beestung lips . . . *I've had wet dreams that didn't come close to this,* the airline steward thought, awed. *In fact, I haven't had one that did.*

He made himself walk to the bar. He made himself order a Cuba Libre. He made himself sit there and drink it. He made himself watch that impossibly beautiful man only out of the corner of his eye. It wasn't easy. He wanted to stare and stare and stare.

Somebody walked up to him. He shook his head, just a little. He would have done that any which way. The other man drew back. If you weren't desperate, or if he wasn't Mr. Wonderful—sometimes even if he was—you didn't go for the first guy who approached you. If you did, you told the world you hadn't had much luck lately.

That was why Gaetan didn't go up to the blond man—who was Mr. Wonderful and then some—right away. He didn't know how long the man had been in the bar, and he didn't want to get shot down just because he was the first to try. The man was so beautiful—those eyes!—Gaetan wanted to ignore all the rules and rituals. He fought temptation. The cost of screwing up here was just too high.

Elaborately casual, a well-built dark man with a ferocious mustache strolled up to the fellow who'd kept Gaetan from making his usual boast. The steward's hand tightened on his rum and Coke. If Muscles scored . . .

But he didn't. After a few brief words, he walked away. His shoulders slumped. Gaetan didn't think the gorgeous man had been bitchy. Try with somebody like that and miss, though, and you couldn't help being bummed.

Heart pounding, Gaetan got up from his bar stool and walked over to the blond man. He hadn't had to worry about rejection for a long time. He was what almost everybody wanted. But the other man was, too, and even more so. If he turned Gaetan down . . . *I'll have to find another bar, that's all.*

"Hello," he said. "How are you?" He let his French accent come out a little more than he usually did. Maybe seeming exotic would help. He could hope so, anyhow.

"Hello, yourself." To Gaetan's surprise, the beautiful man had a trace of an accent, too. It wasn't French. Also to his surprise, he couldn't quite place what it was, and he'd heard every accent under the sun. Whatever it was, it turned English into music, and he hadn't thought that was possible. Then, to his greater surprise still, the other man went on, "I was hoping you would come over."

"Were you?" Joy flamed through Gaetan. This *was* a better town than New York City. People weren't so stuck-up and stuffy here. Suddenly shy in spite of his delight, he added, "I almost didn't have the nerve."

"You? Don't be silly." The other man's laugh had bells in it. He said, "My name's Lingol. What's yours?"

"Lingol?" Gaetan repeated it to be sure he had it right. The man with the sapphire eyes nodded. "I'm Gaetan," the steward said. *We have something in common,* he thought. *We both have odd first names. Isn't that wonderful?* Everything seemed wonderful just then.

They talked for a little while. It seemed to Gaetan that they might have known each other forever. He'd never imagined such easy intimacy with anybody. Afterwards, he didn't remember which of them asked, "My place or yours?"

When they got up and walked out of the bar together, everybody in the place sighed. Gaetan had heard that before. Usually, most of the sighs were for him. Not tonight. He didn't even care—a telling measure of how smitten he was.

* * *

Lazy in the afterglow, Lingol and his new lover sprawled across the bed. He couldn't have been happier if he'd tried for ten years. He felt filled with this world, both metaphorically and literally. Gaetan had been better than he'd expected: not so skilled as an elf, no doubt, but then he'd had only a handful of years to learn, not a span of at least as many centuries. He snatched at every pleasure as if it might be his last, and gave it as if it might be his lover's last.

"Extraordinary," Lingol murmured, and rolled over to kiss him.

"Hey, you were something yourself," Gaetan answered, his features still slack with delight. "Some of that—where did you learn some of that? I've been everywhere. I've been with everybody. Some of that . . ." He shook his head in evident amazement. "Some of what you know, nobody knows."

No elf would have said such a thing. The logical contradiction was too obvious. Gaetan cared nothing for logical contradictions. In his company, neither did Lingol. The elf said, "You know what you know, I know what I know, and one of the things I know is that I'm glad I found you."

Now Gaetan kissed him. "I'm glad I found you. I never imagined . . ." He didn't say what he hadn't imagined, but Lingol had heard that kind of thing a great many times in this world. The folk here were like poorly drawn copies of elves. Among themselves, it didn't matter. When they saw the real thing, when they heard the real thing, when they touched the real thing, they knew it.

Lingol slid down. Gaetan stiffened quite nicely. In Lingol's world, stamina was a given. Not here. This fellow had it, though—had it and to spare. Lingol paused for a moment. "You see?" he said. "You don't need poppers."

"Not with you." Gaetan gasped as the elf resumed, then went on, "You're better than any popper ever made."

"You say the sweetest things," Lingol answered. Gaetan laughed so hard, he lost what Lingol had given him. But that was easily—and enjoyably—repaired.

They went on far into the night.

Gaetan was in love. He'd imagined himself in love heaven only knew how many times before. This, though—this was the real thing. He judged that by the difference between what he felt now and what all the other times had been like. They'd been brass. Some of them had been highly polished brass, and he'd thought for a while they were gold. Now he really had gold, and it showed him what junk he'd been making do with for so long.

He'd never been the sort who walked out of affairs angry. They went on for a little while, and then they ended, and that was how things went. He had fond memories from a lot of them. His address book was fat as a New York City phone directory. Sometimes he'd look through the names and try to match them to faces and cocks in his memory. He could call up some. Others? Well, they must have looked good at the time.

Lingol he knew he'd remember forever. Sheer beauty would have been enough to ensure that. Lingol was beautiful beyond the point of jealousy. Michelangelo would have cried to see him—and, being what he was, no doubt would have tried other things, as well. Lingol's skin was perfect: pale, smooth, soft, more tightly knit than any woman's. The next zit or blackhead or even scrape Gaetan found on it would be the first. He had a body and a face Michelangelo's *David* couldn't have come close to matching.

And as a lover! . . . As Gaetan boasted, he'd been everywhere, done everything, done and been done by everybody. He hadn't thought there was anything he didn't know. He hadn't thought so, but that only proved how little he'd known. Lingol had endurance and finesse he'd never imagined before, and was hung like a horse besides. That just went with all of his other . . . attributes.

And he was a genuinely nice guy. Some of the prettiest people were also some of the nastiest. The steward had seen that more times than he cared to remember. Not Lingol. He smiled. He laughed. He made silly jokes, and laughed at the ones Gaetan made. He acted as if he was seeing San Francisco for the first time. Gaetan knew that couldn't possibly be true, but enjoyed showing off the city all the same—and not just the Castro district, either, but the touristy things like cable cars and Lombard Street and the Golden Gate Bridge and the Japanese garden in Golden Gate Park and the nearby Asian art museum. The pleasure Lingol took in them made Gaetan take fresh pleasure in them, too.

Love? Love!

Gaetan called in all his vacation time and as much leave as he could get away with. The airline wasn't happy with him, but didn't squawk too loud. Up till now, he'd always been reliable as clockwork, and he was good at his job. They didn't want to lose him, and he made it very plain he'd up and quit if they gave him grief about this.

He amazed himself by actually thinking about settling down, getting domestic. He took out his fat, fat address book, looked at it, and started to laugh. When he came into San Francisco, he'd been sure, and even happy, that that would never, ever happen. Him, the ultimate cruiser, putting bars and baths aside for one man? For Lingol, he would have, and in a red-hot minute, too. Love, again.

He knocked on Lingol's door early one evening. They were going to dinner, and then to Finocchio's. Lingol swore he'd never seen the drag queens. Had he chosen that route, his beauty and his flawless skin would have let him put any of them to shame, but that was a different story. Gaetan hadn't been there for a long time. These days, most of the crowd were straight tourists. But the show would be worth watching with Lingol.

He knocked . . . and no one answered. Frowning, he knocked again. From everything he'd seen, you could set your watch by Lingol. Still no answer, though. *"Calisse!"* Gaetan said. He checked the room number to make sure he wasn't doing something stupid like knocking on the wrong door. How Lingol would laugh at that! But he wasn't. He knocked one more time. When he got only silence, worry began to replace annoyance. Lingol was a tourist here, a stranger. If he'd been unlucky . . .

Hurrying back to the elevators, Gaetan tried the house phone across from them. No one in Lingol's room answered. *"Mauvais tabernac!"* Gaetan snarled. He stabbed the DOWN button with altogether needless violence.

He had to stand in line before he got to the front desk, which did nothing to improve his temper. When he did, the desk clerk, a skinny young fellow with close-cropped hair, gave him the glad eye. He barely noticed; he was too upset. He poured out his worries.

"The gentleman in room 761?" the clerk said. "Oh, yes, sir. I remember *him.* Who wouldn't? Let me see. . . ." He flipped through his cards. "Yes, sir. He checked out this morning."

"What?" Gaetan yelped. "That's impossible!"

"I'm afraid it's true, sir. You never can tell with the really pretty ones, or that's been my experience, anyhow," the clerk said. Gaetan, who *was* one of the really pretty ones, had never thought how things might look from the perspective of his less lucky lovers. Now he had to, and didn't much enjoy it. The clerk went on shuffling papers. "Are you the gentleman called, uh, Gaetan?" As English-speakers did most of the time, he made a hash of the name.

"That's me," Gaetan said grimly, not bothering to correct him. "Why?"

"There's a note here for you." The clerk handed him an envelope of hotel stationery. His name was written on it in an elegant, spidery script that could only have belonged to Lingol.

He tore it open. The note inside was in that same almost calligraphic hand. Dear Gaetan, Lingol wrote,

> I am afraid I must go home. I have enjoyed our time together more than I know how to tell you, and I will remember you forever. It seemed better to me to break clean like this than to have a scene and a quarrel and to ruin what we had. Look back on me and remember how we laughed and loved together. This is the most precious thing here or anywhere. I do not think we will meet again, but you are very special to me.

He sighed his name, and then added a P.S.: *I am sorry not to be able to see Finocchio's with you.*

"Are you all right, sir?" the clerk asked.

"No," Gaetan said simply. The best thing he'd ever known, and now it was gone. How was he supposed to go on? Even as he stood there, though, the cynical part of his mind told him he probably would.

For a little while after coming back through the Door, Lingol was a celebrity. That often happened to elves on their return from the other world. New stories were nearly as precious to them as new experiences. And the stories Lingol had to tell of San Francisco and its multifarious pleasures were more than usually juicy. He didn't even need to exaggerate to make them seem as marvelous to others as they had to him while he was enjoying them.

He hadn't had to exaggerate while writing his farewell note to Gaetan, either. Gaetan would have been hopeless as an elf. As a man, he was a marvel, what they called in the other world a pearl of great price. Lingol *did* miss him, *did* wish him well, and expected to be telling stories about him centuries after he'd gone to dust.

Belionora listened to his tales with a certain ironic glint in her eye. "Since you glutted yourself on the one," she said, "have you decided to forswear the other?"

Lingol laughed. "Not likely!" he said. Nor was it—what elf would willingly forswear any part of experience? As well forswear the use of an arm or a leg or an eye.

The elf-woman arched an elegant eyebrow. "I have seen what a talespinner you are," she said. "Deeds count for more than words."

"I have a way to prove it," Lingol said, and before long he did, to his satisfaction and, very evidently, to hers, as well. He ran a hand along the sweet curve of her back and backside. "Do you see?"

She nodded, more seriously than he'd expected. "You've brought back some of the passion, some of the *now,* from the other world to this one. I've known that to happen before, with other elves newly home again. Never quite like this, though, I don't think."

He stroked her again. "I don't think many elves have found over there what I was lucky enough to find. And since you spoke of passion . . ." He kissed her honeyed mouth. They began once more.

Neither of them worried in the least whether she would conceive—one more difference between Lingol's world and the one on the other side of the Door. There, any time a man and a woman lay down together, she might get up with child unless (and sometimes even if) they took elaborate, often enjoyable, precautions. Elves valued lovemaking for its own sake; if the Artist granted an elf-woman a child, that seemed almost a separate miracle.

Rubbers? The mere idea made Lingol want to laugh at the same time as it turned his stomach.

Belionora must have given him a good report after they went their separate ways. He found himself in considerable demand among elf-women for a while afterwards. And his stories, and the way he acted them out, made him more than commonly popular among elves, as well.

"I won't be able to go through the Door for another five hundred years," complained one named Mafindel. Even for an elf, he was notably handsome. "It will probably all be different by then."

"Yes, it probably will," Lingol said. "They're . . . changeable in the other world. But can I give you something to remember Gaetan by? He's so fresh in my memory, you'll hardly know I'm not he."

Mafindel shrugged. "Well, why not? Go ahead, Lingol. Be a *man* for me." The English word, dropped into the pure and beautiful elven-speech, stood out more starkly than the foulest obscenity would have in English.

Lingol did his best. "Well?" he asked when the moaning and writhing were done.

"Not bad," Mafindel said. "Not something I'd want to do every year century after century—too sweaty for that, I think—but every once in a while? No, not bad at all. I may even try to imitate you."

With elves, that was indeed the sincerest form of flattery. Lingol, though, shook his tousled head. "You wouldn't be imitating me," he said, giving credit where it was due. "You'd be imitating Gaetan at one remove."

"It's the only immortality he'll get," Mafindel replied with the half-fearful scorn elves reserved for those who resembled them to some degree but had the misfortune—through their Artist's clumsiness, perhaps?—to be mortal. Mafindel added, "I'll give some of my friends something to remember him by, too."

"That's what I've been doing," Lingol agreed.

And they were righter than they knew.

Gaetan never forgot Lingol. He never stopped looking for him in San Francisco or New York City or West Hollywood or Palm Springs or Key West or whichever other hot spot he happened to find himself in. He never stopped looking, and he never had any luck. Sometimes he would talk about the one that got away, as if he were telling a fish story. A lot of his friends had stories like that, too. They would listen and laugh and buy him another drink.

If he'd drunk enough, he would say, "But he wasn't like that. He was *different.*"

He, too, was righter than he knew. But in some ways, maybe, Lingol hadn't been so *very* different after all.

Even after Gaetan came down sick with one strange illness after another, he kept cruising. He kept looking. He never found what he was looking for. As men went, he was tough. He got whatever last answers he would get just as winter was giving way to spring in the ominous year of 1984.

For Lingol, it all began some years later with night sweats. He woke with the bedclothes soaked and with the feeling that some part of his essence had leached from his body along with the wet, salty flood. The horror he felt each time he woke . . . No one from this world is well equipped to grasp the horror he felt. He had not been young when the folk of this world raised the Pyramids alongside the Nile, and he had not known sickness all the days of his life. Elves knew *of* sickness. *Knowing* sickness was something else again.

Lingol, in fact, did not know he knew sickness. He thought someone had set a curse on him. Celcalad was a wizard famous for cutting to the root of the curses elves aimed at one another in their occasional feuds. Lingol took himself off to see the wizard. He left behind him a number of damp beds and an equal number of very puzzled and even more disgusted innkeepers.

Celcalad heard him out, then murmured a charm. He made a number of passes. The air around Lingol turned blue, then slowly faded to transparency once more. "Well?" Lingol asked eagerly. "What do you see?"

With a small frown, the other elf answered, "Nothing. I am afraid I see nothing."

"Then you are not the wizard you take yourself to be," Lingol said. Normally, he would sooner have bitten out his tongue than spoken so rudely, but he did not feel the way he was used to feeling for years uncounted. Is it any wonder his bodily unease yielded spiritual unease of like magnitude? "Look at me!" he exclaimed. "A blind elf would know I am not as I should be. What else could it be but a curse?"

"I do not know what else it could be." Celcalad's voice was troubled. "I do not see anything else it could be. But I would take oath on the Author's holy name that no one has worked magic against you."

"Perhaps you did not scry deeply enough," Lingol said. "Perhaps a wizard more powerful and more subtle than you has arisen."

"Both these things may be true," Celcalad admitted. "What might you have done to rouse such a wizard against you?"

Elf-feuds were not lightly undertaken. Boredom could end an elf's life. A feud might also. Lives long and free of pain were risked only for the highest—or the darkest—of reasons.

Shrugging, Lingol replied, "I have no idea. I try to get along with everyone. As far as I knew, I was succeeding. None of my lovers has complained of me. And yet . . . I am as you see me."

"Indeed," Celcalad said gravely. "This is unfortunate."

"This is disastrous!" Lingol cried. Celcalad could afford to sound grave. He did not feel as if he had one foot *in* the grave—a comparison that would not have occurred to Lingol had he not been through the Door a few short years earlier. He pointed to Celcalad. "Will you cast a spell of wellness for me? I tried my own, first thing, but it did less than I would have hoped." It had not done much of anything, actually. Lingol preferred not to think about that. He went on, "You, though, being more learned in sorcery . . ."

"I will cast the spell," Celcalad said.

Something in his voice failed to ring true. "But?" Lingol asked. "There is bound to be a *but*. Do not try to tell me otherwise, or I will call you a liar to your face." His bodily misery made him short-tempered and rude.

"There is a *but,*" the wizard agreed. "You are not the first I have seen with a complaint of this sort—not an identical complaint, mind you, but a complaint of this sort. There have been several others—all, strangely enough, in the last few years. I do not understand why this should be so, but so it undoubtedly is."

"How strange," Lingol said, and then, after a moment's thought, "but you still have not explained what the *but* is."

"So I haven't." By Celcalad's somber expression, he would have been happier had Lingol failed to note that. With a sigh, he continued, "I crafted spells of wellness for them, the strongest at my command."

"And?" Lingol asked.

"And they did . . . less than I would have hoped." Celcalad borrowed his words.

Did Celcalad also borrow the worry that lay under the words? By his tone, Lingol feared he did. "Did your spells of wellness do any good at all?" he inquired.

"I am not sure. They did no harm. I am sure of that." The elf-wizard did not want to meet his eyes. When harmlessness was the most he could claim, Lingol could see why he would not.

"If a spell of wellness will not make me right, what will?" Lingol asked with something closer to desperation than elves commonly came.

"I did not say a spell of wellness would not make you right," Celcalad answered. "I only said spells of wellness had done less for others than I would have hoped." *He* spoke like an elf fighting hard to keep desperation out of his voice.

"Cast the spell," Lingol said. "What can be done, let it be done."

"Just as you say." Celcalad bowed to him. The wizard intoned the spell. It was not so very different from the one Lingol had tried in the world on the other side of the Door during his last visit but one. Not so very different—but stronger. The elf could feel that. He himself was not even a journeyman when it came to wizardry. Celcalad knew everything there was to know, or near enough. He did not just use appropriate words and passes—his were *right.* Even as the spell built, Lingol could sense as much.

Celcalad spoke a word of Command. The spell of wellness embraced Lingol in soft warmth. He had needed such spells only a couple of times in all his years. They had fixed whatever small things that had gone awry with him, and fixed them straightaway. He could tell *this* spell was stronger than any he had ever known.

Hope flowed through him as the magic faded. Maybe it was strong enough to overcome whatever strange affliction troubled him. He bowed to Celcalad. "My thanks," he said. "I'll stay here for a little while, I think, so I can tell you how I fare."

"Yes, please do." The wizard nodded wearily. How much of himself had he thrown into that spell? As much as Lingol lost whenever he soaked the sheets? Lingol did not think so. Celcalad continued, "I will want to know how you do, so I can keep refining the spell in case I should need it again." He grimaced. "I had not thought I would need it once. I certainly had not thought I would need it more than once. Now . . . Now, who knows?"

Lingol remembered that the spell had done less than its caster hoped. Evidently, for all its strength, it still *needed* refinement. He almost said as much to Celcalad. But what would the point have been? The wizard was doing what he could. That much was plain. After thanking him again, Lingol walked back to the inn where he was staying.

The short journey was enough to make him fear the spell of wellness had failed. Walking should have been a joy for an elf. Instead, he felt as if he were trudging up a steep slope with three more elves on his back. Sure as sure, whatever oozed from him in the night had not yet been restored.

When he stepped into the inn, he blinked once or twice to let his eyes adjust to the dimmer light. Then he blinked again, surprised to find a familiar face there.

"Belionora!" he exclaimed. "What are you doing here?"

"Hello, Lingol." She nodded to him. "I've come to see Celcalad the wizard. I am . . . not quite right."

He looked at her more closely. She was thinner than he remembered her, and looked tired—something rare for elves who had not undergone some great physical, mental, or spiritual exertion, as Celcalad just had. "How strange," Lingol said. "I've just gone to see him myself. I am . . . not quite right, either."

Belionora's eyes widened. "That *is* strange. I thought it was odd enough when it was only me. But if the two of us—"

"More than the two of us," Lingol broke in. "Celcalad said he had seen several others who are . . . less healthy than they might be." Lingol didn't feel less healthy than he might have. He felt *sick*. Because, like all other elves, he had seen sickness only on the other side of the Door, he had trouble recognizing it when it visited him.

"How can this be?" Belionora asked. "Has some dark sorcerer risen among us?" She shuddered. Long as elves lived, few were left alive from the days when such a thing last came to pass among them. In the world on the other side of the Door, the creatures that walked on two legs had had beetling brow ridges and lacked both chins and foreheads. They had chipped stones. Some of them—the more clever ones—could keep a fire going if they found it, but none had known how to make fire on their own.

"I asked this of Celcalad," Lingol replied. "He said it was possible, but he did not think it likely. His magic could find no trace of curse upon me."

"Did he . . . attempt a spell of wellness?" No wonder Belionora hesitated. If Lingol said yes and that he was cured, then all would also be well with her. But if he said yes and that he remained . . . less healthy than he might, then what did that do to her hopes?

"He attempted one, yes. How much good it has done . . . I don't know yet." Lingol did not want to tell her he felt no better. Telling her that would have dashed his hopes along with hers.

He waited to see if she would ask him whether the wizard had also attempted spells of wellness on any of the several others who had seen him. She did nothing of the kind. Maybe she wanted to ask that directly of Celcalad. Maybe she did not want to ask it at all. Maybe she did not want to know the answer. Maybe she feared she already did, and did not care to have her fears confirmed.

What she did say, with sudden urgency, was, "Sleep with me. When I started feeling this way, I couldn't imagine wanting to ever again, not till I was better. Now, though, with you the same way . . ." Her laugh held something of the desperate defiance that so often informed laughter on the other side of the Door. She might have realized as much, too, for she went on, "Did you ever hear them say, *Misery loves company*?"

"Oh, yes." Lingol nodded. He knew whom she meant. "My place or yours?" he asked. Just for a moment, he thought of Gaetan. But just for a moment—Gaetan, after all, was only a man.

When he and Belionora lay together, that, at least, was all it should have been. They slept—truly slept—in the same bed that night. She coughed in the darkness, and her breathing sounded troubled. He woke drenched in the perspiration that seemed to sap his strength so much more than any mere sweat should have been able to do.

He reached out to touch her, and found she was awake. They clung to each other, as they might have after shipwreck. But on what distant and deadly shore had they washed up together?

* * *

Lingol began to cough, too, and then to have difficulty breathing. A wellness spell did make that torment retreat, but soon afterwards something white and nasty started growing on the inside of his mouth. Another spell of wellness beat it back. For a year or so, Lingol dared hope the curse, or whatever it was, had lifted. Then he broke out in excruciatingly painful blisters on his skin.

He was nowhere near Celcalad when that happened. He could not stand the suffering he would have had to undergo on the journey, so he took his tormented body to the closest spellcaster he could find, an elf-witch named Foriana. She managed to check the blisters. Lingol bowed after the anguish abated. "Many thanks," he told her. "I have never felt anything like that in all my years."

"I am pleased to relieve your pain," Foriana answered. "I am not pleased that you should have it. It is not natural for us. It is not right."

"I should say not!" Lingol exclaimed. "There are times when I feel my poor miserable carcass is nothing but a loaf of bread going moldy. Every time something new sprouts on me, I need another cure." He laughed—it was either that or sob.

"You may be more nearly right than you know. And you *will* know, I am sure, you are not the only elf suffering in this fashion—far from it," Foriana said. Lingol nodded. He did know that, though her *far from it* suggested there might be more sufferers than even he had guessed. She went on, "That such ills should cling to us and cause us harm is not the way it should be. I said that before, did I not?"

"You did," Lingol said. "Not that you needed to—not to me. I already knew."

Foriana nodded, too, more to herself than to him. "Yes, of course you would, and those like you, as well. The ailments from which you and those like you suffer . . . Those are things of this world, like the molds on bread you mentioned. This, I suppose, is why wellness spells are effective against them. But wellness spells of that sort, I am convinced, do not touch the underlying cause of your trouble, the sorcery that allows these normally harmless things to gain power over your body."

"Celcalad is convinced there is no sorcery at the bottom of this affliction," Lingol said. "His charms cannot detect any."

"I know that. I have heard him say as much. I have tried spells of my own, as well." Foriana's red lips narrowed and went paler than was their wont. "I have not yet found any sorcery, either. I admit as much. But it must be there. What else could cause such a dreadful derangement among us?"

"You are the wizard. I hoped you would know," Lingol said.

"I do not. I wish I did," Foriana said. "It is as if we were the folk of the other world, full of sicknesses and plagues and pestilences, as if one of those maladies had come across to this world through the Door." She paused, as if really listening to what she had just said. "Do you suppose such a thing is possible?"

"It has never happened before," Lingol said, and Foriana nodded. To a folk as enduring as the elves, precedent bore a weight unimaginably heavy to mere mortals. Lingol went on, "Besides, from what I saw when I went through the Door not so long ago, such afflictions trouble men and women much less than they did in earlier times."

Foriana sighed and nodded once more. "Yes, I had heard the same thing from others. I look forward to seeing for myself when my turn comes." She looked down at her hands: lovely hands, clever hands, hands that had failed. "No doubt my notion was foolish. It is only that, when one sees trouble with no plain root cause, one begins guessing wildly in the hope that that will do *some* good. Ordinary wizardry seems to have failed. No one can deny or escape that."

Lingol worried more about his own sicknesses. (That was what they were, he thought now, with an angry defiance of the way his people usually tiptoed around such blunt labels when speaking of themselves.) He could not deny or escape those. "Lie with me," he said suddenly, as Belionora had when the two of them found they had both come to visit Celcalad. "It will make things no better, not in the long run, but for a little while. . . . And it will surely make things no worse."

"This is not a usual therapy," Foriana said with a crooked smile. Even that soon slipped. "Yours is not a usual case, either. Far be it from me to deny that—or to deny you what comfort you can find. As you say, it will surely make things no worse."

When Lingol saw Mafindel after a few years, he discovered that, as miserable as his own existence had become, he was still luckier than he might have been. The other elf was scrawny to the point of gauntness, to it and beyond. He moved as if every step pained him. Had Lingol been more familiar with the world on the other side of the Door, had he visited it as student rather than as traveler or tourist, he would have said that Mafindel moved like an old, old man.

As things were, he simply stared in dismay. "By the Artist's holy name," he blurted, "what's happened to you?"

"The same thing that's happened to you, I hear, only rather more of it," Mafindel answered. "My body is doing its best to go to pieces, and its best is turning out to be altogether too good." He shuddered. "I have fits of the runs, bad enough to drive me mad. I can hardly go far from a comfort station. A spell of wellness will cure that, but it always comes back, and it seems to get worse every time."

"I've known some of those," Lingol said sympathetically. It was plain, though, that he hadn't known them so often or so badly as Mafindel. The other elf was a ravaged shadow of his former self.

"The runs aren't the worst part, though," Mafindel said.

"No?" Now apprehension was the dominant note in Lingol's voice. He did not want to know how he could deteriorate more than he already had. And yet, some perversely curious part of him did.

"Oh, no," Mafindel said. "The worst so far was when I started losing my mind. My eyes didn't want to see, my mouth wouldn't shape the words I knew I wanted to say. It was the strangest thing I've ever known, and without a doubt the nastiest. The spell of wellness did seem to cure it, the Artist be praised, and so far it hasn't come back. If it does . . ." He shuddered again.

"What then?" Lingol asked when his friend did not go on.

"I remember a time when we used to think boredom was the worst thing in the world. It was everyone's worst enemy. Some of us perished from it," Mafindel said. Lingol remembered those days, too. They seemed a tattered and all-but-forgotten dream now, or something that had happened to someone else. Mafindel went on, "Well, now we have a worse enemy than boredom." He stared at Lingol, eyes enormous in his thin, drawn face, as if defying him to deny it.

Lingol could not, and knew he could not. "I would dearly love to be bored again. Anything would be better than—this."

"I have had the same thought. I have indeed," Mafindel said. "Anything *would* be better than this. *Anything* would—and so would nothing."

"And I have had that same thought myself," Lingol said quietly. "I have had it—but I did not know anyone else had. I thought it was nothing but my own madness."

"Speak to me not of madness," Mafindel said. "I have met madness. I do not care to meet it again. If I cannot know myself as I ought to be, I would sooner know oblivion than what I suffer now."

"Maybe the wizards will find a cure," Lingol said.

"Maybe." Mafindel's haunted eyes said another word: *No.* "But maybe the cure lies outside wizardry. And if it does, how will we ever uncover it?" He waited; he might have been hoping Lingol could give him some answer that would restore his hope. But Lingol had no answers, even for himself.

Over the years, over the centuries, over the millennia, Lingol had seen every corner of his world. These cliffs in the Green Mountains were no exception. The view was famous—out over the lush valleys in the distance, up to the snowy peaks above and behind, and down to the jagged rocks below. Lingol would rather not have gone there now, would rather not have had occasion to go there now, but not even an elf always got what he wanted. Lingol knew more about that than he had before his last journey through the Door, too.

Mafindel stood near the edge of the cliffs, staring out at the valleys. Along with him and Lingol, Belionora was there, and Celcalad, and a number of his other friends. All elves got to know one another, of course. Had everyone acquainted with Mafindel come hither, the flat ground atop the cliffs could not have held the crowd.

"I do this of my own free will. Indeed, I do it with a glad heart," Mafindel said. Speaking took effort for him. So did standing; he swayed like a skinny sapling in a strong breeze. And skinny he was. The crimson tunic and blue silk trousers he wore hung on him as if made for a much larger elf, though they were his. Had a golden belt not secured those trousers, they would not have stayed up.

"I beg you to wait. I beg you to reconsider," Celcalad said. "We have learned little of what causes these . . . these derangements. In all our years, we have never had to try to learn such a thing. Before too many years have passed, we may come to know much more than we do now."

"No." Mafindel shook his head. "Life has become a burden, a weariness, to me. By all I can see, it will not grow better. It will only grow worse. Perhaps in the end what I suffer will kill me. Perhaps I will only go on as I am, year after year, decade after decade, century after century. What is life nearly eternal worth when it becomes torment nearly eternal? Nothing. No, less than nothing, for to it I prefer nothingness. And nothingness I will have."

He bowed to the friends who had come to bid him farewell. Then, painfully but with great determination, he walked to the very edge. He did not look back. He did not stop. At the edge, he took one determined step more. He went over—and down.

It was a long, long way down. Lingol wondered if he would hear a cry, or hear the impact when Mafindel struck those rocks at the bottom. He heard neither. After a little while, he went to the edge and looked down. Mafindel was only a small splash of blue and crimson. He lay unmoving.

"He is free," Lingol said quietly.

"How I envy him," Belionora said as she came up to stand beside him. She wore more in the way of powder than she or any other elf-woman was in the habit of doing. Then, beneath the pale concealment, he saw a darker mark in front of one ear. Noticing him notice, Belionora turned away and hid her face in her hands.

"I'm sorry. I'm very sorry." Lingol felt ashamed for penetrating the defenses she held up against the world.

"It's not your fault," Belionora said, which was not strictly true, although neither of them knew that. She gathered herself and went on, "I have these horrid purple blotches on my skin. They grow and they grow and . . . From what the wizards say, they grow inside me, too, not just on my skin."

Lingol's stomach did a slow lurch, almost as if he had stepped off into space himself. He said, "Can't the spells of wellness set that to rights?"

"While each spell lasts, it stops the patches from growing," Belionora said bleakly. "That is all it does. When a spell wears off, the patches start again. Before too long, there will be more of them than there is of me—if I don't do something about it first, that is."

"What can you do?" Lingol asked.

"What Mafindel did," she answered. "Then, at least, it will be done." She looked out over the edge of the cliff. Then she looked back at the rest of the elves who had come to say farewell to Mafindel. Most of them were afflicted in one way or another—often in one way *and* another. In a voice not much above a whisper, she said, "I wonder how many of us will be left when all this is over. I wonder whether any of us will be left when all this is over."

"How did it happen?" Lingol said. "How did it begin?"

Belionora shrugged. Even that little motion seemed to pain her, and to weary her. "Who knows?" she said. "And does that really matter any more? It is here."

Lingol could only nod.

* * *

Belionora lingered for another five years before deciding she had suffered as much as she chose to suffer, and that life would get no better for her. Then she, too, repaired to the cliffs in the Green Mountains. Her friends gathered with her, gathered for her. By then, the ceremony had a name. The elves had come to call it a Leavetaking. There had been not a few between Mafindel's time and Belionora's.

Though weak from his latest brush with trouble to his lungs, Lingol made the journey to the cliffs. Carrion birds circled lazily above them. Between Mafindel's time and Belionora's, they had learned their patience would be rewarded.

Among those who came to see Belionora out of her pain were Celcalad and Foriana. The wizard and the witch spent a good deal of time commiserating with each other. Foriana came over to Lingol. "The curse seems to have taken me, as well. I am not as I should be. When I wake in the night, the sheets are soaked with sweat."

He reached out and took her hands in his. The close contact showed him how bony his had grown. He had already known as much, but seeing them next to those of someone healthier—if not healthy any more—drove the point home. "It is the beginning," he agreed somberly. "I am sorry to see you initiated into this mystery."

"Maybe we will learn how to deal with . . . this," she said.

"Maybe we will." Lingol had had that hope, too, when his troubles began. Now? He did not know what he hoped now. For an end, maybe. The times seemed to have swallowed other hopes.

Belionora walked slowly to the edge of the cliff. "I have not much to say," she told the other elves. "Those who have gone before me have already said most of what is worth saying. I do not know what I did to have this happen to me. I do not know what wizard set a curse on me. I do not even know if any wizard set a curse on me. But a curse this is. That I do know. And I know but one way to be free of it. That way I now take, and I take it with a heart full of joy."

As Mafindel and others had before her, she stepped off the edge of the cliff and was gone. One of the carrion birds high in the sky screeched shrilly. The others echoed the call. They would feed soon.

No one went to the cliff's edge and looked down. They had all done that before, at one Leavetaking or another. Instead, almost wordlessly, the elves turned away. Lingol shook his head as he started down from the cliffs.

Continued traffic was beginning to wear a track of bare dirt through the grass there. His shoes scuffed up dust. He hoped it would not set him coughing again. He had done too much of that.

Celcalad fell into step with him when they were nearly down into the flat land again. The wizard said, "On the other side of the Door, I have heard, there is a malady much like the one that afflicts us."

"Foriana wondered if it came from that world. What difference does it make, one way or the other?" Lingol said. Little made any difference to him these days, except whether he felt bad or worse.

"If it does not spring from our world, no wonder our spells hold no power against it," Celcalad said.

"I do not think it matters much to me at this stage of things." Every time Lingol came to the cliffs or to some other convenient spot for another elf's Leavetaking, he came closer to deciding on his own. He often wondered why he had lingered as long as he had. The world was no longer a delight for him. Were he somehow restored, would he ever be foolish enough to complain of boredom? He hoped not, even if he knew he could not be sure. He asked, "Can they do anything for this—if it is this—on the other side of the Door?"

"They can make the afflicted die much more slowly than they would otherwise," Celcalad replied.

Lingol grimaced. "In my view, that is more cruel than doing nothing at all. Truly the Artist who shaped that other world must be vicious or mad."

"It could be so," Celcalad said. "However much they call on Her there, She never answers. Or She may not be there at all. That world may have come together all on its own. How can any of us say?"

"That, too, matters little to me. Nothing much does, not any more." Lingol sighed, and felt the air fighting its way out of his lungs. "How many of us has the curse taken now?"

"Who can say for certain?" Celcalad replied. "Even on the other side of the Door, it often lies idle for years before bursting forth. With us, that time is surely longer, as all times are with us."

"My own time has now grown entirely too long." Lingol sighed again. "And I thought they were approaching civilization, there on the other side of the Door. That little holiday with Gaetan could hardly have been better were he an elf. . . ."

Friends had to help Lingol up to the cliffs. He was determined his Leave-taking should be there. It was the last gesture of respect he could give to

Mafindel and Belionora and others who had gone before him. This latest spell of wellness had done enough to let him see again. There stood Celcalad and Foriana, side by side again. The witch had grown thin: indeed, the curse dwelt within her.

"I am ready," Lingol said. "I am more than ready. I daresay I have waited too long. Had I waited any more, I would not have had the strength to do what I know needs doing." He pointed up to the wheeling carrion birds. "What they will partake of is not me. What is me will live in you, in your memories. Remember me as I was, not as I am. It is the last favor I can ask of you."

He stepped to the edge. He stepped out over the edge. It was wind, all the way down. He remembered Mafindel, as he was. He remembered Belionora, as she was. And, just for the briefest moment, he remembered Gaet

A meditation on the nature of children's literature from **Neil Gaiman**, *who knows something about it. I once sat on a convention panel on fairy tales with Neil, and he ran so many rings around me (and, by and large, the other panelists) that I ended up saying, "Wuh?" It was like being hit by an insight truck.*

He also knows something about writing *children's literature—his* Coraline, *published in 2002, was not only praised and loved by children but highly honored, as well, winning a Bram Stoker Award and the Hugo for best novella.*

The Problem of Susan

Neil Gaiman

She has the dream again that night.

In the dream, she is standing, with her brothers and her sister, on the edge of the battlefield. It is summer, and the grass is a peculiarly vivid shade of green: a wholesome green, like a cricket pitch or the welcoming slope of the South Downs as you make your way north from the coast. There are bodies on the grass. None of the bodies are human; she can see a centaur, its throat slit, on the grass near her. The horse half of it is a vivid chestnut. Its human skin is nut-brown from the sun. She finds herself staring at the horse's penis, wondering about centaurs mating, imagines being kissed by that bearded face. Her eyes flick to the cut throat, and the sticky red-black pool that surrounds it, and she shivers.

Flies buzz about the corpses.

The wildflowers tangle in the grass. They bloomed yesterday for the first time in, how long? A hundred years? A thousand? A hundred thousand? She does not know.

All this was snow, she thinks, as she looks at the battlefield.

Yesterday, all this was snow. Always winter, and never Christmas.

Her sister tugs her hand and points. On the brow of the green hill they stand, deep in conversation. The lion is golden, his hands folded behind his back. The witch is dressed all in white. Right now she is shouting at the lion, who is simply listening. The children cannot make out any of their words, not her cold anger or the lion's thrum-deep replies. The witch's hair is black and shiny; her lips are red.

In her dream she notices these things.

They will finish their conversation soon, the lion and the witch. . . .

* * *

There are things about herself that the professor despises. Her smell, for example. She smells like her grandmother smelled, like old women smell, and for this she cannot forgive herself, so on waking, she bathes in scented water and, naked and towel-dried, dabs several drops of Chanel toilet water beneath her arms and on her neck. It is, she believes, her sole extravagance.

Today she dresses in her dark brown dress suit. She thinks of these as her interview clothes, as opposed to her lecture clothes or her knocking-about-the-house clothes. Now she is in retirement, she wears her knocking-about-the-house clothes more and more. She puts on lipstick.

After breakfast, she washes a milk bottle, places it at her back door. She discovers that next-door's cat has deposited a mouse head, and a paw, on the doormat. It looks as though the mouse is swimming through the coconut matting, as though most of it is submerged. She purses her lips, then she folds her copy of yesterday's *Daily Telegraph,* and she folds and flips the mouse head and the paw into the newspaper, never touching them with her hands.

Today's *Daily Telegraph* is waiting for her in the hall, along with several letters, which she inspects, without opening any of them, and then places on the desk in her tiny study. Since her retirement, she visits her study only to write. Now she walks into the kitchen and seats herself at the old oak table. Her reading glasses hang about her neck, on a silver chain, and she perches them on her nose, and begins with the obituaries.

She does not actually expect to encounter anyone she knows there, but the world is small, and she observes that, perhaps with cruel humour, the obituarists have run a photograph of Peter Burrell Gunn as he was in the early 1950s, and not at all as he was the last time the professor had seen him, at a *Literary Monthly* Christmas party several years before, all gouty and beaky and trembling, and reminding her of nothing so much as a caricature of an owl. In the photograph, he is very beautiful. He looks wild, and noble.

She had spent an evening once kissing him in a summer house: she remembers that very clearly, although she cannot remember for the life of her in which garden the summer house had belonged.

It was, she decides, Charles and Nadia Reid's house in the country. Which meant that it was before Nadia ran away with that Scottish artist, and Charles took the professor with him to Spain, although she was certainly not a professor then. This was many years before people commonly went to Spain for their holidays; it was exotic then. He asked her to marry him, too, and she is no longer certain why she said no, or even if she had entirely said no. He was a pleasant-enough young man, and he took what was left of her virginity on a blanket on a Spanish beach, on a warm spring night. She was twenty years old, and had thought herself so old. . . .

The doorbell chimes, and she puts down the paper, and makes her way to the front door, and opens it.

Her first thought is how young the girl looks.

Her first thought is how old the woman looks. "Professor Hastings?" she says. "I'm Greta Campion. I'm doing the profile on you. For the *Literary Chronicle*."

The older woman stares at her for a moment, vulnerable, and ancient; then she smiles. It's a friendly smile, and Greta warms to her. "Come in, dear," says the professor. "We'll be in the sitting room."

"I brought you this," says Greta. "I baked it myself." She takes the cake tin from her bag, hoping its contents haven't disintegrated en route. "It's a chocolate cake. I read online that you liked them."

The old woman nods, and blinks. "I do," she says. "How kind. This way."

Greta follows her into a comfortable room, is shown to her armchair, and told, firmly, not to move. The professor bustles off and returns with a tray, on which are teacups and saucers, a teapot, a plate of chocolate biscuits, and Greta's chocolate cake.

Tea is poured, and Greta exclaims over the professor's brooch, and then she pulls out her notebook and pen, and a copy of the professor's last book, *A Quest for Meanings in Children's Fiction,* bristling with Post-it notes and scraps of paper. They talk about the early chapters, in which the hypothesis is set forth that there was originally no distinct branch of fiction that was intended only for children, until the Victorian notions of the purity and sanctity of childhood demanded that fiction for children be made . . .

". . . well, pure," says the professor.

"And sanctified?" asks Greta, with a smile.

"And sanctimonious," corrects the old woman. "It is difficult to read *The Water Babies* without wincing."

And then she talks about ways that artists used to draw children—as adults, only smaller, without considering the child's proportions—and how

Grimm's stories were collected for adults and, when the Grimms realised the books were being read in the nursery, were bowdlerized to make them more appropriate. She talks of Perrault's "Sleeping Beauty in the Wood," and of its original coda in which the prince's cannibal ogre mother attempts to frame the Sleeping Beauty for having eaten her own children, and all the while Greta nods and takes notes, and nervously tries to contribute enough to the conversation that the professor will feel that it is a conversation or at least an interview, not a lecture.

"Where," asks Greta, "do you feel your interest in children's fiction came from?"

The professor shakes her head. "Where do any of our interests come from? Where does *your* interest in children's books come from?"

Greta says, "They always seemed the books that were most important to me. The ones that mattered. When I was a kid, and when I grew. I was like Dahl's *Matilda*. . . . Were your family great readers?"

"Not really . . . I say that, it was a long time ago that they died. Were killed. I should say."

"All your family died at the same time? Was this in the war?"

"No, dear. We were evacuees, in the war. This was in a train crash, several years after. I was not there."

"Just like in Lewis's Narnia books," says Greta, and immediately feels like a fool, and an insensitive fool. "I'm sorry. That was a terrible thing to say, wasn't it?"

"Was it, dear?"

Greta can feel herself blushing, and she says, "It's just I remember that sequence so vividly. In *The Last Battle*. Where you learn there was a train crash on the way back to school, and everyone was killed. Except for Susan, of course."

The professor says, "More tea, dear?" and Greta knows that she should leave the subject, but she says, "You know, that used to make me so angry."

"What did, dear?"

"Susan. All the other kids go off to Paradise, and Susan can't go. She's no longer a friend of Narnia because she's too fond of lipsticks and nylons and invitations to parties. I even talked to my English teacher about it, about the problem of Susan, when I was twelve."

She'll leave the subject now, talk about the role of children's fiction in creating the belief systems we adopt as adults, but the professor says "And tell me, dear, what did your teacher say?"

"She said that even though Susan had refused Paradise then, she still had time while she lived to repent."

"Repent *what*?"

"Not believing, I suppose. And the sin of Eve."

The professor cuts herself a slice of chocolate cake. She seems to be remembering. And then she says, "I doubt there was much opportunity for nylons and lipsticks after her family was killed. There certainly wasn't for me. A little money—less than one might imagine—from her parents' estate, to lodge and feed her. No luxuries . . ."

"There must have been something else wrong with Susan," says the young journalist, "something they didn't tell us. Otherwise she wouldn't have been damned like that—denied the Heaven of further up and further in. I mean, all the people she had ever cared for had gone on to their reward, in a world of magic and waterfalls and joy. And she was left behind."

"I don't know about the girl in the books," says the professor, "but remaining behind would also have meant that she was available to identify her brothers' and her little sister's bodies. There were a lot of people dead in that crash. I was taken to a nearby school—it was the first day of term, and they had taken the bodies there. My older brother looked okay. Like he was asleep. The other two were a bit messier."

"I suppose Susan would have seen their bodies, and thought, they're on holidays now. The perfect school holidays. Romping in meadows with talking animals, world without end."

"She might have done. I remember thinking what a great deal of damage a train can do, when it hits another train, to the people who were travelling. I suppose you've never had to identify a body, dear?"

"No."

"That's a blessing. I remember looking at them and thinking, *What if I'm wrong, what if it's not him after all?* My younger brother was decapitated, you know. A god who would punish me for liking nylons and parties by making me walk through that school dining room, with the flies, to identify Ed, well . . . he's enjoying himself a bit too much, isn't he? Like a cat, getting the last ounce of enjoyment out of a mouse. Or a gram of enjoyment, I suppose it must be, these days. I don't know, really."

She trails off. And then, after some time, she says, "I'm sorry, dear. I don't think I can do any more of this today. Perhaps if your editor gives me a ring, we can set a time to finish our conversation."

Greta nods and says of course, and knows in her heart, with a peculiar finality, that they will talk no more.

* * *

That night, the professor climbs the stairs of her house, slowly, painstakingly, floor by floor. She takes sheets and blankets from the airing cupboard and makes up a bed in the spare bedroom, in the back. It is empty but for a wartime austerity dressing table, with a mirror and drawers, an oak bed, and a dusty applewood wardrobe, which contains only coat hangers and a dusty cardboard box. She places a vase on the dressing table, containing purple rhododendron flowers, sticky and vulgar.

She takes from the box in the wardrobe a plastic bag containing four old photographic albums. Then she climbs into the bed that was hers as a child, and lies there between the sheets, looking at the black-and-white photographs, and the sepia photographs, and the handful of unconvincing colour photographs. She looks at her brothers, and her sister, and her parents, and she wonders how they could have been that young, how anybody could have been that young.

After a while she notices that there are several children's books beside the bed, which puzzles her slightly, because she does not believe she keeps books on the bedside table in that room. Nor, she decides, does she have a bedside table. On the top of the pile is an old paperback book—it must be over forty years old: the price on the cover is in shillings. It shows a lion, and two girls twining a daisy chain into its mane.

The professor's lips prickle with shock. And only then does she understand that she is dreaming, for she does not keep those books in the house. Beneath the paperback is a hardback, in its jacket, of a book that, in her dream, she has always wanted to read: *Mary Poppins Brings in the Dawn,* which P. L. Travers had never written while alive.

She picks it up and opens it to the middle, and reads the story waiting for her. Jane and Michael go with Mary Poppins on her day off, to Heaven, and they meet the boy Jesus, who is still slightly scared of Mary Poppins because she was once his nanny, and the Holy Ghost, who complains that he has not been able to get his sheet properly white since Mary Poppins left, and God the Father, who says,

> "There's no making her do anything. Not her. *She's* Mary Poppins."
>
> "But you're God," said Jane. "You created everybody and everything. They have to do what you say."
>
> "Not her," said God the Father once again, and he scratched

his golden beard flecked with white. "I didn't create *her. She's* Mary Poppins."

And the professor stirs in her sleep, and dreams that she is reading her own obituary. It has been a good life, she thinks, as she reads it, discovering her life laid out in black-and-white. Everyone is there. Even the people she had forgotten.

Greta sleeps beside her boyfriend in a small flat in Camden, and she, too, is dreaming.

In the dream, the lion and the witch come down the hill together.

She is standing on the battlefield, holding her sister's hand. She looks up at the golden lion, and the burning amber of his eyes. "He's not a tame lion, is he?" she whispers to her sister, and they shiver.

The witch looks at them all; then she turns to the lion and says, coldly, "I am satisfied with the terms of our agreement. You take the girls: for myself, I shall have the boys."

She understands what must have happened, and she runs, but the beast is upon her before she has covered a dozen paces. The lion eats all of her except her head, in her dream. He leaves the head, and one of her hands, just as a house cat leaves the parts of a mouse it has no desire for, for later, or as a gift.

She wishes that he had eaten her head, then she would not have had to look. Dead eyelids cannot be closed, and she stares, unflinching, at the twisted thing her brothers have become. The great beast ate her little sister more slowly, and it seemed to her, with more relish and pleasure, than it had eaten her; but then, her little sister had always been its favourite.

The witch removes her white robes, revealing a body no less white, with high, small breasts, and nipples so dark, they are almost black. The witch lies back upon the grass, spreads her legs. Beneath her body, the grass becomes rimed with frost.

"Now," she says.

The lion licks her white cleft with its pink tongue, until she can take no more of it, and she pulls its huge mouth to hers, and wraps her icy legs into its golden fur. . . .

Being dead, the eyes in the head on the grass cannot look away. Being dead, they miss nothing.

And when they are done, sweaty and sticky and sated, only then does the lion amble over to the head on the grass, and devour it in its huge mouth, crunching her skull in its powerful jaws, and it is then, only then, that she wakes.

Her heart is pounding. She tries to wake her boyfriend, but he snores and grunts, and will not rouse.

It's true, Greta thinks, irrationally, in the darkness. *She grew up. She carried on. She didn't die. . . .*

She imagines the professor, waking in the night, and listening to the noises coming from the old applewood wardrobe in the corner: to the rustlings of all these gliding ghosts, which might be mistaken for the scurries of mice or rats, and to the padding of enormous velvet paws, and the distant, dangerous music of a hunting horn.

She knows she is being ridiculous, although she will not be surprised when she reads of the professor's demise. *Death comes in the night,* she thinks, before she returns to sleep. *Like a lion.*

The white witch rides naked on the lion's golden back. Its muzzle is spotted with fresh, scarlet blood. Then the vast pinkness of its tongue wipes around its face, and once more it is perfectly clean.

***Orson Scott Card** has earned kudos and awards up the wazoo. What may sometimes get lost in all the hoopla surrounding his best-selling novels (*Ender's Game *and its sequels, and so forth) is what a fine short-story writer he is.*

Witness the following, about one of life's rejects born with no real dreams of his own but blessed with a very special talent.

Keeper of Lost Dreams

Orson Scott Card

Mack Street was not born. He was, in the words of the immortal bard, "from the womb untimely ripped."

Unfortunely, there was no evil Macbeth that needed slaying by someone who was not "of woman born." Still, Mack Street always knew that his life had a purpose—perhaps a great one, perhaps a small one, but a purpose all the same. How else could he explain the fact that he was alive at all?

He did not know why his mother decided to abort him, or why she waited so long. Was the abortion a spiteful vengeance when his father left her only a few months before their baby's due date? Was she merely indecisive, and it took her seven months to make up her mind to get rid of the kid?

And why, when she realized the appalling fact that he was breathing, perhaps even crying those weak mews of a premature baby, did she take him all the way to Baldwin Park, far from the nearest path, and cover him with leaves so that it would take a miracle for someone to find him and keep him alive?

Still, he *was* found, by a couple of boys in search of a safe place to smoke their first joints. Just before they would have discovered that they had been cheated, and the "weed" was, in fact, merely a weed, a common and slightly nauseating one at that, the smaller boy saw the pile of leaves move, and he pulled them away to reveal a naked baby that looked too small to be real.

The bigger boy insisted that it *wasn't* real, or at least wasn't human. "Everybody know that baby coyotes look human," he said.

"You telling me this one gone grow up to be a niggah coyote?" said the smaller boy.

"Come on," said the bigger boy. "Do the smoke first, then we tell somebody about the baby."

"If it do us like it do my big brother, we ain't gone tell nobody nothing for about half a day. This is a tiny baby, he gonna die."

"Little dick like that, he ain't no niggah," said the bigger boy, but already he was putting the supposed weed back in the Ziploc bag. "You want to take him somewhere, you do it without old Raymo. I don't want nobody asking me questions when I got a bag of weed on me."

"Bag of weed, your mama's boogers," said the smaller boy. "I bet they rolled up broccoli or something anyway, they ain't gone give *us* nothing."

"Don't you go talking about my mama's boogers, Ceese."

Ceese picked up the baby, and it wiggled and mewed and he thought, Just like a baby kitten, and then he remembered how Raymo once took a baby kitten and stepped on its head just to see it squish. Ceese decided not to stick around, even though the thing with the kitten was a couple of years ago and Raymo had puked his guts out and threw the brain-covered shoe away and got a licking for "losing" it. You just never knew what Raymo was going to do. As his mama often told him at the top of her voice, he wasn't the kind of guy who ever seemed to "learn his lesson."

So Ceese took off with the aborted baby and ran all the way home and when he showed it to *his* mama and she screamed and ran next door and woke up Miz Smitcher, who was a night-shift nurse, and Miz Smitcher called the emergency room to alert them, and then put Ceese, still holding the baby, in the backseat of her Civic, belted him in, and drove like a crazy woman all the way to the hospital, cussing the whole time about how people ought to have a license to own a uterus.

"People so crazy, they won't let them buy a gun can go right out and make a baby without asking anybody's permission, and when they *get* a baby, they just throw it away."

Then Miz Smitcher had a sudden ugly thought and leaned over the seat to glare at Ceese. "That ain't *your* baby, is it, boy?"

"Watch the road, dammit!" yelled Ceese, seeing how the big truck in front of them had come to a stop and Miz Smitcher hadn't.

Miz Smitcher slammed on the brake so fast that Ceese got flung forward till his chin smacked against the seat, and of course the baby had already flown out of his hands, bounced off the back of the front seat, and dropped like a rock onto the floor.

"It's dead!" screamed Ceese.

"Pick it up, you coprocephalic!" shouted Miz Smitcher.

Ceese leaned over and picked up the baby.

"Is it all right?" said Miz Smitcher.

"Ain't you gone ask if *I'm* all right?" demanded Ceese.

"I *know* you all right, cause you giving me sass and acting stupid! Now what about that baby!"

"He's breathing," said Ceese. "You got so many McDonald's wrappers on the floor, I guess he didn't hit all that hard."

"That baby plain determined not to die," said Miz Smitcher. She flipped off the people behind her, who were honking their brains out. Then she turned on her blinkers like she thought that would make her car an ambulance, caught up with the truck, whipped around it, and kept on going at top speed till she lurched to a stop in the turnaround at the emergency entrance.

Which is how Mack Street happened not to die under a pile of leaves in Baldwin Park, and instead got fostered out to Ceese's neighborhood.

Well, technically, he was fostered to Miz Smitcher, who took to calling him her little miracle, though more likely she felt guilty about jamming the brakes and throwing him onto the floor and she wanted to make sure that if there was some brain damage or something, she'd be able to make it up to him.

But Miz Smitcher worked nights and slept days, and baby Mack slept nights and yelled his lungs out while she was trying to sleep, so it turned out he was sort of fostered to whatever mother was home and willing to take him. Not a one of them took him to heart the way Miz Smitcher did, so mostly he just lay around until somebody remembered to feed him or wipe his butt, except when somebody's kid decided he'd be a great baby doll or a cool squirmy football and incorporated him into a game.

Some folks said that that was why Miz Smitcher gave him the last name Street—because he was raised by most every family on the block. Wasn't a soul asked, and so not a soul was told, that Street was Miz Smitcher's last name before she got married and divorced, and Mack was the nickname of her favorite uncle. Mack didn't find it out till after she died and he went through her things. She just wasn't much of a talker or a self-explainer. If she loved you, you'd have to guess it from her cooking and buying clothes for you, 'cause you'd never know it from a word or a touch.

Still, despite the lack of affection in Mack's life, he certainly didn't lack for stimulation. Being fed mud pies or flying through the air as a forward pass is bound to keep a baby somewhat alert. By the time he started school, he was pretty much fearless. He'd take any dare, seeing as how there was nothing he could be asked to eat or do that he hadn't already eaten or done worse. "There's an angel watching over that boy," said Miz Smitcher, when somebody told her of another of the crazy things Mack did.

Dare-taking was what he did to win a place, however strange it was, among the kids at school. It wasn't where he lived.

For Mack, the real excitement in his life came in dreams. It wasn't till he was seven years old that he first found out that other people dreamed only when they were asleep. For Mack, dreams had a way of popping up day or night. It was the reason the other kids sometimes saw him slow down in the middle of a game and go sort of slack-jawed, staring off into space. When that happened, kids would just say, "Mack's gone," and go off and continue their game without him.

Most dreams he could shrug off and pay no heed to—they weren't worth missing out on recess time or getting barked at by grumpy teachers in school, the kind who actually expected their lessons to be listened to.

But some dreams captivated him, even though he didn't understand them.

There was one in particular; it started when Mack was ten. He was in a vehicle—he wasn't sure it was a car, because a car shouldn't be able to drive on roads like this. It started out on a dirt road, with ragged-looked trees around, kind of a dry California kind of woods. The road began to sink down while the ground stayed level on both sides, till they were dirt walls or steep hills, and sometimes buttes. And the road began to get rocky, only the rocks were all the size of cobblestones, rounded like river rocks, and they hurtled along—Mack and whoever else was in the vehicle—as if the rocks were pavement.

The rocks glistened black in the sunlight, like they'd been wet recently. The cobbly road started to go up again, steeper and steeper, and then it narrowed suddenly and they were almost jammed in between high cliffs with a thin trickly waterfall coming from the crease where the cliffs joined together.

So they backed out—and here was where Mack knew it wasn't him driving, because he didn't know how to back a car. If it was a car.

Backed out and headed down until the canyon was wide enough that they could turn around, and then they rushed along until they found the place where they had gone wrong. When the road reached the lowest point, there was a narrow passage off to the left leading farther down, and now

Mack realized that this wasn't no road—this was a river that just happened to be dry. And the second he thought of that, he heard distant thunder, and he knew it was raining up in the high hills and that little trickle of a waterfall was about to become a torrent, and there'd be water coming down the other branch of the river, too, and here they were trapped in this narrow canyon barely wide enough for their vehicle, and it was going to fill up with water and throw them down the canyon, bashing against the cliffs, rounding them off just like one of the river rocks.

Sure enough here comes the water, and it's just as bad as he thought, spinning head over heels, getting slammed this way and that, and out the windows all he can see is roiling water and stones and then the dead bodies of the other people in the vehicle as they got washed out and crushed and broken against the canyon walls and suddenly . . .

The vehicle shoots out into open space, and there's no cliffs anymore, just air on every side and a lake below him and the vehicle plunges into the lake and sinks lower and lower and Mack thinks, I got to get out of here, but he can't find a way to open it, not a door, not a window. Deeper and deeper until the vehicle comes to rest on the bottom of the lake with fish swimming up and bumping into the windows and then a naked woman comes up, not sexy or anything, just naked because she never heard of clothes, she swims up and looks at him and smiles and when she touches the window, it breaks and the water slowly oozes in and surrounds him and he swims out and she kisses his cheek and says, Welcome home, I missed you so much.

Mack didn't have to take a psychology class to guess what this dream was about. It was about getting born way too soon. It was about getting to the lowest point, completely alone, and then he'd find his mother, she'd come to him and open the door and let him come back into her life.

He believed his dream so much that he was sure he knew now what his mother looked like, skin so black it was almost blue, but with a thinnish nose, like those men and women of Sudan in the *African Peoples* book at school. Maybe I *am* African, he thought. Not African American, like the other black kids in his class, but truly African without a drop of white in him.

But then why would his mother have thrown him away?

Maybe it wasn't his mother. Maybe she was drugged and the baby was taken out of her and carried off and hidden and she doesn't even know he was ever alive, but Mack knew he would find her someday, because the dream was so real, it had to be true.

Later he told the dream to a therapist—the one they sent him to about his "seizures," as they called those trances when he stopped to watch a dream. The therapist listened and nodded wisely and then explained to him, "Mack, dreams come from deep inside you, some chain of meaning so deep, it has no words or pictures, so your brain dresses it up in pictures that it already knows. So from deep inside there's this idea of going down a passage that's both a river and a road, so your brain makes it into a canyon and when it starts to push you and push you, your brain puts water in the dream, forcing you out, and when the deep inner story says that you plunge out into air, then you see it as a plunge out of a canyon, and then who comes and saves you? Your mother."

"So you're saying this is the way my brain makes sense of my memory of being born," said Mack.

"That's one possible interpretation."

"There's another?"

"I haven't thought of it yet, but there might be."

"But it's my mother, anyway, like I always thought."

"I believe that in dreams, if it looks like your mother and you think it's your mother, it's your mother."

"Cool," said Mack. All he cared about was that now he knew what his mother looked like. Mack was as black as they come, but his mother was even blacker, and that was cool. But if she was underwater, then that wasn't so cool. He hoped that his dream didn't mean that she was drowned. Maybe it just meant she swam a lot.

Or maybe it didn't mean a damn thing.

That was the only one of his strong dreams in which he felt like himself, though, and the therapist didn't have any explanation for that. "What do you mean, you don't feel like yourself?"

"I mean that in the dreams, I'm not me. Except that one about the road that turns out to be a river."

"Well, who are you then?"

"Somebody different every time."

"Tell me about those dreams," the therapist said.

"I can't," said Mack. "That wouldn't be right."

"What do you mean? You can tell me anything."

"I can tell you *my* dreams," said Mack. "But these ones ain't mine."

The therapist thought that was totally crazy reasoning. "They're in your head, Mack. That makes them yours!"

Mack couldn't explain why, but he knew that the therapist was wrong. They weren't his dreams.

When he dreamed about finding himself as a baby, about his hands reaching down and picking up this infant, he knew it wasn't his dream, it was Ceese's. Ceese still lived in the neighborhood, but he didn't have much to do with Mack—it was Raymo who told the story all the time about how he and Ceese found Mack. The way Raymo told it, Ceese wanted to leave the baby and smoke weed, but Raymo insisted that they take the baby back and save its life, making out how he was the hero. But in the dream that came into Mack's mind, he saw the real story, how Ceese was the one who did the saving, and Raymo wanted to leave the baby there in the leaves.

But Mack didn't talk to anybody about his dream of the true story, because they'd think he was crazy. Not that they didn't already, but Mack knew that if they got to thinking he was *really* crazy, they'd lock him away somewhere. And the worst part of *that* idea was, what kind of dreams would they stick in his head there in the crazy house?

'Cause Mack knew it was other people putting these dreams into his mind. Most of the time, he didn't know whose dream he was having, though some of them, he knew they had to come from a teacher, and others, he had a pretty good guess who in the neighborhood was having this dream.

The thing was, he didn't know if they actually had the same dream, at least not exactly the way he saw it. Because the dreams he saw, they were always so sad that if other people really knew they had such dreams inside them, how could they get through a single day without crying?

Mack didn't cry for them, though. Because it wasn't his dream.

Like the Johnsons, the ones whose daughter got brain-damaged when she half-drowned in their waterbed, Mack didn't know if the dream he caught from their house was Mr. Johnson's or Mrs. Johnson's or maybe it was Tamika's, a dream left over from back when she was a pretty girl who lived for swimming. In the dream she was diving and swimming in a pool of water in the jungle, with a waterfall, like in a movie. She kept diving deeper and deeper and then one time when she came up, there was a thick plastic barrier on the top of the water and she was scared for just a second, but then she saw that her daddy and mommy were lying on top of the plastic and she poked them and they woke right up and saw her and smiled at her and pulled open the plastic and lifted her out.

If Mack hadn't known something about Tamika's story—or at least the story Mr. Johnson told about how it happened, before they took him off to jail—he might have thought this was just another version of his own dream of being born. Maybe he would have thought, this is how birth dreams come to folks who weren't aborted and left to die in the park under a bunch of leaves.

But instead he saw it as maybe Mr. Johnson's dream of how he wished it had happened, instead of having Tamika trapped under the water all that time till cells in her brain started dying before he realized where she was and cut into the mattress and pulled her out. If only he'd found her right away, the first time she bumped into him from inside the waterbed.

Or maybe it was Mrs. Johnson's dream, since she never felt her daughter inside the mattress at all. Maybe it's how *she* wished it had happened, both of them feeling her poking them so they believed it right away and got her out in time.

Or maybe it was Tamika's dream. Maybe this was how she remembered it, in the confusion of her damaged brain. Diving and swimming, deeper and deeper, until she came up inside her parents' waterbed and they did indeed pull her out and hug her and fuss over her and kiss her like in the dream. The hug and kiss of CPR, but to Tamika, maybe that's what love felt like now.

The thing is, it was a good dream. Maybe when he woke up from it, Mr. Johnson cried—if he was the one who dreamed it. But it made Mack feel good. The diving and swimming were wonderful. And so was the opening of the plastic barrier and the mother and father waiting to hug the swimming girl.

After Mack talked to the therapist, even though he never told this dream, he tried to think of it the way the therapist did. This dream has a mother in it, and a father, so maybe it's really my own dream about a mother and father, only I think it *isn't* my dream because my real mother and father rejected me. So I had this deep dream about opening up a barrier and finding myself surrounded with loves and kisses only on top of that dream, my brain supplied some of the details from the real story of how Tamika got half-drowned in the waterbed. Maybe it's all me, and I'm just sort of twisted up about who's inside my own head.

Around and around Mack went, thinking about how his brain worked—or didn't work—and why he had these dreams, and how he might be getting dreams sent to him from other people.

Until the day when Yo Yo moved in to Baldwin Hills.

She wasn't down in the flat, where Mack lived, and all his friends. She bought a house up in the hills, near the top of the winding road that led to the very place in the park where Mack had been found. She had doctors and lawyers and big-shot accountants and a movie agent and a semi-famous director living on her street. There was a lot of money there, and expensive cars, and fine tailored suits and evening gowns, and people with responsibilities.

But Yo Yo—or Yolanda White, as she was listed in the phone book—she wasn't like them. She wasn't trying to look respectable like those other folks, who, as Raymo said, were trying to "get everything white folks had in the hopes that white folks won't be able to tell the difference, which wasn't *never* gone happen." Yo Yo rode a motorcycle—a big old hog of a cycle, which made noise like a train as she spiraled up the winding roads at any hour of the day or night. Yo Yo didn't wear those fine fashions, she was in jeans so tight around a body so sleek and lush, it made teenage boys like Mack fantasize about the day the threads would give way and those jeans just peel open like a split banana skin and she'd wheel that bike on over and get off it all naked with the jeans spilling on down and she'd say, "Teenage boy with concupiscent eyes, I wonder if you'd like to take a ride with me."

That wasn't no *dream,* Mack knew, that was just him wishing. Yo Yo had that effect on a boy, and Mack wasn't so strange he could get confused about the difference between his wishes and Yo Yo's dream.

He knew Yo Yo's dream when it came to him. In fact, he'd pretty much been waiting for it, since he was familiar with all the regular dreams in his neighborhood, and the ones that turned up only at school—all the deep dreams that kept coming back the same. He noticed easy enough when the new dream came, on a night when that motorcycle echoed through the neighborhood and somebody shouted out a string of ugly words that probably woke more babies than the motorcycle he was cussing about.

The new dream was a hero dream, and in it he was a girl—which was always a sure sign to him that it was *not* his own dream. He definitely wasn't one of those girls-trapped-in-a-boy's-body. But in the dream, this girl had on tight jeans, and Mack sure liked how they felt on him. He liked how the horse felt between his legs when he rode—even though when he came out of the dream, he knew that in the real world it was a motorcycle and not a horse.

In the dream, Yo Yo—because that's who it had to be—she rode a powerful horse through a prairie, with herds of cattle grazing in the shade of scattered trees, or drinking from shallow streams. But the sky wasn't the shining blue of cowboy country; it was sick yellow and brown, like the worst day of smog all wrapped up in a dust storm.

And up in that smog, there was something flying, something ugly and awful, and Yo Yo knew that she had to fight that thing and kill it, or it was going to snatch up all the cattle, one by one or ten by ten, and carry them away and eat them and spit out the bones. In the dream Mack saw that mountain of bones, and perched on top of it a creature like a banana slug, it was so filthy and slimy and thick, only after creeping and sliming around awhile on top of the pile of bones, it unfolded a huge pair of wings like a moth and took off up into the smoky sky in search of more because it was always hungry.

The thing is, through that whole dream, Yo Yo wasn't alone. It drove Mack crazy because, try as he might, he couldn't bend the dream, couldn't make the girl turn her head and see who it was riding with her. Sometimes Mack thought the other person was on the horse behind her, and sometimes he thought the other person was flying alongside, like a bird, or running like a dog. Whoever or whatever it was, however, it was always just out of sight.

And Mack couldn't help but think: Maybe it's me.

Maybe she needs me, and that's why I'm seeing this dream.

Because in the dream, when the girl rode up to the mountain of old bones, and the huge slug spread its wings and flew, and it was time to kill it or give up and let it devour the whole herd, the girl suddenly realized that she didn't have a gun or a spear or even so much as a rock to throw. Somehow she had lost her weapon—though in the dream Mack never noticed her having a weapon in the first place. She was unarmed, and the flying slug was spiraling down at her, and then suddenly the bird or dog or man who was with her, he—or it—leapt at the monster. Always it was visible only out of the corner of her eye, so Mack couldn't see who it was or whether the monster killed it or whether it sank its teeth or a beak or a knife into the beast. Because just at the moment when Yo Yo was turning to look, the dream stopped.

Not like regular dreams, which would fade into wakefulness. Nor was it like Mack's other waking dreams, which he gradually felt slipping away until they were gone. No, this dream, when it ended, ended quick, as if he had suddenly been shoved out of a door into the real world. He'd blink his eyes, still turning his head to see . . . nothing. Except maybe some of his friends laughing and saying, "Mack's back!"

For both these reasons—Mack's fantasies of Yolanda on the motorcycle, Mack's hope that somehow it might be him accompanying Yolanda on horseback to face the slug with her—he keyed in on her as the meaning of his life. Because of her dream, he wasn't just an abortion-gone-wrong, an accidental survivor. He was born to be here in the flat of Baldwin Hills as Yo Yo's bike roared up the street and into the mountain. He was born to love her. He was born to serve her. He was born to die for her in the jaws of the giant slug, if that's what she needed from him.

So Mack didn't miss a single whisper as the adults began to work themselves up about the "problem" in the neighborhood. Somebody complained to the police about the noise, but then word got around that Yolanda's bike had passed the noise test, which only got them angrier.

"If that machine isn't loud enough to get confiscated, then why do we have noise pollution laws in the first place?" demanded Miz Smitcher.

"If we can't get rid of the bike," said Ceese's mom, "then we have to get rid of the girl."

"There's no way she *owns* that house," said Old Lady James. "Hoochie mama like that, how could she pay for it? Some man's keeping her."

"That's the old Parson house," said Miz Smitcher. "Mr. Parson was blind and deaf when they carted him off to the old folks' home, and Mrs. Parson was out of there like a shot. You think *she's* keeping that Yo Yo?"

The suggestions came thick and fast then. Maybe she's squatting there, and the Parsons—or the new owners, if there are any—don't even know she's living in their house.

Maybe she really *is* a hoochie mama, but she makes so much money at it, she actually bought the house cash. "And paid for it in quarters," cackled Old Lady James, "like a straight-up two-bit ho!"

Maybe she's a niece of Mr. Parson and they just weren't able to say no to her.

Maybe she's the girlfriend of a drug lord who bought the house to keep her in it. ("Drug lords can afford better-looking women than that!" sniped Ceese's mom.)

But after all the speculation, the answer was simple enough. Hershey LeBlanc, a lawyer who lived four doors down from her and swore the koi in his pond went insane from the noise of her motorcycle, looked up the deed, and found that the house did indeed belong to Yolanda White, who paid for it with one big fat check. "But the deed has covenant," LeBlanc announced triumphantly.

"A covenant?" asked Miz Smitcher.

"A restriction," said LeBlanc. "Left over from years and years ago, when this was a white neighborhood."

"Oh, my lord," said Ceese's mom. "The deed says the house can never be sold to a black person, is that it?"

"Well, to be precise, it specified a 'colored person,' " said LeBlanc.

"Those things don't hold up in court anymore," said Miz Smitcher. "Not for years."

"Besides," said Old Lady James. "Half the houses up there must have covenants like that, or used to."

"And how hypocritical would we have to be to try to throw her out of her house on account of she's *colored,*" hooted Ceese's mom. "I mean, this whole neighborhood is as black as God's armpit, for crying out loud."

"As black as God's armpit!" cackled Old Lady James. "That is the most racist thing I ever heard."

"If that's the most racist thing you ever heard," said Ceese's mom, "then you went deaf a lot younger than I thought."

"We won't kick her out because she's black," said Leblanc. "We'll nullify the sale because the deed still had that covenant and she didn't challenge it. We'll sue her because she left the racist covenant in her deed, which is an offense to the whole neighborhood."

"So she'll just change the deed and strike out the covenant," said Ceese's mom.

"But by then she'll know we want her out of here," said LeBlanc. "Maybe she'll just sell it."

"To a white family, I'll bet!" said Miz Smitcher. "After all, her deed forbids her to sell to a 'colored family.' "

They all had a good, nasty laugh over that. But when he left, Hershey LeBlanc vowed that he'd find one legal pretext or another to get her out of the neighborhood—or at least stop the loud motorcycle noise at all hours.

That's how it was that Mack found himself walking up the long winding avenue that spiraled into the mountain. He didn't go up there much, once he had satisfied his curiosity about the spot where he had been found—not that he was sure where that spot was, since Raymo and Ceese couldn't agree with each other about where it was, nor did either of them pick the same place twice. And ever since he had become so fascinated with Yo Yo, he had made it a point *not* to go look at her house, because the last thing he wanted to be when he grew up was a stalker.

Today's visit wouldn't be stalking, though. He had heard her bike roar in at four a.m., so he imagined that noon on summer Wednesday should be just about right for a sixteen-year-old dream-ridden crazy boy from the flat of Baldwin Hills to go knocking on Yolanda White's door.

Except there was a locked gate in the fence.

Ordinarily that sort of thing was no barrier to Mack. He and his friends weren't even slowed down, let alone stopped, by little things like fences as they roamed the neighborhood. He could be over this simple white-painted wrought-iron fence in five seconds—less, if he had a running start.

But it wouldn't be such a good start to the conversation if she came to the door and demanded to know how he got into her yard.

So Mack walked right on past the house—eyeing it surreptitiously, but seeing not a sign of life—and kept on up the avenue till he reached the edge of the park. He stood there looking down into the basin where rainwater collected. When it rained heavily, all the runoff from this high valley would pour down into the basin, and there was a tall standing drainpipe, which, when the basin got deep enough, would carry away the water through a big pipe that ran under the street. That's what kept the whole street from becoming a river in every rainstorm.

And that pipe was the place that Mack thought of as his birthplace. Not that he really believed that his mother had been lying right there when some abortionist pulled him out of her. But whenever he saw that pipe, he felt something powerful flowing out of it, like the blood rushing through his body, and he knew that whatever it was that made him Mack Street was still connected to this basin, to that pipe. It was because of whatever flowed from that pipe that he hadn't died up there, buried in leaves. That's what he believed, because it made more sense than believing that his whole life was just a dumb accident.

He was contemplating that pipe, that basin, the underbrush and the leaves that collected there, when he heard the unmistakable sound of a motorcycle engine revving up.

He had waited too long.

He whirled around and raced down the road—even though he had clear memories of running down a hill when he was three and falling and skinning his knees and hands so bad that Miz Smitcher actually cried when she saw the injury. He threw himself onto the mercy of gravity, forcing his legs to stay ahead of his body so he didn't fall over and skid sixty yards. The automatic gate in the driveway was opening when he reached it and hurled himself against it like a bug on a windshield.

Yo Yo was just easing the bike down the driveway when Mack suddenly appeared, clinging to her gate. She stopped and looked at him, and he must have seemed pretty pathetic or something, because she busted out laughing and killed the motor.

The silence was louder than the engine had been.

"Well?" said Yo Yo. "Did you want to say something, or are you just hoping they make bashing-your-face-into-a-moving-gate an Olympic event?"

"I wanted to talk to you," said Mack. "I got to warn you."

"What, somebody sent their crazy teenage boy to tell me to stop riding my bike?"

Mack was astonished. "How did you know I was crazy?"

She just broke up laughing. Practically fell off the bike. "Peel yourself off my gate, and come in here," she said. "I been looking for a crazy boy, and I guess I just found him."

Two minutes later, there he was inside her house, sitting on her floor because there really wasn't a stick of furniture in the living room apart from the thronelike chair on which she sat and the lamp beside it—not even a TV or boom box or anything, just a chair, a lamp, and a stack of books.

He blurted out everything he'd heard them saying about her, excepting only the remark about the quarters. How the covenant excluded black people so she couldn't live there, or maybe she couldn't live there because she didn't change the deed, but anyway it was all about the bike and they were really mad and she'd better do something or they'd cause her a lot of trouble.

"Why you telling me this, boy?"

Well, now, that had him stumped. Not that he didn't know the reason, but he couldn't say, Because I love you. It would hurt too much when she laughed at him for loving a grown woman like her.

"I like your bike," he said.

She laughed anyway. "Want to ride it?"

"Don't got a license."

"Yeah, but that would only matter if I cared." She got up and left the room and came back with two helmets. "Either one of these fit onto that huge head of yours?"

Mack didn't even mind her saying that, since it was true—he always had to set the plastic tabs on the back of a baseball cap to the last notch, and even then it would perch on his head like an egg.

But one of the helmets fit him, or at least he could force it on past his ears, and in no time he was sitting on the bike as she showed him the controls, how to clutch and shift gears, how to speed up, how to brake. "Miz White," he said, "I can't make my hands and feet do four different things at the same time."

"In the first place," she said, "Miz White is my mama. I'm Yolanda. Yo

Yo if I feel like letting you call me that to my face. In the second place, look how stupid most motorcycle riders look. I can promise you, they really are that dumb, and if *they* can ride, so can you. So let's go through it again, and you show me that you know what your hands and feet are good for."

Five minutes later, after a few pathetic false starts, Mack found himself riding Yo Yo's motorcycle down the driveway and out the gate, with Yo Yo herself sitting behind him with her arms around his waist and her breasts pressing into his back and the bike vibrating so much, he couldn't hardly see. He drove slow, and when he came out of the driveway, he turned right, uphill, toward the basin.

He drove fast enough that the bike kept its balance, but not a bit faster. And when he got to the top, he slowed down and stopped.

Yolanda reached around him and turned the key and the engine shut off.

"Now *that* was about the saddest excuse for a bike ride I've ever had," she said. "A man gets on a bike, he's supposed to feel the power of it, he's supposed to pour on the speed."

Ashamed, all he could say was, "Sorry."

"Don't tell me you didn't *want* to go fast."

"Course I did," said Mack.

"I've heard about you, crazy boy. I've heard you take any dare anybody ever gives you, and you're not afraid of a damn thing."

Mack nodded, wondering how his school reputation ever reached a grown-up, especially one that all the other grown-ups hated. It occurred to him that he might not be the first kid to be on her bike with her body pressed up close, and that made him angry and sad and foolish-feeling.

"So how come you were scared to go fast on this bike? It's made for speed, Sneed!"

" 'Cause if I crashed the bike," said Mack, "*you* might get hurt."

She just sat there for a second, then got off the bike and came around the front of it and stood there leaning on the handle and looking in his eyes. "Is that some line you use or something?"

Mack didn't know what she meant by that.

"Because if it isn't, it should be. It's the first line I've heard from a man in a long time that didn't make me want to puke. In fact, it made me want to kiss you."

And being Yo Yo, she reached right out and peeled the helmet off his head, which wasn't easy—for a second or two he thought he might lose an ear in the process—but the helmet came off eventually, and his ears stayed where they belonged, and she reached out and took his head between her hands to kiss him right on the lips and then . . .

She stopped.

The expression on her face changed.

The hands holding his head slacked and then pulled away.

"Lord Jesus be my Savior," she whispered. "It can't be you."

Mack didn't know what she meant by that, but for one brilliant, wonderful, terrible second he thought: She's my mother. She must have been about thirteen when she had me aborted, that's something I never thought about, that maybe she was just a child. But she never knew I was alive till she put her hands on my head and then she somehow knew, maybe she felt the dream inside me, she *knew* I was her baby.

But right along with that thought came another one: I got all hot and hard for my own *mama* and that makes me about the sickest bastard in Baldwin Hills.

And he tried to get off the cycle to get away from her, but then realized that if he was standing up instead of sitting down she'd *see* just what had been on his mind when he thought she was going to kiss him, so he sat back down, and then she said, "No, baby, no. I'm not your mama. Whoever that poor woman was, she ain't me."

Was she reading his mind?

"No, I don't read minds," she said. "I just know *men* so well, I can read their faces."

"No," he said. "Don't lie to me."

"Okay," she said. "I read minds sometimes. Or more like I read souls. And when I put my hands on your head, I saw something inside your mind."

"What did you see?" asked Mack.

"I saw that you're filled with love."

With love or *something,* thought Mack.

"I saw that this spot is holy ground to you," she said.

And he trembled that she could have seen such a thing, just by touching him. Or did she have the story from Ceese or Raymo?

"And I saw that you're the one who found my lost dream."

"What do you mean?" he asked.

"My dream," she said. "When I was a little girl, when it was still horses I wanted to ride, back when I didn't know black girls didn't grow up to ride horses. I dreamed a dream of riding, but then I got older and I stopped having that dream. It was so long lost that I'd forgotten I even had it, though now I can see that my riding this bike must have been like a distant echo of it. Only when I put my hands on your head, after I heard the love crying out from your heart, and after I felt the holiness of this place inside you, then I saw a dream, and it was my dream, and you been dreaming it for me, keeping it for me all these years."

"No, ma'am," said Mack. "I only started dreaming it once you moved here."

"Well, now, that's sweet," she said. "I guess it was inside me all along, only lost. But either way, it's you that found it, and you that brought it back to me, and that makes you my friend for life, Mack Avenue."

"Mack Street," said Mack.

"I always give my friends a new name," she said.

"I'd rather you gave me that kiss."

She laughed, and she kissed him right on the mouth, and it wasn't no auntie kiss, and it wasn't quick. But even so, it also wasn't the kiss she would have given him before she found her dream inside his head, and he knew it, and he was just a little disappointed.

"I'm a minister, you know," she said.

"I didn't know that."

"Well, nobody else does, either," she said. "Because I haven't found the God I want to preach about. But I'm wondering right here if I ain't some kind of John the Baptist, looking around for Jesus. Because you, Mack Avenue, you're the Keeper of Lost Dreams, and that's a God that's been needed in this world for a long time."

"But it's a bad dream," said Mack.

"No, it's not," she said. "It's the best dream of my whole life. It's the dream I love best."

"But there's that monster. That slug with wings."

"And I've got to kill it," she said, "and I don't have any weapons. I know all that. It's my dream, you know."

"But doesn't that scare you?"

"No, sir," said Yo Yo. "Why do you have to ask? In my dream, have you ever felt me be afraid?"

He realized, when she asked, that he'd never felt a speck of fear in her.

A car screeched to a halt. Slowly Mack brought himself out of gazing into Yo Yo's eyes and turned to see Miz Smitcher slamming the door of the car and stalking toward Yo Yo with murder in her eyes.

"Who do you think you are, getting my boy up on that monster and letting him drive it! He got no driver's license, you crazy bitch!"

"Watch who you calling a crazy bitch," said Yolanda mildly. "If I really *was* a crazy bitch, you wouldn't have the balls to call me that."

Miz Smitcher turned to Mack. "You get off that bike, Mack Street, and get in that car."

Mack turned to Yolanda. What should I do? he wanted to ask her.

She grinned at him. "I'll see you later, Mack Avenue."

"No, you won't!" screeched Miz Smitcher. "You come within twenty yards of him, and I'll have you in jail for corrupting a minor! You hear me? There's laws protecting young boys from predatory women like you!"

"Mama bird," said Yolanda, "I got no plans to steal away your little chick."

"I'll have you out of this neighborhood, you and that bike! Now I see you using that thing to lure young boys into your den of depradation!"

Yolanda laughed out loud. "A woman with tits like mine, why would I ever need a bike to lure boys!"

That was so outrageous that even Miz Smitcher couldn't think of a thing to say, and Miz Smitcher *never* couldn't think of something to say. Instead she grabbed Mack by the wrist as he was getting off the bike and nearly made him lose his balance as she dragged him to the car and shoved him in through the driver's side with a push so hard, he smacked the top of his head on the glass on the other side. And in no time she had that car turned around and headed down the hill, but Mack could still hear Yo Yo's laughter behind him.

"She's a minister," he said.

"You shut up," said Miz Smitcher. "You ain't thinking straight and you *won't* be thinking straight for about two hours after having that woman's arms around you and her *kissing* you."

Mack was outraged. "You mean somebody *called* you?"

"Well, I didn't have no psychic vision if *that's* what you're thinking!"

"She's a minister, Miz Smitcher, it was a . . . a Christian kiss."

"Well, there's a billion Christians in this world, and most of them got started with a kiss like that. So you're not to go near her again, you hear me? I'll get her out of this neighborhood if I have to buy a gun and shoot that bike."

"All right," said Mack.

"You agreeing with me, just like that?"

"Yes, ma'am."

"Well, now I know you're lying. A boy your age doesn't just say yes ma'am about staying away from a woman like that."

Mack was thinking like crazy, trying to find a way to get Miz Smitcher out of this rage she was in. And then he got it. "Miz Smitcher, I just thought maybe she was my mama. Maybe she come back here to look and see what become of her baby."

That was it. That was the answer. Because all of a sudden Miz Smitcher's eyes got all teary and she pulled the car over in front of the neighbor's house and just hugged him to her and said, "Oh, you poor baby, of course you'd think she was your mama, her looking like she does. Exactly the kind of woman who'd have an abortion and leave the baby in the woods."

That wasn't exactly what Mack had meant, but it would do.

"So you didn't have the hots for her, you thought she was your *mama*!" Miz Smitcher began to laugh and put the car back in gear and drove the thirty yards to the curb in front of her house and by the time she got the car parked, she was laughing so hard, tears were coming down her face and Mack half expected the windshield wipers to come on.

Two things stuck with Mack from that car ride with Miz Smitcher. First one was, that was the first time he could ever remember her hugging him. Second thing was, You tell somebody something they want to hear, and they'll believe it even if it's the biggest old lie you ever made up.

He promised her everything she asked him to promise—that he'd never ride that bike again, that he'd never go to That Woman's house again, that he'd never talk to her again, that he'd never even *think* of her again. The only true thing he said to her was when she made him say, "I know she could not possibly be my mama."

That night he halfway hoped he'd dream Yolanda's dream, but he didn't. He picked up half a dozen other dreams, including one that he thought might be Miz Smitcher's, and which he never watched all the way through. Yolanda's dream never came, but in the morning he realized, Well of course I didn't dream her dream and I never will again, because I gave it back to her and now it's for *her* again.

But I still got my own dream, he thought. Nothing yesterday was really much like that dream of roads and rocks and cliffs and floods, except I was running down the street like hurtling along the canyon, and at the end of it, a woman reached out and held my head and kissed me and she tasted sweet as love.

***Ray Feist** has been a giant in the fantasy field for so long that it's hard to remember a time when there was just J. R. R. Tolkein and a few others to turn to for his kind of epic mastery. His book* Magician, *which introduced Pug to the world, remains a marvelous read, as do all of his subsequent books, including numerous best-sellers.*

See my headnote to "Blood, Oak, Iron" for Janny Wurts's myriad talents; the one I left out, deliberately, was her marvelous talent for collaboration.

Watchfire

Raymond E. Feist and Janny Wurts

That bitter day in December, a rain verging on snow pattered down and blurred the newsprint of the late professor's obituary. Old Jake held the sodden newspaper over his head. Sheltered beneath that untrustworthy roof, he scraped at an itch under his filthy shirt. From the dim gray of the alley, he watched the professor's daughter cart another box of yellowed, curled paper toward the trash pile heaped by the curb. Shouting obscenities to an impatient landlord, unseen through the opened door, she banged the box down. Her faux pearls rattled against her jangling gold bracelets. Dust puffed, and a cardboard seam split.

Jake grumbled an oath through his chattering teeth. Wait too long, and the box would become just as wet as the others he'd hoped to snatch earlier. The frigid rain was light but persistent, and worsening by the minute.

From the open door, the daughter's protests reached a shrieking climax. "I'm not paying for another month! We just need one more day. How could I give notice? I'm not on the lease! The old man couldn't; he was comatose in the hospital, fercrissakes! What, you think he should have seen the stroke coming and called you just in case?"

Whatever the curmudgeon landlord replied, the door slammed. Jake darted forward on broomstick legs, his wet trousers slapping at his ankles. He bent, snatched with gnarled, red hands, and clutched the burst carton to his hollow breast. Dry fuel for a miserable night would spare him from shivering over the steam in a sewer grate.

The unrelenting rain chased him the length of the alley, getting heavier by the minute. Jake dripped like a dog as he scuttled. If not for the fact that old Gran needed help, he would have forsaken his effort several hours ago.

But Gran hated shelters. She refused to go in, and another hard night would worsen the dry cough that plagued her. Their fire in the old drum by the warehouse required feeding, and the rain made such scavenging difficult. From shop front, to overhang, to the weeping, iced boughs of the bare sycamore trees in the park, Jake lugged the box of old papers. He picked his way over the derelict railroad tracks, past yesterday's sodden newspapers. The glossy page of a soaked fashion ad watched him pass with smeared eyes. Jake shivered in the wind, and he hurried under the runoff that spilled in tinsel streams through the leaks in the overpass.

There, deeper puddles forced him to wade. Before his eyes, the sleet turned to snow, blowing across his view. The sight reminded Jake of the little glass globe that had stood on his father's desk. In the sanctum of a stern and distant man, that was the one object of joy to the child: a little train station caught in a blizzard each time his small hand shook the ball. No matter how miserable Jake felt today, the remembrance gave pleasure when seeing snow the first time every year.

"Could be a white Christmas," he thought. The date must be soon, though he couldn't rightly remember which day of the week the holiday fell on. He was cold to the bone, beneath his torn jacket, by the time he ducked under the roof of the loading dock at the back of the abandoned warehouse.

Old Gran sat tucked in her grease-stained trench coat, her ragged mittens clenched over tucked knees. She was sucking a soda straw between her gapped teeth, rocking and muttering as always. Her filmed eyes would be seeing something other than snowfall, since her babble today bore little semblance to reason.

Jake greeted her anyway and hunkered down next to the rusted five-hundred-gallon drum. The blaze he had left had subsided to ash. The untended flames had burned out quickly. With Gran's singsong nonsense filling his ears, he unfolded his chilled hands and started to roll up the wastepaper claimed from the dead.

The wet bothered his arthritis. Jake dismissed his discomfort, faced with Gran's plight. "At least I still can see," he mumbled. The old woman insisted she wasn't blind, but he pretty much had to lead her wherever she went.

Fate seemed to conspire to keep them together, and the time when she hadn't been with him often felt distant and dim. Jake could recall earlier days, if he had a mind to, the high life he had led before he was homeless, and brought to this low estate.

He had been someone once—an investor uptown. People had seen him as a lion among sheep, a king of the Financial District. The career had finally cost him his marriage. "Trust issues," said the psychologist who had billed him two hundred an hour but failed to straighten him out. His children lived on the far side of the country, and his last conversation with his son had cut off with the same, angry line, to sober up and stop asking for money. Jake couldn't remember the last time they spoke.

" *'How sharper than a serpent's tooth it is*

To have a thankless child.' "

A quotation from *King Lear*; Jake found it ironic. He could still recite Shakespeare, but not call to mind the name of his latest grandson. Jason, or Justin, or Joshua—something that began with *J*. His children had little to thank him for. An absentee father, he had seldom contacted them after the divorce. He'd paid for their college and had his secretary send gifts of money on birthdays and at Christmas. But he missed his daughter's graduation from college when an important merger threatened to fall through.

Then the younger set took over on Wall Street. The junk bond kids edged in on the game, then came the dot-com screwup—Jake had watched his client list shrink. Scared, he lived the fast life in the company of younger women, spending lavishly on gifts, jet-set travel, wild parties, and drinking. A lot of drinking.

His boss told him his services were no longer needed. At first, he feigned confidence; it was just a little slump. He was king, he'd come back. Then his lawyer phoned about a tax audit. The feds took everything: the car, the town house, the Rolex, the Chippendale furnishings, even the designer clothing. Jake had hidden some money. He lived in a rental for a while, but never could get beyond the first interview. Soon the friends who'd lent cash refused all his phone calls.

Jake swiped at the moisture that dripped down his face, glancing up to see if the roof leaked. It didn't. Chiding, he snapped, "That's why you don't want to remember, old fool."

Nothing mattered, now, except feeding the fire.

The folders at the front of the box contained packets of type-scripted letters. The old professor had been meticulously neat. His filing was chronological. The earlier years had been done on a manual machine, with an antiquated ink ribbon. Jake began with the correspondence, since the loose sheaves would be quicker to catch in the whipping gusts.

"Here, Gran," he soothed through her monotonous patter, "I'll have us toasty in no time."

The crabbed old woman stopped speaking. She spat out her straw to suck on her lips. Her face was age-spotted and sad. Snags of yellowish hair poked from under a ski hat so filthy, the color could only be guessed at.

Aware of her unnerving, cloudy-blind eyes, watching each move as though sighted, Jake blotted his sore fingers. He pawed in his pocket to fish out his matches, a half-used book scrounged from the gutter and kept dry in a plastic bag. There were only four left, not a cheerful predicament. During unpleasant weather, the coffee shops would run a man out the door. No matter that he was down on his luck, and just needing a book of matches. "For customers, only," was always the answer.

Jake crumpled a letter and struck the first flame in the shelter of his bent knees. The old professor had been an organized man. Each topic had also been alphabetized. From the folder marked ESOTERICA, MILLENNIUM, the fire chewed through the address of someone named Nathanson.

Its progress singed a black ring through the words, "next séance, and Charles plans to bring that artifact from the northern burial."

"Damn queer old professor," Jake mused to himself. The obituary had stated the fellow had been ancient, remarkably spry at 102. If doctors of history toyed with the occult, no wonder the coot's landlord had been more than anxious to clear out the place at his death. To judge by the degree of hysterical shouting, maybe the fellow had been the sort who would rush to call in an exorcist. Get rid of the spirits! Jake chuckled. As though something other than money determined a man's fate in the world.

He fed in the letters to Nellis, about twenty of them; then Norris, Owens, Patterson, Peters, Potter, Purcell, and Quincy. Soon the blaze cast a ruddy glow over Gran's hollowed cheeks and sallow complexion. A spark like lit sulfur seemed to stare back from the pearly film of her cataracts.

Jake looked on her kindly. Every inch of her wizened face was familiar to him by now. Perhaps the oddest fact of his roller-coaster life was his closeness to this old woman. The morning he'd met her remained strangely clear. He'd been crouched in the Dumpster behind Isaac's Deli, digging through yesterday's garbage, when a stick had banged the side, and a shout had echoed over the rim. "Iggy will find us if we don't run, quick!"

Everyone in the neighborhood knew that crazy Iggy would beat a man to death just because he felt ornery. Though Jake heard no sign of the crazy man's yelling, he had scrambled out and found Gran there, waiting, her eyes like dull pearls and her trench coat as timelessly soiled. "If you want to get warm," she had said, "come with me, Jake."

He hadn't bothered to ask how she knew about Iggy, or question why she used his name. Then, he'd assumed she'd seen him around. Now, he knew that she often had hunches. She'd led him to a barrel fire some of the boys had started on the vacant lot at the corner of Stanhope and Granger. He and Gran spent that first night standing together, listening to everyone's stories of better days. After that, Jake had never been parted from her for more than a couple of hours.

His odd devotion to her was sad, in a way. Had Jake felt nearly as close to his wife, he might have salvaged his marriage. Instead of despair and bad choices, he could have abandoned the glitz of high finance and tried finding something productive. He need not have crawled into a bottle to die, tending fires for a mumbling old woman.

Jake sighed. *"Such is the power of love."* Aware of Gran watching, he shook his head. He could not imagine her as a young woman, still knew almost nothing about her. The need to ask questions had never arisen. She'd settled into his life by existing.

Jake stretched his holed shoes toward the warmth, his chapped knuckles laced under damp sleeve cuffs. *"A dry night,"* he thought mournfully, *"is less chill than a wet one."* He hated to forgo a possible handout to avoid being soaked and frozen. Yet as ice piled up on the sidewalks, the last-minute shoppers would be clutching umbrellas. Running for trains, burdened down with their packages, everyone hastened home, anxious to wrap up their gifts. Christmas charity aside, the ankle-deep slush made people reluctant to pause to give change. Old Man Weather had taught Jake the hard way that most all you got was drenched to the skin, pounding the pavement during a snowstorm.

"It's winter solstice," said Gran, breaking into his misery. "The longest night of the longest year, and our time is nearly upon us."

Jake didn't know what she meant by that nonsense. Dawn would be a long time in coming. He could spend tonight cold, lulled to sleep by Gran's mumbling, or else suffer the puking crazies who scratched themselves and banged elbows all night at the church shelter. Couldn't really find any rest there, sleeping with one eye open. Too often, some fool thought you had something worth stealing. Better to be chilled than get bullied for a couple of matches stuffed in a baggie.

Already run through the *Ws*, Jake nursed in his hoard of wooden slats, pried out of a torn-up sofa. He listened to Gran cough behind her frayed sleeve and watched the gray leak out of the world, while the sparkling snow fell, lit peach by the glare of the sodium lamp.

Jake drowsed to the drone of Gran's patter. The wind dusted drifts through the loading dock, masking the oil stains on the asphalt. The flames flattened and danced in the rusty drum, consuming the last file, a fat sheaf tied up with string. The letters had been written by a person named Xavier. The handwriting was steep and narrow, and almost illegible. Jake fumbled the leaves, overcome by the chill, while the fire-cast shadows loomed in on him.

The last sheets were marked with a cipher that looked written down in old blood. Jake shivered. Whatever correspondence the professor pursued, his colleagues seemed otherworldly. At least, no one these days sent letters spattered with what looked like soot-flecked wax from a candle. Jake shoved the packet deep into the fire. The hiss as the papers flared up fell on silence. Old Gran had gone quiet. Her fogged-marble eyes peered into the dark. Lips working, she spoke without voice.

The Z folder crumpled up into flames. The box was now two-thirds empty. Since the next papers were clippings from newspapers, and the inks would create choking smoke, Jake passed them over. He reached for the first of six yellow legal pads, marked WORKINGS in the professor's fussed hand. Their lined pages were written in his crabbed script. Old enough to have been inscribed with a fountain pen. There were also odd diagrams scored in India ink with a compass. The straight lines had been done with a draftsman's instruments, before innovation replaced ruling pens with the modern Rapidograph.

Jake started to crank the pad into a roll, when old Gran broke out of her stupor.

"Don't burn those."

Jake startled. "Why not? Would you rather be cold?"

Gran rocked, her eerie gaze on his face. "Don't," she repeated. "Two worlds will cross, but a minute from now. It's the spells in that box make the gateways."

"Nonsense," snapped Jake. He flipped the pad's pages. "You can barely see! How can you read this?"

"I don't read words," Gran said, matter-of-fact. Her crabbed finger pointed through her holed glove. "What's written there lies outside of language. Might not read words, but I understand energy. Had a shop, once, where I did spiritual counseling. I know what I smell, on the ethers."

"Crazy old woman!" Jake sighed, exasperated. "Next thing, you'll tell me you're seeing Jesus. Or Satan. At least, that's what you ran on about last week." He shrugged, about to toss the pad into the flames, when the wind gusted hard in his face. The leaves flipped in his hands like an opened book, to lay bare an intricate drawing. Jake clutched the pad, frightened, as his sight became trapped in the mazelike array of fine lines.

Gran was chanting. Her words seemed joined by others, an echo in languages drawn from across time and distance. Jake's head whirled with dizziness. Darkness bloomed over his peripheral vision. The vortex loomed larger and swallowed him whole. Like a leaf, he spun into nothing.

The chanting blurred into a roaring like wind. From very far off, old Gran's words resounded like echoes bounced down a long corridor. "It's a gate spell, I told you. Two worlds will meet. The truth in your heart must now renew them. . . ."

Like a titanic fist, some force slammed Jake through . . . What? A barrier? One second he had been holding a tablet and listening to Gran's senseless drivel. The next moment he reeled as though someone had tackled him from behind. He did not recall landing.

Yet, he now lay facedown on an icy stone floor, his sight black as he reeled with dizziness. For a moment, eyes closed, he wondered if he'd struck his head. Odd sensations coursed through his body. His mind whirled with images and a slipstream of sounds. A child laughed somewhere. He smelled cloves and cinnamon. Then the clear sensation of a melting kiss brushed his cheek. The touch recalled a girl he had known as a child. He felt overwhelmed by a bittersweet sadness.

He remembered how cotton candy had tasted at the state fair, and the huge hand of his uncle, clasping his wrist. But this time, the grip felt unpleasantly tight. He struggled, lost in a strain of oldies music—the soundtrack from the movie that had played as he lost his virginity to Merry Ann Velásquez at the drive-in. They had knocked elbows and banged knees, wrestling and panting to tug off their clothing in the backseat of his older brother's '63 Chevrolet Impala.

Jake smelled flowers and recalled Hawaii.

Voices spoke, snatches of conversation replayed from his past, tantalizingly vivid and close. He groped after phrases that faded away before he quite managed to grasp them.

Then someone murmured, "Hold him. He wakes."

Jake did not recognize who had spoken. If his eyes were open, he still could not see. Hands gripped his body. Jake struggled to move. The effort came to nothing, like trying to move while still dreaming. Enveloped in a sudden, soft warmth, he felt a damp cloth brush his face, infused with a fragrance more sweet than vanilla.

His sight cleared all at once.

He was not by the warehouse. There was no snow. Torches threw flickering shadows inside a round room, and three strangely dressed figures loomed over him. Jake gasped for air. His lungs ached, as though he had been holding his breath for too long, and his body was starving for oxygen. Frantic and scared, he tried to reach up, but his arms were strapped to his sides, and his legs and ankles seemed to be bound.

"Gently," someone reassured him. Her fingers clasped his shoulder with comfort, and her young face seemed calm as she smiled at him. "You will be fine in a moment."

Jake realized he was wrapped in a thick woven blanket, tight enough that his limbs could not move. Still light-headed, as yet unable to speak, he panted as more people tenderly lifted him. They bore him to a table, while he snatched frantic impressions of his surroundings. Nothing made sense. Torches were set in brackets on walls that were fashioned of unmortared stone. The faces of strangers moved in and out of the limited field of his vision.

One man and several women, each kindly and smiling, as if trying to reassure him that everything would be fine. Jake stared at their odd clothes and their primitive jewelry incised with carvings of stylized animals.

The woman who had addressed him before leaned over and cupped his face. "Close your eyes for a moment. Let your head stop spinning. Then we will know whether you are the one, Jacob. If you are, then all will become clear to you."

Jacob? Only his grandmother had called him that. Eyes closed, reeling into somnolent reverie, Jake relaxed. The blanket around him was infused with exotic oils, pungently floral and spicy. The confusion of rich scents was pleasing, not unlike his memories of selecting perfume as a gift, at an upscale department store.

He heard chanting in the background, muted and strange, a rising and falling of unison voices. The sound seemed to soothe and sustain him. Then careful hands started unwrapping the blanket. Drifting in a fog between sleep and waking, he sensed the constricting cloth loosening. As the covering was tugged down and away from his flesh, the brisk air flushed his skin into chill bumps.

More intimate touches brushed down his body, eased by the residual oil. The arousal that stirred between his bare legs shocked through his lingering lassitude. He had not felt *that* in a very long time! Eyes open, he glanced down. His shrinking embarrassment gave way to shock. That wasn't his body! He pushed off the hands that attempted to steady him and shoved upright in stark disbelief. He stared at himself. His stomach was flat. His arms had no age spots, and his legs had not been that firmly muscled since he had trained for collegiate track in his early twenties.

Jake touched his face, felt no lines or wrinkles. Stunned breathless, ignoring the reverent attendants who were urging him to lie down, he looked at his hands. Gone were the gnarled joints riddled with arthritis, the liver spots, and the bulging veins roped through parchment skin. He flexed his fingers, amazed at their strength. Running his palm over his forearms and chest, he battled his wheeling senses.

"Breathe slowly," urged the man at his shoulder. "You'll adjust in another moment."

"We're not here to distress you." The women who clinked with jade bracelets came forward, offering an emerald robe with gold thread and embroidered with symbols he almost recognized. The interlocked motif of circles and squares seemed to be oddly familiar.

Jake accepted the garment. Intensely aware of her presence, made self-conscious and flushed by his state of nakedness, he avoided the eyes of the young women who stood in silent attendance behind her. He fumbled with the strange clasps on the robe, defeated by lingering dizziness.

"Let me help," said the woman. Her smile stayed friendly. More mature than the rest, she had dark hair shot with grey, secured at her nape with a net made of yarn. Her high forehead, straight nose, full lips and strong jaw made her handsome rather than beautiful. She carried herself with aplomb, her figure firm underneath a lighter green robe than the one Jake had been given to wear.

Beyond numb, he nodded, then raised his arms, letting her sort out the folds and arrange the intricate fastenings. The cloth slipped easily over his body, fitting him at the shoulders and waist as though it had been made to measure. When she clipped the last hook, his light-headedness passed. Unasked, he pushed off the table. His legs were steady, even powerful again, and his poor eyesight was restored back to its youthful clarity.

Each shadow was crisp. The flame-lit room was without blurring and double lines. Jake hadn't seen with such vibrant detail since his last pair of eyeglasses had broken. The place where he stood seemed medieval, or older, its stone walls softened with tapestries. Their pattern showed forests, and animals by a stream leaping with fish and swimming waterfowl. An iron brazier burned in an alcove. The square window was large and shuttered with wood, and drafty, as though it lacked glazing. The door was too low to pass through without ducking, a wooden panel fitted with hand-forged hinges and a crude latch.

The strange woman and her coterie of attendants surrounded Jake, as if waiting. Both women and men wore the same, flowing robes. The antique fastenings were polished bone, the cloth hand-woven, but without the intricate patterns sewn into the one allotted to Jake. As though to ease his speechless confusion, the dark-haired woman suppressed a smile. "You're wanting a mirror?"

At Jake's nod, she spoke to a younger man, who opened a chest at the side of the room. He withdrew a round object the size of a shield and held up the frame so that Jake could gaze at his reflection. The front was not fashioned from silvered glass, but a sheet of buffed metal, perhaps tin or some alloy that had a faint golden sheen. Its rippled imperfections revealed a face Jake did not recognize for his own.

Not himself, as a young man, with his sandy, thin eyebrows and the weak chin his ex-wife had complained of, but the way he had secretly wished he might look, had he been born clean-cut and handsome. The features he saw did not suggest a hard life or a loser's character. The man who looked back into his searching eyes appeared confident, even courageous. Jake reached up and touched the reflection, just to make sure. His black hair was thick. His eyes were not bloodshot or clouded. He saw no trace of dissipated skin, or dark circles, or the flush of the long-term alcoholic. He fought tears, overcome. Of all the delusions he had endured at the bottom of a bottle of whiskey, this one was the most cruel.

He backed up, sat down on the table and said, "This can't be real."

"Bless the day!" the dark-haired woman exclaimed, while her attendants smiled with radiant joy, and exclaimed with bursting amazement. "Behold! Fate is answered. He is the Doubter!"

The maidens pressed forward and crowded about him, beckoning and laughing with eagerness. "Come. There is little time before midnight."

"Trust us, Jacob," the dark-haired matron assured. "No harm will come of your stay here."

Jake stood. Still confounded, he chuckled. "If I'm going to dream of being young again, where are the playmates and the Jacuzzi?" As the woman opened the door, and the maidens prodded him on with soft hands, he shrugged and let himself be cajoled along. "Given the surroundings, maybe I should have said harem girls and moonlit bathing pools?"

"Come," said the woman, her smile unfazed by his boorish remark.

Jake followed her into a vaulted hallway, lit by torches set into ring sconces. The guttering flames threw warm light on stone walls in the draft that coiled through the chill passage. A second hallway branched off from the first, leading up a low incline to another floor, where a spiral staircase climbed into a massive round tower. The scale of the building dwarfed anything Jake had seen in his visits to ancient cathedrals. This dream was so real! The stair left him breathless. He marveled at how vibrant everything felt, smelled, and, he suspected, would taste, if one of the maidens should offer him something to drink. Over and over, he flexed his hands. Their pain-free joints and natural strength raised a thrill like intoxication. He was vital again, and bursting with health. With nothing but misery left when he awoke, he resolved to savor each moment.

At the top of the tower, he was shown into a hall twice the size of the earlier chamber. There his party was greeted by an ancient gray-haired man. Still erect, the fellow was powerfully built. He wore a heraldic surcoat overtop of fine chain mail and an engraved silver gorget. Beneath the embroidered hem of the cloth, he wore metal grieves and high-top boots of black leather.

As Jake was brought forward, the man clasped his hands to his breast and bowed. "I am the Sentinel."

Jake glanced aside, unsure of himself. Since no one else seemed inclined to speak, he tried to respond to the courtesy. "I'm Jake."

"You are well known to us, Jacob Moran." The Sentinel intoned with theatrical gravity, "We welcome you as the Doubter."

"What am I doing here?" Jake asked, determined to play along with the delusion. *"If you're having weird dreams,"* he thought to himself, *"why the hell not enjoy it?"*

"Your role is one of the three preordained by the working of fate," explained the older woman who had ushered him to the room. "I am Roslyn, Keeper of the Tower, first among those who are chosen. These behind are my acolytes. In time, as their predecessor, I shall appoint one of them to stand in my place."

Jake smiled without humor. "How nice for all of you, but I missed the rehearsal. Can someone tell me what role I'm expected to take here?"

"I can, Jake." She spoke from behind. Jake spun and regarded a stunning young woman, who must have just made her entry. She was slender and comely, her movement like willow as she crossed the wax-polished floor. Hair like gleaming mahogany had been piled in combs at the crown of her head. She approached, a proud creature, her chin pertly raised. Her taut figure was draped in a flowing red robe, embroidered with patterns of gold wire. More gold flickered and danced to her movement. Her ears, her wrists, and her delicate, bare ankles all glinted with tiny gold chains, each one set with drops of citrine and ruby. A train of attendants trailed at her heels. An erect, haughty crone followed two fair-haired young men, then two more fresh-faced maidens in scarlet.

The ancient among them bowed her head before Jake. "I am Janeal, Minder of the Flame, and these behind me are my acolytes."

Jake gave her his title as Doubter, for courtesy, but could not keep his eyes from the exquisite woman who had led in the procession. She had a hauntingly familiar quality about her. More than striking beauty, and beyond a complexion that glowed like a Victorian painting, Jake recognized the precise slant of her cheekbones and the way she carried her chin. The warmth of her glance, as she watched, seemed to know him. Her eyes were brown, flecked with hints of gold. Her smile all but made his breath stop, as she stepped into place and reached out to him.

Her warm hands gathered his. The chain dangle earrings gleamed at her neck, like a delicate fall of gold rain. "How do you feel, Jake?"

His pulse raced at her most casual touch. Deep-seated feelings welled up, and time seemed to pause, while the workings of memory faltered. Jake experienced a sharp pang of longing—an unbridled desire that rushed through him and lifted his spirit to exultation. He groped after a remembrance so fiercely treasured, its beauty and loss threatened to overwhelm him. Something seemed so profoundly familiar, *so real,* that he verged upon tears for the wonder. Almost speechless, the original question forgotten, he whispered. "My lady, who are you?"

With the firelight glimmering in her eyes, she also seemed flushed by emotion. "I told you we had discovered the gate spell."

Jake's heart skipped. He stared at her unlined face, those clear eyes, and a body erect in the unblemished bloom of youth. As though his entire reality turned over, he knew every curve of her features. *"Gran?"*

Then the Sentinel was at his side, hands clasped, and bowing to acknowledge her presence. "Lady Grania, I am the Sentinel."

She inclined her head. "I know you, my lord."

"You are most welcome, Fire Bringer. The ritual must begin, quickly."

Jake said, "Okay, so I'm probably dying of hypothermia right now, and this is my last delusional dream. But before I go, tell me what's going on, Gran."

"Don't speak." She touched a fingertip to his lips. "We have so little time."

"Less than an hour," the Sentinel said. "You are come just in time." He ushered them on toward a narrow, arched doorway carved into patterns of oak leaves.

"An hour before what?" Jake resisted, unsettled as the other parties and their acolytes swept forward and fell in beside and behind him.

"Midnight," Gran answered. "It's the last winter solstice of the century, my dear." Her urgent grasp tugged him forward.

"Ah . . . the millennium was celebrated some time ago, Gran." Flushed and aching, dizzy with the allure of her scent, Jake could not stop himself being drawn along toward the doorway. He could no more have let go of Gran's hand than he could have refused air, were he drowning. "I may have been piss-drunk most of the time, but I still remember what year it is."

Grania squeezed his fingers. "Not everyone keeps the same calendar, Jake."

The Sentinel reached the doorway, then positioned himself to the left. "It is I who shall watch at the threshold," he said.

"I bear the key." The Keeper of the Tower unlocked the door, then assumed her place to the right.

"Mine, the task to tend the flame that ignites," the Watcher of the Fire pronounced as she took her position behind them.

Grania paused at the threshold. Vivid as desire itself, she presented Jake to those gathered. "I, the Fire Bringer, shall return the Doubter upon the hour appointed."

Before Jake could protest, her grasp drew him onward. They crossed the dark threshold. Their step ventured into a cold, windy night. Together, they mounted a staircase. The flight led them up onto the open turret, and there, they emerged, alone.

A huge brazier of iron stood at the center of a white stone pattern of circles. It was lit by a scanty bed of coals and a flame burned down to a flickering thread.

No other light burned. The surrounding castle was a squat edifice of gray stones set amid windy darkness. No stars blazed above, and no moon. Jake couldn't smell rain or see the lay of the land. The night closed like jet ice about them.

"Where are we?" he asked.

Gran raised his chilled fingers, laid them against her warm neck. "Where does not matter. No people live here, except those involved with the ritual." Her intimate whisper tickled his ear as she slipped her arms around him. Her piled hair rested against his throat, and her softness melted against him. Aware of his hard nakedness under this robe, Jake caught his breath. He embraced her slim shoulders, unable to think, as she clasped him close and leaned into him.

"What's happening?" The warmth of her presence burned him through, while the ceaseless wind keened in his ears. The surrounding darkness seemed thick, and alive, as though living shapes coiled within it. Despite Gran's vivid heat, and his burning desire, Jake felt the hair bristle in warning on the back of his arms and neck. "What are those?" he whispered, afraid lest the dream of her should transform into terror and nightmare.

"You stand on the edge of the Chaos, Jake." Gran's voice scarcely cut through the frigid, cold wind. "This castle stands as the Portal, at the crossroad between the Worlds of the Dark and the Light. That's where we live, Jake."

He laughed. At once, the cheap theatrics seemed foolish. "New Jersey? You say that's the World of Light?"

"And New York, Bombay, London, Rio, all of Earth, Jake. We come from the place of reason, where order and the laws of nature you know stay inside their patterned design. But order takes power, Jake. Entropy seeks to rule. When the fire burns down, Chaos requires no effort to birth its renewal."

Fire caught in Gran's rubies as she gestured toward the fathomless blackness and the unseen shapes whirling about them. "Here, you behold the rising of Chaos, at the Portal of Mystery where two worlds collide. Out of mystery, a man can wake nightmare or dream of beauty. He can spark the fire and rise to claim mastery, or he can despair and fall into madness."

Jake flung out a hand and brushed the stone merlon. Icy stone skinned his fingers. Gran's breath brushed his neck, just as joltingly real. A dying streamer of smoke from the brazier whirled around him, thick with the scent of burned herbs. "This cannot be real," he said, turning to face her. "It's only a dream, Gran. We're not in a castle. I'm lying on the floor of a warehouse on the west side of the Hudson, freezing next to a barrel full of burning papers. You're . . ." He paused, wrenched by grief. "If you were really you, I'd be holding a blind old woman in a trench coat, muttering nonsense and coughing." Wistful, he reached up and tugged out her comb, then tangled his grasp in the cascade of hair that spilled over his hands and wrists. "This is called wish fulfillment, a fantasy. We long to be young. I want a beautiful woman to love me. Gran. . . ." His voice choked. He fought through his upwelling emotions. "I wish we were real. I wish I had a second chance."

Her face tilted. She kissed him. He clung to her, desperate. Her mouth tasted of cloves, and the feel of her warmed him like fine wine, intoxicating his senses. Through her hair, through her skin, he felt her wild pulse as a drumbeat entwined with his own. Then her fingers were working to unfasten his robe.

"Sweet Jesus," he gasped. Her touch seared his skin. "This is too exquisite to be happening."

Her laughter sang through his thundering blood. "You are the Doubter, who will not believe, though a thousand times you have loved me. You have been a baker, and I your wife. Once you were a minister's son, and I, a young member of his congregation. We have been milkmaid and plowman; fiddler and dancer; a blacksmith and a girl in a hayloft. Our roles in the World of Light have no meaning. We meet there, but here, once in a lifetime, our true natures emerge." The last fastening breached, she drew off his robe, exposing him to the elements. Amid bitter cold, his body ignited to the power of her enticement.

Then she let her robe fall away. The glimmer of the brazier traced over her jewelry, sparkling at wrist, ear, and ankle. Against the black night, her flawless form seemed to hold the beginning and end of the world. Jake's chest constricted. She was magnificent in her youth, breasts curved to his hand with exquisite perfection. Her lean waist and taut poise were a dancer's.

Jake drew her into his arms, as a dream. No woman in life could be all that he physically desired, or share the enduring bond he had made with a half-witless old woman. The shrilling wind, and the feral forms darting amid the darkness—none of them could be real.

"Don't think, Jake. Not now. Save your doubting for later." Gran caught his wrist between urgent fingers. "Each hundred years, we meet for this hour. We have lived countless lives and will live countless more, linked by a fate old as time. The chosen call us, and we come together to restore the balance between order and Chaos. The Keeper of the Tower and the Sentinel hold the space while we strike the spark of rebirth."

That moment, the thin flame in the brazier flicked out, reduced to a flickering coal. "Come to me, Jake. The hour is upon us."

"What hour?" Jake shivered. Despite her warmth pressed close to his flank, the bitter, black chill gripped his innards. Undying cold knifed him down to the bone and threatened to tear him asunder.

"Look at me!" said Grania. "I am the Fire Bringer, Jake. This place serves the balance between dark and light. It anchors the boundary between Chaos and order, and ours is the task to drive back the night and rekindle the Watchfire before midnight."

Her face barely an inch from his own, she murmured, "Please, Jake. We have done this, now and forever."

"By dreaming?" His incredulous whisper caught in his throat as her tender hands stroked his flanks.

"By love and death." She kissed his lips, gripped him hard, and leaned into him, igniting his scalding response.

Overturned by a frenzy of passion, he folded her into his arms. Twined together, they burned, incandescent. He never felt the harsh cold of the stones. She gave herself, and he took her, cradled amid their discarded robes, and consumed by a love that welded their forms and remade them as one. Her skin was branding velvet, laid over his own. Every yielding touch drank his raw power. Her scent in his nostrils, her taste in his mouth, and the tidal surge of her movement swept Jake beyond awareness of thought and reason. Empty of care, beyond conscious will, he joined with her in the darkness.

Together, they forged an ecstatic joy that bordered upon the sublime.

They lay, more than flesh, more than mind, more than spirit, until Jake felt as though he hung poised on a pinnacle. Beyond time, at the edge of pure knowledge and certainty, he trembled, while in the howling of the wind, the coal burned down to a cinder. On the brink of encountering the clarity he had thirsted to find all his life, Jake pulled back.

Grania rolled with his movement and straddled him, arched like a bow at the verge of explosive, climactic release. Afraid, he cried out, convinced he had failed her. Through darkness, and loss, and the scream of the elements, he battled the agony of his uncertainty.

Her smile was bittersweet. "My love, fear for nothing. You have lived your destiny. For doubt is what binds the two worlds to balance. You fear the pure light as much as you shrink from the fall of absolute darkness. The curse and the blessing of your human race is to never know one or the other."

"But why?" Jake's shout entangled with the piercing peak of her passion.

Crying out, she dug her grip into his shoulder. "Because it is ordained!"

Suddenly she burned.

Jake shouted again, in terror and pain. Alone, he reached out in a desperate effort to bind her ephemeral form to him. Yet her woman's flesh burned to nothing and left him with emptiness between his locked hands. Bereft of the most profound joy he had known, he groped. Insane with grief, he longed to burn and stay with her. Yet the conflagration she had become slipped through his fingers and did not consume him.

She was gone. In her place a pillar of fire rose upward above his prone body. He lay trembling and spent, reduced by its blaze, while her voice brushed his mind as a whisper. *"Until next time, beloved."*

The flame scoured the top of the tower like daylight, then settled into the brazier. Jake rolled over. The stone circles were empty, but for himself, and two rumpled robes. He shoved himself to his feet, stumbled to the wall, and looked outward.

The dark and the wind had been utterly banished. Under transparent sky, no light burned except the fire that blazed at his back in the brazier. Around the castle of naked, gray rock, he saw nothing but brilliance, thrown back at him as from a mirror.

Jake heard the approach of footsteps behind. He turned around, saw the Watcher of the Flame, and another, strange man, clad in the same clothes as the Sentinel. This one was vigorous, blond haired and young, barely approaching his prime. Both paused by the brazier. The man bowed with reverence, while the Watcher came forward, as though to take Jake by the hand. "A new cycle has started. Grania's part is done. Mine is beginning. Yours is yet to reach fulfillment."

Jake stared at the brazier, too wretched with loss to accept his experience without cynicism. "What became of the Sentinel?"

"I am he," said the boy. "We all play our roles. And for each of us, there is a price."

The Watcher of the Flame retrieved the rose-colored robe and smoothed the crushed folds of the fabric. "The Fire Bringer finds joy but once in her life. For myself, I must bide here with the tower's Keeper, guarding this fire, until death leaves my charge to a successor."

Jake stared, too shaken to care for the fact that he was still trembling and naked. "And for me?"

"To never know, Doubter," the Sentinel replied. "To never know either the light, or the dark, or what lies at the heart of all mystery. My part is to watch for the final sign. You alone can reseal the portal between worlds, after the rekindling ritual."

Jake drew in a breath. Before he could speak, the Watcher reached out and covered his eyes with her fingers.

* * *

Jake jerked awake to the cold light of dawn, a policeman shaking his shoulder. The officer was a stocky young man. His gloved hand hovered next to his baton, anticipation against an old drunk waking up combative. "You all right, sir?" he asked.

Aching inside and out, Jake stirred from his stupor. As if something beautiful beyond comprehension had been ripped from his soul, he blinked bleary eyes and groaned. Every ache in his body protested the movement as he sat up. His hands were numb. He tucked them under his ragged sleeves, embarrassed by the familiar swollen joints, the liver spots, and enlarged veins.

The pinched contempt on the officer's face let him know he was the same derelict as he had been the night before. The clarity of the dream was fast fading, washed out by the glare off the snow. The tastes, the smells, the rich tapestry of experience clouded over, minute by minute.

Jake glanced down and noticed the overturned box. The professor's notes had been kicked to one side, while two paramedics bent next to a gurney. On the stretcher beside them lay Gran.

"Dead," commented one. "Limbs are cold as stone. Probably been gone hours."

"Natural causes?" The officer sounded bored.

"You're wanting to leave us the paperwork, I suppose?" The man wearing the ambulance logo sighed, then covered the dead woman's face with a blanket. "The Office of the Medical Examiner will have the last word, though I'd say hypothermia got her."

Jake swallowed. "I didn't let the fire go out." But he had. The blaze in the drum was burned down to ash. He shook his head, plagued by the fuzzy memory, of a Watchfire lit on the far side of a gate, burning bright in the care of the Keeper. Almost, he felt the eyes of the Sentinel, watching him from a portal that stood between worlds.

"Old Gran didn't freeze," he complained as the police officer relentlessly prodded him onto his feet. "She gave her life to rekindle the balance, and for that, you could treat her respectfully."

The policeman rolled his eyes at his partner, a young woman with a nose nipped with cold, who shrugged back with jagged impatience. She ducked into the warm patrol car and reached for the radio to call the DOA in. Last night had been busy. The homicide detectives could not afford to waste time, and what was another old homeless woman, frozen to death in the street? Both cops were more than anxious to be done with official proceedings.

"Did you know her?" the male officer inquired. "Anything about the deceased that might help us to locate her family?"

Jake gave the name he recalled from his dream. "Grania. She never mentioned any last name. She once had a shop where she did psychic counseling. That's all the history she ever told me." While the paramedic loaded her covered remains into the back of the ambulance, Jake struggled to reconcile his conflicted thoughts. "She had greatness in her, more than you know," he said on a lame note of misery.

Through the burst of radio crackle, as the female officer received the response from the station, the policeman regarded Jake closely. "You don't look well, sir. You need a trip to the hospital?"

Jake shook his head. "I'm not sick. Just cold." But he knew the drill. He still had to stand while a paramedic came over and checked to make sure of his vitals.

"I'll have to take you in to the shelter," the male officer insisted. "You can't stay here. It's too cold, and this warehouse is private property. The owner has the place up for sale, and doesn't want street people loitering."

Jake bundled his jacket around his raw bones. He nodded, then watched for his moment to bolt. Since he was not ill or injured, the paramedics moved off and slammed the ambulance doors.

While the laden vehicle started up and drove off, Jake scuttled into the gloom and splashed through the railway underpass. The squad car could never follow him there, and the officers balked at the wading puddle. They shouted just once, and kept their dry shoes, finally letting him go.

The snow had stopped. Ice and water lay everywhere, reflecting the dull sky of daybreak. Jake limped along, breathlessly wheezing and aching from his brief sprint. He knew if he begged by the stairs to the subway, someone might give him some change.

Then he could get drunk, and numb his grief for old Gran, and forget all about unsettling rituals, and portals that led into nowhere. Whether or not the world was the same, he didn't like having weird dreams. Tonight, the shelter might not seem so bad, even if the soup came with sermons.

Beside the old drum where his fire had burned, a crushed cardboard box lay beside the soaked notes that had opened the gate into mystery. The squad car's tread crushed the inked cipher to pulp, while Jake shuffled his way down the rustled rail siding, musing aloud to himself.

"Funny damn dreams. Seem so real while you're sleeping, then come the dawn, they just fade away into nothing." The aches in his joints were more reliable than any delusion brought on by the cold.

The last thought was dismissed, of gold chains and bright rubies, and a kiss that had kindled a fire. Unaware that his lack of belief closed the ritual, or that his doubt maintained the seal on the portal that guarded the balance between Chaos and Light, Jake considered which busy corner would offer his best chance for panhandling.

Life went on as it had, though the ache for Gran lingered, and a sense of deep loss weighed his heart for the rest of his days.

***Peter Schneider** has worn many hats in the publishing world. I wish he would write more, but his day job, as well as his stewardship of Hill House publishers, keeps him from doing so. Our loss.*

I love his sense of humor, reminiscent of the National Lampoon, and hope you do, too.

Tots

Peter Schneider

It is 2:45 a.m., in the parking lot of the massive superstore shopping centers that have sprung up like a series of mushrooms across the country. But the action at this time of the morning isn't in the Barnes & Noble or Home Depot—it's in an isolated corner of the lot, surrounded on two sides by security fencing and hemmed in on the remaining sides by a variety of vehicles, circled like wagons and facing inward with their headlights shining. The halogen illumination reveals a ring, roughly twelve feet in diameter, crudely outlined on the pavement with a can of purple spray paint. Outside the circle perhaps fifty or sixty people, mostly men but including a smattering of well-dressed women, stand and watch. Money changes hands here—big money. But their attention right now is on the two combatants standing within the ring, long and deadly sicklelike blades strapped securely to their right arms. One fighter takes a tentative step in the direction of his foe and raises his hand in preparation to strike. He'll have to get in closer, however—his four-year-old arms aren't long enough to deliver a killing blow from such a distance.

This is the world of totfighting.

Totfights are the latest craze to hit the parking lots of malls and churches across a broad swath of the southern states—though lately they've been seen as far north as Ohio and as far east as Virginia. The rules are simple: two four-year-old boys toddle into the circular arena—only one toddles out alive.

Many aficionados of the sport see it as a logical extension of the vastly more popular cockfighting—though truth be told, totfighting probably originated long before mankind had domesticated roosters.

It took me several months to make the necessary contacts to gain admission to the inner sancta of totfighting. Needless to say, most of the names in this article have been changed.

One of the leading exponents of this bloody sport will identify himself only as "Charles Reilly of 14 Ellwood Court, Macon, Georgia." "Totfighting has gotten a real bad name lately," muses Reilly as he leans back into the Naugahyde-y comfort of the battered La-Z-Boy in the bar area of his Winnebago. "And that's too bad, 'cause there ain't nobody I love better than my boys. Ain't that right, fellers?" he yells out to the seven or eight well-developed toddlers playing a spirited game of Candyland on the floor of the motor home. But they're too involved in their game to take any notice of the man they call "Pops." Reilly laughs as he opens another can of Mr. Pibb, pours out about half of it into a well-used spittoon next to the chair, and then tops the can up with Midori melon-flavored liqueur. "I got to hand it to them boys. They sure learn fast. That's the first thing I teach 'em—don't pay no attention to people yelling at you outside the circle, 'cause the minute you look up, you'll get a lollipop [the commonly used term for the six inches of highly honed forged steel] right across your throat."

I ask Reilly if he doesn't see any irony in the fact that by the next day at least one or two of these boys could be dead, buried in a shallow grave in the weeds behind a Denny's restaurant whose parking lot served as the arena the night before.

He responds to my question with a glare and a defiant gulp. "You listen here, mister," he says slowly and deliberately, brandishing the can as if it were one of his tots' lollipops. "There is no one in God's great world that loves these boys more than I do. You think I stand out there on bitter cold nights in some godforsaken parking lot and don't worry like hell that one of 'em ain't goin' to come home that night?" He turns his head away and wipes at his eyes with a stained shirtsleeve.

I consider bringing up the fact that he stands to lose several thousand dollars when one of his kids doesn't make it out of that circle, but then decide to retreat to a safer topic. I ask Reilly to explain the various and arcane rules that govern totfighting.

"Well, that's sure a good question," he says, leaning back in his La-Z-Boy and loosening the belt of his TuffSkin jeans. "But afore you can understand the *how* of totfighting, you gotta understand the *why*." Reilly pauses for a minute as he guzzles the last drops from his Midori-and-Mr. Pibb. "It all started back in the fifties—the name of the game back then was monkey-fighting. Now these aren't just any chimps you'd find in someone's garage—these were real warriors—Jamaican Massacre-Macques, bred real special by them potheads down in the islands. Now you put two of these fellers in a ring, and put some razor-sharp Eye-talian switchblades in their hairy little hands . . . Why, it wouldn't be thirty seconds afore one of 'em'd be lying there dead. Now that may not sound like fun to you in-tee-leckchuals but boy oh boy, you could make some good scratch on them monkeys. Now it wasn't always like that, to be sure . . . the real money didn't start showing up until that ol' Shirley Booth got into the act.

"Shirley Booth?" I interject. "The actress? The star of *Come Back, Little Sheba*?"

"I don't know nuthin' 'bout no E-gyptians," Reilly snorts. "I'm talkin' 'bout *Hazel*. You remember her, right? That hot little maid from the TV show. Or mebbe you're too young to 'member gettin' a stiffy when she walked into the room and said, 'Yes, Mr. B.?' Hoo-boy, that lady had class, lemme tell you!

"Anyway, Shirley was one of the first ones to start bettin' big money on the knife-fightin' monkeys. And there for a while it got so that nobody wanted to put their 'feller' up against Shirley's guy, Lloyd. I mean, this monkey was mean as the day is long. You even looked at him wrong, he'd be up on your shoulders a-gnawin' at yer jugular like a cat eats tomatoes. So Shirley, she's bettin' all her *Hazel* money like there was no tomorrow—she was rakin' in some pretty big green. But she didn't count on ol' Reilly, that's for shore. I did some lookin' around, usin' my noggin, you see," he says, tapping his temple. "I found one o' them labs where they was 'sperimentin' on monkeys with some kind o' atomic stuff. I slipped a few bills to one of the guys working there, and that night he left a cage outside the door. When I opened that cage up, out came the damndest thing I ever saw—it was a monkey, all right, but it didn't have no hair on it—looked kinda naked, ya know? But more important, he had big ol' sharp teeth comin' every which way out of his mouth. I called him Mr. Menick, after my poor old gramps who died the month before—may he rest in peace." Mr. Pibb can still in hand, Reilly makes a sloppy sign of the cross, and some of the viscous contents of the can slops out onto his shirt.

"Anyway, the next night I took Mr. Menick to Shirley's mansion. She'd offered twenty-five Gs to anyone whose monkey could take down Lloyd. Well, we went down in the basement and put them fellers in the ring. Old

Lloyd pulled out his blade and started circlin' around Mr. Menick, lookin' at him like he was easy pickin's—but Mr. Menick just sat there, all quiet like, lookin' like he was smilin' with all those teeth. Lloyd started to make his move, and then *wham*—all we could see was what looked like a red snowstorm with them teeth a-whirlin' and blood a-flyin'. Ten seconds later Lloyd was just a mess o' meat on the floor and Mr. Menick had jumped up into my arms, a-cooin' and strokin' my hair. Well, that did it for ol' Shirley—she hit the bottle hard that night and never looked back. Last I heard she was sellin' her tail out in Wichita, dressin' up in her old *Hazel* apron for old winos who 'membered the show."

"Mr. Reilly," I ask, "this is all fascinating, but what does it have to do with totfighting?"

"I'm gettin' there, son," he replies. "You wanted to know how this whole thing started, right? Well, I'm tellin' you. Anyhoo, in about six months Mr. Menick and I had cleaned the clocks of every monkey fighter west of the Mississippi. I had me a roll o' dough that could choke a horse. Then, one night I was over at my daughter's house, and I was playin' around with one of her kids—a little four-year-old called Teddy. I started cuffin' him around the head some 'cause he was bitin' my leg. Man, that kid turned mean in a split second—started whalin' at me with his fists and bitin' me all over. I never saw a kid so riled up. As I was washin' out my wounds later on, it was like a lightbulb comin' on in my head. If folks would pay big money to watch monkeys fight, you can bet yer life they'd pay even bigger money to watch kids fight.

"Two weeks later I'd put together a stable of tots and taught 'em how to jab and stab and dance round the ring like they was that Muhammad Ali guy. Finally, Teddy got so good that I decided to put him in the ring with Mr. Menick. At first Teddy just wanted to play—'Nice Mr. Monkey,' he says holding out his hand. But Mr. Menick wasn't havin' none of that—he jumped up and cut a big gash in Teddy's shoulder. Teddy looks at the blood runnin' down his favorite shirt, then he throws back his head and starts screamin' 'I-yi-yi-yi-yi-yi-yi,' and then he goes to town on Mr. Menick. Next thing you know, he's cut off that damn monkey's tail. Mr. Menick, he just looked up at me, and I swear that hate was pourin' outta his eyes at me. Then he leaped up to the window, smashed it with his elbow, and ran off into the night. Teddy just looked at me with a big smile on his face and said, 'Bad monkey-man gone.' And that, my friend," Reilly exclaims, slapping his knee, "is how this whole damn thing got started."

I look up from my rapidly filling notebook. "One thing my readers will want to know, Mr. Reilly, is just how you choose your tots. Will any four-year-old make a good fighter? Or do you have some sort of system to identify the best candidates?"

"Well, son, lemme tell you 'bout that. The most important thing you gotta know is that pedigree is the most critical element in any 'chick's' value. If'n you're buying a chick for ten grand, then you're gonna want to know what kind of stock he came from. Our records go back at least three or four generations. We don't take just any little kid—they've got to have what we call a 'spirited' background before we make the decision to bring 'em in. I mean, the difference between manslaughter and a second-degree murder conviction in a child's parentage can mean the difference of two grand, easy. And believe me, we don't just put 'em in the circle cold. There's at least two months of intensive training that goes into these boys before they step one little toe over that purple line. Weight training, reflexology, all that stuff.

"Another thing," says Reilly as he pops open another Mr. Pibb, "is that we have certain ironclad rules. First and foremost is, a chick cannot step foot in that ring until the day he turns four years old. And for those who make it to their fifth birthday, that's the last day they fight. Why, we've had kids crying and throwin' tantrums cause they wanna fight some more but they can't 'cause they're too old. There're rules and regulations, just like in any other sport, bud, and when the birth certificate says they're five, then that's it, no matter how damn good a fighter they are. Now there's been some talk about putting together a senior league, and I for one think it's a good idea. But you know how contrary some people can get about changin' the rules."

I ask Reilly what kind of future awaits those boys lucky enough to make it to their fifth birthdays, after almost a quarter of their short lives have been spent maiming and killing their peers. Reilly stares at me with incredulity.

"Why, son, I can't believe you'd ask me that. These boys have got the right stuff, you bet your mama, and there's just thousands of companies out there waitin' to pick these kids up when they're of age. Why, I can't believe that there's any company out there that wouldn't want a former chick as one of their top guys. I mean, these kids have proved themselves where it counts. If you're the head of some *Fortune* 500 company and you're lookin' to hire a new Sales VP, then who're you gonna pick? The kid who's spent his whole life bein' pampered and given stuff and never had to fight for what's his? Or the kid who knows what it's like to be out there and get things done?"

At this point one of the boys toddles up to Reilly and tugs on his pant leg. "What you want, Rocky?" the man says with undisguised affection in his voice. "You want another soda pop, you go right ahead and take it out of the fridge."

"No, sir," replies the boy in the sweet tones of a four-year-old. "I gotta go make mess." Reilly laughs, then heaves his bulk out of the chair and leads Rocky to the bathroom. "I swear, I love these little buggers like there's no tomorrow. Now 'member, son, you gotta start takin' care of this yourself, 'cause you ain't allowed no Pampers in the circle. That's called 'unfair padding advantage.' " Reilly then turns to me and says, "Okay, mister, I hope you wrote everything down in that little book o' yours 'cause we got a match comin' up tonight and we gotta get ready. You gonna be there, right?"

I stand up and stow the notebook in my briefcase, as Reilly stands there tousling the hair of the smiling little boy who may or may not live to see the sun rise tomorrow morning.

"I wouldn't miss it for the world," I say.

The match that night is held in a JC Penney parking lot in Abingdon, Maryland. Cars start showing up around 1:30 a.m., and within half an hour there are perhaps one hundred people milling around the purple ring illuminated by the glare of headlights. I start for a moment when I see a group of policemen approach, but I soon realize that they're there for the show. Large wads of cash exchange hands all around me. I politely decline when I'm approached by a fresh-faced young girl who asks me if "I want any action."

Finally the crowd quiets as Reilly strides to the center of the ring, pulling little Rocky along by the arm. "I got ten grand tonight, people," he exclaims, "and I'm puttin' it all behind this little warrior. Now we was supposed to be fightin' Joltin' Joshua right about now, but he hasn't showed up. Probly dumped a load o' Mars bars in his britches when he found out he'd be fightin' Rocky here," Reilly snorts in laughter. "So I got any takers? Anybody brave enough to put their tot in the ring with Rocky?"

An excited buzz rises from the throng as a small, cowled figure emerges into the ring. He pulls back the hood of his robe and the crowd falls silent. One woman shrieks, and an older fellow with the face of a basset hound yells, "God-damn, that is the ugliest kid I ever seen in my life!"

And indeed, the challenger *is* a particularly grotesque specimen—his nose is a bulblike monstrosity, resembling a muzzle. His brow is immense, bulging over his beady little eyes like some infant Neanderthal. Reilly turns to look at the newcomer and then, I swear, his jaw drops to his chest. "What the hell . . . ," he mutters, and then a glint of recognition flashes in his eyes. "Why, this ain't no tot," he yells. "This here is. . . ."

Reilly's next words are soundless, for his larynx—indeed, his entire throat—has suddenly been slashed into what looks like a julienne salad. At the same moment Rocky bursts into tears as he pulls at Reilly's arm, crying, "I don't wanna fight that boy, Pops. He's too mean and ugly." The blur of the challenger's whirling blade ceases, and the crowd gazes upon the grisly tableau—the sobbing child, Reilly's slowly crumpling corpse, and the grinning, tooth-studded simian face of the misshapen figure—for indeed, it is now apparent that it is not human, but some sort of ape. And then, in a flash, Mr. Menick (or so I assume) leaps from the ring into the crowd where, once again, he vanishes into the night.

Hours later, as I sit in my car scribbling the last of my story, the parking lot is once again a vacant plain. The first few rays of the rising sun are reflected in the puddles of water left by the hoses used to scrub away the purple ring and the remains of Reilly. The only vehicle present other than my own is the battered Winnebago sitting a few spaces over. The stillness of the morning is suddenly broken by a child's wail, soon joined by other cries of hunger and dirty diapers, all echoing from the windows of the motor home.

I snap my notebook shut, take a deep breath, and leave the car to walk over to the Winnie. I open the door, and a miasma of sour milk, Midori, and diaper pails hit me in the face. I can go no farther.

As I hurry back to my car, I hear the hesitant steps of little feet hitting the pavement behind me. "Mister, oh mister," come the soft, bleating voices of little boys. "Where's Pops, mister?"

The starter catches, the engine roars to life, and I pull out, heading toward the mall exit.

I do not look into the rearview mirror.

Jeff **Ford** *is incredibly easy to like, in a business where writers' egos often preclude, or limit, friendship. What I'm trying to say is that even though he's one heck of a writer, he's also one heck of a nice guy.*

His fiction is startling and wonderful, with a grace and charm all Jeff's own. He won a World Fantasy Award for his debut novel, The Physiognomy, *a* New York Times *Notable Book; other titles featuring Physiognomist Cley include* Memoranda *and* The Beyond.

Jupiter's Skull

Jeffrey Ford

Mrs. Strellop had a little shop called Thanatos in the Bolukuchet district at the south end of a cobbled street facing the canal. On evenings in late summer, for those few breezy weeks preceding the monsoons, she would fix her door ajar with a large, dismorphic skull and sit by the entrance, inviting in passersby for a cup of foxglove tea.

She was a handsome woman of advanced years with a long braid the color of iron that she wound around her neck twice and tucked into the front of her loose blouse between her breasts. Her wrinkles—the crow's-feet at the edges of her eyes, the lines descending from the corners of her lips—belied her charm more so than her age and were in no way at odds with the youthful beauty of her elegant hands or the glint in her green eyes.

She wore loose garments—wraps and tunics and sometimes a shawl—all fixed with glitter and sequin designs. Her earrings were thin hoops of crystal that caught the light of the candles positioned about her shop and transformed it into stars on the dark draperies that covered the walls. Her only other piece of jewelry was a ring on the left middle finger that held no precious stone, but instead the polished eyetooth of a man who was said to have once betrayed her.

That tea she served, redolent of the digitalis, slowed the heart and tinged the mind with a dreamlike effect that seemed to negate the passage of time, so that, after a single cup and what seemed a brief conversation, I would look up and notice the sun rising out over the treetops of the forest beyond the waterway. The sudden realization of a new day would place me back in reality, and invariably I would turn to her and ask, "What exactly were we discussing?"

She would smile, eyes closed, and shoo me home with a weary wave of the back of her hand. "A pleasant week then, Mrs. Strellop," I'd say. She would offer me the same and, as I stepped into the street, add the rejoinder, "Good days are ahead, Jonsi." It was only later, while lying in the cot in my small room over Meager's Glass Works, listening to the morning wind and the distant tolling of the bell over in the Dunzwell district, that I would try in vain to piece together what she had told me through the night. With all my concentration, I could bring up only slivers of her tales, and these I could not see but only feel the irritation of like thistle spines in my memory. The effort to do even this exhausted me beyond reason, and when I finally awoke later on, it was with an indistinct and transient belief, like a morning mist already evaporating, that my dreams had brought me closer to a recounting of her words than any conscious effort. In truth, every atom of these baroque nightmares was completely lost to me.

Like Mrs. Strellop, I had also known betrayal and was drawn to the Bolukuchet the way the others who wandered the world with a hole in the heart were, as if by a great magnet that attracted emptiness. The majority of us had a little bit of money, at least enough to live comfortably, and those who didn't, worked at some lazy job from ten in the morning till three in the afternoon when the café opened and generous old Munchter served the first round for free. I had originally landed in that purgatorial quadrant of a crumbling town on the banks of the muddy Meerswal with the ridiculous idea that I might, in my middle years, revive my youthful interest in poetry. Though I jotted down some words upon waking each morning, the writing was, in all honesty, a dodge.

Mrs. Strellop owned a shop the way I wrote poetry, for although she trafficked in talk and that mischievous tea, they came free of charge. There was no product or service I could readily discern. I knew very little about her, save for the fact that she was the first one to welcome me to the district. Ever since then, I'd gone by her place from time to time for a sip of oblivion and a session of amnesia therapy. I never saw her that the sun wasn't in its descent, and I saw her most just prior to the autumn rains. It was Munchter who told me about the ring she wore. I inquired, "What sort of betrayal?" "What difference does it make?" he replied, and then with a shrug, denoting something close to sympathy, refilled my glass for free.

There were many engaging personalities I could have written about in the Bolukuchet. In fact, there were as many as there were individuals living there, for everyone had a tale they were reluctant to tell, a past heightened to mythos by the ingredients of Time, Distance and the distorting forces of exquisite lassitude. We wandered the narrow alleyways, sat, smoking, in darkened doorways, leaned lazily on the rusting, floral designed railings of second-story verandas, like spectral characters in the mind of an aged novelist impotent to envision what happens next.

It is a certainty that nothing good ever transpired in the district, for that would be a contradiction to its idiosyncratic metaphysics of gravity, but nothing terribly dreadful happened either, until, of course, this. On a windy afternoon of dust devils and darkening skies, two days before the monsoon struck, the body was discovered by Maylee, the new prostitute recently in the employ of Mother Carushe. Mrs. Strellop had hired the young woman to fetch fresh fruit and vegetables each day from the barge that docked at the canal quay three streets up. When Maylee, carrying a basket of fresh carrots and white egg plant, pushed open the door to Thanatos, she was met by a ghastly sight. Eyes popping, blackened tongue lolling, Mrs. Strellop, draped in a plum wrap decorated with quartz chips in a design of the constellation of the goat, sat slumped back in her chair, one beautiful hand holding an empty vial that it was later determined had contained a draught of cyanide and the other clutching the doorstop skull in her lap.

She was buried quickly, before the rains would have made the digging impossible, and the next day the entire district turned out at Munchter's for a sort of informal wake of testimony and tearful besottment. We shared tales and descriptions of her, and, after my third Lime Plunge, I must have told everyone of her usual parting phrase to me, "Good days are ahead, Jonsi." It had been suggested to me by Mother Carushe that I compose a eulogy in the form of a poem in her honor and though it was begun, I could never find the words to finish it. Instead, the bargeman, Bill Hokel, played a dirge on his mouth organ. When the last mournful note had wavered away, there was a moment of silence before we heard the rain begin its patter on the corrugated tin of the roof. In that brief span, I wondered if Mrs. Strellop's taking her own life was an act of courage or cowardice.

The rain was cold and unforgiving. For the first two days of the monthlong downpour, I simply sat on the veranda of my small apartment, drinking and smoking, and watched as the large, relentless droplets decimated the last white blossoms of the trailing vine that grew like a net over the facade of the abandoned fish market across the street. Mushrooms sprouted out of stucco, and great grey seagoing birds huddled under the overhangs, heads beneath wings as if ashamed not to be flying. At times the wind was wild, lifting pieces of roof tile off the old buildings and buffeting off course anyone unlucky enough to be out on the street. On the second morning, Munchter trudged beneath me and I called to him, but it was obvious he could not hear my voice above the howl of the wind.

With the death of Mrs. Strellop, my usual feeling of blankness gave way to a kind of depressive loneliness. I knew others in the district much better, but she and her tea and our nightlong sessions had always centered me enough in order to keep that damnable sense of desire at bay. I wouldn't have gone so far as to call it therapy, because as I understand it, the therapist does the listening. It was she who always talked, telling me those long intricate stories I would never remember. Somehow, they worked their way into my system invisibly, without a trace, and alleviated me of any judgment concerning the state of stasis that was my life.

On the third day of the rain, I was awakened by a knock upon my door. I knew it couldn't be Meager come up from the shop below to share a cup of coffee and peruse my latest fragment of verse, since he always went west for the drowned month and gave his two assistants off as well. I dressed and answered the door. Standing on the landing of the rickety wooden stairs that led up from the back of the Glass Works, drenched to the skin, was Maylee. Her usually wavy locks (Mother Carushe knew a thing or two about hair fashion) were slicked and stringy from the downpour, making her already large eyes more prominent. Her fair complexion had a bluish tinge, and she was shivering. I stepped back and let her in.

As soon as the door was closed, I went into the back room and brought a blanket to wrap around her shoulders. She thanked me, her teeth still chattering, and I ushered her over to a chair at the small table near the veranda. Shutting the glass doors to keep the chill off her, I then sat down in the opposite seat. Before I could speak, she lifted a small leather pouch with a drawstring onto the table.

"From Mrs. Strellop," she said.

"How so?" I asked.

"She told me many times, especially in her last weeks, that if anything should happen to her, I should give this to you."

"What's in it?"

She shook her head.

I reached out and grabbed the satchel, pulling it along the table toward me. As I undid the drawstring, Maylee said to me, "Would you like me to leave?"

I laughed, "No, at least get warmed up before going back out in it."

She nodded, looking relieved.

Then I opened the pouch, and a familiar scent wafted up. I lifted the bag and held it to my nose for a moment. "Foxglove tea," I said with a smile.

"Oh, yes," said Maylee, leading me to believe that she had tasted the strange brew.

"Shall I make some now? It might warm you a little."

"Please," she said.

I went immediately over to my stove, got a fire going, and put a kettle of water on. As I filled the big copper tea ball, I noticed for the first time that the stuff was multicolored, made up of flecks of red and yellow, a pale green and some minuscule blue nuggets, suggesting that there were other ingredients in it beside the dried petals of its namesake. It struck me then that perhaps there was no foxglove in it at all, that it had just been a name the missus had assigned it.

I rejoined Maylee at the table while waiting for the water to boil. "You knew Mrs. Strellop quite well didn't you?" I asked, lifting my cigarettes off the tabletop. I offered one to her, and she accepted. Striking a match, I lit my own and then reached across to share the flame.

She took a drag and nodded. "I saw her every day. I would bring her vegetables from the barge that comes down from the farm country. She gave me three dollars for my effort, which I had to give to Mother Carushe, but then she would also give me a cup of this tea. 'Just for you, my dear,' she'd say."

"That tea is something, isn't it?" I asked, laughing.

"I'd take the tea and sit with her for an hour. She always had some story to tell. It was so relaxing. But when it was time for me to leave, I could never remember a single word she had spoken."

"You don't have to tell me. I sat whole nights with her and can't recall a blessed thing."

"I think she was a witch," said Maylee.

I laughed, but this time she didn't. "What makes you say that?" I asked.

"When I would return home from taking the vegetables to Thanatos in the afternoon, Mother would bless me with a special holy water she kept in a bottle that had the shape of a saint before accepting the three dollars. Then she would take the bills and put them in the ice box for a day before spending them. I think she was afraid of Mrs. Strellop."

"If you don't mind my asking, how is it working for Mother Carushe?" I said, trying to hide behind my cigarette. I thought for a moment I had offended Maylee, but then I realized she was really considering my question.

"I have been in the district for only six months, and . . . May I be frank with you, Mr. Jonsi?"

"Please," I said, "just Jonsi, no mister necessary. And there is nothing left in the world that will offend me. I'm not after the details; I just like to hear how others live. You know, sort of as a barometer for my own life."

"Well, I and the other three young women who work for Mother, we are supposed to be prostitutes—no sense in trying to dress it up. Not the life I had at one time envisioned for myself. There was a period when I had designs on being an actress and saw myself delivering great speeches from the stage. I might even have had some talent for it, but I allowed myself to be drawn away from my dream by a loathsome man who eventually left me stranded and broke."

"I can commiserate," I said.

"But that's all in the past. One needs to survive. But, sir, there is something wrong with the gentlemen of the Bolukuchet," she said.

"What do you mean?" I asked, feeling some vague offense.

"I have had only five commissions so far in the time I have been here, and every one of them . . ." Here she grinned slightly and stubbed out her cigarette. "Limp as dishrags."

I couldn't help but laugh, for a variety of reasons.

"Yes, they have money and they have an idea they would like to spend time with me, but when I get close to them, they back away. Instead of me taking them in hand, they want to hold my hand. And they are paying astronomical sums for this. One fellow, last month, had me simply sleep for an hour in the bed next to him. He never laid a finger on me. When I got up to leave, he sniffed the pillow where my head had been and started crying."

"An interesting observation," I said.

"Granted, I have been with only five of them, but I sense it, a plague of deep sorrow, shall we say?"

Luckily, the water came to a boil then and I got up and prepared us each a cup. The perfumed-forest aroma of it was comforting, and for the first time since the rains started, I felt a measure of peace. Maylee and I did not speak while taking the tea. She stared at the table, and I at the pressed tin design of the ceiling. During this long pause, the sound of the rain changed from monotonous to beautiful. Out on the street someone yelled. I closed my eyes and remembered the cool of the evening, sitting in the doorway of Thanatos, watching the patterns of fireflies at the edge of the forest across the canal. Mrs. Strellop's voice started in my memory and then spiraled down through the center of my being, leaving a sense of calm in its wake.

I rested my cup on the table, empty, just as Maylee did hers. She looked over at me, her eyes not half so big anymore, and smiled.

"And Mrs. Strellop told me that you are a poet," she said, her words having slowed to a drawl.

I laughed and shook my head. "I sniff the pillow of poetry and weep," I told her, preparing to forge forward with an honest recitation of my own days to even the account, but she abruptly cut me off.

"—Wait," she said, and held up her hand. "That is the first time I ever remembered something Mrs. Strellop had told me." She breathed deeply. "What a sense of relief."

"I can imagine, believe me," I said, and clapped for her.

"Oh, my god, there's something else, something else," she nearly yelled, squirming in her seat. "That odd skull she had. Do you remember it?"

"Of course," I said.

"She called it Jupiter."

I scanned my memory, and sure enough, yes, in that moment, I remembered her telling me the same. That crumb of information shifted like a grain in a sand pile, and with the insignificant revelation something else became clear to me. "My turn," I said. She looked on excitedly. "He was a throwback, not quite a man—"

"Or more than a man," she said quickly. "Did they not find him in a mountain valley in the range that overlooked her village?"

I pushed my chair back from the table. "The old hunter Fergus brought him back from an expedition into the clouds. From the altitude to which he climbed he could see the planets clearly, and Jupiter watched him like an eye the night he captured the strange lad in a trap that was a hole dug like a grave and covered with flimsy branches." For the last half a sentence, she recited the words with me.

We sat for a moment in stunned silence, and then she said, "I feel lightheaded . . . but not dizzy. Like I'm waking up."

"Every time you voice a string of Mrs. Strellop's words," I said, "the next comes into my mind."

"Yes," she said, "like a magician pulling scarves from his pocket."

"What now?" I asked.

"Fergus believed him to be more ape than human."

"He brought Jupiter back to the village and put him on display in a cage made of branches lashed with lanyards."

"Each of the townspeople paid a silver coin to see him; covered from top to toe with a reddish brown fuzz, cranium like a cathedral, thumbs on his feet and jutting jaw," she said, staring at the wall as if the cage were there and she were seeing him. She shook her head sadly.

"For a time he was a renowned attraction and many came to view him," I added.

Maylee sighed. "And then, like everything—for some, even life, itself—the sense of wonder wore off."

"Fergus spent so much time with the wild boy that he came to realize he was more human than ape, and the lad learned to read and write and speak perfectly."

"He was no longer confined to the cage," she said, as if reading from a book, "but went about in human clothes, helping the aged hunter, now racked with arthritis, get through his days."

"Actually," I said, as if setting her straight, "this Jupiter, this beast boy, was quite a prodigy. Fergus taught him to carve wood with a knife, and the hairy apprentice created a likeness of his master, his father, from a log of oak that stood six feet tall and perfectly mirrored the hunter."

Maylee did not immediately reply, and for a moment, I feared she had lost the thread of events, until she finally blurted out, "Then Jupiter grew, tall and strong. . . ."

"Like this," I said, and not even knowing what I was about, stood up as if carved from words and animated only by the story. I thrust my chest out and flexed my biceps. My bottom jaw pushed forward, and, furrowing my brow, I bent my knees slightly and took slow big steps in a circle.

"That's him," she said. "But then Fergus died."

I felt the air leave me as if I'd been punched in the stomach, and, retaining my simulation of Jupiter, I hung my head and slouched forward. "And the boy was set adrift in an alien world," I said.

"Your eyes," said Maylee.

I could feel the tears on my cheeks. "Time passed," I said, and, with this, sat down and lit two cigarettes, passing one to my guest. We smoked in silence, time passing, but I felt the persistence of the tale like a slight pressure behind my eyes, in my solar plexus. The tea had me in its fog. The light from the lamps appeared unnaturally diffuse, and I heard, whisper soft, traces of a children's choir emanating from my ears. Still, one small part of me clung to reason, and in that thimble of rational self, I trembled with wonder and fear at what was happening.

Maylee stubbed out her cigarette and said, "After Jupiter buried Fergus, he set about making the bottom floor of the old man's home into a shop from which to sell his remarkable carvings."

Her words again initiated the story, which broke open inside of me like the monsoon, washing away any volition on my part. I stood and assumed my primate pose. "He created beautiful objects with his knife," I said. "Animals of the forest so lifelike, customers swore they moved, circus acrobats whose hands clasped the trapeze, monsters full of dignity and courage." My fingers wriggled with the grace of snakes as I turned and carved an invisible figurine.

"The people of the town remained wary of Jupiter, afraid of his size and skeptical of his intelligence. To them he was either a horrid freak or the result of a deal with the devil, but never human," she said, and slowly stood.

She turned her back on me and took two steps as I added, "They did not mind him so much as long as he remained in his shop, a curiosity to visit every now and then and buy a gift from for the holidays or a wedding, but they did not want him on the streets. For his part, Jupiter longed for companionship, someone with whom to discuss what he had read, the mundane events of his every day."

"He felt their distrust for him on the street, so one day he hired a young woman to bring him groceries from the market each afternoon. Her name was Zel Strellop, a kind girl, unafraid of Jupiter's demeanor and enchanted by his craft," said Maylee, dropping the grey blanket from her shoulders and spreading her arms wide as if breaking free from a cocoon.

I could almost see a young Mrs. Strellop in the features of Maylee, and I wondered if to her I appeared as Jupiter. The story possessed us yet more fully, and although we continued to tell it as we spoke, we began simulating every little action our two characters might have undertaken. I noticed that when she told the words of Zel, her voice changed, becoming higher and lighter, and that my own words, when quoting Jupiter, were far more bass than I was accustomed to. For the exposition, our voices remained our own. We moved in and around the apartment, no longer allowing the table to separate us.

There was a series of meetings between the wood carver and the young woman, and they grew increasingly interested in each other. I felt the flame of attraction spark to life in my chest, felt weak in the knees as Maylee as Zel Strellop approached, lightly touched my arm, whispered a secret to me, and finally kissed me for the first time, gently on the lips. I wanted it to continue, but Maylee broke it off and fled to the stove that stood in for Zel's parents' house.

"And then," said I, "Jupiter wrote her a poem to express his love for her," and I walked over and sat hunched at my writing desk. My knife hand reached for the pen. I lifted it and wrote rapidly.

When the sun is high
I watch out the window
for a cloud of dust in the distance,
you on the path,
bringing me oranges, melons and plums.
My impatience is sharp
And carves your likeness
on every moment.

The instant I had penned the last word, Maylee swept the paper away and pressed it to her breast. I stood and turned to face her. "And they kissed more heatedly," she said, and we did.

"His apelike hands swept across the curves of her body," I said from the corner of my mouth, our lips still pressed, and they did.

She stepped back, and in one fluid motion lifted her damp dress off over her head. "Zel disrobed in a fit of passion," she said, breathing heavily.

When she stooped to remove her undergarments, I undid my trousers and let them drop to the floor, not forgetting to add, "He grew brave in his desire and followed her example."

Maylee left me and went back to the table. Over her shoulder, she verily shouted, "There was no bed, so they made do on his workbench." With this, she bent forward and with one sweep of her arm sent the teacups and ashtray and cigarettes onto the floor.

"He approached her from behind," I said.

"His member was pulsing with all the energy he'd brought with him from the mountain," she said.

I looked down, and even in my fog was surprised to see that she was right.

"She gasped as he entered her," she gasped.

I tried to say, "With slow thrusts, he vented his passion," but it sounded as a series of short grunts.

Maylee missed a line or two, herself, in which she was to have described Zel's own pleasure, I'm certain, but filled in with panting and a protracted groan.

For a span of time, I was lost to my life, my role in the story, transported beyond the Bolukuchet, flying somewhere above the rain.

As I pulled out of her, Maylee said, "Time passed," and reached down to grab the cigarettes and ashtray off the floor. We lit up and took our seats at the table, both still heaving from the encounter.

When we had managed to catch our breath, she said, "The townspeople started to become wary of the arrangement between Zel and Jupiter. She was spending far too much time out at his shop. Something about her look had changed."

"Late one afternoon," I said, "Jupiter was visited by the sheriff, a man who had been close friends with old Fergus. He warned Jupiter that people were suspicious and if he wanted the best for Zel, he should leave town immediately."

"Yes," said Maylee, "but what he did not know was that the sheriff had also, that very evening, warned Zel to stay away from Jupiter. As soon as it got dark, though, she sneaked out and made for his shop."

We both stood at this point and each walked halfway around the table to meet face-to-face. "She confronted him as he was clasping shut his suitcase," I said.

"Where are you going?" asked Zel.

"I must leave," said Jupiter.

"I'm coming with you," she said.

"No, you can't," he told her. "It will end in tragedy."

"I'm coming," screamed Maylee, with all the pain of injustice and loss.

"He simply shook his head, tears in his eyes," I said.

"Her anger at the world turned to rage."

"She struck out at him," I said, but did not see Maylee's fist coursing through the air. Her punch landed square on the right side of my mouth. I staggered back and then fell to my knees. My lip was split and I could taste blood. I spit, and a tooth came with it out onto the wooden floor. "He betrayed her," I said, my hand covering my mouth.

Maylee bent over and lifted the tooth, her eyes widening as if it glinted like a diamond. She looked up at me. "Because he loved her," she said.

With this, the spell instantly lifted, more rapidly than a curtain closing, with the speed of falling rain, and, without conversation, we both staggered to the bed and fell into a bottomless sleep.

In the morning, I woke to find her gone, but her scent remained upon the pillow. What I remembered most clearly from the bizarre play we had enacted the previous day was that when she had struck me, in the moment or two when I thought I might pass out, I had realized I must leave the district.

That afternoon, after hurriedly packing and leaving much behind, I left the Bolukuchet and traveled for many days back to the city. At first the change was frightening, and I moved through the days like a somnambulist directed by commands that came from my dreams. Somehow I managed to make all the right moves, and it was not long before a memory of my life prior to the Bolukuchet returned to me and I began to feel at home in my new surroundings.

As soon as I had established myself, gotten a place and employment, I wrote to Maylee, care of Mother Carushe, to see if I could persuade her to join me. Oddly enough, all my letters, more than three dozen, returned unopened with an explanation that the address could not be located. I sent another batch to Munchter's café, to Meager's, and the results were precisely the same.

In fact, no matter whom I asked or what inquiries I made at libraries or post offices, no one had ever heard of the Bolukuchet. Although my new life was fast paced and the basic excitement and wonder of mere existence had mysteriously returned to me, I missed my old friends and the tired, decrepit district. Luckily, I had taken with me the pouch of foxglove tea. At first I imbibed it to try to discover how exactly Zel Strellop had come by Jupiter's skull, but that part of the story was not to be mine. I did, though, revisit my memories of nights at Munchter's, the fireflies in the forest across the canal, Meager showing me the finest prism he had ever created and the blizzard of color with which it filled the room, the soulful tunes of Bill Hokel's mouth organ, et cetera. When these visions came to me, I made them into poems. Years passed and I had enough to collect into a book, which was miraculously published. Its title—*Jupiter's Skull.*

The book won great renown, and I was asked to give readings at colleges and in libraries and coffee shops. When I was interviewed, the question most often asked was, "How did you dream up a place like the Bolukuchet?" I would answer every time that I had lived there, which would cause the interviewer to smirk or smile as if we were complicit in the lie I was telling.

Many years later, on a rainy night, I gave a reading at a local bookstore. Afterward, as was my practice, I sat at a table and one by one people who'd purchased a copy of my book would come forward and I would sign it and chat with them briefly. At the end of a modest line, a woman stepped forward. Before I looked up to take in her face, she said to me, "I bet you could use a Lime Plunge right now."

She had my attention instantly. She was rather plain but pleasant looking in her appearance, brown hair, medium build, late middle age, dressed in a yellow rain coat. "Last week I was in Munchter's," she said.

"Finally," I said, "someone who's been to the district."

"I know," she told me, "out here it's as if it never existed."

She told me that Munchter and Meager and the rest of the old crew were still fine, and that she had read my book and I had captured them perfectly.

"Did you know a young woman, Maylee?" I asked.

"Oh, yes, not so young, really. She owned a little shop, Thanatos, over near the canal. Very long, grey hair, wrapped twice around her neck? I went there often and had tea with her. We rarely used her first name, though. She preferred Mrs. Strellop. I'm sorry to tell you that she passed away only a few days before I left."

"By her own hand?" I asked.

"Why, yes. I wasn't going to say, but I believe it was cyanide."

"And the skull?"

"A woman's skull? Zel, was the name she had for it. Apparently there was an entire story associated with the thing."

"I see," I said.

Before this woman left, she shook my hand, and when she smiled, I noticed the gap from a missing tooth. "Well," she said, "it's good to be back from the district." Then she left the store, and I watched through the window as she disappeared into the rain.

*"**Terry Bisson**, formerly a Kentuckian who lived in N.Y., is now a New Yorker who lives in California. He is the author of numerous SF short stories and novels, some of which have won awards. 'Death's Door' represents his first incursion into fantasy since he was bodily ejected from the field in 1987, following an ugly dust-up with the shade of H. P. Lovecraft."*

So writes Terry himself, after I asked for a few words on what he's been up to, and damned if I can improve on it.

Death's Door

Terry Bisson

Her back was broken. Henry knew it as soon as he saw her trying to crawl out of the street, her hind legs useless.

"Daddy Daddy Daddy!" screamed Carnelia, often called Carny, but not today; not on this awful day in every child's life when, Henry knew, Death is discovered.

"Come here, Carnelia, honey," he said, scooping his seven-year-old daughter into his arms. She was light, and seemed even lighter, as if Death's heavy presence had given wings to Life.

But Marge wasn't dead yet. She was still pulling herself toward the curb, her hind legs twisted in a strange shape that made her look less like a dog than like a giant squid that was somehow no longer giant and no longer squid.

"Daddy, Daddy!"

"She's been hit by a car, honey," Henry said. As if Carnelia hadn't seen the whole thing.

"They were going too fast," said Carnelia, and for the first time Henry saw the ambulance, pulled up at the curb, the light still flashing; and the young black man in the long white EMS coat running across the street toward him.

Oddly, he ran right past the dog, Marge. I'm already thinking of her as the dog, thought Henry.

"The dog ran out in front of me," the young man said. "I couldn't stop. We are on our way to—"

"It's okay," said Henry. "Go. It wasn't your fault, I'm sure."

He set his daughter down and followed the EMS guy to the middle of the street. Marge was still trying to make her way toward the curb, as if hoping that once there she would be restored somehow.

"Go," Henry said again.

Her eyes were open and her tongue was hanging out. Bubbles of blood appeared on her black lips and nose. One was big, and it lasted a long time. Henry kept hoping it would disappear before Carnelia got there, but it didn't.

"She's going to die! She's going to die!"

Henry stood up and put his arms around his daughter's shoulders; she felt enormously, alarmingly frail. "Yes, honey," he said, gathering her to him. "Now do this for me, and for her: Run into the house and get that big box out of the garage, the one the lawn thing came in."

"What for?"

"She needs a place. Just do it, okay?"

Carnelia ran off. Marge was lying on the strip of grass between the curb and the sidewalk, eyes closed, waiting for the transformation that was about to come over her: Death, the Redeemer. It would make her whole again.

"Is she going to be all right?" Carnelia asked breathlessly. She was towing the box behind her, and had picked up two more of the neighborhood kids.

"No, honey," Henry said, kneeling down. "She is going to die. Marge was hit by the ambulance, and it's all over for her. Help me now."

The ambulance was driving off, light spinning. Henry eased the dog into the box. He carried the box into the garage and placed it on the floor under his tool bench.

"Now get her some water," he said. "Bring her a blanket, from that box by the door. Not that one. She's going to die. It's okay; all things die."

Carnelia began to cry again. "This is the blanket she likes."

"Okay, then. Now let's leave her alone. Dogs like to die in private."

"How do you know?"

"I just know." Henry knew because he had done the same thing with his dog, Dallie, thirty-one years before.

"If I leave her, she'll die."

"She's going to die, honey. All things die, It's the way things are."

"I don't like things then!"

"All things have to die, honey. Even things we love."

Not exactly true, as it turned out. Not that day. For that was the day that Death's Door closed.

* * *

"Damn," said Shaheem as he drove off. One dog down, but hopefully a human saved.

Then when he saw her on her apartment floor, he wondered if it was in fact an even trade. The woman was at least ninety years old. About the size and weight of a wet raincoat.

He and his partner loaded her onto the gurney and were easing her down the stairs when a familiar face appeared in the door below.

Is this a big story? Shaheem wondered. He recognized the face from TV. But there was no TV crew following. Ted Graeme was here to see about his mother.

"Mother?" Graeme said. He kissed her finely wrinkled face, aware that he was being watched. He was used to being watched. He was, after all, the anchor on the *Nightly News*.

"Mother?"

No answer. Not a flicker of interest or recognition.

Maybe this will be it, Graeme thought. It would be a blessing. She was his mother but everyone had their time, and she had been miserable since his father had died twelve—was it really twelve?—years before.

Tiny strokes had been chipping away at her, piece by piece. It was a cruel way to go.

"Mother?"

Still no answer.

"You want to ride with her?" asked the EMS guy.

"It's okay," said Graeme. "I'll follow. You're taking her to Midcity, right?"

"Whatever you say, Mr. Graeme."

"We're running late, sir," said Hippolyte. He was the new producer of the *Nightly News*. Secretly, Graeme called him Still-Polite.

"I'm having a family crisis," Graeme said. "Did the warden call?"

"It's all set up," said Hipp. That was what his friends called him. He was a white man with dreadlocks, and Graeme had to remember not to smile whenever he looked at him. Times were changing. Times were always changing.

"I need to stay in the city," said Graeme. "I think Karin should go in my place."

Hipp looked surprised. "For real?"

"Definitely for real," said Graeme, picking up the phone. The most controversial execution in years, and he would have to miss it. "I'm calling her now."

"I'll prep her," said Hipp. "Meanwhile, we have a big story. A plane went down outside Paris, at Charles DeGaulle."

"God. Not another Concorde?"

"Worse. A 777."

It was the one thing they weren't prepared for. Survival. As Jean-Claude poked through the wreckage, he found bodies and parts of bodies. The ones that were whole, or even partly whole, were still alive.

"My wife, my wife!" One man was cut almost in half; his entrails were falling out all over his cheap suit, but he was still alive, asking about his wife in bad African French.

"We're looking for her," Jean-Claude said, even though it wasn't true. They were looking for parts of her, for parts of all of them.

"Bring her to me, *s'il vous plaît*. Let me see her before I die."

"Oui."

Jean-Claude waited for the man to close his eyes, but he didn't. Jean-Claude resisted the impulse to reach out and close them for him. People were screaming all around him.

"They're all burned," said Bruno, his second in command. "They come to pieces when we pull them out, but they won't stop screaming."

"I'll help load them up," said Jean-Claude.

When he got back to the African, he was still alive, still clutching his entrails.

"Load him up," said Jean-Claude. *"Mon Dieu,"* he said to Bruno. "This is the worst yet. An air disaster with hundreds of survivors."

Karin had managed to sound concerned on the phone, but Graeme knew she was pleased. Covering this execution was her big chance. He didn't mind. He would have felt the same. He had once been young and on the make.

He found his mother in the ICU.

"She's still breathing," the doctor said.

"She has a DNR," said Graeme, squeezing his mother's tiny, fluttering, birdlike hand. "It's on her chart."

"I know," said the doctor. "We haven't got her on life support. We couldn't anyway."

"What do you mean?"

"We have an overload today. Lots of serious injuries."

"A bad day?"

"No more than usual, it's just that everyone is surviving." He hurried off.

"I'll be back," Graeme said, kissing his mother's parchment cheek. He hurried out to the lot, beeping his car on the run. With Karin gone, he would have to put together the six-o'clock broadcast all by himself.

"She's suffering," Emily said to Henry when they were alone in the kitchen.

"Carnelia or Marge?"

"Both, damn it! Carny can learn about death without watching her dog die."

"Marge has a right to die at home, with dignity, and not in some vet's office," said Henry. "And as far as Carnelia's concerned, it's not just about learning. It's about going through the changes. She was terribly upset this afternoon. She'll grieve tomorrow. Right now she's fascinated. Death is fascinating as well as terrifying."

"I work with death every day, remember?" Emily said. But she was coming around. She told him about her day while he cut up the salad, being careful to avoid his fingertips. Emily worked as a pediatric nurse in a preemie ward. "Today I thought death was on a holiday," she said. "Today not a single baby died."

"Not a one?"

"You get a day like that every once in a while," Emily said. "I suppose it's a reward for the others."

It was dark. She had expected the darkness, but not the light. The light was for the gullible, the light toward which you floated when you were dead. But here she was, floating toward it.

There were others, like herself. They were specks, sparks. So many. I had not thought that death had undone so many. Floating toward the light. They were rising together.

Then they were slowing. So this is what it's like, she thought. She was surprised. She hadn't thought it would be like anything.

Karin found herself eating too many doughnuts, provided by Krispy Kreme. Tasteless but tasty, she thought. Too tasty. You have to watch your weight when you're on TV. It shows up first in the face.

She put the doughnut away and followed the victim's family into the viewing room. Under the new protocol, the execution was set for sundown. It gave it the appearance of inevitability, almost of a natural death. She wondered if it made it any easier for the condemned.

The guards were already strapping Berry to the gurney. Karin wondered if he would get a cigarette.

Apparently not.

"Do you have any last words?" asked the warden.

"You know I do," said Berry. He turned toward the window, which Karin had been assured was one-way. Still, she wanted to hide her face.

"You are murdering an innocent man," he said.

"Can you go on?"

The producer had heard about Graeme's mother.

"Sure," Graeme said, "but thanks for asking." As he sat down at his desk, an intern handed him the stories. Hipp had sorted them well. Start with the light, ease into the dark.

"Good news on the home front," Graeme began. "Billy Crystal came home from the hospital in Palm Springs, apparently recovered from the stroke that many thought spelled the end of the aging comedian's spectacular sixty-year career. Doctors are cautiously optimistic."

He turned the page.

"Rescue attempts are continuing in the Paris air crash. There are two hundred fifty-five casualties, passengers and crew, most with serious injuries but as yet, miraculously, no deaths. In Lahore, India, UN authorities are investigating what appears to be the worst massacre in recent history. . . ."

"You have to prepare yourself for this," Krishna said.

"I have seen it before," said Paolo.

"No, you haven't," Krishna said.

He led the stocky UN rep through the gate into the temple yard where the worshipers had been surprised. The massacre had been done the old way, with swords. People had been hacked to pieces. Arms and legs were lying on the ground, like spare parts. Bodies lay in heaps, their faces slashed into grim simulacra of red mouths. But that wasn't the horror.

"Jesu!" said Paolo.

The horror was that they were all alive.

The warden himself pulled the switch. There was no sudden killer voltage, no sprung trap, just a slow IV drip—and a peaceful surrender.

The condemned man closed his eyes, and the small crowd sighed with pleasure. Relatives and colleagues of the man he said he hadn't killed. Of course they all say that, Karin thought; and as she did, she realized she had been holding her breath.

Berry kicked: once, twice, and then lay still.

There was a long moment of silence, and then they all stood, reaching for their bags and the ID cards that would let them out of the prison.

Then, as one, they all stopped at the door and looked behind them.

The dead man had just opened his eyes.

The next morning Marge was still alive. Henry put his hand on her side, expecting cold, and felt her breathing. He considered for a moment telling Carnelia that the dog had died anyway, but she would insist on seeing the body before going off to school.

And there she was in the garage door. "Maybe she's going to be all right," she said, kneeling to pet the dog. "Don't die."

"She needs to die," said Henry. "She has massive internal injuries, her back is broken. She wants to be alone and die in peace."

"And you have to go to school," said Emily, gently pulling her daughter to her feet and leading her out of the garage.

"It was horrible," said Karin on her cell phone. "They had to administer the stuff twice, and he still wouldn't die. They made us leave. We're outside in the parking lot."

"That means there's no story," said Graeme. "Maybe you should head back."

"Not yet, please," said Karin. "They have to finish it somehow. That's our story. How's your mother?"

"Hanging in there," said Graeme. She had been moved into the ward with twenty others, all terminal; six of them with gunshot wounds.

"Did I tell you that I knew your mother? She was my English prof at Northwestern. She was a wonderful teacher."

"I know; you told me."

"She wouldn't let us call her Dr. Graeme. It had to be just Ruth. She made Milton come alive."

Coming alive is no longer the problem, thought Graeme.

"You may have to start with a hard story," said Hipp. "We have an earthquake in Lima, just coming off the wire. Seven point six on the Richter scale."

"Jesus," said Graeme, already reshuffling his papers.

So many lights. Sparks. They were still rising, but they had stopped up "above."

Above?

She floated into the cloud, a cloud of sparks. What had seemed like light now seemed like darkness.

Now she could see the light. It was a thin line, like a horizon. She had been watching it for what seemed hours, days? Years? If only she could remember her name.

The sparks were clustered around the bright line, like bugs around a light. She was one of them.

"I got this thing from the military," said Carlos in breathless Spanish. "It's like sonar. You can pick up sounds. In case anyone buried under the ruins is still alive."

"Not likely," said Eduardo. All around there was nothing but rubble, and the screaming of sirens. The business district had been leveled. God knows what it's like in the favelas. "What about the injured?"

"They're flooding the hospital," said Carlos. "More than we're prepared for. Central sent me to look for those who are buried alive, now that we have a way to locate them."

"Let's go, then," said Eduardo. "I've got two crews and two backhoes. Just point us to the most likely."

"That's the problem," said Carlos, taking off the earphones.

"What do you mean?"

Instead of answering, Carols handed Eduardo the earphones and scanned the pickup wand in a circle, around the ruined horizon.

Eduardo didn't even have to put them on. The noise was deafening. Knocks, screams, cries for help or at least mercy. It was as if an entire city had been buried—alive.

"A scooper," muttered Shaheem. He hated scoopers, and what was the rush?

But he was a pro; he turned on the light.

The police were gathered around the bottom of 122 Broadway.

The crowd was still there, held back by yellow tape. He had to push his way through.

"She stood on the ledge and took off her clothes," one of the cops told him. "A sure way to gather a crowd. The guys were trying to talk her down when she just stepped off backward, like this." He stepped back off the curb to illustrate.

Shaheem looked up at the ledge, twenty-two stories up. Two cops were still there: one taking photos, one just looking down.

The scooper had hit headfirst on the concrete, and blood was spattered around for twenty feet, some of it high on the plate glass of Broadway Jewelry. Her head was flat on one side, as big as a watermelon, and when Shaheem knelt down beside her to unroll the body bag, she whispered, "I'm sorry."

Carnelia had sat up with Marge until nine before going to bed. Henry was sure the dog would be dead by morning, but she was still breathing.

The blanket was stiff with blood that had leaked out of her mouth and nose and anus. Henry stuffed it into the trash, then went back into the house. He was surprised to find Emily dressed for work.

"I thought you had the day off. I thought you said—"

"None of the preemies are dying, but we have another problem," she said. "ER is overflowing."

"Overflowing?"

"Everyone they bring in is hanging on," she said. "The halls are filled with stretchers. Midcity has placed us all on call. It's worse than the stadium collapse."

After she left, Henry took a plastic bag out to the garage. Carnelia would be home from school in a few hours. He pulled the bag over Marge's head and sealed it around her neck with duct tape. It moved in and out, slowly at first; then more and more slowly.

He didn't want to watch, so he went back inside and turned on the TV.

The news was disturbing.

". . . unprecedented meeting of the Security Council with the International Red Cross," read Graeme, editing Hipp's clumsy copy on the fly. He had rushed in from the hospital where his mother was in a dim hallway with 126 other people, some of them screaming, others as quiet as herself.

". . . confirms that no one has died, anywhere in the world, for the past thirty-six hours."

He cut to the tape. "It's statistically improbable and medically impossible," said a talking head in a white coat. "People are surviving unsurvivable accidents."

Hipp nodded. Graeme came back on the air.

"And now we take you to Cold Spring State Prison, where our own Karin Glass is waiting for . . ."

Won Lee was taking a picture of Hong Kong harbor with his new digital camera when he felt the deck tip under his feet. Irrationally, it was his camera that he reached for as he began to skid across the deck. He almost caught a stanchion, but the crush of falling, flailing bodies pushed him into the water.

It was cold and the camera was gone. It was dark and he held his breath for as long as he could, then gave up and felt the cold water filling his lungs, almost as satisfying as air. Then it wasn't so cold anymore. Drifting down was like flying. He spread his arms, or felt them spread. He felt himself slip into the soft muck at the bottom of the harbor.

He waited to die. He could see sparks, all around. Had the ferry caught fire? The mud was cold, then not so cold. It all seemed to be taking a long time.

Someone settled beside him. Was it his wife? There was no light, but he could make out a face, the eyes wide open like his own. Was it a man or a woman?

It didn't seem to matter. Something was picking at his hand, uncovering little white bones. He watched and waited. It all seemed to be taking a long time.

". . . governor promises an investigation," said Karin. Her hands were shaking; she tried to hide it.

She had been allowed to see Berry, but not to speak with him. He was still in critical condition, not breathing.

". . . after the last-minute arrival of the DNA test establishing his innocence," she said. She held up the microphone to pick up the chants from the demonstrators. "Meanwhile, the demonstrators outside the prison are calling for the DA's blood, in a dramatic and ironic role reversal."

My best line, she thought. I'll bet that fucking Graeme cuts it.

There were so many sparks. The thin line of light was almost invisible. It was like Milton's blindness, she thought; there was plenty to see in the darkness. More than she had ever dreamed possible.

It had been a surprise, then a disappointment. Now she wanted to see what was on the other side. But there was no other side.

Only a thin line of light.

The sparks formed a cloud around it, like smoke. So many: I had not thought that death had undone so many. They were swarming and she was swarming with them, forward and back, filling the darkness so that the darkness was lighter than the thin line of light.

She wished she could remember her name.

"I'll be late," said Emily on the phone. "They're putting us on extra shifts."

"I know. It's on TV."

"Something very very weird is going on. The hospital is filled with people who shouldn't be alive. One man who took a shotgun blast in the mouth."

"It's a big story," said Henry. "It's on the news."

"Hey, I even saw what's-his-name, from the *Nightly News*. His mother is here. There's a whole hall filled with old people who have been taken off life support, waiting to die. Is Carny home?"

"Soon."

"Is Marge—over?"

"Yes. I'm sure." He told her about the plastic bag.

After he hung up, he went to the garage. He didn't want Carnelia to see the plastic bag.

The bag was no longer going in and out. It had been almost two hours.

He unpeeled the tape and pulled off the bag. He hid it under the blanket in the trash. Marge's eyes were closed. She wasn't stiff yet. He curled her as neatly as possible in the bloodstained box and changed the blanket.

He was tucking it around her when she licked his hand.

"Berry's just one person," said Graeme. "We need you here."

"Please," said Karin. "This is the biggest story of the year. An innocent man almost executed."

"He's still alive?"

"He's on life support," said Karin, "Unlike all the others, who don't need it. Maybe he doesn't either. But I need to stay here for when he wakes up."

"Well, okay, but stay by the phone."

She laughed. "The phone stays by me. How's your mother? Ruth?"

"I haven't heard from the hospital. They said they would call. Meanwhile we just got word from the pound that dogs aren't dying either. Cats, yes."

"Figures," said Karin, who had a dog. "Graeme, what in the world do you think is going on?"

The Cedars was almost empty. The sound on the TV was off but the text scrolling across gave the story:

NO DEATHS, WORLDWIDE. NO REPORTED DEATHS IN . . .

"Weird, huh?" said the bartender, setting down a cold Heineken. "Where you been?"

"I've worked three shifts straight," said Shaheem. "Who do you think is hauling all those people into the hospital? They used to wait for the guys from the funeral home."

"My girlfriend's into astrology," said the bartender. "She says it's a collusion or something of the planets, never happened before. Unpresidential."

"Unprecedented," said Shaheem.

"But that's fantasy," said the bartender. "Me, I'm a believer in science."

"Whatever that means."

"Science is numbers." The bartender pulled a magazine up from behind the bar. "Ever read *Discover*? This month is about the population explosion."

"Implosion, you mean," said Shaheem. "Guess I could do another."

The bartender set another Heineken on the bar. " More people means more deaths," he said. "It says here that more people die now every day than during World War Two. Just of natural causes, plus all the little wars and disasters and shit."

"Not anymore," said Shaheem. He told him about the scooper.

"Maybe death is getting behind," said the bartender. "Temporary overload. No way to process them all. Nowhere to put them."

"Does *Discover* tell you what to do?" asked Shaheem. He was not expecting an answer.

"Just wait," said the bartender. "It'll sort itself out. Things always do."

"You wish," said Shaheem. I wish, we wish, we all wish. "Ever thought you'd see the living waiting for death?"

The line of light was getting thicker. It was now a band of light. The sparks were flying through, extinguished by the light. She watched, breathless, bodiless, and saw that she was getting closer.

Or was the band getting wider? It was the same thing. So many sparks, all rising. She wished she could remember her name.

"It's for you," said Hipp. He handed the phone to Graeme as he picked up another.

The phones were all ringing at once.

"When is Karin coming back?" Hipp asked, over his shoulder. "We have to start putting the news together."

"I'll call her," said Graeme. "That was the hospital."

"Oh." Then Hipp saw that he was smiling.

"My mother just died."

Henry had quit smoking six months ago, but he knew where half a pack was hidden, in his old coat. He smoked two waiting for Carnelia to get home.

There was something on TV, but he kept the sound off. It was too weird. It was a worldwide crisis. But the most important thing was the crisis here at home.

Then he heard wailing, and he realized that Carnelia had gone straight to the garage.

He found her wrapping Marge in the blanket. She dried her eyes with a corner. "Marge died, Daddy. Can we bury her in the yard?"

Henry unwrapped the dog. Her eyes were open. There was no mistaking that peaceful look.

"Of course I will, honey."

"Will you dig a nice hole? Why are you smiling, Daddy?"

"Because, Carny. I'm not."

So much light. There it was, all of a sudden, lots of it. Extinguishing the sparks, one by one, like raindrops in the sea.

Ruth, that was it!

Then it wasn't.

"Thanks for hurrying back," said Graeme, "I'm going to pick up my mother. I want to do it myself."

"I understand," said Karin.

"Lead with your big story," said Graeme. "The man they almost executed."

Karin was taking off her coat and combing her hair at the same time. "It's a bigger story now," she said. She held up her cell phone. "Berry died twelve minutes ago."

"Oh, shit."

"I'll try to get a statement from the governor."

"And last words."

"He was in a coma," Karin said. "I'll go with the last words we had from the beginning: 'You are murdering an innocent man.' "

Joe Lansdale, who has a shelf full of awards, including numerous Stokers and an Edgar, is one heck of a Renaissance man. Besides his dark fantasy and suspense tales, novels and comic scripts, he's written straight and hybrid things that could fit just about any other genre and a few that haven't been invented yet. His work is marked by humor, (often) violence, and a moral center and sense of outrage as firm and dead-on as Mark Twain's.

Joe's written so many things that are favorites that it's hard to make room for the following, which conquers a brand new area for him: the children's book. It's an amazing feat—and my fervent hope is that somewhere up the line this story will appear as a separate entity: a picture book.

In the meantime, children's literature will never be the same.

Bill, the Little Steam Shovel

Joe R. Lansdale

Bill the Little Steam Shovel was very excited. He was getting a fresh coat of blue paint from Dave the Steam Shovel Man in the morning, and the thought of that made him so happy, he secreted oil through his metal. He had been sitting idle in the big garage since he had been made, and he was ready to go out into the world to do his first job.

The first of many.

He was going to move big mounds of dirt and big piles of rocks. He was going to make basements for schools and hospitals. He was going to clear land for playgrounds so good little boys and good little girls would have a place for swings and merry-go-rounds and teeter-totters. He was going to move big trees and flatten hills so farmers could grow good food for the good little boys and girls to eat. He was going to clear land for churches and synagogues and cathedrals and mosques and buildings for the worship of Vishnu, Voudan, and such.

He was so happy.

So eager.

He hoped he wouldn't fuck up.

At night, all alone in the big garage, he thought about a lot of things. The work he wanted to do. How well he wanted to do it. The new coat of paint he was going to get. And sometimes he slept and had the dreams. Thinking about the dreams made his metal turn cold and his manifold blow leaky air.

What was happening to him on those long nights in the dark corner of the garage, waiting for his coat of paint and his working orders, was unclear to him. He knew only that he didn't like it and the dreams came to him no matter how much he thought about the good things, and the dreams were about falling great distances and they were about the dark. A dark so black, stygian was as bright as fresh-lit candle. One moment he seemed to be on solid support; the next, he was in midair, and down he would go, sailing through the empty blackness, and when he hit the ground, it was like, suddenly he was as flexible as an accordion, all his metal wadded and crunched, his steam shovel knocked all the way back to his ass end. Dave the Steam Shovel Man, crunched in the cab, was squirting out like a big bag of busted transmission fluid.

Then he would pop awake, snapping on his head beams, disturbing others in the garage, and from time to time, Butch the Big Pissed-Off Steam Shovel would throb his engine and laugh.

"You just a big Tinker Toy," Butch would say.

Bill wasn't sure what a Tinker Toy was, but he didn't like the sound of it. But he didn't say anything, because Butch would whip his ass. Something Butch would remind him of in his next wheezing breath.

"I could beat you to a pile of metal flakes with my shovel. You just a big Tinker Toy."

There was one thing that Bill thought about that helped him through the long nights, even when he had the dreams. And that was Miss Maudie. The little gold steam shovel with the great head beams that perked high and the little tailpipe that looked so . . . Well, there was no other way he could think of it. . . . So open and inviting, dark and warm and full of dismissed steam that could curl around your dipstick like . . . No. That was vulgar and Miss Maudie would certainly not think of him that way. She was too classy. Too fine. Bill thanked all the metal in Steam Shovel Heaven that she was made the way she was.

Oh, but Heaven forbid, and in the name of Jayzus the Steam Shovel Who Had Died for His Sins and all Steam Shovels' sins by allowing himself to be worked to a frazzle and run off a cliff by a lot of uncaring machines of the old religion, in his name, he shouldn't think such things.

He was a good little steam shovel. Good little steam shovels didn't think about that sort of business, about dipping their oil sticks down good-little-girl steam shovels' tailpipes, even if it probably felt damn good. The Great Steam Shovel in the Sky on the Great Expanse of Red Clay, and Jayzus and the Holy Roller Ghost, would know his thoughts, and it would be a mark against him, and when it was his time to be before the door of the Big Garage in the Sky, he would not meet his maker justified, but would be sent way down there to the scrap heap, where flames leaped and metal was scorched and melted, twisted and crushed, but never died.

Besides, why would anyone as neat and bright with such big head beams and that fine tailpipe think of him? He didn't even have his coat of paint yet. Here he was, brand-new, but not painted. He was gray as a stormcloud and just sitting, having never done work before. And he was a cheap machine at that, made from cheap parts: melted toasters, vacuums, refrigerators and such.

Maudie looked to be made from high-quality steel, like Butch, who eyed her and growled at her from time to time and made her flutter. Happily or fearfully, Bill could not determine. Perhaps both.

But Bill was just a cheap little machine made to do good hard work for all the good little children in the world, and the men and women who made him—

Then Bill saw his Dave.

Dave came into the building, slid the doorway open to let in the morning air, went to a corner of the garage, moved something on the front of his pants and took out his little poker and let fly with steaming water, going, "Ooooooh, yeah, the pause that refreshes, the envy of all racehorses."

Now I know why it stinks in here, Bill thought. Hadn't seen that before, but now I have. He's letting juice out of himself. Smells worse than transmission fluid, oil, or windshield cleaner. Don't the Daves get an oil change?

Dave went out again, came back with a paint gun and a big canister of blue paint fastened to it. He started right in on Bill.

"How's that, Bill?" Dave said, "How's that feel?"

Bill cranked his motor and purred.

"Oh, yeah, now you're digging it," Dave said.

Dave used several canisters, and soon Bill was as blue as the sky. Or, at least he'd always heard that the sky was blue when the pollution was light. He spent all his time in the garage, where he was built and where he had set for months, listening to the other steam shovels and diggers and such, so he didn't know blue from green. He was just a little machine with an eager engine and a desire to do good, and Dave had promised to paint him blue, so he figured the color on him, the paint coming out of the sprayer, must be blue, and it must be the color of the sky.

When Dave finished with the paint, he brought out a big handheld dryer and went over Bill with that. The dryer felt warm on Bill's metal, and when that was done, Dave took a long bristly device and poked it down his steam pipe and made Bill jump a little.

"Easy, boy. You'll get used to this."

The bristle worked inside to clean him, but Bill knew he wasn't dirty. This made him wonder about Dave, him doing this, smiling while he did, poking fast as he could in the ole pipe. But, then again, it did feel pretty good.

When Dave finished, he said, "When you go to work, little fella, make me proud."

On the way out, Dave stopped by Miss Maudie, bent and looked up her tailpipe, said, "Clean. Really clean," and departed.

That day, because of the new coat of paint, the finishing touch, Bill thought he would be sent to work. Dave had said so. But no. The day went by and the other steam shovels, including Miss Maudie, went out to do their work, but he remained inside, fresh and blue and unused.

That night, when the steam shovels returned, he was still in his place, and they, tired, weaving their shovels and dragging their treads, were hosed down by the other Daves, rubbed with rags and oiled and put away for the night.

What's wrong with me? thought Bill.

Why are they not using me to build roads and schools and churches and synagogues and all that shit?

What's up with that?

Night came and shadows fell through the windows and made the barn dark. Bill squatted on his treads in the gloom and tried not to cry. He was so disappointed. And with the night, he was scared.

He hated the dark. And he hated the dreams, and he knew if he slept, they would come.

But if he didn't sleep, how would that be?

What if they called him out tomorrow? He'd be too tuckered to shovel. He had to sleep. Had to.

And he tried.

And did . . .

Down in the motor functions, where the oil squeezed slow and the little rotors turned and the fans hummed and the coals burned, down there, way down there in the constantly fed nuclear pellet fire, Bill dreamed.

And the dream was a blossom of blackness, and he was falling, fast, so fast. Then he hit and his engine screamed. His lights popped on. Then Butch's lights popped on, and there was a hum of Butch's motor, and a clunk of treads, and pretty soon, Butch was beside him.

"You just a big Tinker Toy, and you starting to make me really mad, little squirt. You wrecking Butch's sleep. And Butch, he don't like it. He don't like it some at all, you diggin' on that, Tinker Toy? Well . . . No, you don't dig at all, do you, little friend? You sit and sit and soon rust and rust. If you live that long. You scream that engine again, you gonna wake up with a crowd of mechanics around you. Understand?"

"Yes, sir," Bill said.

"Good. Now . . ." And to emphasize, Butch lifted his shovel and rubbed it against Bill's side, made a scratch that ran all the way from Bill's cab to his treads. ". . . there's a little taste of what may be the appetizer to a big ole dinner. Dig? Oh, wrong term for you. You don't dig at all. You're too little."

"I may be little, but I'm willing to work," Bill said. "I want to build schools and churches and—"

"Shut the fuck up, Billy. Hear me, little bitty Billy. You just a big Tinker Toy."

"I . . ."

"Hear me?"

"Yes, sir."

"That's better, oil squirt."

"Leabe 'em alone, ya ole clunk of paper clips."

Lights were coming toward them, along with a rattling sound, like loose bolts and creaky hinges in a bucket, and soon, close up, Bill saw that it was Gabe the Wise Old Steam Shovel. His paint had gone gray, and his shovel wobbled and leaned a bit to the left, and his treads were frayed, but his head beams were still bright.

"You talking to me, Four Cylinder?" Butch said. "If that many work."

"Gid the fug away from him," Gabe said, "or I'll slap duh gohtdamn steam out of ya."

Butch laughed.

"You do any slapping, old shovel, your shovel will come off. You barely running on treads now, you greasy box of parts."

"Kizz muh ass," Gabe said.

"Won't poison myself with that idea," Butch said. "Gonna let you go, 'cause you so old, you make the stone wheel look like it a modern invention. You do, you know."

Chuckling under the roar of his engine, Butch motored off.

Gabe lifted up on one tread and let fly a steam fart that sounded like a howitzer.

"Thad's whad you can do wid yer gohtdamn stone wheel, ya big hunk of bolt-suckin', leakin', steamin' pile of—"

"Please," Bill said. "There's a lady nearby."

Bill rolled his head lamps toward Miss Maudie, who sat with her beams on, awakened by the commotion.

"Oh," Gabe said. "Sorry, girlie. Gid a liddle worked up sometimes."

"Excuse us for the bother," Bill said to Miss Maudie.

"That's all right," she said, and the sound of her motor made Bill feel a tightening in his joints and a gurgle in his transmission fluid. She blinked her headlights, then shut them down, with, "But I do need the sleep."

"Sure," Bill said. "Of course." And he could feel a tingling in his lines and parts that wasn't just fluid circulation.

"Yah ain't eben giddin' none, and you done exhaust-whipped," Gabe said.

"Sshhhhhh," Bill said, letting out a soft puff of steam. "You'll embarrass her . . . and me . . . and Butch will come back and scratch me again, or beat me. . . . But thanks. Thanks for taking up for me."

"Ain't nuthin'. Jes wand to sleep muhself. So shud up. 'Sides, don't like to see some medal-assed whippersnapper bullyin' a liddle steam fard like yerself. Now, go to sleep."

"Sure," Bill said. "Thanks again."

"Nothin' to id," Gabe said. "And kid, you're habbin' dreams, right? I hear ya moanin' yer engine."

"I am. The same dream."

"Whad is id?"

Bill told him.

"Huuummmm," Gabe said. "Pud my thinker on thad one. I'm a preddy smart fugger, say so myself. . . . But in the meantime, ya want to git them dreams outta yer had, least a lidde. What ya do, ya close yer eyes, and ya think of yerself ridin' Miss Maudie's tailpipe like yer trying to climb a gohtdamn straid-up incline without any treads. Gid me? That'll put yer liddle nut of a fire in a gohtdamn happy place, thad's whad I'm tryin' to tell ya."

"Don't say that."

"Done said."

And with that, Gabe chuckled dryly and rattled off to leave Bill with the shadows and his dreams.

* * *

Inside Bill, the little nuclear pellet fed the fire that fed the coals that heated the water and fed the steam, and once again, Bill dreamed.

He first dreamed of a fine warm place with soft light and he dreamed of mounting Maudie, his dipstick out, riding her tailpipe like he was going up a steep incline. It was a good dream, and he felt a kind of release, as if all his steam had been blown out and all his oils and fluids had been sucked from him. It was a feeling like he could collapse into a heap of smoking metal, and it felt good, this dream, but when it was over, he dreamed of falling again, and falling from way up and down fast, striking the ground, going to pieces, squashing Dave this way and that. And when he awoke, panting heavy through his steam pipe, he found that in his sleep, during the dream about Maudie, he had squirted transmission fluid all over the floor.

(Or had it happened out of fear?)

He was glad it was dark. He was so embarrassed.

Bill looked about, but in the dark all he could see were the shapes of the other shovels. He glanced where Maudie's shape was. She was still and her lights were shut up tight behind their shields.

Near the wall, where Butch stayed, he heard Butch snoring, the air blowing up through his steam pipe in a loud masculine way. The big bruiser even snored like a thug.

Rest of the night, Bill tried to stay awake, to neither have the bad dream or to think of Maudie, but think of her he did, but this time, differently, not mounting her tailpipe as if trying to push up an incredible incline, but side by side with her, motoring along, the two of them blowing a common tune through their whistles, her turning her shovel to him, lifting it, and underneath, her bright red rubber bumper was parting to meet with his . . . and kiss.

But that wasn't going to happen.

He was never going to kiss Maudie or mount her tailpipe.

And, the way it looked now, he was never going to build schools and churches and such for all those children, and what did he care?

Little bastards. They didn't need that stuff anyway.

Then daylight came through the windows of the garage and turned the floor bright, like a fresh lube spill, and for a moment, Bill was renewed and hopeful and willing.

* * *

A bunch of Daves came into the garage and each of them climbed onto a steam shovel, and Bill, hoping, hoping so hard he thought he might just start his own engine and drive out of there, saw his Dave approaching.

His Dave climbed inside his little cabin and touched the controls, and Bill's motor roared. Bill felt his pistons throbbing with excitement, felt oil growing warm and coursing through his tubes and wetting up his machinery. When Dave turned him around and drove him out of the garage, he was so proud, he thought he might blow a gasket.

Outside he saw sunlight shining bright off his blue shovel and he could feel the ground and gravel crunching beneath his treads, and to his left and right were the others, rolling along in line, off to work.

His dream had come true.

They motored to the site and begin to dig. It was a location that would provide space for a large apartment complex, and it was next to another large apartment complex, right across from two other large apartment complexes and a row of fast-food joints, out of which came a steady stream of Daves who didn't drive steam shovels.

The site was currently a patch of woods, a bunch of beautiful trees full of happy singing birds and squirrels at play. But fuck that. Bill and his fellow shovels were at work.

The steam shovels rode in and pushed that shit down, dug up the roots and pushed it in a pile to burn. Birds flew away and squirrels scampered for safety. Eggs in fallen birds' nests were crunched beneath their treads.

The machines dug deep and pushed the dirt until anything that was rich with natural compost was completely scraped up and mounded, revealing clay beneath, red as a scraped wound. Half the patch of woods was scratched away in no time, and Bill was scraping with the rest as hard as he could, knocking some of his bright blue paint off on roots and rocks. But he didn't mind. Those were battle scars.

In the cockpit, he heard Dave say, "Now we're talking. Lookin' good. Fucking trees. Goddamn birds. Shitting squirrels."

About noon they stopped so the Daves could climb down and gather up and eat food and drink from the little black boxes they carried.

Bill, parked by Gabe, said, "Gabe. What about all the birds and squirrels and little animals? What about them?"

"Fug em," said Gabe. "They're all gone, who'll gib a shid? Can't fret over somethin' ain't around, can ya kid? 'Sides, whad's 'em fuggers ever done fer ya?"

"Well . . ."

"Nothin'. Not a gohtdamn thang."

"Well, yeah, I guess . . . But, gee, Gabe, what happens when all the world is scraped down, and they don't need us?"

"Aw, we'll push down ole buildings, scrape 'em down red to the clay, and they'll build some new shid. Always somethin' fer us to fug up so stuff can be built again. Don't fret, kid."

"But, don't the children need trees for shade, and don't trees help make the air fresh? . . ."

"Don't believe thad shid. Tree is a tree is a tree. 'Em liddle chilren, shid, them fuggers can wear a hat and breathe through an oxygen mask for all I care. . . . Hey, saw yer greasy spot when ya rolled out this mornin'. Kinda had ya one of 'em night time squirdaramas, didn't ya?"

Bill felt embarrassed. "Well, I . . ."

"Fug it. It's normal. Thinkin' bout thad liddle cuddie over 'ere, weren't ya, son?"

Bill looked where Maudie was at rest, next to the last line of trees. She looked bright and gold, and even with dirt and clay on her shovel, she had a kind of charm, a sweetness. And a nice tailpipe.

"Well, said Gabe, "ya was thinking 'bout it, wadn't you? That's why ya squirded yer juice."

"I suppose."

"Gohtdamn, boy. Ain't no spose to it. Thad's all right. Thad's natural. Ought to try and talk ya up some of thad, thad's what I'm trying to tell ya. Was younger, ya can bet I'd be sportin' around her, throbbin' my engine, whippin' muh shovel. Muh old dipstick pokin' up under muh hood. Hell, all I can do these days is use id to check muh oil."

"I was wondering about that, Gabe. If the dipstick is under the hood, and the . . . well, you know, the lady's tail pipe is where tail pipes are . . . How does that work, Gabe?"

Gabe laughed. "Ya kiddin', ain't ya? Naw, gohtdamnit, ya ain't. Well, son, on the old underbelly is another panel, and ya get stiff and pokey, it hits the hood, but when ya want to do the deed, ya see, ya led thad little section underneath ya pop open, stick lowers, and, well, son, ya'll figure it out. Promise. Figured out in ya sleep, didn't ya? Old parts and lines knew whad to do without no thinkin' on yer part."

"I didn't say I was going to do anything—"

"—shid, boy. Aint' nothin' wrong wid wantin' a piece of tailpipe. Oh, and I been thinkin' on yer dream, and I know someone might be able to help ya on thad. Can figure it . . . But later. Here come duh Daves. Time ta gid wid it."

They went back to work, and pretty soon Dave said to Bill, "Bill, we got a big old stubborn tree that just won't go, and we got to push it down so we can scrape the clay. I think you're ready for it. Am I right? Are you ready?"

Bill rumbled his engine and whistled air through his steam pipe in response.

"All right, you little shovel, let's do 'er."

And away they went. Bill lifted his shovel and poked it out, and Dave guided him to the tree. It was a big old tree and round enough that four men with their hands linked couldn't have surrounded it. Must have been hundreds of years old, but Bill, he was determined it wasn't going to get a day older.

He put out his shovel and began to push. He pushed hard, giving it all he had. He revved up his engine and whistled his steam and dug in with his treads and . . .

The tree didn't move.

He revved up higher and pushed and pushed and . . .

Nothing.

He might as well have had his engine turned off and be sitting in the garage with a tread up his exhaust.

He pushed harder, and . . .

He cut one. A big one. It came out of his exhaust with a kind of *blat-blat-blat* sound.

Bill couldn't believe it. He had cut a fart to end all farts, and right in front of Dave and all the other steam shovels. He turned one of his head beams slowly, looked to his right, and there was Maudie. She was so shocked, the split in her front bumper hung open, showing her gear-cog teeth (all perfect and shiny), and Bill, he wanted to just run off a cliff. But there weren't any cliffs. Just that big tree standing upright in front of him, and he hadn't done anymore than crack a little bark.

"Well," said Bill's Dave, "this is just too much for you. We'll have to get a bigger and better machine. One that can do the job. And we might want to cut back on that cheap transmission fluid, boy."

Dave backed Bill off from the tree, stood up in the cab and called out, "You better bring in Butch. This is a job for a real steam shovel."

Bill felt his body droop on its treads. His shovel hit the ground with a thud.

He was not only a weakling and a farter, but he was also being beat out by his worst enemy.

Butch revved his engine and threw out his shiny shovel and went up against the tree, and at first Bill thought: Well, he won't do it either.

The tree stood firm, not moving, and then, suddenly, it began to lean and lean and lean, and there was a cracking sound, then a cry of roots and timber like the sound of something being jerked from its womb, and the great tree went down, the roots popping up, clay flying from them in red clunks.

Butch backed off, lifted his shovel, and with a sort of slide, treaded back to the center of the workforce.

Bill saw Maudie turn and look to him, and her bumper was split wide again. But this time, she was smiling.

Back in the barn, Bill sat alone as the windows turned dark. Gabe came rolling over.

"Ya all right, son?"

"I guess."

"Damn, boy. Can't believe ya farded. Thad one knocked a bird out of a tree, gabe us all an oil stink ya wouldn't believe. A fard like that, ya must hab passed into another dimension for a while. Yer gohtdamn head beams crossed, ya cut wind so hard."

"Gee, thanks."

"Ah, don't led it bother you. I led fards all the time. And sometime on purpose. . . . Big old tree like thad, it ain't for a kid. I couldn't do it. Well, in my day I could."

"Young as me?"

"Oh, yeah. Damn, what a fard."

"Please, Gabe. Don't mention it anymore."

"All right. But, son, it was a champion."

Bill sighed.

"Ya know, I told ya I had someone could tell ya 'bout dem dreams yer always having?"

"Yes."

"Well, I'm gonna bring him over. Sid tight."

Gabe rolled away, and a moment later, Bill saw him return with an old gray steam shovel who had steam coming up from between his bumpers. When he got closer, Bill saw that it wasn't steam at all; he was smoking a metal pipe stuffed with old oily shop rags.

"This is Professor Zoob," Gabe said.

"Ah, how are you, ma boy?"

"Fine . . . I guess. Why haven't I seen you before?"

"I am in the back of the garage, yes. I hang there and do little jobs. Push garbage about. But I am old, and they do not call me out much. I would think, soon, I will be for the scrap machine, yes. I have been around for many years, I have, and was driven by a student of much psychology. He studied in my cockpit during his breaks, yes. And when he did, he read aloud from his books, and I listened. I learned much. I learned much about dreams, I did."

"Really?"

"Yes. And before we analyze them, might I say, that I heard about today, about your trouble with the tree and the tremendous fart."

"From Gabe, I suppose."

"Oh, from everyone. It was quite some joke, it was."

"Grand."

"But, if you will tell me your dreams, let me consider on it, maybe I can help you understand."

"I don't know."

"Sure. Sure. Try me."

"Well, there's only one that concerns me, really scares me."

Zoob puffed his pipe faster, sending up a haze of smoke.

"That really stinks," Bill said. "And isn't that bad for you?"

"Of course, but at my age, why would I give a shit? I use a seven percent solution of oil and transmission fluid. The rags burn slower, and in their haze, I think big thinks, I do. And could it stink any worse than the whopper you cut loose with today, huh?"

"I'll never live that down, will I?"

"Won't be easy," Gabe said.

"The dream?" Zoob said.

Bill told him about the dream, about the darkness and the falling and the smashing, and Zoob said, "When you are falling. What is it you smell?"

"Smell?"

"Yes. Do you smell anything? Hear anything? Taste anything?"

"Why, no. It's a dream."

"Ah, but there are dreams where one can hear or smell or taste. Have you not had the dreams about the lady steam shovels, and how that feels and smells and tastes, with the afterbite of steam on the tailpipe, huh, have you not?"

"I . . . I suppose."

"Yes, of course, you can. You can smell things in a dream if there is something to smell."

"Hope ya can't smell thad fard in one," Gabe said. "Thad would peel duh paint right off."

"That's enough," Bill said.

"Well, then, my little friend, think this, do you remember anything in the darkness of your dream? Anything at all? Anything in the shadows?"

"No."

"Ah, then we must resort to the hypnotism."

"What?"

"Hypnotism. Now," Zoob said, rolling back a pace. "I'm going to swing my shovel back and forth, and I want you to watch, listen only to the sound of my voice, and watch the shovel please. There is a small silver spot scraped near the center of it, and that's what I want you to concentrate on. . . . Ready?"

Bill watched the shovel swing back and forth, and Zoob said soothing things and no one mentioned the fart and pretty soon Bill was feeling sleepy, a little dizzy, as if he might fall over; then he felt like he was in a tunnel, and the only light in the tunnel was the shiny spot on Zoob's shovel, and the tunnel was swaying, and then it went still, and there was just the spot before him, like a beacon, and Zoob's voice, easy and soft and suggestive.

"Now, Little Bill, you are in the dream. All dark. Tell me now, what is happening in this falling dream? Tell me."

"Well, let me see. It's dark. . . . That's it. It's dark."

"Listen carefully, Little Bill. You are in this bad dream. And it's dark—"

"And you're in there wid thad fard," Gabe said, and chuckled.

"Silence, Gabe," Zoob said. "No more with the fart . . . Now, you are in the bad dream, in the dark, and you are falling. Are you there, Little Bill?"

"Yes," Bill said. And he was in the dream, all right. And it was dark. No little scrape of light visible. And he was falling. And he felt the old fear rise up out of the darkness and come over him in a rush.

"Shit," Bill said.

"Now," said Zoob, "you are falling, and you are feeling the shit feeling, and I want you to slow this fall, and I want you to look about you. . . .

It's all right. You'll be all right. You should not be scared this time. We have control over this dream, you and I, and you are falling slow and you can take the time to look about. You look about you now, and you listen, and you tell Zoob what it is you see and hear, or smell. You tell me everything, Little Bill, yes."

"Yes . . . I . . . I am falling, and it's dark, and I'm scared and I can see to my right that there's a shape."

"What is this shape?"

"I . . . I don't know."

"Yes. Yes, you do. We stop the fall. You hang in midair. You study the shape and it is— ?"

"It's a . . . It's a Dave."

"A Dave, huh? Ah-hah. Go on, Little Bill."

"He's standing in the shadows. . . . He's getting around fine in the dark—"

"He familiar with the place," Zoob said.

"Yes, it's his home. There are all kinds of machines and gadgets there."

"Like what?"

"A refrigerator, and there's a little light. I guess I didn't notice it before. The Dave is opening the refrigerator and taking something out and the light is coming from there."

"The refrigerator light," Zoob said. "He's getting food. They are always with the food, which is why, over the years, you got the same driver, his ass gets heavy. It makes them blow up like a hot valve. But, go on, Little Bill."

"He's turning, his elbow is hitting something. . . . Something on the stove, and it's falling off."

"What is it?"

"I don't know."

"Take yourself some closer."

"I don't want to."

"It is quite all right, Little Bill. Go closer."

"It's a waffle iron."

"No shit?"

"Yes, sir."

"It is a waffle iron. Now that is some confusing business. . . . Ah, ah . . . Okay, what else do you see, Little Bill?"

"Nothing. It's all gone black."

"Wake up."

Bill opened his head lamps.

"Wow," he said.

"Ain't that some shit?" Zoob said. "One time, in the mirror, I hypnotize myself into thinking I am one big chicken. Tried to roost on top of the garage, but ended up pushing down the wall. Oh, the Daves were mad that day."

"But . . . What about me?"

"You are the waffle iron."

"Beg pardon."

"The waffle iron and many things. Old metals. Busted parts. They were melted down to make you, and the memories of before, they are in the metal. Are at least certain memories. Like the fall. That was traumatic, and the memory, a little metal ghost, it stayed with the metal. The waffle iron, it must have become part of the painframe that holds your memories. That is it, Little Bill. You remember the fall, and therefore, you dream of it and you fear it."

"But I'm not the waffle iron. And now that I know, it'll go away. Right?"

"Nah. You have to work through it."

"How do I do that?"

"Don't know."

"But you're the professor."

"Well, I call myself that. But this, this is up to you, Little Bill. You have to sort of cinch up the old transmission and deal with it. And yes, knowing the source. That will help. You must overcome your fears, and when you do, the dreams will stop."

Professor Zoob turned and rumpled away on his treads. Gabe said, "See, told ya he could help ya. . . . How about thad? Yer a sissy 'cause ya got a mashed waffle iron inside ya. Ain't thad some shid? I'm glad I was made from good medal. Well, going to gid a lube job, if you know what I mean, so, hang tight, kid, and good luck."

"Thanks, Gabe, I think," Bill said, and Gabe went away.

Sitting alone in the corner, his shovel dipped, his head beams to the wall, Bill was surprised to feel a soft metallic touch. He turned, and there was Maudie.

"I know you were embarrassed today, Bill, but I want you to know, it's only natural. A lot of fluid in the system, exertion. I wouldn't feel too bad."

"Well, I do. . . . And you were laughing."

"Yeah. Well, it was funny. On the outside, anyway. From your point of view, not so funny. It was just so loud and long, and that look on your face . . . I wasn't laughing because I think you're a loser. I mean, a fart like that, it kind of embarrasses everyone, and you're always glad it's the other guy, but don't feel too bad. I puked once. Oil all over the place, and there was a big chunk of rust in it. I was so humiliated."

"Really?"

"Really."

"Was it before I came here?"

"I was here a few days before you, and yes, it was."

"Did everyone see it?"

"No. Only me, but I was still embarrassed."

"That's not exactly the same."

"No. Yours was more humiliating, I admit, but, still, I was embarrassed, if just to myself. I mean yours was right out in front of God and everybody. . . ."

"Yes. I know. Maudie, I'm going to go right to it. Is there anyway you and me could get together?"

"You mean, together together?"

"I just want to get to know you. I like you. I'm not a bad guy. . . ."

"I like you too."

"Really?"

"Sure. Everyone in the barn, except Butch, says you're nice."

"No shit?"

"No shit."

"Well, that's swell, Maudie. Maybe, you know, sometime, after work, we could get together in the far corner of the garage. Maybe get our oil changed or something. Watch a little TV in the rec room afterwards. There's a car-chase movie on, the big new one about car wrecks and the fire department, *Lots of Cars and a Dozen Hoses*."

"Oh, those cars. I've seen previews. They're so sexy. So are the fire trucks. That's some metal the cars are built from, isn't it?"

"Actually, I don't know if cars and steam shovels go together—"

"Ah, jealous already, and we haven't even had our first date."

"I guess . . . a little. I mean, how do you compete with movie cars?"

"That's cute. . . . Long as it doesn't get out of hand. And listen, those movie cars, they're always being remade and rebuffed, and they don't really run as fast as they show in the movie. I'm looking for the real deal, and you're the real deal, I think. I'd sure like to find out for sure."

"Gee, Maudie. That's swell."

"Remember, about the tree. That was a big one. It would take someone like Butch to push it over. For heaven's sake, Bill, he's three times your size. It's not your fault."

"Yeah . . . Yeah, you're right."

"You might want to drink a little less transmission fluid, though, you're gonna be straining that hard. I mean . . . You know?"

"Sure. Of course. Good advice."

"See you later."

"Tomorrow? After work?"

"It's a date."

That night Bill slept and he dreamed, but it was not the dream about falling. Zoob had really helped him, and probably had no idea how much. In his dream, he thought of Maudie. And it was a good dream, and they were warm and close and friendly, and spent quality time together, watching TV, having their oil changed, and, in the end, he mounted her like he was climbing an incline to a Rocky Mountain trailer park entrance.

But just as he was about to finish, he cut another one.

He awoke in a sweat.

He had swapped one bad dream for another.

He wasn't falling anymore, but now he was afraid he was going to cut a big one at an opportune moment.

But, hell, he had about as much chance of mounting Maudie, having any kind of relationship with her, as a bird had of finding a tree in a Taco Bell parking lot.

Morning came, and Bill tried to put a good face on it, smiled his rubber bumpers wide when he saw the beautiful Maudie being driven out of the barn. She waved her radio antennae at him, and he waved his back, and she was gone, out into the sunlight.

For a long moment, Bill feared he was not going to get another chance. Steam shovel after steam shovel was rolled outside, and still he sat. No Dave to drive him.

But then, finally, his Dave showed up.

Dave came and climbed up on him. Bill cranked the engine without giving Dave time to do it.

"Wow, you're raring to go," Dave said. "Sorry I was late. Wife felt frisky. Since that happens about once every six months, had to take advantage of it."

They rolled outside, and the sun was bright against the concrete. The team of shovels went past where they had worked before, started motoring along the road, puffing steam, cracking gravel under their treads.

They rolled along until the road rose up and the mountains gathered around them, and still they went up. Bill felt a strain in his motor, and he took a deep breath of steam, squirted it out, hunkered down and dug in with his treads. Up he went, carrying his Dave high and deep into the mountains along the concrete road. Bill tried not to look to his right, toward the edge of the road and the great fall that was there. The feelings he had in the dreams came back when he did. His insides trembled like a piston was blown. His nuclear pellets, his gas and oil engine, his backup steam engine, all seemed to miss a beat as they went up. And up. And up.

The road narrowed, and finally they came to where the road turned to clay, then ended up against the mountain.

Bill realized this was a spot where other shovels had been working. It was wide here. You could put four steam shovels across, digging. Digging open the mountain so the road could keep going up and Daves and their Sallys could ride in their cars carrying all their little Daves and Sallys.

Bill was not first in line, but well behind the first four that went to work, Butch and Maudie among them. Dave pulled him in line with three other shovels and killed his motor. Bill watched Maudie as she worked, the way the sun hit the metal of her shiny ass, the way her tailpipe wiggled, and he was amazed and grateful for her fine construction.

He watched Butch dig and toss the dirt, and was impressed in spite of himself. What a powerful machine. He liked the way the cables rolled under his metal skin and the way he could lie back on the rear of his treads and lift himself up. And he liked the way Butch cussed as he worked, digging, insulting the mountain.

He looked around and saw Gabe working alongside the road, on little jobs, like making the road wider for more concrete to be laid. He thought of Zoob, back in the barn. Did he wish he were out here, digging?

Most likely.

It was the dream of every good construction shovel.

The digging went on, and the day got hotter. His metal grew warm, and he could feel the oils, the liquids inside of him, starting to grow warm and loose. He lifted his head beams and looked at the sky. A single bird soared against it, and the blue of the sky faded as a cloud of pollution, the sign of progress, rolled across it, gray as a cobwebbed garage corner. He thought, If I could shoot a rifle, like a Dave, I bet I could pop that goddamn bird.

Then Dave started his motor again.

Now Bill and three others took the place of the four who had been in line. As Maudie rolled past him, she winked a headlight. Then Butch rolled past him, said, "You just a Tinker Toy."

Bill gritted his gears and went up against the mountain with the other three, and he began to dig. He thought, Dig, boy, dig. And don't cut one. Die before you do that. Dig. Dig this mountain down. Dig like you want to flatten the entire earth. Which, actually, seemed like a fairly noble ambition. Making all the world flat and covered in concrete.

But then what would he do?

Why, tear up the concrete, of course. As Gabe had said. It had to wear out, crack and buckle. Tear it up and scrape it into piles and let them put down more concrete. Oh, yes, Gabe was right. This was the life. Fuck the earth. Fuck the wildlife. Fuck it all. To dig was to live.

And so he dug and he dug, then, suddenly, Dave was wheeling him about. He thought at first he had done something wrong, but realized he was growing low on power. That he had to pull back, like the first four. Maybe get a new pellet to refire the steam. That was it. He had done fine.

He smiled as he clattered tiredly back through the line and another four moved up.

So the day went, three rows of four, taking turns, twelve steam shovels working against the mountain, and Gabe working the side of the road. And finally, midday, the Daves pulled back all the shovels and stopped, had them set alongside the road.

The Daves went about checking oil and fluids and such, and old Gabe, he was sent up to the front to shovel the bits of dirt that remained, scraping it down to the clay, which was a job that made him happy.

Then, the mountain came down.

It came down with a slight rumble, then a big rumble, and Bill looked up and saw Gabe look up, and as the mountain went over, Gabe and Bill could hear the sound of metal bending; then there was nothing but a great dust cloud.

Butch, who was behind him now, rolled forward suddenly, without benefit of his Dave, said, "Man, did you see that shit there? Old Gabe, he done fucked now. One less old geezer in the garage. And that ain't bad."

Bill wheeled. He swung his shovel and hit Butch with everything he had. And Butch—well, it didn't bother him much. Butch swung his shovel too, and just as it hit Bill, making Bill slide back on his treads, Bill heard Maudie's voice.

"You got to get Gabe out from under there, boys. You got to."

"Ain't gonna dig him out unless I got to," said Butch. "He nothing to me, he ain't."

"You're right, Maudie," said Bill, and he hummed up his engine and rolled forward. His Dave tried to work the controls, to make Bill do what he wanted, but Bill ignored him. I got free will, he thought. I can do what I want, and he went at the dirt and began to dig. He dug and he dug, and eventually he saw a bit of scarred metal, and he dug faster, and finally, finally, there was Gabe.

Or what was left of him. He was squashed, and his old shovel had been knocked completely off. Oil dribbled all over the earth.

"Gabe!" Bill said.

Weak as a busted oil line, Gabe said, "Thanks, boy. But ain't no use. I'm a goner. Fugged from bucket to ass end."

And he was.

They brought in a wrecker and took Gabe away, down the hill. That night when they rolled back in the garage, Bill found that Gabe had been dismantled and stacked. Tomorrow, he went to the furnace to be melted down, and reformed.

"It's another life," Maudie said. "He'll be melted into some other kind of machinery. It's not over for him."

"It won't be him," Bill said.

"And there's his soul, it's gone to the sky. That can't be changed. Can't be taken away from him. A residue remains. Isn't it in the manual that residuals can remain?"

Bill thought about the ghost inside him, the residual of the waffle iron. And then he thought about heaven.

"What's heaven like, Maudie? What do you think it's like?"

"Flat. Lots of concrete. But everyday, new hills pop up, and new trees, and they have to be taken down. And we'll be there, just like all the others that have gone before us and will come after us."

"Will Butch be there?"

"I don't think so. I think he gets the other place."

"Gabe was just an old guy," Bill said. "A good old guy."

"I know. Don't look at him anymore."

Zoob rolled up. He said, "I am sorry, Bill. He was good, he was. I miss him already."

"Me too," Bill said.

"I wish you the best of a night you could have," Zoob said. "Gabe, he is all through with the pain. The ache in the bolts and the hinges. Maybe he's lucky. I think maybe I could wish it was me, you see."

"No way," Bill said.

"Thank you. And I wish you, and the lady, good night."

"Good night," Bill and Maudie said in unison.

They rolled away together, went to the dark shadows on the far side of the garage. Maudie swung her shovel so that it draped over Bill's back. Her bumper parted and pressed to his, and they kissed. And kissed again. Soon they were holding each other, stroking metal, and then, heaven above and flatten all earth, he was behind her, and down came the oil stick, and then came the loving.

Afterwards, they sat low on their treads together in the shadows and slid open their side traps and dropped their oil tubes into a fine vat of thirty weight, sucked it up together.

"I . . . I don't know what happened there . . . ," Bill said.

"What happened was wonderful," Maudie said. "I haven't felt that good since . . . Well, I haven't felt that good."

"Neither have I," he said.

That night, Little Bill did not have the bad dreams.

Next morning the Daves came and rolled out all the steam shovels, drove them back up into the mountains. Today, Bill was not as aware of the heights. He felt strong and wanted at the mountain.

They came to where they had stopped working, where Gabe had been crushed, and spread into groups of four. He was in the first group. To his left was Maudie, to her left, Glen, an older steam shovel. And to Bill's right, Butch, who was next to the ledge that fell away into what semed like eternity.

"I gonna show you how to work today, Tinker Toy," said Butch. "Gabe, he done gone now. Ain't here to take up for you. Not that it mattered none, but who wants to beat up an old steam shovel?"

"You don't mind threatening to beat up a smaller shovel than you," Bill said with a kind of newfound bravado, thinking, getting tailpipe made you crazy, made you brave. "I was your size, you might not be so tough."

Butch narrowed his head lamps.

"You pushing, little Tinker Toy. I gonna show you how to work. And, I may show you a thing or two other than that, you hear me?"

"Like I give an oil squirt."

Butch said, "I think maybe you been getting a little business, a little of the golden steam shovel's tail business, and it's making you think you a man, little Tinker Toy, you know what I mean? You ain't no man. You just a Tinker Toy."

Bill shoved Butch. It was sudden. Butch was actually knocked to the side a pace, near the mountain's edge.

"Hey," Butch said.

"Stop it," Bill's Dave said. "I came here to work. What are you shovels doing?"

"I remember that you did that, Tinker Toy," Butch said.

"Hope you do," Bill said.

They began to dig, and everything went well. The mountain moved for them. The dirt was mounded to the side away from the ledge, and some of it was put behind them and carried down the hill and away by other shovels. Zoob was working the edges of the road, doing the soft jobs, the way Gabe had been, though even more slowly.

They worked on and on and the sun rose high and grew hot and made their metal warm and finally very warm, and then hot as the top of a stove. Their metal shone like a newly minted coin in the sunlight, and their well-oiled shovels and treads worked beautifully and tore apart the mountain, and somewhere, inside the mountain, as if the mountain had had enough, a vein of rock that ran all the way to the summit quivered and quaked and let go, and the huge tip of the mountain, like a peaked hat knocked over by a high wind, tumbled down on the four working shovels below.

One moment there was the sun; then there was the darkness. Bill could feel the pressure of the dirt and the rocks pushing down on him. Then, below him the ground moved, and he went down into it. Amazingly, he slipped down at an angle, and down, down, down, as he slid into a weak place in the mountain, a natural tunnel filled with soft dirt. He began to slide back into that. And a rock, dislodged, shot out and stuck in front of him, stopped the progress of falling rock from above.

It gave Bill a bit of space.

He could move his shovel, as a Dave might move his elbow if he were inside a tow sack. He moved the shovel, and some dirt shook. He began to move it back and forth. More dirt shifted. Finally he grabbed the great rock and gave it all he had. The rock moved and dirt came in, but Bill rocked back on his treads and the dirt flowed around him like black water.

He kept working that shovel, and it made a sound like it was trying to let go of clotted oil in the lines. Still, Bill shoveled, lifting it a bit up and down, a little from side to side. Finally, he had traction, and he was moving the dirt. And he was going up that incline, climbing it the way he'd climbed the sweet golden Maudie the night before. He put that image in his head and kept at it, and pretty soon the image was as tight in his head as a screwed-down bolt.

Up he went. Up. And finally there was light.

And he realized his Dave was gone. Probably washed away in the rock and dirt, covered up and crushed like an aluminum oil can.

On the surface, he found the shovels and the Daves digging at the mountain furiously. As he rose out of the ground like a metal mole, the Daves cheered and the engines revved their motors.

He lifted his shovel high.

But it was a short-lived triumph.

He saw that the mountain had come down in such a way that it had covered Maudie and Butch.

Glen had survived it all. His shovel had been knocked off, and one of his treads was slightly dislodged, but already a huge wrecker had come for him and he was being hooked up even as Bill looked.

As Bill watched the wrecker take Glen away, he realized he didn't feel so good and his vision was blurry. There was dirt inside his busted right head lamp, and it was partially covering his line of vision. Inside, way down deep, he felt as if a bag of bolts and gears had been randomly mixed and tossed into a paint shaker. When he moved, he squeaked and clanked and he hurt near the right hinge of his shovel like a Dave had been at him with a welding torch.

Bill hunkered down on his treads and tore at the mountain. Tried to dig where he had last seen Maudie, but he couldn't be sure she was there. Maybe, like him, she had been washed down into a soft part of the ground. He dug and he dug, and finally he saw metal. He revved his engine, and other shovels came. They dug and dug and pretty soon they saw the shiny gold metal of the beautiful Maudie, less beautiful now. Dented and scratched gray in strips, her shovel dangling by one bolt.

Bill hooked his shovel around her and pulled her out. And as he did, he saw behind her a roof of rocks supported by a wall of rock slabs, and in there, crushed down but alive (he could see the headlights blinking) was Butch. When Maudie came out, the dirt went down. Butch went out of sight.

Bill sighed air through his manifold.

Maybe he was dead. The bastard.

The shovels were slowing down behind him. They had Maudie out, and no one was working that hard for Butch, and Bill could understand that. . . .

But, damn it, Butch was a steam shovel. He was a worker. And he had been caught in the storm of the mountain-fall while on the job. And though Bill thought it might be nice to just let the mountain crush him, he just couldn't do it. That wasn't the way it was in the manual. Machines helped machines. Machines helped the Daves.

Bill went at it again, digging, digging, and pretty soon the other shovels were helping, and the dirt began to move.

When it was clear enough, they could see Butch in there. He was much shorter than before, his metal rippled in the center, and above him, supported on two wobbly slabs of rock, was a much bigger slab of rock. It looked as if it were large enough to build a subdivision on.

Bill moved in close and tried to pull Butch out, but it was like trying to work a greasy bolt out of an engine with a coat hanger tipped with chewing gum. Touch and go.

Butch was moaning with pain as the tugging tore at his metal. "I've lost my crankshaft," he said. "And my oil pan's loose. I can feel it sliding around inside."

"Don't move," Bill said. He dug a space close to the edge of the mountain, and within a short time he found he could scrunch in there. One tread was hanging halfway over the edge, and he could hear rock tumbling down the side of the mountain, and feel it sliding out from under his treads. He felt himself slipping a little. For a moment, the old dream came back, flashed before his inner head lamps, and he was falling, and he was scared.

He shook it off.

He looked out and he saw Maudie. She was banged up, but she was going to be okay. Nothing a few tools, a blowtorch and paint couldn't fix. She looked at him, and her lights came on and her bumper parted in a smile, showing that pretty gear work inside, slightly dusty. It gave him strength. He scrunched back farther. Being smaller, he could fit right in beside Butch.

"What in the world will you be doing, my boy?"

It was old Zoob. He had slid up close to the opening. The old steam shovel bent down on its creaky treads and eyed Bill with his head lamps.

"Why are you in there, my boy? Let the rock crush this one, the big hunk of scrap metal."

"He was on the job," Bill said. "He's one of us."

"I think he's not worth it some at all—that is what I think."

"You may be right," Bill said.

"Hey," Butch said. "I'm right here."

Bill brought his shovel up and touched the great slab above him. He hunkered down on his treads and flexed his metal, and lifted with the shovel.

And the great rock moved.

Shovel God in Heaven, and praise Jayzus, but Bill felt strong. He pushed. And he pushed with his shovel, and he felt the bolts that hinged it go tight as a pair of Vise-Grips, but he pushed up anyway.

And that rock moved some more.

"Pull . . . him . . . out," Bill said.

They came forward, two big steam shovels, and they reached in and got hold of Butch, started pulling.

Bill, looking at Maudie, suddenly felt weak. He could feel his hydraulic fluid starting to eke out, could hear it hissing as it erupted through the tubes.

"Oh, shit," Bill said.

Then there was pain.

Sharp. Quick.

And he was flying along through darkness, and ahead of him was a great tunnel lit by a white light. He could see himself flying along, treads working, but touching nothing, and a flock of birds and scampering squirrels and insects and fish and snakes and possums and raccoons and bears, and all manner of wildlife, was rushing along beside him, as well as a flying waffle iron.

And he felt good and happy and fulfilled.

He rushed faster and the light grew brighter, and the animals and insects were sucked forward as if by a vacuum cleaner, and then, just as he was about to go into the brightest and warmest part of the light—

He saw Gabe.

Gabe was blocking his path.

Gabe rammed up against him.

"Gohtdamnit, boy. Not yet. Id's not yer time just now. Ain't far off. But not yet. Got to finish whad yer doin', son."

There was a rush of wind and light as Bill fled back along the tunnel and the light went dark. Then he was standing there, with that great slab of rock on his shovel, and he saw Maudie looking at him, and that look in her eyes was worth all the agony in his shovel, worth the tubes he was splitting, the fluids he was draining.

The shovels tugged at Butch, and slowly, he came free.

Bill couldn't see him now. Couldn't see much of anything. Maudie and Zoob, the other shovels—they were a blur.

"Is . . . he . . . out?" Bill asked.

"He is," Maudie said.

"I love you, Maudie," Bill said.

"And I love you. Oh, no, Bill. Hold on. We'll prop it up and pull you out."

"Too late. I'm . . . a hero . . . aren't I?"

"You are," Maudie said. "Oh, no, Bill. Hold on."

"You'll always remember me?"

Oil slipped from between the edges of her head lamps, rolled down her metal face, over her rubber mouth, as she said, "I will."

"So will I," said Butch. "You ain't no Tinker Toy, after all. You a better man than me. Than anyone I know."

"Nice knowing you some, kid," said Zoob.

And the great slab of rock came down.

It was like an explosion when it hit. Bill felt himself being crushed, washed sideways over the side of the cliff. For a moment he felt the old fear, and it was a fear worth having now, for, in fact, he was falling.

But he didn't keep the fear. Didn't hold on to it.

He was a goner. He knew it. But he was a hero too. And as he fell, he looked up, saw the shadow of the great rock slab falling after him. He chuckled deep inside his gears, yelled, "Geronimo!"

Then he hit the ground. His shovel, which was hanging by a strand of metal, came completely off and spun away. His head lamps went out. There was darkness.

Along with the sound of the great rock falling, a sound like wind through what was left of the world's pines.

"One, one thousand," Bill said, counting the fall of the rock. "Two, one thousand . . ."

Of course, he never heard it when it struck, but—

—down that long black tunnel he went again, and it gave up its blackness to a warm light, and there in the light, fleeing along with him, were more birds and insects and snakes and all manner of wildlife whose homes he had destroyed, and that damn waffle iron, whose soul had been caught up inside him, and he thought, Shit, that wasn't good of me, doing that to the birds and the squirrels and such, but here I go anyway, because this must be heaven, it feels so good, so bright and warm, and he could see Gabe up ahead, beckoning him forward with his shovel.

Then he realized Gabe was whole again. He hadn't thought about that before. In fact, Bill thought, I'm whole again. Bright and shiny with paint blue as the sky.

Now Gabe was beside him. They flowed forward.

Gabe said, "Ya know, stuff I told ya aboud all dem gohtdamn birds and such?"

"Yeah," Bill said.

"I was wrong. But the Shovel Ghawd, he don't gib a shid. We is his, and he is ours. He knows what kind of fuel pump is in a good machine's chest, and boy, you and me, we got good ones."

Then, they were sucked into the total light of paradise.

Joe Lansdale, on deck, writing about "Sleepover," by Al Sarrantonio.

I've written introductions for Al before, and because of this, it might seem I do so out of friendship.

You're right. We've known each other a long time. So I'm glad to do it.

But I also do it because Al is a great short-story writer, one of the most underappreciated in the business, and I'm a fan.

This story will show you why.

What follows is like being inside a broken kaleidoscope, bursting with colors, sharp edges. Add to that a Bradbury-esque feel for childhood, the suspicions of childhood, and what you have is a creepy little tale that'll make certain parts of your anatomy pucker.

—J. R. L. (Hisownself)

Sleepover

Al Sarrantonio

"Chickens were green," he said.

"They weren't," she answered. "They were yellow. Frogs were green."

"That's the sky," he said, grinning slyly to himself. He had a secret grin even when his lips didn't smile. "The sky was green. Grass was blue."

She shook her head back and forth, almost violently. "You got 'em mixed up, Ty. It's the other way round. Grass was green, sky blue."

"It was the way I say," he replied, and his eyes were hard enough that he meant it.

"No, little brother, it was the way I remember." Her voice dropped to a whisper, and she looked at the ground. "I think it was. . . ."

They were on a plain of black smooth glass. Where the sky—which was maroon and devoid of clouds—met the horizon, there was a faint curved thin fuzzy line, like a charcoal-drawn heat wave. The temperature never seemed to change, though sometimes Ty complained of being cold at night. Willa pressed up near him when this happened, but always reluctantly. There was a part of her that was sure he claimed cold just to get attention.

Ty was seven, as close as Willa could remember. He had been seven when they woke up one morning in this place that had, during the night, replaced the second-floor bedroom of cousin Carla's big white house with the white picket fence. Sometimes Willa had trouble remembering some things about the white house now—such as if the garage doors had needed painting or not, or if the mailbox post at the road was crooked or straight.

But there were other things that Willa did remember—the sharpness of the red metal flag on the mailbox, which felt like it might cut your finger when you raised it to tell the mailman there was mail to be taken, or the tart ammonia smell of the cat-litter box when it hadn't been cleaned, or the way Aunt Erin and Uncle Bill's smiles lit up their faces when cousin Carla said something clever. She remembered Carla's science project, the working windmill, with its gold first-place ribbon hanging from it (it had been gold, hadn't it?—Ty would now say it had been tan, or orange)—that was displayed prominently on the fireplace mantel.

But she couldn't remember if the fireplace bricks had been red or white.

"I'm hungry again," Ty said, and this time Willa knew he was looking for nothing but attention. They hadn't been hungry since they had found themselves here. They hadn't gotten dirty, or had to brush their teeth, or even had to go to the bathroom.

Which had led Willa to conclude—

"And we're not dead!" Ty said, reaching over to jab her in the ribs. "We're just . . . *here*!"

"And where is that?" Willa responded.

Ty began to cry, true frightened sobs, which made Willa pleased and then, instantly, sorry. She reached over to brush the hair away from his forehead. "It's all right," she whispered, "We're not dead."

But he was consumed by one of his out-of-control times, and he clung to her, shivering. She could feel the wetness of his tears against the skin of her arm, soaking through the upper cuff of her nightdress.

"Ty, it's all right—"

"No it's not, it's not! We're dead, we're *dead*!"

"I was only joking—"

"You were right, you were right! We're *dead dead dead*!"

The arm that wrapped around Ty began to tremble, and Willa felt her own tears rising, though she kept them down.

"There's only one other thing we could be," she said in the faintest of voices, and only to herself.

A while later, the light show began, as it did every night before sleep came.

First came the yellow streaks, which crossed in parallel pairs overhead, cutting the maroon sky in half. Then the maroon sky split into two parts, like an overhead dome opening, and the darkest sky Willa had ever seen met the black glass plain, and they could see nothing. But this lasted only a moment, not enough to keep them in darkness: for the lights of what looked like a billion stars came on overhead, coming brighter and brighter like novae until their light merged into one overwhelming brilliance like the Sun. They were blinded by the light and closed their eyes, seeing a round retinal afterimage against the insides of their lids, and when they opened their eyes again, the world was as it had been, with maroon sky and black glass underfoot and the fine line of fuzziness at the horizon.

"I'm sleepy," Ty said, and curled up on the black glass and closed his eyes, which is what he always did after the light show. Willa fought it but also found herself tired, and then they slept, and always when they woke up they expected to find themselves back in their sleeping bags in cousin Carla's bedroom in the white two-story house that, Willa was almost sure, needed painting and had an old clock in the kitchen that had a crack in the face and was a little fast.

But always, for nine sleep periods now, they found themselves here.

After this, the tenth sleep period, the same thing happened.

Only—

Something was different this time.

They were not alone.

In the near distance were two shapes huddled on the ground, one of which began to wail.

Ty roused himself and looked at them wide-eyed. "The sky was blue, I'm *pretty* sure . . . ," he whispered.

"Yes," Willa said, though she wasn't positive anymore. In her own dreams the white house had been gray, the clock in the kitchen a minute slow.

The two figures saw them and began to approach, at first tentatively, then running.

"Help us!" the one in front sobbed.

Willa held on to Ty, and the two of them stood waiting.

The two figures stopped ten feet away.

They were children: two girls, younger than Ty. One had blond hair and the other's hair was red, curly all over.

They stared at Ty and Willa, then looked up at the sky, then back at Ty and Willa.

The red-haired one began to moan, but the other one got out, "Where *are* we?"

"Where *were* you?" Willa asked. "Before you came here?"

"In bed!" She had a breathy, annoying voice. "Asleep!"

"Where?" Willa demanded.

"At Janna's house!" Seeing the probing look on Willa's face, she rushed on desperately: "In Kentucky! In the U.S. of A.!"

"What were you doing at Janna's house, in Kentucky?" Willa persisted, almost unkindly. "Why were you there?"

"We were having a sleepover!" the breathy girl answered, and then she too began to cry.

Ty joined them.

"Be quiet!" Willa shouted, staring sharply at Ty and then at the newcomers.

All but the red-haired girl complied.

Willa looked at Ty. "They were in Kentucky. We were in New Hampshire. That means nothing."

Tears threatened again, but Ty kept them down. "The sky *was* blue," he insisted quietly.

"You're sisters?" Willa asked the breathy girl.

She nodded, studying the sky with frightened eyes. She said, "How do we get back?"

Willa gave her a long steady look. "You don't." She turned to Ty, her back to the two new children, and said in a whisper, so only he could hear: "I know what happened."

There were pooling tears in Willa's eyes, which frightened Ty more than anything up till now.

The nightly light show was ending. Willa opened her eyes, still seeing a vestige of fading sun image. The two little girls, Eva and Em, were rubbing their own eyes, sitting Indian-style twenty feet away, where Willa had ordered them to be. Willa watched Eva, the blond-haired one, curl up on the floor and then Em nest into her like a sleeping cat.

In a few moments they were both breathing shallowly, eyes closed.

Willa waited another full minute, fighting the urge to sleep, and then shook Ty gently awake beside her.

He stirred, sought continued sleep, then rubbed his eyes and sat up.

"All right," he said, yawning and stretching. "Tell me."

"This is the truth," Willa answered. She had decided not to cry, and kept her voice steady and low. "Do you remember the night we sneaked down after bedtime and spied on Mother and Father through the stair rails while they sat at the dining room table with a bottle of wine?"

Ty was concentrating, his brow furrowed. "The dining room was brown."

"It was *white,*" Willa said. "Do you remember holding your hands over your ears, because you didn't like what they were saying?"

"The dining room *was* white," Ty abruptly agreed, and then a further amazed spark of remembrance touched his face. He put his hands to his ears for a moment, then lowered them. "They said . . ."

"They said that some people should never have children."

His eyes widened with a faint catch of breath. "I *remember* . . ."

"They talked about how good it had been before we came along, how much they missed those days."

Ty's mouth dropped open in wonder. "*Yes . . .*"

Willa said sharply, with conviction: "They found a way to send us here."

Sudden anger boiled up in Ty's face. "That's not true! They would never do that!"

Twenty feet away, the two little girls stirred, and Willa said calmly, "If you don't quiet down, I won't tell you the rest."

Ty fought to hold his rage: he made fists, counted to ten, but at the end of it he still wanted to scream and cry.

Willa warned, "Be quiet."

Another count of ten, and Ty snuffled. "Tell me."

Willa took a halting breath. Her eyes held a faraway look, as if she were staring at a place she didn't want to believe had existed, but knew had been real. "They wanted to be alone again. They would never kill us or drive us out into the country and abandon us, or put us on a bus with no identification and just enough money for one-way tickets. But in the back of their minds, they knew that if they ever had the chance to make us go away without hurting us, they would take it."

Willa was gazing over Ty's head, her voice flat with shocked belief. "And they found a way. . . ."

Ty's anger returned. He stood up, yelling, "They would *never* do that to us! Dad would never do that to *me*! He helped me build a model airplane! He taught me how to throw a baseball! And mother taught me how to tie my shoelaces!" His face was livid with anger and fear. "They *loved* us!"

The two little girls were awake, holding on to one another.

Willa said, "They loved us because they *had* to. But I'm talking about what people really want, in the center of their hearts. Haven't you always felt it, Ty? When they went away on vacations together and left us at cousin Carla's? The way they looked at each other even when we were with them?"

Willa's eyes were haunted. "Haven't you always felt that the two of them had no room for four?"

"I don't believe you!"

Em, the one with red hair, began to wail, and her sister, the breathy one, sobbed, "Stop talking! It's time for sleep!"

Willa continued, "Did you ever watch the way Uncle Bill and Aunt Erin looked at cousin Carla? They never had those thoughts. They were *meant* to have children. Their hearts were big enough."

"Sleep!" the breathy one insisted, curling down to troubled slumber beside her sister.

Willa ignored them. She was staring hard into a place of remembrance that was fading. "That night," she said to Ty, "when you put your hands over your ears, Mother's face got a strange look on it, and she told Father she'd found a way."

"You're lying!"

Willa gave a single, strangled sob. "And when she brought us to the sleepover at cousin Carla's, she had that same look on her face."

"I won't believe you!" Now Ty clung to her and closed his eyes, and shivered. "I'd rather be dead. . . ."

Suddenly—so suddenly it made her gasp—Willa wasn't sure if Aunt Erin's kitchen had had a clock in it after all.

Or even what a clock was.

Ty moaned, "*No* . . ."

And then he closed his eyes.

Willa whispered, stroking his hair, "We'll have to make a new life here."

She stifled an abrupt, overpowering yawn.

Beside her, Ty was asleep, still trembling. This time he wasn't looking for attention. Willa lowered him gently to the hard obsidian surface and lay down beside him.

She looked over at Eva and Em.

"And now, other parents know the way. . . ."

She snuggled close to her brother and closed her eyes.

* * *

She awoke to a wailing moan transcending the sadness of Limbo, and a world filled with children.

Beside her, Ty sat up and rubbed his eyes.

"Chickens were green," he said.

Willa answered, without hesitation, "Yes."

***Gene Wolfe** grew up in Houston, Texas, and attended Edgar Allan Poe Elementary School before, eventually, graduating from the University of Houston with a degree in mechanical engineering. He's the author of many novels, among them* The Book of the New Sun *and, more recently,* The Book of the Short Sun, *which begins a trilogy completed with* On Blue's Waters *and* In Green's Jungles. *His short fiction has been gathered in five highly regarded collections, the most recent being* Strange Travelers. *He has won two Nebula Awards, three World Fantasy Awards, the British Science Fiction Award, and the British Fantasy Award.*

Enjoy this gem from the master.

GOLDEN CITY FAR

Gene Wolfe

This is what William Wachter wrote in his spiral notebook during study hall, the first day.

Funny dream last night. I was standing on a beach. I looked out, shading my eyes, and I could not see a thing. It was like a big fog bank was over the ocean way far away so that everything sort of faded white. A gull flew over me and screeched, and I thought, *Well, not that way.*

So I turned north, and there was a long level stretch and big mountains. I should not have been able to see past them, but I could. It was not like the mountains could be looked through. It was like the thing I was seeing on the other side was higher than they were so that I saw it over the tops. It was really far away and looked small, but it was just beautiful, gold towers, all sizes and shapes with flags on them. Yellow flags, purple, blue, green, and white ones. I thought, *Well, there it is.* I had to go there. I cannot explain it, but I knew I had to get to that city and once I did nothing else would matter because I would have done everything I was supposed to do, and everything would be OK forever.

I started walking, and I was not thinking about how far it was at all, just that it was really nice that I had found out what I was supposed to do. Instead of thrashing around for years, I had it. It did not matter how far it was, just that every step got me closer.

Cool!

He could not think of anything else to write, but only of the golden towers, and how the flags had stood out stiffly from them so that he had known there was a hard wind blowing where the towers were, and he would like that wind.

Someone passed him a note. He let it fall to the floor unread.

Mrs. Durkin took him by the shoulder, and he jerked.

"Billy?"

It was hard to remember where he was, but he said, "Yes, ma'am?"

"The bell rang, Billy. All the other kids have gone. Were you asleep?"

Thinking that she meant when he had seen the towers and the flags, he repeated, "Yes, ma'am."

"Daydreaming. Well, you're at the right age for it, but the period's over."

He stood up. "I should have done my homework in here. I guess I did, some of it. I want to get to bed early."

The sea was to his left, the ground beneath his feet great stones, or shale, or soft sand. The mountains, which had appeared distant the night before, were so remote as to be almost invisible, and often vanished behind dunes covered with sparse sea oats. There was a breeze from the sea, and though the scudding clouds looked threatening, it did not rain or snow. He was neither hungry nor thirsty, and was conscious of being neither hungry nor thirsty. It seemed to him that he had been walking a long while, not hours or days or years, but simply a long while—time as it had been before anyone had thought of such things as years or centuries.

He climbed dunes and rough, low hills, and beyond the last found an inlet blocking his progress; long before he reached the point near which she lay, he had seen the woman on the rock in the water. She was beautiful, and naked save for her hair; and her skin was as white as milk. In one hand, she held a shining yellow apple.

He stopped and stood staring at her, and when a hundred breaths had come and gone, he sat down on a different rock and stared some more. Her eyes opened; each time he met her gaze, he felt lost in their depths.

"You may kiss me and eat one bite of my apple," she told him. "One bite, no more."

He was frightened, and shook his head.

"One bite will let you understand everything." Her voice was music. "Two bites would let you understand more than everything, and more than everything is too much."

He backed away.

The sun peeped from between clouds, bathing her with black gold. "What color is my hair?"

Perhaps its black was only shadow. Perhaps its gold was only sunlight. He said, "Nobody has hair like that."

"I do." She smiled, and her lips were as red as coral, and her teeth were sharp and gleaming white. "Men have found themselves in difficulties after biting my apple."

He nodded, certain it was true.

"But kiss me, and you may do anything you wish."

"I wouldn't be able to stop," he told her, and turned and ran.

He woke sweating, threw off the covers, and got out of bed. The house was dark and quiet. The alarm clock meant to wake him for school said five minutes past four. He carried his books and notebooks to the dining-room table, turned on the light, and began to study.

In study hall that afternoon, he wrote this in his spiral notebook.

> One time Mr. Bates said how do you know this is real? Maybe what you dream is really real and this is a dream. How can you tell? People argued about it, but I did not because I knew the answer. It is because what you dream is different every night. Waking up you are wherever you went to sleep. Last night it was kind of the same as before, but different because the city was gone. Anyhow I could not see it. I met this girl who tried to get me to say what color her hair was, only I could not. She wanted to kiss me and I ran off.

He made a small round dot for the final period, and read over what he had written. It seemed inadequate, and he added, "I would like to go back."

He stopped upon the summit of a hill higher than most, and turned for a last look. She was standing on her rock now, sparsely robed in hair like fire that cast shadows upon her white flesh that were as black as paint. One hand held up her shining apple. When she saw he was watching her, she raised the other, kissed it, and blew the kiss to him.

For one brief instant, he saw it fluttering toward him like a butterfly of cellophane. It touched his lips, soft and throbbing and redolent of the flowers that bloom under the sea. He shook, and could not stop.

A long time after that, when she and her inlet were many hills behind him and he had long since stopped trembling, he saw a black-and-white dog. It had a long and tangled coat, a long and feathery tail, and ears that would not stand up quite straight. He had never had a dog, but the people next door had a dog very much like that, a dog named Shep. He played with Shep now and then, and he whistled now.

The dog turned to look at him, pricking up the ears that would not quite stand up straight. It was some distance away but came trotting toward him, and he himself trotted to meet it, and stroked its head and rubbed its ears. After that the two of them went on together (the dog trotting at his heels) climbing and descending hills, which gradually became less lofty and less rugged, sometimes catching glimpses of the sea to their left, where waves flashed in sunshine like mirrors, or stalked from darkling sea to darkling land like an army of ghosts.

The alarm clock was ringing tinnily. He got up and shut it off, stretched, and looked out the window. There were leaves, mostly brown, on the broken sidewalk in front of the house. He tried to remember whether they had been there the day before, and decided they had not.

Later, as William shuffled through the leaves, Shep joined him and accompanied him to the bus stop. He petted Shep and declared him to be a good dog, and found something strange in the way Shep looked at him, some quality that slipped away no matter how hard he tried to grasp it.

On the bus he told Carl Kilby, "He looked right at me. Usually they don't want to look you in the face. That was weird!" Carl, who had no idea what he was talking about, grunted.

In study hall . . .

> Last night I found this dog that looked exactly like Shep. Maybe it was him. He was a nice dog and we were way out in a pretty lonely spot. (I did not even see the ocean toward the end.) So I was glad to have the dog. Only what was he doing way out there? He was just walking along like me when I saw him.
>
> I have never had the same dream three nights. Not even two

that I can remember.

"Billy?"

Well, if it happens tonight, too, I hope the dog is still there.

Mrs. Durkin touched his shoulder. "The period's over, Billy."

"Just a minute," he said. "I want to get this down."

A kiss chased me and landed on my face.

It was inadequate, and he knew it; but with Mrs. Durkin standing beside him, it was the best he could do. He shut his notebook and stood up. "I'm sorry, Mrs. Durkin."

She smiled. "The other kids rush out at the bell. It's kind of nice to have one who isn't eager to leave."

He nodded, which seemed safe, backed away, and went to his next class.

The dog was still there, lying down as if waiting for him. The weather the same. The city he had seen had been on the other side of the mountains—he felt certain of that, and he could see the mountains far away, a low blue rampart.

He and the dog walked on together until the dog said, "Chief?"

"God bless you!" he told it, and leaned down a little to pat its head.

"Chief, would you maybe like a drink?"

It seemed entirely natural, but somehow deep underneath it did *not* seem natural. Not surprised but somehow (deep underneath) thrown a little off balance, he said, "Sure, if you would."

"There's a nice spring not far from here," the dog said. "Cold water, with a sort of drink-me-and-be-lucky flavor. I could show you."

He said, "Sure," but when they had gone some distance, he added, "I guess you've been here before."

"Huh-uh," the dog said.

"Okay, then how do you know about this place?"

"I smell it." When they had climbed another hill and the spring was in sight, the dog added, "It might not work for me. Only for you."

The dog drank the water just the same, running ahead of him and lapping fast. There was a pool in the rocks, not too wide to jump over, from which a rill ran. He went to the other side and knelt. I've never drunk out of a dog's bowl, he thought, so this is a first.

It was good water, as the dog had promised it would be, cold and fresh. He had no idea what luck was supposed to taste like, so he tried to analyze the flavor, which was very faint. It was a taste of rocks and pines and chill winds, he decided, with just a little touch of sunshine on snow.

"Does he always follow you like that, Bill?"

Sue Sumner was blond and beautiful, and he knew he was apt to stammer like a retard; he also knew he had to answer. He said, "No, just yesterday and today. He's a nice dog, but I don't know why he comes to the stop with me."

She smiled. "You ought to take him on the bus."

"I'd like to," he said, and realized as he spoke that it was true. "I'd like to take him to school with me."

"Like Mary and her little lamb."

He grinned. "Sure. I've been laughed at before. It didn't hurt much, and it hasn't killed me yet."

It was Friday, which meant assembly instead of study hall. He would save his dream in memory, he decided, and write it down in study hall Monday, with his weekend dreams, if there were any. "Probably won't be," he told himself.

From his notebook . . .

> The craziest thing happened yesterday. We got back from church and I went up to change back. I was putting on my jeans, and there was this bird singing outside. Singing lyrics. I thought this is crazy, birds don't sing words, and I tried to remember how they really did sing. I could remember the tune, but it seemed like I could not remember the words. I kept telling myself there were not any. I put on a CD, loud, and pretty soon the bird flew away. Now I cannot remember what the bird sang, and I would like to. Something about him and his wife (it rhymed with life, I remember that) building a house and don't come around because we will not let you in.
>
> OK, I went outside and right away the Pekars' dog started fol-

lowing me. I thought my gosh it is going to turn into The Dream—the hills, the rocks, the dwarf on the horse and all that, and I am crazy. So I walked about three blocks with Pekar's dog along the whole time.

We got to the park and I sat down on a bench and petted the dog some, and I said, Listen, this is serious, so can you really talk? And he looked right at me the way he does and said yep. What is your name, I said, and he said Shep. I was going to ask if he remembered the naked lady with the hair, only he had not been with me when that happened. So I asked about the lucky water we drank, did he remember that? He said yep. He says he cannot talk to other people at all, only to me and other dogs. The dwarf said all that stuff about the writing on the scabbard and the writing on the blade, and I was not sure I remembered it. I still am not. So I asked him about that and he said he—

"Billy, will you run an errand for me, please?"

He looked up and shut his notebook. "Sure, Mrs. Durkin."

"Thank you. Wait just a moment while I write this note." She wrote rapidly, not scribbling but small, neat, businesslike script. When she had finished, she folded the paper, put it in an envelope, sealed the envelope, and wrote MR. HOFF on it. "Mr. Hoff is an assistant principal. You know that, I'm sure."

"Yes, ma'am."

"I'd like you take this to him, Billy, and I want you to wait for a reply, written or oral. If the bell rings before you get it, you are not to go to your next class. You are to wait for that reply. Leave your books here. I'll give you a note excusing you when you come back for them."

He explained about waiting to Mr. Hoff when he handed him the envelope; Mr. Hoff looked slightly baffled but told him to wait in the outer office.

Sue Sumner sat with him on the bus going home. Sue got off with him, too, although it was not her regular stop. Shep had been waiting at the stop, and she petted Shep until the other kids had gone. Then she said, "What's bothering you, Bill?"

"You could tell, huh?"

"I talked to you twice, and you didn't hear me. At first I thought you were ditching me—"

"I wouldn't do that!"

"The second time I saw that you were just so deep inside yourself. . . ."

He nodded.

"Now you look like you're too big to cry. What is it?"

"First period." He cleared his throat. "I won't be there. I've got to go to the office. Are you going to tell everybody?"

She shook her head. She was wearing a guy's shirt, jeans, and very little makeup; and she was so lovely it hurt to look at her.

"I've got to talk to the psychologist. They think I'm crazy."

She put her hand on his shoulder. "You're not. You'll be fine."

He shrugged. "I think I'm crazy, too. I have crazy dreams."

"Everybody has crazy dreams."

"Not like this. Not the same thing, night after night."

"About me?" She smiled.

"Yeah. Kind of. How did you know?"

She smiled again, impishly. "Maybe I'll tell you, and maybe I won't."

They began to walk. He said, "Shep and I will walk you home."

"I kind of thought you would."

"Maybe I could leave the house a little early tomorrow and go over to your stop and wait there with you?"

Her hand found his. "I kind of thought you might do that, too. Tell me about your dreams."

"It's all kinds of stuff, only it's always about this place way far off. The gold towers. They're the color of your hair. Don't get mad."

"I'm not mad."

"Me and Shep are trying to get there. Shep can talk."

She squeezed his hand.

"I've got this sword. It's a beautiful sword, and there's writing on the scabbard and writing on the blade. The writing on the scabbard is important. Really, really important."

"Are you making this up?"

He shook his head. "If I was, it wouldn't be so scary. The writing on the blade is more important than the writing on the scabbard, but you have to read the scabbard, all of it, before you read the blade. It's all very hard to read because the writing's really old-fashioned. Shep can't read it at all, but I can a little. Last night I was able to make out the first three words."

"I bet you couldn't remember them this morning."

"Sure I can." He spoke the words.

There was an old woman in a rocking chair on the porch of a house they were passing. She called, "Hello, Sue. Hello, young man."

Sue stared, then smiled. "Hi, Aunt Dinah." (It seemed to him that there had been some slight obstruction in Sue's throat.)

"Would you and your young man like to come in for some iced tea?"

"Next time, Aunt Dinah. I've got to get home and do my homework."

A middle-aged man with glasses came out of the house and spoke to Aunt Dinah. She smiled at this man, and said, "I live here with you, sir." When she turned back to them, she said, "That's a fine young man you've got there, Sue. Hold on to him."

When they were a block past that house, he said, "We're going across these hills, Sue. Shep and me are. We found this girl, a beautiful girl with long black hair. Something had her foot, and it was pulling her into a hole, and—"

"I don't want to hear any more about your dreams," Sue said softly. "Not right now. Let's just walk for a while. Not talking."

He nodded. This was Spruce Street, and there was a house there where the people had actually planted spruce trees between the street and the sidewalk. He did not know the people; but he had always felt sure he would like them if he ever met them, because of that. Three houses down, a sleek Mercedes sedan was parked at the curb. He had seen it before, although he did not know the owner. He stared at it as they passed, because it looked different—different in a warm and friendly way, as though it knew him and liked him.

They had turned onto Twenty-third and walked another block before he figured it out. The Mercedes had always looked like something that would never be in his reach. Now it looked as if it was, as if it was a car he could own any time he decided he really wanted one.

Sue said, "I'm ready to talk now, Bill. Is that all right?"

He nodded. "I'm ready to listen."

"There were two things I had to say." She paused, small white teeth gnawing at her lower lip. "They are important, both of them, and I knew I ought to say them both. Only I couldn't figure out which one I ought to say first. I think I have, now. Have you ever been like that?"

He nodded again. "I usually get it wrong."

"I don't believe you." She smiled very suddenly, and it was as though the sun had burst from behind a cloud. "Here's the first one. Do you know why high school is so important?"

"I think you'd better tell me."

"It's not because it's where you learn History or Home Ec. It's not even because it's where you get ready for college. It's because it's where some people—the people who aren't going to be left behind—decide what they want to do with their lives."

He said, "My brother decided he was going into the navy."

"Yes. Exactly. And I've decided. Have you?"

He shook his head.

"What I'm going to do is you, Bill." Her voice was low but intense. "I'm going to stick with you. I think you're going to stick with me, too. I'll see to it. But if you don't, I'm going to stick with you anyway. On the bus I thought maybe you were going to try to ditch me. Remember that?"

"I would never ditch you," he said, and meant it.

"Well, even if you do, I'll still be around. That's the first thing I wanted to say—the thing I decided ought to come first. Now I've said it, and I feel a lot better."

"So do I." He discovered that he was smiling. "You know, I've got this problem, and it felt really, really important. But it isn't. Not anymore."

She smiled. "That's right."

"I was thinking how to tell my parents. That was the part that really had me worried—how could I put part of it off onto them. I didn't think of it like that, but that's what it was. Well, I'm not going to. Why should they worry, when maybe they don't have to? If that school psychologist wants them to know, she can tell them herself. 'Oh, by the way, Mrs. Wachter, your son is crazy.' Let's see how she likes it."

"Here's the other thing I have to tell you," Sue Sumner said; her voice was so low that he could scarcely hear her. "That used to be Aunt Dinah's house, back there. But Aunt Dinah's dead."

The sky had not changed. The sun that was always to their left was to his left still. The racing clouds raced on, with more after them, and more after them, a marathon for clouds in which a hundred thousand were competing.

It must never change here, he thought. Then he realized that all his dreams had taken little time here, no more than a few hours.

The black-haired girl was still sitting on the ground, rubbing a slender white ankle that showed the livid mark of a clawed hand.

Soil wet with blood still clung to the blade of his sword. He wiped it with dry grass, wishing for rags and a can of oil. Reminding himself not to read the blade—not that he could have if he had wanted to.

The girl looked up at him, and her eyes were large and dark, forest pools seen by moonlight. "Not many men would have thought to do that," she said. Her voice was music, dark and low. "And no other man would have dared."

"I'm just glad it worked," he said. "What happened?"

For a moment she smiled. (When she smiled he felt he would have followed her to the end of the world.) "I didn't see the hole, that's all. The grass hid it."

He nodded and sat near her, though not too near. Shep lay down at his feet.

"I wasn't looking. I should have been looking, but I wasn't. It's my own fault. I might as well say that right now, because it's the truth and I'll never be at peace until I admit it. I hate stupid, careless people. But I was stupid and careless. Do you try to tell the truth?"

"Mostly, yes."

"I try constantly, but I lie and lie. It's my nature." She smiled again. "I have to keep fighting it, and though I fight it all the time, I don't fight hard enough."

He recalled something his biology teacher had told him. "DNA is destiny."

"You're a wizard, aren't you." It was more accusation than question.

"No," he told her. "No, I'm not."

"Oh yes, you are." The smile teased her mouth; it was a small mouth, and its perfect lips were very red. "You've cast a spell on me, because I lie and lie but when I said you were a wizard that was the truth. How old are you? Really?"

He could not remember.

"You wizards can make yourselves young again. I know that, but I don't care. You're *my* wizard, and you saved me, and I love you. Now you look modest and say you love me too."

He tried.

She gave her ankle a final rub. "I *wish* this mark would go away. I know it won't, but I wish it would."

Rising, Shep licked it once, shook his head, and backed away.

"Your name is—?"

"Bill."

She cocked her head. "Are you making fun of me, Bill?"

"No," he told her. "I wouldn't make fun of you. Not ever." He meant it.

"My name is Biltis." She rose effortlessly, and he stood up hurriedly. She took his hands in hers. "They'll want to know who my lover is, and I'll say Bill, and they'll laugh at me. Don't you feel sorry for me? Look! I've lost a slipper! Am I not richly deserving of your pity?"

"Maybe it's still down in there," he said, and knelt, and was about to thrust his hand into the hole.

"Don't!" She seized his shoulders, pulling him back. "I was only joking! Y-y-you . . ."

Surprised, he turned to look at her. Her crimson lips were trembling, the great, dark pools moist with tears.

"You mustn't! They're down there. You mustn't reach into holes, or go into caves or—or go down in wells or cisterns. Nothing like that, ever again. They never forget and they never forgive. Oh, Bill!"

She was in his arms. He clasped her trembling body, astonished to find it small and light. He kissed her cheek, and neck, and their lips met.

"Come in and sit down, Billy." The woman behind the desk was dark, heavy, and middle-aged, with a warmth in her voice that made him want to like her.

"Are you really the psychologist?"

"Uh-huh. You were expectin' Dr. Gluck, I bet. She left at the end of the last term. I'm Dr. Grimes." Dr. Grimes smiled broadly. "Why don't you sit right there? I don't bite."

He did, on the edge of a chair more comfortable than most school chairs.

"Do you like bein' Billy? Would you rather be William?"

"Bill," he said. "I like people to call me Bill. Is that all right?"

"Sure, Bill. Bill, I'm goin' to start right off tellin' you somethin' I ought not to tell you at all. I like havin' you here. I been counselin' for close to twenty years now. That's what I do—I'm a counselor. And it's almost always drugs or liquor. Or stealin'. Here at this school, it's been drugs, up to now. Nothin' else. Let me tell you, Bill, a person gets awfully, awfully tired of drugs. And liquor. And stealin'. So I'm real glad to see you."

He waited.

"I got this notebook they took away from you." She opened the file folder on her desk and held it up. "I read it. Probably you mind, but I had to or else I wouldn't have known what was bein' talked about. You see? I wouldn't have known what kind of things to say, either. Maybe you'd like it back?"

He nodded.

She put it down in front of him. "I'll tell you what I thought when I was readin' it. About that dog and the li'l bird singin' and all. I thought, why, this boy's got a real imagination! I told you about those drug people I got to talk to all the time. And the liquor people, too, and the stealin' people. All them. They haven't got—you know why people steal, Bill?"

He shrugged. "They want the stuff, I guess."

"You guess wrong. You ever see stuff you wanted? In a store or anythin'?"

"Sure."

"Uh-huh. You steal it?"

"No." He shook his head. "No, I didn't."

"They do. They take it. They take it 'cause they can't imagine anythin' will happen. They do that maybe a hundred times, and then they get caught. Only next time they can't imagine they're goin' to get caught *this* time. Why are you smilin'?"

"You reminded me of somebody. Not somebody real."

"On the TV?" She was watching him narrowly.

"No." He sensed that he had been cornered and would be cornered again. It would be best, surely, to tell the truth to this friendly woman and try to get her on his side. "In a dream I've been having. That's all."

"You like her. You wouldn't have smiled like that if you didn't. Is she pretty?"

He nodded.

" 'Bout how tall?"

"Up to my chin." He touched it.

"That's in real high heels, I bet."

"No, ma'am. Barefoot."

"Uh-huh. Hasn't got no clothes?"

It was going to be complicated. He said slowly, "She wasn't barefoot to start with. She had slippers, like. Really beautiful slippers with jewels on them. Only she lost one, so she took the other one off. She has on a—a dress with a long skirt. It comes down nearly to her feet. It's gold and red, and has jewels on it, all over."

He waved his hands, trying to indicate the patterns. "It's really, really pretty."

Dr. Grimes was nodding. "I bet she smells good, too."

He was glad to confirm it. "You're right, she smells wonderful."

"You smell things in this dream?"

He hesitated. "Well, I smelled her. And I smell the wind sometimes, the freshness of it. Or the ocean, when it was blowing off the ocean."

"You ever kiss this girl?"

"Biltis." He felt himself flushing. "Her name's Biltis. We laughed about it."

He waited for Dr. Grimes to speak, but she did not.

"I didn't really kiss her. She kissed me."

"Uh-huh. What happened after?"

"She whistled. I didn't think a girl could ever whistle that loud, but she did. She whistled, and this big bird came down. It looked like an eagle, kind of, but it was bigger and had a longer neck. It had a bridle and reins. You know? Those long leather things you steer with?"

Dr. Grimes nodded. "Uh-huh, I know what reins are."

"And she got on it and it flew away." He closed his eyes, remembering. "Only it talked to me a little first."

"This big bird did."

"Yeah. It said I better not hurt her. But I wouldn't. Then it flew away, and she waved. Waved to me."

"I see. That was real nice, wasn't it?"

He nodded. "I won't ever forget it."

"Maybe you'll see her again." Dr. Grimes was watching him closely.

"I don't know."

"Do you want to, Bill?"

"I don't know that either. She scared me, a little."

Dr. Grimes nodded. "Sure. You ever see her when you weren't sleepin'?"

"I don't think so."

"Only you're not sure?"

"No," he said. "No, I haven't."

"All right. I want to talk about awake now, Bill. Funny things happen to everybody, sometimes. I know funny things happen to *me*. Like just last Wednesday I saw a li'l boy that looked just like a certain li'l boy I had gone to school with—like he never had grown up, and here he was, just the same. Anythin' like that happen to you?"

He shook his head.

"Oh, I bet. You know there was somethin'. Tell me now."

He cleared his throat. "Well, I had walked over to somebody's house, and I was coming back. Shep and me."

"Shep."

He nodded.

"Can I ask why you walked over to this house, Bill?"

"Well, it seemed like I ought to. She got off at my stop. Off the bus."

"Uh-huh."

"So I had walked her over to her house. We talked. You know?"

Dr. Grimes chuckled. "She likes you, Bill. If she didn't like you, what's she gettin' off at your stop for? And you like her. If you didn't, what you walkin' her home for?"

"Yeah, I guess. Well, I was coming back home, and Sue's—this girl's aunt Dinah came out of her house and stopped me. She's an old lady, and she's not really this one girl's aunt. She was a friend of this girl's grandmother's."

"I got it. What she say, Bill?"

"She said she needed a big, big favor. She said she owed me already, but she needed another favor, a big one. Shep didn't like her."

Dr. Grimes leaned forward, her face serious. "Did she want you to do somethin' bad, Bill?"

"I don't think so. She just said that this girl's family probably has some pictures of her when she was young. Of Aunt Dinah. Now she'd like to have them, and would I see if I could get them for her. As many as I could. I said all right, but Shep says—I mean he doesn't like her. I don't think he likes me being mixed up with her."

"Shep's your dog?"

"No, ma'am."

"But he's a dog. Does he really talk, Bill?"

It was easier because he had just said it. "No, ma'am."

"You goin' to try to get the pictures?"

"Yes, ma'am. I asked this girl, and she said she'd look and bring them to school today, any she found. If she's got any, I'll take them over after school."

"That's not a bad thin' you're doin', tryin' to help out a old woman like that."

"No, ma'am," he said, "but I thought it was pretty weird. Why didn't she just phone Sue's mom?"

* * *

When they got off the bus that afternoon, he dropped his books at his house and put on Sue's backpack for the walk over to hers. The pictures, faded black-and-white snapshots, were in a white envelope in the pocket of his shirt, under his sweater.

There were more leaves on the sidewalk today; the maples had turned to scarlet and gold, and a bush in somebody's yard to a deep, rich crimson. "In my dream," he said, "where I've got that sword?"

She looked at him sidelong.

"It's beautiful. It's just so beautiful, I can't hardly stand it sometimes. But it's just brown hills and purple mountains way, way off. And the blue sky, with the white clouds moving fast across it. What makes it so pretty is the way I feel about it. I see everything, and I see how great it is. The big bird with the girl riding him, and her hair and her scarf blowing out behind her. She waved, like this, and she had a gold bracelet on her wrist. The sun hit it, and it was the most beautiful thing I ever saw in my life."

"I don't think I like her," Sue said.

"Aunt Dinah?"

"This girl in your dream."

"Oh. I'm not sure I do either. But what I started out to say was that I'm getting to see things here the same way as there. That's really, really beautiful, like I said. But here it's beautiful, too. More beautiful than there, really. Biltis is beautiful. She really is, and her dress is really pretty, and her jewelry didn't just cost a lot, it's like looking at stars. But you're more beautiful than Biltis is."

Quickly, Sue turned again to look at him.

"If your dress was as pretty as hers and you had jewelry as nice as hers is, you'd be homecoming queen and she'd be a maid of honor. You know what I mean?"

Sue took his hand, and that was answer enough.

"So I've been thinking. Pretty soon I might be able to do that. Give you a dress that was so beautiful people would just stop and stare, and jewelry."

Shep said, "Good!" though Sue seemed not to hear him.

"I've been thinking about other stuff, too."

"Have you, Bill?"

"Yeah. Lots of things." He took the white envelope from his pocket. "Like I'd like to show her to you. Show you Biltis, if I could. If I was good in art, the way you are, maybe I could draw her. I'm not, but I can show you pretty close, just the same."

He took out a photograph.

"Like this. The sharp chin, and the little mouth. The big eyes, especially."

"That's Aunt Dinah," Sue told him. "Aunt Dinah, when she was about twenty."

"I know," he said.

"Anyway, she can't really be dead, can she?"

Shep growled softly, deep in his throat.

"I figured it out," Sue continued, "while I was looking for those pictures. See, my mother didn't want me going over there, so she told me Aunt Dinah was dead so I wouldn't. We went to some funeral, some old lady's, and when we got home she told me it was Aunt Dinah. I think I was in kindergarten then. Doesn't that make sense, Bill?"

"Sure," he said.

"I mean, you said she came out and stopped you on the street. Ghosts don't do that."

"I guess not."

"She didn't want to talk to me, because she knew my mother was mad. And she couldn't phone the house."

He said, "Right."

"But maybe you could get them for her. See? That's the only way everything fits."

He said, "We've still got to take her the pictures."

Sue nodded. "Yes, we do. That's why I brought them. I don't know what my mother was so mad about, and it was a long time ago anyway. You ought to forgive people after a while, unless it's something really bad. Dogs are good at that. We ought to learn from them."

She leaned down to pet Shep. "What about the big Social Studies test tomorrow? Have you been studying?"

"Yeah," he said, "only I missed class today. I had to talk to the shrink."

"It wasn't bad, we just reviewed Europe. Would you like me to fill you in a little, when we get to my house? I mean, I'll just tell my mother you weren't in class today, so I'm going to tell you what we talked about."

"Sure!" He smiled. "I've been hoping I could get you to do that. Boy! Am I lucky!"

"Okay. Suppose you got to go to Paris. Give me three or four things you'd like to see there."

He was silent for a moment, concentrating. "The big art museum."

"The Louvre. Ms. Fournier will give you a lot better grade if you use the French name. She teaches French, too."

"I know," he said.

They had reached the house. Still holding the snapshots Sue had brought to school, he climbed four steps to the porch and rang the bell.

"Maybe she won't be home," Sue said from the foot of the steps. "You could just leave them in the mailbox, Bill."

"I'm going out for football." He looked back at her, grinning. "Football players don't just leave them in the mailbox."

He rang again, hearing heavy male footsteps from inside the house.

Sue joined him on the porch. Her deliciously rounded chin was up, but she took his left arm and held it tightly.

A rumpled man opened the door and asked what they wanted.

"My mother had these . . ." Sue's voice faded away. "Tell him, Bill."

He nodded, and held them out. "There's an old lady living with you, I think her name's Dinah?"

The rumpled man shook his head. "There's no old lady living here, son. Forget it!" His face was hard and a trifle stupid, the face of a man whom life had defeated, who could not understand why he had been defeated so easily.

Bill said, "But you know who I mean. I promised her I'd bring her these pictures if I could, and—"

"Do you know her? You knew her name, so you've got to. You tell her to get out of my house and quit bothering me and my family."

Sue's grasp tightened. "Bill . . ."

"It's her house," he told the rumpled man, "or anyhow she thinks it is. She thought it was hers, probably, a long time before you were born, mister. I'll tell her what you said if I ever see her again, but I'm going to give you some advice right now. Take these pictures and don't tear them up or anything. Leave them someplace where they'll be easy for her to find. On the mantel or someplace like that. Let go of my arm for a minute, Sue."

He turned over the white envelope, took a pencil from his pocket, wrote *Dinah/Biltis* on the front, and handed the envelope to the rumpled man in the doorway. "That might help. I don't know, but it might. I'd do it if I were you."

After supper that evening, Ray Wachter asked his son why he was studying so hard, saying, "You've been at those books for a couple of hours now. Is it anything I can help you with?"

"Just Social Studies." He closed the book and looked up. "But I'm going out for football—"

"You are?"

"Yeah. It's sort of too late. Almost too late, but I just decided today. You've got to keep your grades up, or they won't let you play."

Ray Wachter tried to conceal the pride he felt; he was a simple man, but not an unintelligent one. "They might not let you play a lot anyway, Bill. You're not a junior, you know. Don't get your hopes too high."

"Well, this is the first big test in Social Studies, and I'm not too hot in that." Two words from the scabbard popped into his mind, and he pronounced them almost automatically.

"What the hell was that?" Ray Wachter took off his glasses, as if their lenses could somehow block hearing.

"What language, you mean?" Bill tilted his chair back, yawned, and stretched. "No language of this world, sir, nor do I know its proper name. I suppose it's nearer to Chaldean than anything else we have here."

"You're a funny kid, Bill."

He smiled. "Only too often, sir. I fall over my own feet, I know." When his father had gone, he murmured to himself, "I think it must mean, 'Let me be numbered among the learned.' "

He and the dog tramped over the plain, mile upon mile. There seemed to be no convenient way for him to wear the sword. He had tried thrusting its scabbard through his belt, but it slipped and tripped him, and proved to be much less convenient than carrying it, and the long blade it held, over his shoulder.

"Dark," Shep said.

"Pretty dark, yes. Do you mean that night is coming?"

"Yep."

"We ought to have a tent or something." He searched his pockets. "I don't even have anything we could use to start a fire, and there's nothing out here to burn except grass."

Shep said nothing.

"This is a little like a Jack London story. But I don't like that story and have no intention of repeating it. Are you getting tired?"

"Nope."

"Then we should keep walking, for a while at least. Why did she blow her kiss at me, Shep? Who was she, anyway?"

Shep said nothing.

"That's right, you never saw her. I don't mean Biltis, I mean the woman on the rock by the sea. She had an apple, a gold one. She wanted me to bite it, but you can't bite gold."

"Nope?"

"Nope. It's a soft metal, but not soft enough to bite, except for very thin gold leaf. They used to coat costly pills with that."

"Spring."

"This weather? Perhaps you're right, but it seems like fall to me. Very early spring, possibly."

"Water. I smell it. Smells strong."

He smiled. "Then it's probably not good to drink."

"Good water."

"If you say so. I'm learned now, or think I may be, but being learned isn't the same as being wise—I'm wise enough to know that, anyway. Wise enough to trust a dog's judgment of what he smells."

The wolf-wind that had driven the clouds before it like terrified sheep had come down to earth. It ruffled his hair and raced beneath his shirt. He shivered, conscious for the first time of both thirst and cold.

"Talking of water brings us back to the woman on the coast," he told Shep to distract himself from his discomfort. "Let's assume she's someone famous, or anyway someone known. A woman as lovely as she is and as mysterious as she is could hardly stay unknown for long. If we list what we know about her, we may find a clue to her identity."

Shep glanced up at him. "If you say so, Chief."

"*Prima*." He shivered again, and strove to walk a trifle faster. "She was on a rock in the sea. I'm tempted to say by the sea; but it was actually in the sea, although not very far out."

"Okay," Shep said.

"*Secunda*, she was nude. Both these seem to indicate that she had come up out of the sea. People on land wear clothing to keep off the sun and to keep warm." (At that moment he dearly wished his own would keep him warmer.) "People in the sea have no need to keep off the sun and cannot be warmed by ordinary clothing.

"*Tertia*, she was strikingly beautiful.

"And *quarta*, she held the golden apple I have already mentioned. That covers it, I think."

Shep made a small noise that might, or might not, have been of assent.

"You're quite right. There is more. *Quinta*, she had extraordinary hair. It seemed black and blond together. Not black in places and blond in others, but both at once. *Sexta*—a suggestive ordinal, Shep—wishing to give a blessing or something of the kind, she kissed."

"Did she, Chief?"

"Yes. Yes, indeed, she did. And if it was not her kiss that made me aware of the speech of animals, what did?"

They walked on in silence for a time. At length he said, "Do we know of any famous female who would appear to fit our description of her? It seems to me we do. We can call her Venus, or Aphrodite, or even Ishtar. She was born of the sea. Paris awarded her the golden prize called the Apple of Discord. She is the goddess of love, and we cannot understand any animal until we love it. Furthermore—"

"Over there!" Shep raced away.

The spring, when they found it, was wide and deep, and its water was clearer than any diamond. Shep drank, and Bill drank, too, and marveled, by the sun's dying light, to see the cold, crystalline water welling from deep in the earth. It raced away as a noisy brook, narrow but by no stretch of the word feeble.

"Neither am I," he told Shep. "That water made me feel much stronger. I suppose I was becoming weak from thirst, and perhaps from hunger, too."

He drank again, and the strength he knew was a strength he had never known before.

From his notebook . . .

> Dr. Grimes has returned this to me. She wants me to record my dreams as I did earlier, and to show it to her at our next session. I will comply.
>
> Last night Shep steered me to a spring of strength. We drank from it. I felt much stronger and tested my strength by throwing stones, some so large I was astonished to find I could lift them. Shep ran as fast as my stones flew, which I think remarkable. (This morning he ran alongside our bus, following Sue and me to school. I believe he is out on the athletic field.)
>
> When I grew bored, we sat beside the spring, I laboring to puzzle out the inscriptions on the scabbard by the dying light. The days must be longer there, or perhaps it is only that we move

> faster. I read each group of symbols again and again, if it can be called reading. Slowly, terribly slowly, the meanings of a few words creep into my mind. There are some I could pronounce if I dared, though I have no notion (or little) of what they may mean. There are others that I understand, or believe I may understand somewhat, although I have little or no idea of their pronunciation. It is a slow process, and one that may never bear fruit.
>
> And yet these spells are only a distraction, however hermetic they may be. What has happened to me? That is the question. Why do I find myself in that barren land each night? What land is it in which thaumaturgic springs rise from barren ground?

"I want you to stay for a minute or two after the bell, Billy. Will you do that?"

His heart sank, but he nodded. "Yes, Ms. Fournier."

The bell rang even as he spoke. As the rest of the class trooped out, she smiled and motioned for him to join her at her desk.

"That essay of yours on the Louvre—I would have been amazed to see it from an undergraduate at Yale or Princeton, and delighted to receive it from a grad student. To get it here . . . Well, there simply are no words. I'm overjoyed. Flabbergasted. *Être noyé. Muet comme un poison.* Was it really a lodge in the Dark Ages? A place where they hunted wolves?"

"Oui, Madame," he said *"c'était comme les jours du Roi Dagobert."* Seeing her expression, he reverted to English and remained there.

"I shouldn't let you sign up this late," the coach told him. "I wouldn't, if we weren't short. What position do you play?"

"Whatever position or positions you want me to play, sir."

The coach grunted. "Damn right. Where do you think you might be good?"

"Nowhere, probably. But I'll try."

"Okay, we'll try you on the line. I want you to get down like this, see? One hand on the ground. That's good. When I count three, come straight at me as hard as you can. Don't use your hands but try to go through me. Try to knock me over. One—two—*three*!"

It was as though the coach were not in truth a man at all, but a sort of inflated figure, a man-shaped balloon to be shouldered aside.

* * *

Sue Sumner was sitting in the living room, chatting with his mother, when he came home. "I knew you'd be late because of football practice," she said, "but I didn't want to miss our walk. Is that all right?"

He nodded, speechless.

His mother said, "You're going to have supper at Sue's house, Billy. She phoned home, and then I talked with Mrs. Sumner myself. She'll be very glad to have you—she's looking forward to getting to know you. Pot roast. Are you hungry?"

He nodded again, suddenly aware that he was ravenous.

"Your father's so proud of you! What position will you play? I want to be able to tell him when he gets home."

"Linebacker."

"Well, try to catch a lot of passes."

Outside, they petted Shep. "Your mom has no idea what a linebacker does, Bill."

He grinned. "Yes, I know."

"Do you want me to tell her? You know, just girl-to-girl, when I get a chance?"

He looked down at Shep, who said quite distinctly, "Yep."

"Yes, I do. She may actually be interested now that I'm playing."

"Do you think they'll really let you? Play? I know a lot of guys just scrimmage with the team for the first year."

It was a good question, and he considered it for a block or more. "Yes," he said. "I'm going to have a tough time of it because I'm so new. Young men who have been on the team for what they consider a long while are not going to like my playing, and they'll like it even less if I start. But I believe I'll play, and even that I'll start."

"Don't count on starting," Sue said. "I wouldn't want you to be disappointed."

"Thank you. 'What if the rose-streak of morning pale and depart in a passion of tears? Once to have hoped is no matter for scorning. Love once, even love's disappointment endears. A minute's success pays the failure of years.' "

"Why, Bill! That's beautiful!"

He nodded. "It should be—it's Robert Browning. Can I tell you what I've been thinking?"

"I wish you would."

"I was thinking that football might just be a letdown. For me, for my parents, and for you. But it wouldn't matter, because you were here waiting for me when I got home from practice. What difference could football make after that? You were here, and it meant I had won. Practice and games are just bother. Busyness."

"Oh, Bill!" She took his hand.

"So after that, I thought what if you hadn't been here. And it hit me—it hit me very hard—that millions of other men will come home, and can't even hope that you might be there, waiting, the way you were for me. That even if you hadn't been there, I would be privileged like nobody else on earth, because I could hope—really hope, not deluding myself—that you might be. That love's disappointments are better than success in other things."

He cleared his throat. "I realize I haven't expressed myself very well. But that's how my mind was running, and naturally I thought of Browning then, as anybody would."

"Can I tell you what I'm thinking now?"

He nodded. "Of course."

"I'm thinking what a jerk I was. I rode that bus for three solid weeks before I realized what was on it with me. That my whole future was sitting across the aisle, or three seats in back. What a jerk!"

He sighed, and could find no more words.

"Look sharp," Shep whined.

They were approaching the house at which he had left the snapshots, when a breathtaking brunette threw open its door. She was carrying a blue-and-silver jacket, and she held it up for their inspection before running across the porch and down the steps to meet them. "Remember me?"

He nodded. "Certainly."

Smiling, she held out her hand to Sue. "I'm Dinah—Dinah Biltis. I just want to give Bill this. It's cold, and he'll need it." She turned to him, holding the jacket open. "Here, take off that backpack and put your arm in."

He did.

"It's too big for him," Sue said, "and besides—"

"Bill's bigger than you know. Do you like it, Bill?"

"Yes," he said. "Very much." It was loose, but not excessively so. He lifted his arms to admire the sleeves: blue leather with silver slashes.

Without warning Dinah kissed him. At the next moment, she was fleeing back up the steps and into the house. He got out a handkerchief and wiped his mouth thoughtfully.

"Wow!" Shep barked. "Wow, Chief!"

Sue sighed. "I'm supposed to fly into a jealous rage, I think. Isn't that how it's supposed to go?"

He was snapping the jacket closed. "I have no idea."

"I think it is. Are you going to keep the jacket?"

"For the time being anyway."

"Suppose I asked you to give it back?"

He considered. "I'd want to know why. If you had a good reason, I'd do it."

"Suppose I didn't have any reason at all?"

Shouldering her backpack again, he began to walk. "I wouldn't do it. You told me what you had been thinking, a minute ago. Can I tell you what I'm thinking now?"

For an instant her eyes found his face, although she did not turn her head. She nodded without speaking.

"I've already got a mother. She's a good mother, and I love her. I need you, not another mother."

"If I say one more thing, will you get mad?"

"Nope," Shep told her.

"That's a letter jacket. You're not supposed to wear one unless you've lettered."

"There's no letter on it."

"Guys who've lettered are going to take it away just the same, Bill."

He grinned. "Then you'll have won. What's wrong with that?"

"Do you remember Grandma's friend Dinah?" Sue asked her mother over pot roast.

"Oh, my goodness! Yes, indeed—Auntie Dinah. I haven't thought about her in years and years."

Chick said, "Was she the one that collected shawls? You used to talk about her, Mom." Chick was Sue's brother.

Sue's mother nodded. "That's right. I don't believe you ever knew her, though."

"You will," Sue told her brother. "She's back."

Sue's mother picked up the green beans. "Won't you have some more, Bill?"

He thanked her and took a second helping.

Sue said, "You probably didn't notice how old-fashioned her clothes were, Bill. That dark dress and those black stockings. Jet beads. They didn't really shout it, but they were the kind of clothes people wore—I don't know. A long time ago."

He chewed and swallowed, and sipped milk. No one spoke, and at last he said, "They were in one of the pictures. She will have new ones next time, I think."

"Can she do that?"

He shrugged. "My jacket wasn't in those pictures."

"Take it off!" Seth Thompkins demanded, and Doug Douglas grabbed him from behind.

"Sure," he said. "If you want it, I'll let you have it."

Doug relaxed somewhat. Bill slipped out of the jacket, kicked Doug, and hit the back of Doug's neck when Doug doubled up.

Seth's right knocked him off balance, and Seth's left caught him under the cheekbone. He hit Seth in the pit of the stomach, knocking him sprawling.

Martha Novick had stopped to watch.

"People on television talk a lot when they fight." He picked up his letter jacket and dusted it with his hand. "I don't think it's ever really like that. You're too busy."

"I guess I ought to tell Mr. Hoff," Martha said, "only I'm not going to."

He thanked her.

"Did you hurt them bad, Bill?"

"I don't think so," he told her. "They'll get up when I'm gone."

Dr. Grimes closed the notebook and smiled at him. "This is interesting stuff, Bill. Did you really dream it?"

He nodded.

"Armor that looked like your school jacket?"

"Somewhat like it," he said. "Not exactly. Do you care?"

Dr. Grimes nodded.

"All right. My school jacket's blue and silver. You must have seen them."

She nodded again.

"This is a short black leather coat. It's not blue or silver at all—the leather isn't, I mean. But it has steel rings sewn on it, and steel plates across the chest. Some of the steel plates and rings have been blued. Heat blued, I suppose. Do you know how to blue steel?"

"I couldn't do it," Dr. Grimes said, "but I've seen it. Sure, Bill."

"The rest have been polished bright. They'll rust, I'm sure, unless I keep them shined and oiled. So will the blue ones. But I'm going to do the best I can to take care of them. I'll put a little can of oil and a rag in my jacket pockets tonight before I go to bed."

She cocked her head. "Will that work?"

"I don't know. I believe it may."

"Uh-huh. You tell me, if it does. You been fightin'?"

He smiled. "You get around, don't you?"

"You goin' to law school when you get out of here?"

"Why do you ask?"

" 'Cause you answer a question with a question when you don't want to talk. That's a lawyer trick, and lawyers make real good money if they're good. I don't get around a-tall, Bill. I just sit here in my office, talkin' and writin' down and answerin' the phone. But people come and tell me stuff. Got a li'l bruise on that sweet face, too. You really kick that one boy?"

He nodded. "Are you goin' to report me?"

"Huh-uh. Maybe somebody will. I don't know, Bill. But not me."

"I kicked him, and they would have kicked me if they'd gotten a chance. We weren't boxing, we were fighting. How can you play fair, when you're not playing?"

"You're on the football team now."

He nodded.

"Goin' to start against Pershing. That's what I heard."

"The coach hasn't said that to me. I can play halfback and linebacker—or at least he says I can—and I've been practicing those positions. I just hope I get in the game."

"Uh-huh." She smiled. "I was married to a football player, one time. Dee-troit Lions. I used to go to all the games back then, and I still watch a lot. On the TV, you know. You know what they tell me about you, Bill?"

He shook his head.

"They say you always catch a pass. Two men coverin' you. Three. It don't matter. You always catch it."

"I've been lucky."

"Uh-huh. Ms. Fournier, she says you're a genius. You been lucky there, too, I guess."

"I don't think so."

Dr. Grimes sat in silence for half a minute, regarding him. At last she said, "If a boy's too smart, the other boys don't like that, do they? Maybe he was just lucky, but if he'd been luckier he would have missed a question. Maybe two. I ever tell you I like you?"

He nodded.

"I do, Bill. First time I talked to you, you seem like such a nice kid, and you got a good imagination. Now you seem like a nice man with a real good education and a kid's face. That first one was interestin'. This one here, this is real interestin'."

"You're wrong," he said.

"I get up in the mornin', and I want to come to work. That's because of you. How am I wrong, Bill? Tell me."

He rose, sensing that the period was nearly over. "You think I've grown up, somehow, inside. I haven't. I know a lot more than I did, because I've been trying to decipher the runes on the scabbard. But I'm still Bill Wachter, and I'm still young. Inside. 'When all the world is young, lad, and all the trees are green, and every goose a swan, lad, and every lass a queen. Then hey for boot and horse, lad, and round the world away. Young blood must have its course, lad, and every dog his day.' "

Dr. Grimes only watched him with thoughtful eyes; so when a second, and two, had ticked past, he turned and went out into the hall.

She said nothing to stop him, and he was ten paces from her door when the bell rang.

Sue and a tall, smiling man in a checked sport coat were waiting for him when he left the locker room after the game. "This is Mr. Archer," Sue said. "He's going to take us to Perry's for a bite, if that's all right with you, Bill. Is it?"

He smiled. "Do you want to go?"

"Not if you don't."

"Then I do," he said, and her hand slipped into his.

Mr. Archer's car was a red Park Avenue Ultra with tinted windows. "You two sit in back," he told them. "It'll take twenty minutes or so, and I can't talk worth a damn when I'm driving."

Mr. Archer got in and tilted the rearview mirror up; and Bill opened the door for Sue, and got in himself on the other side. By the time that they had left Veterans Avenue behind, and with it the last traffic of the game, his hand had slid beneath her sweater and under the waistband of her skirt.

She was prim and ladylike when Archer opened the door of the car for her; but she left as soon as Perry's headwaiter had seated them, to repair her makeup in the rest room.

"Beautiful girl," Mr. Archer said appreciatively. "You know her long, Bill?"

"Yes and no." Although he had held the restaurant's door for them both like a gentleman, and had pulled out Sue's chair for her (beating the headwaiter to it by one tenth of one second), his mind was still whirling. "We rode the same bus last year, and she was in my homeroom and some of my classes. It was the fourth week of the school year before we got to be close friends." He cleared his throat. "September twenty-second."

Archer smiled. "You remember the exact day."

"Certainly."

"You didn't play last year, did you? I don't think freshmen are eligible."

He shook his head, trying to recall his freshman year. Things had been so different then. So very, very different. So very much worse. "No," he said. "You're correct, they aren't, and I wouldn't have gone out anyway."

"She couldn't have known you'd be a star."

"She didn't even know I'd go out. That day—the day we really noticed each other—I hadn't decided to do it. Or even thought about it, really."

"Sue didn't tell you what I do." Mr. Archer took a card folder from a pocket of his sport coat, fished out a card, and laid it on the table between them. "I'm an assistant coach, just like that card says. I coach offense, and I go to high-school games whenever I get the chance, Bill, hoping to spot some real talent. Mostly I don't."

"In that case," he said slowly, "it was very nice of you to take us out like this."

A waiter came; Mr. Archer ordered a John Collins and two Diet Cokes.

"There are fifty players on each team this early in the season," Mr. Archer said, "so a hundred altogether. Why am I being nice to you?"

"I suppose because my parents weren't there. I ought to explain that. They wanted to come, but I begged them not to. I was afraid I wouldn't get to play at all, and that if I did I'd play badly."

Returning, Sue said, "You didn't, Bill. You made the Panthers look like monkeys out there."

Mr. Archer said, "The score was twenty zip. Who scored all three touchdowns?"

"I was lucky, that's all."

"Five times I saw you catch passes that ought to have been incompletions. Three times I saw you catch passes that should have been interceptions."

A waitress brought their drinks.

"You know the three times rule, Bill? Once, that's an accident. Twice, that's a coinkydink. Three times, that's enemy action. You were the—what school was that, Bill? Who were you playing?"

"Pershing." She had gripped his leg under the table and was squeezing hard, probably as hard as she could, but he had no idea why.

"You were Pershing's enemy," Mr. Archer said. "An enemy they couldn't handle. You weren't watching their coach, but I was—I used to coach high school myself. He was chewing nails and spitting them at his players."

"Bill," Sue whispered, "for just a minute I have to talk to you."

"So do I," Archer told her. "I need to tell him about some of the scholarships we've got. But all my talking will take quite a while, and maybe you won't. I'll go wash my hands."

Over his shoulder he added, "If you want nachos or anything, just order. Steaks. Whatever. On me."

Sue leaned closer, her voice almost inaudible. "Our waitress. Did you look at her, Bill?"

He shook his head.

"It's Dinah."

Back in the Park Avenue Ultra, Mr. Archer asked where they wanted to go. Sue said, "Where Edison and Cottonwood cross. It's a white house, two stories, with a big porch. Okay, Bill?"

"We ought to take you home first."

"No way. You won't tell your folks a thing. Take us to Bill's house, Mr. Archer. Where I said. His mom and dad shouldn't find out he's a hero from the paper."

"Sue . . ."

Archer said, "You're afraid I'll go in and buttonhole your parents. You want some time to think it over yourself first. Am I right, Bill?"

He was not, but Bill said he was.

"I understand, and I won't do it. Listen, Bill, I want to tell you something and I want you to remember it. I was all-city quarterback once, back before you were born. Where you are now? I've been there, too. I know what it's like. You keep my card and I'll talk to you again in a few days."

* * *

"Your folks are nice," Sue said as he walked her home. "They let me tell them all that stuff before they told us they'd been listening on the radio. Did you notice?"

He nodded.

"College games get on TV. State's always do, around here, because there are so many grads. Mr. Archer didn't say that, so I'll say it now. Just something to think about, Bill."

"I am."

Sue glanced at him, then away. "Here's something else. My mom is a very good mother, but she works really hard. She has to be at work at seven, and when she gets home, she has to clean and cook. I help as much as I can, and so does Chick. But she does most of it."

This time it was Shep who said, "Sure."

Sue did not seem to notice. "So she won't have listened to the game, Bill. I'm sorry, but she won't. I mean, I'll tell her tomorrow. But she won't have heard much about it on the radio."

He said, "That's good."

"In fact, she'll be in bed asleep by the time we get there. That's something else to think about, Bill."

Bill thought.

The hills were behind them, the plain ahead of them, flat and featureless, an empty expanse of dry brown grass across which a chill wind moaned. He had given the leather coat with its steel rings to Sue; its shoulders were too big for her and its sleeves too long, but that was good and the leather kept out the wind. "Where are we going?" she said.

He pointed. "See those mountains? There's a city, a golden city, on the other side. We're going there."

"What for?"

"Because it's the only place to go. You can go there, or you can die here. That's all the choices we have." He paused, considering. "I can't make you go there. I'd have to hit you or something, and tie you up when I slept, and I won't do that. Maybe there's something over that way, or over there. I don't know, and if you want to go look, I'll go with you. But—"

"I'm going where you're going, Bill." Sue's voice was firm. "I've already told you that. Only I've got a lot of questions."

"I haven't got any answers," he said.

There was a wild cry high overhead, as lonely and inhuman as the keening of a hawk. They looked up and saw the great bird that had uttered it sailing through ragged clouds, and watched it circle and descend. "That's Biltis," he said. "Maybe she'll help us."

> "She gave Sue a wand with which she can start fires," he wrote in his notebook the next day,
>
> and said we would come to a river, and that there would be a cave in the bank which we were not to enter on any account.
>
> Sue clasped my arm and said, "He belongs to me!" but Biltis only laughed and said I belonged to both of them, and that I had from the beginning.

"Come on in, Bill, and shut the door." Dr. Grimes waved toward a chair. "This here is Dr. Hayes. Dr. Hayes was my teacher a long time ago. Over there's Ms. Biltis from the School Board. I told them I wanted to get Dr. Hayes to consult, and they said okay, but they had to have somebody here to see what was goin' on. So that's Ms. Biltis."

Dinah said, "Bill and I have met already. Hi, Bill."

He said hi in return.

Dr. Hayes asked, "Does he always bring the dog, Tacey?"

Dr. Grimes shook her head. "He talks about it, but I never did see it before. Is that Shep, Bill?"

He nodded.

Dinah said, "It's contrary to our regulations to have a dog in the building or on school property unless it's a guide dog for the blind. In this case, the Board's willing to make an exception."

"That's good," Dr. Grimes said.

Dr. Hayes shaped a steeple from his fingers. "Why did you bring your dog today, Bill?"

"He's not really my dog," Bill said, "he's my lawyer."

Dr. Grimes looked surprised. Dinah laughed; she had a pretty laugh, and it made him feel better to hear it.

Dr. Hayes's expression did not change in the least. "I'm not sure I understand. Perhaps you'd better explain."

"I don't mean he's a real lawyer. He hasn't passed the bar. But I felt I needed someone to advise me, and I know Shep's smart and that he's on my side."

"I'm on your side, too, Bill."

Dr. Grimes said, "So am I, Bill. I thought you knew that."

Dinah grinned; it was an attractive grin, and full of mischief. "We of the Board are always on the side of the students."

"But you're over there." Bill gestured. "And Shep and I are over here."

"I can fix that." Dinah got up and moved her chair so that she sat on his left and Shep on his right.

Dr. Hayes nodded to her. "Is there a statement you wish to make on behalf of the School Board before I begin?"

Dinah shook her head. "I'll reserve it."

"I would prefer that you not interrupt. Quite frankly, your presence poses a threat to the exploratory examination I wish to undertake. Interruptions may render it futile."

"What about the dog?" Dinah smiled.

Shep said, "Nope."

"If the dog proves to be an impediment, we'll dismiss with it, although I doubt that will be necessary."

Bill said, "I'm missing Social Studies."

Dr. Hayes nodded again. "We're aware of it, and we've discussed it with your teacher. She says you have already earned an A, that you know much more of the subject than her course is designed to teach her students. What day of the week is this, Bill?"

"Monday."

"Correct. And the date?"

"October fifth."

"Also correct. We are in a building of some sort. Do you know what building it is?"

"Kennedy Consolidated."

"And why are you here, Bill?"

He stroked Shep's head, at which Shep said, "Dunno."

"Bill?" Dr. Hayes sounded polite but wary.

"I was thinking, sir. I could offer three or four explanations, but I don't have much confidence in any of them. The truth is that I don't know. Why am I?"

"In order that you can provide those explanations, for one thing. Will you?"

Dr. Grimes said, "You see, Bill, what you say to us is goin' to be a whole lot more help than anythin' we could say to you. You been sittin' in some class with a teacher, day after day, I know. This's kinda like that, only you're the teacher now, and me and Ms. Biltis and Dr. Hayes, we're the class you're teachin'."

Shep said, "Go ahead, Chief."

"All right." He paused to collect his thoughts. "I've been writing down my dreams in study hall. You told me to do that, but I was doing it before you told me, and Mrs. Durkin read my notebook over my shoulder and decided that I was psychotic. She likes me, but she still thinks I'm psychotic. She feels sorry for me."

Dr. Hayes said, "We all do, Bill."

"Not me," Dr. Grimes said. "Bill can take care of himself. I only wish he'd help me understand him more, 'cause I don't. I don't indeed."

Dinah grinned again. "Me neither. I feel sorry—"

The telephone rang. Dr. Grimes picked it up and said, "Counselin'. Oh, hello, Sue. You know I never have met you, but I've heard a sight about you from this nice Bill Wachter. He thinks you got angel wings, you know that?

"Why, no.

"Now don't you worry. I got my 'pointment book right here. Maybe two o'clock tomorrow?

"That's good. No, don't you worry none 'bout Shep. I got him right here. I been talkin' to him my own self." Dr. Grimes laughed. "Course he hasn't said much back, Sue. But maybe he will. What he say to you?

"That's good. That Shep's a good sensible dog, Sue. Don't you worry. You come see me tomorrow."

Dr. Grimes's smile faded as she hung up. "Shep's been talkin' to Sue, too, Dr. Hayes. Sue's Bill's girlfriend."

Dinah said, "One of them."

"He didn't say nothin' bad, only wantin' to know where Bill was. So she told him and he went off. She'd like to see me, but the door was closed—just a minute ago, I guess—so she called from the phone in the cafeteria. Yes, Bill? You want to say somethin'?"

He nodded. "I've been pondering the speech of animals. It's not that the kiss that flew to me suddenly made animals talk. It's that the kiss let me understand what they were saying. Love is at the root of it. The more you love anyone or anything, the better you understand it. She kissed me, and I kissed Sue, and that may be the reason Sue understands Shep now."

"I got a cat I call Catcat," Dr. Grimes said. "I don't understand Catcat very good, but that Catcat understands *me* backward and forward, too. She likes me more than I like her. That what you're sayin'?"

Shep said, "Yep."

Dinah said, "I'm going to interrupt here. Bill promised us several explanations and has delivered only one, that the Durkin woman thinks he's psychotic. I would like to hear the others. Also I want to say that I understand Shep perfectly—not that he's said much, but what he has said has been in plain Doggish, which is quite different from doggerel. If the student who called understands him, too, she's no crazier than I am."

Dr. Hayes and Dr. Grimes stared at her.

"Bill's never kissed me. Is that supposed to make a difference? I've kissed him, though."

Dr. Hayes leaned toward Dr. Grimes. "I seem to be losing control of the situation, Tacey. My apologies."

"I guess you see now why I wanted you?"

Nodding, he turned to Dinah. "I take it you're a friend of Bill's family, Ms. Biltis?"

"Why, no. I don't know Bill's parents at all."

Bill cleared his throat. "She wants another explanation, and one just occurred to me. Would anyone like to hear it?"

Dinah said, "I would, Bill." And Dr. Grimes nodded.

"I don't credit this one either," Bill said. "I should make that clear. But I find it interesting." He held up his notebook. "Before I met Biltis, I met a dwarf on horseback. Perhaps it would be more accurate to say that I was overtaken by him. It's all in here."

He paused, inviting them to read his notebook if they cared to. No one spoke.

"He gave me a sword. I want to call it an enchanted sword, and perhaps it is. Certainly the spells on the scabbard are magical, and doubtless those engraved on the blade are magical, as well. I can read the spells on the scabbard somewhat. I read them badly and quite slowly, but eventually I can puzzle them out. Sue and Shep cannot read them at all."

Dr. Hayes said, "Do you feel that these enchantments explain your presence here, Bill? That the casting of a spell has compelled you to come, perhaps?"

He shook his head. "Not exactly. First of all, they are spells, not enchantments. That is to say, they're words of magical import. One merely speaks them, and no chanting is required, although I would think that many chants were required for the sword that was to bear so much magic."

Dinah giggled.

"Of course I have asked myself many times why such a sword should be given to me."

Dr. Grimes said, "It was your dream, Bill. You don't think that's reason a-plenty?"

"That's like saying that all islands are inhabited because all the islands from which we've received reports are." He shrugged. "I've had many dreams in which I wasn't given an enchanted sword, or a sword of any kind. If—"

Dr. Hayes interrupted him. "Do you feel a connection between this sword and your penis, Bill?"

He laughed, and so did Dinah.

Dr. Grimes said, "What do you think that sword might be connected to, Bill, 'sides this dwarf? Comin' from a dwarf, I know why Dr. Hayes said what he did, and lots of people think like that. How do you think? What does this sword you got in your dream make you think about?"

"Biltis," he said. As he spoke, Dinah slipped her hand into his.

"Is that the girl in your dream that rides that bird? I told Dr. Hayes about her, and maybe he'd like to read about her, too, by and by."

Dr. Hayes said, "Perhaps I would, Tacey. Perhaps I should."

"I think so. Why does this sword make you think 'bout her, Bill?"

He looked from Dr. Grimes to Dinah, and back again. "I think that Biltis must be a princess or a queen. Something of that kind, in any case—a woman with a lot of power. I told you about the fire wand."

Dr. Grimes nodded.

"The wand proves that she has magical possessions, and can afford to give them away almost casually. When Sue and Shep and I went into the cave—she had told us not to, but we went anyway, because Sue wanted to get out of the wind. We were attacked, and Sue's wand was at least as important as my sword and Shep's teeth in beating our attackers back and getting the three of us out alive."

Dr. Grimes nodded again, encouragingly. "It was a good thing you got it, Bill."

"It was a good thing Sue did, or we would probably have been killed. And Biltis gave it to her. Sue is jealous of Biltis, but I don't think Biltis is jealous of Sue."

Dinah said, "Neither do I."

"Sue wants to keep me," he continued, "but Biltis feels she already has me, and I think she may be right. When I made the thing that had her by the foot release her, she told me very seriously that I must beware of underground places. I didn't trust her warning then, not wholly. I should have."

Dr. Grimes leaned toward him. "You think that tells why you're here now, Bill?"

"Indirectly. Why did the dwarf give me the sword?"

Dr. Hayes said, "It's your dream, Bill, not ours. Why did he?"

"I don't know, of course. I can only guess. But my guess is that he did it because he had been ordered to—ordered by Biltis. When people talk of kings and queens, princes and princesses these days, it's as stock figures in märchen—pictures in a nineteenth-century book that everyone is too busy to read. But I think that Biltis is a real queen, and real queens have subjects, hundreds of thousands of them, even in a small kingdom. Tens of millions in one the size of England. If a queen with real power had a sword written over with spells she couldn't read, she would look for someone who could, wouldn't she? And get him to read them for her?"

"Right, Chief," Shep said.

"It's your dream, Bill," Dr. Hayes repeated.

He nodded. "I'm not supposed to be explaining my dream, though, am I? I'm supposed to be explaining this—why you got me here. Very well. Suppose you got me here to tell you about the spells on the sword?"

Dinah said, "You've left something out. Perhaps you didn't think of it. Why didn't Biltis simply bring you the sword and ask you to read it?"

He shrugged. "You should know better than I. Possibly because I couldn't. I can read it only very slowly, and when I try, it's usually when we're going to camp, or rest for a while. To read it, I have to be able to see it, and we didn't have any way to make a fire until you gave Sue the wand. Now we'll have a fire and I may be able to puzzle out the writing by firelight."

He turned to speak to Dr. Hayes and Dr. Grimes. "Tell me something, please, and be just as honest as you can. It will mean nothing to you, but it's important to me. Haven't either of you noticed that Ms. Biltis here and the woman in my dream have the same name?"

"What are you talking about?" Dr. Hayes asked.

Dr. Grimes said gently, "They're not the same, Bill. This lady here's Ms. Biltis from the School Board, and the one in your dream is," she referred to her notes, "Biltis."

Bill turned back to Dinah. "So that's the way it is."

"Yes." She gave him her impish smile. "Don't worry. It won't hurt them."

"I wasn't worried," he said.

"Careful," Shep muttered.

"I have a sword," Dinah told Dr. Grimes. "It's out in my car. I'd like to bring it in and show it to Bill, if no one objects."

Dr. Grimes looked to Dr. Hayes, who said, "What do you think, Tacey? Is he apt to become violent?"

Dr. Grimes shook her head. "He's always been just as nice as pie, 'cept playin' that football, and he's generally just catchin' passes and runnin' then. You want to cut anybody, Bill?"

"No," he said. "Certainly not."

Dinah had already gone, seeming almost to have melted away.

"Somebody goin' to ask you to read that sword, you think, Bill?"

He nodded.

"Me, too. You goin' to do it?"

"I don't know yet."

Dr. Hayes said, "Do you really think that there may be writing on it, Tacey? An engraved blade? Something of that sort?"

"I guess we'll see. Bill thinks she's the same as the lady in his dream, and I see why. She does act sort of like it. You think she got that mark on her foot, Bill?"

He nodded.

"I been wantin' to ask you 'bout that. The first time you seen her, she had her foot down in that hole?"

"Correct."

"She do that on purpose?"

Shep said, "Yep."

"Bill?"

"I don't know. Shep thinks so. If it was intentional, it may have been to explain a preexisting mark on her ankle."

"A birthmark, like," Dr. Grimes told Dr. Hayes. "You can see it through her nylons if you look close."

He shook his head. "You're being drawn into the patient's delusional system, Tacey."

"Okay, maybe I wasn't seein' nothin'. Maybe it was just a shadow. What you think, Bill? You 'gree with Dr. Hayes?"

Shep said, "Nope."

Dr. Hayes murmured, "You must know, deep inside, that there is no such mark, Bill."

" 'I am Sir Oracle. When I ope my mouth, let no dog bark.' " He smiled. "Another possibility is that she wanted to warn me about the underground creatures—the cavern-folk, or demons, or whatever we choose to call them. If she wanted to show me—not merely tell me—that they are real and dangerous, she chose a good way to do it."

"Only you went in that cave anyhow," Dr. Grimes said. "Can I see your book?"

He passed it to her, and she flipped it open.

Dr. Hayes said, "Some of the teachers here don't think your dreams are real dreams, Bill. They don't believe that they are dreams and not daydreams, in other words. Does that surprise you?"

"Yes," he said, "I didn't know they knew about them. Mrs. Durkin has been talking in the teachers' lounge, I suppose."

"Are they real dreams, Bill?"

"I don't believe so. I don't believe they're daydreams either."

Dinah returned, shutting the door behind her. "Here it is." She held up a package loosely wrapped in brown paper. "I got it from a company in Georgia." She unwrapped it, ripping the paper. "I had them send it UPS Overnight. It cost a little more, but it was worth it."

A glittering hilt protruded from a sheath of unadorned black leather.

"Here, Bill. I'll hold this part, and you can pull it out."

He looked to Dr. Grimes for permission. She nodded, and he drew the gleaming double-edged blade clear of the sheath.

Dr. Hayes said, "Is that the sword you've been telling us about, Bill?"

He rose, weighing the sword in his hand.

Dr. Grimes said, "That isn't a magic sword at all, is it, Bill?"

He moved the sword, not thrusting or slashing with it, only testing its weight and balance.

"There's writin' on the blade up close to that handle," Dr. Grimes continued. "I been tryin' to read it, only I can't. Not from here."

" 'Made in India,' " Bill said absently.

Dr. Grimes laughed. "It can't be no magic sword if it's made there, can it, Bill?"

Dinah sniffed. "It's my sword, and I think it's a very nice sword."

"It feels well in the hand," Bill said, "and I can't believe that anyone would waste so much good workmanship on poor steel." He seemed to be talking to himself.

Dr. Hayes said, "But not a magic sword. I hope you agree, Bill?"

"I do." He looked up. "It is becoming a magic sword, however."

Shep said, "Good!"

"Because I'm holding it. Magic is flowing from me into the sword. I didn't know that could happen, but it can."

Dr. Hayes looked at Dr. Grimes, who said, "Bill, I know you're just havin' fun, but you're makin' Dr. Hayes here think you got something really wrong with you. It's not nice to fool people that way, and you could get in a lot of trouble just doin' it."

"Because I said that?" He smiled. "Why is the Holy Grail holy, Dr. Hayes? Why does it perform miracles? It is the cup used by Christ at the Last Supper."

"Perhaps you can tell me, Bill."

"You don't know. Dr. Grimes?"

She shook her head.

"Because something—not magic, let's call it divinity—flowed from Him into the cup. We know that sort of thing happened, because once, when a sick woman touched Him, He said He had felt the power leave Him. *Dynamin* is the word employed in the Greek gospel—power, might. I might guess at the Aramaic word Christ actually employed, but I won't. Such things should not be guessed at. For me the word is *lygros*."

A glow like the light from blazing wood wrapped the blade of the sword as he pronounced *lygros*.

"The magical power of death, the power to kill," he whispered.

There was a knock at the door.

"You put that away, Bill," Dr. Grimes told him sharply.

He ignored her.

Dinah called, "Come in!"

The door opened, and Ms. Fournier looked in with a worried smile. "Sue Sumner isn't in here, is she, Dr. Grimes?"

Shep said, "Nope."

"One of the students told me she wanted to talk to you, and I thought—I hoped . . ."

Dr. Grimes said, "I haven't seen her, Ms. Fournier. She's in my book for tomorrow."

"The chem lab supplies are stored in the basement," Ms. Fournier continued, "I suppose you know that. Mr. Boggs sent her for some—oh!"

Shep had bounded past her, closely followed by Bill, sword in hand. With a murmured, "Excuse me," Dinah followed him, kicking off her high heels to run before she was three steps down the corridor.

"Me, too, honey." Heavier as well as older, Dr. Grimes required most of the doorway.

"Pardon me," Dr. Hayes said. He was holding his pipe; although it contained no tobacco, he thrust it resolutely into his mouth and clamped it with his jaw before striding away.

"I looked!" Ms. Fournier called after him. "So did Mr. Boggs! She's not there!"

They caught up with Bill and Shep in the furnace room, where Hector Fuente turned from his unsuccessful argument with Bill to demand, "What're you doing here, lady?"

"I'm Dinah Biltis from the School Board," Dinah explained. "We're here to rescue Sue Sumner, if there's enough of her left to rescue."

"You got to have a pass."

"And I do. I'll show it to you in a moment. Have you looked in there, Bill? That iron door?"

He had not seen it. He lifted the steel bar and threw it aside.

It burst open, nearly knocking him down. The first hideous thing that rushed past him was not quite a corpse or a bear. The next had four legs and a multitude of arms, with an eye at the end of each. His first cut severed two, and they writhed on the floor like snakes. Others seized him; he broke their grip and drove his blade into the bulky, faintly human body. For perhaps five seconds, its death throes made it more dangerous than it had been in life.

Someone was shooting, the shots loud and fast in the enclosed space of the furnace room. He scrambled to his feet, reclaimed his sword, and saw Shep writhing and snapping in the jaws of a nightmare cat with foot-long fangs. With her back to the furnace, Dinah was firing a small automatic. Her last shot came as he took his first step, and the slide locked back. His blade bit the big cat's neck as though it had rushed into battle of itself, dragging him behind it. He felt it grate on vertebrae and cut free, severing the throat and the jugular veins, saw the great cat's jaws relax and the pitiful thing that dragged itself free of them and was so soon soaked by its own spurting blood.

Laying aside his sword, he embraced the dying dog. "Shep! Oh, my God, Shep!"

Dinah bent over them both, her empty gun still in her hand.

"Can't we heal him somehow, Biltis?"

She said, "You can, if you want to," and he repeated the words he had spoken once before, when he and Sue had walked past a certain house, whispering them into Shep's ear. The light of his blade shone through the clotting blood at that moment, purer than sunshine.

* * *

The three of them found Sue two miles underground and killed the things that had been guarding her. He wanted to carry her, but she insisted (her voice shaking and sharp with fear) that she could walk. Walk she did, though she leaned heavily on his arm.

Shep scouted ahead, sniffing the air and whining in his eagerness to be gone. After the first quarter mile, Dinah said, "This little flashlight's just about gone, Bill. See how yellow it is?"

"Yes. Out brief candle, and all that. Can we get back without it?"

"I think so. Remember the light from your sword? Do that again."

"I didn't think you saw that," he said.

"I see a lot. Do it again."

He muttered to himself, and when Sue released his arm, he fingered the blade; and a sapphire light crept up and down that deep central groove some call the blood gutter, and spread to the edges after a minute or two, and trailed, by the time they had gone another quarter mile, from the point. He relaxed a little then, and hugged Sue, and tried to make the hug say that they would make it—that she would see the sky again.

"Don't let them get me, Bill." It was a whisper from her mind, yet clear as speech. "Oh, please! Don't let them get me."

"I won't," he said, and prayed that he could keep the promise. "Are you on our side, Biltis? Really, really on our side?"

"Certainly," she said, and grinned.

Sue said, "You shot them. You wouldn't have, if you weren't on our side, would you?"

Dinah did not bother to reply.

"She wouldn't, would she, Bill?"

"Of course not," he said, "but I don't understand how she did it. Her gun was empty before we came in here."

"I had a spare magazine in my purse, that's all."

"One magazine?"

Dinah nodded. "Just one."

As they walked on (he with an arm about Sue's waist, she weeping and stumbling), he wondered whether Dinah had been telling the truth. She had sounded as though she might be lying, and it inclined him to trust her; she had been careful with her voice when she said she was from the school board.

The iron door was closed and latched. He lifted the latch, but the door would not open. He pounded on it with the hilt of his sword, which did no good at all, and the four of them threw their combined weight against it, which did no good either.

When the rest were exhausted, he went back down the long tunnel, leaving Shep to protect the two women—or perhaps, Dinah and her little gun to protect Sue and Shep. By the fiery light of his blade he found something huge cowering in a crevice; he persuaded it to come out by telling it (entirely truthfully) that he would kill it if it did not.

When the two of them returned to the door, he called out to Dinah not to shoot, saying that the thing came as a friend. "If you will break this down for us," he told it, "we will leave the underground realm forever and trouble it no more. If you will not—or cannot—I will kill you. You've got my word on our departure, and on that, too. Will you try? Or would you rather die here and now?"

The thing lifted the latch as he had, but the door would not open. It threw its weight against it, and it was bigger than any bull.

A crevice of light appeared. Bill put down his sword and got his fingers into it, and spread it as he might have opened the jaws of a crocodile, with veins bulging in his forehead and sweat dripping from his face, and the huge thing he had found throwing its terrible strength against the door again and again until the steel bar bent, and the boxes and barrels, the desks and chairs and tables that had been piled against it gave way.

They rushed out—Shep, Sue, Dinah, and he, climbing and stumbling over the fallen barricade. And the thing came after them, with Bill's sword in its hand; but Shep severed its wrist, Dinah put a bullet into its single eye, and he drove his reclaimed sword between its ribs until the quillons gouged its scales.

They found Drs. Grimes and Hayes dismembering the catlike monster that had seized Shep, and feeding the parts to a hulking old coal furnace, assisted by Hector Fuente and his machete. "They lef' this ol' furnace here for standby when they went to gas," Dr. Grimes explained. "They lef' coal, too. Hector here, he tol' us all 'bout it. This ol' coal furnace, it don't need 'lectricity, so when the 'lectric goes off, like in a ice storm, he can run it to keep the pipes from freezin'."

"It is a great loss to science," Dr. Hayes added, "but it is not *my* science. Besides, we would be accused of faking our evidence—the inevitable result of such discoveries."

Dinah said, "They shut the door on us, Bill, and barred it, and piled all that stuff in front of us. Shall we kill them?"

He shook his head.

The four of them went up the stairs and out onto the athletic field, past the volleyball court and the tennis court, and onto the field on which the football team would practice after school.

"It's so g-good to be o-outside." Sue was trembling. "Look! There's good old Juniper Street. It—it d-doesn't look the way it did, not to me. It looks like a toy under somebody's Christmas tree. B-but it's Juniper, and I love it. I always will, after—after that. Don't you love it, too, B-Bill?" Her eyes had filled with tears.

"I do," he said, though he was not looking at it. "See the hardware store? And Philips Fabrics?"

As Sue nodded, Dinah whistled shrilly; a huge black bird plummeted toward earth at the sound of that whistle, a minute dot that became a hurtling thunderbolt. They watched it land (barked at by Shep), watched Dinah mount, and waved good-bye.

"Who is she, Bill?"

He shrugged. "Who am I? Who are you?"

"Bill's girl," Sue replied.

Repeating those words to himself, he turned to look at her. Her eyes were of the blue light he had seen upon his sword, her disheveled hair the gold of the towers; the tilt of her nose and the curve of her smudged cheek filled him with a longing so intense that he dared not kiss her.

"Are you sure, Sue?" He had struggled to control his voice, and failed.

She nodded without speaking.

"Then I want you to look higher than the hardware store and the fabric store."

He watched her. "No, higher. Off into the distance. What do you see?"

"Mountains!" Her eyes were wide. " Bill, those are mountains! There aren't any mountains around here. There aren't any mountains like those for a thousand miles."

"That's right." He began to walk again.

"You're going?"

" Yes," he said. "I'm going."

"Then I'm going with you."

Once they had left the town behind, the mountains were no longer impossibly distant. "One thing for sure," Sue said, "nothing will ever scare me after what happened today."

Shep wagged his tail in agreement. "Me, too! Right, Chief?"

William Wachter shrugged. "I have a feeling that this was the easy part," he said.

COPYRIGHTS